THANKS, B

For a moment, the great covered park was what it had been when Hansen first saw it: bright, clean, and filled with thousands of healthy people, though their faces were now streaked with tears and terror. Then it changed again, and Hansen saw an armored vehicle that must have weighed hundreds of tonnes.

The tank glided toward Hansen. It sprouted missile batteries and guns. The folk of Diamond keened and clutched one another, keeping their faces down and their eyes closed.

There was no place to run. Hansen picked up the chair—extruded plastic, light if not quite flimsy . . . and probably just as effective as any other man-portable weapon against a monster like the tank which bore down on him now. Hansen swung his piece of furniture at a vision block on the upper left of the tank's bowslope.

The plastic chair whistled at and through the knobbly armor without touching anything material save the air. Hansen overbalanced and almost fell.

"Oh, Mr. Hansen . . . ," someone murmured behind him. Hansen turned. Lea was staring at the chair in the visitor's hands.

Hansen put the chair down carefully, feeling embarrassed.

"Oh, Mr. Hansen," Lea repeated. "I'm so sorry." She stepped closer to him and reached out her hand. Hansen felt—cold wasn't the word, but a sensation as deep as if freezing water were drawing all the warmth out of his body. There was a thin film between Hansen and everything around him.

"We're so sorry," she said through a corridor of mirrors. "It isn't a fault in you, Mr. Hansen, but weapons don't exist here in Diamond."

She raised onto her toes to kiss him. He couldn't feel her lips. Everything was becoming gray.

"And you are a weapon. . . ," whispered words that were only a shadow in Hansen's mind as he felt the structure of Diamond interpenetrate him completely and leave only nothingness.

NORTHWORLD
TRILOGY

David Drake

NORTHWORLD TRILOGY

Northworld ©1990, *Northworld: Vengeance* ©1991, *Northworld: Justice* ©1992 by David Drake

A Baen Book

Baen Publishing Enterprises
P.O. Box 1403
Riverdale, NY 10471

ISBN: 0-671-57787-5

Cover art by Patrick Turner

First Baen printing, March 1999

Distributed by Simon & Schuster
1230 Avenue of the Americas
New York, NY 10020

Printed in the United States of America

Northworld

For Toni Weisskopf
who, like the Black Prince,
won her spurs among scenes of butchery.

Chapter One

Hansen saw the blast bubble like an orange puffball above the building roofs three kilometers away. He stuck his head out the side-window of his chauffeured aircar and heard the *whump!* over the rush of wind.

"Don't get us above—" Hansen started to say, but the car was already sideslipping to lose altitude and take them the rest of the distance to the crime site in the shelter of the buildings. The drivers who rotated through Commissioner Hansen's duty list were the best in Special Units. This one, a human named Krupchak, didn't want to enter the sight radius of the bandits' heavy weaponry any more than Hansen did.

Hansen's visor was split into three screens: the top showing the view from one of the units already at the crime site; the center clear for normal sight; and the bottom running a closed loop from the incident that set up the current situation. Hansen's own viewpoint showed nothing but faces from the ground traffic gaping upward at the aircar which howled above them with its emergency flashers fluttering at eye-dazzling speed.

The Civic Patrolmen on-site were busy blocking streets and trying to evacuate civilians already in what was clearly a combat zone. They weren't interested in the building at 212 Kokori Street where the bandits had holed up, except to keep from being blown away by the shots spitting—and sometimes slamming—from the top story of that structure.

Hansen set his remote to one of his own Special Units teams which had already arrived. Hansen's people (some of them female and not a few of them inhuman despite the complaints from bigots) were for the moment setting up fields of fire to block the bandits if they tried to escape. They were ready and willing to make a frontal assault if the Commissioner gave them that order.

The target was a fortress. Special Units would make a frontal assault on it over Commissioner Hansen's dead body.

1

Literally.

The structure was part of a row of cheap two- and three-story apartment buildings built long before the twenty-nine-year old Hansen was born. The windows of the top floor now bulged with the soap-bubble iridescence of a forcefield. A white Civic Patrol hoverscoot stood abandoned outside the building's front entrance.

Kokori Street wasn't a slum. The Consensus of Planets didn't permit slums in or around the capitals of any of its 1200 worlds; and besides, there were few real slums anywhere on Annunciation. Still, though there wasn't any trash in the street, the buildings' cast facades were dingy and sculpted in curves which flowed according to tastes superseded decades before.

The district's residents generally staffed the lower tiers of the city's service industries—but they *had* jobs, because residence in a planetary capital for periods longer than three months required that a household member be gainfully employed. Here on Annunciation, the Consensus fiat was enforced by the Civic Patrol—backed up by Special Units if necessary.

Ousting unemployed squatters could be a nasty job, but the worst casualties were usually a broken nose or a wrenched knee. *This* job was uniquely dangerous, but there was nobody in Hansen's section (and few enough in the Civic Patrol) who wasn't glad to have it.

The Solbarth Gang. It had to be Solbarth, the criminal whose genius was equalled by his ruthlessness. Inhuman ruthlessness, the news reports said; and this time the news reports were precisely correct.

One of Hansen's people was trying to get an update on the situation within 212 Kokori. Behind a Civic Patrol forcefield barricade parked a nondescript van. A SpyFly the size, shape and color of a large cigar burred from within the vehicle.

The little reconnaissance drone was scarcely visible until it arced to within a meter of the building's sidewall. There it exploded as ropes of scintillance.

Whoever was inside had an electronic flyswatter; which figured, if it was Solbarth.

A man jumped from a second-floor window, stumbled, and ran three steps toward the portable forcefield one of Hansen's units had set up at the intersection kitty-corner from the target building. A black sphincter dilated in the villains' protective screen. A blue-white flash cut the runner's legs from under him, long before he reached safety.

The body thrashed.

Just a civilian caught in something that was none of his business. Would've been smarter to hide under the bed until it was all over. But then, if Special Units opened up with the kind of firepower necessary to overwhelm the gang's forcefield, the whole block would melt into a bubbling crater.

That wasn't going to happen.

"Support," Hansen said, cueing the artificial intelligence in his helmet. "Is the building's climate control in metal ducts?"

A green light winked even as the Commissioner's last syllable rose in an interrogative.

The AI had accessed the data from Central Records; probably out of Building Inspection, but the exact provenance of the information didn't matter. Every scrap of data about this building, its residents—and the villains believed to be holed up here—had been sucked into a huge electronic suspense file within seconds of when the shooting started. Any extant knowledge that Hansen might need waited at the tip of his tongue.

The trouble was, quite of lot of what Hansen needed to know would be available only in the after-action report on the operation; and Commissioner Hansen might or might not be alive to examine the data then.

"Top to Orange Three," he ordered, letting the AI punch him through the chatter of the unit he'd just watched launch the SpyFly. "Put one into the building's ventilation system. Use a One-Star."

The 1° class drones were old and slow, but they had double-capacity powerpacks and were rugged enough to airdrop with their lift fans shut down.

"Sir, they've turned off the air system 'n the louvers 're down!" the Orange Three team leader replied in a voice half a tone higher than normal.

"Then it'll take the SpyFly a bloody while to burn through the louvers, won't it?" Hansen snarled. "So get on the bloody job!"

"Hang on, sir," his driver warned. The aircar bounced to a dynamic halt behind the forcefield barricade at the intersection.

A streak of flame washed from the villains' hideout. The portable forcefield pulsed like a rainbow, but it absorbed the burst without strain.

Regular police fired a sparkle of stun needles, but the temporary opening in the villains' forcefield had already closed. The Special Units teams held their fire the way they'd been ordered to do.

Polarized light cast a blue wash over everything on the other side of the barricade. The legless man halfway to the intersection had stopped twitching. Another plasma bolt licked from the far side of the building, silhouetting the roof moldings with its brief radiance.

Hansen glanced at the video loop running across the bottom of his visor. It displayed the sensor log of the patrolman who'd arrived to investigate a reported domestic disturbance.

The cop had been a little fellow and young, to judge from the image of him recorded in reflection from the building's front door as he entered. He was whistling something tuneless between his teeth. As he climbed the stairs, he checked the needle stunner in his holster.

He'd been a little nervous, but not nearly as nervous as he should've been.

It was all a mistake. The reported loud argument had been in District 9, not here in District 7. An administrative screw-up that normally would've meant, at worst, that a family argument blossomed into violence because the uniformed man who could've stopped it had been sent to the wrong place.

No sign of a domestic argument now. Knuckles rapping on a doorpanel; *Who's there?* muffled by the thick panel, and "Civic Patrol! Open up!" sharply from the cop whose equipment was recording events and transmitting the log back to his district sub-station; standard operating procedure.

Maybe if the patrolman had been a little less forceful in his request—

But that was second-guessing the man on the spot, and Hansen wasn't going to speak ill of the dead.

The video image of the door opened. Before the figure within was more than a blur, the universe dissolved in a plasma flare that the victim didn't have time to understand.

Hansen got out of his vehicle. The air smelled burned, from the forcefield and the weapons the villains were using; from the hellfire dancing in the Commissioner's mind.

His jaws hurt. He'd been clenching them as he watched the patrolman die. Hansen's muttered order cleared his visor of both the remote and the recorded images, but the fatal plasma burst continued to blaze a dirty white in memory.

Bad luck for the cop, knocking on the wrong door. And very bad luck indeed for Solbarth.

Four Special Units personnel squatted behind the forcefield they'd stretched between their vehicles. Two sighted over plasma weapons; one had a wide-muzzled projectile launcher; and the fourth, the team leader, carried the forcefield controls, a pistol, and long knives in both of her boots. They were all dressed in light-scattering camouflage uniforms which blurred their outlines and hid anything that an opponent could use for an aiming point.

The team members kept their faces rigidly to the front, pretending they didn't know the Commissioner was standing behind them. "Pink Two to Top," Hansen heard the leader say. "Are we clear to fire?"

The question didn't come to Hansen through the commo net, because the Commissioner's AI blocked out all the idle chatter that would otherwise have distracted him from the real business of solving the problem.

Hansen stepped over to the team leader, put a hand on her shoulder, and said, "We'll get where we're going, Pink Two. Don't worry."

"Sorry, sir," one of the plasma gunners said, though the reason *he* thought he needed to apologize was beyond Hansen's understanding.

Nobody needed to apologize. No matter how good your training was, no matter how much on-line experience you had, there were going to be tics and glitches in a real crisis. People said things, people forgot SOP . . . sometimes people shot when they shouldn't've, and even *that* was forgivable if you survived it.

Training went only so far. Situations like this went right down into the reptilian core of the brain.

With his fingers still resting on Pink Two's shoulder, Hansen said, "Support. Give me a fast three-sixty of the target site. Left side only."

Hansen's artificial intelligence began walking him visually around the apartment building. Remote images from other police personnel were remoted to the left half of the Commissioner's visor, changing every ten seconds to proceed around the site in a counterclockwise direction.

A patrolman in an apartment to Hansen's right poured a stream of stun needles toward the gang's hideout. There were brief sparkles on the forcefield and occasionally a puff of dust from the plastic facade. Raindrops would have been more effective than the one-gram needles were at this range.

On a roof halfway down the block, Special Units personnel stripped the tarpaulin from the 4-cm plasma weapon they'd just manhandled from an armored personnel carrier. Two other teams watched tensely from behind the forcefield they'd erected to shelter the gun installation. They knew the weapon could probably batter through the villains' protective screen; but they knew also that the sidescatter of powerful bolts hitting powerful armor was likely to incinerate every unshielded object within a kilometer of impact.

Ten seconds later a white aircar picked out with gold braid skidded to a halt behind a forcefield manned by Civic Patrol personnel. Holloway, Chief of the Capital Police, got out. He was still trying to seal his bemedaled uniform blouse over his fat belly.

An aide lifted a pair of slug-throwing hunting rifles out of the car and handed one to Holloway. Both men aimed as a police technician spun narrow loopholes in the protective forcefield so that his superiors could fire at the hideout.

No one but Special Units personnel was permitted to use deadly force. No one.

The AI cycled to the next image around the circle. Hansen's mouth was open to bark an order that Holloway, even Holloway, would obey—*or else*—when his right eye saw a whorl gape in the villains' forcefield. Solbarth must be using tuned elements so that merely presenting a weapon opened his shield wide enough to fire. *That* sort of hardware was too expensive even for Special Units.

And the weapon being aimed in Hansen's direction this time wasn't a plasma gun.

"Watch it!" he screamed, and, "Down!" to the personnel near him who thought their forcefield protected them from the villains' fire.

Hansen flattened, pushing the team leader out of her crouch and hoping the three men had sense enough to obey without asking questions. There was a flash from the momentary hole in Solbarth's protective bubble.

A ten-kilo war rocket arched down on a trail of thin smoke.

The missile skimmed the top of the police forcefield—which would have halted it harmlessly—and detonated in thunder on the pavement behind Hansen and his people.

The blast hurled the Commissioner's car—was the driver clear?—onto its side. The pavement shattered. Howling shards of missile casing pocked facades for twenty meters in every direction. Bits that struck the inner face of the forcefield hissed and melted as their kinetic energy was transformed into heat.

Hansen's ears rang. The men around him were all right, and his driver was getting out of the aircar with a dazed look on his face.

A rifle bullet whacked the hideout's facade and ricocheted over Hansen's head.

Hansen took a deep breath. "Top to all units," he said in a voice that rattled like tin in his own ears. "Cease firing. All units cease firing. I am Commissioner Hansen, and this site is under the jurisdiction of Special—"

Three bullets smacked the villains' forcefield where it bulged from one of the third-floor windows. The projectiles melted in showers of white sparks. The muzzle blasts of the rifles echoed down the corridor of building fronts like a burst of automatic fire.

"I say again, cease fire," Hansen ordered. "Special Units personnel, enforce my orders by whatever—"

The left half of Hansen's visor had cycled back to a view of Chief Holloway just as the fat man's body rocked back under the recoil of his powerful rifle. Hansen fully expected one of his people to stitch the Chief's ass with stun needles, but he hadn't said that.

Actually, he hadn't gotten the order completely out of his mouth before the back of Chief Holloway's limousine geysered metal and plastic, then collapsed in flames. Somebody from Special Units had put a plasma round into the vehicle.

Well, Hansen's personal motto was that no means were excessive if they got the job done. Holloway hurled the rifle away and curled up in a ball. His aide tried to shield the Chief's body, but the disparity in size of the men made the attempt ludicrous.

The delicate flicker of stun needles hitting the villains' forcefield stopped also.

Hansen stood up. A black spot in the center of a window spat plasma at him. He flinched as the bolt coruscated fifty centimeters from his face.

He drew his own pistol. "Pink Two," he said, wishing he could remember the woman's name. "Get ready to open the screen for me."

"You'll shoot, sir?" the team leader asked.

"For me, damn you!" Hansen shouted. "Me! Not a gun!"

He'd have to apologize later.

"Yessir."

He'd been this scared before, so scared that his palms sweated and muscle tremors made the fine hairs on the surface of his skin crawl. Sure, he'd been this scared.

But he'd never been *more* scared.

"Now," Hansen said very softly. He leaped forward as the forcefield collapsed momentarily to pass his body.

It was thirty meters to the front of the building. Hansen had covered half the distance in ten quick strides when a hole like Hell's anus spun in the bulging forcefield above him.

The Commissioner's pistol snapped two high-velocity projectiles through the opening before the villain within could fire. The mirror of the protective forcefield dulled momentarily as its inner face absorbed the plasma bolt triggered in a dying convulsion.

Hansen was doing *this* job because he wouldn't order any of his people to do it, and because it had to be him anyway.

But nobody in Special Units was better qualified to handle it, either.

Motes of plastic drifted in the sunlight beneath 212 Kokori, bits snapped from the facade by stun needles and shrapnel from the villains' own weaponry. They had one hell of an arsenal in there. This wasn't a police action, it was a war . . . or at any rate, it'd degenerate into a war if Hansen's try here failed.

Hansen looked back the way he'd come. Squat figures, mere shadows behind the polarized sheets of forcefields, waited with mechanical passivity.

He was panting, as much from tension as from the sprint. The villains' forcefield bulged from the windows above him. It was driven hard enough to reflect light, not merely shadow it. Solbarth must have his own fusion generator. . . .

But even Solbarth couldn't fight the Consensus.

"Support," Hansen said. "Give me a lower-quadrant remote from the four-centimeter's guns—"

The sight picture, broad field in acquisition mode, from the crew-served weapon directly across from 212 inset a quarter of Hansen's visor. He could see himself as a tiny figure in the corner of the image, staring at the bulging fortress above him.

"—ight," Hansen's mouth said, completing the order that the AI had already obeyed.

He heard the *crack!* of a plasma weapon firing somewhere from the back of the building, but there was no time to worry about that now.

"Solbarth!" he shouted. He tilted his visor up, losing the panoramic image that he'd need for warning if—

"Solbarth!" Hansen shouted again, his voice no longer muffled by the shield in front of it. "This is Commissioner Hansen. I'm giving you a chance."

"Kommissar?" said the voice that Hansen's artificial intelligence had passed to his ear. "Orange Three. We've got the SpyFly in position outside the last set of louvers. Do you want us to burn through?"

"We don't need a chance from you, Hansen," called a cold, clear voice from a window on the third floor. "You'll be old and gray before we run out of supplies."

"Orange Three, not yet," Hansen muttered. He desperately wanted images from within the hideout, but he knew that this reconnaissance drone would be zapped like the others if it left its protective screen of metal too soon.

Hansen cocked his visor at a 45° angle, open enough for him to shout past it. He peered at the distorted quadrant of panorama—which his AI immediately reconfigured to meet its master's needs.

And why the hell hadn't he been smart enough to *tell* the machine to do that?

"Solbarth, I'm offering you your lives," Hansen said. He could hear other muffled voices from the lower floors of 212 Kokori, civilians praying or weeping into their shielding hands. "It's more than—"

The helmet beeped to warn Hansen and flashed a red carat over the remoted image on his visor, but his gunhand was already rising, pointing—taking up the slack on the trigger. An arm thrust a wide-mouthed mob gun through the window five meters above the Commissioner's head.

Hansen fired twice. The villain's weapon rang and bounced off the bloody transom before dropping to the street. There was a bullet hole through its bell muzzle, and a separate hole through the wrist which the screaming gunman jerked back within the forcefield.

"You won't open *this* can with the toys you've brought out so far, Hansen," Solbarth said, as calmly as if the wounded man's whimpering was only the whisper of wind. "When you *do* requisition what you'd require . . . if you do . . . then this whole district will be radioactive for a decade."

The bare skin of Hansen's hand and chin stung from the whiplash muzzle blasts of his pistol. The shadows of Special Units stirred restively behind their forcefields.

"Solbarth," he called, "if you don't surrender to me *now*, I'll have the building cut away beneath you. For all I know, your forcefield may hold; but that won't matter to you, because you and everything else inside the field're going to be shaking around like the beans in a maraca as you drop into the sub-basement."

The silence was so deep that Hansen could feel the pulse of the villains' forcefield through the fabric of the building.

"The lower floors are full of civilians," Solbarth said. Hansen thought he heard a tremor of color in the gang leader's voice, though 'emotion' would have been too strong a word for it.

"Solbarth," Hansen said, "I know you . . . and you know me.

This is a Special Units operation. I answer to *no one* until it's complete. And I promise you, Solbarth, that I'll do exactly what I told you I'd do."

Very softly, almost subvocalizing, he added, "Orange Three, go ahead. Support, switch my remote."

"A starship," the cold voice demanded. "A starship and your word that we'll be allowed to take it and leave, Hansen."

"Your lives, Solbarth," the Commissioner repeated flatly. "And the rest of your lives to spend on whatever hellhole or prison asteroid the Consensus chooses to send you. But I promise you your lives."

The remote quadrant of Hansen's visor suddenly melted into an image of the gang's hideout. All the interior walls of the third story had been removed. The cases of food and water suggested that Solbarth hadn't been entirely bluffing when he'd said they could withstand a siege.

Not years, though. Not the dozen males and three females still moving.

A corpse had been dragged into the center of the room. The moaning man, his right hand hanging by a scrap of skin, still huddled beneath the window at which Hansen had shot him.

The female who'd just gotten up from the protective-systems console to join the argument was a Mirzathian, skeletally thin and over two meters tall. The SpyFly whose sensors were recording the scene made a bright pip on the holographic screen the Mirzathian was supposed to be minding. The touch of a key could have pulsed the drone's electronics fatally, but neither the Mirzathian nor any of the other gang members had time to spend on that now.

Solbarth was a male of average height, with a pale complexion and features of perfect beauty. He was wearing a loose-fitting suit of rather better quality than the clothing of most residents of District 7. He moved languidly, but Hansen's practiced eye could still identify the bulge of a pistol high on Solbarth's right hip.

When Hansen wore a business suit, that was where his own holster rode.

"He won't really spare us!" the Mirzathian shouted.

"He won't really blast all them civvies!" a heavy man with a shoulder-stocked plasma weapon boomed simultaneously.

"He didn't come here," Solbarth said mildly, *"here—"* he gestured down in the direction of Hansen, standing beneath the overhang "—to lie to us. He's Hansen, and he's quite mad . . . but I think he's telling the truth."

"Look, whadda we got to lose?" whined another gunman. "Look, they blast us or we wind up drinkin' our own piss 'n starvin', right? So whadda they do to us worse if we *do* chuck it in now?"

"Wait," said Solbarth.

He leaned closer to the window above Hansen and called, "Commissioner, there's something that you don't know about me. How can I trust—"

"I don't know that you're an android, Solbarth?" Hansen said. His words echoed uneasily, in his ears and weakly through the radio link from the SpyFly that had penetrated the hideout. "Sure I do. The offer stands."

"*You* promise," Solbarth said forcefully. "But the Consensus wipes androids that vary from parameters, Hansen. You can't promise for the Consensus."

Hansen wiped the lower half of his face with his left hand. Sweat glistened on his skin, but his mouth was as dry as the pavement.

"Solbarth," he said, "you're a murdering bastard and I'd've strangled you with my own hands if I could. But I'm Hansen, I'm Special Units, and here I'm in charge. For this moment, I *am* all twelve hundred worlds of the Consensus."

He took a deep breath. "They can fire me for making this deal if they like. But the Consensus will stand by my deal . . . or by god, Solbarth, the Consensus will deal with me. On my honor."

The image of Solbarth turned to face his henchmen. "I think," he said with delicate insouciance, "that we should take the offer."

"*I* say you're fucking crazy!" the Mirzathian snarled. She snatched up an antitank launcher and leaned toward the window.

Hansen wasn't sure he'd ever seen a man draw and fire as swiftly as Solbarth did . . . though Solbarth wasn't technically a man. The contents of the Mirzathian's skull splashed the inner face of the forcefield and sputtered. With their velocity scrubbed away, bits of bone and fried blood tumbled out the window and fluttered past Hansen to the sidewalk.

There were two more shots from within the hideout; the heavy man collapsed around the plasma weapon cradled in his arms. Either he'd been planning to use it, or he'd looked like he had . . . or, not improbably, Solbarth was making a point to the remainder of his gang in the most vivid fashion possible.

Other weapons clattered to the floor of the hideout. A small man covered his face with his hands and cried, "I'm clean! I'm clean! Don't shoot me!"

"Hansen!" Solbarth called without turning his eyes from his fellow villains. "We accept your offer. Warn your men that we're coming out!"

The android's left hand keyed a series of commands into the protective systems console. The window above Hansen gave an electronic whine. The forcefield went translucent an instant before it vanished altogether.

"All units, hold your fire," Hansen said. "The subjects are surrendering. I repeat, the subjects are surrendering. Blue teams, prepare to secure the prisoners. Orange teams, be ready to move in with the medical staff. There's a wounded prisoner, and we won't know about the residents here until we check."

The SpyFly showed Solbarth gesturing the last of his subordinates down the stairs with a negligent wave of his pistol. The slim android set the weapon carefully on the floor, bowed toward the closed heating duct whose paint had blistered when the SpyFly burned through a hole for its sensors, and left the room.

Hansen couldn't tell whether or not the bow was ironic. Perhaps not.

"Blue teams," Hansen said, "I want you to accompany the prisoners to the detention center after you turn them over to the Civic Patrol. There'll be no accidents along the way."

He swallowed. "Whatever it takes, there'll be no accidents."

Six Special Units personnel jogged from their positions in the building across Kokori Street. They held both nets and electronic restraints.

The first of Solbarth's men poked his head through the entrance door. His mouth was bent into a smile like the rictus of the last stages of tetanus, and his eyes were glazed with fear. Blue One gestured to the villain as though he were a dog to be petted.

The man glanced aside at Hansen, then bolted into the arms of the personnel waiting to immobilize him. A second gang member scuttled out behind the first.

Hansen was still holding his pistol. He tried to holster it, but his hand was shaking too much for him to manage that operation. Swearing under his breath, he set the weapon down on the sidewalk in front of him and clasped his hands together.

There was commotion at the intersection where Hansen's car lay on its side, but he couldn't tell what was happening since the portable forcefields were still—properly—in place.

Chief Holloway waddled down Kokori Street from the other direction, at the head of a contingent of Civic Patrolmen. Holloway's white uniform was streaked and blackened. His face was maroon. Blood pressure might prove fatal though the nearby plasma bolt had not.

Most of the villains had left the building. Blue One was giving crisp orders to the Civic Patrolmen arriving to accept prisoners cocooned in restraining nets. Some civilians poked their heads from the lower-floor windows, able now to savor the adventure they'd survived . . . and how close it'd been, might they never know!

Hansen was tired. He was as tired as he ever remembered being.

"Kommissar!" cried the team leader whose concern was obvious despite compression of the radio signal and the minute speakers in Hansen's helmet. "This is Pink Two, and something's—"

The warning crunched to silence, though Hansen could vaguely hear Pink Two continuing to shout behind the barrier.

"Commissioner Hansen," said a voice more mechanical than any machine needed to be in a day that AIs could manufacture surds and sonants with greater life than those of any rhetoric teacher. "You are summoned by the Consensus."

Something—a spindle of black *fuzz*, taller than a man—drifted through the forcefield blocking the intersection. There was another spindle beside the first.

Hansen had never seen anything like them.

The portable forcefield sputtered and vanished.

"Not now," Hansen said. The sweat on his palms was suddenly cold. "I've got to—"

Hansen's visor went opaque. His helmet was dead, screens and speakers alike. He took the helmet off.

His hands no longer shook. He didn't glance down toward his pistol, but his toe, with a motion that might have been only a twitch, located the weapon precisely.

Solbarth stepped from the entranceway. The android froze, his blank eyes taking in Hansen and the creatures which slid toward the Commissioner at a walking pace.

The two spindles were hazily transparent. An aircar—Hansen's own aircar, torn but upright again—drifted along behind the creatures, a hand's breadth above the pavement.

No one was aboard the vehicle. Krupchak, the driver, gaped at Hansen from beside the personnel of Pink Two.

"Commissioner Hansen, please get in the car," said the mechanical voice.

It sounded exactly as it had before, even though Hansen was no longer wearing his helmet.

"I had the authority at this site," Hansen said hoarsely. "You have no grounds to remove me without a hearing."

The spindles moved to either side of him. Hansen's skin tingled. Close up they still looked transparent, but he thought he saw something *in* the black tendrils as well as between them.

The vehicle's power door opened. "Commissioner Hansen," the voice repeated, "please get in the car."

Hansen obeyed, shifting his foot slightly so that he didn't scuff the pistol. One of his people would take care of it. . . .

Fifty meters away, Chief Holloway licked his lips. He looked as though he were watching a pornographic display.

The door shut after Hansen. The two spindles drifted through the plastic panels, into the driver's compartment. Hansen didn't see them fold or shrink, but their peaks didn't quite brush the vehicle's blast-pocked headliner.

"Sir, should we—" shouted one of the Special Units personnel as he leaned from a roof with his plasma weapon half-pointed.

"*No!*" Hansen cried. He stuck his head out the shattered side window and shouted, "No, everybody get on with your duties."

He didn't know what was going on, but he knew that it wouldn't be helped if his own people started shooting.

The aircar slid in a tight circle and accelerated as it started to rise.

"I have full authority from the Consensus for everything I've done here," Hansen said, knowing that in truth, he'd always claimed whatever authority he needed to get a job done and trusted that he could make it stick after the fact.

That had always worked. Until now.

"The Consensus is not interested in your actions here, Commissioner Hansen," said the voice. The words sounded in the Commissioner's mind, seeming to have nothing to do with the creatures which were escorting him. "The Consensus has need of you on a planet called Northworld."

The car had risen to 300 meters and was moving at a speed that made the wind howl through the many shrapnel holes. Other air traffic was avoiding their arrow-straight rush.

Hansen frowned. "What's Northworld?" he muttered.

The creatures—or the voice—must have been able to hear him despite wind noise, because Hansen's mind rasped with the words, "The Consensus will inform you of what you need to know, Commissioner Hansen. In good time."

For the first time in his life, Commissioner Nils Hansen realized that there might be more to the Consensus of Worlds than simply the bureaucracy of control of which he himself was a part.

Chapter Two

North came out of the Matrix, gasping and wheezing as he always did.

Hanging in the Matrix, the world that connected the Eight Worlds, was like drowning in ice water. The infinite series of minute events forced itself into his being, through him; chilling his flesh, freezing him, threatening to grind *him* out of existence in an avalanche of nine-times-simultaneous discrete realities.

It would almost be better not to be a god.

"But that is a lie, North," said Dowson with the dry precision which was all that remained to him since emotion had been cut out of him with his body.

"Who are you to speak of truth and lies, Dowson?" North said. "All you know are facts."

"Facts are all there is to know, North," replied the disembodied brain suspended in a vat of nutrient. The words washed across North to ring coldly within his skull, but they were not as cold as the Matrix. . . .

He shuddered again and looked up at the roof of his palace, shards of sunlight frozen into groins and vaulting that could cover an army.

"There's another one coming," North said. "From outside, from the Consensus."

The liquid flowing through Dowson's vat kept up the same soft susurrus it had whispered for ages. "What will you do with these?" asked the non-voice as colored waves which sprang from a cone of ice beside the vat. "Find them a plane of their own?"

"There *are* no unoccupied planes, Dowson!"

"None that you know of, North," the brain replied. "None that I know of either."

For a moment, North imagined that the pause was one of sadness, but Dowson's words were as emotionless as ever when he continued, "Send them to the lizardmen, then. Let them destroy one another."

North's laughter bellowed out in response to the bitter joke. The sunlit building trembled and quivered with shadows. North stretched his long, sinewy arms high above his head, and the air cleared.

"The others will need to know," Dowson warned.

"The others will want to know," North corrected. "I'll summon them."

His right hand twisted in the air. Motes of light sprang away as though condensing from the atmosphere; a score of sparkling blips that drifted in widening circles until they touched the walls of the palace, spat, and vanished on their missions.

"They're only sending one this time," North said, trying to control the shudder which remembering the Matrix induced in him. "A man."

"You'll kill him?" Dowson asked, carelessly, uncaringly.

"His name is Hansen," said North. "And he will serve my purposes."

zoomed up on the screen. One of the two twitched toward Hansen
as its antennae blurred and just as suspiciously as those of its
companions.

Hand on your gun, sir, a voice said in the middle of
Hansen's brain.

Chapter Three

Hansen's car was speeding toward a large building on what
had been the outskirts of the capital twenty years before. Now
it was a bland residential district, not dissimilar to the one from
which Solbarth had spun his webs of theft and murder.

The building was marked as Consensus property on the maps
Hansen had viewed in the course of his duties, but there were
many Consensus buildings in any planetary capital. A warehouse,
Hansen had thought; and he would still think the great three-
story block was a warehouse, except—

Except that two *creatures* had ordered the Commissioner of
Special Units into an aircar that they were driving straight into
the front wall of the building.

Hansen opened his mouth to protest—and closed it again,
because there was nothing he could say that the spindles didn't
know already.

The warehouse was an old one, built of clay and a plasticizer
which hardened after extrusion. That technique created a solid
structure of surpassing ugliness even when new.

The aircar was about to hit the dark dun building at 200 kph.
The smear Hansen made would scarcely be distinguishable from
the stains and earth tones already an indelible part of the wall's
texture.

He forced his muscles to relax. So be it. A pedestrian in the
street looked up in amazement.

The aircar shot through the 'wall.' Hansen felt a momentary
chill. They were in a lighted tunnel whose circular sides made
the drive fans rumble.

"Where are we?" Hansen demanded. The noise of the damaged
car was even worse in this enclosure than it had been in the open
air, but he knew the spindles could hear him if they wanted to.

No answer rang in his mind. They shot past a pair of cross-
tunnels. Half a dozen workmen carrying unrecognizable tools

glanced up at the aircar. One of the faces turned toward Hansen was inhuman: blue, scaled, and as expressionless as those of its companions.

"Where are we *going*?" Hansen cried. He didn't even expect an answer.

He'd been a powerful man, a few minutes ago. In some ways—in some circumstances—the most powerful man on Annunciation.

He looked at the things beside him in the car and wondered whether any man in the Consensus really had power.

The spindles were shrinking. When Hansen first saw the creatures, they had been taller than he was; now they were only about the length of his thigh. They sputtered like electronics on the verge of failure, and the scenes within the fabric of their bodies were becoming increasingly clear.

Hansen looked away.

The tunnel ended in a white-tiled rotunda which appeared so abruptly that Hansen felt the car braking before his eyes focused on the change in scenery. Two figures waited for them, both human—

Not human. Both of the figures were male androids. One was as beautiful as the dawn, while the other was a squat, hideous travesty of humanity with thick, twisted limbs. They might very well have come out of the same production batch.

The rotunda had a high, domed ceiling. There were eight archways leading from it—all of them closed by bronze doors, including the arch by which the aircar had just entered.

"Please get out, Commissioner Hansen," said the voice in Hansen's skull. The aircar bobbled a few centimeters above the floor instead of settling with the shut-down fans.

"This way, please, sir," said the handsome android. He had to shout to be heard over the racket the car made.

The android was speaking with his mouth. At least *that* was a change for the better. . . .

Hansen got out of the vehicle. It sped off into—through— another doorway.

The spindles who'd escorted the Commissioner had shrunk to hand's breadth height. They were giving off sounds of sizzling, fiery anger as they disappeared.

The rotunda was almost silent when they and the aircar were gone.

"This will only take a moment, sir," said the misshapen android, raising the flared nozzle of the apparatus he carried. "Please hold still."

"What are you—"

"Please hold still," said the handsome android as the nozzle hissed an opalescent bubble which wobbled and grew without detaching itself from the apparatus. The android reached around Hansen and guided the edges of the bubble like a couturier with a swatch of cloth.

"Now, sir," said the ugly android, "if you'll step carefully onto this . . . ?"

Hansen lifted his feet so that he was standing on the doubled thickness of the bubble's lower edge.

He understood, now. They were blowing him a temporary atmosphere suit, a membrane of polarized permeability. Oxygen could pass in, while carbon dioxide and other waste gasses passed out no matter what the composition of the encircling atmosphere.

A useful tool for chemical emergencies or even fires, though the membrane didn't block heat. Temporary suits could keep people alive in hard vacuum for as long as the oxygen level within the bubble remained at a breathable level.

The hideous android smiled as he continued to extrude the material. Hansen supposed the expression was meant to be friendly.

The handsome attendant took a palm-sized device from his belt. He gathered the flattened bubble over Hansen's head in his slim hands and touched the edges with the tool, mating them with a faint sputter.

The seam was a quiver of light when Hansen moved and made the bubble tremble. His mind told him falsely that his lungs had to struggle to breathe. He controlled his expression, but he could feel his heart rate rise.

"That's right, sir," said the ugly attendant. "Now, if you'll just walk this way . . . ?"

The attendant had shut off his apparatus. Now he gestured toward one of the archways. His skin had the utter pallor that some androids tried to conceal with cosmetics; but whatever his skin color, this creature couldn't have been anything that sprang from a human womb.

Hansen obeyed, walking deliberately so that the flexible membrane could billow ahead of his motion. He could see and hear normally, except for a slight shimmer in the air and the hint of distortion at the seam.

The Commissioner's senses were overloaded with hormones from the gunfight, from the capture that should have been the crown of his career no matter how much longer he served the Consensus—

From all that had happened since.

"Why is this happening to me?" Hansen shouted. "Why are you doing this?"

The handsome attendant shook his head blandly. He'd put the sealing device back into its belt pouch. "Don't worry, sir," he said. "Just step through the portal."

Would the bronze doorleaves open, or would—

Hansen stepped through what had seemed to be solid metal. There was an instant of chill. He thought he saw the crystalline pattern of the atoms themselves, but then he was through the door and standing in a darkness more intense than that of the core of his brain.

Light bloomed, a flush of pink so faint that for an instant Hansen thought the illumination was an accident of his optic nerves—synapses tripping to relieve the oppressive black.

The color was real. He could see again.

Almost-color sublimed in all directions from a stalagmite of ice that grew out of a floor as smooth as a bearing race. Hansen couldn't see any walls, but the ball of light—fading as it expanded—swelled across a dozen other cones of ice.

Hansen braced himself. When the pink glow touched him, a voice in his mind said, "There has been a crime, Commissioner Hansen."

Other stalagmites were scaling away drifts of color as weak as the nimbus of sunlight about a butterfly's wings. Each was a separate pastel, each so pale that only by comparison could they be differentiated.

"I don't belong here!" Hansen cried. "If there's been a crime, let me out of here and I'll deal with it."

Hansen could see that there was no door behind him now, nothing but vacancy and a plain like a mirror.

Green ambiance washed over him. "There was a world," said a different voice in his mind, mellifluous and a trifle arch. "It had been charted. Humans could live there, we thought—"

Orange light. A voice like a whip. "The Consensus thought. Captain Rolls led a unit to do a final examination. They—"

Pink neutrality again: "They vanished. A crime has been committed."

Motes of light drifted upward like fog without finding a ceiling. Hansen tested the floor with his toes. It was solid, unyielding. It felt cold, even through his boots and the double insulating layers of his airsuit.

Almost all of the cones were glowing now as they discharged their burdens of thought and near-light.

"Listen and learn, Commissioner Hansen," said blue certainty in the Commissioner's mind. "We sent another team under Captain North, trusted personnel who had dealt with crises on a dozen other worlds to be colonized. Faithful—"

"Faithful servants of the Consensus," quivered a red voice. It reminded Hansen of the lip-smacking tones of politicians who demanded tough measures but who'd never stood in an alley after a firefight and realized how little there was to a human being after the life goes out of him. "North had cleansed worlds, seeded them—changed weather patterns, raised continents, crushed all opposition to the Con—"

"The Consensus," whispered violet. "North reported that he had succeeded again, that we should send a colony at once, that all was prepared for settlement. He said that we should call the planet Northworld, that it was his right that the planet receive his name."

Blue fog drifted over Hansen. "We sent the colony, because—"

"—because he was a faithful servant," rejoined the red tones. "Ruthless and skillful, a servant to the needs of the Consensus. But North and his team had not returned from the planet, as they reported, and the new colony—"

"The planet vanished," said pink light. "There has been a crime, Commissioner Hansen. The colony has been stolen, the planet has been stolen."

"Northworld has been stolen," thundered Hansen's mind in the organ tones of all dozen shades of light at once. "You will determine why, and you will cure the problem."

The plain on which Hansen stood was boundless, but he no longer thought it was empty. There were shapes in the far distance, hinted bulks as huge as storms on a gas giant.

"This is nothing to do with me," Hansen cried with fatalistic recklessness. "The colony wasn't sent from Annunciation, North wasn't—*was he?*—from here. I have my duties. Let me return to my duties."

Light like yellow sunshine washed over him. If glaciers could laugh, the sensation in Hansen's mind would have been that cold laughter. "Your duties are to the Consensus, Commissioner Hansen," said a voice. "The Consensus demands that you deal with this event. You have been chosen from among—"

"From among many," said violet light. "From among all the planets of the Consensus, from all the peoples. . . ."

"Records have been searched," said the cold blue voice. "The Lomeri settled the world in past ages—"

"The lizardfolk settled Northworld in past ages," said pink, "but no Lomeri were there when the exploration unit arrived. There has been—"

"There has been a crime, Commissioner Hansen," purred a pastel so faint that it might have been either brown or mauve. "When Rolls' exploration unit landed, they found a waterworld with necklaces of islands—"

"Island necklaces and no other land," the yellow light said. "But North reported a world with 46% of the surface area land."

"And now the world is gone and North is gone, and they have taken with them the colony," said pink. "There has been a crime, and you must solve it—"

"*Cure* the crime," insisted the red voice. "Deal with the criminals with the full rigor of the Consensus, for the will of the Consensus is the law of the universe—"

"For all the universe except Northworld," resumed blue. "*That* world does not recognize the Consensus, nor do the Lomeri—"

"The Lomeri who were lizards and who have been dust," rasped the orange voice, "for a thousand millennia before there were men. And before the Lomeri there were other settlements, we are sure of it—"

"The Consensus is sure," whispered violet, "though that past is a far past even for the Consensus."

"Far even for us. . . ." the voices of color murmured in unison.

Hansen felt the chamber shiver like a sigh. His feet were becoming cold, and it was not merely his imagination that the membrane around him sagged. It was voiding the carbon dioxide Hansen exhaled without a corresponding influx of oxygen.

"This isn't my job," Hansen said. "I don't—"

He paused. He was at the center of a glowing ambiance that continued to expand indefinitely, like the ball of plasma generated by a nuclear weapon between the stars.

"Send a fleet, s-sirs," he continued, afraid to choose a term for the entities which spoke here with him. "I'm a man, a cop. I don't find planets. You need a—"

"There was a fleet," said a voice as scales of light shimmered away from the brown/mauve stalagmite. "A fleet and a fleet—"

"—and a fleet," echoed the pink voice. "Humans in the first fleet, and they vanished—"

"Though drones," said blue, "had penetrated the area where Northworld should have been, and the drones reported nothing. Therefore we sent—"

"The Consensus sent a second fleet," said the red voice, "crewed by androids and ready to destroy anything it met in the dead zone, the region—"

"The region that had flouted our majesty, our Consensus," resumed the violet voice. "And when the androids vanished without warning, without report, we sent a third fleet that was a great machine in itself but which lived and thought, though—"

"Though not as men think, and not part of the Consensus," chuckled the yellow voice. "And it vanished, Commissioner Hansen, as though it had never been . . . and though machines that are no more than machines ignore the area and pass through it."

Hansen felt the pressure of thoughts, of words, all around him. The airsuit was no protection. His whole body was becoming numb.

"Fleets have failed," said the red light, "so we are sending you. We will arm you, Commissioner Hansen—"

"But the fleets were armed," shivered tones of deep green light. "You will be alone, so you may penetrate the defenses unnoticed—"

"Penetrate the mystery . . . ," brown/mauve murmured.

"You are the best for the task," boomed all the colors together. "On all the planets of the Consensus, in all the Consensus."

You are resourceful/Commissioner Hansen is resourceful/The Kommissar is resourceful, rasped/purred/said the voices pounding Hansen's mind.

And then, in a single thought so smooth and steely that it could have been Hansen's own—and perhaps it *was* Hansen's own thought—

"Commissioner Nils Hansen will execute the will of the Consensus. . . ."

Chapter Four

The light through the varied crystalline roofplanes was brilliant without being dazzling. Some of the score of figures seated around the walls used the rays to ornament themselves; others formed the light into shrouds and hulked as shadows within opalescent beauty that hid their features better than darkness could have done.

North sat in the high seat and glowered at his peers. His left eye didn't track with his right; there were limits to power, even North's power, and the freezing paths of the Matrix had exacted a price as he learned them.

"This latest probe by the outsiders doesn't matter," said Rolls from his place near the doorway. He was almost as tall as North and enough heavier than the man in the high seat to look soft . . . until one looked more closely. "Any of us can take care of that—"

"My *pleasure*," said Rao. A smile of anticipation licked over his broad, dark face.

The curtain of light beside Rao rinsed away for a moment as Ngoya reached over to stroke her husband's thick wrist and silence him. Rao wasn't interested in—wasn't capable of understanding—what Rolls and many others of the team regarded as major issues. Ngoya was often embarrassed for her husband, since she in turn failed to see that Rao's single-minded simplicity was also his greatest strength.

"What matters," said Miyoko, pointing an index finger at North to emphasize her words, "is the threat to Diamond. You can't think of sending this invader to Diamond until we at least understand—"

"We don't *know* there's a threat," objected Saburo, not so much in disagreement as to calm his sister. He glanced uneasily at North, trying to read meaning into the craggy patience of the man who had led both his own team and the exploration unit of which Saburo was a member ever since—

27

But 'since' implied duration. . . . Saburo composed his mind, then his face, and nodded apology to Rolls.

"There is a threat to Diamond," said Rolls, "whether or not we can see where it comes from."

He looked up at North, then across the hall to Eisner, and continued, "I'll admit that *I* can't see the source of the threat."

Eisner nodded her crisp agreement; North and North's face said nothing.

"I don't see what the problem is," Penny said. "I don't see why we're here at all."

Penny was playing with her appearance. As she spoke, she changed from a petite redhead in her early twenties to a tall, black-haired beauty whose face promised experience as well as passion . . . and back again to the redhead. A curtain of light provided a mirror, and the jewel on Penny's breast glowed with the power it gave her desires.

"On Diamond," Eisner said—in another of the attempts to inform which exasperated her fellows as much as Penny's care of her physical form bothered Eisner— "the inhabitants—"

"Yes, yes, I know," Penny snapped, briefly flirting with an older image, still redheaded. "They're having nightmares, terrible nightmares, and that's all very sad—but there *can't* be anything really wrong going to happen with them, because we're the only ones who can touch them or Ruby."

She looked around the room challengingly. "And if we did, the balance would fail, and we'd all—"

Penny made a moue of distaste and a dismissive gesture with fingers which for the moment were long and aristocratic. "Not that anybody would *do* that."

Fortin stretched and smiled. His white skin and perfect features were a legacy of his android mother, but the twisted subtlety of his mind was his own . . . if not from the genes of North his father.

"Who can fault the wisdom of our Penny?" Fortin said. His lilting sarcasm cut all the deeper because what Penny said *was* true, though none of them doubted the reality of the danger except Penny, who didn't care; and Rao, who couldn't imagine it; and Dowson, who saw no threat in the Matrix and who lacked the fleshly baggage of emotions from which to create a hobgoblin that the data didn't support.

"I still don't think we should chance setting an intruder down in Diamond until we have a better idea of what's going on," Rolls said calmly.

"Of course," said Eisner as much to herself as to the assembly, "if the intruder were put in Diamond, we might learn more about the threat—"

"We might learn he *was* the threat!" Miyoko snapped. "Put him in Ruby. They'll take care of him!"

"Or set him on the plane of the Lomeri," her brother added. "So long as he's coming from outside the Matrix, we have absolute control of his destination. It makes no sense to take a risk—" he nodded to Miyoko "—even though the risk is still speculative."

"We'll set the intruder in Diamond," said North, speaking for the first time during the assembly he had called, "because only in Diamond can we be sure that all of his weapons will be stripped from him—" he smiled "—without harm."

"What do we care about hurting him?" Rao asked. "I mean, it's all right with me, but he's just an outsider. Isn't he?"

He looked around his fellows to make sure that there wasn't some point he had missed. Ngoya patted his arm.

North nodded. "I understand your position, my friend," he said, "but I've seen far enough into the Matrix to be sure that this Hansen is no threat to Diamond."

"But still—" said Miyoko.

"And I," North continued, "have my own reasons for wanting him unharmed for the time. Surely *I* needn't be the one to apologize for not killing, eh?"

"Well, do what you want, then," said Penny, who had finally fixed on slight, red-haired youthfulness. "You're going to anyway. I don't see why you even bothered to call us here."

Fortin began to laugh, because Penny was again perfectly correct. . . .

Rolls waited to meet Eisner in the doorway of North's palace as they left the assembly. She smiled at him, but the expression went no deeper than her thin lips.

"He sees something in the Matrix," she said, flicking her head back to indicate their leader and late host. "Do you?"

Eisner's hair was the color of a gray-draggled mouse; a few

wisps which had escaped from her tight bun wobbled abstractedly.

Rolls shrugged. "North plays games," he said. "If there were something to see, you or I would know it. But still. . . ."

Neither of them spoke for a moment. Their eyes glanced over their fellows leaving the assembly; some of them concerned, some not.

Rao had hitched to his cart a pair of frilled ceratopsians from the plane where the Lomeri ruled. Most of the beasts which whim led others to ride or drive gave the dinosaurs a wide berth, but Saburo's huge hog-like dinohyid exchanged angry grunts and foot-stampings with Rao's much larger animals.

Eisner nodded. "Good day," she said and turned.

"Let me take you back," Rolls said. "You don't need to walk."

"I don't *need* to do anything," the woman corrected crisply. "None of us do." Eisner was thin and looked small at the moment, but only Rao and North failed to shrink when they stood next to Rolls.

"But yes," she added. "All right, I don't need to walk."

Rolls whickered to his giant stag and let it nuzzle his hand for a moment before he mounted. The beast had cast its horns and looked oddly naked. Still, it was awkward to bridle a creature whose horns spread a meter and a half to either side.

Everything was whim—for Rolls, for all of them since North had discovered the turning of the Matrix which gave them each whatever they most wanted. . . .

Rolls leaned over and lifted Eisner up ahead of him. The stag's spine was higher and sharper than a horse's, so the saddleframe had to be built out stiffly to give a comfortable seat. Horses were better adapted as riding animals, aircars were a far more efficient way to get around; but the most *practical* means of transportation for Rolls, for any of them, was the choice that provided the most amusement—and a practical level of aggravation.

It had been hard at first to imagine that there were any negative aspects to godlike power.

Eisner tried to straddle the spine the way Rolls did, but he turned her side-saddle and put his arm around the small of her waist to support her. She met his eyes and said coolly, "Still your games, Rolls? You might have learned by now."

Rolls shrugged. "The saddle was designed for me, so you'll find this more comfortable, Eisner," he said. "More practical, if you wish."

He clucked to the stag. It turned obediently and slid by the fourth stride into the long-legged canter that Rolls found its most comfortable pace.

Eisner sniffed, but she didn't object further to Rolls' touch. Neither did her abdominal muscles soften beneath his hand.

Rolls kept the contact well within the bounds of what was necessary for the task. His easy-going charm was effective because a real concern for others underlay it.

Rolls smiled to himself. One might almost say that concern for others ruled him.

The grassland swept by beneath the stag's measured paces. The rounded roofline of Eisner's palace appeared in the near distance.

"Do you remember," Rolls said, "when duration had meaning?"

Eisner shifted to meet his eyes; her left thigh slid over his. "Time still has meaning, Rolls," she said. "Time means everything dies. Even us. . . ."

Eisner had looked older than her years when Rolls' unit arrived on the planet it was to survey. Power had not given her youth, neither in her face nor in the mind which, more than age, had shaped the lines of that face.

Obedient to its training rather than specific command, the stag drew up before Eisner's palace, a windowless dome. Rolls held out an arm like a steel bar to support the woman as she lowered herself to the ground.

She looked up at him and said, "We created Diamond and Ruby as bubble universes, bound into the Matrix by our united minds."

Rolls nodded. "A whim," he said. "A desire to create the perfection that we—"

He swung his leg over the saddle and lowered himself beside Eisner "—fail to achieve in ourselves."

Rolls pretended to be unaware of the wariness in the woman's eyes at the implication that he intended to enter her palace.

She grimaced. "All right," she said and stepped toward the door. It opened in response to her presence. Eisner kept no human servants.

"If one of *us* destroys Diamond," she continued, "our minds fall out of balance with the Matrix and . . . All of us. But only we can harm Diamond."

"If that were the case," Rolls said as he ducked to follow Eisner, "then Diamond wouldn't be in any danger. As perhaps it is not."

Though the ceilings within Eisner's dwelling were full height, the woman had pointedly constructed the door transom to clear her head by a centimeter. Eisner had few visitors; and, she would have said, little need for them.

"There's Fortin," Eisner said as she turned. "Fortin is insane." The door behind Rolls remained open, a reminder and invitation to him to leave.

"Fortin is very clever," Rolls said. "And yes, he's usually destructively clever. But he doesn't want to die before his time, Eisner. All our time."

He looked at the books, racked in a jumble of varied sizes and bindings. Computers were a better way to access information, and the Matrix itself was all knowledge if one had the patience to prowl its twisted, freezing pathways. Eisner used both, constantly, because there was no end to learning . . . but books were a symbol, and symbols had a particular reality here on Northworld.

"There's something we don't see . . . ," Eisner murmured.

"We're changing, Eisner," the man said as he watched his hostess through the corners of his eyes.

"We don't change," Eisner snapped, crossing her arms over her chest as she turned her back on Rolls. Her breasts, as unremarkable as her face and hair, were hidden beneath the loose folds of the coveralls she habitually wore. "We're old and we're getting older, but we don't *change*. We don't have the power to change ourselves—"

Rolls touched the woman's shoulder. "You know what I mean," he said.

"—except for Penny with her necklace," Eisner continued. Her voice, never particularly attractive, cut the phrase like a hacksaw. "She can change."

"Penny got what she wanted," Rolls said. Rather than try to turn Eisner to face him, he stepped around her.

"You have—" He gestured with his left hand. "You wanted

knowledge. You wouldn't trade that for Penny's necklace, would you?"

"No, no," Eisner agreed, forcing herself to lower her arms, though she met her guest's eyes only for a moment. "I have exactly what I want, of course. . . ."

"But we don't have to limit ourselves to one thing," Rolls said. "Eisner, we have *all* powers, we're like gods. But we're focusing down to—" his hand described an empty circle "—to caricatures, like Penny and her appearance."

"And her men, you mean!" Eisner said.

Rolls' expression softened to see the pain in the woman's eyes. "That's all part of the same thing, Eisner," he said gently. "You know that. There's no reason that we can't change things back. Become—"

He reached out slowly, his fingers curled to cup Eisner's breast. "—complete human beings again."

Eisner slapped his hand away and turned her back again. "I don't want that!" she said.

In a voice almost too faint to hear, she added, "And you don't want me, not really."

"I *do* want you," Rolls said. "I want you to be—"

"Go on!" Eisner said, facing Rolls to gesture imperiously toward the door. "Get out. Your sympathy is quite unnecessary."

"Whatever you wish," the big man said as he obeyed; but he paused, hunched in the doorway, to add over his shoulder, "There's still time to change, Eisner."

As the door swung closed behind him, Rolls heard her cry, "There's nothing to change!"

There was no doubt in her voice; but Rolls thought he heard sadness.

Chapter Five

"There are no abnormal emanations from the target zone," said the artificial intelligence controlling Hansen's intrusion capsule.

In its current mode, the capsule's radiation on all spectra was as close to zero as Consensus technology could arrange. That meant Hansen had no radar, no lasers—no emission rangefinding of any sort. He was dependent on the target to reveal itself when the intrusion capsule got close enough.

If North had managed to blank out a planet as thoroughly as Consensus scientists had shielded this capsule, the two were going to intersect with what would seem to be a hell of a jolt from Hansen's side.

"On a dark stormy night . . . ," Hansen sang.

Hansen had a pleasant voice, but he couldn't carry a tune even on a good day.

". . . as the train rattled on. . . ."

A good day was one on which Hansen wasn't scared and strapped into a seat with only the dim blue numerals of the console to illuminate his surroundings. In low-observable mode, the AI shut down all non-essentials so that there was as little energy as possible to be trapped within the hull as heat.

It was out of his hands. There was nothing to expect from the next few moments except death, and there wasn't a damned thing he could do about it. He'd been shot at before, but it wasn't like that. Then he'd had a gun in his hand or at least the chance of getting to a gun. . . .

". . . one young man with a babe in his arms," Hansen sang tunelessly, "who sat there with a bowed down head."

His palms were sweaty, his skin prickled, and he figured he knew now what it was like to be under artillery fire where life or death were at the whim of entities in the invisible distance.

"The calculated time of arrival is five seconds—" said the artificial intelligence.

There was no lack of data for the calculations—

"Four—"

—because the Consensus handlers had watched three fleets vanish at the intersection point.

"Three—"

The voices in the mist might think an intrusion capsule—

"Two—"

—could slip through where a fleet couldn't, but Hansen didn't believe that.

"One—"

If it wasn't impact and instantaneous death waiting, what—

"N—" said the artificial intelligence, the first grunt of "Now!" before it cut off and the console display went dead black.

Hansen listened to the sound of blood coursing through the veins of his ears.

The next line of the song went, 'The innocent one began crying just then . . .' Hansen would've kept singing to show the bastards *somewhere* that being trapped in limbo until his air supply failed didn't terrify him; but his mouth was too dry to form the words.

The hull of the capsule quivered. One of the hull plates shifted like a shingle that had rotted away from the staple holding it to the wall.

Light bathed Hansen through a crack that widened as the plate fell off completely. The capsule's three-layer coating of absorptive materials had already sloughed like the carcase of a beached jellyfish.

The console displays were still dead.

Hansen should've been dead also. The amount of heat or other radiation it would take to make the capsule disintegrate would carbonize a human being before he knew what was happening.

Not that Hansen *did* know what was happening.

Three more hull plates fell away, clanging against one another and, more mutedly, on the ground beneath.

Hansen still couldn't see much, just blue sky with some impressive cumulus clouds in the distance. He hit the quick-release plate in the center of his restraints and rose with a neutral look on his face.

Hansen was more than 200 meters in the air, on top of a huge building. He was looking out over the neat patterns of farmland, and—

The floor of the intrusion capsule gave way and dropped Hansen thirty centimeters to the ground. That shouldn't've been unexpected, the way the upper hull was crumbling, but *every*damnthing was a surprise just now. The read-outs and touch-sensitive panels on the console all had a frosted look as though they were withering under extreme heat.

Particularly surprising was the fact that he was alive.

The capsule had—landed?—on a promenade around the building's roof. Behind Hansen was the quarter-sphere sheltering the audience section of a 3,000-seat odeum.

Two men and a woman came from a door in the back of the much smaller quarter-sphere intended to cover the performers. Apart from miniature figures in the fields below, these were the first living beings Hansen had seen since a trio of androids strapped him into the intrusion capsule.

"Can we help you, sir?" called the older man in the center of the group.

Hansen stepped out of the collapsing ruin of his capsule. The fallen hull plates had a porous look, and the monomolecular carbon frame members were beginning to sag under their own weight. He'd envisioned a lot of possibilities for what would happen on this mission, but not this one.

Not anything as survivable as this one, if it came to that.

He bent his mouth into a pleasant smile to match that of his questioner and said, "Ah, my name's Hansen. Ah, this is going to sound silly, but is this Northworld?"

Hansen wore what looked like standard exploration-unit coveralls until you checked at the level of the weave and found the battery of hidden weapons and sensors. Besides the coveralls, he had a satchel holding three separate changes of clothes, each one a direct copy—in appearance—of an outfit that one of the later colonists was known to have carried to Northworld.

His options didn't include sandals and loose, flowing robes cinched at the waist with a belt of soft fabric—which is what the three locals greeting him wore.

"Well, that isn't our name for it, Mr. Hansen," said the other man—still older than Hansen by a decade, if appearance was anything to judge by. "We call it Diamond, but since we believe we're in a spacetime bubble of our own, we may well be a minority in our opinion."

"We're so *glad* to see you," said the young woman who touched Hansen's arm in a gesture of welcome and perhaps reassurance—for one or both of them. "We'd been afraid that it was, you know . . . something to do with the Passages."

Her fingertips felt warm even through the cloth. She had long brown hair and was very attractive, primarily because of her lively expression.

This place might well *be* a bubble of phased spacetime; certainly it wasn't Northworld, a barren wilderness until its settlement three standard months before. The crops below had been in the ground longer than that, and Hansen couldn't even guess how long it must have taken to construct the city-sized building on which he now stood.

"You were expecting me, then?" Hansen asked, keeping his tone mild. The promenade was paved with a rubbery layer that responded comfortably beneath his boots.

"Well, not you precisely," said the old man.

"My name is Dana, by the way," interjected the younger man. "And these are Gorley—" the other man "—and Lea."

"And as Lea said," Gorley went on, "we're delighted you're here—"

"Both for yourself," added Lea, "and because you're not. . . ." Her face quirked in embarrassment, and her hand squeezed Hansen's biceps.

"But particularly for yourself, Mr. Hansen," the older man went on. "We never received a visitor before."

"As to whether we knew you were coming," said Dana, "and please—you mustn't take this as an insult—but. . . ."

"You are disruptive, you see," explained the woman. "Here in Diamond, because of the, ah. . . ."

"Well," said the older man, "your weapons, Mr. Hansen."

He pointed with the paired index and middle fingers of his left hand toward the remains of the intrusion capsule—now a silhouette in ash as if a quantity of cardboard had been burned on the promenade. "I'm afraid that the vehicle in which you arrived was itself a weapon."

All three of the local citizens looked apologetic. "And you see," the younger man finished, "weapons don't exist in Diamond."

"Anything can be—" Hansen snapped before he got control of his tongue. Even if what he'd been about to say were true— and it certainly *was* true where he came from that anything could be used as a weapon if the will to do so existed—that wasn't an attitude he wanted to stress to his present hosts.

"But with the weapons gone," Lea said, "we hope that *you'll* be able to stay. Would you like to see the village?"

"Or perhaps you're hungry/he's hungry?" the men said in near unison.

"I—" said Hansen. He looked at his hosts and decided to be perfectly honest—because he didn't have enough information to lie; and anyway, because he preferred the truth.

"I'm not hungry," he said. "But I'd like to get out there—" he gestured toward the surrounding fields "—just to prove this isn't some kind of stage set."

Lea giggled and hugged herself closer to Hansen. Both men smiled also. "Of course, of course," Dana murmured.

"And I'm wondering a little where everyone else is . . . ?" Hansen added.

Contact with Lea wasn't as pleasant as it should've been, because Hansen noticed his coveralls gave too easily at the pressure of her soft body. The equipment woven into Hansen's garments seemed to have vanished. His intrusion capsule was now fluff which drifted over the edge of the building on the light breeze.

"We didn't want you to worry," said Dana.

"We thought you might be startled by a crowd," said Gorley.

"But *everyone* wants to meet you," said Lea, "not just here but everywhere in Diamond."

As she spoke, an aircar curved neatly around the odeum from a landing site on the opposite edge of the roof. Simultaneously, loosely organized groups of people began approaching from either direction along the promenade.

All the newcomers, including the vehicle's driver, dressed in a similar fashion, but there was wide variety in the color and textures of their garments. The crowds contained many children, some of them infants being carried or led carefully by the hand by their parents.

"Hello, Mr. Hansen," called a little boy, waving a small bouquet.

The aircar touched on the walkway near Hansen and rotated slightly to face its nose outward toward the edge of the roof before it settled finally. The vehicle hummed instead of howling; Hansen couldn't see fan ducts.

These might be gentle people, but they weren't stupid—and they weren't without technology. The whole city-building—very likely the whole of Diamond, planet or universe or whatever it was, was listening to what Hansen said and reacting to it immediately.

"We thought you might prefer to ride," said Lea, nodding toward the car.

"Though we can take the elevators if you'd like," said Dana.

"Or walk," said Gorley. "We'd be more than happy to walk with you."

The old man looked fit enough to manage the walk despite his age, but Hansen wasn't sure *he* wanted to try the long staircases, even going down.

The crowds had halted a comfortable, non-threatening ten meters from Hansen and his companions. More people were still coming around the curves of the promenade.

"No, the car'll be fine," Hansen said, letting Lea guide him into the open vehicle.

"Goodby, Mr. Hansen!" called the little boy, waving enthusiastically.

"We'll have a proper gathering in the common area later," Gorley said.

"If that's all right with you, Mr. Hansen, of course," Dana interjected.

"Yeah, I . . . ," said Hansen. He didn't know enough to ask questions.

"But everyone's so excited," Lea said. "We all wanted to see you in person as soon as we could."

The car lifted to clear the turbulence around the building's edge, then dropped in a curve toward the fields. The irrigation ditches between rows of grain were dry at the moment, but a large reservoir reflected the cloud-piled sky in the near distance, ready to flood the ditches if needed.

"How long has Diamond been settled?" Hansen asked.

The driver throttled back, slowing the car as he steered for a dike between fields. The vehicle was admirably quiet, but it seemed to have surplus power even with five of its six seats filled by adults.

"Our records go back ten thousand years," said Dana.

"What?" Hansen snarled. "That's three times as long as there've been human spacecraft!"

"We didn't mean to distress you, Mr. Hansen," Lea said softly.

"You understand, of course," said Gorley with an apologetic look, "that time within our bubble—if our scientists are correct—doesn't necessarily travel at the same rate as that of the outside universe . . . of which our ancestors may have been a part."

"Though," Dana said, "we don't have any record of existence anywhere but here, in Diamond."

"I'm sorry," Hansen said.

It bothered him that these people kept apologizing to him when hell, either he was at fault or nobody was. He got out of the car and walked toward the rows of grain.

Diamond wasn't an elaborate stage set. Hansen's boots sank into the turned earth. The air was fresh with the scents of growth, and a cloud of small insects rose from the shade beneath the leaves as he reached into the grain.

The crop was still green, the grainheads unformed. Hansen stroked the fine-haired leaves.

His outfitters had given him a ruby ring in a massive gold setting for the middle finger of his right hand. The stone was now as dull as a chip of cement, and Hansen was quite sure that the one-shot laser which the ruby focused no longer functioned.

He turned back to his hosts. They had waited beside the car in attitudes of hopeful attentiveness.

"Do you have criminals on Diamond?" he asked abruptly.

"Oh, no, Mr. Hansen," Lea replied.

Hansen smiled lopsidedly. "Then I'm damned if I know what good I could ever be to you," he said as he took his seat in the car again. "But I guess I'm here anyway."

"Oh, Mr. Hansen," Gorley said, "you can't imagine how wonderful it is to us to have a visitor! We weren't sure that it was possible to enter or leave Diamond."

"May we return to the village, then?" Dana asked. "Or perhaps you'd like to see the animals?"

"The village is fine with me," Hansen said. There was a mild low-frequency vibration through the frame of the aircar for a moment as the driver raised his power. "You know, I'd sort of figured you were vegetarians."

"Ah, well, we are," explained Gorley diffidently. "But we use milk and wool, you see."

The car climbed as swiftly as it had dropped minutes before; he'd been right about the vehicle having plenty of power. "You've been trying to get out of your bubble, then?" he asked.

"Oh, goodness, no!" said Dana in amazement. He blushed in embarrassment. "I *am* sorry. We just—we're happy here."

"It's the knowledge that we miss," explained Gorley. "It's all very well to speculate about our existence, but proof that there *is* an outside universe is quite marvelous."

Lea bent close and kissed Hansen's cheek. "We do hope you'll be comfortable in Diamond."

Instead of returning to the section of promenade where Hansen's capsule had appeared, the aircar circled the building and dropped onto a purpose-built docking area where hundreds of similar vehicles were already parked. "The community is gathering in the common area," Gorley said. "That seemed simplest."

"But if it makes you uncomfortable to be on display, even briefly," Dana said, "of course your peaceful enjoyment is far more important to us."

"To all of us," Lea agreed and nestled closer to her guest.

There was a bank of at least twenty elevators, each of them sized to hold half a dozen people. Cages and shafts alike were of a material whose crystalline transparency had been slightly dulled by dust and use. Again, Diamond hadn't been somehow raised as an elaborate hoax to fool Hansen.

The aircar's driver waved and got into a separate cage. Hansen didn't see the controls—or, for that matter, the elevator's drive and suspension apparatus—but he and his three guides dropped to a level forty meters beneath the roofline and got off when the door rotated open.

The whole area was open except for the eight massive pillars which housed the elevators as well as supporting the building's upper stories. Plants grew around the outer edges and a lightshaft in the center.

The ten-meter ceiling kept the space from looking packed, but it was full of people who waved and cheered when Hansen got off the elevator. He wasn't sure he'd ever seen a crowd that big with a *happy* ambiance to it.

"We have a little dais built for you, if you don't mind," Dana said, bending close to speak directly into Hansen's ear.

Lea gripped his hand with friendly firmness as she led him to up a short flight of steps to a chair on a plastic platform. "If you could say a few words, that would be wonderful," the young woman said as she motioned Hansen to the seat.

Even so they weren't all going to be able to see, Hansen thought; and then he noticed that the crowd of gaily-clad citizens was moving in a clockwise rotation, bringing forward those from the other side of the huge room and taking away those who'd already gotten a close look at their visitor. There was no apparent pushing or concern.

"Ah—" he said.

The room stilled save for the whisper of sandals on the tile flooring.

He certainly wasn't going to sit. He felt like an idiot. Lea started down the steps. Hansen grimaced, wishing he'd grabbed her earlier so that he at least wouldn't be alone here in his— 'ignorance' was an insufficient word for how he felt.

"Ah," he repeated, "ah, I don't know how I came to be here, but I hope that—"

The sunlight through the open sides of the common area dimmed as though shutters had been drawn all around the building. People screamed.

Hansen glanced around him. The threat was everything but palpable, and he was exposed on top of the dais.

He was in his element.

Short-boled palms and bromeliads fringed the exterior of the common area. While the sky beyond darkened in pulses like the throbbing surf, the broadleafed plants were sucked into shadowy, fanged silhouettes. The sun brightened again, and the normal foliage returned.

Shadow humans appeared in the common area when the plants grew serpent doubles also.

Amid the crowd's weeping and wordless cries, Hansen heard from hundreds of throats *a Passage/another Passage* . . . and over and over again, *May it be swift/May it end/end/end*. . . .

For a moment, the great covered park was what it had been when Hansen first saw it: bright, clean, and filled with thousands of healthy people, though their faces were now streaked with tears and terror. Then it changed again, and Hansen saw an armored vehicle that must have weighed hundreds of tonnes.

The tank glided toward Hansen in a false silence while the shadow figures and vegetation shuddered with the noise that such a monster must have made in any medium denser than vacuum. It sprouted missile batteries, guns, and swatches of wire mesh which could have been either antennas or a form of defense.

The tank proceeded at a walking pace which nothing in the park or its own shadow world slowed or affected.

The folk of Diamond keened and clutched one another, keeping their faces down and their eyes closed.

There was no place to run. Hansen picked up the chair— extruded plastic, light if not quite flimsy . . . and probably just as effective as any other man-portable weapon against a monster like the tank which bore down on him now.

Lenses and vision blocks winked with gray highlights that didn't come from the sun of Diamond. None of the tank's guns were aimed at Hansen, but attachment lugs on the bowslope would gore him back until he and they sailed off the edge of the building. Even on the dais, he had to look up to see the top of the turret and the multiple weapons' cupolas.

Hansen swung his piece of furniture at a vision block on the upper left of the bowslope.

The plastic chair whistled at and through the knobbly armor without touching anything material save the air. Hansen overbalanced and almost fell of the front of the dais. Daylight had returned, and with it the rich, soft colors of Diamond.

"Oh, Mr. Hansen . . . ," someone murmured behind him. Hansen turned. Lea had started up the steps to the dais again and paused, staring at the chair in the visitor's hands.

Anything's a weapon if you want it to be one.

Hansen put the chair down carefully, feeling embarrassed . . . though there wasn't any need to, god knew. What he'd done made as much sense as anything could in a crazy situation like that.

"Oh, Mr. Hansen," Leas repeated. "I'm so sorry."

She stepped closer to him and reached out her hand. Hansen glanced over his shoulder; the whole crowd was watching him, but there was an evident sadness in everyone's eyes.

What he'd done made sense where Hansen came from; but this was Diamond.

He felt—cold wasn't the word, but a sensation as deep as if freezing water were drawing all the warmth out of his body. There was a thin film between Hansen and everything around him. He felt the pressure of Lea's hand but not its warmth.

"We're so sorry," she said through a corridor of mirrors. "It isn't a fault in you, Mr. Hansen, but weapons don't exist here in Diamond."

She raised onto her toes to kiss him. He couldn't feel her lips. Everything was becoming gray. He remembered the capsule in which he'd arrived, ash that divided into dust motes as a breeze swept it gently from the promenade.

"Goodby, Mr. Hansen. . . ." called a distant, childish voice.

"And you are a weapon . . . ," whispered words that were only a shadow in Hansen's mind as he felt the structure of Diamond interpenetrate him completely and leave only nothingness.

Chapter Six

Rolls found Fortin with his back to an outcrop, looking down the slope and through the shimmering discontinuity to a forest on the Open Lands, the surface which could be reached from any of Northworld's other planes. Armed figures groped among the dimensionally-distant trees, an army searching for the foe with whom it would fight to decide . . . nothing or everything, a matter of perception.

Fortin was tossing pebbles. They quivered when they struck the discontinuity. Fortin's arm wasn't strong enough to hit the warriors from his vantage point, but his tiny missiles flicked snow from the tree branches.

"Planning to visit the colonists?" Rolls said, seating himself beside Fortin. North's son had surely seen him climbing from the valley below; if he chose to ignore Rolls' approach, that was merely a ploy—and as such to be ignored.

"Perhaps," said Fortin without looking around.

He threw another stone. It sparkled and switched planes. By adjusting their vision, the two men could focus on either the stream a thousand meters below in their reality or the snow-wrapped forest and ignorant army. "Do you care, Rolls?"

Rolls chuckled. Seen from this angle, Fortin's face had the cool perfection of a well-struck medal. "What you plan is no concern of mine, Fortin," he said. "You know where my interests lie."

Fortin turned at last to face him. "Whatever I do," he said, "you'll know."

Rolls shifted slightly. "That's right," he agreed easily. "You— do things. I observe. Eisner learns."

The granite ledge on which they sat was flaking; Rolls reached beneath his buttocks to sweep aside some sharp-edged bits. Fortin picked up one of them, looked at it, and dropped it again instead of flinging it through the dimensional barrier.

"Why are you here?" he demanded.

Rolls smiled. "I'd like," he said, "to borrow Penny's necklace."

Fortin began to laugh. He had a tenor voice, as smoothly pleasant as his features—and as cool. "Then you'd better ask Penny, hadn't you?" he said, looking down for the stone he'd just cast aside.

"I thought perhaps you might help me," said Rolls.

"Did you?" the half-android remarked without interest. His index finger dug at the ledge, trying idly to worry another bit loose.

"I . . . want to borrow it for only a moment," Rolls said, trying to keep his voice clear of the concern he was beginning to feel. He had no way to coerce Fortin, and a claim on the halfling's friendship would be as empty as claiming to be a friend of the Matrix itself.

Though the Matrix was not perverse.

"It's nothing to me how long you want it," Fortin said. "Or what you want it for." He met Rolls' eyes again.

Rolls grinned. He was willing to bargain with Fortin; for a moment, though, he'd been afraid that there was nothing he could provide that the other wanted.

He should have known better. Schemes filled Fortin the way maggots did a three-days corpse. There was sure to be a scheme which impinged on Rolls or what Rolls could do. . . .

"Yes," Rolls said, "I can see that." He settled himself against the crag, closing his eyes to feel the sunlight warm their lids.

"I've been thinking of visiting Ruby, you know," said Fortin in a voice as coolly distant as if it came through the dimensional barrier. "It seems to me that Ruby might have something to do with the problem of nightmares on Diamond."

"Waking nightmares," Rolls said, opening his eyes and looking without expression at his smaller companion. "Yes, you might very well be right."

"But I would rather," Fortin continued, picking his words with the care of a climber negotiating a cliff face, "that my visit to Ruby didn't come to North's attention. My father doesn't—"

A look of fury momentarily transfigured Fortin's face, though his features were no less perfect for the purity of the emotion they displayed. "My father doesn't trust me."

Rolls laughed, an easy, deep-throated sound. "Nobody trusts you, Fortin," he said.

The anger left Fortin's visage, leaving behind a coldness like the blue heart of a glacier. "Because my mother was an android," he said.

"Because you're Fortin," Rolls said, still smiling. He'd never been a good liar, and acceding to godlike powers had leached away even the impulse to say less than the absolute truth as he saw it.

And Rolls saw very clearly indeed.

"Maybe it's in the genes," he added, his expression untroubled by Fortin's wintry glare. "After all, Fortin, nobody really trusts North, either."

Fortin turned away. He drew in a deep breath and pretended to look for another chip of stone to throw.

"I can't prevent North from seeing whatever he chooses to see," Rolls said. "But he observes for reasons . . . and I observe because it's my life."

For a moment, a look as bleak as a snowfield wavered across Rolls' soft, handsome features.

"*I* won't be the one to inform your father that you're visiting Ruby," he said.

Below and beyond them, scouts rejoined the army. A trumpet call quavered through the discontinuity and the wind skirling past the crag.

"All right," Fortin said. His voice and visage were carelessly without expression again. "If you can occupy Penny outside her room—and without her necklace—for half an hour, say—"

Rolls chuckled again. "That should be possible," he agreed.

"—then I'll see about 'borrowing' it for you."

There were two armies visible now. To the men on the crag, they seemed to be fighting as though mirrored in the flat surface of a pond.

Chapter Seven

Hansen felt the shock of landing before he knew he was alive. The ground was solid enough to knock his breath away.

He could see again. He still existed—or existed again.

Hansen hadn't fallen far. In fact, he'd just gotten his feet tangled during the moment—or however long; maybe he didn't want to think about that—during which Diamond forced itself through the space of Hansen's being. The sun *here* was a little past midpoint.

He was on a forty-meter bluff, overlooking a considerable floodplain forested with scrub conifers as well as willows. The river which had carved the bluff was now an occasional glint through the trees a kilometer away. On the far horizon was a conical mountain from which trailed wisps of yellow vapor.

There was snow on the leaf mould and in the creviced bark of the trees around Hansen, but the air didn't seem particularly cold. A fieldmouse gnawed audibly nearby, rotating a pinecone with tiny forepaws to bring hidden seeds in range of the glittering incisors.

Hansen wasn't on Diamond. He could be quite sure of that, because riders carrying lances and crossbows were picking their way from left to right through the trees below.

A trumpet called from nearby to the right. A living creature out of sight on the left answered the horn with its own louder, angry echo. Two of the riders turned their shaggy, big-headed ponies and trotted back the way they'd come. Their fellows, perhaps a dozen of them, checked their weapons and resumed their careful progress through the trees.

Hansen looked at his laser ring. The stone remained as dull as it had been on Diamond, and even the metal had the false sheen of plastic.

The band crumbled as he tried to work the ring off his finger. He dropped the bits on the snowy ground in disgust.

One of the horsemen below took a curved trumpet from beneath his fur jacket, set it to his lips, and blew a three-note call.

Hansen sighed. He wasn't trained to survive alone in the woods. The sooner he brought himself to the attention of the men below, the better . . . though of course, 'better' might amount to a swift death instead of a slow surrender to cold and hunger.

"Don't be a fool, Hansen," squeaked the fieldmouse. "Swear yourself to my service. You'll never survive here without my help."

Hansen rubbed the trunk of one of the pines. The outer surface of the bark rasped as it ground away beneath the ball of his thumb, exposing the russet layer within.

"Mice talk here, then?" Hansen said conversationally. So long as he squeezed the treetrunk, he could keep himself from slamming his fist into it in frustration at this further madness from which he was now sure he would never escape. . . .

"Faugh!" the mouse said. "Such a form is useful when I visit the Open Lands. You might not even think me alive in your terms, Hansen."

The little creature tossed the cone aside. Half the scales had been nibbled into fibrous sprays. They looked like the blades of a turbine whose epoxy matrix had disintegrated under stress.

"I'm a machine," said the mouse, cleaning its whiskers with its paws. "You can call me Walker. On my plane of Northworld the sun is red, and even the shoals of horseshoe crabs which used to couple on gravel beaches have died. There is no life besides me and my fellows—if we live."

Another horn blew; a second group of horsemen rode into sight among the trees below. Several crossbows fired. The flat *snap!* of the bows' discharge sounded like treelimbs cracking under the weight of ice.

Men shouted. Hansen didn't see anyone fall, but the conifers hid most of the details.

He was shivering; perhaps it was the cold. "You're a time traveler, then?" he said to the fieldmouse. The beast's left eye was as dull as the ruby which had powdered like chalk as Hansen removed his ring.

"You still think in terms of duration, Hansen," Walker said. "Don't. This is Northworld."

He paused for a moment to lick the creamy fur of his belly in firm, even strokes of his tongue. "I'm from a different plane of the Matrix. There are—" the mouse voice took on a didactic singsong "—eight worldplanes of the Matrix, and the Matrix which is a world. But those who live *in* the Matrix are mad."

The riders on both sides were falling back. A riderless pony rushed to and fro among the trees, neighing and shaking cascades of snow from the branches.

Men on foot, stepping heavily with the weight of the full armor they wore, moved through the forest in a ragged array. They didn't appear to be armed, but whenever one brushed a low treelimb, wood and snow spluttered away in a blue crackle.

Similar pops of electronic lightning suggested that more armored footmen were approaching from the other direction, but the line of contact would be at some distance to the right of Hansen's present vantage point. He began walking in that direction, keeping a grip on saplings because he was paying less attention than he ought to the bluff's edge.

Walker hopped along beside him. "Swear yourself to my service, Hansen," piped the fieldmouse voice. "You're nothing and nobody without my guidance. But be warned: oaths have power on Northworld."

Scores of fur-clad horsemen like those who'd acted as skirmishers followed a few meters behind the ragged line of footmen. The latter's armor was painted in brilliant colors, no two patterns alike. Hansen estimated that there were about 150 men in the force advancing from his left, with only a third of them in armor; but the trees made certain counting impossible.

Several horns called. Fifty or sixty equally garish armored men came into sight from the trees to the right.

A small gray bird, crested like a titmouse, landed on a branch beside Hansen. It rapped the seed in its beak three times to break it open. The bird's head flicked as it swallowed the kernel, letting the husk flutter over the edge of the bluff.

"That's the army of Golsingh the Peacegiver," the bird said, twitching its beak in the direction of the newcomers. "Those others there—" it bobbed in the direction of the force to Hansen's left "—they're Count Lopez' men, though he's bedridden and can't lead them."

Hansen looked at the bird. One of its eyes was bright; the other had the yellow, frosted look of weathered marble.

"My word *always* counts, Walker," Hansen said harshly. "I'm not giving it to you."

Lopez' mounted force suddenly sallied through the loose ranks of his armored footmen. Snow and dirt flew from beneath the hooves of the ponies.

When the riders were twenty meters short of leading clot of Golsingh's footmen, crossbows snapped on both sides. Several of Lopez' men tumbled from their saddles, but their own missiles were directed at the armored footmen.

It appeared to Hansen that the quarrels sizzled and dropped just short of the armor. Several, probably metal-shafted, vanished in showers of orange sparks.

A single footman stumbled, then fell backward in the snow. His heels drummed briefly. The fletching of a missile projected from his left armpit.

Walker made a *tsk-tsk-tsk* sound, as dismissive now as if he were in human guise. His beak sawed in the direction of the fallen man. "A hireling," the bird explained. "Shoddy armor; no chance at all."

He turned his one bright eye on Hansen. "But more chance than you have, Kommissar. Unless you put yourself under my control and direction."

Hansen gathered a blob of saliva on his tongue. He grimaced and swallowed instead of spitting.

Golsingh's lancers had also ridden through the loose array of their own footmen and were struggling with mounted opponents in a chaos of shouting and ringing metal. Hansen couldn't imagine how the fur-clad riders told one another apart after the first shock had mixed their lines.

The foremost group of Golsingh's footmen, twenty or so of them, broke into a stumbling run. Their leader was a huge man in red and gold armor. The nearest horsemen bellowed afresh and tried to disengage.

The man in red and gold pointed his right arm and splayed the middle and index fingers of his gauntleted hand. A blue-white arc snapped in a ten-meter parabola from the fingers with a noise like sawing stone. It touched three horsemen in a long whiplash curve, igniting their garments and cleaving away the head of one man as surely as an axe could have done.

Hansen was sure that at least one of the victims had come from Golsingh's side.

"That's Taddeusz, Golsingh's foster father," Walker said with another avian sniff. "The warchief as well. He thinks that war is for warriors, and freemen are more trouble than use."

Taddeusz and his clot of footmen—warriors—continued to pound forward. Saplings burst into flame when arcs touched them in broad slashes, but the freemen had spurred their ponies out of the way so that no more of them fell.

A gap was opening between Taddeusz' group and the nearest of the remaining friendly forces. A few other warriors began to trot from Golsingh's line, but they seemed motivated by personal excitement rather than a desire to hit the enemy as a coordinated force.

Taddeusz and a green-armored warrior from Lopez' army plodded together with a rippling crash of electrical discharges. They met in an alder thicket. Hansen couldn't see the moment of contact, but lightning swept the slender stems away in time for him to watch the Lopez warrior pivot on his right foot and fall.

There was a black, serpentine scar across the green breastplate. Smoke or steam oozed from the neck joint of the armor.

Taddeusz strode on. His arc was condensed to a quaver that reached less than a meter from his gauntlet. Another of Lopez' warriors cut at the war chief with an arc extended into a whiplash. It popped and sizzled, wrapping Taddeusz in its blue fire; clumps of snow puddled around the red and gold boots.

Taddeusz took a step and another step, each in slow motion as though he were walking in the surf. His opponent suddenly tried to back-pedal. He was too late. Taddeusz' right arm slashed, and the dense electrical flux from his gauntlet sheared into his opponent's helmet.

Circuits blew all through the damaged suit. Taddeusz blanked his arc for an instant, then snapped it back to life as he moved on.

His victim toppled. A wedge-shaped cut bubbled halfway through the sphere of the helmet, as though it had been struck by something more material than directed lightning.

A dozen fires struggled fitfully among the scrub trees. Sapless wood tried to sustain ignition temperature against the cold and snow.

Hansen moved sideways to keep Taddeusz in view. A crevice in the face of the bluff blocked him.

He cursed. It was three meters across. There was crumbling soil on the opposite side, but also saplings that'd provide handholds if he needed them.

A rocky, 70° slope jolted down to the embattled floodplain if he missed his hold.

Hansen jumped, knocking the saplings away with his chest as he landed a safe meter beyond them. A twig cut his cheek. He was beginning to feel the cold.

Lopez' men were closing on Taddeusz from all sides. A dozen or so of Golsingh's men still followed their warchief. They closed up and formed a circle as Lopez' resistance stiffened. Smoldering armor lay along the course they'd cut into the enemy, the detritus of their success.

You could get more organization by rolling two handsful of marbles together.

"Damned fools!" Hansen snarled. "If that's all they know about war, they oughta stick to knitting."

He wasn't aware that he'd spoken aloud until a red squirrel balanced on a branch above him took the half-gnawed hickory nut from its jaws and said, "They know that they are warriors and heroes, Hansen. Since you know nothing of Northworld, you must give your life into my keeping."

"Go away," Hansen said, restraining an urge to sweep Walker over the bluff edge.

He concentrated on the fight instead. He'd felt a fierce rush of anger—but he knew his emotion was directed at the *butchery*, the *stupidity* going on below.

Hansen was a craftsman, and controlled violence was his trade. The armies below were composed of murderous buffoons.

Two of Lopez' men moved against Taddeusz simultaneously. Taddeusz cut at the one on his right; the warrior tried to block the warchief's arc with his own. There was a moment of explosive dazzle and a shriek like that of bearings freezing up. The warrior attacking Taddeusz from the left slashed at the warchief's helmet.

Taddeusz stumbled. The opponent to his right staggered away. The man's red-striped armor had lost the sheen of electronic polish, but the fellow managed to run three steps before he fell. A pair of fur-clad freemen leaped from their ponies and started dragging the warrior to a safer distance.

One of Taddeusz' party leaped between the warchief and his opponent's descending stroke. Both warriors froze as their arcs crossed. Another of Lopez' men punched Taddeusz' defender in the side with an arc which blazed on entry and was still spluttering when a finger's breadth of it poked through the opposite side of the armor.

Taddeusz got to his feet. Only two of his men were still standing; both of them promptly fell under multiple attacks. The warchief cut low, severing the thigh of the nearest opponent.

Two of Lopez' men struck at Taddeusz from behind and the side. He spun, sparkling like a thermite fire but still moving with deadly precision. His short-curving arc carved through a helmet and the arm a desperate warrior had raised for protection.

Taddeusz extended his arc into a blue dazzle ripping a full three meters from his hand. He slashed it through the air as he turned and turned again, clearing the area around him. He was ringed by at least twenty of Lopez' warriors, but each time some of them moved to attack, the warchief's sudden movements sent them scampering away.

The remainder of Golsingh's army had begun to catch up with their warchief. Several of Lopez' warriors turned to meet the new threat. Hansen's nostrils wrinkled with the sharp bite of ozone, even at his distance above the fight.

There was something else. Something quivered on the verge of visibility across the battlefield. Black shutters opening, or a great crow splaying its wingfeathers between the sun and death below. . . .

But not quite.

A warrior in silver armor raised his right gauntlet toward Taddeusz, palm outward.

The warchief's arc lashed toward the man. Before the cut could land, an unconfined discharge leaped from the silver gauntlet to Taddeusz' chest.

The thunderous report sounded like a transformer exploding.

Both suits of armor lost their luster. Taddeusz' arc-weapon shrank to an afterimage on Hansen's retinas. Lopez' men moved in for the kill.

The remainder of Golsingh's army, lead by a figure in royal blue, swept across the circle of their opponents. One of Lopez' warriors paused in the middle of a stroke aimed at Taddeusz and tried to run. Several others were struck down from behind.

Warriors began kneeling with their arms raised. Lopez' freemen hopped back onto their ponies and trotted away, harassed by Golsingh's horsemen.

Hansen noticed that the arc which touched the man in silver met no more resistance than it would from as sapling. It cut the warrior in two at mid-chest.

Walker tossed away the remains of his nut and sniffed. "The first rule of war," he chittered superciliously, "is never to fire a bolt. It takes minutes for your suit to build up power again."

Lopez' men were taking off their armor. The suits opened down the left side like gigantic clamshells. Each suit's arms and legs remained attached to the backplate, but the helmet and body armor split to allow the warrior access to his suit.

Dismounted freemen knelt beside Golsingh's fallen warriors. In some cases the victim was able to stand after he'd been lifted out of his armor.

Golsingh's baggage train arrived at the battlefield in a bedlam of trumpets and crackling brush.

"Well, I'll be damned," Hansen muttered.

"You'll surely be lost unless you put yourself under my protection," the squirrel retorted primly. "You would have joined Lopez' army just before the fight, wouldn't you? And where would you be *now*?"

There was a remuda of saddled ponies in Golsingh's train, but the baggage animals were elephants covered with long black hair. Their tusks had been sawn off close to the jaw and capped with copper bands.

The beasts would've been mammoths, if Hansen were standing on Earth a million years before . . . and very possibly they were mammoths here on Northworld—whatever nightmare Northworld turned out to be.

The animals were guided and accompanied by a hundred or

more men on foot—but certainly not warriors. Whereas the freemen were dressed in furs, not infrequently picked out by streamers of bright cloth, this lot looked like so many bales of dingy rags plodding through the snow.

Hansen looked at the squirrel. "Servants?" he said.

Walker flicked the brush of his tail. "Slaves," he replied.

Most of Golsingh's men were getting out of their armor also. Pairs of slaves attended each warrior and carried the empty suits to bags of rope netting hanging from the flanks of the mammoths.

Hansen was shivering uncontrollably. He looked at the slope, wondering whether he could climb down directly in his present state or if he needed to find a gentler descent.

The warrior who'd worn the royal blue armor stretched as he stepped clear of his suit, then walked over to join Taddeusz. The warchief's armor had for the most part regained the luster it lost when the bolt of raw energy struck it. There was a black star-burst in the center of the gold and scarlet plastron.

"King Golsingh," Walker said. "He has dreams, but he's too soft to make anything of them."

Slaves were stripping the corpses of warriors; no one seemed to pay any attention to the handful of dead freemen. Birds were already circling the battlefield. The corpses of Golsingh's men were laid over a pile of faggots sawn by the few warriors still wearing their suits. Lopez' men lay where they'd fallen.

All the armor, damaged as well as whole, was loaded onto the mammoths who stamped angrily and hooted at the smell of blood. A score of Lopez' warriors had been captured. They were herded together, under guard by freemen, and watched the proceedings with evident disquiet.

It wasn't going to get warmer on the bluff, and the drop wasn't likely to become less steep. Hansen lowered himself over the edge, keeping a grip on a treebole until his boots found purchase. So far, so—

"You're a fool," the squirrel chittered. "They'll pay no attention to you. Or worse."

Hansen glanced over his shoulder. Warriors were mounting the ponies brought on leads, and the line of mammoths was plodding off in the direction from which it had come.

Taddeusz and Golsingh were arguing. The warchief shouted an order. One of the warriors still wearing armor stepped toward the line of prisoners.

One of Hansen's boots slipped. He dropped a step, then slid twenty meters in a half-controlled rush.

Hansen didn't have to be watching to know what the vicious sizzle of an arc weapon meant. Because the captured warriors had no helmets to muffle their voices, their screams were clearly audible. Crows called in raucous answer.

Halfway down the slope, a fair-sized pine grew in a crevice. The bluff below that point was at a fairly safe angle. Hansen let himself slide, angling to catch the tree and hoping that Diamond hadn't rotted the tough fabric of his coveralls the way it had his weapons.

It was a near thing in another way: he almost slid past the tree. The bark tore his palms as he grabbed and the shock strained his shoulder muscles, but those were small prices to pay for not fetching up against the granite outcrop twenty meters further down.

Bits of rock pattered as Hansen clung to the tree and panted. Golsingh had just mounted his pony. He said something to Taddeusz and pointed toward Hansen.

The pyre piled with the corpses of the winning side was ablaze and beginning to roar. The bodies of the captives smoldered on the snow. Birds were landing on them.

Taddeusz shouted a series of orders. A pair of lancers rode toward the warchief. The warrior who'd just acted as executioner halted in the process of getting out of his armor.

Hansen dropped to the plain in a series of calculated hops, knoll to rock to clump of trees stunted by periodic flooding.

He flexed feeling back into his hands, but he'd never been much good without weapons. Anyway, if it came to a real fight, he was more meat for the crows.

"Lord Taddeusz!" Hansen shouted. "Lord Golsingh, I'm a traveler from a far land, drawn to your excellence."

He hoped the locals here spoke Standard. The colonists of course had . . . and the folk of Diamond, albeit accented . . . and the mouse/bird/squirrel that called itself Walker, for whatever *that* was worth.

The clear solidity of the sky and trees pressed in on Hansen. If all this was real, then what was he?

"Who are you, then?" Golsingh called in Standard, walking his pony a few strides closer to Hansen.

The beast sidled, presenting its left shoulder to Hansen as it advanced. The king frowned and tugged at the left rein, turning the pony's head without straightening its approach.

Golsingh was of average height, though he looked small next to his warchief. Taddeusz might better have mounted a mammoth than the pony which struggled beneath his weight. The king's neck and hands were well-muscled, but his swarthy face had a fine bone structure. Hansen got the impression of a slight man who had trained himself to athletic prowess.

Whereas Taddeusz was a bear . . . and Nils Hansen was a hound, with flat muscles and a hound's utter disdain for the way cats play instead of killing.

Hansen smiled, and he probably shouldn't have, because Taddeusz said brusquely to a freeman, "Kill him!"

The man lowered his lance and clucked to his pony. Hansen continued to walk forward. A short pine tree just ahead and to his right was the best shelter available. He'd run for it when the lancer charged, but until then—

"Stop!" Golsingh shouted to the freeman. Hansen halted also, unwilling to look as though he were disobeying a royal command.

"Taddeusz," Golsingh continued, "remember that I am your king."

"Excellency," replied the big man, "I'm just—"

"The battle is over," Golsingh snapped. "*I* am king, and I will give the orders now."

Taddeusz nodded in contrition. "I apologize, my son," he said. "I had only your safety in mind."

Golsingh smiled. "As always, foster father," he agreed, nodding back to the bigger man as a mark of honor.

Both men had enveloped themselves in fur cloaks and caps when they took off their armor, so it was hard for Hansen to judge their ages at twenty meters' distance. Golsingh was probably in his mid twenties, Taddeusz two decades older. The warchief's weathered complexion and grizzled russet hair would look much the same when the man was in his sixties, but the brutal force he'd displayed during the battle suggested a lower limit to his age.

Or else Taddeusz had been Hell itself on a battlefield when he *was* in his prime.

"Lord Golsingh," Hansen said, "I'm a, ah, a warrior who's come from the far reaches of—" *why not?* "—Annunciation to, ah, join Your Excellence."

"Is this a joke?" said Golsingh, looking at his foster father with a puzzled expression. One of the slave attendants who huddled as they awaited their masters' pleasure began to laugh.

A crow glided from a treetop and landed nearby on the one corpse the victors hadn't bothered to strip: the warrior whose armor hadn't stopped a crossbow bolt. The bird cawed in amusement, fixing Hansen with its one bright eye.

"Yes, he's probably Lopez' buffoon looking for a new place," Taddeusz said. He added in dismissal—no longer angry, because the intruder was no longer worth his anger, "Go back to your master and tell him to have himself at Peace Rock within a tennight or we'll burn him and everyone else in his miserable village alive."

Taddeusz and Golsingh both wheeled their ponies.

Hansen's face went flat. "If you're looking for a buffoon," he shouted to the riders' backs, "then you could start with the fool who led your right flank into that half-assed charge. It was god's own luck he didn't lose you a battle you should've had on a platter!"

The horsemen drew up; Taddeusz' pony stutter-stepped as the warchief twisted to look over his shoulder. The freemen lifted the lances they'd laid crosswise on their pommels for carriage.

"I'll handle this, Excellency," Taddeusz said.

The wall-eyed crow danced from one foot to the other on the dead man's chest, clicking its beak in mockery.

"I tell you I'm a warrior!" Hansen said. "I can help you more than you imagine in planning your next battle."

"You lot," Taddeusz said, pointing to the four slaves. "Serve him out."

He nodded to Golsingh again. "Come along, Excellence," he said. "We don't want to fall too far behind the column. You never know what's lurking in these woods."

The horsemen trotted off together, spurning clods of mud and snow behind them. The slaves, drawing single-edged knives from beneath their rags, moved toward Hansen.

"A warrior has armor and attendants," cawed Walker. If the slaves heard the words, they gave no sign of it. "What do you have except your own foolishness, Kommissar?"

The riders were out of sight among the trees. "Look," Hansen said to the slaves. "This isn't your problem. Why don't you guys just wait a few minutes—"

The nearest of the slaves rushed him.

Hansen scampered back. The knife looked dull, but its wielder slashed with enough enthusiasm to manage the job if he got close enough.

"Look," Hansen called, "somebody's going to get—"

"I git his boots!" the slave cried to his fellows. All four of them were plodding after Hansen at the best speed their rag-wrapped feet could manage on the slushy ground.

Hansen jogged in the direction Lopez' surviving freemen had retreated. Only his mind was cold now. The defeated men had scattered equipment as they fled, and—

A shadow sailed past his head with a caw and a snap of its wings. It landed on a fallen branch ten meters ahead, then hopped so that its black beak was toward Hansen.

Walker's claws rested not on a branch, but rather on the stock of a crossbow. . . .

"You don't deserve help!" the crow called as it sprang airborne an instant before Hansen snatched up the weapon.

"I don't *need* help, Walker!" Hansen snapped as he turned to face his pursuers.

And that was true enough. He would've found something. Though maybe not this crossbow, a little off the track he was following and half-buried in snow. . . .

The slaves paused doubtfully when their victim turned to face them.

"Naw, it's all right," said the one in the lead. "It ain't cocked, and anyhow, he don't have arrows."

Hansen lunged, smashing the speaker in the face with the crossbow's fore-end, then using the tips of the bow to right and left like a pickaxe to the chests of the next two slaves. The second stroke caught only rags as the target leaped backward, squawling in justified terror.

The crossbow weighed over ten kilos, combining a meter-long hardwood stock with a stiff steel bow. Anybody who doubted Hansen was armed with *that* in his hands was a fool and a—

Hansen buttstroked the man with the broken face, knocking him over the body of his fellow. The other two slaves were running. Hansen ran after them.

—dead man.

"Oh, you're a fine warrior to fight slaves!" Walker cried. "Are you proud of yourself, now?"

Hansen stopped. His legs were trembling, and he could only breathe in great sobs.

Walker was right. There'd been four of them . . . but trash like that wasn't what he'd trained for, *lived* for.

Hansen began walking back toward the battlefield, getting control of his adrenalin-charged muscles by moving them. When he was sure the surviving slaves were gone for good, he dropped the bloody crossbow.

The suit of abandoned armor was still where it had fallen. The crow lighted on it as Hansen approached.

"I can show you where a fine suit, a king's armor, can be had," Walker said. "Do my will and I'll reward you."

"Will this work?" Hansen demanded.

He knelt beside the body. The casing appeared to be mild steel, though there had to be complex electronics within. There was a single large catch, directly beneath the crossbow bolt projecting from the left armpit.

"Badly," Walker cawed, hopping to a sapling so slender that it bobbed beneath the crow's weight. "You won't dare face a real warrior in flimsy junk like this."

The helmet was a featureless ball. From a distance, Hansen had assumed there were concealed eye and breathing slits. He'd been wrong.

"Don't tell me what I dare," Hansen said. He released the sidecatch and flopped the suit open.

The man within had voided his bowels as he died. The stench hung in the cool air like a pond of sewage.

Hansen pulled the dead man from the armor with as much

dignity as his need for haste and the corpse's stiffening limbs permitted.

The warrior had been old, with a pepper-and-salt moustache and only a fringe of hair on his head. The bolt was through his lungs, and he'd hemorrhaged badly from his mouth and nostrils. At least they were much of a size, Hansen and the dead man. . . .

"How do I make it work?" he grunted as he lifted the body clear.

Walker stopped preening his lustrous, blue-black feathers for a moment. "The suit powers up when it closes over a man," he said disinterestedly. "A living man, that is. But you're a fool to trust yourself to it, Hansen."

Hansen clucked in irritation. The suit could be stood empty on its spread legs—the warriors he'd watched had stripped in an upright position—but the piece was too heavy for Hansen to lift alone. It'd better have servos to multiply the effect of its wearer's motions.

He braced his hands on the edges of the thorax armor and thrust his booted feet into the leg openings simultaneously. *They put their pants on one leg at a time . . .* , he thought with a grim smile.

The armor still stank. He lay back in it and fitted his arms into the arms of the suit. It'd stink worse in a few minutes if Hansen died in it also; and the smell would matter just as little either way.

"Walker!" he said. Would he be able to speak and hear with the suit closed up? "How do I make it throw an arc?"

The crow cocked its head. "Point your fingers and say 'Cut,' " it said. "Spread them wider to lengthen it."

Artificial intelligence controlled, then. How did you get AI and crude feudalism together? "And to fire a bolt?"

"The first rule of—"

"*Bird!*"

"*Caawk!*" Walker said. Then, "Point your palm and say 'Shoot.' "

Hansen closed the armor. When the latch clicked, a display lighted in front of his eyes and tiny fans began circulating the foul air.

He got up. The visual display was streaked with raster lines and seemed to be compressing 180° into the width his eyes would normally allot to ninety.

"Reduce field fifty percent," Hansen said automatically, before his conscious mind could remind him that this crude unit might not have verbal controls—or any controls at all.

The forest expanded to normal width and depth—a narrow window on the world, but the best display for walking.

Fast walking, if he could manage it. He had a lot of time to make up.

He took a step, then another, and raised his pace into a clumsy jog. There was enough delay in the suit's response to Hansen's movements that he thought at first he was going to topple. The dynamic rigidity of the joints was just great enough to save him from that embarrassment.

All exposed points of his body began to chafe. The armor was lined with suede at some points, with hide at others, and for some of its area with cloth scarcely better than the rags in which the slaves were clothed.

Hansen could feel a finger of cold air below his left arm, where the arrow-hole marked the suit. He didn't think he'd have to worry about arrows, though—

But that reminded him. As he clumped along, following the muddy, surprisingly narrow, track the mammoths squeezed into the bottom land, he thrust out his right arm, pointed his fingers, and said, "Cut!"

An arc—blacked-out on Hansen's display—sizzled from his gauntlet. It licked a small pinetree into resinous flame.

Hansen fell on his face. When his suit shot out the arc, the legs didn't have enough power remaining to drive him at the speed he expected.

The arc continued to lash the leaf mould into sluggish fire. *How did he—* "Stop!" Hansen shouted. "Quit!"

The weapon cut off.

Hansen didn't see Walker as he got up again, but from the closeness of the voice, the crow must have been sitting on his shoulder as it said, "A better suit would not have done that. A royal suit, like that which I offer you as my servant, could strike with both hands and still run faster than an unarmored man."

"I'll manage," Hansen said.

He began to jog again, then broke into a measured trot. He was flaying the skin from his knees, shoulders, and jutting hip bones.

He'd worn hard suits before, but rarely—and even less often in a gravity well. Motors in the armor's joints carried the weight and drove it in response to Hansen's muscles; but the muscles had to initiate the movements, and there was always a minuscule delay. He felt as if he were trying to run in a bath of soap bubbles—except that soap bubbles wouldn't've galled him.

Hansen concentrated on each next stride. His display fogged with his gasping exhalations. He didn't notice that the trail was rising until he broke out of the trees and saw, on ground that rose still higher across a swale, a palisaded village from which rose the smoke of scores of hearths.

The riders and mammoths of Golsingh's train straggled across the low ground, halfway down and halfway up the other side. A freeman at the rear of the line blew his curved horn furiously, pointing toward Hansen with his free hand.

Three of the warriors around Golsingh and Taddeusz at the bottom of the swale began getting into their armor.

Hansen slowed cautiously. He visualized himself skidding on his faceplate toward the men he wanted to impress; the image diverted some of his tension into a laugh.

A thought occurred to him. He centered the arming warriors in his display and muttered, "Visor, plus ten."

Hansen's helmet immediately gave him the requested magnification. The images were fuzzy, but he could see that the warrior donning the red-silver-blue armor was an octoroon, and that all three were powerful fellows of about Hansen's own twenty-nine years.

"Resume normal vision," he said, sucking his lips between his front teeth as he considered the situation.

This armor was crudely built, but it had a surprising range of capacities. Hansen was fairly certain that the warriors who'd struggled so clumsily in battle didn't know or didn't care about most of the things their suits could do. That gave him an advantage.

God knew that he was going to need one.

"Lord Golsingh!" Hansen shouted as he strolled toward the

waiting army. His armor quivered with the amplified sound of his voice. "I came here to serve you. If there's no place in your service at the moment, then I'll empty one for myself!"

Hansen didn't know anything about the culture of Northworld—but he knew organizations and pecking orders. He'd failed at the start with this lot because they didn't respect him. He wasn't going to fail again because of a lack of arrogance.

After all, it wasn't as though arrogance didn't come naturally to him.

The three warriors had their armor on, now. The suits were painted in patterns of black and silver; red, silver, and blue; and lime green with a phoenix emblazoned in gold on the plastron. All three men were big, and their armor was of obviously high quality.

As opposed to what Hansen was wearing: a piece of junk which had once been striped orange and blue, but which now was marked more by rust than by paint.

The shaggy line of mammoths continued slog onward, but horsemen as well as most of the slaves began to collect at the bottom of the swale. It was the only place for a kilometer in any direction where there was enough flat, clear space to serve for a dueling ground.

Hansen walked on, matching his pace to that of the baggage train. The mammoths moved deceptively fast, covering two meters with each slow stride. Their droppings steamed in the mud, offering Hansen's lungs a tang of crushed hay.

Golsingh's army waited for Hansen. Most of the riders had dismounted, though the king and Taddeusz still sat on their ponies, looking over the heads of the three warriors in brilliant armor.

"That's Villiers' suit," somebody announced. "He's stolen Villiers' suit off his body."

"Cut," said Hansen. An arc spurted at an angle from his right hand. His fingers adjusted its length to quiver just above the muddy ground. He continued to walk forward against his suit's greater resistance.

"Villiers never did anything right," another voice guffawed. "Not even die."

"Lord Golsingh," Hansen shouted twenty meters from the

armored warriors, "I challenge whatever champion you choose for a place in your service."

Taddeusz turned to Golsingh. "This is a slave," the warchief said.

"He's dressed as a warrior," Golsingh responded, quirking a smile at Hansen. "And of course he boasts like a warrior." The king had short, curling hair and a down-turned moustache. "I think he deserves to die like one."

Taddeusz shrugged. "Zieborn," he said. "Kill him."

The warrior wearing a phoenix stepped forward. A long arc sprang from his right gauntlet and swung toward Hansen in a curve.

Hansen stopped dead. He squeezed his right index and middle fingers together so that the arc at their tip shrank to a coating like St. Elmo's Fire, the greatest flux density of which his suit was capable. He felt a tingle in his right arm as he blocked the attack, but it was Zieborn's arc which failed momentarily with a pop.

The bigger, better-armed warrior boomed a curse. He stepped forward with his arc-weapon ablaze again, shortened to the length of his forearm.

"Off!" Hansen ordered his own AI and lunged toward his opponent with all his suit's power concentrated on movement.

Zieborn must have expected Hansen to back-pedal—or flee, subliminally thinking of the armor as the poor excuse for a warrior who'd worn the suit most recently and died in it. Golsingh's champion swiped horizontally.

Hansen was already within his opponent's guard. He grabbed Zieborn's right wrist with his left hand, shouted "Cut!" to his AI, and carved upward in a shower of sparks from belly to throat.

The painted phoenix sputtered away from the armor in a gout of ash and gold leaf. The underlying metal pitted but did not burn.

Zieborn's electronic armor was proof to the worst punishment Hansen's arc could deliver; and the other man's arm was forcing his weapon toward Hansen's face.

"Off!" cried Hansen and shifted his suit's full strength into his grip on Zieborn's right wrist.

Hansen had survived because he was very quick and—when he had to be—very strong. He was very possibly stronger than the king's champion now, just as he'd out-thought the man and jumped into a clinch before the other could respond.

And it didn't matter, because the crucial factor was the amount of power available to the armor—not to the human muscles within the suit.

Hansen's display overloaded with the intensity of the sizzling arc and blacked out. The weapon made a sound like a crow laughing. Its negative image forced itself inexorably toward Hansen's eyes like the tongue of a dragon.

He braced his right hand against Zieborn's armored neck and pushed, with no effect on what the warrior was doing. If Hansen twisted away and tried to run, his opponent's arc would extend and cut collops from the back of Hansen's flimsy suit. So—

Receptors crackled and a quadrant of Hansen's display went dead. The edge of Zieborn's tight weapon had touched Hansen's helmet.

"*Shoot!*" Hansen cried. The jolt left him blind, deafened, and tingling all over as if he'd been living in the heart of the lightning.

But Zieborn's snarling arc hadn't come through his helmet, destroying Hansen's eyes with a metallic plasma even before the electricity itself converted flesh to traceries of carbon.

Hansen reached down to his left side, forcing his suit unaided against the friction of all its powerless joints. He tugged the catch open, then pulled the plastron away from the backplate. Sunlight flooded in.

So did the smell of burned flesh.

There was a babble of voices, angry or amazed in tone, but Hansen didn't bother to process the words until he'd struggled free of the armor. Being trapped in the suit with its ventilation system and all receptors as dead as so many bricks was a more claustrophobic feeling than he had expected.

But Zieborn was dead too. His suit had lost its luster, and in the center of its neck joint was a hole no larger than a worm bores in an apple. Smoke drooled from the hole and from the louvered vents beneath the arms. That was why the air smelled like a bad barbeque.

The other two armored warriors waited impassively, but a freeman pointed his crossbow at the center of Hansen's chest. The quarrel had a four-lobed steel head.

"Put that fucker down or I'll feed it up your asshole!" Hansen snarled. The menace of his voice slapped the freeman back a pace, lifting his weapon as his mouth fell open.

Hansen's suit and his opponent's remained frozen and upright where they stood. A chickadee fluttered by so close that a wing brushed the hair which sweat plastered to Hansen's head. It lighted on top of Zieborn's helmet and said in a tiny voice that only Hansen seemed to hear, "The second rule of war is that in war, there are no rules."

"Lord Gol—" Hansen said. His voice broke. His throat was dry, dry as bleached bones.

"Lord Golsingh," he said, "I claim a place with you."

"We know nothing of this—" Taddeusz said to his king with a face as red as a wolf's tongue.

"And I claim," Hansen continued in a rasping, savage voice, "the armor of this man I killed in fair combat."

"We know," said Golsingh to his foster father, "that he can fight."

The king looked down from his pony toward Hansen and went on, "Your first request is granted . . . Hansen, wasn't it?"

Hansen nodded. He wondered if he was expected to bow.

"Your second request is not granted," Golsingh continued with a cool, vaguely detached expression. "Zieborn's armor goes to his eldest son, as is proper."

Hansen felt his face harden. He'd learned the importance of good equipment here, if he'd learned nothing else this day.

"But I think you've proved your right to a suit of comparable quality from the loot we took from Lopez," Golsingh went on. He glanced toward the curve of his retainers.

"Get him a horse, someone," the king snapped imperiously. "And get this gear loaded up. The women are probably worried about what's going on."

A pair of slaves pushed forward with a saddled pony, perhaps the one Zieborn had ridden until he was ordered to deal with the intruder.

"Oh," Golsingh said, "and bring Villiers' suit as well. It doesn't seem to have been as valueless as we'd assumed."

Chapter Eight

One of the human servants held up a mirror of polished ice. Fortin checked the set of his saucer hat, adjusted the brim slightly, and stepped into the discontinuity around which the central hall of his palace was built.

On the other side of *this* twig of the Matrix lay a swamp shadowed by giant ferns in the plane which his ancestors—

—his mother's ancestors—

—inhabited. This time, however, Fortin's destination was not so much a part *of* the Matrix as apart *from* it. For a moment, Fortin heard the boom of something in a warm pool swelling its throat in a mating call, while his eyes were still locked with those of his servant, impassive until the Master was well and truly gone.

Fortin let his mind step sideways . . .

And his feet were on solid ground, beneath the sullen sky of Ruby. A company of soldiers in battledress stood at attention before Fortin. The guns of a dozen huge armored vehicles were trained on him without even a vague attempt to be discreet about their caution.

A communications specialist stood beside the officer in command of the drawn-up company. The officer keyed the handset flexed to the com-spec's radio and said, "This is Bonecrack Three. The Inspector General has arrived. Out."

The officer stepped forward and saluted Fortin sharply. "Sir!" he said. "I'm Major Brenehan, in charge of your escort. We're very glad to have you with us again."

Fortin responded a deliberately languid salute which he knew would infuriate Brenehan—infuriate anyone in Ruby, with its total dedication to precision and lethal efficiency. He wanted their help, but he couldn't keep from insulting them. It made him *hate* himself—

But then, Fortin hated himself anyway, most of the time. At least most of the time.

69

He smiled at Brenehan, flicked a non-existent bit of dust from the breast of his uniform, and said, "Very good, Major. I wish to confer with the High Council at their earliest convenience."

"Yes sir," said Brenehan. "At once, sir."

The major took the handset again and began speaking a series of codewords into it. The infantrymen remained at attention.

The tanks continued to point their main guns at the spot where Fortin had appeared, and where he continued to stand.

There was a pause in the radio conversation.

"You're very security conscious," Fortin said with a smile.

Brenehan looked as if the visitor had commented on the fact that they didn't smear their faces with pigshit. "Yes sir," he said guardedly. "We are. Of course."

The radio chattered to Brenehan. He replied in a series of precise monosyllables, his eyes on Fortin. Finally he nodded and returned the handset to the com-spec.

"Very good, sir," the major said. "If you'll come with me, we'll take you to the meeting site."

The infantry fell out of formation in response to an order Fortin didn't notice. Brenehan nodded toward an armored personnel carrier grounded behind the troops, then began striding to the vehicle without looking around to see if the visitor were following.

"What if I wanted to meet the Council at General Headquarters?" Fortin asked, speaking louder in order to be heard over the rising note of the APC's lift engines.

"I don't think that will be necessary, sir," Major Brenehan said.

He offered Fortin the jumpseat near the door, where the commanding officer usually sat. A platoon of infantry piled aboard the vehicle behind them. The remainder of the company loaded onto the other three APCs. They took off with a roar of fans even as the last trooper slammed the door behind her.

There was a joystick attached to the seat. Fortin gripped it and toggled the switch that should give him a full holographic display—where they were, where they were going, and maps of any other region of Ruby he chose to view.

Nothing happened. Very security conscious, even with the Inspector General. . . .

"But if I *did* want to visit General Headquarters?" Fortin pressed, knowing that it was his self-destructive impulse working again.

"You'd have to take that up with the Council itself, sir," said Brenehan. He stood beside the seat which would normally have been his, bracing himself against the armored ceiling as the vehicle pitched and bucked. The soldiers facing outward in a double line were robotically impassive as they checked and rechecked their weapons and other gear.

Fortin smiled at him. "I'm impressed by the way you always pick up my arrival," he said.

"Well, sir," Major Brenehan replied with a smile of satisfaction, "any disruption to Ruby is a potential threat. And even you, sir, if you'll pardon my saying so . . . are a disruption."

The flight to the rendezvous point took twenty minutes, but Fortin suspected that part of the time was spent in direction changes which only security required. The instant the car touched down, its sidewalls hinged flat with a *bang/bang* and the platoon of infantry lunged out with their rifles and multi-discharge energy weapons pointed. The accompanying APCs had also grounded and were disgorging their troops.

They'd landed on a volcanic plain, patterned in grays and greens by lichen. Other troops were already in position, nestled into crevices between the ropes of cold lava. Fortin noted that the waiting troops were equipped with crew-served weapons as well as the lighter hardware which his escort/guard carried.

There was no sign of the Council, just troops.

Fortin rose with dignity and walked toward the other position. Brenehan's men—the Inspector General's men—ported arms and fell in to either side of him. Some of the devices being pointed at Fortin were scanners rather than weapons, peering into the visitor and his equipment to make sure no threat was intended.

There was no question about where the priorities in Ruby lay: the Council was greater than the Inspector General—but Security was greatest of all.

A colonel stood, gestured Fortin within the perimeter, and spoke into a radio like that which followed Brenehan. Then he saluted Fortin and said, "Good to have you with us, sir. It'll be just a moment more."

There was a heavy drumming from the western sky. Another squadron of armored personnel carriers swept in low and fast. Most of the APCs landed in the near distance, but one crossed the perimeter and dropped only meters from where Fortin stood. Its fans blew hot grit across his face and uniform.

A door in the side of the vehicle opened. The uniformed woman within looked like a hatchetfaced leprechaun. "Sir?" she said. "We've brought a mobile command post. If you'd care to join us?"

Fortin stepped inside and met the stares of the five members of the Council who waited in a formal at-ease posture around a central table/display console. The ceiling of the command-post vehicle was twenty centimeters higher than that of a standard APC; even Marshal Czerny, as tall and thin as North himself, bent forward only slightly.

Marshals Czerny, Kerchuk, Tadley—the tiny, sharp-featured woman—Moro, and Stein. They wore the gorgets of their supreme rank, but their camouflaged battledress contrasted with the pearl gray of Fortin's parade uniform.

The arrogance of those in Ruby amused Fortin—and frightened him. *If you'd care to join us?* after they'd danced him to their tune—and would continue, in one way or another, no matter what the Inspector General said, to do whatever they felt was necessary.

He could order the Council to commit suicide *now*, in front of him without explanation—and they would obey. But if his orders threatened Ruby, or might threaten Ruby—if the Inspector General absolutely required to be taken to General Headquarters . . . then obedience would be very slow indeed, and all possible administrative means would be taken beforehand to limit the potential damage.

Arrogance, but the arrogance of duty. Nothing came before that: not life, and certainly not the Inspector General. The folk of Ruby *believed* with a frightening intensity, while their visitor believed in no one, in nothing, except perhaps in his own godlike cleverness.

"Sit down, comrades," Fortin said, gesturing his hosts to the seats around the display but continuing to stand himself. "I have a technical problem for you."

He smiled with chill humor. "I think you might find it amusing."

Czerny nodded sharply, part agreement, part prodding.

"Let us postulate for the moment," Fortin continued, "that Ruby is a segment of phased spacetime in a larger universe—"

"Yes, yes," Stein murmured. "We accept that."

"—but that you are balanced *within* the matrix of that universe with a precisely opposite bubble universe."

Moro's chubby fingers were gliding across his keypad. The air before him quivered with a holographic display, intelligible only from the aspect of the intended user's eyes. "Balanced in what sense, sir?" he asked/demanded briskly.

"In every sense, Marshal Moro," Fortin replied.

"Our military equals, then?" Tadley said.

"Quite the contrary," said Fortin, reveling in the glow of interest replacing caution in the eyes of those watching him. "Your *opposites* in the arts of war. Your perfect balance."

A gust of wind traced across the lava flats, curling fiercely enough to make the vehicle tremble. Wisps of air with a sulphurous tang crept through the vehicle's climate control.

"So . . . ," said Moro, his fingers still, then dancing again. "So. . . ."

"If such a target existed," said Fortin, "how would you go about attacking it?" He smiled again.

"A number of the possibilities which occur to me now . . . ," said Kerchuk. His voice was rich and cultured in contrast to his scarred, brutal face; he had only one arm.

". . . would involve support for the operation from outside Ruby," he continued. "Are we to postulate that, sir? And if so, what are the param—"

"Under no circumstances are you to postulate outside assistance, Marshal Kerchuk," Fortin said sharply. "This operation is to be planned for execution by resources available within Ruby alone."

"On the face of it," said Moro as he stared at his display rather than the visitor, "an impossible task. The operational unit's first requirement, of course, would seem to be exiting from Ruby—from the universe."

"And even if that problem could be solved—" said Stein.

"It *can* be solved," interjected Tadley. "A way can be found."

Stein looked at her. "Your confidence does credit to your optimism, Marshal," he said caustically. He raised his eyes to Fortin again. "Even were that problem solved, if we and this postulated target are *truly* in balance—"

"Then it will flee through general spacetime at precisely the rate at which our operational unit pursues," said Kerchuk with a broken-toothed grin. "An interesting problem indeed."

"There's also the difficulty of *locating* the target," Stein mused aloud.

"No difficulty at all," Tadley snapped decisively. "If they're really our—other selves, shall we say—then locating us locates them as well."

Even Stein and Moro nodded agreement with that.

"If I may ask, Inspector General . . . ," said Marshal Czerny in a voice like stones rubbing. "What is the purpose of this proposed attack?"

Fortin hesitated a moment. "The total destruction of the objective," he said crisply.

"Yes," said Czerny, licking his lips. "I supposed it might be that."

"This will take study," Tadley said. "We'll refer it to Contingency Planning and see what they come up with."

"I think," said Marshal Czerny, "that the matter will go directly to the Battle Center rather than Contingency. Although we will treat it as contingent unless and until we receive an execution order."

He raised an eyebrow toward Fortin.

Fortin smiled again. "Yes, that will do quite well," he said. "I'll return to see what you have determined."

He paused. "It's necessary to identify all potential threats in order to defend against them, of course," he added.

"Of course," murmured the voices around the display.

All of them were grinning like sharks. All six of them.

Chapter Nine

"Welcome to Peace Rock," said Malcolm, the powerfully built warrior who'd worn the red-blue-silver armor as he'd watched over Hansen's duel with the late Zieborn. Malcolm had a *café au lait* complexion and a rich baritone voice that was musical even in its sarcasm.

A mammoth raised its trunk and hooted loudly as it walked through the gate in the outer 'defenses,' merely a wooden palisade. But then, stone and reinforced concrete would be no better protection against the warriors' arc weapons.

"It was Blood Rock under Golsingh's old man," said Shill, who seemed to be one of Malcolm's hangers-on; a crabbed, older warrior one short step up from Villiers, whose corpse and armor had been abandoned on the field. "Golsingh changed it, because he's gonna bring peace to the whole kingdom. *He* says."

"Don't matter," said Maharg, a hulking young warrior and also under Malcolm's vague protection. "There's plenty work for us while he's bringin' peace."

"This is the capital?" Hansen said. "This is the *king's* capital?"

Peace Rock was a village of mud streets and houses whose thatched roofs arched over meter-high drystone foundations. It stank of beasts—mammoths, ponies, and huge bison with polled horns, stabled within stone fences—and of excrement, obviously from the population as well as from their livestock. Women and children, their varied status indicated by the quality of their clothing, greeted the returning army.

Peace Rock's only substantial building was in the center of the community: a hall forty meters long and almost half that in breadth. Hansen judged the roof to be ten meters high at the peak, but its thatched expanse swept down to waist height at either side. Smoke from an open hearth boiled out beneath both end gables.

Slaves had begun unloading the mammoths and collecting

75

the ponies for feed and grooming. Many of the freemen were disappearing into squalid huts with women in tow. Nothing like an afternoon of slaughter to bring men to the need for reaffirming life in the most basic fashion possible. . . .

Hansen nodded to the hall. Dozens of male and female servants—and a pair of young women too beautiful and beautifully dressed to be less than nobles—waited at the entrance to greet Golsingh and Taddeusz.

"Is that Golsingh's palace, then?" he asked the trio of warriors whom he'd permitted to take him under their wing.

"That's the hall," said Malcolm. "You'll sleep there, until you find a woman with a hut of her own."

He looked sharply at Hansen. "Why, do you do it differently in Annunciation?"

Hansen shrugged. "Not really," he said noncommittally.

His coveralls had lasted the run and struggle in the battlesuit, but they weren't sufficient garb for a winter evening. Where the skin was chafed, Hansen's limbs burned in the cold. He was going to need additional clothing—furs, like those the freemen and warriors wore—heat, and food, all very quickly, or exposure was going to finish what Zieborn had attempted.

The richly-dressed blond woman put her arms around Golsingh and kissed him. As if that slipped the leashes of the others gathered before the hall, the servant women broke ranks into the returning warriors like a covey of quail lifting.

Malcolm patted Shill and Maharg on the shoulder and said, "Later, gents." He strode forward and lifted a buxom redhead off her feet as she threw herself into his arms. A touch of embroidered hem showed beneath her fur cloak.

"Lucky bastard," Shill muttered, but there was more pride than envy in his voice.

"We'll do all right," Maharg said, looking around the crowd. "'specially tonight, since there'll be some bunks cold otherwise."

A woman with an infant at her breast and a child of three clinging to her dress suddenly began to wail in heartbreak. Maharg watched her, flat-eyed.

The black-haired noblewoman took Taddeusz' hands in hers and dipped her head. The warchief bowed back to her.

Hansen frowned. "His wife?" he said. "Taddeusz' wife, I mean?"

"Krita," explained Shill. "His daughter. Don't touch her."

"Won't have much choice 'bout touching her at battle practice," said Maharg with a note of gloomy memory. "Fancies herself a real warmaiden. Wouldn't be surprised she goes for one of North's Searchers."

"North?" said Hansen, suddenly shocked by memory of the mission that had sent him *here*. "There's a man named North here?"

"No, no," said Shill in aged peevishness. "The god North. Where did you say you came from?"

"Look," said Hansen, "if I don't get near a fire, it won't *matter* where I came from. Can we go inside? Somewhere?"

Maharg shrugged. "Why not?" he said and stamped toward the entrance to the hall.

Golsingh, Taddeusz, and the women who'd greeted them were already going in, talking with animation. The blond paused for a moment in the doorway and looked back over her shoulder at Hansen.

"Unn, the king's wife," said Shill grimly. "And if she don't wear armor much the way Krita does, don't let that fool you. She's a tough one too. And she don't want anybody tryin' t' put one over on Golsingh."

Hansen snorted. "If Golsingh wanted to listen to me," he said, "I just might make him a real king. But I don't guess that'll happen."

The interior of the hall was dimmer than the twilight outside, but it was warm—which was rapidly becoming the only thing in the world that Hansen cared about.

The center of the long room was a hearth. Board cubicles, each with its own door, ran down either sidewall. Between the hearth and the cubicles, a U of trestle tables was arranged with benches on their wall side. Two carved chairs supplied the cross-table at the far end in place of a bench.

The whole thing was barbaric and pre-technological; whereas the warriors' armor was extremely sophisticated—though idiosyncratic.

And there was a god named North somewhere, for a man-hunter named Hansen to find and to deal with.

Golsingh and Taddeusz seated themselves on the two chairs.

To Hansen's surprise, Krita and Unn took cups of jeweled metal from servants and offered them to the leaders instead of joining them at the table.

The face of Golsingh's blond wife was as cool as the surface of a forest pond which hides all the life beneath its reflection. Taddeusz' dark daughter Krita had high cheekbones and eyes like fire glinting from a hatchet blade. She wore a sleeveless tunic of blue brocade, cinched with a belt of gold. Her sinewy arms had calluses at the wrists and elbows, places where Hansen's armor had rubbed him raw.

Hansen had been busy enough taking stock of his new surroundings that he hadn't paid attention to the way his companions hesitated beside him while other warriors seated themselves at the benches. Servants stood on the inner side of the U—where the hearth must've been damned uncomfortable against their calves. They were slicing joints and ladling stewed vegetables onto plates.

Shill muttered something and scuttled toward a bench about halfway between the chairs and the door. Hansen followed, hungry enough not to realize that something beyond open seating was involved.

Maharg hung back. "Malcolm's not here," he said.

The benches were filling. Shill glanced over his shoulder, hesitated—but carried out his original intent. Maharg grimaced as he seated himself to the older man's right—throne—side; and Hansen squeezed in beside Maharg.

"How do I get proper clothi—" Hansen began as a female servant set a plate covered with broiled meat—half-burned, half-raw—and stewed vegetables before him.

The man to Hansen's right turned and gripped him by the ear. "What do *you* think you're doing here, you slave's whelp?" the man demanded.

The corner of Hansen's eye placed the carving knife—too far—and the serving fork—just right, as the servant froze in surprise. The warrior who held him was big, young, and very angry. Hansen didn't know the etiquette at Peace Rock, but he did know that in a fraction of a second, Nils Hansen would be discussing the matter with the survivors, over the body of the man beside him.

"I think," said Malcolm, taking the other man by both ears from behind, "that he's the guy who took your brother one-on-one, Letzing. Which you—" Letzing's fingers relaxed as Malcolm twisted "—couldn't've managed in a million years. So what're *you* doing up-bench of him?"

Malcolm lifted Letzing deliberately from his seat. Everyone in the hall was watching, but no one attempted to interfere.

Letzing stumbled as Malcolm walked him backward off the bench. "You wouldn't do this to me if my brother were here!" he cried out unexpectedly.

Malcolm let him go and said brutally, "Zieborn's not here. He's dead. Want to try me tomorrow and join him? Want to try me tonight?"

Letzing was broader than Malcolm and almost as tall, but you didn't need Hansen's experience to realize that it would be the contest of the axe and the firelog if Letzing accepted the challenge.

Letzing knew that too. He turned away and stamped across to a seat on the other side of the hall—and well down the bench. Malcolm took his place, looked at Hansen, and said, "Well, we're the bold lad, aren't we? But if Maharg doesn't mind, I certainly don't."

Maharg forked a slice of meat into his mouth and said mushily, "Aw, it don't matter. I figured I'd let him sit beside you this once, is all."

The meat was unseasoned, tough, and cut into larger chunks than Hansen was used to putting in his mouth. He chewed and stared at Maharg until the powerfully built young man met his eyes.

Hansen swallowed. "And then again," he said deliberately, "maybe this is how it's going to stay."

Maharg flushed and took a spoonful of turnips and potatoes. He didn't reply.

Malcolm guffawed and accepted the cup handed him by the redheaded woman he'd embraced on returning. "Quite the lad," he repeated.

The food was not so much bad as boring, and the beer that was the only available drink had a musty undertaste. Still, Hansen was hungry enough to have chopped a piece of one of the draft

mammoths if nothing else were available. He concentrated
happily on his meal.

While the warriors ate, slaves carried suits of armor into the
hall and placed each in one of the cubicles along the sidewalls.
Malcolm nudged Hansen and said, "That's yours," pointing to
the quartet of slaves who had just entered with a russet and
black suit.

"The arm's cut off," Hansen said, trying to keep the concern
out of his voice.

"Don't worry," Malcolm explained. "It's a good suit. We'll carry
it to Vasque the Smith tomorrow and get it repaired."

"It's a *damned* good suit," muttered Shill.

Maharg turned on the old warrior and snarled, "So why didn't
you ever challenge Zieborn and get a suit just as good, ha?"

"Maharg," said Malcolm quietly.

"Yeah, well," said the younger man as he went back to his
food.

Taddeusz' daughter took a silver pitcher of beer from a servant
and walked down the runway between the fire and table. Her
soft shoes made no sound on the hall's puncheon floor. Golsingh,
Unn and—with dawning fury—Taddeusz watched her progress.

She stopped in front of Hansen. He looked up in surprise.

"Krita!" the warchief shouted.

Krita bent and filled Hansen's cup.

"I want to meet the new hero," she said in a clear voice that
rang in the sudden silence. "The wolf in Villiers' clothing."

"Some would say," Unn called with equal clarity down the
length of the table, "that it's a coward's part to slay a man with
a bolt."

Hansen went cold. He looked in Unn's direction, but he saw
nothing except a blur of blond hair and his own cold fury.
"Zieborn wouldn't say that, milady," he said loudly.

A warrior across the hall snorted. "That's tellin' her, buddy!"
he shouted. The whole room rocked with laughter as heavy fists
pounded the tables in amusement.

Krita raised an eyebrow and walked back to the other end of
the room.

Taddeusz stood up. The hall quieted.

"I served my king this day as no other man has done," the

warchief boomed in what Hansen realized after a moment was a set speech. "Alone I strode among my king's enemies—" *nearly true, and nothing for a sensible man to boast about* "—and smote them down by the scores. Cerausi, the warchief of Count Lopez, a mighty hero, dared stand against me. His armor was silver and blue. He struck at me—"

Hansen began to nod. He was exhausted; the fire warmed him, and much of his blood supply was in his belly, converting the heavy meal into strength for the morrow.

He looked around covertly to see how the other warriors were reacting to Taddeusz' speech. They were just as tired as Hansen, and most of them had been much less sparing with the beer. Several had already collapsed in place. Servants worried the plates and remains of food out from under them.

Hansen heard dogs yelping outside, but at least they weren't being allowed in the hall during the meal as he'd rather expected would be the case. Reassured that the worst he was likely to do would be within the bounds of propriety here, Hansen slid his dish out of the way and concentrated on keeping awake.

After Taddeusz finished his speech, the warrior at the head of the bench to the king's left rose and rambled off on a boast of his own. No one seemed to listen to him—or, for that matter, to any of the warriors who followed him with equally boring harangues. As soon as one warrior sat down, the next—across the hall—got up, even if they'd been snoring on the table a moment before.

It was noticeable that the farther down the benches the speakers were, the shorter and less circumstantial their boasts tended to be.

The man across from Hansen stopped in the middle of a sentence that hadn't seemed to be going anywhere. He didn't so much sit down as flop when his legs gave way. A servant handed him a refilled cup.

Maharg elbowed Hansen. "Well, go on!" he said.

"But—" Hansen said. He stood, shaking his head to clear it. All right, he hadn't been in the battle, and he wasn't going to brag about killing Zieborn . . . or anybody else. Zieborn hadn't been the first, or the twenty-first; but that had been the job of Special Units.

"I won't tell you what I've done," Hansen said, raising his voice over the sound of snores and servants clearing dishes. "That's little enough so far, here in your country. And I won't boast about what I'm going to do in the next battle or the next hundred battles. But—"

Hansen turned to the cross-table. Taddeusz was—no, the warchief *wasn't* asleep, for his eyes snapped firmly shut when Hansen stared at him. Golsingh was watching; and Krita, and Unn. . . .

"But Lord Golsingh, if it's your true desire to bring peace to all your kingdom—peace that stands, not a battle here and a feud there, always and forever, for you to stamp out and go on to the next—"

The king was nodding. The women's faces didn't change.

"Then I can show you how to do it."

"That isn't a warrior's part!" Taddeusz shouted, raising his head from his crossed arms. Golsingh looked at him with a frown.

"I'll do a warrior's job when there's fighting," Hansen snapped. "But I'll let you do a king's job, Lord Golsingh—if you really want that!"

He sat down abruptly, before he said too much—if he hadn't already. The beer's unpleasant taste covered a surprising kick.

Another warrior rose and maundered unintelligibly.

Hansen fell asleep while the last warriors spoke.

Clashing metal—a dropped cup—awakened him. The hearth had burned to coals, but there was still enough light to see forms hunched at the tables. Half the room was empty, but many of the warriors were continuing to drink and mumble to one another.

"Malcolm, where do I bunk?" Hansen asked, hoping he'd correctly identified the man to his right.

A servant stepped between the coals and Hansen. "More beer, hero?" she asked.

Not a servant. Krita.

"No," Hansen said curtly. "And you can call me a hero when you believe it yourself. Not now."

The black-haired woman laughed. "How good are you, Hansen?" she asked.

"Good enough," he said. "As good as I—"

He paused. "I'll tell you this, lady," he said in sudden decision. "I'm the best there is. That's how good I am."

He turned his back on her throaty chuckle. He was pretty sure he remembered which cubicle he'd seen them carry the russet and black armor into.

Malcolm put a hand on Hansen's shoulder. "That one," he said, pointing to a doorway.

"Thanks."

"Quite the lad," Malcolm said. "You know, boy—"

Hansen paused at the doorway and looked back.

"—I'm not sure I'm going to want to know you," Malcolm finished.

And he chuckled as he sat down on his bench again, but Hansen was pretty sure the comment had been more than a joke.

Chapter Ten

There was just enough sunlight percolating through the walls of the bed cubicle for Hansen to see his breath in a chill cloud.

Hansen straightened his arms; the heavy fur bedclothes resisted. He groaned and swung himself out of bed at once, because it wasn't going to get better—and if he didn't have the guts to face the morning, any morning, then he'd spent his life in a variety of the wrong businesses.

The parts of Hansen's body that didn't ache jabbed when he made them move. Twenty-nine was too old for this crap; he ought to leave it for the new crop of bright-eyed nineteen-year-olds who healed fast, who didn't know how badly they could get hurt—

Who hadn't seen enough other people die to realize that they would be among that number very soon themselves.

On the other hand, Taddeusz had been in the heart of the battle, and he was damned near old enough to be Hansen's father. Which probably proved that older didn't necessarily mean wiser . . . and that Hansen wouldn't be ready to hang it up at Taddeusz' age either.

Things had bitten him in the night. Hansen told himself he'd get used to that. He'd better. The jakes here were an open pit with a crossbar and a perfunctory windbreak—damned cold last night, and he'd get used to that too; though he figured either to find or invent a chamber pot before evening.

Hansen's battlesuit stared blankly at him from the foot of his bed.

Hansen opened the door of his cubicle to let in more light. The latch was a bar set in heavy staples, an unexpectedly sturdy arrangement given the flimsy construction of the bed chamber itself. Slaves, sweeping the night's debris into the hearth with straw brooms, dropped their voices when they saw one of the warriors was up—and chattered again when they saw it was Hansen.

Only Hansen. Well, he'd been a newbie before, in the Civic Patrol and later when he transferred to Special Units. If he survived the next few months, he'd have as much respect as he wanted.

Hansen examined his new battlesuit. It was a noticeably solider unit than the one from which he'd ejected Villiers' corpse. The difference was not so much in the weight of the metal—equating mass with sturdiness was an error out of which he'd trained himself long before—but in the fit of the various sections.

The lining was thick suede. It wouldn't keep his skin from chafing, but it was probably as good a material as could be found for the purpose here. Hansen found to his surprise that it wasn't slick with dry, clotted blood down the left side, because the arc that burned off the former owner's arm had also cauterized the blood vessels.

The severed piece lay on the floor in front of the rest of the suit. Hansen rotated it in his hands, looking at the line of bubbled metal and the core of integrated circuits, shattered and blackened by high-temperature cutting.

Repairing *this* wasn't a job for a smith on a feudal backwater. It would require technicians of exceptional competence—

And by watching the work done, Hansen might just find the path to North and the answers the Consensus had sent him to find.

The door of the cubicle next to Hansen's opened. "You look cheerful," said Malcolm, though the way he said it indicated that he'd noticed more than humor in Hansen's grin.

"What are you doing here?" Hansen asked in surprise. "I assumed you'd be . . ."

"Nancy, you mean?" Malcolm said with a smile of his own. His features were as perfect as his voice, and his tawny complexion looked almost golden in the diffused sunlight. "I was on duty last night—we sleep night and night in the hall, here at Peace Rock. Taddeusz is very firm about that."

Hansen nodded. "Something we can agree on," he said.

Malcolm smiled more broadly. "It isn't considered good form to entertain your friends in your chamber here," he went on. "But it's been known to happen, particularly the night after a battle."

"You, ah . . . ," Hansen said. "I'm not sure . . . do you have formal ranks here? That is, what's *your* rank, for instance?"

"Where do I sit at table, do you mean?" said Malcolm with a puzzled expression. "But you saw—"

He grinned again. "Ah, you drank more than I thought. I've been on the lower end of the left side, but after yesterday's battle I'd decided to move to the middle—even before you put yourself in my train."

So that was why Malcolm had been so friendly. He was himself an ambitious outsider, trying to build status by increasing the number of warriors under his protection.

"Not everybody would say I was a desirable supporter," Hansen commented aloud.

"Not everyone would," Malcolm agreed, nodding. "What do you say, my bold laddie?"

Hansen met the veteran's eyes and said, very deliberately, "I say that in a year, you'll be sitting in Taddeusz' seat. If you want to."

Malcolm looked around sharply to see if any of the slaves were within earshot—a precaution Hansen had taken before he spoke.

"I think you've just convinced me that the others are the smart ones," Malcolm said.

He nodded toward the damaged armor. "Let's get your suit repaired," he added. "And let's you not talk about things that don't concern either of us."

"All right," said Hansen. He got a grip on the suit. "Where do we go with—"

Malcolm swatted his hands aside. "Where do you come from?" he said in amazement.

He turned to the cleaning crew. "Hey!" he called. "You lot! Get over here and carry Lord Hansen's armor to the smithy."

Good humored again—Hansen's stated plans had frightened Malcolm, but the notion of a warrior doing scut work had offended him—the veteran warrior smiled and said to Hansen, "There should be some furs in Alyn's chest—at the head of the bed."

He gestured into the bed cubicle. "Knock the lock off if there is one. Alyn won't mind where he is now, whether North took his soul or Hell did."

There were furs—and they smelled—but they were warm

and the bright sunlight was cheering, although not particularly warm. Hansen wondered idly what season he'd arrived in. It wasn't a question he thought it'd be a good idea to ask.

The smithy turned out to be a long shed against the back of the palisade. Wicker baskets of rock—ore, presumably, but not smelted metals—were piled around the walls. There wasn't a hearth in front of the building as Hansen had expected, and the open fire within was no more than necessary for heat.

Four grunting slaves set the armor just inside the doorway. A fifth started to lay down the arm he carried, but Malcolm stopped him with a snap of his fingers. "Not yet," he said. "Vasque, we have a project for you."

There were already three men in the smithy: a bald old fellow with a wizened face, and two lads in their late 'teens. The old man was seated. One of the youths stood, looking uncertain, and the other lay on a couch, snoring stertorously, beside a table heaped with sand and gravel.

The old man glared. "Then it'll have to wait."

"Wrong, Vasque," said Malcolm. "The king directs that Lord Hansen here be outfitted properly. The king's honor is involved."

"Faugh," muttered Vasque. He stepped to the suit and ran his fingers over first the plastron, then the sheared metal along the cut. The sleeping youth was muttering to himself.

Hansen couldn't judge the status of the smith and his apprentices. Vasque wore a gorgeously-embroidered tunic—though there was a cracked leather apron over it. Even the youths were dressed rather better than many of the warriors.

"Not much of a suit," Vasque said. "Dilmun's work, I wouldn't be surprised, and he was never much."

"Dilmun's good enough to dress the Lord of Thrasey," said Malcolm. "And as for this suit, there were three arcs on it together before it failed."

"On a good day, I suppose Dilmun might be all right," Vasque admitted grudgingly. He took the severed arm from the slave and worked the elbow joint with his hands as he peered at the cut. "Well, we'll see."

The sleeping youth groaned loudly and threw out an arm. After a moment, his eyes opened. The other apprentice helped him sit up on the couch.

Vasque handed the arm back. "Go on, boy, go on," he said to the apprentice, making shooing motions with his hands. "There's king's work to be done."

He turned to the slaves. "Lay it down by the couch, you. I'll take care of it now."

As the slaves laid the damaged suit full-length on the floor, the two youths positioned the arm by it so that the cut ends joined. Vasque himself stepped outside. He came back with his leather apron laden with bits of ore.

"Might need more than this," the old man muttered, "but I think not, I think not. . . ." He arranged his chips and pebbles around the severed arm with as much care as a florist creating a wedding bouquet.

As the master smith worked, the apprentices poked into rubble piled on the table. The youth who'd been sleeping came up with the forearm of a battlesuit. The rock heaped over it was pebble-sized on top, but the portion around the piece itself was fine dust that made Hansen sneeze.

Vasque lay down on the couch the apprentice had vacated. One of the youths took a polished locket on a thong from around his neck.

"Keep back, boy . . . ," the smith murmured.

His eyes, focused on dustmotes dancing in the light, glazed and closed. The apprentices watched with critical interest, while the slaves gaped with amazement as great as that which Hansen tried to conceal.

Asking what in hell was going on would be just as bad an idea as trying to learn what the season of the year was. Besides, Diamond had come pretty close to Hansen's idea of what heaven would be—right down to the fact there'd been no room for *him* there.

That meant Hell wasn't a word he wanted to take in vain on Northworld either.

Vasque was shuddering in his sleep. Hansen gestured toward him. "Is he any good?" he asked Malcolm in an undertone.

"You won't wake him," said Malcolm in a normal voice, as though that were the only reason someone would want to discuss the matter in a whisper. "And yeah, he's very good."

The veteran smiled impishly. "Almost as good as Dilmun, I'd say. You'll have a suit to be proud of."

Malcolm took the piece of armor from the apprentices and looked at it critically. "Who's this for?" he demanded suddenly.

The youth who'd been on the couch said, "Well, it's for stock, milord."

"For practice," added his fellow.

On closer examination, Hansen saw that the portion of armor wasn't complete. It was shorter than most adult male forearms; and, while there was a raised border on the wrist end where the piece would join the gauntlet, there was no corresponding reinforcement toward the elbow. The core of circuitry in a ceramic matrix was white against the heavy metal of the exterior and the lighter cladding of the inner face.

Malcolm handed the piece back. "Keep practicing," he said coldly.

The ore shifted around Hansen's suit. The chunks on top of the pile slid as dust puffed away. As Hansen watched, a fist-sized lump he thought was magnetite crumbled as though in a hammermill. Bits of it drifted down through the interstices of the pebbles beneath it.

One of the apprentices bobbed his head in approval. "Look, he must be four centimeters away from the join," he said. "Great extension!"

Malcolm sniffed. "The important part," he said, ostensibly to Hansen, "isn't how far a smith can reach through the Matrix for material but how well he stitches the result together. *That's* the craftsmanship that keeps you and me alive, Lord Hansen."

"That and skill," Hansen remarked coolly.

He hadn't seen Walker since the duel the day before. That was someone whom he could question without worrying about raised eyebrows.

Of course, while Walker could be a machine from the end of time, as he claimed; or simply a series of talking birds and animals, as he appeared—the likelihood was that the little voice was an aspect of Hansen's psychosis, like everything else around him. Maybe Commissioner Nils Hansen had been shot in the head as he ran toward Solbarth's hideout. . . .

Half the gravel piled on the shoulder of the battlesuit powdered and slipped to a flatter angle of repose.

Vasque shuddered like a swimmer coming out of cold water.

His apprentices stepped toward him, one of them with a skin of wine or mead, but the older man waved them away. "There!" he gasped. "There, Lord Malcolm. Tell me about Dilmun *now*."

"Although," he added as he got to his feet and only then accepted the container of drink, "I checked the whole suit while I was in the Matrix, and it's not so very bad after all. . . ."

"How do we test it?" Hansen asked.

Malcolm smiled. "I get my suit," he said, "we go out to the practice ground . . . and I see just how good you are, laddie."

It wasn't an especially nice smile; but then, neither was the grin that bared Hansen's teeth.

Chapter Eleven

The practice ground was outside the palisade, on a broad, flat stretch of meadow that had been trampled to gluey mud. A bad surface for comfort, but one which accurately reflected the sort of filthy conditions in which wars had been fought from time immemorial. There were fir posts set up at three-meter intervals around the perimeter; many of them had been burned in half.

Hansen was already pleased with his new armor. His displays were crisper by an order of magnitude than those of Villiers' suit, and the limbs moved in response to Hansen's movements without nearly as much lag time.

Of course, getting there and being able to see what he was doing were by no means half the battle.

No other warriors were on the practice ground, but Hansen and Malcolm had attracted a scattering of spectators, both freemen and slaves, on their walk from the hall. A female slave called an offer that Hansen didn't quite catch, but the laughter of the others hinted at the nature of the words.

"All right," said Malcolm. "Let's make sure we're both on practice setting, shall we?" The words had buzzing undertones as they reached Hansen through the speaker in Malcolm's helmet and the headphones in Hansen's.

The veteran's right gauntlet sprouted an arc. He turned and slashed. The weapon scarred a post to the heartwood but didn't blast it apart the way Hansen had seen trees disintegrated during the battle.

He could guess, but: "What's the codeword on your suits?" he asked.

"Huh?" Malcolm responded like a bumblebee. "Practice, of course. I thought that was standard everywhere?"

"Practice," Hansen said, then, "Cut." His arc sizzled into the post, cross-cutting Malcolm's mark to within a degree of perpendicular.

He smiled. Malcolm cut at his head.

Hansen hadn't expected the attack—*my fault*, his mind cursed as he threw himself backward and tried to raise his arc weapon to block Malcolm's. He didn't succeed in either attempt. Malcolm's arc slipped under Hansen's flailing guard and cut across his neck joint.

Hansen's armor froze. His display vanished and left him in blackness lighted only by the afterimages on his retinas.

He wasn't dead. He could feel his heart beating in claustrophobic fear.

"Well," demanded Malcolm's distorted voice, "reset your suit."

Ah. . . . "Reset," said Hansen, hoping that was the key word—though he was becoming increasingly impressed by the flexibility of the suit's artificial intelligence. Light dawned—literally. Hansen's display flooded him with images of morning. He saw Malcolm waiting a pace back, arms akimbo.

Hansen flexed his left gauntlet and cried, "Cut!" as he lunged. Malcolm shifted and slashed down at his attacker, but he hadn't been expecting Hansen to strike from the left. Hansen's thrust struck home at the veteran's hip joint.

There was a shower of sparks. Hansen's arc snuffed unexpectedly, but Malcolm's suit went dull and his empty gauntlet quivered to a halt in mid-stroke.

Hansen had fallen into a three-point stance. He pushed himself erect and backed a step, waiting for Malcolm to reset his armor. "Cut," he muttered, flexing his right hand to be ready for the next attack.

This was work, was heavy exercise. His armor weighed over a hundred kilos. Though that wasn't dead weight so long as it was powered up, inertia gave the suit the resistance of a brick wall for the instant before its servos took over the work from Hansen's muscles.

A long arc twinkled from Malcolm's gauntlet. In practice mode, the discharges were at only a fraction of war power, and interlocks cut off the weapon as soon as its touch had shut down an opponent's armor. It was at least as safe as fighting with buttoned epees, though no doubt accidents could happen.

And it was a good time to explore the capacities of the armor itself.

"Display energy levels," Hansen ordered, wondering what the artificial intelligence would make of the command—and delighted to see Malcolm's suit not as painted steel but as a mosaic in which the visual spectrum mapped electrical activity across the surface of the suit.

The arc sprouting from the veteran's right hand pulsed from indigo through violet. The gauntlet itself was a bright blue, while the remainder of Malcolm's limbs and torso rippled mostly in the yellow and green. The helmet peak was nearly orange, and another orange blotch wavered across the plastron generally at mid-chest level.

It looked like . . .

"Off!" Hansen said, and the hot spot on Malcolm's armor vanished as soon as Hansen's weapon did.

God almighty! Malcolm's artificial intelligence tracked Hansen's arc—and raised the defensive charge of the spot the AI thought most at risk.

The veteran's knee joints streaked orange as power fed to the servos. Malcolm started a lunge but Hansen, alerted by the display, drove forward to anticipate the attack. His left hand slid along Malcolm's right wrist and forearm, and his right hand speared toward the veteran's throat.

Forgot the arc.

"Cut!" and the crackle of harmless sparks ended almost as soon as they'd begun. Malcolm fell over as his circuit breakers tripped. His suit blurred into the dull red background.

Hansen stepped back and reformatted to standard optical display. He was taking deep, gasping breaths. His suit's air system strained between each wheezing exhalation to clear condensate from the displays.

The surface of Malcolm's armor quivered as the veteran reset it. There was no definable change from a suit that was powered up to cold one, but the difference in appearance was as great as that between a living man and a fresh corpse.

Malcolm rose to a four-limbed crouch but paused there. "How did you do that?" he asked.

"It's the display," Hansen explained. His suit's steel casing vibrated every time he spoke. "Look, let's stop this for a minute and I'll show—"

Malcolm gave a brief nod of his armored head. The spectators were turning their heads. Hansen turned also and saw the figure in gleaming black armor striding down the path from the settlement.

"Show *me* what you can do, stranger," the figure called.

Ordered. *Small—as much shorter than Hansen as he was shorter than Malcolm. Wasn't in the battle the day before. A battlesuit of exceptional quality. . . .*

"If you wish it, milord," Hansen said deliberately as the black figure stepped through the line of posts that marked the edge of the practice ground.

"Not 'milord,' you fool!" the figure's harsh mechanical voice snarled. An arc sprang from the right gauntlet.

"Display energy levels," Hansen murmured. The figure before him shimmered in cold blue. *This was going to be . . .*

"Yes, milady," he said aloud. "Krita."

Instead of striding toward Hansen, Krita's hand twisted and shot her arc across the four meters separating them. He didn't have time to think about defense before his displays went dark and left him with his own moist breath.

"Reset," Hansen muttered. "Cut."

He spread his fingers, giving him a broad fan of spluttering discharge. Krita waited, spurting and shrinking the weapon vertically from her right hand. At its peak, the discharge fountained ten meters in the air.

A very good suit indeed.

Hansen stepped forward. Krita's weapon lashed down at him. He caught the blow and shrank his own arc to a tight ball as he took another step—

The arc from Krita's left gauntlet slashed across his knees.

Falling in a dead battlesuit was very similar to being rolled off the porch in a garbage can. It wasn't likely to be fatal. . . .

"Reset. Cut."

Default setting on Hansen's display was standard optical. He didn't bother to switch it over to show energy levels; Krita's battlesuit operated at such a high order that there'd been no significant change in the display when she attacked.

Although—

Hansen rose to a crouch and lunged forward as if to tackle his opponent around the knees. He thought that by leading with his helmet, the focus of his electronic armor, he might be able to get close enough to use his own arc effectively.

A contemptuous sweep of Krita's hand swatted him down. His scalp and the back of his neck tingled, even at the arc's reduced charge level. Hansen grounded face first.

He squatted. His display was fuzzy. He wiped the faceplate of his helmet with his steel palm.

Blobs of mud dribbled from his gauntlet like raindrops blowing across the windshield of a moving vehicle. His display cleared. The suit's electronic defenses worked on fouling; they just took a little time.

Krita laughed. She stood three meters from Hansen with her hands on her hips.

Hansen had cut his chin, and he thought his nose was bleeding. "Cut," he said, flexing his right hand. He snapped the long arc across his opponent's ankles.

Mud hissed away as steam and dust. Krita laughed again, without moving.

"Off," Hansen said and lifted the palm of his left gauntlet toward the woman's throat as he charged.

At this range, a bolt might or might not have been effective enough to end the duel; one had, after all, shut down Taddeusz' battlesuit under similar conditions. Krita'd probably watched Hansen kill Zieborn; certainly she'd had an opportunity to finger the hole the stranger burned through Zieborn's armor and life. . . .

The threat shocked her into a defensive response: limbs rigid, arc weapons shut down; her AI concentrating all the suit's energies on the point the bolt would strike.

There was no bolt. Hansen hit the woman with a crash like anvils meeting, gripping her by both wrists. Even at this range the black battlesuit was probably proof against Hansen's arc—

But his mass and the momentum of his rush carried her backward a half-step until Hansen twisted and threw her over his knee. Krita skidded a meter in slick mud, her limbs flailing.

Hansen stepped back and let his arms hang at his sides. There was no way he could prevent Taddeusz' daughter from taking whatever revenge she chose, but by standing braced he could at least keep from falling over again when she tripped out his circuit breakers.

Krita got up. Her suit streamed mud as if she were under a firehose.

Black fury. . . .

She turned and stamped back toward the palisade. One of the fir posts was in her path. Instead of changing direction, she lashed out with an arc that exploded the base of the post into blazing splinters. A patch of mud hardened to scorched adobe.

Malcolm split his armor and twisted his torso free. "My, my, my," he murmured, watching Krita go.

Hansen opened his own suit also. The outside air turned his sweat into a cold bath. His breath rattled through his open mouth; he hoped his nose wasn't broken.

"My, my," Malcolm repeated. He looked at Hansen. "You know," he said wonderingly. "I think you deserve each other."

"Why wasn't she fighting?" Hansen asked. "You know, yesterday?"

Malcolm looked at him oddly. "Women don't go to war," he said. "Not . . . not here." His face hardened. "Not anywhere I want to be, either."

Hansen withdrew his arms from the battlesuit and massaged his shoulders. The woman in black armor had disappeared into the palisade.

"That's a waste," he said, though it wasn't quite what he meant; and anyway, he wasn't sure what he meant. Cultural factors didn't make a lot of sense here on Northworld—or anywhere else Nils Hansen had been or heard of.

"North has his Searchers," Malcolm said, "and if it were in our Krita's gift, she'd be one of them, you bet."

"Searchers?" Hansen said.

His mind was suddenly back in gear. While he fought Krita, he'd been locked into the notion that only the next microsecond mattered. "Searchers. That's the—black shutters opening and closing? During the battle yesterday?"

"Black wings, yeah," Malcolm agreed, wary again. "Some people say that, I've heard. Nothing I know about myself."

His mouth quirked in a false smile. "Nothing I like to talk about much, to tell the truth."

So there was a way to North . . . maybe.

Hansen thrust his hands back through the armholes and prepared to close his suit over him again. "All right," he said. "Let's get to it. There's a lot I need to learn about this suit before I use it for real."

Malcolm laughed. "Well, you don't have very long to manage that, do you?"

Hansen started to pull the clamshell shut. "Eh?" he said as he strained against the dead weight of the armor. It gave slowly, pivoting like the door of a cell across his view of Malcolm.

"Didn't you know?" called the veteran's voice. "The Lord of Thrasey defied Golsingh also. We'll be—"

Hansen's suit slammed shut. His display flickered to life, and the conclusion of Malcolm's statement buzzed with static.

"—fighting him in three days."

Chapter Twelve

The palace in which Penny lived was a thing of curves and pointed turrets joined by sweeping walkways. Balconies jutted from beneath arched windows, and flagstaffs streamed pennons in the breeze. The walls were slabs of pink marble with pearly inclusions, while the grilles and railings were pure yellow gold.

A central spire, slim and twice the height of any other portion of the palace, swelled at the top into an onion-domed suite.

"I always find it breathtaking," said Rolls dryly from the saddle of his giant elk.

"Indeed, my lord," said Fortin. He walked at Rolls' left stirrup and wore Roll's livery as though he were one of thirty human retainers accompanying their master on his visit to Penny.

Rolls looked down at the half android. They'd chosen slouch hats and capes of bright orange velvet for the retainers on this operation, a costume which hid the wearers' form and features. Penny's human servants wouldn't recognize Fortin, but she herself would if she saw him clearly. Even now that they'd reached the critical stage, Rolls remained sure that there was little chance of that happening.

Trumpeters on the lower balconies of the palace blew a greeting in sequential notes while flags of gold on pink—matching their livery—fluttered from their instruments.

The gate was also golden. The doorleaves, molded with cavorting cherubs, opened with glassy precision as Rolls and his entourage approached them. Hundreds of Penny's servants were drawn up in the entrance hall.

Rolls dismounted. Like his retainers, he wore orange—but briefs that were little more than a jockstrap and matching sandals. He'd been proud of his body before—before North, before godhead. If he was past his first youth and carrying ten kilos more than ideal, then it still was a body that justified pride.

For the moment, the important thing was that all eyes be on him and not on his servants—as was proper in any case.

The trumpet calls ended when Rolls and his entourage entered the hall. String instruments played by hidden servitors took up a melody so saccharine that Fortin murmured to Rolls, "Now the little cupids fly down from the ceiling, don't they?"

The entrance hall had coffered walls with tall sconces on the verticals and mirrors on the sunken central panels. Another set of great doors stood at the top of a pink marble staircase at the far end of the hall.

The music built to a crescendo. The pulses of light rising through the transparent sconces dimmed.

Rolls continued to walk forward. His servants fell off to either side and milled behind the lines of Penny's pink-clad folk. "Good luck," he murmured as the caped-and-hatted figure to his immediate left broke away.

"Good luck to *you*, my friend," Fortin whispered back. "Our Penny expects her standards to be met. . . ."

When Rolls passed the center of the room, the gold doors above the staircase swung open in silent majesty. The vague, mirrored glows of the sconces exaggerated the vast size of the hall.

Penny stood at the head of the stairs, a statuesque vision of beauty and passion. Her hair was black, her complexion as white as bleached flour. Penny's dress and elbow-length gloves were the same brilliant scarlet as her lips, and a single bright jewel gleamed at her throat.

"Greetings, Lord Rolls," Penny called in a throaty contralto. "It has been long since you visited us."

She pouted. In the same voice, but with utterly different intonation she added, "I thought you didn't like me any more."

"You know how jealous I am, my darling," Rolls said as he advanced to the foot of the stairs.

In this outfit, with his hairy, muscular body, he looked like an apeman approaching the mistress of the plantation. Penny would probably find the contrast piquant.

"But I found I couldn't keep myself away from you."

Of course, Penny found most things piquant when they touched on her areas of interest.

She extended a gloved hand to him. "You know the others

mean nothing to me, darling," she said—and giggled, spoiling the effect.

Rolls took the first of the six steps normally, swung his long leg up the next two together, and mounted to the landing in a rush as Penny threw open her arms and allowed him to sweep her off her feet in a passionate embrace.

"Oh, Rolls," she murmured with her eyes closed. "You know I've missed you, honey."

It bothered Rolls that sometimes he had the feeling that Penny was much more intelligent than she seemed. Than she *played*, forming herself into a one-dimensional caricature. . . .

But then, that was what they all did, since godhead, unless they fought the tendency the way Rolls did.

And perhaps even if they did fight.

Rolls nodded upward and lifted his eyebrows. "Ah, can we . . . ?" he asked. The strings had resumed playing, but in whispered undertones of sweetness.

"I thought you'd never ask," said Penny haughtily.

She linked her arm with his and led him back through the gold columns. The doors closed behind them, shutting off the music and the sound of servants chattering as soon as their masters' backs were turned.

The room beyond the doors was a circular foyer, not as large as the entrance hall but huge in its own right. The floor was paved with marble. Around the walls roses had been trained into secluded arbors. Light flooded through high windows.

Rolls' bright sandals whisked on the stone as he led his hostess toward the transparent lift across the room.

Penny glanced down at herself. "How do you like this?" she asked critically.

Rolls paused and kissed her, resting his left hand on her shoulder and his right, caressingly, in the small of her back. In this form, Penny was supple and tall enough that her head reached his chin when they both stood erect.

"Now?" she said, urgent, questioning, hopeful. "Or in the roses?"

She nodded. As she did so, a pair of servants entered the foyer through a door hidden in the foliage, saw their mistress and her guest, and bolted back out of sight.

"No," Rolls said. He didn't have to fake the interest in his voice. "I have an idea."

He led her by the hand to the lift tube, their strides lengthening with each step.

The lift appeared to be an empty three-meter shaft until Rolls and Penny stood on it. The air beneath their feet hardened and they began to rise. A foreshortened figure in pink livery walked across the foyer, unaware of their rising presence.

Penny stroked Rolls' bulging groin. "I thought perhaps . . . ," she said, and as she spoke the figure in the air beside Rolls was shorter, slender, and nude except for the necklace.

"Or even—something unusual?" and she was fat, though her breasts were heavy rather than pendulous. Her hair was black for a moment, then blond, and finally a rich chestnut. She cocked an eyebrow at Rolls.

The lift rose through the ceiling of the foyer and into the shaft of the central tower. Individual rooms opened onto a hall which circled the shaft.

There were railings here. The lift was for Penny, her peers, and those whom her whim chose. It was a straight drop to marble for any ordinary human servant who stepped into the shaft.

Rolls leaned forward and kissed one of the dark nipples, letting it swell under his tongue. "No," he said as he straightened, "I don't think quite . . . ."

Penny licked her lips. She let her body tremble through changes, one after the other, and as she did so her fingers reached under the waistband of Rolls' briefs.

The lift had risen past the servants' quarters, though a spiral staircase circled the shaft. The floors at this height were mostly open rooms whose furnishings were decorated with flounces and lace. Balconies bulged from the other walls.

"What I would like," Rolls said carefully, "is *you*, Penny."

They glided to a halt at the top of the tower. The dome was several times the diameter of the spire that supported it. Its floor area was divided into four suites, each with its own door off the lift shaft.

"Well, of course!" Penny said, throwing open a door into a huge bedroom furnished mostly in white fur. The outer wall was crystal and brilliant in the sunlight.

She looked at her companion in sudden surmise. "Oh . . ." she said. "This old thing?"

The woman before Rolls was suddenly a short, slightly overweight nineteen-year-old, with curly blond hair and pale areolae.

Rolls took Penny's left breast in his hand and kissed her hard on the lips. He stepped back and pulled down his briefs.

"You," he said. He smiled broadly. "On the balcony. But you, not the necklace."

Penny's tongue touched her lips again. Her hands rose and paused around the almost invisibly fine filament that supported the jewel that was all she now wore. Then she lifted it off in a convulsive motion and tossed it toward a dresser whose mirror and cosmetics were needless frills here—like most of this palace, like most of their lives, all of them.

The only change in the woman's appearance was that a mole sprouted on the side of her left breast. Its pigmentation was darker than that of the nipple.

"Come and get me, then," Penny giggled.

She turned and scampered toward the circular balcony. The crystalline panels slid open as she approached.

Rolls followed. It was necessary that he let her run partway around the dome before he caught her.

But he was as ready to catch her as she was to be caught.

Chapter Thirteen

"I hurt," said Hansen, "all over."

He kneaded his thighs viciously as he walked. At least fighting in a battlesuit didn't leave hands cramped the way Hansen's fierce grip on a gun butt invariably did.

Malcolm raised an eyebrow. "You look like you're in shape," he said. "It was a good workout, but . . ."

Hansen checked the double quartet of slaves sullenly carrying the warriors' armor. Malcolm had dragooned the nearest spectators without hesitation when he and Hansen agreed that they didn't feel like walking their own suits back up the half kilometer to the palisade. Furthermore, the train of slaves stumbling along behind them was an excuse for Hansen to walk slowly—and spare his aching legs.

"Yeah, well," Hansen said. "I'm in shape, all right—but I don't have the muscles for this *particular* job. Every piece of equipment you use—and that's as true of a rake as it is of a battlesuit—it takes a little different set of muscles."

A calculated risk.

"But—" said the veteran.

Hansen gripped Malcolm's right hand with his own left. Because of the tan Annunciation's sun had given Hansen, their skin was almost the same shade.

That wouldn't be true long—if he lived.

"Listen, Malcolm," he said. "Where I come from, we don't fight with battlesuits. We've got other weapons, that's all. It doesn't mean I'm not a warrior."

The two men continued to walk, hand in hand. Malcolm's expression was unreadable. Then he broke into a smile and said, "No, I don't doubt that you're a warrior."

He clapped Hansen on the back. "If Zieborn wasn't enough proof," he added, "what you did to me this morning surely is. You'll have to teach me some of those tricks."

They'd reached the palisade. The odor of Peace Rock assailed them, though the fact the citadel was on high ground meant there was *some* drainage.

Hansen nodded seriously. "I'll teach you all of them," he said. "There's still a lot to learn about this armor, and everything I learn, you and, you know, the others. They'll have to learn too, Maharg and Shill."

Malcolm sniffed. "Maybe Maharg," he said, concentrating on his feet. There were boardwalks between the huts, but many sections had sunk down into the mud.

"Both of them," Hansen said. "And later, all the rest after we've shown them that it works. We'll start this afternoon."

Malcolm laughed and strode ahead of his companion. "*You* can play with your armor this afternoon, laddie," he called back over his shoulder. "Nancy and I have some other exercises in mind—particularly seeings as I may get my balls whacked off in three days time!"

There was food being served in the hall. Hansen made do with beer, a slab of cheese and a wedge—torn rather than cut— from a round loaf of bread. Shill and Maharg had cornered Malcolm, though Malcolm continued to slake his thirst without apparent interest in what his hangers-on were saying.

Hansen decided to leave them all alone for the moment. He made sure that his battlesuit was stowed properly, then walked outdoors, munching on his bread.

There were a number of new warriors in the citadel. Some of the men had traveled with their own retinue of freemen, slaves, and baggage mammoths. The king was going to war, the king was hiring warriors.

Most of the would-be recruits lacked even their own battlesuit. Old men like Shill, youngsters like Maharg, with too little skill, training and luck to have won their own equipment.

Golsingh would pack them into whatever equipment he had available. One of those hungry-looking fellows would certainly be wearing Villiers' old suit when Taddeusz led the army out in two days' time.

And maybe the hireling would get lucky; but more likely, the new occupant would wind up the same way Villiers had, dead and forgotten almost before his corpse had frozen in the winter night.

Grit from the flour mill scrunched between Hansen's teeth. He liked the flavor of the bread, though. There were a lot of things he liked about Northworld; and a few he was quite sure that he was going to change, whatever else he did here—if he survived.

Hansen stepped into the smithy, now crowded with new arrivals whose battlesuits required repairs. He'd been fortunate in his timing. A few hours later, after these recruits had arrived and been issued units which needed repair, Hansen wouldn't've had the time he needed to practice with the unfamiliar hardware.

One of apprentices lay on the couch in the center of the shed. Ore was piled on the chest of the armor beside him.

Vasque was arguing with three warriors, each of whom stood beside what Hansen was coming to recognize as a (damaged) battlesuit of reasonable quality. Meanwhile, several lower-status warriors were trying to badger the other apprentice, though the boy was obviously too exhausted even to give coherent answers to the demands being fired at him.

Hansen moved in. "You lot," he snapped. "Get out of the way. You'll be taken care of in good time—better time than you deserve, at any rate."

He sat down beside the apprentice. The hired warriors backed unwillingly, but Hansen's assumption of rank made that rank real among these newcomers—and perhaps generally real in the Peace Rock pecking order.

There were slaves standing against the walls of the single room. Hansen pointed at one and said, "Beer! Something to drink. Now!"

The slave scurried off. People—lower-status people—didn't argue about orders here on Northworld. Of course, Special Units personnel hadn't argued with Commissioner Hansen, either.

As an afterthought, Hansen offered the apprentice a chunk of his bread. The boy took it and began to worry at a corner, not so much out of hunger as in an apparent need to do whatever was put directly in front of him.

"Just how is it that you work on armor?" Hansen asked, pitching his voice reassuringly but glaring at the other warriors to keep them at a distance. "How do you know how to design the circuit architecture, for instance?"

"Uh?" said the apprentice. His eyes were dull with exhaustion. Whatever was involved in fixing battlesuits, it certainly wasn't work that did itself. "Archi . . . ?"

He blinked and focused on Hansen. The warrior's patient interest brought the youth back to the present and the ability to think.

"I go into the Matrix," he said, "and I find the piece I'm supposed to work on. Where it's different from the Matrix, I move things so that it fits. I don't—".

The slave reappeared with a skin of liquid. Hansen took the container and passed it directly to the apprentice. While the youth drank greedily, Hansen asked, "What do you mean by 'the Matrix'?"

It couldn't be whatever Walker had talked about, dimensions and planes of spacetime. . . .

"Well, you know . . . ," the apprentice said. "Though you're not a smith. . . ." His brow furrowed. "It's the way everything's put together, you know, *inside*.

"You're hypnotized, and the first time you need a master to guide you, but it's like—" He gestured with his hands. Beer splashed from the neck of the skin. "—feeling your way through shadows even then."

Hansen nodded gently, to show that he was interested without interrupting the flow of words.

"And it's clearer each time," the young smith said with increasing animation, "but it's still like, you know, kneading mud and ash together into the shape of the armor. Even the master—" he gestured toward Vasque.

His voice lowered conspiratorially. "Even the greatest masters," the apprentice whispered to Hansen, "I don't think *they* see really clear. But the closer you can mold the workpiece into the Matrix—"

"Mold it in your dreams, you mean?"

The youth shook his head.

"It's not a dream," he said firmly. "It's entering the Matrix. And it's real—" He grinned and lifted a section of thigh armor from the table behind his bench. "—as this is."

He handed the piece to Hansen. It was dense and unquestionably real.

Hansen grinned back. *And then again, it might be exactly what Walker had meant; but if it was, it didn't help Hansen a lot.*

"Thanks," he said as he got up. "I figured I ought to know something about the hardware, since my life depends on it now."

And *that* was no more than the truth.

Hansen thought he might find Shill and Maharg in the hall, so he wasn't surprised to see them at the building's entrance.

He *hadn't* expected to see Malcolm stamping toward the pair from one of the huts, tying the sash of his vivid tunic and glowering like a stormcloud. A female slave skipped along the boardwalk behind Malcolm, eyes bright with anticipation.

"I thought I'd take you two out for a little practice," Hansen said to Shill and Maharg while Malcolm was still three strides away. The words were an instinctive game to prove that he was both innocent and ignorant of whatever was going on.

"What in the *hell* is going on?" Malcolm snarled.

"Nothin'," Maharg mumbled. He was rubbing his face. His nose had bled a rusty wedge into his moustache and beard.

"There's a new lot in from the East," Shill said. " 'Bout a dozen of 'em all together."

"Seven, yeah," said Malcolm. Hansen noted the way the veteran's anger vanished as though he'd closed a door over it.

Malcolm glanced toward the hall. Sounds of laughter and a snatch of song came though the half-open doors. "Go on."

"Bastards think they're tough," Maharg said. His voice caught.

Because Maharg was so big, it was hard to remember that he was only about sixteen standard years. That didn't make him less dangerous—more dangerous, maybe—but it meant that his emotions were still on the roller-coaster of youth.

Right now, Hansen thought he might be about to cry.

"They are tough," Malcolm said coldly. "Go on."

"They threw bones at him!" Shill said. "He was braggin' about what he'd do in the next fight, and they started throwin' bones at him. And *me!*"

"You bloody damned fools," Hansen said, before Malcolm could speak. The words were so close to those the veteran *would* have spoken that Malcolm blinked to hear them from another mouth.

Hansen pointed at Shill. "You sent for him, didn't you? Grabbed a slave—" the woman who'd followed Malcolm from his ladyfriend's lodging hovered nearby "—and sent her to roust your boss?"

"Well, I thought—"

"If you'd bloody *thought*," Hansen snarled, his arms at his sides and his face leaning close to that of the old warrior, "then you'd've known the best way to get out of this without a loss of status was to pretend it didn't happen. What d'ye expect? That Malcolm's going in there—"

He pointed at the door with his index and middle fingers together. "—and mop up your dozen tough bastards himself?"

"Wuzzn't that many," Maharg muttered, lifting his nose high, then lowering it again despite the fact that it continued to bleed. "Fuck this. I oughta go to Frekka. They're hiring there."

Malcolm's face hardened. "No true warrior would take service under merchants," he said.

"They got good armor fer *their* people," Shill said. "They know how a warrior oughta be treated."

"Merchants' armor!" Malcolm snapped. "All turned out the same."

"Sure, that's easy for *you* ta say," sniffled Shill. "You got a first-class outfit, you do. But how about somebody like me what never had no luck?"

"You've just had your luck," Hansen said. "You met me. Now, go on in there, one at a time so nobody thinks we're starting anything—which we're not—and get your armor. I'm going to teach you how to use it."

The two hirelings, the old man and the near boy, gave Hansen identical looks of sheeplike defiance. Then Shill spit into the mud, rubbed his lips, and said, "I s'pose practice wouldn't hurt none, with a battle coming up."

He peered through the doorway, then ducked inside.

"You coming with us?" Hansen asked Malcolm.

The veteran shook his head curtly. "No," he said. "No."

But ten steps down the walkway toward his girlfriend's dwelling, Malcolm turned and called, "Maybe later. Maybe."

❖   ❖   ❖

Hansen took a critical look at his two companions on the practice field. He understood Shill's bitter reference to armor now: the hirelings wore junk, little better than the suit in which Villiers had died.

Maharg's suit might originally have been of respectable quality, but that was in the ancient past. Now the plastron was crudely patched, and the legs had sections of varied diameter where stock pieces had been spliced in to repair damage.

Shill's armor didn't even have a distinguished pedigree. It was a collection of bits of flimsy apprentice work, welded together by another apprentice. The join lines were obvious, despite Shill's attempt to hide them with a pattern of horizontal black and yellow stripes.

"How did you guys survive the battle?" Hansen asked in genuine wonder. "Did you stick close to Malcolm?"

"Well, we were . . . ," Shill said, the electronics robbing his voice of the embarrassment Hansen was sure was present. "You know, we watched his back."

"I fought a guy," said Maharg. "He didn't, you know . . . he didn't want to get real close."

And his armor wouldn't've been an improvement over Maharg's present suit if the boy had managed to bring him down. There were a majority of hirelings like these in every army, fodder for the leavening of principal warriors.

That would change.

"Then you were smart," Hansen said harshly, "because if you'd tried to be heroes before, you'd be dead. But now—" he pointed his finger at one man, then the other "—you're going to do things exactly the way I tell you."

"Why?" said Maharg bluntly.

"Because I'm going to make you a baron, boy," Hansen said, glad for the harshness the helmet speaker put into his voice.

He turned his head to the older man. "And you, Shill," he added, "because I'll make you rich. Without me you'll be slopping hogs in a few years, unless you get chopped despite the way you try to dodge around keeping outa trouble."

The blank face of Hansen's battlesuit couldn't smile. He clapped the men on the shoulders instead and said, "Come on, let's find a quiet corner where I can teach you what these suits can do. Even *your* suits."

The practice ground was several hectares in size, plenty of room even now when most of the warriors in Peace Rock were involved in either practicing for the coming battle or proving their prowess to Taddeusz and the cluster of high-ranking warriors around him.

Hansen faced a post on the end as far from the warchief as possible.

"All right," he lectured. "Your suits have both identification and designator capacity. Say, 'Mark friendlies blue.' "

"Huh?"

In Hansen's display, azure crests spiked from the top of the hirelings' helmets. "Just do it!" he snapped. "Do you remember what I said about obeying orders?"

The warriors looked at one another. "Oh . . . ," murmured one of them. "I din't know it could do that."

"Right," said Hansen dryly. "Now, the AI can also designate. The way we're going to win—the way we're going to *survive*, I want you to be very clear on that—is by all three of us striking together. I'm going to mark the target with a flashing white light. When the light changes to red, we all three hit it. Together, that's very important to overload the hostile system."

"I don' unnerstand," said both the hirelings.

"Bring your arcs up," Hansen said. "Practice, cut . . . ," and his right gauntlet quivered with the vibrating power that shimmered in it. It was an insidiously pleasant feeling, the power of life and death in a glittering package. . . .

"Now, watch."

Hansen centered the post in his helmet display and said, "Mark."

A pulsing white corona gleamed on the electronic image of the post in his display and that of his two trainees, though the scene wouldn't've changed to naked eyes.

"Strike!" and he slashed his arc weapon forward into the red glare marking the post, cutting the wood in a blaze of sparks and flying fibers—

While Shill and Maharg stood, with faces that were probably as blankly incomprehending as the painted fronts of their battlesuits.

Hansen straightened. "Now," he said calmly, "let's try something different. Maharg, I want you to hit the post when I yell 'Strike,' do you understand?"

"Ah . . . All right."

"Mark," said Hansen, lighting the post on their screens. "Strike."

Maharg feinted clumsily. Hansen's arc hit him from behind. The young warrior toppled to the mud.

"Not next year, not next second," Hansen said. "When I give you an order, you do it *now*. Do you understand?"

Maharg started to get up. "You bas—" he growled.

Hansen waited a beat for Maharg to get far enough off the ground that hitting it again would be a useful lesson. Then he slapped Maharg down.

"I am going to make you a real warrior," Hansen said to the youth's prone form. "I'm going to make you a baron, just as I said. But you're not going to argue, you're going to take orders. Do you—"

"You bas—"

Hansen's arc lashed out again.

"Nobody's ever given a shit for you, boy!" he said. He was shouting. "Nobody! But *I* care, and I'm going to make you what you want to be if I have to kill you first! Do you understand? Do you?"

The recumbent suit twitched into life again. "Yessir," Maharg said.

"All right," Hansen said. He was trying to keep the adrenalin shudder out of his voice. He wasn't successful. "Get up and watch how Shill does it."

He turned toward the post. Smoke trembled from a few splinters Hansen had knocked away with his earlier cut. "Mark," he said.

Chapter Fourteen

By late afternoon, Shill and Maharg had gotten surprisingly adept at obeying Hansen's orders. On their own, with the pair of them engaging Hansen, things didn't work as well.

When Maharg was *ad hoc* leader, he tended to strike before he remembered to call the designator to his partner. Shill, on the other hand, dithered. His command to '*Strike!*' was always followed by Maharg's lunge—but usually not by Shill's.

Still, this was only the first day of training. When it came to the real thing against the Thrasey forces, Hansen would be there to give the orders—unless he got his head burned off.

In which case, he couldn't pretend he much cared what happened afterward.

By the time Hansen led his tiny force back across the field, Taddeusz had been joined by Golsingh—in boots, breeches, and a fur cloak. A group of warriors were going through exercises before them.

"That's the lot what made trouble in the hall," Shill grumbled. He angled his steps to pass a little further to the side of the seven warriors.

"Hold up," said Hansen. A thought struck him.

"Group secure communications," he said, then, "Can you two hear me now?"

"Hey, that's real clear," said Maharg. His own voice was much crisper than it had been on straight audio between the suits.

"Shill?"

"Huh? Yeah, I kin hear."

"When I tell you to report," Hansen said in a controlled voice, "you report. Understood?"

"Whatever," Shill muttered.

"Right," Hansen said. "Now, are you guys up for some serious play? Trying out what we just learned on our friends there?"

"You think we can take *them*?" Maharg demanded.

"Designate hostile forces green," Hansen said and watched spikes of bottle green dance from the helmets of the warriors from the 'East,' wherever that was.

He was getting to like his suit. It would've been useful to have back on Annunciation, where he belonged. . . .

But that was for later. "No," he said aloud. "I think they'll kick our butts, frankly. But it'll give us some practice that we need."

Neither of the juniors spoke for a moment. Then Maharg said, "Hell, I've had my butt kicked before. Once more don' matter."

"Then stick close to me," Hansen said. "Remember your orders. And for god's sake, when it starts, *don't* quit till they're all down or we are!"

"Cut!"

The three warriors stepped forward in line abreast. If Hansen looked to either side he would have seen an underling with a blue spike on his helmet, but for now he was taking that on trust.

"Mark," he said with the seeming leader of the Easterners centered in his display.

The fellow was sparring with two of his own men. His suit was clearly a cut above the one Hansen wore, while two more of the Eastern warriors were almost as well equipped. The other four wore scrapings of the same general quality as Shill and Maharg—but there *were* four of them.

The leader paused. "You see, Lord Golsingh?" he boomed. "I claim the right of prowess to command your left wing!"

"Normal speech," Hansen ordered his AI. His face prickled with sweat, as if this were real, not a game. They were three meters from the Eastern leader.

"I'd always heard that no Easterner had any balls!" he shouted. "I don't think you seven can fight us three *real* men! Wanna try?"

"You—" the Eastern leader gasped in a choking voice. The arc bloomed from his hand.

"Strike!" shouted Hansen, and they struck, by *god* they did, all three together and the Easterner, off-balance with his pivot, toppled to the mud while Hansen cried, "Mark! Strike!"

Only Shill and Hansen that time, because Hansen had turned a hair to his right and blocked Maharg with his body, but the Easterner dropped, not one of the dangerous pair but he fell in front of one of those, tripping his fellow. Hansen struck into the tangled suits, no time to mark and command.

But his two fellows struck with him anyway, guided by the arc without a designator, as if Maharg could think and Shill could act—but they could, because he'd told them they could or because the gods were good or maybe because men like a leader to follow because it's so much simpler than thinking.

Maharg took the arc of the remaining Eastern champion squarely on the crest of his helmet and dropped. Hansen stepped close and hacked at the man, but the Easterner was both fast and experienced, catching Hansen's arc with his own.

Hansen's right arm shuddered as if he'd grabbed a live AC line. He grabbed the Easterner's wrist with his free hand. As he did so, a sickly arc snaked past his helmet—Shill striking from behind him with a skill born of practice.

The Easterner's weapon dimmed as his AI drained power from it to boost the defenses against the fresh threat.

Hansen struck home and slung his opponent to the side as dead weight.

Two of the remaining Easterners made a convulsive rush at Shill, putting the old man between them and Hansen. Shill screamed momentarily; then his microphone shut down with the rest of his suit's power.

Hansen chopped right, then left. The last Easterner stood like a statue six meters away, too surprised or frightened to take any action.

A kid who froze, or a man as old as Shill who's forgotten this is only play. . . .

Hansen's arc lengthened and took the warrior in the chest. The Easterner turned sluggishly to run. Hansen stepped forward until his weapon was close enough to overwhelm his opponent's armor and drop him.

He stopped, panting heavily.

"You treacherous slimy bastard," rasped the amplified voice of the Eastern leader, rising to his feet.

Now that his suit was reset, mud was coursing off the painted metal with almost the enthusiasm that it had from Krita's armor under similar circumstances. "Now I'm going to kill you."

The dense flux that shot from the leader's right gauntlet wasn't a practice weapon.

"Battle status," Hansen ordered his AI, raising his arc in guard. He'd thought Krita might kill him, but it hadn't crossed his mind that this fellow would take a defeat personally enough to commit murder in front of Golsingh himself.

Because it surely was murder, Hansen going one-on-one with a suit as good as this fellow's. Maybe somebody would—

"Hey!" shouted the king. "Stop that! We need—"

The Easterner cut at Hansen's head. Hansen blocked the blow. His display flickered with the strain, even though the arcs crossed two meters from the attacker's gauntlet.

"Taddeusz! Stop them!" Golsingh ordered.

Hansen backpedaled, praying that he wouldn't trip over a warrior sprawled on the ground behind him. His display would give him a 360° view if he wanted it, but he was afraid the distortion would be more dangerous than the chance of an obstacle.

"Let them play, milord," the warchief replied with the casual certainty of a man who knows that he's wearing a battlesuit and his king is not. "I have doubts about both of them. More than doubts about the—"

"Hey!" boomed an amplified voice.

A warrior strode onto the field behind the Easterner. *Red-blue-silver battlesuit—*

"Watch him, Malcolm!" Hansen shouted. "He's nut—"

The Easterner spun like a dancer, slashing at Malcolm's head. Malcolm got his arc up in time, but the shock of meeting knocked him to his knees.

Hansen stepped forward and cut at the Easterner's live gauntlet. All three armored warriors froze like a group of statuary as sparks roared and dazzled in all directions.

The Eastern leader's suit was of very high quality. The artificial intelligences controlling the other two suits had to drain all power from their servos to prevent the Easterner's arc from finishing Malcolm. A patch of mud beneath the trio began to harden as full-power discharges lashed across it.

Hansen leaned forward and reached out with his left hand, moving against the dead weight and stiffness of his suit.

The Easterner's weapon was slowly driving down Malcolm's guard. Hansen's right gauntlet had grown hot, and his air system reeked with the odor of suede as the lining charred.

Hansen unlatched the Easterner's suit, shutting off the arc and the defensive charges instantly. Malcolm's straining arm slashed upward when the resistance was released, plowing across the Easterner's plastron in a glare of burning metal.

The Easterner fell face-down. Steam gouted as mud cooled the glowing mass where his chest had been. Malcolm tried to rise—and failed; then tried to open his own battlesuit. His gauntlet pawed in the general direction of the latch without quite touching it.

Hansen found the latch of his own suit by closing his eyes and letting instinct guide his desperate hand. He swung open the front of his clamshell and paused, too exhausted to go further until the pain of his burning right hand goaded him to drag his arms out of their casings.

He stared, dull-eyed, at the steaming ruin of the Eastern leader.

The ruin also of Hansen's hopes for a first-class battlesuit. The steel which sheathed the electronics had a good deal of mechanical strength, but against the full wrath of an arc weapon it might as well have been so much tissue paper. Malcolm had burned the Easterner out of his suit's chest cavity, and in so doing had irreparably ruined the plastron itself.

Oh, the piece could be repaired in time—though certainly not in time for battle against the Lord of Thrasey. But the battlesuit would never be as good as it had been before the damage, not even in the unlikely event that the repairs were done by a smith as skillful as the original builder.

"Well, I said I had my doubts, milord," Taddeusz said. "Lamullo will command the left wing as usual."

Golsingh nodded. "Shall we go back to the hall now?" he said. "I hope there's been a message from Frekka about the suits we ordered."

The king and warchief turned their backs. Hansen swore quietly, trying to gather up enough strength to get out of his armor. Maharg and Shill had stripped and were aiding Malcolm.

Golsingh's blond wife had accompanied her husband to the practice field. Hansen blinked to see her staring at him. Her face didn't change as he met her eyes, then turned and walked on with the other nobles.

Chapter Fifteen

Fortin waited a moment for other members of Rolls' entourage to form around him in an alcove of the entrance hall. When the six big men had done so as planned, Fortin squatted down and reversed his cloak to bring the pink side out.

There was a white beret under his slouch hat. He kicked off his black boots, replaced them with pink sandals, and pulled up white tights to cover his legs as he rose.

The last item of Fortin's disguise was the pink violin, hidden beneath his cloak with the sandals.

At the moment Rolls swept Penny into his arms at the far end of the hall, Fortin stepped through the mirrored door at the back of alcove. He was an unremarkable flash of pink in the event that any of Penny's servants noticed him at all.

Three women were chattering among themselves in the corridor. They paused when Fortin appeared, then resumed their discussion in marginally lower tones as the newcomer ignored them. Fortin strode down the hall in the opposite direction.

Fortin knew the layout of Penny's palace better than . . . probably better than anyone else, even Penny's servants, because they grew old and died. Penny herself neither knew nor cared about the intricacies of the mansion constructed to her whim. Her focus was narrower—and very different.

A squad from the kitchen staff, looking more than usually silly with their fluffy uniforms grease-spattered, wheeled trolleys of food up one of the side-corridors as Fortin passed. They paid no attention to him.

The food would be served to Rolls' retainers in one of the many refectories on the lower level of the palace. No one would notice that there was one fewer of the men in orange livery than had been admitted to the hall.

A garden of palmettos was planted beneath the staircase at

117

the end of the main corridor. A prismatic slit window high in
the wall above provided the plants with sufficient light for growth.
Fortin checked over his shoulder to make sure nobody could
see him, then tossed his balled cloak behind a screen of the
broad, feathery leaves. Penny's upper level servants didn't wear
overgarments.

Fortin skipped briskly up the stairs.

A doorway opened immediately off the spiral staircase; on
the other side would be an arbor in the palace rotunda. Fortin
reached to open the door, but paused with his hand on the knob.

There were voices from the other side of the panel; male
and female servants, several of each. Nothing that would concern
Penny, of course, so long her needs were attended. . . .

Fortin laughed silently and continued up the stairs that now
spiraled within one of the flying buttresses. He had more
important things in mind than disturbing an orgy—or joining
it.

His sandals *whick-whick-whick*ed on the stone treads with
the regularity of a metronome.

They all hated Fortin, but they needed him as well. For tasks
like this, for the tricks that no other *god* could accomplish. . . .

And that made them hate him all the more; but they had to
bear his presence unless they were willing to destroy themselves
as well, for the Matrix was balance. If the others slew Fortin,
then they let their own lives out in the same stream of blood.

If Diamond were destroyed—

If Fortin were to destroy Diamond—

Then Fortin's fellows, who hated him because he was half
android—which they despised—and half North, whom they
wisely feared . . . then Fortin's fellows might slay him in their
ungoverned rage and bring down all this near perfection which
they ruled. Which would be the best trick of all, surely.

The staircase ended in a finial at the top of the buttress. Fortin
peeked out. No one was in sight.

A railed walkway circled the top of the rotunda, more to add
golden glitter to the appearance than for safety needs. Beyond
the railing, Fortin could see fairy-castle turrets, each streaming
with bright flags, studding the outer walls of the palace.

Still hidden in the finial, because there were windows in the spire overlooking the rotunda roof, Fortin stripped down to his pink jockstrap and sandals. He strode out, wearing an expression as arrogant as the bulge of his groin.

In the flare of the central spire was an unobtrusive door. It opened to Fortin's touch. The corridor beyond was decorated with plaster cherubs, roses, and swags in case Penny herself chose to use it. In all likelihood, nobody passed through the hall except the maintenance crews who swept and polished the roof.

And Fortin. Now.

He ignored the stairs around the elevator shaft. A trio of servants stepped from a room across the way, carrying bundles of bedclothing. One of them saw Fortin, and they ducked out of sight again.

Their mistress had the power of life and death, so there was risk to a servant whom Penny noticed—but not much risk, because death didn't interest Penny very much.

Their real danger came from the savage whim of a human promoted to the mistress' bed. Such a one had Penny's ear and power—until she tired and cast him out. Out, nowhere; perhaps to menial service, perhaps back to a grubby village in the Open Lands where he'd been born; perhaps to a void in the Matrix, for Penny had her notions too, and in bed alone she could be interested for good or ill.

No sensible servant wanted contact with a doomed man who might wish to destroy as much as he could before his own inevitable end.

Fortin walked into the lift shaft and began to rise. Not because he was one of Penny's favorites, as those who watched from behind half-opened doors thought; but because Fortin too was a god.

He wondered if Penny hated and despised herself. Probably not. She wasn't perceptive enough to realize that she should, that they all should.

Fortin got off the lift at the top level, where the spire swelled into the huge, gilded egg of Penny's private suite.

Maids were straightening one of the great rooms. They peered at Fortin through the open door. One giggled. They were nude except for wisps of white gauze in their hair and a similar tracery of pink around their hips.

Fortin stared at them coldly. "This isn't for you," he said, jutting his hips forward to emphasize his words.

The girls' bright, scrubbed faces changed. One of them quickly closed the door.

Fortin entered the white angora room that was Penny's particular favorite. He paused when he heard laughter, but the balcony door was open and the sounds came through it.

The necklace was on a dresser. Fortin fingered the stone for a moment. It was warm, blood hot, even though it must have been several minutes since Penny tossed it aside to get on with a variation of the one matter that interested her more than her own appearance.

Fortin slipped the transparent strap over his head and let the jewel bounce against his own chest. For a moment he looked at himself in the dresser's triple mirror and saw the form of Rolls, complete with the first hint of a paunch rolling over the cord of his orange jockstrap.

And again, a muscular stud with sullen, swarthy features, not Fortin but any one of a thousand men who'd gained Penny's attention in an existence where duration no longer had meaning. The jewel concealed itself.

Fortin looked toward the balcony door. It stood open at an angle. Reflected in its crystal surface, ghostly against the cloud-streaked sky beyond, he saw Rolls and Penny.

The palace's mistress was leaning her whole torso out over the top rail. Her chubby calves intertwined with the railing's vertical supports, and Rolls' great hands gripped her breasts.

Penny cried in delight as Rolls stroked into her again from behind, and again, and again.

A risky position, even with Rolls' strength and Penny's own undoubted athleticism. But what was even godhead without risk?

There was no expression on Fortin's face as he stepped into the lift shaft. He would leave the palace as a faceless member of Rolls' entourage and hand over the necklace as soon as they were clear.

When Rolls was done with it, Fortin would slip the necklace back here.

And Fortin would revisit Ruby.

Chapter Sixteen

In order to accommodate the influx of recruits drawn by rumors of war, the tables were butted end to end. They were clear of food, now, and the night's serious drinking had begun.

Hansen squeezed the shoulders of the men to either side of him, Malcolm and Maharg; muttered, "Wish me luck"; and ducked under the trestles to reach the service walkway between tables and hearth.

"Hey!" called one of his fellows. A husky woman with pitchers in either hand stopped so abruptly that some of her beer sloshed, but Hansen strode directly toward Golsingh at the crosstable.

He'd learned by now that Taddeusz wasn't going to permit an underling—particularly Hansen—to approach the king if he could help it. With the table between them, the warchief *couldn't* prevent the contact, unless he was willing to lower himself and his dignity by crawling under the trestles the way Hansen had done.

Malcolm sat less than a third of the way down the left bench now. Most of the recruits were gutter-sweepings, not respectable warriors. Good warriors were going elsewhere. That was one of the things Hansen had learned in talking with Malcolm and his fellows.

Servants fluttered out of Hansen's way. At the head table, Unn and Krita stared at him. The face of Taddeusz' daughter was flushed from the hearth, but Unn's pale skin was perfect except for a smudge of ash on her forehead.

Krita smiled, filled a square-bottomed cup of mammoth ivory, and handed it to Hansen without a word. He took it, startled out of his focus on what he was about to say to the king.

"Ah, Your Highness," he blurted.

"That's the servants' side of the table!" Taddeusz snarled. He'd started to rise when his daughter offered the cup to Hansen, but his chair and the table trammeled the abrupt action. He fell back. "Get out of there—and *away* from here!"

121

"I am His highness' servant," Hansen said, thinking of what he'd told Walker and smiling inside at his own duplicity.

But—he didn't *trust* the squirrel/titmouse/crow, and he didn't understand enough about what Walker was trying to do to protect himself. Hansen thought he understood Golsingh—and the other factors in *this* equation—well enough, certainly better than the actors did themselves.

Which didn't mean that Hansen was safe. Just that he knew the name of the lion into whose jaws he was sticking his head.

"Sir," he said, looking at the king and ignoring the way Taddeusz twisted his chair sideways so that he could get up, "if you'll let me talk with you, I can serve you better. Maybe—"

He bobbed his beard-stubbled chin toward the warchief with "—better than anybody else. Which may be why they're afraid of letting me talk."

"You—" Taddeusz bellowed, lifting his goblet of silver-mounted rock crystal. He might have thrown it, except that Krita stepped between her father and Hansen.

"Sit down, foster father," Golsingh said. Taddeusz remained frozen in a posture of agonized fury.

"Sit down!" cracked the king's voice.

"Yes, milord," Taddeusz muttered. He sank down as if in a state of exhaustion.

"Milord," said Hansen, wondering what the other warriors in the hall were making of this, "your father and your father's father were kings, but they didn't rule further than their armies could march in three days—and that only when their armies *were* marching. Is that correct?"

"We have the submission of a hundred lords!" Taddeusz snapped. "You're talking nonsense!"

"And those hundred lords fight each other, one pair or another of them every day, every year. They'll send you tribute, and they'll send a message of congratulation when you win a victory, but they won't send troops to join yours when you march—"

"Some—" said Golsingh with a frown.

"—unless you're marching by their keep on the way, with enough force to burn the place around their ears," Hansen continued, speaking with the same brutal frankness that had gathered him enemies regularly during his decade in Consensus bureaucracy.

That had its advantages too. His enemies had made sure Hansen was sent where it was hot; and, since he'd survived, he'd been promoted rapidly into the shoes of officers who hadn't.

"Do you want tribute and the name?" Hansen said. "Or do you really want peace—Golsingh the Peacegiver?"

The warchief shook his head in frustration. "The business of a king is war," he said. "And power. Milord, it's unkingly—unmanly, I'd almost say—to talk of imposing peace. The gods don't approve."

Golsingh's youthful features hardened. "I'm king here," he said sharply to his foster father. "The gods can rule in their heavens, but—"

He turned to face Hansen. His face was suffused with a hot passion not so very different from what roiled unseen in Hansen's mind.

"Yes," Golsingh said, "it's peace I want. A peace in which a man—a woman!—can walk from one end of my kingdom to the other and never be molested. A peace in which a purse can lie in the center of the road for a year and no one will steal it. *That's* what I want!"

Taddeusz got up. "My son," he said, "you're tempting the gods. I hope you think better of your words before it's too late."

The warchief's voice was firm with sadness and anger, but he was no longer trying to shout down the discussion. Taddeusz stalked out of the hall, his felt boots cushioning the beat of his heels on the puncheon floor.

Krita turned to watch him go. Hansen had been aware of the warmth of her body ever since she'd interposed between him and her father, although she'd moved a step away afterwards.

Hansen swallowed the beer in his cup with a surge of thirst and reaction.

"Milord," he said, "then the way isn't to fight each lordling who defies you. You've got to take Frekka, make it your capital, and use the trading wealth to build an army that—"

"Frekka?" said Golsingh. "Frekka? Don't be silly. My ancestors have lived at Peace Rock for generations, and—"

"Sir, your—"

"—and besides," Golsingh continued in his royal voice, "Frekka is already a part of the kingdom."

"Then why is the shipment of armor you're expecting—you *need*—for your expedition delayed?" Hansen retorted sharply. "And why are the merchants of Frekka paying subsidies under the table to whichever of your barons looks least trustworthy?"

"You don't know that!" Golsingh snapped.

"Everybody knows that," Hansen said with flat brutality. "We have the choice of pretending not to believe the report of every traveler who's come from Thrasey or Frekka in the past month. But we don't have the option of not *knowing* it."

"Why would they *do* that?" the king said in a suddenly gentler voice.

He set down the cup he'd been playing with and kneaded his cheeks with the fingers of both hands. "I'll give them safe roads for their commerce. That's one of the main things that I want for the kingdom, for everyone."

"You'll give them a king they have to obey," Hansen said simply. "The caravans from Frekka are safe enough on the roads now."

"But they have to hire guards to—" Golsingh protested. He caught himself. "Oh."

"Yeah," said Hansen. "That's what I've heard, too. That the Syndics of Frekka have more warriors in their hire now than you do."

He started to drink, remembered that he'd finished the beer in his mug—and found it full again. Unn smiled coldly and bobbed the silver pitcher in her hand.

"The Frekka merchants want the same sort of kingdom as you do, Lord Golsingh," Hansen said. "The only thing is, they want to be the rulers of it."

"Did you come here from Frekka, then?" Unn asked unexpectedly.

Hansen looked at her. "No, milady," he said. "I came from much farther away than that. And—"

He swigged beer in order to settle his thoughts before he finished the statement. "And I think it helps to come from a distance, sometimes, when you look at a problem."

Unn leaned forward to fill her husband's agate cup. There was nothing in her expression to suggest that she'd heard or spoken in the past moments.

"Lord Golsingh," Hansen said earnestly. "Give me five men

of my choosing for the battle against Thrasey. Tell them to do exactly what I say for the next two days of training, and the same in the battle. And I'll *win* the battle for you."

"Don't be absurd!" Golsingh snapped with more anger than the request itself involved. "I'll do nothing of the sort. A nothing like you, with no pedigree and no war honors anybody's heard of!"

I asked him to do something that even he can't order these stiff-necked warriors to do and be obeyed, Hansen realized.

"And anyway . . . ," Golsingh added in a very different voice. "Even if I were to—do what you suggest. You'd never . . ."

The king looked down at his hands, then up so that he faced Krita but watched Hansen out of the corners of his eyes. "You'd never be able to do what you say. Would you?"

Hansen smiled his dragon smile at Golsingh. "One of these days, milord," he said, "you and I are going to find a way for you to give me what *I* want . . . and then I'll give you the kingdom you want."

He turned to go back to his seat, then turned again. "That's if we both live long enough, milord," he added.

Golsingh's face was expressionless. But Krita was smiling ferally . . . and so was Unn.

Chapter Seventeen

The cold of Ruby's winter was shocking. The wind drove ice crystals like miniature scalpels through the close weave of the Inspector General's dress uniform.

The company of infantry drawn up at attention wore coveralls the color of dirty snow. The faces of the troops were as impassive as the armored bows of the tanks among the stunted fir trees, aiming their guns at Fortin.

An officer wearing a patch over her right eye stepped forward and saluted. "Sir!" she said. "I'm Major Fernandez, in charge of your escort. The High Council has already been briefed. They're proceeding to a rendezvous point."

Warts and knobs studded the tanks: weapons and sensors and defenses of various sorts. Snow collected on the angles and aided the camouflage of the huge vehicles, instead of melting from warm metal as Fortin would have expected. The shielding which hid the tanks from thermal imagers was obviously of exceptional quality.

As was every other facet of weaponry and mayhem in Ruby.

"Very good, Major Fernandez," Fortin replied without bothering to salute at all. He strode toward the nearest armored personnel carrier. "Let's get started then, shall we?"

The troops broke for their vehicles with a shout at Fernandez' order. Their noise didn't completely mask the whine of the hydraulic motors rotating the tank turrets so that their guns tracked the Inspector General to the millimeter as he walked.

A visitor to Ruby was a potential threat. North the War God was sacrosanct in Ruby, but security was greater even than North.

Though there was no wind to bite within the vehicle, the metal frame of Fortin's seat was cold. The APC made a lumbering take-off and turned hard to starboard.

Fortin smiled. If he'd really cared to know where he was being taken, the artificial intelligence woven into the metal braid of his uniform would have told him.

Neither where nor how they were going mattered. Nonetheless, Fortin was amused to know that his hosts would follow a unique course to a unique location; a location that shared with previous meeting places only the fact that it was a barren wasteland as far as possible from anything of significance to the security of Ruby.

"Brace yourself, please, sir," said Fernandez, locking the Inspector General onto his jumpseat with a powerful arm as the APC descended abruptly. She was missing two fingers as well as the eye.

Fortin's stomach squirmed with a feeling of queasy pleasure, like that he felt when he realized the tanks' big guns were tracking him and might at any instant blast him to vapor. It wasn't danger which provided that almost sexual thrill, but rather the thought that there might suddenly be a universe in which he didn't exist.

The drive engines howled to full power, buffeting the vehicle with echoes reflected from narrow walls to either side. Motion stopped except for engine vibration; then the APC dropped the last centimeter to the ground.

Fernandez slammed open the vehicle's hatch with the same motion in which her other arm released the Inspector General. He stepped out.

The sidewalls of the APC hadn't dropped because there wasn't room for them to do so within the narrow gorge in which the vehicle had landed. Two infantrymen were facing Fortin with automatic rifles leveled. Twenty meters above on the rim of the canyon were a pair of tripod-mounted plasma weapons whose bolts could devour the armored personnel carrier itself if circumstances required.

A colonel behind the infantrymen said, "All right, port arms." As the men obeyed, the colonel went on, "This way, sir. The Council is awaiting you."

The Council's command vehicle was fifty meters away, out of sight behind a kink in the gorge. Snow had drifted over the rim to knee height. High boots were part of the colonel's camouflage uniform, but Fortin wore polished shoes. Snow seeped over the tops of them, and he smiled at the discomfort.

Marshal Czerny leaned out of the side door. "Come aboard,

sir," he said. His voice rasped as though he'd drunk lye, but it was probably just age. "Glad to have you with us again."

Of the five marshals around the table this time, Moro and Stein looked old, and Czerny looked as old as life itself. Tadley and Kerchuk were gone, replaced with a pair of men whose nametags read Breitkopf and Lienau—both of them middle-aged, wolf-lean, and with features that would have looked unusually cruel on sharks.

Fortin was a god to whom duration meant nothing, but duration meant decay and death for the tools he used. Despite the arrogance of the folk of Ruby, they would all die—and they didn't even care about that, so long as the system they served survived.

"Sit down, comrades," the Inspector General ordered. "I've come to see how you've succeeded with the task I posed you."

Fortin knew the answer already. The grins that not even discipline could hide, the wolfish joy in the faces above the gleaming gorgets—those were the signs of success.

The other four marshals looked at Moro. He spread his plump fingers as if to examine his nails and said, "We believe we may have a—theoretical—solution to your problem, yes. We first used the Main Battle Computer to locate the target—"

"Locate the position it would occupy if it actually existed," Breitkopf interjected in a surprisingly smooth voice. "The target is of course beyond even the possibility of actual observation."

"By us," added Stein.

"And quite a pretty problem it was then," Lienau continued, "since we still couldn't hit a point of separate spacetime with which we were in perfect balance."

"That balance was the key," said Marshal Czerny in his cadaverous voice. "Marshal Moro calculated—"

"The Main Battle Computer calculated," said Moro, fluttering his fingers in protest but unable to keep a note of pride out of his voice. "I merely suggested certain parameters."

"Marshal Moro calculated," Breitkopf said, "that the statistical identity of Ruby and the target point could be converted to *physical* identity."

"That if we bring Ruby into phase with the target," Moro amplified, "then we become the target—"

"And displace whatever's there now. Displace it out of the universe," Czerny concluded.

He coughed, lightly at first but growing into a racking series during which his fellows looked studiously at their displays and pretended not to hear.

"You say 'out of the universe,'" Fortin said. "Where, then?"

Lienau smirked. "Somewhere incomprehensible, sir," he said. "Certainly out of play."

"Ruby has been in a dynamic balance with the target—assuming the target exists," Marshal Stein said. "If we displace the target, then *our* segment of phased spacetime remains in static balance within the greater universe."

"Which is perfectly safe, of course," Moro said.

Czerny cleared his throat. No one except Fortin looked at Czerny until the old field marshal managed to say, "The security of Ruby must be our chief goal, of course, sir."

"As it is yours," Breitkopf added, in certainty as complete as his error.

"You say, 'bring into phase,'" the Inspector General said, examining his own perfect fingernails as he spoke. "How would you propose to go about that—if I were to give you the order to proceed?"

"Quite simple, really," Stein explained. "Just a matter of reversing the magnetic pole, Moro thinks."

"The Main Battle Computer indicates that would be the preferred course, yes," Moro agreed absently as his eyes focused on a hologram aligned so that only he could see it. "And the computer would, of course, control the power fed into a planet-wide network which would achieve the switch."

"It would have to take place when our phase was positive," Breitkopf said.

"Otherwise—" He drew his finger across his chrome gorget. There was a smile on his hard face, but madness winked behind his eyes at the thought of taking the action that would destroy Ruby rather than the target.

"So," said Fortin. "Physical preparations have to be made before your plan could be executed?"

Czerny began to laugh, a terrible sound that doubled him over in obvious pain. No one spoke.

Czerny straightened slowly and said, "Extensive preparations are required, sir. And they are already complete."

"We could not be sure when you would visit us again, Inspector General," Moro said. "So we decided to—improve our time while waiting."

"Nothing remains," said Lienau, "but for you to order us to execute the plan."

Fortin felt time stop—for him, for Ruby . . . for all the planes of the Matrix. Paths branched here, and ends approached with absolute finality.

"Very good, comrades," he said. "Execute your plan."

His face twisted. He began to laugh, louder and louder, until his eyes no longer focused for the quivering anticipation in his belly.

Chapter Eighteen

Golsingh's army camped in the forest on first night of the expedition against Thrasey. Hansen saw his breath when he awakened. Snow had drifted onto the furs that covered him, and there was the threat of further snow in the sullen sky.

Slaves were building up the long fires and clattering with food preparation; ponies whickered. Hansen swore, scratched, and got up. He hadn't gotten chilled in his cocoon of heavy furs, but the irregularities of the ground left him stiff and sore.

They were camped in a valley of pine trees shattered two meters in the air. During a grim winter several years before, the trees had been buried in snow to that height. An avalanche blasting down from the crags to the right had sheared off the trunks above the level of the protective snow.

Hansen glanced up uneasily, but the high rocks were mostly bare and seemingly too distant to spawn such a catastrophe anyway.

Which was a reminder to be wary at all times, here no less than when he headed Special Units on Annunciation.

Shill sat on a log by a fire and stared into the mug he held before him. Hansen snapped his fingers at a slave, called, "Something hot to drink!" and seated himself beside the older warrior.

Shill gave him a nervous smile, as though he expected to be kicked. There was a bruise on the older man's forehead from one of the work-outs Hansen had put him through.

"I was wondering," Hansen said as he took the cup a slave brought him, "who was on guard last night?"

"Guard?" repeated Shill. "Guard against what?"

That was exactly the reply Hansen had expected, but he'd been too tired the night before to go into the matter then. When you ache all over, from training and from the unfamiliar exercise of riding a pony, it was easy to tell yourself that everything would

131

be taken care of by the people whose business it was. And anyway, there wasn't anything he could do to change accepted practice.

The second part of the proposition still looked accurate in the grim light of day.

"What if the Lord of Thrasey attacked us at night?" Hansen asked, simply to get a reaction which would represent the attitude of everydamnbody in this sorry excuse for an army.

The older man was honestly puzzled. "Huh?" he said. "Nobody fights at night. And anyway, the battlefield's still a mile ahead. Though I guess we'll have to suit up and walk it," he added glumly, "just in case Thrasey jumps the gun."

Hansen sucked at the contents of his cup. It was fresh mead or perhaps honeyed wine, sweet enough to qualify as food and warm from being mulled in a water-jacketed boiler—which was the most sophisticated device he'd seen on Northworld, apart from the battlesuits.

"So," he said as his mind digested the information. "The time and place of the battle are arranged already? And that's always the case?"

"Sure," the older man agreed with a nod. "How else would you do it?"

He gestured. Trees of considerable size grew on the valley's distant southern slope. A mist hung among their branches, indistinguishable from the bitter smoke hovering over the pine-log fires of the encampment.

"Blazes," Shill said. "We could stumble around for weeks and never find Thrasey—nor the other way either."

A group of freemen were mounting their ponies. When the riders were safely in their saddles, slaves handed them weapons—lever-cocked crossbows or three-meter lances.

Some of the freemen had already ridden off. Scouting appeared to be as disorganized as every other aspect of battle management.

Hansen abruptly slugged back the rest of his drink. "I'm going out with them," he muttered.

"Why d'ye wanna do that?" Shill asked.

"Because I think *somebody* in this army ought to know what's going on," Hansen snapped.

He looked around. "I gave my pony to a couple slaves to off-saddle and feed," he said. "Where would they be now?"

"If you're really going to do that," Shill said, "take one of those." He pointed to the gaggle of freemen, mounting and equipping. "They're saddled already, after all."

"Right, thanks," said Hansen, striding toward the freemen.

The older warrior shook his head in wonderment. "Sometimes I wonder what sorta place you come from," he called.

Hansen turned his head. "That's fair," he retorted. "Because I sure-hell wonder what sort of place I've come!"

The leader of the half-dozen freemen whom Hansen accompanied was named Brian. He was about Hansen's age; a husky, steady man whom Hansen would've been glad to have as a unit leader back on Annunciation.

The remainder of the troop were fire-eaters averaging about nineteen years old, jerking their ponies with heavy hands and boasting about what they were going to do to Thrasey's scouts and warriors. Since freemen were less than cannon-fodder if matched against warriors in battlesuits, Hansen expected their enthusiasm to wane as they approached the enemy, but it made him uneasy to listen to their nonsense.

They rode through the trees, listening to the calls of scouts who'd left before them and sometimes crossing pony tracks in the snow. Half a mile from the encampment, the shallow valley Golsingh's men had followed most of the way from Peace Rock opened onto a broad plain.

The snow was deeper than it had been among the trees. It crushed flat the yellowed grass that would have been several meters high if erect. Sight distances were deceptively short. The open country seemed to stretch for kilometers in every direction, but swells too gentle to be noticed cut visibility to a reality of a few hundred meters.

They crossed a frozen stream. The banks were straight and little more than a meter high, but willows and coarse reeds grew so thickly along the margin that the ponies had to force their way through.

Hansen's mount didn't want to chance wetting its feet. He kicked it repeatedly in the ribs and had just regretted his lack of spurs when the pony decided to cross the narrow stream in a rush that almost unseated him.

Fur hats showed above the hillock beyond the creek. The younger freemen kicked their ponies into a wild gallop, yipping and cheering. Brian followed, calling to his men not to get carried away.

Hansen gripped his saddle with both hands to stay aboard and allowed his pony to gallop along with her fellows. It was unlikely that a rider as unskilled as he was could have controlled the animal anyway.

When the troop reached the top of the hill, they could see two Thrasey riders galloping back toward their encampment, less than a mile away on another rolling peak. One of the Thrasey freemen turned in his saddle and fired his crossbow in the direction of his pursuers. Two of Brian's men responded.

The snap of bowstrings was flat in the open air. None of the missiles came anywhere near a target.

Hansen reined up his pony to take stock. Brian shouted some warnings that showed he understood the danger of the position. Despite that, he and the remainder of the troop of freemen continued to pursue the Thrasey riders.

Other horsemen were coming from the encampment and along the plain to the right.

The Lord of Thrasey's encampment was a straggling thing with no more sign of a berm or other protection than Golsingh's own. The huge black forms of mammoths wandered in small groups, sweeping snow from the prairie with their trunks and lifting bushels of grass into their mouths.

Golsingh's force had carried fodder for their draft animals. The Thrasey army must have packed firewood over the treeless prairie, for a pall of smoke hung above their encampment.

Wan sunlight shone from battlesuits being polished by slaves. There seemed to be a surprising number of the suits.

Probably more than the hundred or so warriors in Golsingh's force this time.

Two riders from the camp joined the pair whom Brian's men were pursuing. The four turned to face their opponents.

The ground between the Thrasey encampment and the relative height from which Hansen watched was flat and almost as perfect for battle as the center of an amphitheatre. The stream closed the left margin, while the right curved out of sight within the slightly higher ground. Hansen had a box seat for the skirmish.

One of the Thrasey freemen raised his crossbow and shot. The black speck of the bolt snapped toward Brian—and on, vanishing in the snowy grass. Hansen thought it was parallax which had made him think the missile had struck, but then Brian swayed in his saddle and flung his lance aside.

The two crossbowmen accompanying Brian were desperately trying to reload their weapons. Their leader must have given an order Hansen couldn't hear for the distance, because he and his whole troop began to trot back the way they'd come.

The Thrasey freemen started to follow. One of Brian's men turned and shook his lance in threat. Another band of horsemen burst through the willows at the creekbed a kilometer away.

Hansen doubted that either side could be sure which party the newcomers supported. The Thrasey patrol began walking its mounts up the gentle slope toward their camp.

Hansen's pony had settled to crop the long grass. It looked up without particular interest as its fellows rejoined.

The younger freemen were flushed and panting. Brian looked sallow. His left sleeve had been torn off, and he clutched his biceps with his right hand.

"Let's see it," Hansen directed, clucking his pony nearer to the wounded man.

"Bastards," Brian muttered.

The clouds had thickened. It was beginning to snow sparse, tiny flakes. The temperature had dropped a degree or two since dawn.

Hansen pried the freeman's fingers from around the deep, ragged tear. The wound was bleeding badly, but the square-headed quarrel hadn't smashed bone or nicked an artery.

With only direct pressure on the arm, Brian would've bled out if an artery were severed. . . .

"Right," said Hansen, squeezing Brian's hand back over the damage. "Is there a—medic, whatever, back in camp?"

"Old Jepson, he sets bones sometimes," one of the freemen said.

"Does he stitch wounds?" Hansen demanded, and the blank expressions he received were the expected answer.

The wounds warriors took on Northworld were usually fatal

and certainly self-cauterized. There was little that even the finest medical facilities of, say, Annunciation could have done for injured warriors except perform limb-grafts. And it wasn't the business of *this* society to worry about wounded freemen and slaves.

"Right. You—" Hansen pointed to the freeman on the strongest pony "—ride back for the camp as fast as you can, and stick your shirt in boiling water. *Fast!*"

"Huh?"

"It'll be the bandage. Now ride, damn you!"

The freeman didn't understand the purpose of the orders, but he heard the death threat in Hansen's voice. He dug the jangling rowels of his spurs into his pony and began to canter back toward the camp.

"I'm all right," Brian said. He kneed his mount into careful motion. "Bastards."

"Sure," agreed Hansen, walking his pony alongside. "One of you," he snapped to the younger freemen, "make sure we're headed straight back."

If he could have trusted his own riding skills, he would have tried to support Brian . . . though the wounded man seemed to be doing pretty well.

Brian's waxy complexion was the main concern. The wound wouldn't be directly fatal, but shock might very well finish the job.

Brian urged his pony into a trot. His reins hung loosely in his left hand.

"Tooley's there," he said loudly, instinctively aware that if he let himself slip into shock and somnolence, he wouldn't come back. "I saw his suit, red and white."

"Naw," objected one of his fellows. Hansen, his knuckles white on the reins, marveled at the way the other men could ride and talk. "He's with Count Rolfe, ain't he?"

"Frekka," said Brian. "He quarreled with Rolfe this summer and went to Frekka. Holroyd and Finch, they hired on with Frekka too. And they're up there."

It was snowing harder, but they were back among the trees now and the needles caught some of the flakes. The trees blocked much of the wan sunlight as well. Hansen looked forward to boosting the light amplitude on his battlesuit's display.

"Finch ain't nothin'," said another man. "An' Holroyd ain't much."

"Tooley's shit hot, though," Brian rejoined. He must be in considerable pain, but he was looking better for the hard ride. "And there's a lot of the buggers. I'd figured sixty, maybe eighty tops at Thrasey if the Lord'd been hiring his ass off."

"There's more 'n that," said one of his men. Despite their youth and indiscipline, these freemen had enough experience—and intelligence, Hansen was realizing—to make them good scouts.

"There's a hundred 'n twenty easy," Brian agreed grimly. The camp was in sight. Warriors were getting into their armor near each of the fires.

"Course," Brian added, "the King 'n Lord Taddeusz, they'll clean 'em up anyhow."

The freeman might have sounded more confident if it weren't for the wound sapping his vitality.

Hansen would have had doubts in any case.

Hansen saw Malcolm's brilliant suit on the left edge of the encampment, closely accompanied by Shill and Maharg.

Low status warriors could be identified as a class—as cannon-fodder—by the amateurish detailing of their armor. That would be easy to cure: buff all the suits down to bare metal and let the artificial intelligence separate friends from foes.

Hansen should've thought of that sooner. It was too late to change for this battle. And it was beginning to look as though that made it simply too late. . . .

He slid from his pony and left the animal to wander as it chose while he opened his armor. He tossed his fur cloak onto the bundle a slave had made of his bedding, then stripped off his fur breeches.

The wind was cold, but the interior of Hansen's battlesuit would be colder than hell until it came up to operating temperature in ten minutes or so. Delaying wasn't going to help matters. Hansen clambered inside and latched the suit over him.

The technological ambiance calmed and reassured him more than he'd expected. Hansen didn't belong in the feudal museum that was Northworld society, but he'd lived the most important parts of his adult life in a battlesuit of one sort or another.

And maybe he was kidding himself about the society as well. He belonged here a lot more clearly than he had on Diamond.

"Remote, quarter, Malcolm," he said, putting his suit through its paces before he needed to use them for real. The upper righthand quadrant of his display showed Hansen, on a reduced scale, what the veteran warrior was seeing.

Malcolm faced Lamullo, the commander of Golsingh's left wing. Lamullo's father had left him an excellent battlesuit, painted in candystripes of bronze and black; but the son had inherited little of his father's aggressive drive. Hansen suspected that Lamullo's lack of ambition was as much the reason Taddeusz supported him as the suit itself was.

It was snowing harder. Hansen pursed his lips and glanced around him—then said, "Mark Golsingh," and let his AI do the work.

A carat pulsing on Hansen's display indicated where the king was hidden at the center of a group of twenty-odd warriors, most of them well equipped.

"Remote quarter Golsingh," Hansen said as he started in that direction. Golsingh and his warchief were listening to Brian say, ". . . and a lot of 'em been at Frekka, Thrasey must've hired 'em away in the last week or two."

The freeman's left arm was in a sling. One of his fellows was standing nearby, ready to support him if needed. Hansen hoped they'd used the—hopefully—sterilized cloth for a bandage, but there was only so much you could do. . . .

The error in the scout's report had no tactical significance, but it made all the strategic difference in this world. The Lord of Thrasey hadn't hired mercenaries from Frekka; they'd been sent as a gift. Hansen was willing to bet his life on that.

Of course, he wouldn't have a life to gamble with further unless things worked out better today than they were likely to.

"That doesn't matter," said Taddeusz contemptuously. "Nobody who'd take service with merchants is of any concern."

Hansen reached the back of the circle of high-ranking warriors. He put a gauntlet on the shoulder of a man, hoping the fellow would make room. The man turned slightly and shoved Hansen away.

"I remember Tooley," Golsingh replied, sounding thoughtful.

"He was here a few years ago. Terrible temper, but ... Not a warrior I would dismiss lightly."

"Command channel," Hansen directed his artificial intelligence.

He shouldn't have access to a commo frequency intended for top-ranking personnel, but there was nobody except Hansen in the whole army who knew how to activate the push, much less lock out middle-rankers like himself.

"Don't worry about—" Taddeusz was saying when Hansen's voice broke in on his earphones with: "Lord Golsingh, I'm sorry to interrupt—"

"Who!" Taddeusz shouted. They all used amplified voice communications instead of the excellent radios built into their suits. "Hansen? Is that—"

"—but I've viewed the battlefield and there's a way we can win this, I think pretty easily, especially with the low light conditions."

An arc blazed up from the center of the group of warriors.

"Taddeusz?" the king said doubtfully.

The circle broke outward like a ripple spreading.

Hansen also began backing away. "Lord Taddeusz, please," he said. "The terrain—"

The warchief's weapon slashed down.

Hansen jumped back. The arc, though attenuated by three meters' distance when it struck him, screeched in Hansen's ears and blurred his display into hash. He fell over.

Taddeusz shut his arc down instead of stepping closer. "If I hear your voice again this day," he said in a distinct tone more threatening than a bellow, "I will kill you. Begone!"

The circle of warriors closed about the leaders again.

Hansen got to his feet. His suit wasn't functionally damaged, but the paint had blistered off most of his breastplate.

He'd been this angry before.

He began walking toward Malcolm and the left wing.

He'd been this angry before. He always felt better when he'd killed something. As he would very soon.

Trumpets across the camp blew. A freeman near Lamullo took his own horn out from under his cloak and responded with a two-note call.

Cold and distant as the wind, other trumpets answered from the Thrasey encampment.

The sky was sullen. The upper left arm of Hansen's suit had been repaired, but he hadn't thought to replace the suede liner. Each time his skin touched the casing, the steel felt like a burn.

Warriors were moving out in clumps, forming a line of sorts.

"Maharg," Hansen said. "Shill. Come with me. We've got a battle to win."

Sometimes when Hansen felt the way he did now he slammed the heel of his hand into a wall. His battlesuit would knock over the stump of any of the nearby trees.

He clashed his palms together. The shock of power-driven steel against steel rang through the nearest warriors, turning a dozen faceless helmets toward him.

"For people who don't deserve it any damn way," Hansen added bitterly; though the good lord knew he should've been used to it by now.

Shill and Maharg swayed in their tracks. Hansen looked at Malcolm and said, "Malcolm. Come with us. You go out there like the rest—"

He nodded, uncertain whether the gesture was distinguishable while he wore armor. "—and you'll just get yourself chopped up. There's too many of them."

"Come along, you lot," Lamullo called over his shoulder. The gaggle of armored men was drifting into the woods. Freemen on ponies were intermixed with the warriors for the moment.

"No," said Malcolm. Then, sharply, "No!"

But instead of moving immediately to join the rest of the left wing, he pointed to Shill and Maharg and said, "You two. You can go with him if you want to. You—do what he says, all right? Do what the laddie says. But I can't."

Malcolm turned and followed Lamullo with long, clashing strides.

"Remote, quarter, Malcolm," Hansen ordered his AI. "Local unit, secure communications."

He grinned invisibly at Shill and Maharg who quivered between frightening alternatives. "Come on then, guys," Hansen said. "We've got a battle to win."

Chapter Nineteen

Hansen lead his little unit into the bed of the stream. Here, the watercourse was little more than washed stones, ice, and the brown, hollow stems of frozen reeds.

Trumpets called frequently, but Hansen now realized the cries were more generally for the amusement of the freemen with the horns than they were signals or commands. Warriors argued with what their king told them directly—or ignored him, if they had Taddeusz' stature, at any rate. They weren't going to take directions passed by members of the lower orders.

One of the hobbled draft mammoths joined in with a series of piercing shrieks, as meaningful and perhaps as musical as the human notes.

"This isn't taking us toward the battlefield," Maharg said. They were all stumbling and patting their hands on the bank to keep from falling down. "They'll . . . Taddeusz, he'll give us the chop for deserting like this."

"We're going to get to the battle," Hansen said. "The streambed curves around, no problem."

He hoped it did. If this wasn't the same creek, he was going to have some explaining to do.

Though not, he suspected, to Golsingh.

"We're gonna get there late, though," Shill said with an undertone of . . . 'satisfaction' might be too strong a word. Might be.

Hansen crashed on. So long as the others' suits didn't have to power their arcs or electronic defenses, they could match his more efficient unit stride for stride. It can't have been a pleasant march, but it wasn't for their leader either.

They were getting out into the prairie, where herds of mammoths had kept the grassland open with their destructive feeding. The stream banks were a little deeper.

Hansen could see nothing directly beyond the reeds and alders. His quadrant of Malcolm's display showed the main line of

141

Golsingh's army straggling up the hill which overlooked the chosen battlefield. Their footing had been much better, and they were, as Shill had said, well in advance of Hansen's unit.

They didn't look like an army, though. The warriors were in blobs and clumps, with potentially dangerous gaps all along the line. They had no more organization than bits of popcorn strung into a necklace by a kindergartner.

Taddeusz, with a dozen or so followers, was far in the lead on the right flank. Just as he had been during the battle against Count Lopez.

Taddeusz hadn't learned a damned thing. Which figured.

Hansen used his artificial intelligence to identify the players. Even without the compression of the remote display, he would have found it difficult to tell one set of painted armor from the next.

The sky hadn't brightened since dawn, and the snow was falling thicker.

"Mark friendlies blue," Hansen muttered, watching tags flicker across the quadrant. If he looked behind him, he'd see the same markers of blue light on the helmets of Shill and Maharg.

"You two," he ordered. "Say 'Mark friendlies blue' the way I told you in training."

"We did that," Shill grumbled. "Back to the camp."

Good lord, they were learning!

"Any chance we could siddown and rest?" Shill asked abruptly. The microphone in his helmet picked up his panting breath. "I won't be good fer shit if I don't get a breather."

"When were you ever good fer shit, Shill?" Maharg gibed.

"If we rest now, there won't be anything to do but count the corpses by the time we get where we're going," Hansen said. His body felt as though he'd spent the morning as a tackling dummy.

"Suits me," the older man muttered; but he kept up, and they all kept going despite the fact that the water was now knee deep. Occasionally they broke through the ice, then tripped on hidden rocks.

The banks were waist high and slightly undercut. Willow roots provided solid handholds for Hansen and his men when their feet slipped.

Malcolm had reached the top of the hillock. Through the veteran's eyes, Hansen saw freemen shout thinly and charge in the center of the plain. The Thrasey riders were badly outnumbered. They fell back immediately behind the oncoming row of warriors.

Crossbowmen banged bolts toward the freemen and occasionally at the warriors as well. Hits sparkled vainly on the battlesuits.

The forces of the Lord of Thrasey outnumbered Golsingh's by at least twenty warriors.

On the far right flank, a knot of men under Taddeusz charged the Thrasey line at a lumbering run. They were a good hundred meters ahead of the king's more regular array in the center, while Lamullo's left wing was echeloned back about the same distance behind Golsingh's division.

And, thanks to the rough going and the way the creek meandered, Hansen's pitiful unit was just about that far behind the left wing. It made good geometry but bad war.

"Come on," Hansen snarled. He started running. If that stupid bastard of a warchief could do it, so could he.

Shill fell headlong. Hansen turned, but Maharg was already helping the older warrior to his feet. They pounded down the creek like enraged hippos, striking sparks from the rocks and cursing monotonously into their microphones.

The Thrasey right wing was thrown forward also, so the forces engaged along their full lengths more or less simultaneously. Rippling arc weapons reflected between the ground and the low clouds.

Hansen noticed a phenomenon which had escaped him during the forest battle of the previous week: at the moment of contact, each battleline spread into two lines. The well-armored champions engaged one another in the front ranks, while lesser folk in scruffy, cobbled-together armor hung back a pace or two.

Malcolm snapped his arc at a warrior in black and white from four meters out. His opponent blocked the stroke and replied with a cut of his own. Armor of the quality of either suit was impervious at that distance, but neither man seemed inclined to close for the moment. Three other warriors flanked the Thrasey champion—from a step back.

Malcolm was missing the support of Shill and Maharg. Not that his juniors did anything, not really; but they were there. . . .

Hansen fell down. Shill put out a hand, but Hansen grabbed a tree root and jerked himself upright by it.

At the edge of Malcolm's display, Hansen saw Lamullo being pressed hard by a warrior in red and white. *Tooley, the one with a terrible temper but nobody you'd wish to see on the other side*.

Lamullo was blocking his opponent's strokes adequately, but he seemed unable to counterattack. After each parry he stepped backward.

Malcolm rushed his man with a shout. The Thrasey champion dodged back and collided with one of his own supporters. Malcolm's arc crackled the length of his opponent's outflung left arm, glancing but shearing also in a fountain of sparks.

The Thrasey warrior staggered in the opposite direction and fell. One of his retinue stepped over the champion to guard him. Malcolm cut vertically. The other warrior caught the arc on his own weapon, but he didn't have the power to stop it from sizzling into and halfway through his helmet.

Malcolm slashed to his right, taking the second member of the retinue on the hip joint and crumpling him like a sheet of heated polyethylene.

The third low-status warrior turned to run. Malcolm's arc sliced off his feet at the ankles.

Hansen swore. He'd seen in the swirling action what Malcolm didn't have the time or inclination to notice.

"Hold up!" Hansen snarled to his men. He thrust his arm into the reeds to clear a sight line. The growth was too thick. His arc scythed down the reeds in a cloud of steam.

They hadn't come as far as he'd intended, but the battle itself had moved toward them. Hansen was slightly behind the right flank of the Thrasey line. The nearest warrior was twenty meters away, watching his front, and the nearest actual fighting was ten meters beyond that.

Tooley jumped over the Lamullo's body and bore down on Malcolm with a roar.

"All right," said Hansen, cool again. "Let's go."

He gripped a willow trunk and started to drag himself up. The roots pulled out in a shower of dirt.

"Here," said Maharg, making a stirrup of his hands. Hansen stepped into it and felt the other warrior's battlesuit lift him. Shill followed by the same route, then bent and with Hansen jerked Maharg to the top of the bank.

A pair of Thrasey freemen watched with amazement as the three warriors appeared from the dense growth. They rode into the battleline, shouting a warning.

A warrior—it looked like one of the Thrasey side—cut them both down with as little hesitation as Hansen had shown when he cleared his sight line.

"Remember . . . ," said Hansen. He didn't feel the aches and battering he'd just given his body, but his forearms were quivering with adrenalin. "When the marker goes red, everybody hits 'im together."

But Hansen took the nearest Thrasey warrior himself, cutting the man so deeply through the shoulderblades that the arc crackled out through the flimsy plastron before Hansen shut it off.

They dropped three of their opponents before the fourth man even turned around. The warriors hanging back behind the real engagement weren't well equipped anyway.

Maharg's arc froze the fourth man. Hansen swatted away the fellow's life with something near contempt, as though he were scraping cow manure from his glove.

They struck the front rank, unaware and from behind; three of the Thrasey champions went down under the multiple attacks as easily as the hirelings had.

The air stank of ozone and burned flesh. The snow softened the outlines of the bodies, but it couldn't hide the smells of death.

Golsingh's collapsing line stiffened. Several of the more formidable surviving warriors on the left wing fell in with Hansen and his crew. They were turning the Thrasey flank.

Tooley screamed an amplified challenge as he lunged toward Hansen. His arc was a dense blue-white, even though it was extended more than a meter.

Malcolm must be dead.

"Strike!" Hansen shouted with his arc hovering just above his right gauntlet. He stepped close, the opposite of what he wanted to do and—with luck—not what Tooley expected.

Shill and Maharg had jumped back from Tooley's furious rush. Hansen was alone.

Hansen knew he couldn't block Tooley's weapon, even with his own flux as dense as his suit could produce. He caught Tooley's downward slash and held it momentarily while his body twisted out of the way.

Their armor clanged together. Tooley's arc carved into the sod explosively, covering both men in a veil of steam. Hansen's right arm was numb. His chest shuddered as he tried desperately to hold his opponent's weapon aside.

Something crackled past at the lower edge of Hansen's vision—an arc, Maharg stepping in to cut at Tooley's hip joint. Red and white paint blistered in the dancing arc, but the electronic armor held—

Until Shill squeezed between Hansen and Maharg. The old man thrust home at the core of the younger warrior's attack, and Tooley's battlesuit failed with a *crack!* that blew a doughnut of soot and steam across the field.

Tooley fell backward. Hansen started to topple onto the corpse. Shill braced him for a moment until Maharg could grab Hansen's shoulders and lift him upright.

Hansen tried to raise his right arm. He watched with amazement as the limb obeyed, but he still had no sensation from the shoulder on down. His chest felt cold and he was shuddering.

The battle paused. The warriors who'd followed Tooley, and those men of Golsingh's whose opponents had fallen in the flank attack, waited uncertainly. Hansen was trying to get his breath.

Malcolm got to his feet behind the Thrasey warriors. His helmet and plastron had been seared black by Tooley's arc. It was only by the red-blue-silver bands on his arms and legs that he could be identified. He hacked down the nearest man from behind.

"General freq!" Hansen gasped to his AI. "Come on, you bastards! Golsingh and Peace!"

He wasn't sure that was the best battlecry for *this* place, but peace was the brightest hope Hansen himself could imagine just now.

And he knew there'd be no peace on this field until every one of the Thrasey warriors was down.

"Strike!" with his display centered on a Thrasey warrior whose arc quivered first toward Hansen's unit, then toward Malcolm.

Hansen slashed; Shill and Maharg cut, together and within a fraction of a second of their leader's stroke. The warrior's helmet burned as Malcolm chopped down the man beside him.

"Come on!"

The whole Thrasey flank collapsed. Warriors turned and ran as Golsingh's troops swept toward them from the front and side simultaneously.

"No-'count merchant kissers!" Malcolm bawled as he strode down the line he was crumpling. "Frekka-paid cowards!"

They didn't look like cowards a minute ago, Hansen thought as he tried to keep up with the veteran.

But the prejudice against merchants' hirelings must be as great *among* those hirelings as it was among warriors who hadn't decided to accept Frekka's offers. So long as they were led by a champion of Tooley's stature, they stood and fought; with their leader down, there was no sign of the willingness Count Lopez' men had shown to fight on after the battle was clearly lost.

Despite the success of Hansen's flanking movement, the battle *wasn't* clearly lost for the Thrasey forces.

The central division around a figure in blue and silver armor ("The Lord of Thrasey," answered a feminine voice when Hansen asked his AI for an identification) had surged into the gap between Golsingh and the headlong advance of Taddeusz' unit. The king had avoided being surrounded only by falling back, and the Lord of Thrasey was pushing him hard.

A dozen Thrasey warriors faced around to meet the threat from the collapsing flank. The foremost were champions from the lord's personal bodyguard, and even the warriors of their retinues, falling into place behind them, looked reasonably well equipped.

Malcolm slowed and stopped five paces from the new line. The rush of easy winners behind him halted at the appearance of a real enemy again.

Hansen put a hand on the veteran's shoulder. "Malcolm," he said. "I'll lead and you back—"

Malcolm pushed Hansen aside with a clang.

A maelstrom of arcs snarled around the leaders. The Lord

of Thrasey had led the remainder of his bodyguard in a rush to overwhelm Golsingh before the king's left flank could rescue him.

The melee blazed like the lightning which swirls in the funnel of a tornado, flinging battlesuits and bits of battlesuit out from its lethal core. Golsingh stood in his blue armor and struck with deadly effect, but the warriors to either side of him dropped.

Malcolm shouted wordlessly and charged the waiting line.

"Strike with Malcolm!" Hansen snarled as he lurched forward beside the veteran.

Malcolm's arc crossed with that of a fellow whose armor was decorated in orange swirls. Hansen feinted toward the next Thrasey warrior to the left, then struck at the shoulder of Malcolm's man. The armor burned, flinging the limb in one direction as the man's body toppled in the other.

Maharg parried the thrust of the left-hand warrior and went to his knees with the searing force of the fellow's arc. Hansen's sideways sweep drove the Thrasey warrior back. Maharg stayed down, shaking his head.

The Thrasey survivors backed. Some of Golsingh's warriors pressed forward.

"What are you doing?" Malcolm demanded. "He was mine!"

"Winning!" Hansen snarled back on straight audio. "D'ye want to die? We'll all die if we don't cut the king loose, 'n that means teamwork!"

Malcolm lunged forward, thrusting. His arc slipped past the guard and through the plastron of a warrior hesitating between facing Malcolm and joining the attack on Golsingh. The man was dead and falling, but Hansen struck him anyway because he was moving with the stroke and it was better to follow through than to change his rhythm.

Shill chopped at the body as he followed Malcolm and Hansen. His arc cut at the ankles of the next Thrasey warrior as his betters—as his *fellows*—whipsawed the victim through both shoulder pieces.

The last of Golsingh's bodyguards fell. Three of the four men with the Lord of Thrasey, all of them champions, turned and faced the threat from the flank.

Thrasey and his remaining warrior slashed at the king. The

warrior got home with a blast of sparks that blistered blotches of paint away from Golsingh's helmet.

Malcolm cut at a guard wearing black and white checks. The Thrasey warrior thrust back, not at Malcolm but at Hansen lunging in to double the stroke. Hansen's display blurred and all his hair stood out straight as his muscles twitched.

He almost fell as his display shrank back into bright focus. All three of the Thrasey bodyguards held their blocking position. One of the Golsingh's left-wing warriors had fallen between them and Malcolm.

Two meters away, the Lord of Thrasey was body to body with Golsingh. Their arcs were locked in a shower of blue fire. The warrior with the Lord of Thrasey had lifted his rippling arc weapon for the final blow.

"Come on," Hansen gasped as he jumped forward. The check-armored warrior parried his cut.

Their armor crashed together, jarring the Thrasey warrior back a half step before the power of his better suit stopped Hansen's rush and began bending him over. Malcolm was dueling with another bodyguard, and there was no chance that—

Shill stepped between Hansen and Malcolm with his palm outstretched. His bolt struck the Lord of Thrasey at the join of his backplate and helmet. Malcolm's opponent swiped sideways, cutting through both knees of Shill's powerless suit.

Golsingh neatly decapitated the Lord of Thrasey.

Shill toppled forward. The bodyguard struggling with Hansen doubled up as Maharg stabbed him through the belly.

Hansen's AI tagged all the figures still standing with the spike of blue light. Friendlies, they were all friendlies. Malcolm had finished his opponent when the fool struck down Shill, and Golsingh was hacking with an intensity that was more vengeance than caution at the smoldering ruins of the warrior who'd almost killed him.

Hansen unlatched his suit. He opened the heavy clamshell with hysterical strength that belied his exhausted weakness of moments before. The snowy air was a club, but his body was already shuddering.

The smell of burned meat was even worse when he jerked open Shill's battlesuit.

Shill's eyes were closed, but his nostrils flared as he breathed.

He wouldn't be breathing long. The wounds were cauterized by the arc that made them, but the shock of the high voltage and double amputation would certainly be fatal.

Freemen rode in to join the warriors at the moment of victory.

"Furs!" Hansen screamed. His voice cracked. "Furs! Here! Now, goddam you!"

"Fin'ly broke my way," Shill whispered. He was smiling. "Didja see him go down? I killed the fuckin' Lord a Thrasey!"

A freeman leaped from his pony and draped his cloak over Hansen's shoulders. Hansen snatched it off and tucked it around Shill, still cradled in the back half of his armor.

Maharg knelt beside them. "You all right, sir?" he asked. "You all right?"

"Old Shill fin'ly . . . ," Shill said.

His eyes opened. The old man's pupils were a brilliant blue that Hansen hadn't noticed before.

"Old Shill fin'ly had some luck!" Shill gasped.

His chest arched. A convulsion drove the remainder of his breath out in a long rattling cough that continued several seconds after the light had gone out of the blue eyes.

Maharg shook Hansen by the shoulders. "Sir?" he said. "Are you all right? You're crying."

Chapter Twenty

"Well, Lord Golsingh," said the warrior named Audemar, "if you pass your right to Thrasey's armor, then the suit should properly go to me."

"We've been over this, Audemar," Golsingh said. His voice was so quiet that Hansen barely heard it over the scrunch of his spade.

"He shouldn't be doing that," Taddeusz grumbled. "It isn't a warrior's business to work with his hands."

"He did a warrior's business this day, foster father."

Hansen freed another block of turf. A pair of slaves set it on a tarpaulin with three others. They lifted the edges of the cloth to carry the lot to the growing mound.

Hansen positioned the spade, then slid it down through the sod. He wriggled the T-handle to clear pebbles caught among the grassroots.

"But when Lamullo fell," Audemar said, "I was the senior warrior in the left division. Therefore I should have the leader's share of booty taken by the—"

"Shut up, Audemar," Taddeusz said.

"Lord Malcolm sits at my left now in banquet, Audemar," Golsingh said. His tone was growing sharper and thinner, like a blade being drawn from a cane scabbard.

There weren't any proper stones with which to raise a mound here, but turf would last as long. More fitting for Shill, besides. Shill hadn't had the harshness of rock; but he'd endured nonetheless.

"Ah, sir?" said Maharg. He looked older now, but that might be only exhaustion. "Would it be all right if I, ah . . . if I dug one myself?"

Hansen straightened, leaving the spade upright in the cut. He gestured toward the handle. "Keep the corners square," he said, massaging his lower back with both hands.

He looked around critically. "We've probably got enough by now."

There were thirty slaves lifting sod for the mound, but the straggling rectangle Hansen had cut in the prairie was twice the area of what any of the others had managed. Well, the slaves were working because it was their life to work—and their lives if they didn't. Hansen cut sod because—

The mound was two meters high, an oval proportioned eight to three across the axes, much like the proportions of a sleeping man.

"Hope he likes it," Hansen said.

Maharg levered the strip of turf loose and stepped back so that the slaves could remove it. "Shill?" he said. "I dunno."

The young warrior knuckled his forehead. The fine hairs on the back of his right hand had crinkled when the surge of an opponent's arc overloaded his battlesuit. "I never figured North's Searchers'd, you know, be interested in Shill."

He looked at Hansen. It wasn't just exhaustion: Maharg had aged. "Nor me neither," he added. "Though with the new armor, that might change. Thanks to you."

"You earned it," Hansen said. "Shill did too."

He looked toward the sky. It was cold, and the wind made his vision blur.

"I recognize your right to appoint whomsoever you please to positions of honor, your majesty," Audemar said, his voice hoarse with suppressed anger.

"If you choose to make a warrior of limited status your left wing commander—and your new Lord of Thrasey!" Audemar bit the words out "—then that is your option, and I only hope you don't regret it soon. But—"

The sun was low. Because there was a thin slice of clear sky near the horizon, the landscape was brighter than it had been this day before.

Malcolm turned from the battlesuit which stood upright at the head of the mound and walked toward the group around the king.

"—that's for the *future*," Audemar continued. He was about fifty years old, of middle height, and soft rather than precisely fat. "At the time the booty was taken, *I* was in charge—"

Hansen watched with no expression for a moment, then jerked the spade from the soil and also walked toward the king. Maharg was beside him.

"—and that means that the Lord of Thrasey's armor is mine by right unless you claim it yourself. It's a royal suit and even after repairs it will be superior to mine. Theref—"

Malcolm gripped Audemar by the shoulder with his left hand and spun the older man so that his cheek was in position for Malcolm's broad right palm. The slap sounded like a treelimb breaking.

Audemar would have fallen, but Malcolm continued to hold him. The backhand bloodied Audemar's nose.

Taddeusz started to move. Golsingh stopped him with a raised hand. "Wait," the king said.

Hansen let the spade lie down along his right leg again.

"Listen, you bastard," Malcolm said. He and the man he held were about of a weight, but Malcolm's fury gave bulk to his greater height. "If you'd been worth shit yourself, we wouldn't've had to bury Shill today, would we?"

"That old man was noth—" and the rest of the word vanished in a spray of blood from Audemar's lips as Malcolm slapped him again.

Golsingh stepped between them. "That's enough," he said mildly. His head turned to Audemar. "Audemar," he went on in a tone of thin steel. "You have been informed of my decision. Further objection to it will be treason. Do you understand?"

Audemar spun and walked off. His steps were uncertain.

"Very good," said Golsingh. The king's eyes met Hansen's. "Then we'll return to last night's encampment and set off for Peace Rock in the morning. There's no point in trying to travel any distance now."

Hansen nodded. "Yes, milord," he said.

His throat was dry. He set the edge of the spade on the ground and drove it in a hand's breadth, so that a slave could easily find it.

"Let's go find somebody with a skin of beer," Malcolm said to Hansen and Maharg. His voice had odd breaks and catches in it, as if he had crumbs in his throat.

At the head of the mound over Shill's dead body, the late sunlight winked on the blue and silver majesty of the Lord of Thrasey's battlesuit.

Chapter Twenty-one

"It's customary after a battle, Lord Hansen . . . ," said Krita as she leaned forward to fill his cup.

The breasts wobbling beneath the scooped neckline of her blouse were fuller than the taut planes of her face and her muscular limbs had led him to expect.

". . . for a warrior to describe his own exploits. Not those of a—friend?"

"Shill was my friend, yes," Hansen said coldly.

"Maybe he didn't have any exploits to describe," suggested Unn. "Is that it, Lord Hansen?"

"Krita, girl," said Taddeusz from the opposite corner of the cross-table, "stop chattering while we're trying to plan. And leave *him* alone anyway."

Krita looked at Unn, balancing the beer pitcher on her hip. She was wearing red again, while Unn's dress was of linen dyed the same rich blue as Shill's eyes.

"I hear," said Krita, as though she hadn't heard her father speak, "that Hansen was one of Lord Malcolm's greatest champions. And we *know* what a hero Malcolm was—"

Krita bent again, this time filling Malcolm's mug.

Hansen thought the new Lord of Thrasey looked flushed, but with Malcolm's complexion it was hard to tell. Besides, the color might come from drink, the hearth, or the fact that Malcolm was now the man sitting to the King's immediate left.

"—don't we?"

She drew her index finger up the back of Malcolm's wrist. He jerked his hand back as though she'd touched him with a branding iron. Taddeusz clutched the arms of his chair.

"Lord Golsingh?" Hansen said loudly to cut through the woman's—the women's—deliberate provocation. "Have you given any thought to what I said about Frekka?"

"Have I realized that you were correct in what you told me

154

before the battle?" Golsingh said with the trace of a smile. "Yes, I have."

He looked to his other side. "And you're of the same opinion now too, aren't you, foster father?"

"That Frekka needs to be put down?" Taddeusz said harshly. "Yes, I'll grant that. Burnt down and sown with salt, *I* say—but you've got your own notions there, too, don't you?"

He glared fiercely at Hansen. His daughter shifted so that her back was to the warchief and her mocking, enticing smile played over Malcolm, Hansen and Maharg.

"We need—" Hansen said.

"*We* need!" Taddeusz snarled.

"Lord Golsingh needs—" Hansen said, raising his voice to shout down the warchief if that were necessary, but Taddeusz was only interjecting "—the trade and manufacture of Frekka to succeed in his plan of unifying his kingdom. What he doesn't need are the present Syndics of Frekka and their games."

Taddeusz drained his goblet. "And Golsingh will take your advice, I suppose?" he said/asked bitterly.

"The king will do as seems good to the king, foster father," Golsingh said in his thin voice.

Taddeusz met his eyes for a moment, then blinked.

"More beer, girl," he growled as he thrust his goblet out to Krita. Unn filled it instead.

"I've looked over your suggestions of which warriors go to Thrasey with Lord Malcolm," Golsingh continued when he was sure his point had been taken.

"And your own requests, Lord Malcolm." He nodded toward Malcolm, who leaned closer in relief at the change of subject. "There are discrepancies." The king smiled. "*Only* discrepancies, I would say. Now. . . ."

The conversation turned to the merits—and otherwise—of warriors Hansen knew only as battlecolors, not names. He relaxed, glad not to have a fight just now. He was bruised and aching, and his eulogy on Shill had drained whatever energy the battle two days ago had left.

Shill died because he trusted Hansen farther than he should have.

Maharg got up from the table. He patted Hansen on the shoulder and said, "Thanks," as he left.

Maharg wasn't on watch tonight, and he'd made a female friend since he came back from the battle a hero. . . . Which was Maharg's doing, not Hansen's, not really; but the boy didn't see it that way.

A female friend. . . .

"We've been wondering, Lord Hansen," said Krita as she refilled the mug that he seemed to have emptied, to his surprise, "whether you're one of those men who don't like women?"

"*What?*" The question sobered him like a bucket of melt-water.

Unn's eyes were amused, Krita's were laughing.

"Since none of the girls say you've," Krita continued, "shall we say—given them the time. That's so, isn't it?"

"I haven't *had* the time!" Hansen snapped, flicking his eyes right and left—and right again, to the cross-table; but thank god the bitch had chosen to keep *this* conversation in a low voice.

He grimaced. "This is the first day since I've, I've been here, that I haven't been training in my battlesuit. *You* know how exhausting that is."

"Are you ashamed of your tastes?" Unn asked coolly. "Some of the male slaves quite like it, we're told. Not that it matters what a slave thinks."

Krita giggled. "Some of the warriors, too. And not the least of them, either. Would you like some names?"

"What I'd like—" said Hansen, standing as he downed the beer in his mug in three quick gulps. And he'd been wondering if *Malcolm* was flushing at this bitch's games! The low firelight was sufficient camouflage now, thank goodness.

"What *I'd* like is a piss and my bed."

He stamped out of the hall for the former; and, much later, having emptied the skin of beer he'd taken from a servant, he returned and found his bed.

Hansen was awakened by the sound of the bar sliding between the staples of his door, locking it from the inside. There was no light at all.

Hansen swung his body erect at the far end of the bed. He didn't get up because his legs were tangled with furs. He'd do himself more trouble than help by the noise he'd make trying to free them.

In Hansen's right hand was an iron pry-bar, half a meter long. He held his breath and the weapon, waiting for the intruder to make his move.

"Do you have the time now, Hansen?" whispered a woman's throaty voice. "Or should I send you one of the serving boys?"

A woman's voice, the smell of a woman. . . . Hansen's body began to shiver.

The plank bed trembled as she rested her hand on it, then sat down. "Are you afraid?" she murmured.

"No," Hansen lied. "Why are you—"

Her fingertips, then her palms, slid through the hairs of his bare chest.

You bet he was afraid of Krita. She was her father's daughter, headstrong and violent—and surely frustrated in a dozen different ways, ready to light a fuze in order to watch the explosion that would follow.

Taddeusz was out in the hall, slumped in drink over the table. If he even dreamed—

But it'd been too long since Hansen made love to a woman. He hooked the pry-bar over the edge of the bed and reached for Krita.

She wore a robe of thick, clinging material. He fumbled with it for a moment.

"Wait," she said, imperious in the darkness, and pushed Hansen's fingers out of the way. Ribbon-ends brushed him as she untied them; then her strong hands pulled his face down to her breasts. Despite her cool demeanor, Krita's heart was beating fiercely and her nipples were already erect.

They made love with a swift violence that embarrassed Hansen—it had been a *long* time—but thrilled the woman to the point that at climax she bit his shoulder to stifle her cries.

He continued to stroke into her, uncertain as to the etiquette of sex here on Northworld—and individuals were more different than cultures, besides.

Krita murmured in question, then fell into the rhythm again.

Her head tossed and she moaned, "Oh Penny bless me . . . oh bless me . . . oh, oh. . . ."

She buried her face in his shoulder again, this time without biting, and began shuddering through a series of multiple climaxes while Hansen thought of Krita's father and the fact her breasts were flatter and broader than they had seemed when he glimpsed them beneath her dress.

"Oh, gods . . . ," she whispered as she let her body go limp. Her fine hair pooled over his hands. He imagined it in the light of the hearth, black with auburn streaks colored by the glowing coals.

"Why did you come here, Hansen?" she asked. Her fingers kneaded the great muscles over his shoulders, then traced down the knobs of his spine.

"Chance," Hansen said in the honesty of the moment.

He realized as he spoke that his honest statement was almost certainly untrue. North and the Consensus were playing a game, and Nils Hansen was one of their pawns.

But *that* truth wasn't one to speak here.

"But I'm probably the only person on this—" *planet*, but he wouldn't say that "—kingdom who can make Golsingh's dreams a reality. And that's what I'm going to do."

"Then you really intend to help the king?" Krita said. She chuckled. "Taddeusz hates you, you know?"

"Yeah, I'd figured that out."

"He thinks you're a deliberate troublemaker."

Her fingertips lightly massaged the place she'd bitten. Hansen felt it burning. She'd broken the skin for sure . . . but it wasn't anything that'd show with his clothes on. "He thinks you were sent by Frekka to bring down the kingdom."

Hansen snorted. "He wouldn't think that," he said, "if he'd been where the *battle* was being decided the other day instead of haring off on a private war of his own. Golsingh'd be cold meat today if it weren't for . . ."

"If it weren't for you?" Krita prompted, challenge in her tone.

"If it weren't for Shill," Hansen said. "And Malcolm. But yeah, I was there too. And your father wasn't."

Her body shifted. "Here," she said. "Lie beside me for a moment. Is there enough room?"

There was, so long as Hansen watched his head. The bed was almost as broad as the cubicle itself, but the sweep of the thatch lowered the ceiling on the outer edge.

She ran a hand down his chest to his groin. Hansen's belly muscles twitched. He was always ticklish, but particularly at times like these.

He was as relaxed as he'd ever been in his life. He began to play with the woman's groin.

"I've heard what happened during the battle," she said. Her vaginal muscles sucked greedily at his finger. "The real stories—*oh*—not just the boasting around the table tonight. Oh. *Oh*. Why do you. Blame yourself. For Shill dying?"

Hansen concentrated on what he was doing. Discipline had gotten him through a lot of bad moments, out of a lot of situations that he'd rather not have been in.

"Because he was my man," he said quietly. "Because he did what I ordered him to do and taught him to do, and doing that got him killed."

"And so he died cursing you?" the woman said. "That's not what *I* heard."

"He didn't know what he was saying at the end," Hansen said.

"Don't believe it!" Krita said harshly. She pulled his face down to her breasts again. "Yes," she murmured, "yessss. . . . Bite them—please, *bite*."

Her fingers were like oaken dowels on the back of his head and neck.

"Shill was sixty years old," she whispered into Hansen's ear. "He'd never been anything. He wouldn't even have had a job here if it weren't for Malcolm, and Taddeusz wanting to keep Malcolm happy even though he doesn't like him."

She'd been manipulating his prick as she spoke. Now she threw her legs over his. The ceiling was in the way. Hansen slid sideways, to where the thatch gave her enough room to mount him.

"You made Shill a warrior, Hansen," she said as she inserted him into herself. "You made him a *man*. If you were a god, you couldn't have served him better."

A fist pounded on the barred door. "Krita?" Taddeusz shouted. "Krita! Come out of there, you little bitch!"

Hansen's hand gripped the end of his pry-bar. "Your idea?" he asked softly.

"Gods no!" the woman gasped as she fumbled for her robe. "No, no. Oh, gods, I'm . . ."

"Hansen, open this door or I'll break it down!" Taddeusz demanded. His fist slammed the panel hard enough to spring the boards. A trickle of yellow lamplight entered the cubicle.

Hansen explored the ceiling with his hand. The thatch was on stringers at half-meter intervals, plenty of room to slip a body through—but there was a mesh of withies above the stringers, and *that* wouldn't pass anything larger than a clenched fist.

"Didn't I say open?" bellowed Taddeusz as the door slammed repeatedly. The bar held but the panel itself began to split.

"Into the suit!" Hansen whispered as he tucked his pry-bar under one of the stringers and lifted, putting his full strength into the motion.

The mass of thatch shifted, but only a few strands of the tough willow-wand netting popped despite his effort. Hansen moved the bar and tried again. Night air gushed through the temporary gaps.

Half a board smashed in from the door. Taddeusz' big hand reached through the rectangle of lamplight and raised the latch.

The woman was out of sight.

Hansen swung to his feet and pulled the door open. He wished he'd had time to dress, but he wished a lot of things right about now. He held the pry-bar loosely at his side.

"What's all this about?" he demanded as Taddeusz pushed him backward and Hansen slammed the heel of his foot down on Taddeusz' instep.

The warchief yelped and halted. The hall behind him was full of people. Nobody in the building could've been drunk enough to sleep through that hammering.

Taddeusz carried one of the freemen's lances, gripping it well ahead of the balance. An awkward weapon.

"Where is she?" he said. "I knew she was here as soon as I went up to the room and found her gone!"

"Look," Hansen said, "there's nobody here. Let's move back and discuss this—"

Taddeusz thrust the lance past Hansen, into the furs piled on the bed. The bed platform splintered. Taddeusz was a strong bastard, no mistake.

"Where *is*—" the warchief said as he stabbed again, a horizontal stroke that pinned the furs against the far wall of the cubicle.

"What's going on here?" Golsingh demanded from somewhere back in the crowd. "Taddeusz?"

"Keep back!" Taddeusz snapped. "This is for me."

He scowled, then brightened with surmise. "In the armor, is—"

Hansen stood with his back against the battlesuit. "If you touch my armor without permission, warrior," he said with terrible distinctness, "I will kill you here and now."

He pointed the end of the pry-bar between Taddeusz' eyes, only a hand's breadth away.

Malcolm forced his way through the doorway. He gripped the warchief's right elbow with both hands. Taddeusz shook himself free with contemptuous ease.

"I'll break your neck anyway," Taddeusz snarled.

His muscles bunched, then froze as a voice crackled from the hollow of the hall saying, "Father! What's the matter with you? Are you mad?"

"Look," said the freeman holding the lamp. He pointed toward the thatch that Hansen's desperate efforts had torn.

Taddeusz turned slowly, then burst out of the bed cubicle like a boar charging hounds.

Malcolm exhaled in relief. Hansen was too focused to feel anything. He pushed his friend from the cubicle behind Taddeusz and followed, pulling the broken door closed behind him.

A dozen animal-fat lamps supplemented the dull glow of the hearth. Krita stood near Golsingh. She wore boots and a fur cape on which the snow was melting.

"Where were you, you whore?" Taddeusz demanded in a thick voice.

"Outside, walking with Unn," his daughter blazed. "If it's any concern to a drunken pig like you!"

"You were not, you slut!" Taddeusz roar as he lurched forward.

Golsingh stepped between father and daughter, saying, "Fos—" and Taddeusz stiff-armed him out of the way.

Never hit a man with your bare hand, a man had once told Hansen. An old man, too old to live but too tough to die.

Hansen raised the pry-bar, measuring the distance to the back of the warchief's skull which wasn't as hard as iron whatever he might think—

A figure in a battlesuit stepped into Taddeusz' path. The warchief crashed into the armor, bounced back, and raised his fist in a gesture so vain that even he understood its absurdity.

Taddeusz twined the fingers of both hands around themselves. He squeezed as though choking a dragon.

The battlesuit was Hansen's own.

Had been Hansen's. He'd claimed Tooley's armor after the battle, and his own suit went to—

Maharg's voice boomed from the battlesuit's amplifier, "Excellency? Are you all right?"

The suit's great steel arm extended toward Golsingh, who was already picking himself up from the floor.

If Krita was here, fully dressed—and she was—*then who in hell had he been fucking?*

Taddeusz knelt before Golsingh.

"Excellency," he said in a voice choked by emotion. "I don't deserve to live. Slay me, but grant my spirit forgiveness for the insult to which my whore of a daughter drove me."

"Don't—here, get up, foster father," Golsingh said uncomfortably. "Come on, we've all been drinking, and we've imagined things tonight, I'm sure."

The warchief arose. He looked even more like a bear when the lamps woke amber highlights from his beard and moustache. "No imagining, Excellency," he said.

Taddeusz turned and pointed to Hansen. "A joke for you, was it? Drag my name through the cesspit?"

"Father!"

"I wish you no disrespect, Lord Taddeusz," Hansen said carefully. The warchief had lost his lance at some time during the scuffling, but he could still break a man's neck with his hands.

"You'll do me none after tomorrow," Taddeusz said heavily. "Lord Hansen, I challenge you. We'll meet tomorrow at midday."

"Foster father, this is not a thing I wish!" the king said sharply.

The big man glanced at him.

"I regret that, Excellency," he said. "But it happens nonetheless. It's a matter of my honor."

Taddeusz glared past Golsingh toward his daughter. She looked away angrily.

Golsingh shrugged. "So be it, then," he said without raising his voice. "But—if you do this thing, against my express will, Lord Taddeusz . . . you will leave Peace Rock and never return. I swear it."

Taddeusz nodded. "So be it, then," he said.

An opening at warchief—just the kind of move that Hansen needed for his reorganization to work, though a bit early, three months later after Malcolm proved himself, that'd be better. . . .

Except that everybody was assuming Hansen, the catalyst of the change, would be dead after tomorrow's duel.

Golsingh looked around the hall bleakly. "Go to your beds," he ordered. "There's been enough harm done this night."

"Wait," said Malcolm. The veteran was wearing boots and a linen nightshift, damp with the snow that had fallen on him when he ran to the hall at the sound of trouble. His body, from chest through hips, was a solid tube of muscle. "You can't set the meeting so soon."

Taddeusz looked from Malcolm to Hansen and snorted dismissively. The big man was no longer angry, just determined. "What's the matter?" he said. "Is your friend afraid to die?"

Hansen smiled. He wasn't sure what the answer to that one was. Too much had happened. Been happening.

"He'll meet you in a tennight," Malcolm insisted. "You can wait that long."

Krita had disappeared, but most of the others in the hall, warriors and servants alike, were listening with interest. Golsingh waited with a hard, emotionless expression which Hansen suspected was a mirror of his own.

Taddeusz shook his head. "The challenged has three days by custom to settle his affairs," he said. "Three days and a half day, then."

Taddeusz looked at Hansen. His visage was that of a man glaring at the turd onto which he'd just stepped. "Or he can run. He can go farther in that time than I'd be willing to chase him."

Malcolm looked at Golsingh. "Excellency? A tennight would—"

The king shook his head. "Lord Taddeusz will have what custom dictates during his remaining stay at Peace Rock," he said coldly. "In three days and a half day, then."

He and the warchief both turned and strode toward the ladder to their chambers above the far end of the hall. They didn't look at one another. When the crowd didn't part quite fast enough, a thrust of Taddeusz' arm slammed a number of people into the wall.

Golsingh turned at the base of the ladder and shouted, "Go to your beds, damn you!"

The crowd scattered to side-chambers and the entrance, murmuring in voices as dim as the glow of the long hearth.

Hansen let out his breath. He was stark naked and the hall was cold. Malcolm stood beside him, and Maharg was returning from having stripped off his armor in his own chamber.

Now that the lamps were gone, the hall was dark. Its framework creaked mournfully as wind pressed the roof.

"Just a second," Hansen said, slipping into his cubicle. He closed the remains of the door before he started exploring the darkness with his hands.

His battlesuit stood ajar. There was no one within the armor, no one hidden in the pile of bedding. The tear in the thatch Hansen had made as camouflage was wider and a real gap, now that somebody with a sharp blade had slashed through the mesh of withies.

The knife must've been in her robe, because it sure wasn't hidden in what she was wearing when Taddeusz started banging on the door. . . .

Hansen started pulling on his coveralls. "Come on in here, then," he said as he reopened the door. It wasn't much privacy, but with Malcolm's cubicle to one side and Maharg's to the other, it would do about as well as anything available.

He couldn't see Malcolm's expression in the darkness, but there was a combination of wonder and regret in the veteran's voice as he fingered the torn thatch and said, "Well, laddie, you've got expensive tastes, haven't you? This time it's your life they've cost you."

"I appreciate your confidence," Hansen snapped.

Maharg was standing like a fireplug in front of the door.

"You did a smart thing, putting your armor on," Hansen said to him. He grimaced. "A lot smarter than anything I did tonight, Malcolm. I know that. Question is, where to we go from here?"

"Your only chance was getting the Thrasey armor," Malcolm said, impressively calm and matter-of-fact. "It's a royal suit, and with a good enough repair job, it might stand up to Taddeusz."

Hansen had seen too many officers flustered when the news they had to report was very bad. That got in the way of solutions . . . and damage limitation, when there were no solutions. But as for what Malcolm was saying—

"I've got armor," Hansen said. "And I wouldn't take Shill's suit if it were that or go naked."

"Shill doesn't need it—"

"*I* don't need a suit!" Hansen snapped. "I've got Tooley's suit. And what's Shill's is Shill's!"

"Oh, it's a good suit, is Tooley's," Malcolm said reasonably, as though unaware of the hard edge glinting from Hansen's tone. "As I know to my cost, having been put down by it—and out, it would have been, without you, laddie—and Maharg here; and without Shill, to whom I owe my life as surely as Golsingh does, I think, but he's still dead."

"There isn't time," said Maharg. "To get to the mound and get back, mebbe. But not to get it fixed, no way. That's a three-day job with the head off, you bet."

"Look—" said Hansen, his anger past.

"No, laddie," said Malcolm, patting his shoulder in the darkness. "You listen, because it's as you said: you're a warrior, but not with battlesuits."

Malcolm sat on the bed, drawing Hansen down beside him. "You think Tooley's armor is good," he continued, "and so it is; but Taddeusz wears a royal suit, and that's to yours as my armor was to Tooley that day that would've been my last without your help. And there will be no help in a duel."

"He took Zieborn down wearing crap," Maharg said. "Villiers' suit, that was crap aginst my old one, even."

"You tricked Zieborn," Malcolm said reasonably, "and very clever it was, laddie; but you won't trick Taddeusz. He watched you then, and for all that he's a bastard, our Taddeusz is as fell and canny a warrior as we'll any of us meet."

"Musta killed more folks 'n bunk in the hall, he must," Maharg agreed sadly.

"So for you to face him . . . ," Malcolm continued. "Remember what it was like for you when Krita matched herself against you—and you wound up wrestling—the *first* time? Now, think what that'll be like with her father and the weapons at full bore."

Maharg snorted with laughter. "Taddeusz's gonna fuck you good!" he quipped.

Hansen found his face grinning even as his mind wondered sourly whether Maharg would think the joke as funny were it his neck on the chopping block.

It also occurred to him that he, and Taddeusz' daughter, and one other woman, were the only people in Peace Rock who didn't believe that Krita had been in Hansen's bed this night.

There was no way Krita could have cut her way through the willow mesh soon enough to reenter the hall fully dressed at the time Hansen saw her. Which might mean his plans and his life were about to end because of half an hour with some slut from the scullery. . . . But he didn't believe that either.

"All right," he said coldly. "What do you see as the options?"

"Run," said Malcolm flatly. "Or die, laddie. Because you're too big to wear *her* suit—"

"If she'd let me borrow it," Hansen said.

"As she might, women being as they are," Malcolm continued. "And too big as well for Golsingh's, or I think he'd have offered it from what I saw on his face. He's a smart man, our king . . . and a hard one, which is much the same at times."

"Thrasey ain't far enough," Maharg said, dropping the words into a silence. "Nowhere Taddeusz might hear. Nowhere in the kingdom."

"And the kingdom will be the worse for it, laddie," Malcolm said softly, "and we'll all be the worse. But that's not so much to bear when you're alive, isn't it?"

Hansen barked out a laugh. "You don't think I owe it to honor to meet the challenge, then?" he asked.

"Taddeusz would think that," said the veteran very carefully. "And it might be that I would think that, were it me whom Taddeusz challenged. But just as being a warrior is different where you come from, laddie . . . I think honor is different as well. Not so?"

Hansen looked at him. There was no light and no expression at all. Maharg drew in his breath.

"Which is not to say," said Malcolm, "that I ever doubted you were a warrior either, you must see."

Hansen relaxed. "Yeah, I guess I do," he said.

He laughed harshly again. "Look," he added, "the main thing I see is that there'll be time after a night's sleep for anything we can figure out to do. And I'll be in better shape to deal with it then."

Malcolm squeezed his shoulder again. He and Maharg went to their own cubicles.

Dawn streamed through the hole in the roof. The weather had finally broken, and the sky was clear.

Hansen raised his head from the cocoon of furs—blinked—snatched up the pry-bar. There was a meter-long snake, probably disturbed from its winter burrow in the thatch, coiled in the open front of his battlesuit.

He got stealthily to his feet. The snake turned its head.

It had one bright eye and a milky globe for the other.

"Well, Hansssen . . . ," Walker said. "Are you ready to be my man for a battlesssuit? For a sssuit that a god would envy, to be my man . . . ?"

Walker's forked tongue flicked and toyed with something scarcely visible, caught in the latch of the armor.

"I'd need it in three days," Hansen said. "Otherwise—"

He took a deep breath and made the decision that his mind had waited till dawn to confirm. "Otherwise I'll fight him with what I've got."

"In no time at all, Hansssen," the snake replied. "I have told you that you musssn't think of duration here, you musssn't. . . ."

Hansen tossed the pry-bar onto his bed. It rang on the planks. "All right," he said. "What do I have to do?"

A ray of sunlight caught the thing Walker was playing with and turned it to a wire of gold. It was a strand of blond hair, long blond hair—

The hair of Golsingh's wife Unn.

Chapter Twenty-two

The door of Eisner's palace slid open as smoothly as oil moving in water.

Eisner laughed humorlessly from within. "You're alone, Rolls?" she asked. "No troupe of jugglers or dancing girls in attendance?"

Rolls ducked as he stepped into the library. He felt but could not hear the door close behind him.

"I don't need to put on side with you, Eisner," he said. "In fact, I walked instead of riding."

"Should I congratulate you for that?" she asked tartly. "We can do anything we please, can't we? We gods." There was bitterness in the final word.

Eisner sat at the hub of a semi-circular desk whose surface, a gorgeous expanse of burl walnut, was covered with various forms of paper.

Books were interfiled with their open edges together, each marking a place in the other, and in worms of six or eight volumes with each spine thrust into the open edge of the next. Cards and sheets of paper, some of them covered with cryptic notes, marked other places. Swathes of gate-fold hardcopy peeked from the stacks of bound volumes.

There was no dust in the room.

Eisner had a collection of bound sheet music open in front of her. Light fell on it from a hidden source, providing perfect illumination.

"Yes, the problem's always been to decide what to do rather than whether or not it's possible," Rolls agreed.

He held his left hand closed. Eisner glanced at it, then back to his face, but for the moment the big man ignored her interest.

"Did you come for a reason?" Eisner demanded.

"My, what a greeting," Rolls said with a rueful smile.

Eisner rubbed her forehead in self-annoyance. "I'm sorry,

Rolls," she said. "With all the time in—" her lips twisted "—in the world, I can certainly talk with a friend. And you've always been as much of a friend as I allowed."

There was a second chair beside the desk, but it too was covered with books and papers. For a moment, Rolls' lips pursed as he considered moving the stacked volumes to the floor. Instead he walked around the end of the desk to look over Eisner's shoulder at the open score.

"What's this, then?" he asked. " *'I wish that I could,' was the man's sad reply, 'But she's dead, in the coach ahead.'* "

Eisner stiffened momentarily, but she recognized that interest rather than amusement prompted the question. Like her, the big man was a watcher, a searcher. . . .

"It—has to do with the last intruder from the Consensus," she said. "I thought there might be an avenue of approach to locating the threat to Diamond."

Rolls nodded, glancing up at the books whose shelves covered all the walls save where low doorways interfered. "Have you thought about what I said, Eisner?" he asked. "About it still being possible for us to be human?"

"We *are* human," she snapped.

Rolls wasn't touching her, but his big form blocked Eisner into her desk alcove. Though he continued to look upward, he shifted to the side as if responding to the nervous anger in the woman behind him.

"I mean," he said gently, still without looking toward her, "that we could resume being fully human. Complete men and women. It's worth taking risks to stay fully human, don't you think?"

"You come closer than most of us, Rolls," Eisner said. The bitterness was back in her voice. "But I . . ."

Rolls turned. When she looked up at his face, she remembered that this big, soft-looking man had led an exploration team, and that he was the one of them who watched against the final day when androids and Lomeri unlocked the pathways of the Matrix and came for long-deferred vengeance.

Risk.

Rolls opened his left hand slowly. His thumb and forefinger held the band that was a shimmer rather than an object, and the jewel below glowed with its own internal fire.

"For one day only," he said as he lowered the necklace over Eisner's head.

"How did you . . . ?" she started. Her voice caught as her mind connected the data it was her life to connect.

And he was right. With Penny's jewel between her breasts—it was worth it.

Eisner stood up. The chair caught the back of her knees. She pushed it away. Her face was changing, and her body filled out as she unsealed the touch-sensitive opening of her coveralls.

Rolls poised, watchful but unwilling to presume even now that Eisner was shrugging out of her single garment.

Nude, she looked at him and then, very deliberately, swept dozens of books onto the floor to clear half of the desk's polished walnut.

"Well, come on, big boy," she said, spreading her arms to Rolls.

Eisner wore the form of a plump, blond woman; a young woman, still in her teens. The necklace dangled brightly across her chest.

There was a noticeable mole on her left breast.

Chapter Twenty-three

The snake rippled down the right arm of the battlesuit and onto the gauntlet, where it shrank and started to vanish. Its single good eye began to glow like a starlit diamond. The tail continued to squirm toward the jewel until all hint of a serpent had disappeared.

"Get into your armor, Hansen," said the mechanical voice of the suit.

Hansen settled himself carefully into his armor. It was awkward to have to back into the suit . . . but thinking of the physical awkwardness took his mind off the real questions.

"Close it, close it," Walker said irritably through the suit.

Hansen was careful to twine the strand of blond hair around his finger rather than leave it to be found in the cubicle. The cold suede was clammy and smelled of the man who'd died in it.

Hansen's screen lighted with a view of the bedchamber. Across the top crawled the message:

TAKE TWO STEPS FORWARD, THEN TURN RIGHT AND STEP

"The bed's in the way," Hansen protested. Though he supposed he could smash through the frame if he needed to.

OBEY glared huge letters as the rest of the holographic display blanked.

Well, he'd taken orders like that when he was a junior, and he by god expected his own people to take orders when *he* gave them.

Nils Hansen, junior volunteer, took two steps forward. His armored legs didn't strike anything. It was disorienting to walk with no view but that of a command, worse than moving blind. He turned and took another step.

Hansen's display suddenly blazed with cold blue lines, branching and linking among themselves into faceted patterns. He no longer felt the pull of gravity, though there was something beneath his feet.

"Walker!" he said sharply. He didn't move either his arms or his legs. He felt as though he were standing in the schematic of a crystal lattice—

Or in a spider web.

A tiny red bead began to crawl along one of the blue lines. The pattern went on—forever, in all directions.

Hansen was alone in a universe of crisp, cold invariance, in which one spark moved.

He opened his mouth again to shout for Walker; closed it; and stepped as if the lines in his display were pathways and the red bead was his guide—

As of course they were, and it was.

Hansen stepped onto a wasteland. He faced a horizon silhouetted by the blur of a red sun. The skeleton of something gigantic lay a little distance from him, its ribs reaching toward the light like the fingers of a drowning man.

Hansen stood on a shingle beach, gravel separated out here by the waves in the unimaginably distant past when this planet had seas. Now there wasn't even an atmosphere: what air remained formed a rime on the pebbles.

The louvers on the battlesuit's air system clicked shut. Their sound reminded him that though the armor sealed for river crossings, it didn't have an air pack to supplement whatever was trapped within its volume.

A crystal the size of a house was trundling slowly toward Hansen on jagged spines. The bases of the spines twisted within the mass until the whole—creature—overbalanced forward, onto other tines which twisted in their turn. The effect was a combination of a sea urchin and an avalanche.

The spines and flats of the crystal reflected and diffracted light from the dying sun, but at the heart of the mass burned the spark of Walker's eye, with more life than the glow on the horizon.

"Was that the Matrix, Walker?" Hansen asked as though he were calm. "Is that what the smiths see when they build armor?"

Walker's laughter clicked in Hansen's earphones. "What you saw was a hologram, a pattern of light, nothing more," the voice said. It sounded . . . not human, but no longer mechanical either. "And what the smiths see, that is in their minds. Patterns also, reflections of the absolute."

Walker was staggering still closer. Light danced: on the fracture planes crossing the spines, and from lines of cleavage within the central mass.

Something that winked on the horizon might have been a form like that of Walker.

"There is a price for seeing the Matrix, Commissioner Hansen," Walker said. The spark in the crystal's core fluctuated as he spoke. "And for seeing *through* the Matrix, there is a very high price."

"This suit doesn't have much air, Walker," Hansen said. The great mass had halted just in front of him. Several of the spines, their glitter streaked by milky flaws, waggled slowly above Hansen.

"You're done with this suit," replied Walker, and the crystal toppled forward.

Hansen braced for the impact, but there was none—no contact, just the utter cessation of movement that he'd felt once before, when his intrusion capsule reached the point in space that should have been Northworld.

Was Northworld.

His display blanked. The only sound was the thump of his heart.

Walker's voice, no longer coming from the earphones, said, "You will keep the artificial intelligence and portions of the sensor suite. You will gain for me access to certain information which the androids have on the plane to which North sent them when they came to investigate. And you will gain the battlesuit which I promised you."

Hansen thought he could see glimmers of light, but perhaps they were merely his optic nerves firing in an attempt to save his sanity from the blackness. "I'll need weapons!" he said.

"You have your mind, Kommissar," Walker said dryly.

There was light and warmth and a splash of brown water as Hansen, limbs flailing, plunged feet first into a swamp.

The air was so saturated that the humidity took the edges off the light of the hot sun overhead. Hansen, wearing his coveralls and a dense skullcap sealed in black plastic—all that remained of a battlesuit that could've withstood anti-tank weapons—was waist deep in mud.

If he wore the entire suit, he'd still be sinking toward whatever passed for bedrock.

The surface was muddy hillocks and ponds—nowhere dry nor deep. Ferns and spike-branched reeds a meter high grew promiscuously across the terrain, but there was no ground cover. Every twenty meters or so sprouted what looked like low trees—but probably weren't, since the branches curling from their tops were lacework similar to the ferns.

Something rose from the squelching mud on the next hillock over. It was a four-legged reptile several meters in length, with a great knobbed sail on its back and a mouthful of fern fronds. There was a collar around its neck.

"And who would *you* be, friend?" muttered Hansen as he stepped out of the pond into which he'd fallen. The creature was obviously an herbivore, but so was a bull.

"It has no personal name," said a crisp voice in his ears, the AI Walker had said he was leaving; and which Hansen had forgotten, like a damned fool, till the machine intelligence stretched a point and recalled itself to his attention. "It is an edaphosaurus from the herd of the android Strombrand."

The edaphosaurus chewed with a sideways rotary motion of its jaws. The skull looked small in comparison to the bulk of the chest and belly, but the vast cone of greenery disappeared rapidly enough down the throat. The beast cocked its head at an angle and sliced off the next installment of ferns, keeping one eye focused on the intruder as it did so.

Hansen squinted, trying to pierce the thick atmosphere. He could only see a hundred meters or so, and the steamy air washed out colors at half that distance. Hot sun on open water and a vast expanse of transpiring foliage. . . .

Another edaphosaurus plodded from the gloom, continuing through the pond in which Hansen had landed. Its feet and belly sent water in all directions. Halfway up the bank the beast stopped, bellowed, and began to claw at its collar with a forepaw. The webbing between its toes was brilliant scarlet.

After a moment of scratching which rotated the collar a quarter turn without dislodging it, the beast resumed its clumsy amble. Something hooted angrily in the direction from which the edaphosaur had come.

"What are the col—" Hansen started to say when a lizard-headed biped carrying a staff and a radio handset bounded through the mud on the herbivore's trail.

"What's *that*?" he snapped instead.

The biped saw Hansen, halted in a crouch that splashed rippling semicircles in the pond, and bolted back the way it had come. In addition to the artifacts in its hands, the lizardman wore a short, off-the-shoulder tunic and a collar similar to that of the edaphosaurus.

"That is a Lomeri slave, one of the herdsmen of Strombrand," replied the artificial intelligence. "There are three herdsmen all told."

The shapes in the mist had mentioned the Lomeri, the lizardfolk, when they'd interviewed Hansen for this mission . . . or the mission that led to the mission which led to *this* mission. But those passing references had implied that the Lomeri were a race of the far past who—

"You are thinking of duration again, Commissioner Hansen," said the voice that was as surely Walker's as it was surely answering a thought Hansen hadn't spoken. "Ignore duration, because it no longer applies."

"Are the Lomeri slaves of the androids here?" Hansen asked. He heard a winding note that could have come from either a living animal or a signal horn. He could run, but the Lomeri obviously knew their way about this swamp better than he ever would.

"These Lomeri are slaves," said what was probably the AI, not Walker, "as some androids are slaves of the Lomeri on the plane they rule. There is passage across the Matrix through the Open Lands, and there is raiding from all sides."

Two different horns answered the first. Certainly signals.

"Is North on a plane?" Hansen demanded. "Can he be reached?"

The visible edaphosaur suddenly closed its jaws with a *clop* so abrupt that half-ingested ferns fell in a fan to the mud. The beast turned and ran off into the mist with an exaggerated side-to-side twisting of its heavy body.

Three lizardmen stepped into sight. Their radios were slung in belt pouches. The staffs they carried were sharpened on both ends.

There was a clicking of electronic laughter in Hansen's ears. "Kommissar, Kommissar," said Walker. "North and Rolls have formed an alliance and merged the planes on which they found themselves. But to visit them through the Matrix requires permission. Which will not be forthcoming if the Lomeri slay you now."

Hansen laughed. He lifted one of the reeds from the mud with a firm pull.

"Oh, they won't kill me, Walker," he said with the comfortable assurance of a man with a short-range task—for a fucking change! "My masters, they sent the best."

Hansen tried twirling the reed. The upward-pointing spikes were each about twenty centimeters long.

The balance changed as mud flew off the root ball. Hansen kept the reed moving as he walked toward the Lomeri by as direct a path as the muddy shore allowed.

"I'm your master now, Commissioner Hansen," Walker said with asperity.

"Translate for me," said Hansen.

"—and if we lose any more of the cattle," said a voice with startling clarity—the helmet excerpted from Hansen's battlesuit contained a first-rate parabolic microphone as well as the artificial intelligence— "then Strombrand'll flay us 'n no mistake."

The lizardmen had halted, chittering among themselves. The skirmish line in which they'd appeared drew together when their quarry started toward them.

"If he gave us decent equipment, they wouldn't fouling stray, would they?" snapped another Lomeri in reply. "So it's his fault."

"It's our hides," the first rejoined.

"Walker," Hansen said. "Can I fix their hardware with the equipment I've got?"

"Yes," said the AI. Its tone was subtly different from Walker's, even though both machine intelligences spoke through the same circuitry.

The Lomeri were slightly taller than Hansen. They were thin and had the dangerous look of figures wound from barbed wire. Patterns of red and orange scales beneath their singlets made them look as though they were on fire.

"Strombrand needs us," said the third lizardman decisively.

"He'll let us off with a beating . . . and it's worth *that* to have red meat again!"

He measured the distance to Hansen—five meters and closing—with a grin on his toothy jaws.

Hansen grinned back. "Oh, but it's not worth trying something that'll get your all four limbs rammed down your throat, is it, boyo?" he said, listening to the speaker in his helmet hiss and clatter with lizardspeak.

He flicked the root end of the reed toward the hungry Lomeri. Water spattered the creature. Instead of blinking, nictitating membranes slid sideways across the large eyeballs.

"Or," continued Hansen, "you could be nice to me and I'll improve your equipment so you won't get a beating ever again."

He darted the reed out, spike-end first, like a Lomeri tongue. The nearest of the creatures flinched back, gripping his staff to his chest.

"Which'll it be, boyos?" Hansen asked.

The Lomeri hunched together, hipshot so that they could all three face the intruder. The AI fed Hansen their whispered words clearly: *How could he . . . Look, he can't be that tough. . . . Did your mother hatch many such fools? He could be anything! Well let's—*

One of the Lomeri—the first one—straightened, took his radio from its holster, and (after a moment's hesitation) tossed it to Hansen.

"Go on, then," the lizardman directed. "Fix it."

Hansen looked at the unit. Its black plastic shell had a dial and a miniature joystick with no other features. A short coil antenna poked from one end.

"Bring it up under your chin," Walker's voice directed. "But continue to watch the Lomeri."

"No fear *that*," Hansen said as he obeyed.

He grinned at the lizardmen. He'd poke the spiky end of his reed in the face of the first to come for him, grab away the creature's staff, and do a quick right and left with the points on the other pair. . . .

Of course, even if the move went precisely as planned, that left the third lizardman chewing Hansen's throat out with teeth made for nothing else.

Half a dozen narrow, jointed pseudopods grew past Hansen's face from the helmet. They were crystal, and it was easy to guess who—rather than what—had extended them.

The glittering tips prodded at the casing. Harsh light spluttered from a miniature laser cutter; then the faceplate lifted in the grip of one pseudopod while the others probed beneath.

The Lomeri backed another step away.

"Pft!" clicked the voice in Hansen's ears. "Junk, only junk."

Hansen's mind split between two realities. He could still see the lizardmen flicking their tongues in nervous pulses, but they seemed to be projected on a flat screen. The forepart of his vision filled with lines and shadows which Hansen's instinct told him were representations, not forms—but were closer to the concept of a Platonic ideal than anything his own senses could show him.

"Walker," he asked, "how does this unit work?"

The vision sharpened. Blotches of shadow broke into fans of lines or vanished.

"It transmits a signal to the collars of the edaphosaurs," Walker replied. "The dial controls the frequency—badly, but I'll improve that. And the joystick determines the amplitude of the signal which the creature's collar feeds to it as pain induced in the main nerve trunk. A goad of sorts, badly made and underpowered."

Hansen licked his own lips. Funny how dry your mouth could get, even in a saturated atmosphere like this.

"Walker?" he said. "Can you boost the power and expand the range that the unit covers?"

"I'm tapping it into the Matrix as a powersource," Walker said. "And yes, Kommissar, while I'm at it I'm adjusting the frequencies so that the unit will also control the collars the herdsmen themselves wear."

There was another electronic chuckle. Hansen's vision returned to normal. The pseudopods resealed the unit and withdrew.

Hansen tossed the unit back to its owner. "Try it," he said. "But watch the power—and if you get to the end of the dial, it'll work on your buddies, too."

The lizardman toyed with the joystick. There was an agonized bellow from deep in the swamp. The Lomeri's finger released the stick.

Distant splashing continued for thirty seconds, then slowed. A second prod was followed by another bellow, much closer. An edaphosaur—the one whose wandering had brought the herdsman to Hansen to begin with—reappeared.

"It *never* worked like that on the cattle," the lizardman muttered in delight.

"Next?" said Hansen.

The Lomeri played with the first sending unit while Hansen worked on the second. Edaphosaurs seemed to have no herd instinct and a tendency to wander. Bleats of pain echoed in all directions as the lizardfolk drove the beasts closer—and, when they were in sight, tortured the sluggish sailbacks for the pleasure of watching them bleat and squirm.

"Now there's only one thing . . . ," Hansen said as he returned the second unit.

Two lizardmen grabbed for it. When one snatched it away, the other jabbed his staff toward his comrade's belly.

Both of the creatures straightened up in screaming pain. The third Lomeri had twitched first the dial, then the joystick of his repaired unit. His laughter had the brittle cruelty of a brick shattering stained glass.

Hansen took the remaining unit as its owner hopped on one leg, trying to raise his head even higher as his clawed hands plucked at the collar which controlled him. The third lizardman threw his joystick back to zero and let both his fellows collapse gasping in the mud.

"The only thing is," Hansen resumed while crystal limbs as angularly misshapen as those of a spider crab reached past his face, "is that in this swamp, the units are going to degrade again. This atmosphere—"

He waved his hand through the miasma of humidity and rotting vegetation "—is going to crud up what it doesn't eat, so you'll need to find somebody to fix your hardware again."

He tossed the third sending unit back to its owner.

The lizardmen looked at one another. The nearest shifted his grip on his pointed staff.

Hansen smiled at him. "I wasn't lying about feeding you yourself either, boyo," he said.

The lizardman shrank back.

"So I think I better leave this with whichever of you wants it," Hansen said. He lifted the helmet from his head, judged the distance, and lobbed it in a high arc that descended directly in the center of the three Lomeri.

Mud gouted as all three creatures jumped for the prize. One grabbed it with both hands and shrugged off the others with a quick twist of his shoulders. He squawked as one of his fellows stabbed him hard enough in the belly that the staff's modest point tented the scaly hide on the victim's back as it tried to exit.

The killer gripped his weapon an instant too long. His uninjured fellow leaped for his throat and clamped it with the jaws that had so impressed Hansen. Blood, as red as a mammal's, sprayed in all directions.

The killer let go of his staff. He tried to pry apart his fellow's jaw hinge, but the teeth had done their work, and his arms were already losing strength.

The surviving lizardman pitched aside the corpse his jaws had nearly decapitated and straightened. He was laughing.

The hideous glee turned in mid-cackle to a shriek that mounted the scale of audibility as the Lomeri struggled with his slave collar. The last sound he made was a clicking grunt, an instant before he toppled face down into the pond. His legs continued to thrash, but no bubbles rose from the water covering his nostrils.

The lizardman with the staff through his guts dropped his sending unit. He bent forward, trying to reach the fallen helmet. His fingers touched it, but he didn't have enough strength remaining to pick it up. His limbs splayed as he fell.

Hansen worked the helmet out from beneath the twitching body. Now that he wasn't wearing it, he could see that there was a single blue diamond where the plastic covered his forehead. "Hello, Walker," he said as he put the helmet on.

An edaphosaur grunted happily. The herd was separating again.

"That was unnecessary," said Walker tartly. "You could have killed them yourself with the first sending unit."

"I've done a lot of unnecessary things," Hansen said. His eyes had no expression, but his palms went cold with the thoughts that flamed through his mind.

"The only ones I regret," he went on, trying to control the

sudden quiver in his voice, "are the people I've killed when I didn't have to."

Hansen looked at the bodies. All of them were still moving. He wondered if they'd squirm till it thundered. "If that lot needed to die," he said, "then they'd die. Their choice."

"Pft," said the voice in his earphones. "But so long as you succeed, I won't object to the technique."

"Can you guide me to Strombrand's place?" Hansen asked.

"Of course."

"Then let's go," Hansen said, rubbing his hands on his coveralls as if trying to burnish the feel of death from his skin. "I think he'll be in the market for somebody to round up his herd for him."

Chapter Twenty-four

Hansen expected a rough palisade around a squalid village, and a sanitation problem worse than that of Peace Rock.

Instead, the high black wall which loomed from the mud and mist was seamless. It had the smooth glint of plastic or surface-sealed concrete. Beyond the wall was a geodesic dome, also black and bulging nearly a hundred meters into the air. The low towers at intervals along the outer wall were too small for living guards—

But just about right for the sensors and weapons of an automatic defense array.

Hansen stopped.

"Go up to the gate and claim admittance as a lone traveler," Walker ordered. "Strombrand should feed and house you for three days."

"Right," said Hansen, keeping his arms at his sides and his hands open toward the sensors. Walker didn't want him dead; that was one of the few things that Hansen *did* know with confidence.

Of course, that didn't mean that his crystal master couldn't misjudge the odds. . . .

"I claim shelter as a traveler!" Hansen shouted to the blank patch of wall that he'd identified as a gate without asking Walker. Though there was no difference in the sheer plastic surface, the mud had been trampled into a trough leading to this point.

The mini-towers to either side buzzed internally.

"Strombrand has the information you want, then?" Hansen asked as they waited.

"Strelbrand controls the data bank," Walker replied. "They are batch brothers, Strelbrand and Strombrand, dextro- and laevo-rotating twins; and it may be that Strombrand can get us access to what his brother holds."

The section of wall slid downward. Two sullen humans wearing slave collars stood inside with a double-headed android. The slaves weren't much cleaner than Hansen—who'd swum a ribbon of muddy water when Walker assured him that there was nothing beneath of a size to concern him.

The android lounged against the inner surface of the wall. He held a bell-mouthed mob gun in his arms.

"Welcome traveler to the palace of the great lord Strombrand," the slaves sing-songed together in Standard.

"Boy, you look a treat," said one of the android's mouths. The other laughed. "C'mon," the first head continued. "I'm s'posed to take you to my father."

His free arm gestured toward the huge dome. His gun continued to point at Hansen's midsection.

The courtyard was mud surfaced, but there were arched pens—or houses—built into the surrounding wall. Dozens of humans worked at various tasks in the courtyard, all of them wearing slave collars.

They glanced sidelong at Hansen. Their expressions were not very different from those on the faces of the Lomeri as the lizardmen discussed their next meal.

"Father?" Hansen whispered as he stamped toward the dome. "Android batches capable of reproduction are destroyed at once."

"Androids that can reproduce are destroyed—or are very carefully controlled, Kommissar," Walker replied. Hansen thought he heard amusement in the tone. "The batches that can reproduce have a level of cunning which is missing from their normal fellows . . . and which is very useful for certain purposes. For your Consensus."

Solbarth. Was Solbarth from the same batch as Strombrand?

"And sometimes very dangerous, when they get loose," Hansen muttered. *But I was better than he was.*

Slaves at the entrance to the dome hosed off Hansen without ceremony. "C'mon, c'mon," one of them ordered. "Turn, won't cha?"

Hansen wasn't in a position to complain about the treatment—and behind him, the android's muddy boots were cleaned the same way.

The interior of the dome was illuminated by the tubes of light along each junction line of the facets. The colors varied from one bar to the next—never bright, never saturated; never quite pleasing. Their mixture threw a muddy ambiance around the hundred or more figures, slaves and androids, in the center of the hall.

"G'wan," said the two-headed android as he prodded Hansen in the back with the mob gun. "Grovel fer the ole man and let's find something t' eat."

You'll grovel for me if you poke me again with that gun, Hansen thought; but that was just for his soul's sake. A scene wouldn't help him get the job done, and doing the job had always been Hansen's goal. It didn't really matter what the job was, so long as it was his to do. . . .

Hansen stepped through the loose crowd. Several of the androids were as perfectly formed as Solbarth had been—physically. Others were hideously misshapen, with extra limbs and multiple heads like Hansen's guide.

The androids dressed in layers of flowing garments and were heavily bedizened with gold and jewels. Some of the human slaves were able to follow the same fashion. The plump man speaking to the android seated on the room's only chair ("Strombrand," Walker said, but that was obvious) wore a gold torque which almost hid the plastic collar which controlled him.

"The herdsmen still haven't reported in, sir," the slave said.

"Well, then raise the amplitude when you ask, Donner!" Strombrand said. "Do I have to tell you everything?"

Strombrand had the normal complement of head and limbs, but no one could have mistaken him for a human. He was brutally massive, literally three times as broad as a normal man. His bare arms were roped with sinew and as thick as flowing basalt; the coiled bracelets he wore would have fit around Hansen's waist.

"But we're already broadcasting at a very high level," Donner protested. "I'm concerned that we'll harm the fools if we raise it again, and you *know* how difficult it is to replace Lomeri."

"If you're talking about the three Lomeri I saw on my way here," Hansen said, stepping toward the throne, "then they're beyond anybody else hurting. They seem to have gotten into a fight and pretty well finished each other off."

"What?" peeped Donner.

"What?" boomed Strombrand, lurching up from his chair. Hansen couldn't help blinking because the motion was so similar to that of an avalanche rumbling toward him.

"Well, it's like I said," Hansen explained. "They'd done each other with spears and teeth, you know."

He shrugged. "There were a couple sailbacks around, which is why I thought of the bodies when you said herdsmen."

"When was this?" the android chieftain demanded. Despite the bestiality of his form, Strombrand's white skin was so smooth that the bars of light lay on it in distinct patches rather than a general blur.

"Three hours, perhaps?" Hansen said. Even without the artificial intelligence—and Walker—Hansen's internal clock could have given the time to within five minutes; but that wasn't anything Strombrand needed to know.

"And the herd's been wandering?" Strombrand boomed. "Well, don't just stand there, Donner! Round up the house slaves and get off after them!"

Sweat beaded on Donner's bald scalp as he wrung his hands together. "Oh, it'll never work," he moaned. "Those *damned* cattle, they *like* to stray, and by the time we get out there in the *mud* they'll all be gone!"

"Did I ask for an opinion?" demanded the android, balling a fist larger than Hansen's head.

"If all you're concerned with is getting back your cattle," Hansen said, "I can call them home for you."

All eyes in the room focused on him.

"Clever, clever Hansen," Walker whispered in his ears.

"Of course," Hansen continued, "there's something I need that you can help me with, Lord Strombrand. Shall we make a pact, you and I?"

The android seated himself again. His right index finger tapped the arm of his throne. It sounded like a maul striking a chopping block.

"What sort of pact?" he asked.

"There's a question I want to ask your brother's data bank," Hansen said. "Will you help me get the chance to ask it?"

Strombrand's great brows drew down in a scowl. "That?" he said. "It's not Strelbrand's, it's all of ours, from when we came here. He'll never give you permission, no matter what I say."

"That's not the deal," Hansen said. "*I* call your cattle back . . . and you use your best efforts to allow me to ask one question of the data bank. Your oath on that?"

"Oaths have power here on Northworld . . . ," Walker said, repeating one of the first things he'd told Hansen on the snow-covered bluff.

Strombrand knuckled his broad jaw. "All right," he said.

The android stood up, more deliberately than he had before but no less threateningly. "But *I'm* not interested in best efforts, stranger. If you don't bring back my whole herd, you'll provide the main course for my dinner tonight. Do you understand?"

"Oh, yes," Hansen said with a cold grin. "I understand you very well, Lord Strombrand."

See to it that you understand me, he thought; and that was not a boast.

Walker's signals prodded the herd of edaphosaurs home while Hansen stood in the muddy courtyard whistling bars from *In the Baggage Coach Ahead*. Later that afternoon as Hansen climbed into an aircar to be taken to the estate of Strombrand's brother, he noticed the chief slave Donner leaning close to one of the sailbacks.

Donner was whistling earnestly, hoping to see some flicker of interest in the reptilian eyes.

Strelbrand's palace was identical to that of his brother.

Strelbrand himself was Strombrand's mirror image; his wife, as broad as either man with two pairs of arms and legs, was still more hideous.

And Strelbrand's reaction to his brother's request was just as Strombrand had warned.

"What?" the seated android boomed. "Is there madness in our batch, Strombrand, that you'd think of asking me this thing? No! No, of *course* not!"

Strombrand was as defensive as a spider in another spider's web. He hunched his shoulders as if accepting a weight. "I'm oathbound to ask you, brother," he said. He didn't look back at Hansen, who stood at his heel.

"Well, then I'm oathbound to tell you you're crazy, brother," Strelbrand said. "You know how much North and his lot'd like to get into that bank!"

"I was oathbound," Strombrand said; *almost* a repetition of his earlier words.

Strelbrand rose to his pillarlike legs. The dais under his throne stood put his head higher than that of his brother. "Tell your oathlord, Strombrand," he said, "that I alone can enter the chamber."

Strelbrand's wife whispered something into his ear.

"And my daughter Acca, of course," the android chieftain added. He grinned like the earth cracking open. "But she can't enter it, because she can't leave, can she?"

The laughter of the crowd followed Strombrand and Hansen back into the courtyard.

"I told you so," the android muttered to the human as they got into the open aircar.

"So you did," agreed Hansen. "So we'll come back tonight, to the tunnel beyond the walls that leads to the chamber holding the data bank."

Strombrand paused. "You know about that?" he said in something between threat and wonder.

"Go on, lift off," replied Hansen. He smiled. "And yes, I know a lot of things. I know that you'll keep your oath to me tonight, don't I?"

Strombrand slammed his throttles against their stops to lift in the muggy air. The monstrous android couldn't possibly have been afraid of the expression he saw on Hansen's face.

The night was as warm and humid as midday. A haze of light seemed to cling to the thick atmosphere. Strombrand set his aircar down on the riverbank with a squelch.

Bubbles from the rotting vegetation rose in a series of muted belches.

They'd landed next to a metal plate two and a half meters in diameter. It would have been almost invisible by daylight, but the mud covering the metal had a faint phosphorescence which emphasized the unnatural circularity. Strelbrand's mansion wasn't far off, but the mist would have hidden it even if the sun were up.

"This is the correct location," Walker whispered approvingly in Hansen's earphones.

"Very good, oath-brother," Hansen said to the huge android. "Now, if you'll just open the tunnel and turn off the protective systems, I'll say we're quits."

Strombrand looked at his passenger. "Who are you?" he growled.

A small lizard in the reed-choked stream raised its head at the sound, then dived beneath the surface with a quick thrust of its broad forelegs.

"I'm the man who whistled your cattle back," said Hansen. "Shall we go?"

Strombrand cursed like thunder and got out. The vehicle slurped from side to side as he moved. He adjusted the sling holding the nozzle of his laser. The powerpack on his back would have required a separate vehicle before a normal man could have moved it.

"If I'd known what you were going to want," the android said, feeling through the muck for the handle, "I'd never have made the oath."

Hansen said nothing.

Insects bumbled into them and buzzed away again: tiny wasps which sipped plant juices for want of nectar in this flowerless world, and biting flies adapted to the cold-blooded sailbacks and their kin, uninterested in the human and android after a preliminary sniff.

Hansen saw iridescent motion against the lights of the instrument panel; he snatched left-handed. Furious wings burred against his palm and closed fingers.

At least he hadn't lost his speed.

The door lifted with a horrible sucking noise. The light from within diffused above the entrance. Strombrand gestured downward. "There you go, then,"

Hansen got out of the vehicle. "After you," he said with a gesture of his own. "You still have to disengage the automatic defenses."

"I didn't promise to die for you!" the android shouted. "If there's a risk, it's yours to take."

"But there isn't any risk for you, Strombrand," Hansen replied mildly, pointing toward the opening with his right index finger. "Because the defenses think you're your brother, so you can turn them off. As you and I both know."

A great-throated carnivore sent a grunting bellow up from deep in the swamp, responding to Strombrand's voice. The big android cursed and plunged into the tunnel.

From outside the entrance, the tunnel appeared to drop straight into the earth. Strombrand was walking as though one edge of the circle were down. With each step, his body rotated another few degrees around the axis of the tunnel.

Golden light from the far end suffused the interior. It winked softly from the android's jewelry and the bright fittings of his laser pack.

Strombrand's broad body shrank faster than distance should have required. Ripples formed between the android and Hansen as though Strombrand were crossing hot sand.

Sparks suddenly enveloped the center of the tunnel. Strombrand paused, lapped in blue fire. He took another step forward and manipulated a switch in the wall. The sparks died away; the curtain which had seemed to fall over the tunnel lifted.

Strombrand continued walking. Hansen slowly released his breath. A second gout of sparks surged over the android so fiercely that the man waiting outside the tunnel felt his own hair lift.

Again Strombrand walked on through. His huge body had shrunk to the size of a marmoset in the center of the golden ambiance.

He reached the end of the tunnel and waved a tiny arm back at Hansen.

"Go," said Walker. "But be careful."

"Go teach your grandmother to suck eggs," Hansen said evenly as he stepped into the tunnel and felt a surge of buoyant energy wrap him.

There was no feeling of vertigo or disorientation as Hansen strode toward Strombrand. Once the human looked over his shoulder to see whether the rotation he'd noticed from the outside was evident from this viewpoint; but there was only mist at the tunnel entrance—and anyway, it was a foolish thing to consider now anyway.

Strombrand grew to his full misshapen enormity. The door behind him was the source of the golden light. He gestured toward it with a hand the size of a power shovel and said, "All right. I've opened the way for you. You and I are quits now."

Hansen opened his left hand. The wasp he held buzzed from him, seeking the light. It touched the surface of the door and disintegrated in a flood of golden radiance.

Hansen smiled. "Open the door for me, oath brother," he said.

Strombrand's shadowed eyes were pools of black fury. He thrust at the center of the door.

There was a loud click. The glow lighting the tunnel shut off, but the door panel swung slightly ajar and a degree of illumination crept around its circular margin.

"My oath is kept," Strombrand said. "Acca will deal with you—but that's no concern of mine."

He strode back along the darkened tunnel without waiting for Hansen's reply.

"It is safe, now," said Walker.

Hansen touched the metal panel gingerly. It was warm and as massive as a vault door—but the android's touch had disengaged its defenses.

Hansen leaned his weight against the doorleaf. For a moment, inertia withstood his thrust; then the circle of light around the panel began to widen.

"Stranger!" Strombrand called from the end of the tunnel. His powerful voice was attenuated by more than distance. "I've opened the way for you. I've kept my oath!"

Hansen looked over his shoulder. The android was sighting down the nozzle of his laser.

"Don't move!" Walker ordered in a tone of absolute command. Hansen froze. His eyes and mouth were open, waiting. . . .

The laser blast was a corkscrew of green light curling down the walls of the tunnel instead of following the straight path along the axis to Hansen's heart. His eyes tracked the bolt's helical progress, though at light speed there should have been no sensory impression except the shock through all his nerves as the center of his chest vaporized. . . .

The blast of coherent light struck and rebounded from the

door between Hansen's chest and right arm. Steam puffed from the sweaty fabric of his sleeve. Because the door was ajar, the bolt caromed a dozen times from the walls of the tunnel as it flashed back to the entrance.

Strombrand's body ignited in a crackling green dazzle. His scream was terrible but very brief.

Hansen blinked and rubbed the bare skin of his cheek which prickled from the actinic glare.

"Walker," he said. "What does she look like? Acca?"

"Does it matter?" the machine voice responded.

Hansen shrugged. "I suppose not."

Walker's laughter clicked. "Go on, Kommissar," he said. "Go on. We've come this far."

Chapter Twenty-five

Hansen stepped into a sun-dappled woodland. It was late spring, and the tips of the fir branches were bright green with new growth. A squirrel chittered wildly as it peered around a treetrunk at the intruder.

Hansen probed at the ground with his finger tips. He touched a yielding surface—but not the mat of needles his eyes told him to expect. He reached for a fir tree and found nothing, only an illusion of light through whose ghostly ambiance his hand gestured.

A tall nude woman ran barefoot past the false trees. Her braided red hair was long enough to fall to the back of her knees when she was at rest. A male cardinal flew from a pollen-bright bunch of cones as she flickered by.

Then the bird and woman were gone. Even the squirrel was silent—and none of them had existed to begin with.

The door had closed behind Hansen. No sign of its presence remained. He licked his lips and walked in the direction the woman's image had taken.

Hansen stepped into a meadow. The grasses waved high over his head. The stems were studded with tiny pastel flowers; birds fluttered among them.

He couldn't tell which way the woman had gone. His body touched nothing as he brushed through the sunlit display.

The woman was walking toward him. The grasses parted for her. A chickadee hopped from a green milkweed pod to her shoulder and back again, calling its brilliant, cheerful song.

The sun burnished golden highlights from her hair, but her skin was the pure white of an android.

Hansen stepped into her path. "Lady?" he called. "Acca?"

The image stepped through him without contact. He turned and ran after it/her onto a drift-swept volcanic plain. Here and there a patch of gray-green lichen grew where winds had scoured snow from the ropy basalt.

192

A golden battlesuit strode across the rock toward Hansen.

He halted. His body wanted to run, but there was nowhere to run. . . .

"Acca," Hansen called. "I've come to you."

Hansen could not only hear the sound of the battlesuit's steps, he could feel the impacts through the springy reality of what appeared to be lava.

The figure was within ten meters of Hansen. It raised its right gauntlet and ripped the air with the lethal blue fountain of its arc—higher than the distance still separating guard and intruder.

"I must kill you," the suit said in a woman's melodious voice.

"There's no must, Acca," Hansen said. He spread his open hands. "You make your own fate. I was sent to you."

The arc cut off. The battlesuit continued to advance, step by measured, armored step.

"I have everything here!" Acca said.

The volcanic waste shimmered into the meadow, the forest; a rocky skerry on which elephant seals roared their challenges back to the tossing surf.

"Now you have everything, Acca," Hansen said. "I was sent to you."

The golden armor halted almost close enough for him to touch it. "You can't leave, now," Acca said.

Hansen nodded. "I don't want to leave, Acca. I was sent to you."

The battlesuit's right arm reached down to the latch and tripped it. Hansen gripped the edge of the heavy plastron and helped pull it open.

The woman inside was the original of the images which Hansen had followed through the images of places.

The spring forest grew about them again.

Acca accepted his hand as she stepped out of the golden armor. She looked him in the eyes and asked, "What do you want?"

"You, Acca," Hansen said. "And to ask one question of the knowledge which you guard."

He smiled. "But first you," he said as he put his arms around her naked, perfect form.

They lay on a beach whose sand had the smooth resilience of rubber beneath them. The light of a full moon turned the sheen of the open battlesuit to silver. Hansen didn't recognize the constellations.

He kissed Acca's throat. She smiled and purred, but her eyes did not open.

"Darling?" he said. "Now I need to look at the data bank."

She raised her hands to his neck.

"Why that?" she murmured. Her fingertips traced the flat muscles of Hansen's shoulders and chest.

Moonlight turned her coppery pubic hair to silver. Hansen touched her groin, very carefully because the past hours had surely caused bruising.

Acca closed her eyes firmly again. She began to breathe in a series of gasps at decreasing intervals. He knelt and took one of her nipples between his teeth gently, tonguing it until her shuddering climax had come and passed.

"Now, darling," he whispered. "The data bank. One question."

Acca moaned softly. She made a gesture toward empty air. A terminal formed there, abruptly as solid as Hansen or the battlesuit standing in rigid majesty.

"Place me in front of it," Walker ordered through the earphones, "and get into the battlesuit. It will fit you."

Hansen kissed the woman's lips and got up. *He'd always done whatever the job required.*

He set his helmet on the ground. The air through his perspiring scalp felt cool and pure.

Acca looked up at him with languid eyes. "Don't play with the suit now," she said. "Come to me. Just hold me."

She smiled. Hansen closed the battlesuit over himself.

The display was diamond hard. Acca stared at him in dawning wonder.

The jewel burning in the center of the plastic helmet had extruded crystalline pseudopods into the casing of the terminal.

"What are you doing?" Acca called. She waved at the terminal, but it ignored her by remaining solid. "Please come out. Please, whoever—"

Walker was growing like a time-lapse image of ice forming in a supersaturated atmosphere. Highlights streaked his crystal limbs, but a single blue spark winked at his heart.

The mass grew above Hansen and about him, distorting his

vision of the surroundings. The universe started to shift.

Very faintly, Hansen heard Acca calling, "Please, whoever you are. Please don't leave me. . . ."

For a moment, Hansen in his golden suit stood on frozen shingle beneath the huge red sun. The crystal surrounding him began to cloud and crack, like ice in shadow on a warm day. Bits dropped from the outer surface of the mass.

"Walker?" Hansen said, outwardly calm but unable to control the jolt of adrenalin that made his limbs quiver.

Walker's form was crumbling to white sand which dribbled across the gravel of the ancient beach. Hansen could still see the blue glint, but it hovered in airless space before him. He was hearing speech and almost words again. . . .

". . . sen, I sum . . ."

The universe shifted again. Bright sunlight, a red and gold battlesuit; muddy ground—

He saw the practice field below Peace Rock. The whole community was standing around the circle of posts to hear Taddeusz issue his formal challenge.

"Appear or wander an outlaw and coward," shouted the warchief's amplified voice, "destined victim for the hand of any man, slave or free. Hansen, I summon you!"

"Display energy levels," Hansen whispered.

The ground was solid beneath his armored boots. He heard the crowd's gasp.

Taddeusz was twenty meters from him. To the sensors on Hansen's new battlesuit, the power levels of even the warchief's royal armor were varied—and vulnerable.

"Cut," Hansen said. His weapon snarled as it traced a line across the mud at Taddeusz' feet.

"You should have learned, Lord Taddeusz," Hansen shouted across the field, "not to summon what you lack the strength to send away."

"Dog spawn!" Taddeusz spat. His rippling arc crossed Hansen's at midpoint between the combatants.

The prickling of incipient overcharge unexpectedly lifted the hair on the warchief's arm.

It must have startled him, but Taddeusz was an old campaigner.

He snatched his weapon back, let it vanish into his gauntlet, and thrust with his left hand.

Hansen saw the charge levels building, but he didn't move to block the stroke. They were still twenty meters apart, and if the armor Hansen had brought from—bought from—Acca couldn't take the impact, he might as well learn it now.

The world roared. Hansen's display lost definition and color, and his every hair—from head to the tiny ones curling on the backs of his big toes—straightened as much as his garments would permit.

Hansen twitched his gauntlet. His arc touched Taddeusz' and cut it, breaking the circuit.

The warchief switched hands. Hansen slashed. Taddeusz' AI shifted power from attack to defense, but his armor's scarlet and gilt burned away in a line from wrist to shoulder.

Hansen let his opponent back a step uncertainly.

"Taddeusz," he said. "You see that I don't need to fear you. Let's stop this now."

Taddeusz lunged forward. The arc fanning from Hansen's gauntlet absorbed the thrust before it touched his golden armor. Hansen twisted his hand and overloaded the weapon close to the warchief's gauntlet.

"Taddeusz!" he shouted. "I haven't touched your daughter. I swear it on my honor!"

He'd've sworn he hadn't touched Unn, Acca, or anybody at all if he'd thought it would prevent an unnecessary killing. But even the truth was useless here. . . .

Taddeusz stepped in, his arc flickering from one gauntlet to the other as the warchief searched for an opening with the skill of long practice and natural talent. Hansen shifted his own broad arc, reading Taddeusz' power shifts to block each threat before it occurred.

Golsingh wore tights and a black velvet doublet as he watched expressionlessly from the sidelines. Unn and Krita stood to either side of him. Malcolm and Maharg were to Krita's left.

The air was bright and warm, so only a few of the spectators were wrapped in furs.

Taddeusz attempted a furious overhead cut. Hansen caught

the stroke and held it, stepping closer while power draining to Taddeusz' weapon froze the warchief's armor.

Hansen's left gauntlet spat a second arc. He thrust surgically, aiming for Taddeusz' ankle. Paint blistered.

The warchief's weapon went dead as his battlesuit overloaded. Hansen stepped back and let Taddeusz fall on his face in the mud.

"Listen to me!" Hansen said. "I don't want to kill you. Stop this nonsense, take your armor off, and let's discuss the good of the kingdom."

Taddeusz rolled to his back. Balled dirt stripped from his red and gold armor as his suit powered up again.

The black scars on the warchief's arm and ankle were a reminder of how badly he was overmatched. Hansen let him rise.

"There'll be no good in this kingdom so long as you live," Taddeusz said. He turned the palm of his right hand toward Hansen.

Hansen brushed his opponent's gauntlet with a low-amplitude arc from his own suit. Taddeusz' bolt was deafening even through the battlesuit, but the touch of Hansen's weapon steered the charge into the ground. Mud, burned to brick and shattered, blew in all directions.

"Taddeusz!" Hansen shouted. He was sweating despite anything his battlesuit's flawless climate control could do. "Don't make me kill—"

The warchief's armor shuddered and gleamed as he reset it again. It was a fine suit, a royal suit. It recovered quickly.

"—you!"

"You're a coward and no man at all!" Taddeusz shouted. "I'm going to kill—"

Hansen's arc slashed at Taddeusz' neck. The red and gold battlesuit resisted in a momentary blaze of blue fire.

Sparks of blazing metal replaced the electrical discharge, white droplets that pattered onto the ground where they raised puffs of steam.

Taddeusz' helmet fell. For a moment the headless battlesuit remained upright. Then it too fell.

Hansen turned to Golsingh. "M-m . . . ," he said.

His voice caught. Somehow during the fighting he'd bloodied his nose.

"My king," he said. "Lord Golsingh. I regret . . . I regret . . ."

Golsingh nodded. Unn was cold-faced, but the scarf in her hands was twisted into a silken rope.

"I regret the death of your foster father," Hansen continued with sudden assurance. "If you permit me, I'll pay you the blood debt in the best way possible."

He took a deep breath. "Make me your warchief in Taddeusz' place, and I'll lay the kingdom at your feet!"

Golsingh nodded. "Yes, Lord Hansen," he said.

He looked around the circle of spectators with eyes as hard as Hansen's own before adding, "And there will be none, I think, to deny the appointment."

Chapter Twenty-six

North was the Matrix. His mind flowed through the shattered pathways like melt-water dancing down the rocks of a cataract. He was all the knowledge in his universe, and it was freezing him.

With the skill of long experience, North's consciousness sifted the rush of chilling, killing data, but there was too much. . . .

A party of Lomeri, riding triceratops and carrying energy weapons, herded long-necked sauropods through a forest of conifers. The trees overtopped even the giant dinosaurs by scores of meters.

Humans in armor powered by energy differentials within the Matrix arrayed themselves outside a port city. It would be a major battle with hundreds of warriors on either side. Hovering over the field, just out of phase with the combatants, was a leash of North's own Searchers. The hard-faced women were ready to transfer the brain patterns of dying warriors into their data banks and bring them back to North.

Crystalline machines stumbled ceaselessly over the barren wastes of a world so old that it forever kept the same face to the huge red sun it circled.

A slave-stealing expedition of androids, as disparate in appearance as a necklace of pearls and broken fragments of oyster shell, poised beside one of the discontinuities between planes. The androids were heavily armed. Across the veil of the discontinuity was scrub woodland and crumbled rockpiles which once had been chimneys. The raiders would have to go far to find human habitations.

Rao took leave of Ngoya. He looked awkward and dismayed at the concern his wife could not completely hide after so many repetitions of the event. He was fully armed, and the vessel in which he would pursue raiders across the Open Lands was a battleship on the scale of a tank. The one human servant who would accompany Rao watched his master with mingled fear of the coming task and impatience to get it over with.

Eisner in the form of Penny braced herself against her desk. She had wrapped her legs around Rolls so that her heels forced him deeper into her.

The people in the common area of a village on Diamond looked up in horror and surmise. A child began to cry but shushed as his mother picked him up. The whole crowd stood, linking hands. Someone began to sing in a quavering voice; the whole park joined in a hymn to love and growth and the sun that follows the rain.

The shadow that fell across Diamond was not from a cloud. There was a subtle shift of energies as molecular vibrations elsewhere in the Matrix changed phase—and reverted, so that sun streamed into the park again, while the uniformed populace of Ruby frowned and checked weapons and tensely watched a sky boiling with auroral discharges.

Ruby snapped fully into vibrational phase with Diamond. The common area went red, then black. Ruby soldiers pounded one another on the back and shouted in triumph, but as black blurred to nothingness, there was no sound except the fading memory of a hymn to life. . . .

North rose from the Matrix in the usual gasping terror of a man bobbing to the surface through icy waters.

"Dead," he whispered. "Killed." His face was terrible.

His last vision from the Matrix was the sight of a tank curvetting in the cloud of red dust its fans raised. It was painting the sky with blasts from its weapons.

Chapter Twenty-seven

A kilometer from the outskirts of Frekka, ages of plodding caravans and grazing had turned the mammoth prairie into a barren waste: dusty now at high summer; muddy in season; and less depressing only in the depths of snow-swept winter because the whole continent was too bleak to contrast.

Part of the dust raised by the hooves of Hansen's pony had settled over him like a yellow drapery; much of the rest seemed to have clogged his throat. Messengers had run ahead when Hansen reached the bridge over the ditch protecting Golsingh's encampment. He was pleased to see that among the friends waiting for him at the flap of the king's tent was Malcolm—holding up a skin of beer.

Golsingh would have traveled in royal state, but Malcolm and Maharg must have had equally hard, dusty rides as they marshaled the other contingents from distant holdings. With luck, though, they'd've had less less difficulty than Hansen had, convincing lordlings to provide the warriors their oath to the king required.

Golsingh helped Hansen from his pony and tried to embrace him while Hansen slurped beer from the spout of Malcolm's flask.

"Any trouble?" Malcolm asked, as though the warchief would have been two days late—and ridden in alone—if there *hadn't* been trouble.

"The messenger arrived warning you'd been delayed, of course," Golsingh said. While the Lord of Thrasey pretended nonchalance, the king feigned reasoned coolness.

Hansen looked at the lowering sun. "The rest're two hours behind me," he said. "They'll be in before sunset."

He'd swallowed the first swig of beer. He rinsed his mouth with the second and spat it on the ground. Better late than never.

"Glockner held us up," he said.

"Said he wouldn't give you the men?" asked Maharg.

"Nothing that straight," Hansen explained. "You know Glockner. Took a day to round up enough baggage mammoths, and then some of them showed up lame. Third day, Glockner and about half the men I'd picked for his share of the muster, they came down with flu or something."

Malcolm shook his head angrily. "Well, we're probably as well off without that tricky bastard," he said. "But after we're done here, I'll go—"

"Oh, he's coming," Hansen said as he drank again. "He's back with the rest. Everybody got healthy faster'n you'd believe when I put my suit on and burned down Glockner's hall."

Maharg and Malcolm laughed. Golsingh's face blanked for a moment, and when he opened his mouth it was to say, "Rough work, Lord Hansen."

"Not as rough as hanging Glockner on a rope of his own guts," Hansen said flatly. "Which was the next step."

He met the king's eyes. "Peace is the desired end, milord . . . but for the moment, I'm your warchief."

Golsingh said nothing for a moment, then clasped Hansen's shoulder again. "Yes, I see that. It's a matter of knowing what to do. And you've proven already that you know better than—" he smiled his hard smile "—I did before our association."

"Figgered you had something like that in mind when you took Glockner fer yerself," Maharg said. "Hell, I coulda handled him."

Hansen grinned. "Yeah," he said, "but you would've made sure they all stayed inside when you burned the hall. This time I wanted his troops more 'n I wanted a lesson for the other barons. Matter of emphasis is all."

"They aren't proper warriors," Golsingh said suddenly. "Frekka's aren't."

He nodded westward, though the walls of Frekka were the better part of a kilometer away, out of sight beyond broken ground. "They wouldn't meet us mid-way for battle."

"They had scuts in armor shootin' bolts at us from the walls, too," Maharg put in. "Won't call 'em warriors."

Hansen's face stiffened. "That sort of game could get real expensive," he said.

"We need Frekka," Golsingh responded sharply, then tried to soften the words with a smile. "You convinced me of that, after all, Lord Hansen. Blasting the city to the ground won't do any good. And after all, we could simply move back out of range until you arrived."

He cleared his throat and smiled again. "Until we'd consolidated our forces."

"We've got warriors on guard at night," Malcolm said. "But I also thought maybe any freeman or slave kills a Frekka scout, then he should get a battlesuit and eat at the bench."

"They show they done it," added Maharg, "by bringin' us the ears."

Golsingh nodded. "That was Marshal Maharg's idea," he said. "And I approved both."

Hansen handed the beer to Malcolm. He kneaded first his buttocks, then his thighs, with his fingers. Hard to tell which parts hurt the most after he'd been in the saddle for most of three weeks, but at least a pony beat walking. A howdah on a mammoth, now . . . But that wasn't done; and anyway, he didn't feel comfortable around the huge beasts even when he was safe in his battlesuit.

"No reason not to go inside," the king said. "I'll have a meal prepared?"

"Sounds good to me," Hansen replied, taking Golsingh's gesture as a directive and ducking under the tent flap.

It bothered him sometimes that he'd knocked his fellows—his friends—so off-balance that they became indecisive as soon as he was around. They—all three of these men, the marshals and the king; and a number of the others he'd trained at Peace Rock and Thrasey over the past six months—could handle the new style of war without difficulty.

They had *done* so; this camp was proof of the fact. But as soon as Hansen appeared, they all stood around with their fingers up their collective ass.

Hansen sat cautiously on a camp chair while slaves bustled with a meal of cold boiled chicken and vegetables.

There was no delaying the real question, because all the royal forces were mustered now. All the help Golsingh was going to get was camped around him at this moment.

"What sort of numbers are we looking at?" Hansen asked.

The king licked his lips. "Many," he said. "I think—perhaps a thousand."

"Shit," said Hansen quietly.

He held a chicken drumstick while he hacked at the thigh joint with his belt knife. The knife didn't hold an edge worth a damn. "Where'd they all come from?"

"There's ships in the harbor," said Maharg. "Pirates."

"They've allied with three or four sea-kings," Malcolm agreed. "The Syndics have equipped the pirates with better armor in exchange for helping defend Frekka."

"Then they're bughouse crazy," Hansen said as he took a mouthful of meat. "People with money always think they can buy people with—" he started to say 'guns' "—weapons. What they buy is masters, if they're not damn careful to pick folks with honor."

None of the other three were touching the food. Either they'd already eaten or something had spoiled their appetite.

The enemy numbers had sure-god spoiled *Hansen's* appetite, though he couldn't let it show. With luck, the royal forces amounted to two and a half, maybe three, hundred warriors.

"They have a number of, I suppose, sailors and craftsmen wearing partial armor," Golsingh said. "The suits cover only the torso and one arm, so they don't really provide any protection; but they still have arc weapons, and they can be turned out much faster than complete suits of even poor quality."

Hansen shrugged. "We didn't expect it'd be easy," he said. "They're crazy to arm the pirates who've been bleedin' *them*, and the poor working scuts *they've* been bleeding, or I miss my bet."

He tossed the chicken bones toward the tent flap. "Anyhow," he added, "crazy or not, they're going to lose."

Hansen said the words because he thought it would cheer up his friends. He found, to his surprise, that he meant them.

"Sir?" called a messenger from beyond the flap of the tent in which Hansen slept alone. "Marshal Malcolm says there's troops coming from the city."

Hansen rolled to his feet, dropping the pry-bar back on his

cot. "Got it," he mumbled as he climbed into the golden battlesuit. His muscles ached, his mouth felt like a wiping rag, and his sinuses were packed with yellow dust and mucus.

And all of that started to clear again with the familiar surge of adrenalin through his body. There'd be plenty of time to hurt later, if he survived.

Hansen's armor latched over him; the world sharpened. He'd set the brightness default to display 100% of normal daylight. The night's waxing moon provided enough light to kill by, but the amplified images were better by several orders of magnitude.

He wondered if the Syndics of Frekka had realized the full potential of their battlesuits. There hadn't been any sign of that in previous clashes with Frekka's hirelings.

The merchants *were* willing to ignore the traditional disdain for fighting at night, but that didn't require so much intelligence as it did a willingness to change the rules when the rules didn't suit them.

The Syndics didn't operate under the morality of shopkeepers, who know their customers and know they have to do business with them tomorrow as well. The leaders of Frekka had graduated to an attitude that'd always been common among the higher reaches of business and finance, when merchants saw a path to heaven through monopoly.

But Golsingh was in the way of that apotheosis; Golsingh, and Golsingh's new warchief. . . .

"Upper quadrant, map display," Hansen ordered his artificial intelligence. "All powered suits."

At the scale of the map, the attackers were a worm of red dots creeping from the blur of the city. The royal camp was a blue sea which brightened as additional warriors scrambled into their armor.

"Camp, secure commo," Hansen said. "All royal elements, do not, I repeat *do not*, leave your positions. Camp Marshals, enforce my command by whatever means necessary."

Half a year hadn't been enough time to turn all the warriors of Golsingh's army into disciplined soldiers. Malcolm might have qualms about striking down over-eager types who threatened to get in the way of the warchief's planned response, but he'd do it.

Maharg wouldn't hesitate an instant before using his new rank and battlesuit on warriors who'd scorned him six months earlier.

"Suit, rank and number of attackers," Hansen asked.

Red holographic figures overlay the map, rating the attackers' armor from Class 3 down to Class 12—a startlingly low quality, presumably indicating the partial suits to which the king had referred. There were fifty-seven all told in the attacking party, with a majority of their equipment in Class 12.

Cold meat for troops who knew what they were doing.

Which most of the royal army didn't—but Hansen didn't need most of the army.

He'd thought of calling the twenty-man command he'd organized under Maharg 'the Guards,' 'the Special Unit,' or the like. . . . But that would have made it a prestige appointment and made it difficult for him to keep out the sort of headstrong champions who had neither aptitude nor interest in learning how to *use* the suits they wore. So instead—

"All elements," Hansen said. "Marshal Maharg and Unit Four will deal with the raid. I'll accompany them. Marshal Malcolm—ah, Malcolm under the guidance of the king—commands the camp until I return."

"Hansen, you're not leaving me here!" Malcolm snapped, identified by his voice, by the tiny purple number on Hansen's display, and by the fact he was speaking on the command channel to which only the king, the marshals, and Hansen himself had access.

"Right!" said Maharg brightly, a usage he'd picked up from Hansen.

"Lord Hansen," said Golsingh, "I must forbid you to go out there. It's quite unnecessary, and you shouldn't be hazarding yourself in the darkness."

"Malcolm," Hansen said, "*shut up* and do your job! Lord Golsingh, with all respect—shut up and let *me* do my job!"

Hansen was panting and his legs quivered. He hadn't moved his body since he closed his armor and got on with the business of organizing the defense.

If he survived, maybe he'd apologize to the friends he'd just insulted. More likely, he'd figure he'd done what needed to be done at the time; which was never grounds for an apology.

"Maharg," Hansen called as he stepped into the open, "have the men ready. I'm on the way."

He forgot to allow for the helmet's bulk when he ducked through the flap. His head pulled the tent down behind him. Hansen's servants scuttled about the wreckage, squealing in concern.

The twenty-man team and their leader knelt just outside the north gate of the encampment. "Suit, tag Unit Four white on all unit displays," Maharg said as Hansen crossed the ditch.

Good, the boy was learning.

"Unit, secure commo," Hansen said as he clasped Maharg's shoulder in recognition.

The map quadrant of Hansen's display showed the attackers several hundred meters to the west of Golsingh's camp, stumbling in single file over the broken terrain. *Definitely* not using their suits' light amplifiers.

"Right," said Hansen. "We're going to take them in the middle. That's where their top people are. Maharg, you take Red Team and push the leaders into the ditch around the camp. I'll chivvy the rear ranks back to Frekka with Blue Team. Everybody clear?"

The response was jumbled, but Hansen's AI threw a gratifying eighteen of twenty-one possible up in the corner of his display.

"And everybody on 100% normal daylight?"

Sixteen *rogers*, followed by five more in mumbled embarrassment.

"Remember, it's just like training," Hansen added. "Except these guys aren't fit to wipe the asses of the people you trained against. Right?"

Rogerrogerroger.

"Let's move!"

Unit Four moved fast in the night, but they had a considerable distance to cover in order to attack perpendicularly to the enemy's line of advance. The Frekka forces halted in a grove of birches two hundred meters from the royal camp. They were bunching up as troops farther back in line reached the leaders.

They really didn't see Death arriving on their left flank until Hansen, twenty meters from a pair of stragglers, said, "Cut!" and the bright snarl of his arc sent Unit Four in at a run.

The first two targets required no more skill than a bandsaw

needs for boards. Only the chests of these Frekka personnel were armored. Their legs burned like torches when the surge of Hansen's arc boiled all the water out of them.

There was an incandescent crackling along Unit Four's line of advance. The least of the men in Hansen's unit wore armor as good as the best suit among the Frekka troops, and trained teamwork would finish what shock had begun.

The trees to the left were aflame. Because of the way the Frekka forces had bunched, Maharg's Red Team had more than a fair share of targets—but Hansen was on the far right of the line, and he wasn't about to screw up an attack plan himself because he got greedy.

A dozen Frekka warriors hesitated on either side of the gully they'd been crossing when Unit Four slaughtered the men marching ahead of them. They turned and ran when Hansen faced them.

"Blue Team," Hansen shouted as he strode after them—*the golden suit had enough power to jump the gully rather than struggling down one side and up the other*—

"Follow m—"

There were two Frekka warriors in the gully as Hansen started to leap it. Their suits were in a class with the first one Golsingh issued to Hansen. An arc slashed across Hansen's crotch as he rose for the jump.

Instead of clearing the obstacle, he crashed into the far bank like a turtle who'd tried to fly.

Hansen's ears rang. The unexpected pain of his nose was as stunning as being struck by a thunderbolt. All around him was a roaring that fused clay into bubbling glass in a blue glare. Over the sound of the arc weapons he could hear men shouting.

Hansen's display turned fuzzy. The upper right quadrant still showed the red dots running toward his own white marker like flies headed for fresh carrion.

The pain of almost-blocked electrical discharges stopped abruptly. Hansen could smell the hair crisped over most of his body, but now the blazing arcs surrounded him at a slight distance. It was as though he rode a bottle through the heart of a tornado.

The red dots vanished. Hansen's display sharpened, but his eyes were too blurred with pain to focus on anything.

"Sir?" called one of the pair of his own men who were trying to lift Hansen upright. "Are you all right? Are you all right?"

Hansen managed to pat one of the men on the back; but it was almost a minute before he felt able to speak again.

Hansen assumed it was another slave entering the tent. He continued sponging at his face, treasuring the sting of cold water, until he heard Golsingh's voice say, "You all may leave. I'll take care of any needs the warchief may have."

Hansen opened his eyes. The slaves scurried out, setting the flames of the oil lamps dancing.

The king wore a sequin-patterned shawl over a pair of light coveralls. His face was serious.

Hansen dabbed at his face again. His nose hurt like hell itself, but he didn't think it was broken.

"I'm all right," he said. It struck him that the king's coveralls were modeled on Hansen's own pair.

Golsingh dipped a finger in the basin of water. "Wouldn't you like it heated?" he asked.

"It's okay."

Hansen wrung out the rag and met the king's eyes as well as his swollen nose would permit. "Lord Golsingh," he said, "I fucked up. I'm sorry."

Golsingh nodded. "Yes," he said, "you did."

The king sat down on the cot, blinked, and moved the pry-bar out from under him.

"Peace is very important to me, Lord Hansen," he said. Hansen went back to mopping his bruised face so that he wouldn't have to meet Golsingh's eyes. "The most important thing in my life."

Golsingh cleared his throat. "The—dream, if you will, that one day the men of this whole continent will be free of the necessity of fighting these interminable, useless wars.

"I suppose," he went on with a rising inflection which indicated he supposed no such thing, "you as a fighting man find that as—unpleasant as Taddeusz did?"

Hansen looked at the king out of the corner of his eyes. "No," he said, "I don't. If I can work myself out of a job here, then . . . then I'll have accomplished something. *Something*."

He shrugged, then barked a laugh. "Anyway," he said,

wondering if Golsingh would understand just what he was admitting, "the job I'm doing at the moment's always been the only important thing to me. That hasn't changed since I wound up here."

"Yes, well . . . ," Golsingh said to his warchief's back. "In a duel, skill and the quality of one's armor are the important; but in a battle, a melee . . . often the better man falls to the lesser."

"I said I fucked up," Hansen said. "That doesn't mean I shouldn't've been out there tonight, it just means that I don't know everything. Yet."

"You've trained the men very well," Golsingh said. "And the Thrasey contingent, of course. We miss your company when you're in Thrasey, you know."

He cleared his throat again. "Unn often asks when you'll be returning. When you're at Thrasey or . . . just away from Peace Rock."

Hansen looked at the king. "Krita's still missing?" he asked.

Golsingh nodded. "Yes," he said. He toyed with his moustache before resuming, "Unn—we—would be very upset if something happened because you'd put yourself in a position that someone else could have handled just as well."

Hansen held the rag over his face and eyes. He wondered if the hot, prickling flush he felt crawling over his skin was visible to the man sitting behind him.

"You see," Golsingh continued softly, "I need you if my—dream of peace is to succeed. And that's more important to me than anything."

"You don't need me," Hansen replied in a thick voice.

He dropped the cloth into the basin and faced the king. "You've learned the important part," he said. "Strike for the head and never mind the little shit, that'll come when the head falls."

Golsingh opened his mouth to speak, but Hansen chopped him off with an abrupt motion of his hand.

"Tactics?" Hansen continued. "Malcolm and Maharg can handle that now. Maybe there's still some tricks they haven't got yet, but they've learned how to *learn*, and that's the important thing.

"You don't *need* me anymore."

The king stood up. His face wore a quiet smile. "Be careful tomorrow," he said. "That's all I ask. We ask."

He walked to the flap, then looked over his shoulder again at Hansen. "After all," he said, "you're also my friend."

Hansen continued to stare at the tent flap long after it had closed behind Golsingh.

Chapter Twenty-eight

"We have to destroy them!" Rao snarled, more to himself than to his peers gathered with him in North's hall. "Ruby destroyed Diamond, so we have to destroy Ruby."

"We mustn't let anger rule us," said Miyoko. She stared at her tented fingers, and her words—like Rao's—were a personal litany.

"We'll destroy Ruby," North said from the high seat. If Rao's anger was volcanic, then North's face was a thundercloud and his words clipped flashes of lightning.

From behind a veil of light Penny snapped pettishly, "We can't do that, we're *linked*. And anyway, it's just one of those things that happens, and I don't think we ought to let ourselves get so upset."

Dowson pointedly dropped the shield of light behind which he usually sheltered to save the sensibilities of his peers. He floated before them, a brain in a tank of oxygenated fluid.

The outer surface sublimed from the cone of colored ice beside him. His words washed across the assemblage: "Our oaths and our selves guarantee the existence of Ruby."

"Forget that!" said Rao as his wife clutched his forearm with tears of concern in her eyes. They all knew the degree of single-mindedness of which Rao was capable, but Ngoya knew her husband best of all. "We guaranteed Diamond, didn't we? And they destroyed it. Ruby *killed* Diamond, so Ruby has to die!"

He started to get up. North's right eye focused on him like the single sharp point of a spear. "Sit," North said.

Rao met North's glare without fear; but he let Ngoya guide him back into his seat.

"Eisner," said North, "do you have any suggestions?"

Eisner, pinch-faced and cold, continued to look straight ahead of her. "Dowson is correct," she said without affect. "The Matrix has its own logic. If we destroy Ruby, we destroy ourselves."

She stopped speaking. Her fingers formed a perfect flat pattern in her lap and her eyes did not blink. No one else said anything.

"Rolls, then?" resumed North with the playful lethality of a cat pawing prey too frightened even to run. "Do you have something to add?"

Rolls looked at him. "I'm not afraid of you, North," he said.

North smiled. "You'd be a fool if that were true, Rolls," he said. "But you're not a fool."

Rolls swallowed. "All right," he said. "The others are of course correct. But yes, we have to avenge Diamond."

"Ruby isn't responsible for anything!" Penny whined. "They just—it's what they do. It's what we *created* them to do, to be. So why are we getting so upset?"

"We aren't talking about justice, Penny," North said in the silky, terrifying voice he'd used from the start of the council. "Merely cause and effect, what was done and what therefore must be done. Isn't that right—"

His head turned like a gun mount rotating. "—Fortin?"

The white android face deliberately turned away. "Whatever you say, dear father," Fortin remarked in the direction of the doorway.

There was a tremor of fear and anticipation in his voice. "You told us that Ruby had to be destroyed, so no doubt you're going to destroy Ruby."

Rao got up again. "Sure," he said. "I'll do it. That murder was the work of Chaos, and we can't compromise with Chaos."

"You idiot!" Saburo cried, the insult bubbling out behind the rush of his own fear. "*You're* Chaos with that attitude. You'll doom yourself and maybe *all* of us if you do that!"

"There's no need of that, Rao," North said without apparent anger. He rose in his seat, craggy and gray and as lethal as a murderer's worn knife. "Fortin is quite right. I'll take care of the matter."

He raised his hand. Black wings began to whisper toward the hall.

The others rose also, walking toward the door in emotions as various as there were individuals.

Rolls looked over his shoulder and called to the terrible man standing before the high seat, "You can't send your Searchers, you know. They can't *enter* Ruby. Only we can do that. Only a god!"

North smiled. His face was as bleak as a frozen gully.

"And if you think to open a path for your machine warriors," Rolls added from the doorway as the others stepped past him, "you can't without disturbing the balance of the whole Matrix. Not even you can do that!"

"Go on, Rolls," North said. "This is mine to deal with now."

"Ruby could defeat your machines!" Rolls cried. "Any number of them! The Matrix—"

North pointed his index finger. "Go now, Rolls," he said.

Rolls plunged out of the crystalline brilliance of the hall. Sunlight on the meadow was warm and gorgeous, but the ice in his marrow didn't want to melt.

The animals on which they'd ridden to the council were excited by their masters' return. Penny looked at the hourglass muscularity of the human who guided the deer pulling her chariot and said, "If you want to know what's *really* bad, I can't find my necklace."

Ngoya turned on her suddenly. "I can't believe even *you* could be so shallow that you'd think your necklace was equivalent to, to the *horror* that passed to a whole world!" the dark woman snapped.

"Easy for you to say," Penny retorted, her face hardening into something unexpectedly shrewd. "If your precious Rao came home in two pieces, would you say that was nothing—" her voice became whiny "—to a whole world?"

Ngoya flushed.

Rao heard his name and turned. "Huh?" he said. "Ngoya, what're you waiting for, anyway?"

"I'm good at finding things, Penny," said Fortin. He sauntered toward her. "Would you like me to try?"

"Good at losing things too," Penny said with a sniff of doubt.

The android formed the thumbs and forefingers of his hands into a square. Within their pale frame, an image began to take shape: ermine fur, a mirrored dresser—behind the dresser, something red and glowing.

Where he'd returned it.

"Look familiar?" Fortin asked nonchalantly.

"It can't be there," Penny breathed. "That was the first place I looked."

Fortin shrugged and pressed his hands together to snuff out the image. "Look again, then," he said. "Or don't. It's all one with me."

Penny leaped into her chariot and shouted orders to her driver.

Fortin caught Rolls' eye and smiled. "Everybody gets what they look for," the half-android said. "Don't they—partner?"

Rolls mounted his restive elk. His face was stony, but Fortin's laughter behind him boiled through his mind like the memory of Diamond dying.

North watched as the light began to scatter and refract in the center of his hall. Black planes, like stress fractures in clear ice, formed and vanished and reappeared in sudden solidity.

A machine and the woman riding it came into phase.

The physical reality had no wings. The machine's slender body stood on oversized, jointed legs like those of a katydid or a cave cricket. The trunk of metal and crystal was slender, barely large enough to form a comfortable saddle for the hard-faced woman who sat astride it.

She dismounted and bowed to North, standing before his high seat. "Master," she said, "you summoned me specially. There is—"

She raised her face; her features were without expression "—someone in the Open Lands you want killed. Shall I get my armor?"

North smiled at his Searcher. "You're very eager, little one," he said approvingly. "But no, not 'killed' this time but a killer."

She nodded again and set her left hand on the saddle pommel, ready to remount.

"Do you believe in god, my dear?" North asked archly, toyingly.

The Searcher blinked. "You are god, Master," she said.

He shook his head. "The only real god *here* is balance," he said, no longer playful. "There is a man needed to preserve balance, throughout the Matrix."

The woman nodded, but without particular interest. Her eyes reflexively examined the structure of her machine, the dragonfly f matter which took her in a bubble of spacetime between the planes of the world, at North's will and by his dispensation.

"Yes, Master," she said. "I'll fetch you his soul."

A beam of light through the ceiling struck her hair. It raised auburn highlights from a tight coil that had seemed black as the heartwood of ebony before the rays pierced it.

North shook his head, smiling. "Not this time," he said. "Not his soul alone."

The Searcher's eyes widened with surprise.

"Mind and body," North continued. "Mind and body and soul, I suppose, if men have souls."

For a moment North's visage was as terrible as the advancing edge of a glacier. The cold fury was not directed at the woman, but she felt herself shrink inside for all her courage.

Then the silent storm passed, and he, smiling again, said, "I chose you in particular, Krita, because he's someone you used to know. . . ."

Chapter Twenty-nine

Golsingh rarely sounded impatient. Because the words were so clipped and precise, Hansen couldn't be sure whether he was hearing an exception when the king said over the command frequency, "If they don't come out soon, we're going in. And I'll build a new port over the ashes of Frekka."

"They're coming out," Malcolm reported from the right flank.

The mid-morning sun fell squarely on the gray stone walls of Frekka, half a kilometer from where Hansen had marshaled the royal army. The ground between the two dipped slightly, no more than one meter in twenty—a swale of no military significance but some interest psychologically.

Painted, polished metal winked from seven gateways as the Syndics' army shambled out of Frekka.

Hansen instinctively used his map display instead of looking to either side to check his forces. Pitiful forces, considered as an army of men: 309 warriors and a thousand or so armed freemen and slaves. As a unit of tanks, it would have been very large, though, and his warriors would be a match for tanks in close terrain. . . .

"Hell *take* 'em," Maharg muttered from the left flank. "There's really a shitload of the bastards."

Golsingh, separated from Hansen in the center of the line by only a score of expectant warriors, said, "Most of them wearing half-suits. Walking corpses, as we know from last night."

Hansen checked the digital readout in his display. His mouth pursed, not that the numbers were news to him.

"Still," he said judiciously, "there's more of them in decent armor than we've got all told."

"Yeah, laddie," said Malcolm. "But they don't have a soul, that lot."

Malcolm was right.

Hansen suddenly realized that he'd spent all his time on

Northworld trying to teach fighting men the difference between soldiers and mere warriors. Warriors were the undisciplined rabble that was good for nothing but dying when it met trained troops. That was an important distinction, but—

There was a difference between a soldier and a merchant, too. You can't simply bean-count your way to victory. Some of the most ruthlessly efficient armies in history had been composed of ex-clerks and shopkeepers . . . but that took training.

Golsingh had Nils Hansen. The Syndics of Frekka had no one but themselves—and no chance.

Still, there surely was a mother-huge lot of the bastards the Syndics had hired.

The wings of the Frekka army began streaming down the gentle slope. A few score of the warriors wore wildly-decorated armor—pirates, brutal and well-accustomed to sudden death, but untrained in the business of attacking enemies who were both prepared and equipped.

The remainder of the flanking units was of half-suited levies, each man staggering under the weight of the plastron and carapace which couldn't protect him against an arc. They were threats only in the way gadflies threatened cavalry, biting from behind and throwing the lines into a confusion more dangerous than the sips of blood they drank.

The advancing forces kept a cautious distance between themselves and either flank of the royal army. The Frekka main body, containing most of the fully-equipped warriors, held their places under the walls of the city.

Merchant logic.

"They think it's going to hurt us to walk all the way to them," Hansen said. "The damned fools. Their men'll shit their pants watching us come at 'em like Juggernaut."

"We await your order, Lord Hansen," Golsingh reminded with the same touch of almost impatience.

"Secure, general commo," Hansen told his AI. "Right. Everybody remember your training. Your job is to keep step with the other guys in your team and kill whoever the team leader designates. Don't worry about your rear, there's people to cover you. Walking pace, don't get hasty. There'll be plenty of time."

Hansen's mouth was dry. There ought to be something inspiring to say, but he couldn't think what it was. His knees were shaking, and all he knew was that he wanted to stop talking and go kill something.

"Move out, guys," he said. "Let's kill 'em all."

The royal army bellowed as its hundreds of armored legs crashed forward. If the sound didn't scare the Syndics, then the poor bastards were stupid as well as ignorant of war.

As his forces advanced, Hansen switched to a 360° field and suppressed the map display. He wouldn't need sharp vision for several minutes, so for the moment the compressed panorama of the whole field was more important.

A party of warriors charged out of the Frekka line, following their instincts instead of orders. When they saw their fellows were standing fast, they paused—a score against oncoming hundreds—and scurried back into line, just as thirty or forty more warriors decided to join their charge. The Syndics' formation was disintegrating while the royal army was still five minutes from slaughter.

The flanks were Hansen's real concern. Those hundreds of half-armed troops could sweep around the royal army like light cavalry, like Hannibal's Numidian horse which plugged the last Roman chance at Cannae. . . .

Hansen's fear was the Syndics' hope, and both proved illusory. Men wearing half-suits were slower and clumsier than warriors whose armor carried its weight with power from the Matrix.

The royal advance slipped past the encircling jaws at two steps a second. Half-armed clerks and artisans staggered after them under the burden of their equipment, concentrating on keeping up—

Until they met the sudden arc-lit scything from the royal troops detailed to meet the expected danger. Unit Four on the left, twenty warriors from Malcolm's brutally-trained Thrasey contingent on the right; picked men whose battlesuits could saw a tree—or a bare leg—at thirty meters.

And did.

Better-equipped pirates charged from either flank with the instinctive reaction of men—even the worst of men—to do *something* when they see their fellows being slaughtered. Some of the pirates wore excellent armor; all of them were experienced killers.

The royal troops butchered them anyway.

One of Maharg's warriors went down in a blaze of sparks when a sea-king with great bronze wings welded onto his helmet struck off his feet. His conqueror died an instant later. Three arcs hacked him simultaneously and continued cutting after the pirate's vivid armor lay in bits on the smoking ground.

That was the only casualty on the left flank. A couple men were down on the right, but so were scores of pirates and nearly a hundred half-armored artisans.

The remainder fled. Golsingh's freemen were sniping at them with crossbows. Hansen could see several clots of slaves, some holding a victim down while others probed his vitals with their knives.

The screams of the dying accompanied the royal army's triumphant rush up the hill toward Frekka.

Hansen switched back to standard display and lit his arc weapon.

Hansen had arrayed the left and central divisions of his army with about two meters between one man and the next to either side. The Frekka warriors covered the same front but at nearly twice the density. Training couldn't change the fact that when the forces closed, many of the royal troops would face the arcs of two or three opponents—and would therefore be killed.

Black wings hovered, though there was nothing in the sky except a shimmer as of heated air.

Directly before Hansen was a figure whose armor was gold like his own, but carved and decorated like a temple frieze; a Syndic rather than a champion. The warriors to either side of the Syndic were veterans wearing battlesuits scarred by the combats they'd won. They braced for the contact, while the man in carved armor hesitated as if to dart back through the gate behind him.

When the lines were twenty meters apart, Hansen ordered, "Left and central divisions, hold in place! Remember your orders! Hold in place. Malcolm, hit 'em!"

The right wing, led by the Thrasey contingent and heavy with the army's better-equipped warriors, formed a dense ball and smashed its way into the Frekka forces. The warriors to their immediate front, trapped between stone and a wall of ripping arcs, could neither fight nor run. A few escaped through the nearest gates. The rest died.

Malcolm turned his unit left and marched it down the twenty-meter corridor between the city and the remainder of the royal army, taking the Frekka line in the flank. The warriors in the rear of Malcolm's division faced around and, merely by threat, scattered the survivors of the Syndics' light forces.

It was like watching a bowling ball roll through chaff.

The execution of Hansen's plan wasn't perfect, though he got a better degree of obedience than he'd expected from warriors he considered half-trained.

Men nerved to kill or die can lock their focus on the target before them, forgetting their training, their orders—their names. Parts of the royal army charged home in a blaze of sparks. Elsewhere, Frekka warriors broke ranks to meet the royal onslaught. In either case, snarling combat drew more troops in from either side.

But the plan worked well enough, because there still was an unshaken royal line at the moment the Syndics realized they no longer had a left flank and their center was beginning to disappear into the same flaming meat-grinder.

The gold-armored Syndic facing Hansen turned and bolted through the gate behind him. All along the line, men wearing richly-decorated battlesuits broke and ran.

"Get 'em!" Hansen bellowed on the general push, but there wouldn't have been any way to hold the warriors of his army longer anyway.

The veterans who'd been guarding the vanished Syndic closed a half-step reflexively. Hansen cut at the first. The warrior's arc caught Hansen's and blocked it, but the overload threw a nimbus of blue haze around the figure and began to blister the paint on his right forearm.

The second bodyguard stepped closer and chopped at Hansen's waist. Hansen was prepared for the stroke and parried it by switching his arc to his left gauntlet.

The first warrior took his release as a gift from providence and lumbered toward the gate. Hansen sheared through the second man's suit at mid-thigh, then caught the first from behind while he was still between the gate towers.

The man's battlesuit was very nearly of royal quality. It lost motive power but held until Hansen swiped his victim to the side with his gauntlet almost in contact with its target.

"Through the walls!" Hansen shouted as he led the nearest of the royal forces through the gate. "Don't spare anybody with a weapon!"

Which wasn't, part of his mind told him with amusement, a very necessary order.

Even this major entryway curved abruptly just inside the gate, and the houses of Frekka leaned over the cobblestoned street. Most of the dwellings had been built at two stories, but they'd been raised by third-floor lofts as expanding business increased the need to house drovers and artisans within the walls.

Thinking of walls. . . .

The Syndics' army had broken, even the right wing which hadn't really been engaged. Frekka warriors massed at the gates the royal army hadn't yet captured. Many of them were trying to climb over the three-meter walls.

Now that their leashes had been slipped, Golsingh's men weren't waiting to go in turn through the gates either.

There were snarls behind Hansen as arcs gnawed the base of the heavy stonework. Quartz popped, mortar blazed as limelight, and fracture lines forced by differential heating shattered the biggest blocks in moments.

Sections of the wall crashed down. Undamaged ashlars from the higher courses bounced crazily, knocking over warriors who weren't quick enough to dodge them.

A roofing tile broke on Hansen's helmet.

He looked up. An old woman wearing a shawl over a dress embroidered with pearls stood on the roof coping. She was lifting a second tile to hurl down at him.

The woman dropped the useless missile and began to scream as the faceless gold helmet turned toward her.

Hansen lowered his gauntlet and smashed through the doorway into the house. The lintel was a 6x6 timber. His helmet struck it squarely. The timber didn't break, but it tore away in a shower of plaster and broken wainscoting.

The stairway was to the left off the front hall. Hansen took the steps one at a time, placing his armored boots directly over the stringers. He still wasn't sure the treads would take the weight of his battlesuit, but they did. . . .

The entrance to the loft was a ladder at the far end of the second-floor hall. The old woman was halfway down it. She saw Hansen coming up the stairs and screamed, trying to scramble back the way she'd come.

Hansen reached the base of the ladder while she was at the top of it. He jerked the heavy frame out of the wall to which it was pegged.

The old woman dangled from the loft opening, bleating like a trapped rabbit. She'd lost her shoes and her thin legs threshed like a drowning swimmer's. She wore black stockings held up by incongruous flowered garters.

Hansen started to laugh. He tossed the ladder aside and caught the woman easily when her arms let go.

"Listen to me," he said, using the amplification of his suit's speakers to overwhelm her terrified cries. "You know where the—the city hall, the headquarters is."

The woman's eyes and mouth clopped shut as the words hammered her. She opened them. "The Palace of Trade?" she asked.

"Right," said Hansen, walking back to the staircase with his prisoner cradled in his left arm. "You're going to guide me there."

He didn't figure he needed to voice a threat. Besides, his heart wouldn't've been in it. This old lady seemed to be the only person in Frekka with any balls.

The street to which Hansen returned was chaos. Royal troops thronged it, some of them coming from the opposite direction in their confusion. A number of the warriors were clumsily draped with loot. Several houses were already burning, sending flakes of dingy white ash down across the street and men.

"Suit," Hansen said to save his AI the trouble of guessing whether it should take the next words as a direction to it. "All elements in line of sight."

Then, "Listen up, you dickheads!"

Every warrior in sight of Hansen stiffened at the radioed command.

"This is your warchief," Hansen continued. "Follow me to the headquarters and we'll take their surrender."

He paused. "And *any* bastard I see with loot after the next thirty seconds, he spends an hour in the latrine pit when I get things sorted out!"

Hansen looked down at the old woman in his arms. She was actually clinging to him.

"Now, madame," he said as quietly as he could and still be heard over the sounds of battle, "let's go to the Palace of Trade. And the quicker we get there, the safer everybody's going to be."

Hansen's armored worm squirmed toward the center of Frekka, directed by the old woman's pointing arm. He started with about twenty warriors and a handful of slaves and freemen, but their numbers increased at every intersection. There were a number of abandoned battlesuits which unarmored members of Hansen's entourage appropriated.

The civilian populace had mostly hidden. Occasionally someone scampered like a rat back into an alley at the warriors' clashing approach. There was no resistance, though several times a Frekka hireling stumbled into Hansen's group and was cut down as he tried to run.

Hansen's passenger spat in the direction of each smoking corpse. "Cowards!" she snarled. "If they'd been men, they'd've met you in the field!"

"Lord Hansen," Golsingh said on the command push. "I'm in a gate tower as you suggested—" 'ordered' would've been a more accurate description of Hansen's tone when they laid their plans before the battle, but Hansen's temper was always short when it was about to hit the fan "—and I can see warriors boarding ships in the harbor."

"Right," said Hansen. The maze of close-built houses and curving streets had left him without a clue as to his location. Was the Palace of Trade near the harbor? Was—

"Right," he repeated. "Broadcast over a general frequency that no warrior will be harmed if he takes off his suit. And— d'ye have a couple other people with you in the tower?"

"Roger, Lord Hansen."

"Right. If any of the ships put out from the dock, have one of your guys fire a bolt at it."

"We can't possibly harm armored warriors at this distance, Lord Hansen," the king protested. "Even my suit doesn't have that much power."

"*Not* you!" Hansen snapped. "I don't want *you* a sitting duck for some slow-learner."

He took a breath. His mouth was dry, while his throat and nasal passages had been scoured by ozone from the omnipresent arc weapons.

"Milord," he said more calmly. It looked like there was a square at the end of the current street. "You can't hurt the armor, but the ships'll burn like tinder . . . and one thing a battlesuit *won't* do is swim. Trust me."

It was a square. Across it was a stone building of four high stories whose corners were raised further by twenty-meter spires. The leaves of the arched central doorway were ajar. Darting through the gap stood the gold-armored Syndic who'd faced Hansen—briefly—outside the walls.

He disappeared inside. The bronze-clad door leaves closed.

"Come on!" Hansen bellowed as he broke into a run. "Don't kill anybody inside until I do!"

Hansen's arc licked the doors from across the courtyard. The bronze blazed green at the first touch. The wood underneath was a better insulator. It flamed up instantly, but the panels might have held until Hansen struck them with his suit's full mass—had not at least twenty more of his men ripped their arcs into the same point as they charged.

The doorleaves blew open in splinters. Hansen, the old woman still in his arms—too terrified to scream, forgotten in the greater need—was the first of the men through their flaming tatters.

Oil lamps hung in brackets from the high ceiling, but their glow was insignificant compared with the hard blue-white arclights quivering from the gauntlets of the battlesuits.

The man Hansen had chased into the hall was climbing out of his armor. He was a fat old fellow, blinking in wide-eyed terror at the killers who'd burst through the doorway behind him.

"Don't!" he whimpered. "Don't! Don't!" He screwed his eyes closed.

He was dressed silk and cloth-of-gold. So were most of the

thirty or forty others, men and women alike, who'd gathered in the building before the enemy arrived. More battlesuits, generally of good quality but covered with rococo decorations, winked in the royal army's weapons. All the suits were open, empty.

The Syndics and their hangers-on had surged for the back door when Hansen's arc blew open the front. They rushed back as abruptly. Hansen raised his weapon, his mouth open in amazement to think that they were about to attack him barehanded when they wouldn't face him with armor.

Another party of warriors burst in through the back door. Maharg's all-crimson suit was in the lead.

"All right!" Maharg thundered. "Who's the boss here?"

"*I* am, Marshal," Hansen boomed back.

"Oh, sorry sir," his abashed junior said on the command channel. "I didn't know—Malcolm, you made it too?"

Malcolm touched the warchief's shoulder. "I've got my Thraseys ringing the building," he said. "That gives us an organized reserve if we need one—which I doubt."

"Right," said Hansen.

He pointed his index finger at the Syndic quivering in his armor like a clam half-drawn from its shell by a crow.

"You," Hansen said. "Are you the Chief Syndic or whatever?"

The fat man opened his eyes, closed them again, and said, "There's no chief. I'm, I'm Bennet."

Something shook in the air. Hansen thought it must be the shock of buildings falling, but no one else seemed to notice the vibration.

"Do you have authority to surrender the city?" Hansen demanded. "Does anyone here have the authority?"

A man from the group Maharg herded back into the room threw himself at Hansen's feet. He was young but already fat and as bald as Shill the day he died.

"We do, we surrender, Lord Golsingh!" he babbled. "We're a quorum! We surrender! Oh gracious king—"

Hansen had an urge to kick the scut away. He repressed it to a shake of his armored boot—which had the desired effect of making the fellow scuttle back with a squeal.

"The king's not here," Hansen said, raising his voice to be

heard over the increasingly loud clatter from all around him, even the stone floor. . . . "As the Warchief of Peace Rock, I accept your surrender on behalf—"

"The king's here!" a man shouted from the doorway. "He's here!"

Hansen turned. Golsingh's splendid blue armor was silhouetted in the arched opening. *Underlings, no matter how respected, do not give commands to monarchs.*

"Your Excellence—" Hansen said, but the sound of the black pinions enveloping him was too loud even for his own ears.

The old woman in the arms of his battlesuit began to scream and point upward. Hansen's viewpoint hung suspended among the chandeliers and quivering stone vaulting.

He could see the empty interior of his armor—and the crypts beneath the building where a score of servants hid among the stored regalia and wine casks for public banquets. The white heart of the planet blazed up at him—

And was gone in weltering images of ice and beasts and huge red sun, which ended in a view of a light-struck hall infinitely greater than the one from which he'd been plucked a timeless moment before.

Hansen's feet were on a black floor as smooth and flawless as polished diamond. Twenty-odd curtains of light ringed the walls.

"Welcome, Hansen, once Commissioner," said the blur at the further end of the hall. "We have a task for you."

Chapter Thirty

It reminded Hansen of the place, the plane, where the lords of the Consensus briefed him.

The resemblance wasn't physical. He stood in a hall of such purity that the walls and roofbeams bent the light without dimming it. The floor beneath him was black but so smooth that Hansen felt he was standing on the soul of nothingness, the ancient ether which science had long denied even as an ideal.

The Palace of Trade had vanished. The Syndics, the conquering warriors in their battlesuits . . . everything except Hansen himself was gone.

The lords of the Consensus had been vast bulks, hinting of whale shapes but vaster even than fluid oceans could support. Here there were dazzles of light along the sides of the hall's empyrean perfection . . . and Hansen knew at an instinctive level that it was the same.

"Fortin," said a voice from the veil of splendor at the end of the room, "you will explain to Hansen his task. As for the others of you—you've seen that I have the situation in hand. Leave it with me, then."

Hansen had heard that voice—that *sort* of voice, he meant, but it went beyond that—before. The fellow outlining the mission, with all the weight of power and certainty behind him, telling others what they *would* do and what they *would not*.

Hansen always thought he'd be that sort of man when he had the rank, but he'd been wrong. *Commissioner* Hansen, and people jumping when he spoke—but he'd never been certain of anything except himself, and he couldn't give a man an order and make it sound like he expected to be obeyed.

Obeyed *or else*, if it came to that; but it was the *or else* Nils Hansen believed in, and that wasn't the same thing at all. . . .

The iridescent curtains were moving, shifting toward the

doorway; moving faster than a man could move over the distance . . . if the distance were as great as if seemed, which instinct suggested it was not.

"Penny?" said the voice of insouciant command. "You've recovered your necklace, I believe?"

"What if I have?" whined a girl's voice, almost close enough for Hansen to touch the speaker though the nearest of the auroral veils was/seemed a hundred meters away. Then the same voice, sulky, "Yeah, Fortin found it for me. Why . . . ?"

"To borrow, as you know. Because of Diamond. Because it's necessary to achieve balance."

For all the assurance with which the male officer spoke, Hansen could read the slightest doubt underlying the words. *This I ask*, the doubt admitted, *and though I would like to command it, I cannot. . . .*

The tone of a man who knows he *must* depend on others, but hopes they won't realize the fact.

Hansen began to smile.

The rainbow veils swept out of the hall like sun-struck sea mist scattered by a breeze. From the mass of them came a male figure, huge, walking toward Hansen with something winking from the fingers of his right hand. As he came closer, he shrank until he stood before the ex-Commissioner as a person no taller than Hansen himself. . . .

But that was not the surprise.

"Solbarth," Hansen said. "What are *you* doing here?"

The pigmentless, beautiful android lost his look of superior disdain for an instant. He glanced toward the single shield of light remaining, the one at the end of the hall from which the commanding voice rang.

"What?" the android said. "I'm not Solbarth. Any Solbarth."

"You're Solbarth," Hansen said. His assurance was suddenly no more than a ploy, a tool luck had offered him to get more information. "You're a criminal, and I captured you on Annunciation."

He grinned. "You haven't forgotten *me*."

The android blinked. "My name is Fortin," he said. "As for being a criminal—I'm a god."

Fortin's laugh barked harshly, falsely. "It may be that you knew a batch sibling of my mother," he said with empty dismissal. "I'm half android, you see."

Laughter boomed from behind the veil of light.

Fortin shook his head to clear away discomfort and settled the mantle of disdain about his visage again.

"No matter," he said. "We've brought you here to restore balance in—"

"*I* brought him here," interrupted the commanding voice.

Fortin smiled. Enunciating as clearly as the notes of a jade bell, he resumed, "My father brought you here to restore balance in the Matrix. You will be inserted into Ruby, a portion of phased spacetime. You'll be disguised—"

Fortin hefted the necklace in his left hand. Hansen had a sudden vision of himself in drag, dripping with jewelry and his hair done up with ruby-studded combs.

"—but they'll be awaiting you. And they'll probably have warning of an impending attack."

The hidden speaker said, "Their threat warning system is very good. On Ruby, everything to do with war is almost ideally good. Wouldn't you say so, Fortin?"

The minuscule fluttering of the android's—half android's—nostrils was the only sign he'd heard the interjection.

"Your task," Fortin continued, "will be to penetrate Ruby's Battle Center. The main computer there has already been programmed to carry out a particular phase shift. You must—"

"No," said Hansen.

Fortin's face froze. "Don't think to cross me, human," he said.

His malevolence would have surprised some listeners; but not Commissioner Hansen, who'd spent three years tracking down one Solbarth, a criminal of almost incredible savagery. . . .

"No," said Hansen. "There's no 'must' from you for me. *You*—"

He tapped out with a fingertip that stopped just short of the android's chest "—can't order me to piss on your boots. Though that I might do for fun."

Laughter rocked and boomed from the end of the hall.

Hansen whirled on the sound.

"D'ye think I'm a gun you can point?" he shouted. "Do you? Well, you're fucking wrong!"

"Do you remember Diamond, Hansen?" the voice asked.

"Where you first entered our continuum . . . not at our request."

It occurred to Nils Hansen that this pair was going to threaten harm to the gentle folk of Diamond unless Hansen did their bidding. An extortionist's trick, a hostage-taker's strategy.

And Hansen would have to react in the only way his soul would permit—kill Fortin, kill the voice behind the curtain of light; kill and keep killing until they killed *him*.

And perhaps the survivors would be less quick to use that gambit again with a man who was every bit as ruthless as they.

Fortin saw the look in Hansen's eyes; something close to an expression of sexual climax suffused the perfect android features. It froze Hansen and sickened him, as if he'd entered a room with murder in mind and found his intended victim eating a plateful of feces.

"This is what happened to Diamond," said the hidden man. "This is what you must avenge, Commissioner Hansen."

The hall vanished. Hansen hung in nothingness surrounded by the common area of the city-building where his capsule had landed. The room was full of standing, singing people, but he saw them as photographic negatives while something else printed through in their place.

Then he was truly among them, seeing Lea and remembering how her body had touched his with a warmth that was no flirtation. There was the little boy who'd waved and called Hansen's name, and—

He saw their flushed faces and the tears streaming down their cheeks as they sang of joy and sunlight.

The sun was a black pit out of which thundered a platoon of tanks rolling *through* the singing innocents rather than over them, grinding away the substance of their universe and not merely their bodies.

In place of the open park was a canyon walled by black houses as massive as coastal forts. Citizens in uniform danced in the street, firing slugs and streaks of ravening light into the air. Through all the celebration, the tanks roared triumphantly.

"You remember Diamond," said the commanding voice. "This is Ruby, which destroyed Diamond. I brought you here, Commissioner Hansen, to destroy Ruby and preserve balance."

The vision was gone, the hymn that was worse than the screams that should have accompanied the descent to some spicule of nothingness and death. . . .

Hansen shuddered uncontrollably. He worked his hands, watching the fingers bend and the skin mottle with strain over the knuckles. "Go on with the briefing," he said.

Fortin laughed. "We thought this was a job you'd be willing to do for us," he said smirkingly.

Hansen looked up. The android stepped away reflexively.

"I won't do anything for you," Hansen said. He spoke very distinctly. "I'll do the job—*this* job. But not for you."

"Which is all we ask . . . Kommissar," said the voice from behind the veil.

Chapter Thirty-one

The figures surrounding him in Fortin's hall of ice weren't hidden by their curtains of light, but Hansen's mind was focused on the insertion ahead.

Gods, humans, or diffracted shimmers, it was all one with him. He barely heard the swarthy, densely muscular man say, "Just how often *do* you visit Ruby, Fortin?"; and that penetrated Hansen's concentration only because of the threat beneath the words.

Fortin's finger tapped the bemedaled breast of the jacket Hansen wore, checking for the slight bulge of Penny's necklace. "All right," he said. "Here's the ring."

Hansen slid the large diamond in a gold band onto the middle finger of his left hand. His finger joints were no larger than the shafts of the phalanges. The ring fit easily, then clamped with a tiny prickling.

"Seconds to insertion," Hansen thought.

"*Forty-seven*," the ring's AI responded, using the nerve pathways of Hansen's body.

"It's connected?" Fortin said nervously.

"It's all fine," Hansen replied. "Look, I'm briefed and ready. Just step back."

"I don't like to see my necklace—on somebody else," murmured one of the spectators.

"And *Fortin!*" another chuckled. "That's a look *you* haven't tried—or have you, dearest?"

"That's not your gunhand, is it?" Fortin fussed. "It won't interfere?"

Hansen glowered at the android face of which his own was for the moment a perfect copy.

"My gunhand," he said distinctly, "is the hand I've got a gun in at the moment."

He flexed his left fist. The artificial intelligence flashed harder

233

echoes of light across the ice and the fawn-gray uniform Hansen
was wearing.

"It won't interfere. Trust me." Hansen's face formed a sort
of smile. "Nothing interferes with that."

"*Five seconds to insertion*," said the machine voice in Hansen's
mind.

"Here we go," Hansen said aloud, stepping toward the
discontinuity as though his briefing officer were not in his way—
and Fortin wasn't; he'd jumped aside as his double strode through
the space.

Hansen began to giggle. He was wondering if the necklace
would hide the stains if he pissed the pants of this beautiful
dress uniform. The thought wasn't the worst way to release
tension at the start of an operation.

He stepped into the faceted blur in the center of the hall
and—

His polished shoe ground down on the gritty red soil of a
drill field. An officer stood in front of a platoon of infantry.
They were drawn up at attention but armed to the teeth. Dust,
blowing across the field from the fans of eight APCs, aided the
excellent camouflage pattern of the troops' fatigues.

The field was scooped from the side of a mesa. On the rim
above, a tank company aimed its weapons toward Hansen. Each
of the two-squad armored personnel carriers mounted a light
cannon in its forward cupola; the guns were centered on Hansen's
chest also, though some of the weapons would have to blast
through the bodies of the infantrymen at attention.

Hansen didn't assume *those* gunners would be any slower to
shoot than the others.

The waiting officer threw Hansen a sharp salute. "Sir!" she
said. "I'm Major Atwater, in charge of your escort. We're very
glad to have you with us again, but I have to warn you that
we're on heightened alert. It's been raised to Threat Level 3."

Hansen returned the salute crisply but brought his arm down
to point at the pair of APCs waiting with their hatches open.
"Then let's get the hell out of an obvious target zone like this,
Major," he snapped.

Major Atwater spun on her heel. She bawled, "First Platoon,
saddle up!" though the formation had disintegrated with troopers

running for their vehicles almost before the first syllable was out of her mouth.

"*The other vehicle is commanded by Lieutenant Filerly,*" Hansen's AI informed him.

The infantry poured aboard the armored personnel carriers with the grace of belted ammo cycling through a machinegun. The APCs lifted to hover half a meter off the ground.

Atwater leaped aboard behind her troops. The hatch of the other vehicle clanged shut. Hansen reached for the equipment belt beneath his coat and followed the major. Within the APC, the crew chief's finger was on the hatch switch.

Hansen threw toward the rear of the troop compartment the contact grenade he'd snatched from his belt. Wearing the uniform and appearance of Major Atwater, he dropped backward out of the closing hatch.

The grenade belched orange from the hatch and the firing ports. Ammo went off in a crashing secondary explosion.

The armored personnel carrier staggered in the air. Hansen rolled to his feet and ran. The blast-ruptured fuel cells burst in a cataclysmic fireball, hurling bodies and other debris in a wide circle.

"Filerly!" Hansen shouted as he ran toward the APC which had taken aboard the other two squads. "Pick me up! The Inspector General's been assassinated!"

The armored personnel carrier, already several meters in the air, did a touch-and-go grounding whose violence proved the driver was nervous. The platoon leader, Lieutenant Filerly, hung out of the re-opened hatch and jerked Hansen aboard.

Hansen grabbed the microphone flexed to the vehicle's radio.

"This is Rainbow 6," he lied, aware of the nervous intensity with which Filerly stared at his CO's scorched fatigues. "Blue, Green and Yellow elements, land and secure the area. I'm taking Red Two to Headquarters immediately to report."

The APC's driver was listening on the general push, because the big vehicle surged forward before Hansen gave him a direct order.

The holographic periscope in the cupola showed the other six vehicles of the escort landing and dropping their side panels to spew troops. Wind scattered black smoke from the puddle of fuel and wreckage.

Hansen rested his fist against the vehicle's computer/ communications console. He felt a faint crunching as his ring chopped a micropathway through the console's casing. The unit began to hum and buzz without Hansen's direct input.

"The officer commanding the Headquarters guard detachment is Colonel al-Kabir," said the artificial intelligence in Hansen's ring. *"He's off duty and asleep at the moment, but he will shortly be roused because of the raised threat level."*

"Have the security police confine al-Kabir to quarters on orders of—of the High Council," Hansen thought. "You can do that?"

"It is done," the AI responded with what Hansen suspected was an electronic sneer.

"You've got his appearance?" Hansen added.

"Full physical details are in the central files," the AI said. *"Of course."*

"All units!" squawked the console unexpectedly. "Threat Level 2 is in effect. Repeat, Threat Level 2 is in effect."

"Ah, Major Atwater?" Filerly said. "We don't have clearance for even the outer HQ Zone when the threat level's above 5."

"I've received the handshake from the headquarters identification unit," the artificial intelligence said. *"It will recognize us as Colonel al-Kabir."*

"Proceed to the main entrance, driver," Hansen ordered coldly. "The High Council has cleared us through because of the information I'm bringing."

Lieutenant Filerly looked at him doubtfully, but it wasn't the business of a Ruby officer to question a direct order.

They were overflying wind-carved badlands at less than ten meters' altitude. The tops of the richly-layered plateaus loomed above the vehicle. Occasionally Hansen caught sight of antennas or a dug-in missile array flashing by beneath them.

"I hope you're—" the platoon leader started to say, and the APC howled out of the ring of miniature buttes into a vast area of ocher dirt, pocked and studded with armaments.

Guns and missile batteries tracked the vehicle, but none of them fired. Hansen glanced sardonically at the lieutenant, wondering what the expression looked like on his present female features.

"Be ready as soon as I'm out of the vehicle," Hansen thought.

"I am ready to act as soon as we are out of the vehicle," the artificial intelligence corrected coldly.

A concrete elevator head that looked like a pillbox stood in the midst of four tanks with their bows facing outward.

"In the middle of the tanks?" the car's driver asked.

"Land in front of the two nearest tanks," Hansen ordered.

Each tank's main armament was a 20-cm laser, augmented by a coaxial automatic cannon and blisters holding a variety of other guns. All the weapons that could bear did so as the APC grounded in a spray of dirt and grit. Hansen reached past the crew chief and pressed the door switch.

The hatch cycled open. Hansen stepped out into the shimmer of dust and heat haze in the guise of a fifty-year-old man with a shaven scalp and a colonel's star-in-square lapel insignia.

"Hey!" cried Lieutenant Filerly, reaching for his holstered pistol as he watched the transformed figure stride toward the elevator door opening in obedience to the command of Hansen's ring.

The AI snapped out a second prepared command to the defense array. Both tank lasers ripped the armored personnel carrier at point-blank range, hurling bits away in the blast and sparkle of the automatic weapons joining the chorus of destruction.

Hansen dived into the elevator cage. The back of his neck and ears stung with the awful radiance bathing Lieutenant Filerly and his vehicle. As the elevator door slammed shut, Hansen saw one of the tanks sliding forward to crush anything remaining in the blaze of slag and fire.

"The entrance guards are under Captain Alsen," the artificial intelligence said.

The cage dropped two levels and stopped at the first support area. A company of shock troops were drawn up behind portable barriers across the corridor in both directions. Their guns tracked Hansen as he got out of the entrance elevator and stepped toward the red-painted door of the shaft beside it.

"Captain Alsen," he ordered crisply, "interdict *all* further entry to HQ region."

"But sir . . . ," the black-helmeted guard officer said. "We've been alerted to expect Field Marshal Yazov soonest."

Hansen set his ring against the keyslot controlling the elevator.

"That message was false, Captain," he said. "The enemy has penetrated our communications system. Any vehicle entering the outer HQ Zone must be destroyed at once."

He felt a minuscule *click* through his ring finger. "I'm reporting to the Citadel at once, as ordered."

"Aye aye——" Alsen was saying before the door slammed shut on the remainder of his words.

The interior of the elevator cage was polished steel. As it plunged downward, Hansen saw that he now looked like a moustached wrestler going to fat. Though he still wore fatigues, they had epaulets and his insignia were the wreathed stars of a field marshal.

"Thank you, ring," he thought.

"There is no need to thank me."

"Does this shaft go all the way to the Citadel?"

"We will drop beneath the Citadel level," the artificial intelligence informed its wearer. *"I've keyed us down to Computation Control."*

Hansen didn't realize how fast the cage was dropping till it slowed and the inertia bent his knees as though he'd jumped off the roof of a building. The door opened.

The walls and ceiling of the corridor were covered by mirrors, seamless except for emergency doors every hundred meters. There was a low-frequency vibration in the air.

"Left," directed Hansen's AI.

There were a number of people already striding up or down the corridor. They wore white smocks, the first citizens of Ruby Hansen had seen without uniforms . . . though the smocks were, now that he thought about it, uniforms also.

The technicians glanced at him as he passed and, though no one challenged him, he could feel them continuing to stare at his mirrored figure as he walked onward.

"How far?" he thought.

"Turn right at the cross-corridor," the ring said instead of answering.

Hansen wasn't as frightened as he should have been. It was like a house-clearing operation. He was moving so fast that he had no time to think about anything except the step he was taking *now*. Move and shoot—and keep it up until there's nothing else moving in the target area. . . .

The mirrors suddenly lost their opacity and opened vistas of

Ruby's surface: missile batteries rising, searching for targets; children too small to bear arms marching in lock-step toward shelters; adults all over the planet grabbing weapons and reporting to battle stations.

Hansen turned the corner. Another figure marched in the mirrored walls to his left and right: Colonel al-Kabir. Smock-garbed technicians stopped and stared.

"How *far*?" Hansen's mind demanded of the artificial intelligence.

"*To the left at the next corridor,*" the machine responded grudgingly. "*And a hundred meters.*"

The reflections of al-Kabir quivered suddenly into Major Atwater, keeping pace with Hansen. If Hansen turned his head, the reflections turned also. . . .

"Sir?" called a technician. "Sir."

Hansen took the corner with a crisp military pivot. He was sweating. Alongside him strode the Inspector General with Fortin's cold, pale features.

Hansen could see the outline of the door he wanted in the wall ahead, but the mirrored reflections beside him shook. The real Nils Hansen flanked the false Field Marshal Yazov.

"Threat Level 1!" screamed a public address system. "Intruder! Intruder!"

Technicians were reaching under their smocks for weapons, but now Hansen was in his element. His left hand hurled a grenade behind him as he screamed, "Shut the crash door!" hoping his AI could react before the grenade did.

The pistol he drew was standard issue for Ruby. Its recoil was heavier than Hansen was used to, but it pointed like an eleventh finger and its bullets were explosive.

The skull of the first technician exploded in a red flash that blew her blond hair in all directions like chair stuffing. Hansen aimed for the center of mass of the second and third techs, dropping them both before they'd cleared their own pistols.

The emergency door clanged shut behind Hansen, then started to reopen as the PA system screamed, "The intruder is operating the electronic controls! Close and lock all doors manu—"

The grenade blast knocked Hansen down, but the part-open door protected him from the fragments that shattered the walls and the humans on the other side of it. He scrambled to his feet, pulling a spool charge from his equipment belt.

The door of the Computation Control room slid halfway open and stopped. Hansen leaped through, unreeling the spool charge behind him. His pistol centered on the forehead of the technician straining against the door's manual control wheel. Only as the door slammed shut again did Hansen fire.

The ballooning horror of the man's face was echoed by the strip of spool charge which detonated under the door's pressure. The multi-dogged valve torqued in the explosion, locking itself inextricably closed.

Technicians holding unfamiliar weapons started from their seats. A line of explosive bullets rang on the back of the wedged door and the floor where Hansen had been an instant earlier.

Hansen's form became that of the headless female technician he'd killed in the hallway. His left hand hurled the last piece of equipment from his belt—a spoofing bomb. It popped, deploying half a dozen miniature projectors.

Black-suited holographic gunmen capered about CompCon, some of them upside down. Technicians gaped and fired. Their bursts destroyed equipment in arcs and implosions, but the blazing gunfire didn't—couldn't—affect the holograms.

There were five technicians within the sealed room. As sickly layers of powder and explosive residues quivered at further muzzle blasts, Hansen moved his body only as much as he needed to get an angle on the next target.

He killed each technician with a single shot. The last of them, screaming in disbelief, pointed her machinepistol at the center of Hansen's chest and continued to squeeze the trigger even as the headless corpse aimed its gun at her left eye. The technician had emptied her weapon before the dancing holograms sputtered and vanished.

"*Quickly,*" said the voice in Hansen's brain as the last technician fell, all but the splash on the wall behind her. "*They're starting to drill through the door.*"

Hansen was holding his breath in a subconscious attempt to keep from vomiting the acid that was the only thing in his stomach. The renewed threat focused him. He looked for an undamaged terminal.

"In the left corner!" snapped the artificial intelligence.

Rather than reload, Hansen snatched an unfired pistol from the holster of the man he'd killed at the door controls and ran to the indicated console. He could hear tools cutting. They were very fast, very organized, the folk of Ruby; very skilled in the arts of war.

He put his ring against the terminal's control board.

Ruby wasn't facing a world of pacifists this time.

Almost simultaneously with the *click* from Hansen's finger, the lights in CompCon dimmed and the sound of electronic whispering hushed. He had his gun out, looking for a target.

"I'm shutting down other functions in order to bring up the matching program again," the AI explained. *"It's no longer in the active memory."*

The sound of computers working resumed at a higher, more insistent, note.

Something appeared in the center of the room—not a tank but the memory of a tank like the one which had ground through the crowd on Diamond while Hansen waited with a chair.

This time he had a better weapon—not the pistol, but the artificial intelligence on his finger which was turning Ruby against itself.

Hansen began to laugh. The electronic ghost disappeared, replaced by a scene from the field where Hansen arrived. Nervous troops were forming a perimeter while officers and non-coms checked the bodies scattered when the APC exploded. A lieutenant had turned over the corpse of Major Atwater. The escort commander had been stripped by the blast, but her features were still recognizable.

"Yes . . . ," the AI whispered to Hansen's mind in satisfaction.

The leaf of the heavy door was beginning to glow a soft rose that brightened into golden radiance.

Hansen began to shudder. He thought at first it was reaction, but then he noticed that the wounds of the dead technicians were beginning to steam in the frigid air.

"What's—" he said and stopped, unable to frame the question lucidly.

"We are repeating the cycle," explained the AI. *"We are putting Ruby in phase with Diamond."*

With where Diamond was *now*.

In the center of the room, the ghost image of a Ruby family huddled in its bunker. The youngest of them was a boy of ten. Their fingers were poised on the controls of the weapon systems poised around and on top of their bunker. They had no target, and their faces were growing pale. . . .

A hollow drill pierced the door to CompCon. Its snout quivered and twisted, seeking Hansen.

Hansen fired first. The charge of his explosive bullet was an orange flash against the yellow-white blaze of the door. He fired twice more, smashing the drill point before it could loose its own lethal greeting.

There was a *bang!* from within the panel itself and the glow dulled to red.

"The door has a self-sealing core," said the AI. *"All the defenses here are redundant. It will hold long enough, I estimate."*

The room was colder than the surface of a dead planet. A second drill began to gnaw at the door.

Another ghost, holding out her hand to him. Lea, surrounded by icy darkness; her hair unbound, her voice—surely her voice, not a memory.

Her voice calling, "No, Hansen, not this. Not for *us*."

But yes, for them. For all the folk whose souls wouldn't let them fight for themselves, who'd rather die than to kill—

That was Diamond's decision, and it did Diamond honor. But the folk of Diamond already knew that Hansen didn't belong with them. . . .

"There . . . ," said the artificial intelligence.

The door to CompCon collapsed in blazing fragments. Hansen fired into the opening, but Ruby was fading and merging with Diamond, spiraling down an icy black helix with nothing at all at the bottom. . . .

Chapter Thirty-two

Hansen's boots clashed on the floor of the light-struck hall. A wisp of smoke trailed from the muzzle of his pistol, but he'd emptied the magazine back in another universe.

The figures seated along the sides of the room were no longer veiled in light. They shouted a mixture of triumph and greeting as they rose and tramped across the adamant to Hansen, their forms shrinking with every step.

"Well done!" boomed the stocky, swarthy man as he clapped Hansen on the back. "Couldn't've done better myself."

"You couldn't have done as well, Rao," said a woman with an oriental face. "Brute force would have failed."

"Rao," Hansen repeated. "From North's team?"

"Once I was," Rao admitted. "Once I was."

Rao's powerful hand closed over the pistol Hansen still held.

"But let me take this, boy," Rao added. "Not the rules, here, you know. Makes some of 'em a little nervous, you see."

Hansen recognized other faces from his briefing on Annunciation. The big man was Rolls, who'd led the initial exploration unit, and—

A plump young woman squeezed through the crowd, using her elbows expertly, and slid her hand beneath Hansen's jacket.

"My necklace?" she demanded. "You have my necklace safe?"

"Uh?" said Hansen. "Sure."

He lifted the gossamer strap; the woman snatched it away as soon as it was clear.

"You're Penny, aren't you?" Hansen asked. "From—"

"Yes," she responded, a regal and statuesque redhead from the moment the jewel dropped over her head. "And you and I *must* see a lot of one another."

The figure seated at the end of the hall had not joined the general throng. He was fully in shadow until the sun moved above the crystal ceiling. A prismatically scattered beam fell across the craggy face in a rainbow.

His right eye blinked. His left did not.

"Walker!" Hansen shouted.

The tall figure stood.

"North," he said, laughing. "But sometimes Walker."

The others backed a few steps away when North spoke. Hansen looked at them, then toward their leader again. "Where is this place?" he asked. "Where are we?"

"North found the path through the Matrix," said a decisively plain woman. Eisner, Hansen thought; one of the exploration unit. "We travel all eight planes of the Matrix, now; and the Matrix itself is the ninth."

"We're gods," said Rolls. "You can think of us that way, Hansen."

There was more in his tone than satisfaction, but Hansen didn't have enough information to guess what the other emotions were.

But the real question—

"What's going to happen to me, then?" Hansen asked.

North began to laugh. Others of the self-proclaimed gods smiled or blinked in surprise.

"You don't understand, do you?" said Fortin with the air of detached amusement that was the attitude Hansen knew to expect of the android.

"Then tell me," Hansen said. He didn't need a gun in his hand to make the words a threat.

Fortin's face chilled. "It's very simple," he said. "Only one of *us* could enter Ruby from the—inside of the Matrix. So we had to make you one of us before we sent you in."

"Welcome to godhead, Kommissar," North said.

His terrible, thunderous laughter echoed through the hall.

Author's Note

The poems of the Poetic Edda (sometimes called the Elder
Edda) cover various aspects of Norse myth, mythic history, and
folklore. They aren't in any sense a structured belief system,
though their odds and ends comprise almost everything known
about ancient Norse beliefs. They were written over a period
of centuries and across the sweep of the Norse world (including
Greenland). Though the subjects are pagan, most of the verses
were put in their final form by Christians.

The disparate pieces were then hammered to fit by an
anonymous Icelandic redactor who was not only Christian but
also remarkably limited both as an editor and as a poet. In
addition, the redactor was missing pieces of some of his poems,
and there is also a large gap in the sole text of his compilation.

Put in short terms, the Poetic Edda is a confusing hodgepodge
which hadn't particularly interested me when I read it twenty
years ago. Anyway, my training was in classical languages and
history, not those of the Norse/Germanic world.

Then in 1986 I took my family to Iceland for a three-week
vacation. While I was there, I picked up a copy of Hollander's
excellent translation of the Poetic Edda and read the verses
among the geography in which they had been compiled and
(in part) written. I found them stunningly evocative.

Iceland's contrasts would probably have had a considerable
effect on me anyway. For example, one day I stood on the largest
glacier in Europe; the next day I was on an active volcano. Similar
stark dichotomies pervade all the physical features of the country.

Iceland was the right place—the right places—to appreciate
the Edda.

I returned with the certainty that I was going to use the Edda
as the basis for my own fiction, though I was damned if I knew
just *how* I was going to do that. I read some secondary materials
(particularly Dumezil and H. R. Ellis Davidson) regarding the

structure and themes of the Norse myths, but that course wasn't productive; not because the authors were wrong, but because their truth wasn't my truth.

So I did what I'd been taught to do by the best teacher I've ever had, Professor Jonathan Goldstein, when I was an undergraduate at Iowa: I went back to the primary sources. I paraphrased the complete Poetic Edda, and took notes on the Prose Edda (or Snorri Edda, written by Snorri Sturluson, Iceland's greatest literary figure, in the thirteenth century) and the Volsung Saga (which covers the material in the missing portion of the Poetic Edda).

Finally I went over the resulting 15,000 words of notes and chose elements which I thought would work in a science fiction novel. Initially I tried to include too much for a single volume, but I kept whittling away at the material until the length seemed satisfactory.

The myths which became major facets of *Northworld* are:

a) the Death and Avenging of Baldr;
b) the Peace of Frothi;
c) the Theft of the Mead of Skaldship; and
d) the relations of Gefjon and Heimdall referred to in the *Lokasenna*.

The above themes are not part of a single episode or cycle within the Eddas. For the sake of my classically-trained soul, I've woven them together in a logical progression; but that progression doesn't exist in the original.

In the present context, I'm a storyteller, not a scholar writing an exegesis on Norse myth; but I *have* tried to reflect the worldview I briefly shared while staring across the smoking basalt wastes of Iceland.

The world of the Eddas was harsh and unforgiving; but it wasn't without nobility. I hope both aspects come through in *Northworld* and the later novels I've planned for the setting.

Dave Drake
Chatham County, N.C.

Vengeance

To my son Jonathan,
who liked the first one.

Chapter One

As Nils Hansen lay on the grass of the grave mound, staring toward the black pines silhouetted against the sunset, he heard a shout in the near distance and the *sring!* of a sword coming out of its scabbard. Hansen jumped up from the warm earth, though he'd come here unarmed and there was no need for him to take a local quarrel as his own anyway.

No external need.

The approach of men on ponies—several men, judging from the voices raised as they yipped to their mounts—had been hidden by the snorts and clicks of the herd of giant peccaries being driven to the stockade at Peace Rock for the night. Vague skyglow glinted on the riders' harness and weapon-edges as they spread to encircle the herdsman.

Three men, one carrying a curved saber and the other pair pointing lances as they walked their ponies forward, Hansen thought as his legs took him into trouble because that was what they'd always done, ever since Nils Hansen was able to stand.

"You keep away from me!" bellowed the herdsman as he pivoted clumsily. He aimed his crossbow at first one of the intruders, then another. "You keep away or I'll shoot!"

Peccaries trailing the main herd grunted and clashed their tusks. The pigs stood belly high to a pony. They were more than dangerous when they chose to be—but for now the beasts were less interested in a fight than they were in the swill awaiting them in the compound. They made way for the riders.

They made way for Hansen as well. With the dusk and the tension, none of the four actors noticed that a fifth man was joining them.

"And what d'ye suppose'll happen then *after* you shoot, boyo?" demanded the rider with a saber.

"Yeah, is that the way Peace Rock treats travelers asking guest rights, pig-smell?" added a lancer.

The riders halted like the spokes of a wheel, each about five meters from the herdsman at the hub.

"I don't have anything to do with guest rights!" cried the herdsman desperately. "You'll have to ask the Lord Waldron!"

The herdsman was trying to face all directions at once, but his real concern was for the lances whose points were already half the distance to his chest.

Hansen knew that was a mistake. The danger wasn't from weapons but rather from the men carrying them. The rider with the saber was the one deciding what would happen next. If Hansen were in the herdsman's place—

He'd shoot the leader at once and take his chances with the other pair. The lancers would run away or at least freeze for the moment it'd take to snatch the saber and the reins of the loose pony—

But Nils Hansen had the advantage of being a killer himself, with training and experience to hone a great natural talent.

"Listen to that!" said one of the lancers. "No respect for travelers nor his master neither! You know, we oughta—"

The peccaries were faint clicks in the distance. The sky had faded enough that whole constellations were visible in the east.

"You ought to learn civil speech," Hansen said, close enough to touch the nearest pony before it shied from his voice, "or the lord won't have any more respect for you than I do—*boyo*."

He'd had to speak up. The jingle of harness as the leader hunched over the neck of his mount meant that the fellow was about to lurch forward and cut the herdsman down from behind.

The leader straightened, trying instinctively to conceal the saber behind his right leg as the lancer nearest to Hansen sawed the reins with his left hand to control the startled pony. For an instant, the herdsman's crossbow pointed at the center of Hansen's chest; then the square-headed bolt twitched sideways to follow the lancer who steadied his mount a few meters away.

"Who the hell are you?" snarled the leader.

"I'm a traveler passing through these parts," said Hansen easily. He watched the teeth glinting in the leader's black beard and, in the corner of his eyes, the wink of the nearer lancehead. "Maybe I'll want to claim guest rights at Peace Rock myself."

Then, because he saw it was about to happen and he liked to tell himself that it wasn't what he wanted, it was never what *he* wanted, Hansen said, "Friends, we don't need a prob—"

The leader said, "Take 'im, Steith!", and the horseman to Hansen's left thrust forward with his lance.

Hansen was already moving, shifting his torso backward by its own depth so that the lancehead grazed Hansen's tunic of blue-dyed linen instead of grating in through one set of ribs and out through the other.

The herdsman shouted and jumped free of the circle. He still waved his crossbow, but the fellow's instincts told him it was a weapon for wolves, not men, and his fingers refused to squeeze the trigger bar.

Hansen gripped the spear shaft with both hands. The wood had been shaped with curve-bladed knives, not by lathe-turning. Hansen could feel the ridges through the calluses of his palms as he tugged.

The rider lurched forward. He dropped the lance to catch himself on the saddle pommel. His pony, slapped alongside the muzzle by the lance shaft, shied again.

Steith shouted as he tried to control his mount. The leader was shouting also, but Steith was between him and Hansen, and the second lancer couldn't seem to decide whether to track Hansen or the yammering herdsman.

Hansen didn't say a word as he slammed the butt of the weapon into Steith.

The lance wasn't fitted with a metal buttspike. Hansen's shoulder muscles were powerful even when he was calm, and now his blood bubbled with adrenaline from fear and rage. He thrust the blunt wooden pole a hand's-breadth deep in Steith's chest, catapulting the man over the cantle of his saddle.

The man with the saber kneed his mount forward as Steith's pony bolted out of the way. The lanceshaft cut an arc in the air as Hansen swapped it end for end. The leader couldn't be sure what had happened in the confused darkness, but he understood the wink of the lancehead centered on his chest. He drew up his mount with a curse.

Steith's pony, panicked by the smell of the pulmonary blood that sprayed its neck and mane, galloped into the forest with a terrified blat of sound. The other lancer shouted, "Abel! Abel! What should—"

"Get the fuck outa here!" the leader replied, yanking the head of his pony to the left and digging in with the same-side spur.

Both riders cantered off, the leader a pony's length ahead of the surviving lancer. The lancer was still bleating demands for an explanation as they disappeared.

"Eat *this!*" cried the herdsman as he aimed his crossbow.

Hansen lifted the crossbow's muzzle with the tip of his lance.

"What?" said the herdsman. "What?" He did not shoot.

The lance trembled like a willow in a windstorm. Hansen threw the weapon down and hugged his arms tight against his chest.

Blood and death stank in the air and in his mind.

The light was gone. The treetops stood out against the sky, but the trunks and the ground and the corpse lying there on its back were only blurs in blackness. Hansen squatted, trying to control his body as hormones burned themselves off in nervous shudders.

"My lord?" said the herdsman as he bent over Hansen. "Were you struck? My lord?"

"Just back off!" Hansen snarled. The herdsman hopped away in terror.

It was the adrenaline. Mostly the adrenaline.

Hansen stood up. "Look, I'm okay now," he said.

His voice had a rasp in it. He must have been shouting. There'd been a lot of noise and confusion; it was hard to keep the sequence of events straight, even though they had just happened.

"My lord," said the herdsman, "I'm Peter. May I guide you to Lord Waldron?"

"At Peace Rock?" Hansen said. He flexed his hands. He'd strained them in the brief moments of his grip on the lance. "Yeah, I'd appreciate that. I could use . . ."

Rest. Food. Some answers.

"Who were those—folk?" he asked aloud. "Has the Peace of Golsingh broken down?"

"Oh, them," said Peter, scornful now that he'd seen the backs of the men who would have killed him.

He'd dropped the crossbow when Hansen struck up the

muzzle. Now he searched for the weapon, finding it beside the narrow track which the hooves of his peccaries had worn. "There's a lot of rovers from Solfygg to the east, recently. Warriors. They stay within the law, mostly, but they go from stead to stead and call out to a duel anybody who looks at them crossways."

Peter set off along the trail. Familiarity and the odor of pig droppings guided his steps where the faint light could not. Hansen followed along. He was glad to be moving again, but the big muscles of his thighs still fluttered with hormones and reaction.

"Those weren't warriors, surely?" he said. The hill ahead of them showed the ragged rim of a stockade, and the air held a tang of woodsmoke.

It didn't seem so very long ago that Hansen had last been in Peace Rock.

"Them warriors?" the herdsman said. "No, just retainers, the sort you'd find who'd follow a rover."

He spat. "A murderer, to give them their proper name. But the rovers now have battlesuits like the gods themselves wear, so they say. With armor like that, they kill whoever it is they call out."

"Do they just?" Hansen murmured too softly for Peter to hear.

He was beginning to tremble again. He should never have come back.

"Peace Rock was the king's seat in the time of the great Golsingh, King Prandia's grandfather, did you know?" the herdsman went on. "Before he moved to Frekka. And even then, his wife—"

"His wife Unn," Hansen said.

He thought only his mind had spoken, but the herdsman looked over at his companion in surprise and said, "Yes, Unn was her name. Do you know the story?"

"Tell me," Hansen said, flexing his broad hands in the darkness.

"Queen Unn asked to be buried here at Peace Rock," Peter said, "because it was here that she learned to love King Golsingh, so they say. That was her grave mound back there where the scuts waylaid us.

"Waylaid *me*," the herdsman corrected, but Hansen's mind was lost in another time.

A party of men, visible only as three bobbing torches, had just issued from the gate of the stockade a hundred meters away. "Peter! Peter, is that you?" one of them bellowed.

"I'm all right, Cayley!" the herdsman shouted back to the search that had been organized when the herd of peccaries returned without him.

"Well, where in North's name have you been?" one of the searchers demanded peevishly.

"She was supposed to be a beautiful woman," Peter said to his silent companion. "Blond hair and eyes the color of the summer sky."

"She was the most beautiful woman I've ever seen," Hansen said; but this time, the whisper was too soft to be overheard except by the pines.

Chapter Two

When the sun rose high enough to penetrate the valley, its light turned the ice-covered pines into dazzles of beauty outside the door of the brothers' lodge.

Sparrow paused with his armload of wood and stared up at the rainbow sparkles. Slats of ice popped and tinkled, dancing down through the lower branches as they melted from the first sun-warmed needles.

The forest would be dangerous today. When tufts of pine needles lost their covering of ice and flicked upward, the strain of their release would provide the final stress on some of the parent branches. Great limbs would crash down to crush anything beneath them—even a mammoth; even a man as powerful as Sparrow the Smith.

Sparrow chuckled. The forest was always dangerous.

"Shut the damned door, will you?" bellowed Gordon from within the lodge.

"Shut it yourself," Sparrow replied as he pivoted through the doorway carefully, because the logs he carried were each longer than the door was wide. "I'm the one who's doing something useful."

Gordon got up to close the door flapping on its leather hinges; Sparrow clumped past him to the lodge's central hearth. Sledd, the third of the brothers, lay stripped to a loincloth on a bench beside the hearth.

Sledd was in a trance. On the side opposite the fire from him was a carefully-arranged pile of scrap and ores. The materials shifted in response to unseen pressures and choosings. Sledd's mind worked within the Matrix, seeking through chaos.

The Matrix was the pattern of all patterns. Events moved in all temporal directions the way a tossed stone sends circular ripples across the two-dimensional surface of a pond. Sledd searched the infinite possibilities for a template that matched the form he wished to create in crystal and metal. When desire meshed with the reality of the Matrix, atoms of raw material realigned themselves into one of the patterns chance could cause them to take—

And an object of great sophistication formed within the pile of rocks and junk.

A man who could find templates within the Matrix was a smith.

A man who could ride the event waves of the Matrix to any reality—who could focus his mind in the raging chaos and form a palace or a world—a man with *that* power was a god.

But short of the gods, there was no smith on Northworld the equal of Sparrow and his brothers; and Sparrow was the greatest of the three.

"We're going to have to replace the hinges," Gordon complained. "I don't think Sledd tanned them through this last time. They're starting to crack already."

"It was a cold winter," Sparrow said without concern. He bent at the knees to lower the wood to the puncheon floor. If he simply opened his arms, the dozen 10-kilo billets would crash and bounce in all directions. "And sometimes the hide has flaws. Even mammoth hide."

The wonders the brothers had created stood or moved about the interior of the lodge.

In the center of the single long room, nine balls of light wove a sphere of intersecting circles around an invisible hub. The balls trailed luminous lines that faded gradually until the next slow circuit renewed them. Smoke from the hearth dimmed the illumination, but the soot that coated the ridge pole and the open gable ends through which the smoke escaped in lieu of a chimney did nothing to tarnish the insubstantial balls themselves.

A water clock hung from the wall opposite Sparrow's bed closet. A simulacrum of a wolf worked from tin lifted its leg to spurt droplets into a crystal cylinder scored to mark the minutes. On cold nights the water would have frozen, save that Gordon had fitted it with heating coils powered by energy differentials within the Matrix itself.

A battlesuit stood before each of the bed closets. Most of the objects the brothers had created were unique, but any smith could find the template for the suits of powered armor with which warriors clashed in dazzling radiance across the face of Northworld. Battlesuits like these, however, approached the ideal of the Matrix as closely as physical objects could do.

Sparrow stepped back from the pile of fresh logs and worked the thong and peg which fastened his cape out of the eyelet on the other side. He shook the garment to clear it of drops of melt water, then tossed it on one of the chests which served for clothing storage as well as benches when the brothers sat.

The cape, lifted whole from a cinnamon bear, was nearly the color of the smith's own hair and beard. Shortly after the brothers came to the valley three years before, Sparrow had strangled the beast with his bare hands when he surprised it raiding one of his snares. His forearms still bore scars from that battle.

Sledd began to murmur, coming out of his trance. Sparrow glanced to see what his brother had been creating, but a pile of reduced ores still covered the object like the crust of clay over a lost-wax casting.

Gordon put another log on the hearth. Sparrow walked over to the shelf built onto the front panel of his bed closet and took from it the mirror he kept there.

The polished bronze surface was a circle only about ten centimeters in diameter. For a moment it showed Sparrow his own face and whiskers, tinted even ruddier by the metal's hue.

The smith's fingers manipulated the controls on the back of the circle. Metallic luster cleared into a scene of figures moving against the brilliant green of summer foliage.

"Gods but it's cold!" Sledd mumbled. "Stoke up the fire, won't you?"

"Sledd," Sparrow said. "Gordon. Look at this."

His brothers' faces blanked as they joined him, one to either side. Sledd reached down to work a cramp out of his right thigh.

"Can you make them bigger?" Gordon asked.

"A little," said Sparrow. His index finger stroked the controls. The face of the nearest figure, a woman with perfect features and long black hair, filled the mirror's small field.

"No one we know," said Gordon as Sparrow panned the image back to capture the surroundings again.

"They're Searchers," said Sledd. "And that's the spring at the foot of this valley."

The other two women were blonds, both of them larger than their black-haired companion. As the Searchers ran down the flower-carpeted slope to the spring, Sparrow shifted the image in his mirror to examine the equipment the women had left on the knoll behind them.

Sledd trembled with the chill of the Matrix. He picked up his brother's cape because it was handy and slipped it over his own shoulders. "What are Searchers doing here?" he said.

"How did you find them?" asked Gordon simultaneously.

"Unless I ask the mirror for something in particular," said Sparrow, "it shows me what's nearby that it thinks will most interest me. The picture is near in time. A few months from now."

Three battlesuits stood on the wooded knoll. Each of the frontal plates which covered the wearer's face and thorax was swung open against the hinges on the left side of the join.

The brothers' eyes narrowed as they surveyed the armor. Even with the image shrunken to fit the mirror, they could see that the suits were of excellent quality.

That was to be expected of battlesuits which clothed the servants of North the War God.

Behind the armor were the mounts which had brought the Searchers to the brothers' valley: electronic dragonflies.

For the moment, at rest with their gear stowed, the fragile-seeming vehicles looked more like long-legged cave crickets. When the gossamer antennas unfolded like wings to shroud the saddle in a bubble of separate spacetime, the Searchers could slip between the worlds of the Matrix.

When they were on North's business, the dragonflies hovered over battlefields, just out of temporal phase with the struggle going on below, while their receptor antennas drank and stored the minds of the dying. Flickering shutters of black radiance marked the Searchers' passage to the humans of the Open Lands.

"Go back to the women," Sledd murmured thickly. "It's been a long time."

"Don't be a fool!" Gordon said. "They're Searchers."

Sparrow adjusted his image. "Why not Searchers?" he said. "They're women too."

The women were splashing one another in the cold water of the spring. They had left their tunics on the bank.

"These are the god's servants," Gordon said. "We can find other women."

"If we want to trek for a week we can find other women," Sledd replied tartly. "And who would we find then worthy to bring back here? Our father is a king!"

"If there's any justice," said Gordon, "our father is freezing in hell."

"*And* his new wife," said Sledd. "*And* their bastard whelps."

One of the women sprang to the bank laughing and ran into the woods. Her companions followed a moment later. The black-haired Searcher was as lithe and compact as lynx.

Sparrow stroked his ginger beard. "The Searchers have lives beyond the god's orders," he said. "These three aren't on North's business now."

His lips pursed. "They won't be on North's business next summer, I mean."

He shifted the image again. The women were picking fruit from a blackberry tangle at the edge of the woods. They reached carefully to avoid scratching their bare flesh.

"If we do," said Gordon cautiously, "we'll have to wear our battlesuits."

"No," said Sparrow.

The black-haired woman flicked a ripe berry at one of her companions. It burst in a purple blotch on flesh so clear that the veins showed blue beneath the surface. The blond laughed and flung back a handful of the fruit.

"Sparrow," Sledd protested, "you're forgetting they're Searchers. If we try to take them unarmed, they'll put their own armor on and cut us down."

Sparrow focused the image down again on the face of the black-haired woman. "No," he said slowly, "I'm not forgetting who they are. But if they're worthy of us, then we have to be worthy of them. We can't force this sort."

Gordon nodded agreement. "Not and live," he said. "We have to sleep sometime ourselves."

Sparrow reached out as though he were going to stroke the woman's smooth, tanned cheek; but his fingers paused just short of the mirror's surface.

"It may be," he said, "that we can convince them of our worth. . . ."

Chapter Three

"Lord Waldron," announced the herdsman in a cracked attempt at grandiloquence, "here is the worthy stranger who saved me from attack by bandits. Ah, and saved your pigs."

In good light—illuminated by the fat-soaked rushes within the Great Hall of Peace Rock, at any rate—Peter was a squat man of sixty or so, twice Hansen's apparent age. He wore a peaked pigskin cap, bristle side in, which he snatched off belatedly as he spoke with his master. Despite the age obvious in the lines of Peter's face, his hair was as black and stiff as the peccary bristles.

"The other pigs, you mean," said the warrior seated to the right, just below Lord Waldron's crosstable. "Phew, man, don't stand so close."

"Arnor," said the lord. "Not now."

Lord Waldron was as old as Peter, though his hair was white. Standing, he would be half a head taller than Hansen. Waldron looked fit rather than active, and there was an aura of intelligent calculation in his eyes as they touched his visitor.

"What do you mean—" Waldron said to his herdsman, before breaking off and shifting his steady gaze to Hansen.

"If you're a traveling warrior who claims guest rights, sir," Waldron said, "then you must tell us your name."

The Great Hall was the same thatch-roofed structure it had been when it was the king's seat in past ages; but because all the circumstances had changed, the physical surroundings seemed different as well.

Most of the bed closets in which the lord's warriors slept had been removed from the long walls. The benches and trestle tables to either side of the central hearth were still occupied at dinner, but only because freemen now sat on the lower benches and ate with the lord and his warriors.

Lord Waldron sat at the crosstable with his wife, a woman as old as he who hennaed her hair. There were only three warriors on each of the parallel benches below them.

Hansen blinked away his memory of the long room filled with over a hundred drunken, shouting warriors. He liked this better, though the other was a more proper milieu for *his* sort.

"My name's Hansen," he said aloud. "And I would be grateful for a meal and a night's lodging, my lord."

"You do claim to be a warrior, don't you?" asked Arnor. He was a big man in his mid-thirties; running now to fat. Judging from where he sat below the lord, Arnor was probably Waldron's chief advisor and leading warrior . . . to the extent that Peace Rock in its present guise had military requirements.

Arnor spoke in a tone whose studious calm attempted to take the sting out of what could easily be construed as an insult; but it was a proper question to a stranger who appeared without a battlesuit or retinue. Arnor, as the lord's champion, had the duty of asking—at the risk of a challenge if Hansen turned out to be a hot-blooded spark who felt his honor had been impugned.

Enough fights had come Hansen's way already without him needing to look for another. He opened his mouth to make a suitably mild reply—

But before he could speak, Peter the herdsman cackled, "A warrior? You bet he is! He killed six bandits with his bare hands. And *they* had swords and lances!"

Everyone stared at the guest.

Hansen chuckled. "There were only three of them," he said. "Two—"

And he paused because his voice broke. All the humor of Peter's overstatement had drained from Nils Hansen's soul when his mind remembered fury as red and real as steel glinting in the dusk.

Something unmeant must have showed in Hansen's face. The lord's wife gasped. Waldron's sudden flatness showed that he too had known battle in his day.

Hansen clamped his palms together. He knew the sweat and trembling would pass in a moment. Just a memory of blood and terror, one of too many memories to count. Soon his mind would scab it over with the rest.

"Two of them rode away," Hansen resumed, forcing the corners of his mouth up into a smile. "Anyway, I wasn't bare handed

after I took the lance from the first . . . but yes, my lord, I'm a
warrior. Though I have no equipment."

Arnor laughed, breaking the ice around the table. "Even on
your telling of it," he remarked, "I'd say your father chose right
when he named you after the god Hansen."

He turned to the crosstable and added, "Milord, let's seat
our friend with us now, and—"

"Yes, of course," said Waldron, nodding.

"And," Arnor continued, "since we've got some spare equipment that might fit him, I wouldn't mind trying him out on the
practice field in the morning. For a regular place in your
household."

"At least if he comes without armor of his own, we know he's
not a rover," said a warrior on the other side of the hearth.

"Do be seated, Hansen," the lord said. His face clouded.
"Armed riders like that, though . . . It means there probably *is*
a rover about."

Lord Waldron hadn't assigned the guest a specific seat. There
were gaps on the benches to separate warriors from the
community's freemen. Hansen noted general relief as he chose
to sit at the end of three warriors on his side of the hall.

Arnor shrugged. "They've missed us so far," he said. He lifted
a drumstick. It had been stewed so long that the meat fell back
on Arnor's plate before it reached his mouth.

A buxom serving woman handed Arnor a torn wedge of bread.
He shoveled meat onto the wedge with the fingers of his other
hand. "Maybe the reception they got from Lord Hansen here'll
make them . . ."

The remainder of the comment was lost in the wad of bread
and chicken.

The two warriors seated down-bench from Arnor were middle-
aged and even less imposing than their leader. They nodded
cautiously to Hansen. The serving woman handed him a plate
of meat and vegetables and a massive pewter tankard of beer.

The fire on the central hearth had been allowed to go out as
soon as the meal was cooked, but woodsmoke lingered to spice
the air which entered through the open gables and chinks in
the low log walls. There were walkways for servants between
the hearth and the lines of tables to either side of it.

The warriors opposite Hansen were much the same as those beside him, though the trio across the hearth appeared to be somewhat younger. Peace Rock wasn't the place a warrior went if he hoped for action.

Hansen drank. The beer was surprisingly good, but the tankard gave it a metallic undertaste.

"Lord Hansen," said Waldron's wife, "was it your parents who named you after the god, or is it a name you chose when you decided to travel?"

"Amelia," said her husband, "we don't quiz strangers."

But Lord Waldron wasn't frowning; and of course the folk here *did* quiz strangers. Anybody who lived in a community as isolated as present-day Peace Rock sought all the entertainment they could get when someone came in from the outer world.

"No, it's the name my parents gave me, lady," Hansen said, carefully limiting himself to a truth he could tell without causing a furor. He added, "I come from far away, and there's no one in this whole kingdom likely to know me."

Arnor leaned forward to look past his two fellows to glare at Hansen.

"Do you come from Solfygg, then?" Peace Rock's champion asked. His voice was harder than Hansen had thought him capable of using.

"I do not," Hansen said flatly. He met Arnor's eyes. "I come from much farther away than that."

To break the discussion, Hansen raised his tankard, drank, and found to his surprise that he had emptied the vessel. *Killing was a dry business, but he never remembered that at the times in between.*

Lady Amelia's sex and position made her arbiter of when to pry and when to ease off on the stranger. Now she said to her husband, "The king should do something about these rovers."

Waldron responded promptly, "If they stay within the law . . . ," and the conversation involved the members of the household while Hansen devoted himself to his meal.

The woman serving on this end of the table was older than Hansen had first thought, somewhere in her mid-thirties. She set a wedge of bread on Hansen's plate and gave him another of the bright-cheeked smiles that had caused him to under-estimate her age.

"My name's Holly, sir," she said. "Will you have more ale?"

Hansen grinned and held out his tankard. "You wouldn't have another wooden masar in the cupboard for me to drink out of, would you?" he asked the big woman as she poured.

Holly paused in surprise. She wore a dress of dark material, cut very low in the bodice. For modesty a handkerchief was pinned to the shoulders of the dress, but the show she provided when she lifted the kerchief to mop her face, as now, was almost professionally intriguing.

"You want to drink from wood like a freeman, milord?" she asked in puzzlement.

"A whim," Hansen said. He grinned over the rim of his mug as he drank.

"Of course, sir!" said the servant as she turned.

Hansen sipped his ale, noting again the bitterness which alcohol leached from the metal. This wasn't the only society in which the wealthy and powerful proved their status by being more conspicuously uncomfortable than lesser folk.

For all that, Peace Rock seemed a happy place now that it had become a backwater. There'd been affection rather than fear in Peter's voice when he addressed his lord, and the muted chatter along the benches at dinner was generally cheerful.

Hansen mopped stewed chicken onto his bread and let the bland dullness of Peace Rock drift around him.

"A masar, milord," said the serving woman, giving Hansen another of her brilliant smiles. She set down a broad elm cup and filled it with a flourish of her pitcher.

They were willing to take him in, Waldron and Arnor and Holly, clearly Holly.

"Call me Hansen," he said, "or I'll start calling you Lady Holly."

Holly giggled and covered her mouth with the lower edge of her pinned kerchief.

Hansen knew he didn't belong here, of course.

But then, Nils Hansen didn't belong much of anywhere; and for the moment, at least, it was good to spend time with people who found their lives happy.

Chapter Four

One, then three armored figures rode their dragonflies out of time. They trembled at the edge of visibility as if they were sliding in and out between the fracture planes of mica schist.

In the millisecond intervals when they were visible, happy laughter caroled from the external speaker of the black battlesuit.

Gordon crouched lower and muttered, "Just like your mirror showed. When and where . . . and especially who."

Sparrow laid a hand the size of an ice-bear's paw on Gordon's shoulder to remind him to be silent.

The dragonflies sharpened into perfect temporal focus. Brush crackled under the weight of the vehicles and their armored riders. There was a brief trail of steam; dew which the sun missed had touched hot metal.

The riders dismounted. The Searcher in black armor reached down to the latch below her right armpit and pulled the front of the battlesuit open. When the latch released, it shut off all the battlesuit's systems—including the servos which ordinarily powered the articulated joints of the armor.

The black-haired woman inside the suit swung the dead weight of the massive frontal armor as easily as if she were a man with triceps twice the size of those of her own trim arms.

Sledd wrinkled his nose; Sparrow's and Gordon's eyes prickled a moment later. The dragonflies ionized air when they appeared. A tendril of ozone drifted twenty meters to where the brothers hid.

The fire-orange battlesuit with bronze highlights opened as well. The blond Searcher inside coughed.

"For North's own sake, Krita!" she complained. "Why can't you let the stink blow off at least? We aren't on a deadline."

"Krita's always on a deadline, Race," said the other of the big blonds, waving her hand back and forth to dissipate the ozone. "She thinks if she runs fast enough, death won't catch her."

Krita laughed again. She pulled herself out of her battlesuit, both legs together—an awkward task that her muscular grace made look easy. She wore a singlet of doeskin; her feet and long legs were bare.

"Come along, Race, Julia," she called as she pushed through the screening brush to reach the flowered slope beyond. "Last one to the water never gets to touch a man again."

The two blonds climbed out of their armor as lithely as Krita. They were both taller than their companion, and they looked softer—the way oak cudgels seem softer than chipped flint.

"*That*," called Race as she and Julia loped along after Krita, "I wouldn't wish on my worst enemy!"

The blonds wore linen shifts. They were already lifting the garments over their heads as they disappeared downhill from the brothers.

Gordon exhaled heavily. "You're right," he said to Sparrow. "It *is* worth it."

"I didn't remember how long it had been," Sledd murmured.

Sparrow said nothing. He was watching the image in his mirror, the shrunken figures of women sprinting down the hundred meters of gentle slope.

The blonds' longer strides made up distance, but Krita held her lead to the sedges where water spilled from the rocks. The three women plunged together into the deep pool in the spring's center. Their clothing lay on the bank.

"Now," said Sparrow as he got up deliberately and walked to the equipment which the Searchers thought they had left concealed.

Sledd ignored the dragonflies on their spindly, wonderfully strong, monocrystalline legs. Instead he caressed one of the battlesuits whose quality he could fully appreciate. The suit's pattern of scarlet, silver, and mauve scales was not painted on, as Sledd had assumed, but rather integral with the outer sheathing.

"I still say we ought of worn our own armor," he said.

"There's nothing I want from those three that I can get with a battlesuit on," Gordon replied.

Some of the nearby foliage was shrivelled. Ozone had bleached the green out of it.

Sparrow bent over Krita's dragonfly, then squatted. There was a set of manual controls on the underside of the saddle's edge. He did not touch them. Instead, the master smith adjusted the image in his mirror to show the same controls.

"What are you doing?" Gordon asked.

"Sledd, don't show yourself," Sparrow grunted absently. The third brother was peering through the brush in the direction the women had gone.

Sledd grimaced and squatted beside Sparrow. "Well, what *are* you doing?" he demanded.

"When the Searchers see us," Sparrow explained, "they'll either run away or they'll attack. We can't keep them from killing us, soon or later, unless we're willing to kill *them*."

Sledd spat. "That'd be crazy," he said.

"Yes," said Sparrow. The image of the dragonfly controls blurred, then focused. There was a subtle difference between reality and the form in the mirror. "But it may be that we can keep them from running."

Sparrow poked a broad finger *through* the surface of his mirror and touched a control switch.

There was a dull pop. The dragonfly beside him vanished, but the image in the mirror remained.

The big man let out a long sigh of relief. "Like that," he said as he rose and moved to the next vehicle.

"Where did you send it?" Gordon asked with a frown. He looked at the black battlesuit standing as a monument to the vanished dragonfly.

"It's still *here*," said Sparrow as he focused his mirror on the controls of Race's dragonfly. "But it isn't now, not quite. It's waiting—"

His finger jabbed. The second vehicle vanished from the brothers' present.

"*They're* waiting in a time state just out of phase with the space around them," Sparrow went on as his mirror blurred and sharpened. "It's in the regular controls; it's where they stay when they ride the battle plains."

"Where Searchers ride," Gordon said.

"Of course Searchers!" Sledd snarled. "We knew that before we started, didn't we?" He shivered in the summer shade.

A trill of laughter echoed from the spring. Sparrow looked at his brothers. "Calm down," he said in a firm voice. "There's risk. We don't have to make the risk worse."

Gordon grimaced. "Sorry," he said. "Sorry."

The last dragonfly puffed out of sight. Sparrow panned the image back momentarily, showing all three of the vehicles still on the knoll . . . with the empty battlesuits, and in the presence of the brothers.

Sledd muttered a curse. He felt in the air where the mirror said a vehicle should be. His hand met nothing, though a stray beam of sunlight danced across the ginger hairs on the backs of his fingers.

Sparrow switched the mirror's image back into a mere reflection in polished metal. He hung the artifact around his neck by a rope whose gold and silver strands were as fine as those of a battlesuit's circuits.

"What do we do now, Sparrow?" Gordon asked. Below, the Searchers giggled like young girls as they climbed from the water to look for berry bushes.

"Now . . . ," said the master smith. He combed absently at his beard as his eyes focused on a possible future. "Now we wait. And hope."

The women chattered as they walked up the slope. There were damp patches on their garments where their skin had not dried when they pulled the clothing on. Krita and Race held hands.

Julia had lifted the hem of her shift to cup a double handful of fresh blackberries. She yelped, then giggled, as a branch whipped back and caught her where the linen would normally have been some protection.

Krita saw the three big men standing beside the battlesuits. They were dressed in breeches and jerkins of tanned leather, crudely sewn but ornamented with metalwork of exquisite quality.

Krita took her hand from Race's and said, "There," in a quiet, charged voice.

Julia shook the berries from her garment. The groups were poised like packs of dogs meeting at the boundary of their ranges . . . or a pack of wolves, and a family of bears.

For a moment, Krita could imagine that it was the men's bulk which hid the dragonflies from her. She edged to the side, and her keen eyesight pricked the life out of that hope.

"We mean you no harm, ladies," Sparrow said. He stepped forward slowly, as though he were taking part in a ritual. He lifted the mirror from his breast. "We hold you in honor."

"We want nothing of you," Race called threateningly. "Do you realize who we are? Do you want the gods to blot away the very memory of you?"

"You are kings' daughters and Searchers, lady," said Gordon. Sparrow took another slow step. His brothers remained as motionless as the empty battlesuits beside which they stood. "But we are the sons of a king ourselves."

"We're smiths like no others that ever lived," said Sledd. "We'll make you wonderful things."

"Where are our vehicles?" Krita asked in a voice like frozen steel.

"You can't catch us, you know!" snapped Julia.

"And if you did," added Race in an unknowing echo of Gordon's words of months before, "then—you'll have to sleep sometime." Her teeth as she smiled were as bright and sharp as those of a predator.

"Your armor is here, ladies," Sparrow said. "You can kill us now if you like. We are a king's sons, and we wish you only honor as our wives."

Sparrow had crossed half the distance separating him from the women. He held the mirror out to Krita and said, "Take it. It's for you."

The sleeveless jerkin showed deep pink scars from the bear's claws on the inside of Sparrow's forearm.

Krita stepped forward with brisk certainty instead of making a quick, rodentlike grab for the dangling object. Her eyes met Sparrow's. She took the mirror, then backed away.

"Give us our vehicles," she said flatly.

"Anything but your dragonflies, Lady Krita," Sparrow said.

The shaggy form of the master smith contrasted sharply with his cultured voice. His pale eyes were calm, but no one could look into them and hope that prayer or threats would make Sparrow draw back from the words he had just spoken.

"Wonders that not even the gods can match," Sledd boasted.
Julia glanced at him. She chuckled.

"Look into the mirror, Lady Krita," Sparrow coaxed. "Yes,
like that. Ask it to show you something—anything, anyone."

Race played with a spot of berry juice on her garment. "You
can make it change by speaking to it?" she asked, flicking her
gaze from the object to its maker.

Krita murmured to the mirror. Its surface blurred.

Sparrow nodded. "Like a battlesuit's controls," he said. "Many
smiths build battlesuits, lady. Only I could have created *that*."

"Well, is it true, Krita?" Julia demanded. "Does it work?"

"Oh, yes, it's true," Krita agreed in a distant voice. There
was a decisive hardness in her expression that been missing
before. She hung the mirror's cord over a bare twig to free her
hands.

"We wish only to honor you as our wives, lady," the master
smith repeated.

Krita barked a short, harsh laugh. All five of the others watched
her.

"Well, girls," Krita said in a bright voice. "We came here to
relax for a while, didn't we?"

She reached down and began deliberately to pull her singlet
over her head.

Race sighed, then smiled at Julia. The blond women lifted
off their shifts. The brothers stepped forward in increasing haste.

Birds chirped and fluttered among the foliage. The mirror
rotated lazily on its cord. Its surface showed the face of Nils
Hansen.

Chapter Five

The door at the low end of the Great Hall banged open. Hansen jumped when instinct tried to throw him under the table to cover.

"Lord Waldron!" bleated Cayley, the watchman from the gate in the stockade. "They're coming, the rover! He's got his armor, and he's got mebbe a dozen riders with him besides mammoths for baggage!"

Lord Waldron rose to his feet with a grim expression. "Silence!" he boomed, quashing the sudden jabber of nervousness throughout the big room.

Lady Amelia raised her knuckles to her lips; most of those in the hall stared raptly at their lord.

A mammoth tethered in the Peace Rock compound screamed welcome to the newcomers it scented.

"Cayley," Lord Waldron said, "go back to the gate and admit them with all honor. Do whatever they tell you to do."

"Right," said Arnor. "Don't argue about anything."

Several of the warriors nodded nervous agreement.

Hansen's face went blank. He didn't understand what was going on, so he watched and listened . . . and waited until he knew enough to act, or until he had to act anyway.

Cayley ducked out of the hall. The door missed the notch of its wooden latch. It slapped the post and swung open again.

A freeman on the lowest bench hopped up to close the panel, then froze in terrified awareness that all the normal rules had changed. He scuttled back to his seat, leaving the door ajar.

"Now for the rest of you," Waldron continued, "there's none of us going to make trouble, do you understand? He wouldn't be coming here unless he had a battlesuit that can mince ours like forcemeat. No matter what he says, we're going to agree with him!"

"He'll leave in a day or two if he can't get a duel out of any of us," Arnor said with a glum shake of his head. "It wouldn't do a bit of good to get killed."

Lady Amelia stood up. Her thin face had flushed; now it was white. "There's seven of you, aren't there?"

Her eyes swept the room, skimming across her husband and the other warriors before resting a moment on Hansen's expressionless visage. "Eight, now. This battlesuit isn't so good that eight of you can't cure him, is it?"

The squeals of the giant peccaries provided a jumbled warp through which baggage mammoths wove their louder, even shriller, calls.

"The Peace of Golsingh gives every man the right to travel through—" Lord Waldron said.

"He's coming here to *kill* you!" Amelia said.

Her control cracked. Hansen saw in her eyes love—and terror for her husband's life.

"He's coming here to fight a duel under the law!" Waldron said sharply. "*If* we give him the excuse. And we're not going to do that."

"Too right," muttered a young warrior. "I didn't hire on to here t' be outlawed for murder."

"Why *did* you promise to serve my husband?" Lady Amelia shouted. "To eat and drink and skulk when your lord is at risk?"

The old woman turned quickly to hide her tears.

Amelia and her husband sat on chairs, not benches. Her seat wobbled as she brushed past it, then rattled back onto its legs. She ran up the stairs to the chambers the lord's immediate family shared above the back of the Great Hall.

The warrior to whom Amelia had spoken hunched his shoulders and stared at the table in front of him.

"She's upset," said Lord Waldron to his retainers. His voice quavered.

He controlled it with an obvious effort and went on, "We're all upset. But remember: stay calm or it's your life. And it may be my life as well."

"We'll get out of this just fine if we all stay calm," Arnor added.

Hansen sucked at his lips. He drank the rest of the ale in his wooden masar, then toyed with the pewter mug again.

Cayley flung the door open. "All hail the noble lord Borley!"

the watchman shouted in a voice pitched even higher than that with which he had warned of the rover's approach. "Come from far Solfygg to claim guest rights with Lord Waldron!"

To Hansen's surprise, when Borley entered—pushing Cayley aside with deliberate brutality—he was already wearing his battlesuit. "That's right!" boomed the warrior's voice through the speaker in the faceplate of his powered armor. "My name's Borley, *Lord* Borley to you lot unless you're willing to challenge me. Any of you man enough for that?"

No one answered. Most of those in the hall grimaced with downcast eyes. Hansen took a tiny sip of ale, just enough to sluice around in an attempt to moisten the dryness of his mouth.

Borley's retainers spilled into the hall behind him. The leader's face was familiar to Hansen: Abel, the black-bearded rider who had turned and run from Hansen's lance.

Abel carried his saber slung over his back where it wouldn't knock against objects when he was dismounted. Several of Borley's other retainers also brought edged weapons into the hall in defiance of custom and courtesy.

Hansen wondered if Abel would recognize him. Probably not. The fading sky had done a better job of lighting the horsemen than it did men on foot, a meter lower in the shadow of the pines. Probably not.

Borley walked toward Lord Waldron at the crosstable at the far end of the room. The rover chose the aisle on the side opposite Hansen to make his deliberate progress. His battlesuit weighed over a hundred kilos. Every time his foot crashed down on the puncheons, sparks jumped from the sole to scar the wood.

The rover's battlesuit was of remarkably high quality, the sort of armor that a king might wear. Just as Lord Waldron had expected. . . . A wandering thug had no business owning equipment like that.

"What's the matter?" snarled Borley's amplified voice. "Dumb insolence, is it? Refusing to greet me with the honor I'm due?"

"Lord Borley," Waldron said promptly, "be welcome to my hall. Sit at my right hand, if you will—or in my own seat."

Arnor had been correct also. None of the warriors in a place like Peace Rock could afford armor that would last more than one swipe in a duel with a royal suit like Borley's.

Borley's retainers poured into the hall behind him. There were eight of them all told, not the dozen Cayley reported.

And not nine, either. Not since the ninth met Hansen.

The retainers split into two groups and pushed into the benches where the leading Peace Rock freemen sat. The locals scrambled to get out of the way, but Borley's men kicked and shoved them anyway.

"You don't mind accommodating my boys, do you, Waldron?" Borley demanded as he continued his slow progress toward the crosstable. "You don't think that maybe because they're the sons of thieves 'n whores that they aren't better than anybody in your lot?"

"Not at all, Lord Borley," Waldron said in a steady voice. "Your servants are welcome to sit wherever they choose in this hall."

Abel climbed into the seat at Hansen's left and jostled him. Hansen met his eyes.

The leader of Borley's retainers was young, smart, and fit, despite a certain puffiness of his features which suggested that drink would catch up with him soon—if a rope didn't. Abel's left thumb and forefinger were missing; the wound had been cauterized with hot iron that left a glistening pink scar.

He opened his mouth to snarl at Hansen but changed his mind. "Give me some room!" he grunted to the man on his own left.

Hansen sipped ale that tasted of metal and bile.

"You know," said the rover, "I'm kinda disappointed in you, Waldron. I'd heard you been telling folks that you're a tough bunch here at Peace Rock. Tougher than me, I'd heard. I figgered you guys'd like to try me in a duel so we could see who was really tough."

Servants were pouring ale into mugs for the newcomers. Holly put a tall jack of tarred leather in front of Abel.

"No, not here, Lord Borley," said Waldron. "There's nobody here as strong and brave as you."

Abel grabbed Holly's wrist as she set the jack down. He gripped the kerchief over her bodice and tore it loose.

Holly tried to stifle a scream.

"You don't mind my boys finding a little entertainment while they're here, do you?" the rover asked in a voice like that of a hog who had learned human speech.

Waldron swallowed. "If that's what pleases you, Lord Borley," he said.

Abel levered one of the woman's heavy breasts out of the dress with his three-fingered hand. Holly squeezed her eyes shut. She was murmuring a prayer.

Hansen's eyes watered. Microswitches in the powered armor must be arcing to leave a trail of ionized air.

"Some of 'em haven't had anything better than a mare t' stick their dick into fer weeks," Borley said. "Course, some of 'em *like* mares."

Hansen's wrist jerked, oversetting his pewter tankard. The half its contents remaining sluiced across the trestles and down over Abel's lap.

The retainer jumped backward with a shout. The bench and the fellow to Abel's left trapped him in the path of the stream.

Holly pulled away to stand in the ashes of the cold hearth, out of reach from either row of benches. Her arms were crossed over her chest; her head was bowed.

Abel stood at a twisted angle between the bench and the table, staring at Hansen.

"Sorry," Hansen said. "I've always been the clumsy sort." He spoke softly, and his voice trembled.

"Fucking moron's the sort you are," Abel muttered; but he sat down again and ostentatiously turned his back toward Hansen.

If Borley had noticed the incident, he made no comment.

"Well, what about you lot?" the rover demanded. He pointed to the warriors on his side of the hearth with the thumb and forefinger of his gauntlet spread—the gesture that would spread a blade of ravening electricity if Borley gave his battlesuit a verbal order to *Cut*! "Think you're as tough as me?"

"Oh, not me/not me/Nobody I know's as tough as you, Lord Borley," the three young warriors chorused. One of them stared at the table, one of them offered the rover a smile as false as a wax doll's, and the third warrior let his eyes dance across the sloping thatch roof of the hall as he spoke.

The tip of Hansen's right index finger traced the rim of his empty mug.

Borley strode across the back of the crosstable. "You've

already told me you're a coward, haven't you, Waldron?" he said.

"That's right, Lord Borley," Waldron said. He faced the door at the far end of the room. His eyes looked like bits of glass. "You're welcome to sit here in my seat for the full three days of your guest rights."

"How about you, then?" Borley demanded as he paused in front of Arnor. "You're the champion of this shitpile, aren't you? Is that your name? Sir Shitpile?"

"That's right, Lord Borley, if you say it is," Arnor said in a choking voice.

"Hell take you all!" the man in armor grumbled in what might have been real disgust. "You really are a lot of dog-turds here, aren't you?"

Hansen hunched over his mug, staring at the pewter but not seeing even that.

"That's right," Arnor said as the two warriors seated below him bobbed agreement. "We're nothing but dog-turds compared to a hero like you, Lord Borley."

The stink of ozone was very close behind Hansen, now.

"Well, what about you, *boy*?" the rover asked. "Do you think I'm tough?"

Hansen neither moved nor spoke. Abel stared at him with a look of avid anticipation.

"I *spoke* to you, boy!" Borley thundered. Hansen's body twitched with the shock as a powered gauntlet gripped his shoulder and spun him to face the rover.

Close up, Hansen could see that the limbs of the battlesuit had been joined to the thorax by a smith less able than the one who constructed the component parts. The lustrous power of those components shone through the painted skulls with which Borley had ornamented the armor.

"I'm a stranger here myself," said Nils Hansen, "so I don't know how tough you are. Where I come from, though, we'd think you were just a blowhard."

The blat of noise from the battlesuit's speaker was inarticulate in its rage. Borley raised his right hand to smash Hansen where he sat.

Hansen grabbed the catch under the rover's armpit and pulled the suit open. For a moment, Borley's broad, droop-moustached face stared out of the unpowered coffin his armor had become as soon as it came unlatched.

Hansen slammed his pewter mug against the rover's forehead. Abel bawled in surprise. He tried to snatch his saber from its sheath. Hansen backhanded the retainer across the temple, knocking him sprawling into his fellows.

Everyone in the hall was shouting. Arnor lifted himself from the bench with a smooth grace that belied his appearance of softness and vanished into the bed closet directly behind him.

Hansen's face was white and staring. He pounded the mug into Borley. Stiff joints kept the depowered battlesuit upright, but the man within slumped forward so that Hansen's fourth blow thudded against the suede which lined the armor.

Gasping with reaction, Hansen stepped back. He tried to survey the rest of what was going on in the Great Hall.

Borley's retainers stood back to back, a tiny clot on either side of the hearth. Those who were armed had drawn their weapons, but there was nothing but fear in their eyes.

Arnor strode out of his bed closet, wearing a tan-and-gray battlesuit. A blue-white arc snapped from his right gauntlet, fluctuating in length from a few centimeters to a meter and a half as Peace Rock's champion spread or closed the gap between his thumb and forefinger.

Extended, the arc quivered close enough to one of Borley's terrified men that his beard began to shrivel.

"All right, you slime!" Arnor shouted. The suit's external speaker gave his voice an eerie resemblance to that of Borley moments before. "Time for you to leave!"

The three retainers standing on Arnor's side of the hall rushed for the door; those across the room followed a half pace later. They paused on the threshold.

Torchlight wavered through the open doorway and winked on metal. The slaves of Peace Rock were gathered outside the hall. They carried hayforks, flails, and iron-shod staves.

Arnor's arc weapon sizzled into a thin ellipse almost four meters long. He crashed a massive step in the direction of Borley's men. They bolted through the door and began screaming as the farm implements landed their first blows.

Abel had knocked over one of the tables as he fell. His face was slack; there were dribbles of blood from his ear and nostrils. For a moment, the stertorous breathing of his master was the only sound to be heard within the Great Hall.

Hansen dropped his mug; it rang on the wooden floor. The metal was as distorted as though it had been hammered on an anvil.

He shouted to the staring faces, "He touched me as if I were a slave, not a warrior. He acted like a dog, and I treated him like a dog deserves."

"Oh, may the gods bless you!" Holly blurted in a high, clear voice.

Lord Waldron and his warriors crowded toward Hansen with their hands outstretched.

Hansen turned and gripped Borley beneath the arms. He dragged the rover out of the legs of his battlesuit, then let the man drop to the puncheons.

"Somebody get him outdoors," Hansen said in a throaty, terrible voice. "He'll void his bowels when he dies, and we don't need the smell in here."

"We didn't need the smell of him alive," said Lord Waldron as he embraced Nils Hansen.

Out in the courtyard, a mammoth screamed at the scent of fresh blood.

Chapter Six

Sparrow ran to the left of the mammoth rather than between the double row of huge footprints. Otherwise he would have to break stride to avoid skidding on broad splotches of the beast's dung. The trail was now so fresh that the pine-scented droppings steamed on a thin bed of snow.

Sparrow and the mammoth were both pacers who matched their strides to the long haul. Krita ran like a deer. She loped and bounded over obstacles, wasting energy that the others conserved by never changing the length or rhythm of their steps. . . .

But the hunters were in sight of the mammoth, now, and Krita was closing the gap while the smith was still a hundred meters behind her.

"Not—" Sparrow shouted as his right heel struck the ground.

"—yet," he boomed out at the completion of the next stride. "Wait!"

Krita would do as her own whim directed. Sparrow shortened his pace by a centimeter, quickened his legs' scissoring by a few heartbeats, and began to draw minusculely nearer to his companion and their prey.

They had no business hunting a mammoth at all, just the two of them. Sparrow and Krita had been checking their trapline when they struck the trail of the beast. It was a lone bull who had passed by so recently that the edges of his footprints in the fresh snow still showed flakes whose individuality had not melted into a blur.

"Come on!" Krita had cried.

She unfastened her cloak and slung it onto the snow as she sprinted off in the unexpected direction. If the smith had not followed, she would have gone on alone.

Sparrow had stripped to the waist as he ran. He still sweated. The air was cold and dry. The tiny snowflakes of the evening

279

before had ceased to fall before midnight, while the temperature continued to drop.

Sparrow would have taken off his fur leggings as well, but that would require him to break stride; and he would not break stride.

The mammoth's ivory tusks gleamed in intervals of sunlight through the pine boughs. As Krita drew nearer, she slanted her course slightly to the right. She was parallel to the beast's haunches and closer than the length of her spear.

Krita still wore her doeskin chemise. Though she was a small woman with a taut, trim body, her breasts were too heavy for her to run comfortably with them unrestrained. She had twisted her belt so that the sheath of her broad-bladed knife waggled like a tail.

Sparrow's quickened stride forced him to suck in deeper breaths. Needles of ice danced in his lungs.

The mammoth paced onward. Its legs moved deceptively slowly, but each step carried the beast another three meters across pine straw and snow. Either the animal was unaware that it was being pursued, or it was too certain of its own black-haired, mountainous strength to pay attention to mere humans.

Krita drew level with the mammoth's right shoulder. She poised the spear above her head.

"Wait!"

Krita stabbed, using the full strength of her upper body. Her left boot anchored the thrust. It slipped on pine needles iced into a mat and kicked the other leg out from under her as well.

Instead of plunging through the forward lobe of her quarry's lung and into the heart, Krita's spear ripped a long gouge across the mammoth's ribs.

The mammoth flared its small ears and pivoted like a dancer. Its trunk lifted. The beast shrieked outrage and fury as Krita tried to roll to her feet.

Sparrow hurled his own long-bladed spear from ten meters away. It sank to the shaft in the roll of fat and gristle on top of the mammoth's head.

"Ho! Mammoth!" Sparrow shouted as he waved his arms.

The beast's eyes glittered beneath its deep brow ridges.

Ignoring Krita, as Sparrow intended it to do, the mammoth strode forward with the inexorable power of an avalanche.

Sparrow turned; and, turning, fell. He didn't feel the impact of the frozen ground because of the molten pain in his lungs.

The mammoth paced forward, right rear and left front legs together. Sunlight flared as Krita swung her heavy knife.

Left rear and right front—

The mammoth staggered and slid down on its left haunch. Sparrow stared up at the ribbed red dome of its palate.

The mammoth trumpeted in raging fury. It tried to turn. Krita, moving behind the huge animal with the grace of an ermine pouncing, cut the beast's other hamstring as well.

Sparrow rose. His spear wobbled high in the air. Its point was in the spongy bone of the mammoth's skull—useless to the hunter and harmless to his prey.

Krita backed away from the beast she had crippled. She set both palms against the trunk of a pine tree and leaned against her arms with her head bowed. Her black hair, loosened by the run, covered her face like a veil of mourning.

With the major tendons to its heels cut, the mammoth was unable to lift its hind legs. It was anchored where it stood as surely as if it had frozen in ice.

Sparrow walked around the beast, just beyond the circle its trunk could lash in desperate attempts to reach him. The mammoth lifted its right foreleg: once, twice . . . and settled again into the pose in which it now knew it would die.

Sparrow met the animal's black, glittering eyes. He blinked before the mammoth did. Sparrow walked the rest of the way to his goal. His vision was beginning to settle, and the air felt cold on his bare, trembling skin.

"I was wrong," Krita said. "I'm sorry."

She did not raise her head. Her chest heaved with the violence of her breaths. Her right shoulder and forearm were scraped where she had struck the frozen ground.

Sparrow found the woman's spear a few paces away in the snow. The tip was dappled with blood. He hefted the weapon, then stepped close to the mammoth from the rear. The gash above its heel was drawn back in a bloody smile by the white, severed ends of the hamstring tendon.

The beast slapped its ears twice, but it did not turn its head.

Sparrow set the point behind the mammoth's shoulder with a craftsman's precision, then drove it home. The steel passed between the ribs with only a faint grating sound, but the mammoth's hide and muscles were thick and its fat was a sucking blanket to clog the stroke.

Sparrow bellowed: with his effort, and in an access of pity. The steel slid in. A meter of the ash shaft followed it. There was a great sigh as the mammoth's settling weight drove the air out of its lungs.

Krita touched his shoulder from behind. "We'd better get back," she said. "Before we freeze."

"Yes," Sparrow agreed without turning.

Krita stepped in front of the smith and kissed him fiercely. "Back to the lodge," she said. "And to bed."

Chapter Seven

In the darkness of his bed closet, Nils Hansen ran his fingertips over the surface of the battlesuit that had been Borley's. An amazing piece of workmanship—except for the joins between limbs and body, and even those were the work of a competent smith.

Enough. The cool solidity of the armor was the last physical sensation Hansen felt as he—a man who had become a god, and who was still very much a man—let his being merge with the Matrix that bound the eight planes of Northworld.

It was like diving into a slush of salt and snow, except that the chill was mental as well as physical. He rode the infinite possibilities spawned by every event, expanding into the future and past together—

Dawn breaks.

Dawn breaks in a solar flare that scours the land and seas of all life.

Dawn never comes and the world hangs in twilight.

—all possible, all real; unbounded—

Except that something blocked and channeled Hansen's course across the event waves.

For an instant without time Hansen struggled, spreading his consciousness across the eight worlds and the Matrix. He knew everything that could be and had been and was . . . and the other moved with him, as fast and as far, immersed in perfect interpenetrating cold without end—

without end

without

Hansen let himself be guided and slammed into individual being. He stood in North's hall of frozen light.

Hansen shook and trembled. It was a grim pleasure to him that the tall, one-eyed man on the High Seat also shuddered with the greater-than-cold.

North straightened from an attempt to hug himself into a fetal ball. He shook his head to clear it, then ran the fingers of both hands through his hair to settle it into smooth gray waves.

North smiled at Hansen, then glanced at the clear container on a stand beside his High Seat. "Well, Dowson," he said, "you should have joined us. We had a very interesting game, Commissioner Hansen and I. Didn't we, Kommissar?"

He smiled again. There was no more humor on North's craggy features than there had been the first time.

A brain floated in fluid within the container. Scales of light sublimed from the outside of the tank and expanded across the hall like the shockwaves of supernovae. As the colors swept through Hansen, his mind heard Dowson's voice say, "There are no games, North. Only the Matrix. Only reality."

"For you, perhaps, Dowson," said North. "But not for the rest of us."

"I'm not your plaything, North," Hansen said. His voice trembled, not so much from the freezing Matrix as with Hansen's need to control his own cold rage. "I was never *that*."

"For all of you, North," whispered a wash of color. "Only reality."

"No . . . ," said North.

His eye bored at Hansen. Hansen stared back as though his heart were hard as an awl.

"Don't interfere with *my* affairs, Kommissar," North said. "In the West Kingdom."

Planes and solids of pure radiance swept around North to form vaults of unimaginable height. His nose, hooked like a raven's beak, flung a hard shadow over his chin as he glared at Hansen.

"The West Kingdom's my own affair, North," the younger man said flatly. "It's been my affair since I was a warrior there with King Golsingh."

North spat. The floor was black and clear in intricate marquetry. His saliva splashed as speckles of blue light.

"Golsingh is dead," said North.

"The Peace of Golsingh isn't dead," Hansen retorted. Then he grinned, and his expression was as stark as the smiles of the one-eyed man. "But you'd like to change that, wouldn't you, North? What do you have against peace?"

North shrugged. "What do you have for it, Commissioner Hansen?" he asked in a reasonable tone. "If there's anyone in the West Kingdom who knew you before, by now they're old and on the point of death."

Color trembled from Dowson's container. "Men die in peace as surely as in war," the brain said. "*We* will die, North."

North's face went hard again. He wore the jumpsuit uniform of the Colonial Bureau of the Consensus of Worlds; his collar tabs bore a field-grade officer's shimmering holograms. "Yes," he said. "Queen Unn died in peace, but she died young for all that."

Hansen shrugged. *Letting them get to you is letting them win.*

"Then just say it's my whim," said Hansen. "I spent my life before I came—here, before I came to Northworld . . . I spent my life keeping the peace."

He could feel his cheek muscles tensing, changing the planes of his face. He must look like a grinning skull. "That's what we called it in the Department of Security, keeping the peace. So I'm going to keep one island of peace here on Northworld, too."

"And if I say you will not . . . Kommissar?" North asked.

Above the men and the tank containing what had been a man, coffers of light shifted down through the spectrum, orange and red and finally a red near to black. A sudden, soundless jolt of ruby lightning raked across the arches.

Hansen laughed. Jets of violet as saturated as the discharges from a Tesla coil ripped from every finial of the vaulted ceiling. Their crackling was scarcely distinguishable from Hansen's laughter.

North laughed as well. The hall brightened to its former purity.

"All right," said the one-eyed man in apparent good humor. "Will you play me a game, Commissioner Nils Hansen? To see whether the Peace of Golsingh will hold . . . or not hold."

"It'll hold," said Hansen.

"I won't interfere," said North. "But if you play, Hansen, you'll play as a man—not a god. If you intervene in the Open Lands as a god, I will crush the West Kingdom so completely that men will whisper when they speak of it. Do you understand?"

Hansen spat. A section of the floor dissolved into blue fire, then reformed. "I hear you talking," Hansen said.

North nodded as if well pleased by the response. "One more thing, Kommissar," he said. "If you play in the Open Lands as a man . . . you can die as a man."

Dowson said, "All men die. . . ." in a veil of light.

Hansen shrugged. "All men die," he said. "I'll play your game."

He raised his arm. In another instant, he would have slipped back into the Matrix, but the one-eyed man called, "Speaking of Queen Unn . . . she died in childbirth, didn't she?"

Hansen looked at North. *He felt nothing at all*—

"Yes, I believe she did," he said.

—*except the urge to kill.*

Then he was gone from North's palace.

North chuckled mirthlessly. Dowson's voice washed over him, saying, "Hansen is not a hard man, North."

North stared at the tank with his one eye. "What do you mean?" he said. "He's a killer. You know that."

Colors—blue and mauve and orange—shimmered away from the tank. "Oh, yes," said Dowson. "But Hansen doesn't plot all the time to win his point."

The ripples of speech continued to expand and fade until they merged with the radiant walls.

North got up from his seat. He turned away from the man in a bottle; the god who had no life except in the Matrix, which was all lives.

"You know I'll need warriors at the end, Dowson," North said. "How am I to find them if there isn't war in the Open Lands? Constant war!"

"Hansen isn't a hard man, North," Dowson's words rang. "But you are a hard man."

North raised his arm. "Then he'll lose our game, won't he, Dowson?" he shouted as he dissolved into the Matrix.

"Perhaps some day he will lose . . . ," whispered the brain through the infinite paths that North followed.

Chapter Eight

Hansen fled through the paths of the Matrix. All times, all knowledge, all possibility; expanding before him as a wilderness of needles hiding one needle.

In a forest valley, three women lay on a flowered hillside and waited for their men to return from hunting. Above them, clouds scudded in a blue summer sky. . . .

One cloud was a bear, Krita thought; and one cloud was a horse.

And one cloud was an electronic dragonfly, sailing through the universe in perfect freedom.

"Forever," Race muttered, and Krita knew that her companions were thinking the same thing that she was.

"We should have gone with them," said Julia.

Krita closed her eyes and let the back of a finger rub the leaf of a violet. The contact was almost too subtle to notice. Her mirror lay flat on her chest, below her breasts, where its metal cord hung when she was upright.

Race snorted. "How many times can you walk a trapline?" she demanded.

"The men like it," said Julia in half protest.

"The men," said Krita, "have their craft. We have—"

She rose to a sitting position and plucked the violet up by its roots. "*This* is what we have," she concluded.

She tossed the flower contemptuously behind her, toward the knoll on which the Searchers had left their vehicles for the last time.

"I miss being able to move," Julia said. "Of course, we could leave here on foot. . . ."

"Oh, aye, that's a *fine* idea," Race said. "Three women with no protector and nothing but what we could carry on our backs— what do you suppose we'd find for a fate then?"

She looked to Krita for support, but the black-haired woman was playing morosely with images in the mirror Sparrow had given her.

"*I* miss the fighting," Race continued. "Where North sent us, we were warriors as good as any man . . . but not on our own, not in any kingdom in the Open Lands."

"What I miss . . . ," Krita said, but she spoke so quietly that the others heard the words as only a sighing breath.

The mirror showed Hansen, looking much as he had when Krita first saw him two years or two lifetimes before. He was seated with a lord and his warriors, as much at rest as a lounging cat—

And, unless Hansen had changed, as willing to leap with his claws out.

"Well what of that?" Race protested. "Sledd gives me as much pleasure as any man I've met . . . but not *forever*! Not with him, not with anybody."

Hansen got up from the bench and walked toward the door of the hall. A chestnut-haired servant, fat and nearly forty, watched him leave with an expression that Krita had seen before.

Krita's lips tightened minutely. The image focused down on the face of the man she had known first as an outcast, then as a warrior. Now as a god.

"There's more to their lives than to ours," Julia said sadly. "There always will be unless they give us back our dragonflies . . . and they won't do that, because they're afraid we'd leave."

"They're right about *that*," Race snorted.

Hansen's face grew as though he were walking toward the back of the mirror. He smiled, a little crooked but warm, not something that a carnivore would offer as it sprang. Krita had seen both expressions on Hansen's face, and both expressions were real.

"Fagh!" Race continued. "If I have to endure this for *another* year—"

Krita bent forward to kiss the surface of the mirror. Her lips met warm lips which returned the kiss.

She jumped up with a cry of blurring emotions. The mirror jounced at the end of its looped cord. Had the mirror not been attached, Krita's convulsive motion would have flung it as far as the spring below.

Race and Julia, warriors both in all but sex, were on their feet. Their senses scanned the placid hillside for the source of Krita's surprise.

"The—it's all right," Krita said. She slipped the cord from around her neck and held the mirror where all three Searchers could view it with ease. Its face quivered with glimpses of clouds, trees, and the women staring at a polished metal surface.

Race and Julia were still and watchful. Krita's visage was transfigured.

"Show us . . . ," Krita said; paused, and continued, "Show us the lodge."

The mirror obediently filled with the image of the rough-hewn building that had been the Searchers' home for the past year. It was roofed with fir shakes, not thatch, because grassy glades were rare this deep in the forest.

"Closer," Krita said.

The image shifted and swelled, centering on a corner where the eaves swept down to knee height above the ground.

"There . . . ," said Krita. The mirror trembled in her left hand, but she controlled the spasm of hope and fear.

Krita reached through the mirror with her right thumb and forefinger. She plucked a weathered, gray splinter from the lowest shake and brought the bits of wood out into sunlight and flowers.

"Show me my dragonfly," Krita said softly.

The mirror focused on a life-sized portion of a dragonfly's manual controls. The image was as sharp as if it were real.

"Oh North . . . ," Julia whispered. "Oh gods."

"We're saved," murmured Race. Her eyes held the soft incandescence of a perfect sexual climax.

Krita reached into the image. Her dragonfly popped into present existence in the brush where she had left it.

"Not North," she said. "But yes, we're saved."

Her companions sprinted up the hillside. Their vehicles appeared on the knoll before the Searchers reached it. . . .

The three women paused for a moment with their dragonflies quivering in the interior of the lodge they had entered through the Matrix. Their battlesuits stood in front of the bed closets the Searchers had shared for a year with the three brothers.

Race and Julia moved quickly to don their armor. Krita hesitated for a moment. She took off the mirror; held it; and then set it on the wooded floor between the armored feet of Sparrow's battlesuit.

Before she put it down for the last time, Krita kissed the rim of the mirror which the greatest smith on Northworld had crafted with consummate skill.

"Yes, of course, all of you go along," Ritter said. "But don't bother me again."

The workroom was partitioned at the center of Keep Greville, the most protected place in the nobleman's communal installation. Even the Duke's own apartments on the level above would be . . .

Chapter Nine

The concubine was oblivious of the skill with which Ritter designed electronic shielding so that it wrapped the tank in his holographic monitor with minimal surface area and no dangerous sidelobes. That wasn't her job.

Her gown was a pale diaphanous blue. It was cut off-the-shoulder and down to the waist, so that one breast was always bare and the dark nipple of the other shifted visibly beneath the folds of the garment when she moved. She took a moment to adjust the strap and give her master time to notice her.

Ritter didn't turn around. He reshaped the force envelope slightly to smooth a concavity that showed orange in the wall of blue-level protection.

"We were wondering, sir," the concubine finally said, "which of us you'd be wanting for tonight?"

Ritter muttered a curse.

"What's that?" he demanded, glancing over his shoulder. The butt of the holstered pistol, no less real for being a symbol of Ritter's status among the lesser nobility, clacked against the chair arm. "What—"

"It's only that the Duke's second lady's giving a party tonight," the concubine said, tumbling the words out rapidly as though their torrent could quench the engineer's possible anger. She was a squat woman, heavy with muscle but perfectly formed on her big-boned design. "And it's getting late, sir, and we were just wondering if some of us could, you know, sir, could go, please?"

"Late?" said Ritter.

Inset over the exterior doorway of Ritter's huge workroom was a screen which showed the water-meadows outside Keep Greville in realtime. He glanced up at it. The sun had set hours before; the light of a full moon silvered the backs of the herd of short-legged rhinoceroses which had come from the swamps to feed.

"Yes, of course, all of you go along," Ritter said. "But don't bother me again!"

The workroom was positioned at the center of Keep Greville, the most protected place in the huge, self-contained installation. Even the Duke's own apartments on the level above would be destroyed before an enemy reached the sanctum of the Duke's chief engineer.

The high ceiling and circuit of the walls could be converted to vision apparatus, so that if Ritter wished, he could pretend to be working in the unspoiled wilderness that existed in past ages before the founding of Keep Greville.

For a time after his skill had won him his present rank, the engineer had done just that; but only for a time. He knew that, whatever his eyes told him, he was held forever within multiple impenetrable shells of force fields and ferroconcrete.

Ritter's immediate work area glowed in the soft, shadowless illumination thrown by an array of micro-spots with optical fiber lenses. The remainder of the room was lighted only by diffusion, instrument tell-tales, and the dim rectangle of the screen above the door out of Ritter's suite.

Occasionally a piece of machinery clopped or gurgled, but for the most part the large chamber was still.

"The frontal slope should be proof to a flux density of three-hundred kilojoules per square centimeter," Ritter muttered, talking himself back into the problem from which the concubine had recalled him. "But the volume of the field generator must be less than . . ."

The engineer's fingers tapped commands even as his voice trailed off. The tank's schematic changed shape, becoming more fishlike; the colored overlay of forcefield modified also.

The concubine had been squat. Ritter himself appeared to be as wide as he was tall, though that was an illusion. He was forty-one years old, but he had looked much the same when he was a decade younger. His massive features would not age appreciably until he was sixty or older.

His hands moved as gracefully as those of a juggler as he controlled the information patterns of his design console.

Ritter paused, waiting for the thought that he needed to form in his mind and, almost as one, to extrude through his fingertips into the display growing in hologram. There was a whisper of sound behind him.

"Will you bitches all—" Ritter bellowed as he spun around in his chair.

Instead of one of his concubines, a man taller and much more slender than Ritter stood two meters behind the engineer's console.

"Who the *hell* are you?" Ritter demanded. Carefully, to avoid calling attention to what he was doing, he shifted his hips forward on the seat cushion.

"My name's Hansen," the stranger said. He wore a one-piece garment of unfamiliar cut. "I've come to make you an offer, Master Ritter."

"I'd like to know just how you *did* come here," Ritter said. He swivelled the chair beneath him carefully with his heel, so that the arm no longer interfered with his gun hand. "I didn't think it was possible for another man to get through the door to my harem."

"I didn't come through your harem," Hansen said easily. "And more important that how I came—"

Ritter snatched the pistol out of its holster. As the muzzle started to rise, Hansen's boot moved in a perfectly-calculated arc and kicked the weapon out of Ritter's hand. The pistol sailed beyond the lighted area and clanged into an ultrasonic density tester.

The engineer lunged up from his chair.

"I wouldn't," said Hansen. His hands were spread at about hip height, and his torso was cocked forward in a slight crouch.

Ritter was twice the stranger's bulk and strong for his size; Hansen held no visible weapon. Ritter looked into Hansen's blank, cold eyes—and sat back in his chair.

Hansen relaxed. "More important than how I came here, Master Ritter," he resumed as if there had been no interruption, "is what I'm able to do for you. I need help, and I'm willing to help you in return."

"What can you offer *me*?" Ritter said. "What can *anybody* offer me that I don't have?"

He gestured with his left hand; lights went up across the whole room. Equipment, both electronic and mechanical, stood in separate cubicles. Racks held flasks of gases, fluids, and powders—as well as armor plate in slabs large enough for full-scale testing.

The workmanship throughout was of the highest quality, and nothing in the complex arrangements appeared to be out of place.

"And there," said Hansen, waving behind him toward the door of Ritter's living quarters, "is every luxury your world can offer . . . but that isn't what you mention when you talk about your status. That's why I want you and not somebody else to help me, Ritter."

"Do you know what power I've got?" the engineer demanded. He stood up and paced toward Hansen. "I could have anybody—outside the Duke's immediate family—executed, Hansen."

Ritter pointed with an index finger as thick as a broomstick. "I could have the Duke's first lady in *my* bed if I demanded it. I'm the best engineer in the world! There's nothing the Duke wouldn't give me to keep me building armaments for him and his soldiers."

Hansen grinned. "Can you leave Keep Greville, Master Ritter?" he asked as softly as a stiletto penetrating silk.

Ritter's face set like flesh-toned concrete. He shrugged. "No," he said.

"Now you can leave," said Hansen. "If you want to come with me."

The engineer did not react.

"You'll need an airpack," Hansen added as though he were unaware of Ritter's hesitation.

Without speaking, Ritter walked to a freestanding cabinet. It opened when his hand approached its latch. He removed an airpack and helmet from the ranks of protective gear.

He looked over his shoulder at Hansen. "Do you want to borrow something?" he asked.

Hansen shook his head. "I won't need it," he said. "For that matter, you won't need the helmet for the time we'll be out. Just a face mask."

Ritter put the helmet back on its shelf and closed the cabinet.

Hansen walked into a nearby cubicle, ducked out of sight, and reappeared. "Here," he said, holding out butt-forward the pistol he had kicked from Ritter's hand. "You won't need this—but there's no reason you shouldn't have it."

Ritter reholstered the weapon impassively. "Where are we going?" he asked.

"To my home," Hansen said, "though I'll take you by the scenic route. I'm going to guide you with my arm. You don't have to do anything except step forward when I do."

Hansen's eyes hardened. "But *don't* panic and run," he went on. "Even if you don't see me for a moment or two. There's nothing along the way that's as bad as being left there with it. And you *will* be left if you run."

"I don't panic," said the engineer. His voice rumbled like a glacier calving icebergs.

"That's good," said Hansen without expression. He put his left arm around—partway around—the big man's shoulders. "Keep the airpack to your face and step for—"

Ritter's right leg swung forward in unison with Hansen's. The air shimmered opaque and *rotated* in a plane that was not one of the normal three dimensions.

Points of light in infinite number surrounded Ritter. For a moment they were chaos, but when he realized the alignment, he saw that all the beads were segments of lines focused on *him*.

They were as cold as the Duke's charity.

Ritter was alone—without the stranger who'd promised to guide him; without even his own powerful body. He was a point in a pattern of intersecting lines, and when he moved (because he had been moving when he entered this limbo without soul or warmth) the lines shifted also and kept him at their focus until—

"You tricked me!" Ritter shouted as his heel shocked down on solid ground. He realized simultaneously that his voice and body worked again, and that his guide had not entrapped him forever in a waste as dead as the circuits of a computer's memory.

Hansen still held him. "What was—" Ritter began before his eyes took in his new surroundings.

"Step," said Hansen.

The soil was frozen and crusted with snow. Ritter had never seen snow, even when he was young and not yet too valuable to be permitted to leave the armored fastness of Keep Greville. He and his guide stood behind one of a pair of lines of men who wore personal armor as they fought one another.

The armored men slashed with electrical arcs which sprang

from their empty gauntlets. Blue-white discharges crackled like ball lightning when they crossed one another, until one of the arcs failed or both combatants stepped back to break the contact.

A pine tree burst into flame as an arc brushed it; then a fighter's armor failed in omnidirectional coruscance. Bits of burning metal and superheated ceramic flew from the heart of a hissing electrical corona.

"Step," Hansen repeated. The pressure of his arm was greater than a man so slender should have been able to exert.

The man whose armor had exploded was toppling forward. His head was missing, and the top of his chest plate still bubbled with the heat of its destruction. Ritter strode—

Into a world of crystal and cold so intense that the surface of Ritter's skin steamed. Around him stood pillars of glass—pillars of glassy ice—figures of ice! They were figures, because Ritter *knew* they moved though they were so glacially slow that he and his guide could wait here an age and see nothing.

"Step," said Hansen, but the engineer was already striding into—

A swamp. Ritter's weight plunged him over his boot tops in muck. The metal fittings of his airpack frosted momentarily as the hot, humid atmosphere thawed them. Drops of dew condensed on each of Ritter's exposed body hairs.

He took the mask away from his face.

"Step," Hansen urged from beside him.

"Wait," said Ritter. He drew in a deep breath redolent of vegetable decay.

This wasn't the swamp outside Keep Greville or any other swamp on Ritter's world. Large trees growing in the distance had branches like the limbs of hydras rather than anything vegetable. Leaves tufted from each of the joints of the meter-high reeds nearby. There was no true ground cover, only flat creeping greenery that looked at first glance like slime.

But after the frozen horror of one moment—one *step*—before, Ritter needed a rest in the familiarity of sucking mud and air as moist as the breath from a steam kettle.

"Those *things* were alive," he muttered to Hansen.

"At one time they were," Hansen agreed. "I suppose you could say they still are."

Watchful though not especially concerned, Hansen's eyes flickered over sheets of still water and the reed tussocks where the mud formed islands. Nothing of significant size moved, but something hidden in the mist bellowed a challenge.

Ritter straightened. "What kind of hell was that?" he demanded.

His guide looked at him with eyes momentarily as bleak as the waste the men were discussing. "The only kind of Hell there is, I think," he said. "Just Hell."

Hansen's mouth moved in what might have been either a grimace or a shiver. "Put your airpack on," he said. "We have to go."

With the mask clasped firmly his face again, Ritter tried to take a step forward. The mud clung to his boot, and he didn't think his leg was moving until the invisible plane rotated him—

Onto a gravel strand under a huge sun hanging motionless on the horizon in perpetual dawn. The vacuum sucked greedily at the waste valve of his airpack. He felt his skin prickle against the pressure of his cells' internal fluids.

There was a wink of blue from a distant corniche. Something with its own light source had moved, because the sun and all it illuminated was dull red.

Hansen's lips moved. Though Ritter could not hear the word, he stepped into—

An upland forest of tall evergreens, and a beast so huge that for the first instant Ritter thought he had appeared next to a gray-green boulder.

The rock sighed with flatulence. Ritter looked up to see, browsing needles fifteen meters above him, a small head . . . on the end of a serpentine neck . . . attached to a ten-tonne body, now upright and hugging the treetrunk with its forelegs to stabilize itself during the meal.

There were dozens or even hundreds of the creatures around him, hidden in plain sight by their size and the cathedral gloom of the forest.

"Step," said his guide, and—

The men were on an island. Its shore was being combed by a breaker kilometers long. The air was fresh with the tang of salt. Sea oats bowed away from the off-shore breeze.

Ritter lowered his face mask. "Were they dangerous?" he asked. "The animals?"

Hansen shrugged. "One of them could have stepped on you, I suppose," he said. "But no real danger from them, no."

He looked over the breakers. A few kilometers out, a storm covered as much of the horizon as the two men could see from where they stood. Lightning quivered in and from the clouds, but the thunder was lost in the constant pulse of breaking waves.

There was more that Hansen wasn't saying. Ritter looked at his guide. "You were worried about carnivores, then?" he pressed. "What is it?"

Hansen shrugged again. "Not the carnivores," he said, "though they could be bad enough on the wrong day. The Lomeri live there on Plane Two. But we weren't there long enough for them to find us."

"I don't know who the Lomeri are," said Ritter. He noticed that he was nearly shouting. Because the surf was omnipresent, it did not seem loud—until he tried to speak over the water's sound.

"Lizardmen," said Hansen, still looking at the flickering horizon. "It doesn't matter. Come, we're almost there."

Ritter thrust his boot forward and felt his heel strike hard—

On the floor of an open-fronted shower stall. Instead of water sluicing down, Ritter's ears sang with harmonics in the audible range as beams of ultrasound bathed him. The mud shook off his clothing as fine dust which hidden vents sucked away.

"Welcome to my home," Hansen said with an expression that appeared both mocking and wry to the point of being bitter. "At any rate, I call it that."

Somewhere in the background, a male voice sang that *Spanish is the loving tongue*, but no humans were visible. The engineer glanced at a couch. It shifted and became broad enough for his massive form.

Ritter stepped out of the shower stall. They were in a circular room whose walls were so clear that only slight vertical discontinuities between the panes of crystalline material proved that the ceiling was not suspended over open air. The furnishings were sparse, though the way the couch returned to its former configuration in the corner of Ritter's eye suggested that flexibility would make up for number.

"*I don't look much like a lover . . . ,*" sang the cracked tenor voice, "*yet I say her love words over. . . .*"

Ritter walked over to the clear wall. The dwelling was built into a sideslope. Their upper-story room was level with a flowered prairie on one side, while on the other it overlooked a valley floor. A breeze drew swathes of shadow through the grass heads below, but there was no sign of large animals for as far as Ritter could see.

He turned abruptly to Hansen. "Where are we?" he demanded.

"In my home," said his guide. "On Northworld."

"No," said Ritter. "Northworld is where we left. Where *I* live."

He frowned, then noticed that his right index finger was playing with the butt of the pistol Hansen had returned to him. He snatched his hand away. "That was the old name, at least," he said. "We call it Earth, now. Most people."

Hansen nodded. "That *is* Northworld," he said, speaking calmly. "So is this, and so were the seven other stops we made. All equally real."

He smiled. "Or equally false, of course," he added. "Take your pick."

Ritter swallowed. He jerked his right hand down again. "I don't—" he said.

His tongue hesitated over 'understand,' then concluded, "—believe you!"

"I don't really care whether you believe me or not, Master Ritter," said Hansen. His look of amusement underscored the truth of what he said. "That's not why I brought you here."

Ritter's mouth opened, then closed. He had spent his life working to the whim of Duke Greville, who was a fool. This man, whatever he might be, was not a fool. . . .

"Go on," said Ritter.

"I brought you here to show you something," Hansen said with a smile of appreciation for his guest's attitude. "I'd like you to copy it for me."

He gestured at a slab of wall. The crystal frosted, then began to seethe with images.

"Why me, Hansen?" Ritter said bluntly.

"Because it has to be done without me manipulating the Matrix directly," explained the slim man with ice-gray eyes. "And there's no one anywhere, anytime, on Northworld who can do that as well as you can, Master Ritter."

The engineer looked from the speaker to the images forming in the wall, then back again. Figures moved inside a room built entirely of natural materials.

"What do you want copied?" Ritter asked.

"One of these," said Hansen as he pointed.

The image in the wall froze. "They're called dragonflies. I want a dragonfly like the ones these Searchers are riding."

Chapter Ten

Sparrow knew the Searchers were gone before he took in the fact that their battlesuits were missing. The lodge felt empty; as empty as a tomb.

The mirror he had given to Krita winked from between the boots of his own armor.

"And except for that damned fox, we'd have another three martens," Gordon grumbled to Sledd as they entered behind their brother. "Hey Julia!"

"They've left," said Sparrow in a quiet voice.

"Race!" called Sledd as he shifted the straps of his pack that doubled in apparent weight as he tried get it off. "Damn. Help me with this, Sparrow."

"They've left us," Sparrow repeated. He didn't move from where he stood when the realization hit him.

"Hey, where's the battlesu . . . ," Gordon began. His voice trailed off. He and Sledd stared at their brother, finally taking in his words.

"They can't have gone!" Sledd insisted. He hunched his shoulders and flexed himself away from the straps of his pack. The bundle of fresh furs hit the floor with a thump.

"Are they walking, then?" said Gordon. "But they took their battlesuits."

"They've found their dragonflies," said Sparrow as certainly as if he had watched the women leave, "and they've ridden away on them."

Sledd ran his fingers over the carved wooden panel of his bed closet. Race's battlesuit had stood there.

"I don't believe—" Sledd began; but he did believe, and his bunched fist slammed through the lindenwood panel with a sound like the first stroke of lightning.

"Why did they . . . ?" Gordon said. He knelt and removed his own pack, thumbs beneath the straps. His eyes were closed in concentration.

301

Gordon couldn't get out the rest of the question; and anyway, the brothers all knew the answer.

Sledd flexed and massaged his right hand as he wandered toward the further end of the room. Objects that he and his brothers had made winked in perfect wonder. A silver cabinet opened for him as he came near. Its trays held every piece of the splendid jewelry he had fashioned for Race.

Sledd kicked at the cabinet morosely.

"It doesn't matter, does it?" he said. "We can go back to the way things were, that was plenty good enough. If we want women, we can always buy time from the nomads down south, the way we did before."

"Wait, there *is* a way!" said Gordon gleefully. "Sparrow, we'll use that mirror of yours to find them again, and then we'll—"

As Gordon spoke, he bent down and reached for the mirror. "—talk with them, conv—"

"No!" said Sparrow, bear huge and bear quick as his bulk slid between his brother and the object. "That's Krita's. Nobody touches it but—"

"You made it!" Sledd objected.

"Nobody but Krita!"

No one spoke for a moment. The beads of light continued their stately dance in the center of the lodge. Their illumination was dimmed by the blaze of sunlight through the east gable and the open door.

"We can still find them, you know," said Gordon, the words coming out faster as the wish clothed itself in the trappings of reality. "We can! They'll go—"

"They'll go back to the gods," said Sledd. He sucked the knuckles of his right hand. "We'll never see or hear of them again."

Sparrow turned slowly, lost in his own thoughts. His pack bumped the bed closet. He absentmindedly twisted one hand behind him to lift the massive weight, then removed the other arm from the unloaded strap.

"They'll want to see their homes, won't they?" Gordon protested. "They'll spend some time back where they were born, now that they're free."

Sparrow opened his bed closet. While the men were gone,

Krita had pinned sprays of fresh flowers to the railing within. The stems had wilted and half the petals were scattered on the bedding.

"That was years ago," Sledd said, but he was commenting on the proposal rather than dismissing it out of hand. "Time isn't the same with the gods."

"It's not so long for Julia," Gordon said. He threw open a clothing chest, choosing quickly among the linens and woolen garments for which the brothers traded on their infrequent journeys to the fringe of the settled world. "Her father was King Tournalits. He may still be alive."

"Race had brothers," Sledd remarked. Though he spoke softly to hide the hope that might tempt fate to deny him, his normally harsh voice trembled with something close to tenderness. "But that was in the far south, Pallaia."

"Then we'll go to Pallaia!" Gordon said. "And to Tournalits' fortress in Armory. If they aren't there, they'll at least visit some time—and we can c-c-convince them. To return."

Sledd opened a chest and began to set out a trading assortment—rings and bracelets and lights brighter than jewels; pots that heated by themselves, and boxes that sang in tones of inhuman purity. The brothers did not keep baggage animals, but their own massive shoulders could carry enough of the products of their craft to buy a duchy.

Gordon paused. "Sparrow?" he said. "Your Krita . . . ?"

Sparrow looked at his brothers. "Oh, she'll come back to me, you know," he said. There was no emotion in his voice. "You go on, yes, look for your, your . . ."

The smith's mind hesitated between 'women' and 'wives.' In the end he chose neither and continued, "You go look for Race and Julia, and maybe you'll find them. But I'll stay here, because I know my Krita will come back to me one day."

Sparrow's brothers stared at him. The master smith's eyes were opaque.

If Sparrow was looking at anything, it was deep within his heart.

But his heart was probably empty as well.

Chapter Eleven

Hansen sat in the empty bed closet to which he had returned, staring at memories. Someone tapped on the door.

He rose from the bed, but the door wasn't barred. He collided with the figure who slipped in as Hansen reached for the lifter.

Contact made his guest a woman whose low bodice was embroidered. The moon rising beyond the opening in the east gable woke a sheen from Holly's chestnut hair.

She closed the door quickly. "I—" she began stiffly, but then the rest of the words came out in a rush, "—wondered if there might be something I could do for you, sir? I owe, we all owe—"

"Oh, nothing like that," Hansen said in surprise, though it *shouldn't* have been surprising.

He always forgot that people thought he was doing things for them. He wasn't. He did what was in front of him, what people forced him to do. It was never what Nils Hansen wanted, just that he was there when it had to be done.

"Oh," said Holly. "Oh, I'm s-s-sorry—"

Air stirred as the servant whipped the cloak back over her front and turned to leave.

"Wait," said Hansen.

He heard her fumbling in the dark for the latch lifter. When she couldn't find it, she slapped the thin doorpanel in frustration.

"Wait," Hansen repeated.

For a moment, Holly resisted the pressure of his hands. Hansen was stronger than the servant, stronger than any woman he had met, and he would not be denied.

"It's all right, really," Holly said in a voice which suggested she believed her own words. "You want someone younger and, and not so fat. I'll tell—"

"No, wait," Hansen murmured.

"Any of the younger ones would be honored, but I said that—"

304

Hansen's arms were around Holly's shoulders. "Stop," he said. He kissed her forehead and felt her relax.

"Just wait," he repeated, and as she turned her face upward, he kissed her on the lips.

"I rattle on when I, when I'm nervous," Holly said. She tugged her cloak open and pulled his right hand to her bosom. "I—what you did for us—"

Hansen bent. Holly was wearing a clean dress, not the one in which she'd been pawed by Abel, but the pattern was similar. He kissed the curve of her right breast, just above the nipple.

"Oh," Holly said. She put her arms around him. "Oh dear."

"But not here," Hansen said, straightening. "I—"

He paused. "There's too many memories."

"Oh . . . ," Holly said in a different tone. "Oh, of course, the killing tonight . . . Oh, I see."

For an instant, Hansen trembled with a vision of Unn shaking her blond hair out in a cascade across her breasts and the firm, pale flesh of her abdomen.

"Yeah," he said. "That's . . ."

He didn't have the heart to continue with the lie, but it was all right. The woman misunderstood as Hansen meant her to do.

"Right," he went on softly. "Ah, don't you have a place of your, your own?"

"The children are—" she muttered, thinking aloud. "But I could move—" She focused on Hansen. "It will take a little time, that's all, but—"

"Wait," Hansen murmured, kissing her lips again as the only practical way of interrupting Holly's nervous flow. "We'll just go walking, shall we? It's a warm night."

Children might mean a husband.

Some questions are none of a third party's business, and no one benefits from the third party asking them.

"Yes, the meadow's lovely with the moon over it," Holly said. She led the way out of the bed closet and into the silent hall. "There's a wicket through the palisade, and there's no watchman there. Not that it . . ."

The mud streets of the village were almost as quiet as the lord's hall had been. Penned animals grunted and gurgled with the noises of digestion, but the beasts showed no interest in the two humans on the board walkways.

The moon was brilliant: full, and halfway now to zenith.

Holly nimbly jumped a gap where streets crossed, then hugged Hansen fiercely as he followed her. "It seems like everything is getting different," she murmured.

"I didn't have anything terribly exotic in mind," he said dryly.

"Silly!" she said, kissing his cheek and striding on toward the gap in the palisade at a quicker pace. "Though that would be . . . I mean, *almost* anything, at least."

The circle of withies intended to loop the wicket closed had rotted away. Holly turned the wooden grating open, then leaned it back against its posts when Hansen had followed her.

"What I really meant was the rovers, of course," she continued. "And the king summoning levies to Frekka for his army."

The meadow was scythed, not cropped by the teeth of animals whose hooves would damage the roots. It had not been long since the last mowing.

"Umm, prickly," Holly said as she bent to brush the stubble. "We'll put my cloak down."

She giggled. "And besides, I don't care!"

The field sloped gradually. By now, irregularities in the ground would hide the couple from anyone looking down from the palisade. Holly paused.

"Lord Waldron has been summoned to Frekka?" Hansen said as his fingers fumbled deliberately with the brooch clasping Holly's cloak.

"No, it's not a full summons," she said as her own hands, gently but firmly, took over the task from Hansen. "Two warriors only from here, that would be Arnor and Cholmsky, I suppose. . . ."

She turned and spread the garment in a graceful motion. She lifted her face to Hansen; the moonlight showed concern in her expression. "Unless you go, milord."

Holly gripped him fiercely before he could decide how to react. "Oh, lord. Something has to be done to stop the rovers. Or—"

She shuddered with reaction. "Or everything will change," she closed simply, and began to unlace the sides of her dress.

If Hansen had ever thought the serving woman was stupid,

he would have been disabused by that simple and accurate assessment of the kingdom's plight.

They knelt on the cloak, then lay on it and one another, changing positions several times. It wasn't love, but it was something both of them needed.

And perhaps in its way it was love.

Chapter Twelve

On the third day that Platt watched the isolated lodge, he got the chance he needed. The smith left, carrying a pack and a hunting crossbow.

Even so, Platt waited an hour before he risked leaving his hiding place in the gorse at the edge of the clearing. So long as he was sober, the spy—the exile—the *outlaw*—was cautious as a fox. Platt had been sober perforce for most of the past three years; and, cautious, he had made sure he was alone on the occasions he had stolen enough liquor to get drunk.

The tendons of Platt's legs complained when he got up. He carefully walked the stiffness out of them in the forest before he attempted the hundred meters of clear area surrounding the lodge. If challenged, he would claim to be a wanderer and lost; the first true, the second very nearly true, for he'd had no idea he would find a dwelling this deep in the forest.

There had been an incident a month before, and the house-holders had hunted him with dogs. Platt had moved fast, because it was his life at stake, and he had deliberately struck off into the wastes; habitation meant support for those chasing and no shelter for their quarry. By the time Platt had lost the pursuit, he had also lost all but the barest notion of his whereabouts.

In the empty nights, with his belt tied to a branch to prevent him falling from his squirrel-nook in a pine tree, Platt had time to reflect on the fact that his life had long ago lost all purpose.

The clearing was a carpet of pine straw near the trees, bare earth as Platt neared the lodge. He had decided to go to the door opposite the one from which the smith had left. The outlaw stepped lightly, careful not to stir the ground cover or leave footprints in the dirt—which fortunately was dry.

Platt's head moved only the slight amount that an honest traveler would look around as he approached haven in the wilderness. His eyes flicked constantly ahead and to the sides, and his ears strained to hear the squeal of a crossbow being cocked behind him.

The smith looked like a powerful man, but the real proof of his strength lay in the size of the crossbow he carried—and cocked with a lever, not a windlass.

But the big man had no reason to believe that his lodge was being watched. It was only chance that Platt had decided to follow the faint trail from the spring at the head of this valley. He'd thought it might be an animal track along which he could set snares to supplement the nuts and berries which had sustained him since he fled.

The lodge had been a surprise. Platt dropped from instinct. It was a hot, still day and the doors in the gable ends were open. The outlaw could see directly down the long room.

Platt could also see wonders of which he had never dreamed, not even when he strutted around the royal court secure in his position and his cunning. Platt was third cousin to King Hermann—

But the child's father had been kin to the king as well; and because Platt had been drunk, he hadn't murdered the witness after he raped her.

"Hello the house," Platt called, too softly to be heard any distance into the forest. The smith's pack had implied a long trek, but Platt never took needless risks.

When he was sober.

The latch string was rawhide, old and cracked. No one had used this door in years.

"Hello?" Platt repeated. He teased the latch open carefully to keep the string from parting.

What had been wonders to the outlaw watching from a distance were unbelievable when he stood within the lodge. They lighted *themselves*, some of them, and the intricate motions of the rest were like a dream of a god's palace. Platt began to shiver with anticipation and—for the first time in three years—hope.

With this to offer King Hermann. . . .

Platt opened the door only wide enough for his thin body to slip through like a mouse squeezing into a cupboard. He looked around in amazement. Half of the devices were beyond his ability to guess their purpose.

In every sweep, Platt's eyes paused at the far door through which the smith might at any moment return.

The moving spirals that lighted the room hung in the air without any physical support. Platt's long knife probed beneath them, hoping to find a wire thinner than hair or a crystal column that passed light as the air itself did.

Nothing. Perhaps there was a support overhead, attached to the ceiling . . . but in the midst of so many marvels, it became easier to accept the truth of the inexplicable.

There were three bed closets. Platt froze as he considered the implications, but instinct assured the outlaw that the lodge was empty though he had seen only one man leave it.

A battlesuit stood open before the nearest closet. Aided by the artificial light overhead, Platt peered at the suit. It was not painted. After a moment's examination, the outlaw realized that paint on armor of this quality would be like paint on a knife blade—defilement, not decoration.

His fingers ran over the glass-smooth joints of the finest battlesuit he had ever seen. Even the mechanical connections were perfect: though the suit was unoccupied and cold, the frontal plate swung as easily as if the hinges were balanced on jewels.

Platt breathed very softly. Many of the articles of the smith's craft were unique; and, because there was nothing with which to compare them, some of Hermann's courtiers would be unable to see their value.

But all warriors understood battlesuits. *Everyone* would see the supernally high quality of this suit.

He started to leave then, because he would gain only further amazement by staying—and Platt, even cunning, grasping Platt, had been bludgeoned to awe by the wonders he had already seen. When the shadow of his body moved, a mirror winked from between the battlesuit's legs.

The outlaw bent down, intrigued more by the placement than by the object itself. He raised the little mirror, though the caution that kept him alive against the odds was screaming that he *must* leave, that the lodge's owner might be anywhere—

The smith's face stared out of the mirror's surface.

Platt screamed like a rabbit as the snare tightens. He spun

with his knife thrusting, knowing that its blade was keen enough to shave; knowing also that a man of the smith's size and strength would snap the intruder's neck like a twig even after being disemboweled.

Platt was alone in the lodge.

The outlaw picked up the mirror again from where terror had flung it. It had not been damaged by its skid along the puncheons—but now it was only a mirror which reflected Platt's terrified face.

But it *had* shown the smith—

As soon as Platt thought of him, the smith's image filled the metal surface again. He was trudging forward stolidly against a background of tree boles. His crossbow was in his arms because it would interfere with his back if he slung it, but he had not bothered to cock the weapon.

The smith was several kilometers away from his lodge, but Platt was watching him.

The outlaw hugged the mirror to his breast for a moment, feeling in the object's hard outline the certainty of his own return to society. Then, cautious even in triumph, he set the mirror back where he had found it.

Platt latched the door behind him carefully as he left—for the time being—the lodge and the objects of wonderful craftsmanship within it.

Chapter Thirteen

Ritter scowled grudgingly at the craftsmanship of the dragonfly which he viewed through the window of Hansen's house/palace/eyrie.

"This isn't going to be easy, you know," the engineer said. "I'll need the vehicle itself to examine."

"Yeah," said Hansen. "We'll go get it."

Ritter frowned. "How long can I keep it?" he asked.

"As long as you need," Hansen replied with a shrug. He looked out through the panes to the east, toward the horizon of gently waving grass. "Duration doesn't matter here."

The exterior of Hansen's dwelling was of cast plastic with windows of preternatural clarity. North had told him that the building had no soul, but it was the architecture to which Hansen had become accustomed when he was a security officer on a far world, in a distant time.

Besides, Hansen wasn't sure that he had a soul either. If he did, then he shouldn't have felt empty inside most of the time.

"But won't the owner miss it?" Ritter protested. He knelt beside the perfect image and took an electronic magnifier from his sleeve pocket.

The dragonfly's control module *was* a seamless monomer casting, at least down to the level the portable unit could magnify. He'd probably have to cut—and that meant analyzing the material so he could learn how to weld it before he started to dismantle the dragonfly.

"It'll go back to the niche in time where Krita finds it again, never fear," Hansen explained. There was movement on the horizon, not just the grass bending and rising in its slow dance with the wind.

"It's not going to be easy," Ritter repeated as he spot-checked radiation from various points on the vehicle while it was at rest. "And I'll have to take it back to my own laboratory. . . ."

The squat engineer looked up, half expecting to be told that he must perform the work *here*, away from his familiar equipment and support structure—

Which would give Ritter the excuse he needed to bow out of the project and go home to what he knew.

Hansen turned and nodded, "Yeah, I assumed you'd want to do that," he agreed without concern. "Though I could duplicate your equipment here, if you'd prefer."

"No, I . . . ," Ritter said. "I'll be all right, back in my lab. No one questions what *I*'m working on."

He was afraid of the unknown. Every human being feared the unknown.

But Chief Engineer Ritter wasn't so frightened of learning the unexpected that he would refuse a unique opportunity.

Ritter resumed his preliminary examination of the dragonfly by measuring the dielectric potential across ten centimeters of the casing material. For the readings to be valid, the 'window' had to be as transparent across the whole spectrum as it was in the optical wavelengths. . . .

Hansen opened the door and looked out to the east. He could barely hear the clatter of the swans' pinions, but the car they drew was hidden behind the cloud of feathers rowing against the air.

"Just so long," he said to Ritter, "as you can do the job."

"Matter is matter," the engineer grunted. "I can analyze it; and if anybody can build it, then *I* can copy what he did."

He scowled at the reading he'd just taken. He checked it against similar lengths of the control panel and a leg strut, then swore in appreciation.

"All right," Ritter said, "I've seen enough to know that it's no good me fooling around with pocket instruments on a project like this. You deliver—"

His eyes focused past Hansen's shoulder. "What in *hell* is that?" he demanded.

Hansen laughed with some amusement but no humor. "My visitor, you mean?" he said, following the engineer's eyes. "She drops by when she has nothing better to do . . . and tries to do *me*."

The swan car swept in a circle that brought it to a halt broadside before the men. Between fifty and a hundred of the birds had been somehow harnessed to the gold lacework vehicle.

The swans held their positions well enough in flight, but as soon as they settled, they began to hiss at one another like a knot of vipers.

The driver was a haughty youth with broad shoulders, a wasp waist, and a pointed black moustache which perfectly matched the color of the jock strap that was his only garment. He glanced at Hansen, then Ritter, sniffed, and began polishing the slim-spoked wheels with a chamois rag.

Ritter blinked in amazement at the queenly woman who descended from the car.

She was tall, and her hair and clinging dress were both the exact color of the golden car. When she moved, for instants that were almost subliminally brief, the dress seemed to vanish and leave her—except for the jewel between her breasts—as perfectly naked as she was perfectly formed.

Hansen slid open a crystal door. "Hello, Penny," he said with the wry smile of a man who'd been impressed despite himself. "You know, I've been meaning to ask you—how do you train those birds?"

Penny waved a languid hand. "It's taken care of for me," she said in a voice of studied culture.

Then she looked over her shoulder at the swan car and snapped in a very different tone, "Myron! Move it away, won't you? How is anyone supposed to think with all that racket?"

Ritter expected the driver to react sullenly, if at all. He knew the type, and they weren't all male.

Instead, Myron dropped his chammy and touched the controls—electronic, not mechanical reins, the engineer saw. The birds settled into the traces and began to beat their wings in unison.

Whatever else Penny might be, this surly young stud behaved as if she held his life in the palm of her hand.

Which meant that she probably did.

The car trundled off a few hundred meters, where the swans' noise was lost in the breeze.

"I have an idea you'll like, Hansen," the woman resumed in her false cultured tones again. "And I promise that you won't believe how *much* you like it until you've tried. . . ."

She touched Hansen's chin with long, perfect fingers and turned his face to a three-quarter profile.

Hansen disengaged Penny's hand. "I'm busy, Penny," he said.

"Do you want me dark haired?" she asked.

Light struck from the jewel on her breast and abruptly she *was* dark, with hair like a rippling ebony carving and lips a fuller, darker red to match. "You know that time doesn't matter here, whatever you're doing. Busy doesn't exist for us."

"I'm always going to be too busy for you, Penny," Hansen said. "I wish you could understand that."

His face hardened into the expression Ritter had seen momentarily when Hansen kicked the pistol from his hand. "I'd appreciate the offer more," he went on, "if I didn't know you'd say the same thing to a Shetland pony you hadn't met before."

Penny sniffed. She didn't appear to be upset by the insult. "You don't know what you're missing," she said.

Her jewel flashed. She changed again, her body rather than merely her hair and features. Ritter's mouth was dry. Now Penny was a heavy, shorter woman whose chestnut hair had flecks of gray.

"I watch you with other women, you know," she said archly to Hansen.

He laughed. "I can't stop you," he said.

"I can *be* those other women," Penny said with a sudden fierce edge. "Look at me, Hansen! I can be—"

The jewel winked. Penny was blond, not quite so tall as before, not quite so statuesque, and Hansen shouted, "*No!*" as his fist rose mantis-quick for a blow that would crumble bone—

Penny was a teenage girl, not unattractive, who wore coveralls of gray synthetic and an expression of blended fear and desire.

Hansen squeezed his right fist with the fingers of his left hand. "Penny," he whispered to the ground in a ragged voice, "don't show me Unn again. Don't."

He looked up at the girl. She simultaneously shifted to the woman's form in which she had arrived.

"It isn't just a body, Penny," Hansen went on, his voice filling to its normal timbre. "And it especially isn't just that body."

"You're wrong, you know," Penny said, without rancor but flatly certain; as certain as Hansen was in his own belief.

She turned and looked Ritter up and down appraisingly. "Your slave's from Plane Five, isn't he?" she said. "They're all such squatty fellows."

Ritter had seen men eye women that way—Duke Greville, for instance, whether the woman was a new concubine or the daughter of a peer; but it was a surprise to see the look on a woman's face.

"He's not a slave," said Hansen easily. "We're helping one another. Partners."

Ritter didn't stare devouringly at women. A unique piece of equipment—like the dragonflies waiting across a dimensional window—might elicit the same expression from him, he supposed.

"I haven't had one of your type for . . . ," Penny said, walking around the engineer as if he were a garment displayed on a mannequin. She giggled. "There *I* go, talking about duration."

Ritter rotated to face her. The jewel on her breast twinkled. At each flash, Penny was a different female form. Each time, along with changes in hair color and facial features, she was slightly shorter and a few kilos heavier—tending toward the somatotype with which the engineer was familiar.

"Turn around," Penny said sharply, making a brusque gesture with her hand. "I want to see your profile."

"Go to hell," said Ritter. He turned his back on her and knelt to study the dragonfly again.

The sonic imager he carried lacked power to penetrate the casing material. He'd need the full-scale X-ray equipment of his lab, and—

The woman giggled again and leaned over Ritter's shoulder. One bare, heavy breast lay on the back of his neck; the nipple of the other brushed his right biceps. "What's your name, then?" she asked coyly.

Ritter stood up slowly and turned.

"Penny," said Hansen in a dangerous voice, "he's under my protection."

"I'm not going to hurt him, you know," Penny replied with a touch of steel herself. "Just the opposite."

"My name's Ritter," Ritter said. "I'm an engineer."

The form Penny had settled on—for the moment—was that

of a twenty-year-old woman, five centimeters shorter than the engineer. She had red hair—nearly orange on her head, duller and mixed with brown on her armpits and pubic triangle. Her body was thick, but powerful muscles dimpled the fat sheathing her hips and thighs.

Apart from the jewel, she was completely nude.

"Penny, we have business to take care of," Hansen said in a tone that thinned as he noticed the way Ritter met the woman's eyes.

Penny put a hand on the engineer's shoulder. She turned to Hansen and said haughtily, "What's the matter? Is he really your slave after all, and you control his breeding rights?"

Hansen took a deep breath. "Master Ritter?" he said, letting the context serve as the remainder of the question.

Ritter touched his lip with the point of his tongue. He didn't understand the powers of the people he was dealing with; but he didn't doubt that those powers went beyond the ability to appear and disappear, went beyond the capacity to change shape.

Went possibly to life, and certainly to death.

"Duration really doesn't matter?" he asked. "Time spent here doesn't mean time taken away from the job?"

"No problem," Hansen said. He gave Ritter a genuine grin. "Go have fun, partner."

The engineer ran his hand over the plane which displayed the dragonfly, careful to avoid touching the curved surface.

"*This*," he said to his guide, "is the kind of fun I've never had before."

He looked at Penny. "All right, lady," he said. "I'll go for a ride with you, if that's what you want."

Hansen smiled. "I want to talk to Penny alone for a moment, Ritter," he said. "If you could—"

"I'll tell Myron to bring the car by," Ritter said with a grin of his own, pride and anticipation. "Let's see if he gives me a hard time."

He stalked off, a powerful man wearing bright, loose clothing that bulged with equipment. Very sure of himself, of his ability and of his manhood.

Hansen's smile faded as he transferred his attention to Penny.

Before the expression was wholly gone, it had become a leopard's snarl.

"He's my responsibility, Penny," Hansen said. "If you get—"

"I won't hurt him!" the woman blazed.

"We can't bring the dead to life, Penny," Hansen continued as inexorably as a train on rails. "If you do something in a fit of pique that can't be undone, then I'll come after you. Do you understand?"

"You'd bring down the Matrix if you did," Penny said. "All of us. All of Northworld."

"Do you doubt me, Penny?" Hansen said in what was barely a whisper.

"No," the woman said. For a moment there was nothing in her eyes but calm intelligence. "I don't doubt you at all, Hansen. There won't be a problem."

Penny took the man's hard right hand between both of hers, raised it, and kissed the tip of Hansen's trigger finger.

She turned to meet the swan car. Her driver cringed like a whipped puppy in front of the big engineer as they approached Hansen's house.

Chapter Fourteen

A temporary stage had been erected before the House of Audience in the center of Frekka. The rest of the stone-flagged square was filled with warriors summoned from all across the kingdom and their attendants.

"You really wanted to be sent with the royal levy, didn't you, Hansen?" Arnor asked. His voice was tinged with wonder and a little bitterness.

Sunlight had not yet burned off the chill fog. The waiting men coughed and grumbled and spat.

"Sure," said Hansen, shrugging to bring the collar of his fur cloak tighter against his ears. "I'm a warrior, so I want to go where the fighting is. Right?"

He gave his companion a thin smile. "Didn't you want to come, Arnor?"

"Now stop milling around, gentlemen!" ordered the only person on the stage at the moment, a brightly-dressed usher. "King Prandia will be out to address you momentarily."

"Then you ponce off someplace else and get the king out here where he belongs!" snarled a lord with good lungs and too much rank to cool his heels willingly.

"It's my duty," Arnor muttered. "I'm the champion of Peace Rock, and the lord himself is too old to attend the levy."

"You could say it's my duty too," said Hansen as he eyed the crowd.

There seemed to be about a hundred warriors present. Close up, a warrior's bearing distinguished him from his freeman attendants even when the warrior wasn't wearing his powered armor. In diffuse light and a mixed crowd, though, it was hard to be sure.

"Anyway," Hansen added, "I've got the best battlesuit in the hall. Thanks to my benefactor, the Solfygg rover."

The House of Audience was a tall building with spires at the

319

corners; it antedated the year two generations ago that Frekka became the royal capital. Four trumpeters stepped out of the front door. Their trumpets were slender cones, each with a broad flange soldered onto the bell more for appearance than to affect sound quality.

Three of the instrumentalists managed a clear fanfare, but fog had gotten into the throat of the fourth man. His call sputtered. Even at best, the echoes from the old buildings surrounding the square were thin on this dismal morning.

"A bad omen," Arnor muttered.

"Balls," said Hansen in sudden anger. "Men make their own luck!"

Warriors in battlesuits shifted to block the streets entering the square. Instead of individual paint schemes on their armor, these men wore only patterns of stripes on their right arms. The color and width of the stripe indicated the warriors' unit and rank within it.

Professionals. The standing army—the Royal Household— of the West Kingdom.

"Hail to King Prandia the Just!" cried the usher. He hopped off the stage as a stocky, fortyish man mounted the steps behind him.

Prandia wore hose and a puffed black doublet that would crush flat without discomfort when a battlesuit closed over it. The spangles on his beret were as likely jewels as they were metal sparklers, but neither the cap nor the rest of his garb made any concessions to the cold.

Prandia's breath plumed from his nostrils as he eyed the assembly. Warriors in fur tried to control their shivering.

"Hail, King Prandia!" chorused the crowd.

A number of people cheered with genuine affection. The interest of a few warriors was primarily on the armored professionals who now surrounded the square.

That only meant that Prandia the Just wasn't Prandia the Sucker.

The king's skin was pale and he had blue eyes. He looked nothing at all like his grandfather, Golsingh the Peacegiver . . . though his coloring was very similar to that of his grandmother.

Queen Unn.

"Lords and warriors of my kingdom," Prandia said. His tenor voice carried across the square with surprising power. "The Duke of Colimore, my friend and son-in-law—"

Breath fluffed again from Prandia's nostrils. He drew in a deep breath and continued, "The Duke of Colimore has been murdered with all his family by Ontell . . . who was his counselor, and claimed to be his friend."

"Happened at midsummer," Arnor muttered to Hansen. "Ontell's got a way about him, but he's mean as a snake inside."

"Ontell has usurped Colimore," Prandia continued as coldly as though he had not just mentioned his daughter's murder, "though the duchy is of my kingdom and in my gift. It would appear that Ontell is receiving support from the King of Solfygg . . . but that will be a matter for another time, after we do justice in Colimore."

"Princess Unn was the apple of her father's eye," Arnor said. "She was the prettiest little thing you ever saw."

"Was she indeed?" Hansen said. His lips were as pale as bone.

"I will not be leading you against Colimore in person," Prandia continued. "That duty will be performed by my marshal, the Duke of Thrasey, who will handle it ably and professionally—"

The tremors which shook the king's body could have been a reaction to the cold, but Hansen was shaking also within his furs.

"As I do not trust myself to do," the king added, getting control of his voice midway through the clause.

"Because the kingdom has been at peace during my reign and that of my father," Prandia went on in his original cold, powerful tones, "it is necessary to organize you gentlemen of the levy for the first time. To that end, your battlesuits have been set within the House of Assembly."

The king gestured at the building behind him. The crowd murmured. Warriors were considering the matter of greatest concern to them: their status within the first army of the West Kingdom in generations.

"Please enter the building—only warriors!" Prandia said, raising his voice to a sufficient degree. "Enter the building and stand beside your own armor. Duke Maharg and several of his champions will speak with each of you individually before making their assignments."

"Duke *Maharg* of Thrasey?" Hansen said to Arnor as the push to the House of Assembly's doors began. "How old is he?"

"Hmm?" said Arnor. He eyed the rush doubtfully, then settled back to let the crowd thin before he moved toward the hall himself. "Maharg? Oh, he's the king's age. They were raised together when Prandia was fostered by the first duke, that was Malcolm, Maharg's father."

"What . . . ?" Hansen began. He sucked his lips between his teeth for a moment. "What happened to the old duke, then?"

"Well," said Arnor, "I think he's still alive, though he must be older than the hills. He abdicated in favor of his son, oh, must be ten years ago."

The square around them was full of chattering freemen, but all the nearby warriors had made their way to the queue snaking around both edges of the stage. Prandia looked down and caught Hansen's eye for a moment.

"I guess we better go," Hansen said to his companion. They moved ahead. Freemen jumped out of the way of their greater status.

"Why were you wondering about old Malcolm?" Arnor asked.

"Oh . . . ," said Hansen. He could feel the eyes of the king focused on his back, but he did not look up as he passed the stage. "I used to know him, a long time ago."

The champion snorted. "As young as you are?" he said.

They had reached the doors of the House of Assembly. Voices and hardware echoed within. Warriors looked for their battlesuits and objected to where the armor had been placed, as though a preliminary sorting had already occurred.

"If you did," Arnor added, "you must've been just a boy."

Chapter Fifteen

A puppy yowled pitiably as Bran and Brech, the king's twin boys, held its hind legs in the fire.

From the look of King Hermann and Stella, his hard-eyed queen, they would willingly be treating Platt as their six-year-olds were the dog.

"Like nothing you ever dreamed of seeing, excellency," Platt whined.

The outlaw knelt in front of the royal chairs with his forehead to the floor. When he spoke, dust and ash puffed away from his nervous lips. "Lights that hang in the air and move. A mirror that shows far places."

"Pah!" said Salem, a young baron who'd joined Hermann's council since Platt was outlawed. "His breath fouls your hall, majesty. Let me stop it for good."

"Armor fit for the gods to wear!" Platt wailed against the flagstones.

"Wait," said King Hermann.

The outlaw exhaled bubblingly in relief.

Platt had taken the only chance he would ever have of being rehabilitated; but it had looked, and it might still be, that he had lost that final necessary toss of the dice. Unless the king believed Platt's story, the outlaw had nothing to trade for his life; and even before his exile, Platt's word had done little to compel belief.

"But I'll lead you there!" Platt whined to the scorn echoing in his own mind.

"For pity's sake, Hermann," said Stella in a voice like chilled steel. "Tell him to get up out of that ridiculous pose."

Her tongue clicked against the roof of her mouth. "Or kill him. That might be better."

"All right," said the king. "Get up. For now."

Platt scrambled to his feet. He bobbed and touched his forehead to each of the hard, sneering faces around him.

The thrones were on one end of the large, rectangular audience chamber. Hermann's councillors stood to either side with their uniquely-decorated battlesuits behind them as identification and insignia of rank.

The barons hated one another; but they hated Platt more. If the king had suggested it, they would all have cooperated to drown the outlaw in a cesspit.

There was a huge hooded fireplace in each of the sidewalls, cold now except for the fire the twins had lighted for their fun. During the morning levee, the chamber would be filled by suppliants; but Platt had been brought to the king in late afternoon, when Princess Miriam and her ladies in waiting used the room's acoustics for their lute playing.

King Hermann was forty and fleshy rather than fat. His queen was younger by ten years, but she had never been beautiful or even striking, in the positive sense. Her eyes were intelligent and cruel. Very cruel.

"Milord, he lives alone on the northern edge of your kingdom, deep in the forest, and he has treasures beyond belief, I swear to you," Platt said quickly. The words tumbled out like a cascade of smooth, stream-washed pebbles. "He's a smith, and he makes wonders, not just battlesuits. But his battlesuit is, milord, I can't describe its perfection—but I can show you. For my life."

There was a sudden crash and screeching from among the girls on the opposite end of the chamber. Princess Miriam lashed at a servant with her lute.

"How *dare* you not serve me first?" Miriam shrieked. Fragments of the sound chamber of her instrument flew. She swung again. A string twanged.

The servant, a girl little younger than the fourteen-year-old princess, hunched on the floor. She was afraid to run or even raise her arms to shield against the blows. A platter of candied fruit lay scattered over the stones.

The six ladies in waiting sat rigidly on their stools as if they too were pieces of furniture.

"Miriam, my dear," called the queen in a peremptory voice. "Keep your voice down, please."

The princess looked at the broken neck of her lute and the

bits of sound chamber dangling from the strings. She kicked the servant and hissed, "See what you did? Get out of here!"

The servant ran, scuttling the first few steps hunched over like a frog. The puppy had also escaped from the twins during the commotion. It moved with surprising speed on its two good legs and waited until it was beyond the doorway to begin yowling again.

Baron Tealer, an old man and kin by marriage to the girl who caused Platt's exile, cleared his throat. "If this place is in the forest, milord," he said, "then it's not in your kingdom. Our writ doesn't run through the uninhabited wastelands."

"If there's someone living there," said Hermann as he stroked his pointed beard, "then it's not uninhabited."

The king smiled at his manicured hand. "And if there's such wealth there, Tealer," he continued, "then it must be royal wealth, mustn't it?"

Several of the barons shrugged a grudging acceptance of what they saw would be King Hermann's decision.

Stella looked at her husband. "Hermann," she said.

"My dear?" Even the king looked uncomfortable when he heard that tone of voice.

"If you're going to rob a man of such power, a smith . . . ," the queen said deliberately, "make sure you kill him as well. You'll remember that, won't you?"

"I'm his king and he owes me tribute," Hermann muttered without meeting his wife's eyes. "That isn't stealing."

Chapter Sixteen

"Did you think I'd stolen him, Hansen?" Penny called in a tone of harsh challenge as Ritter brought the aircar to a halt in front of Hansen's dwelling.

Hansen noted that the engineer flared the ducted fans fore and aft so that they wouldn't spray grit over Hansen's legs as the car settled. Ritter was a good man; an amazingly good man.

But then, Nils Hansen always needed the best when there was a job *he* couldn't do.

"Master Ritter isn't a chattel you could steal, Penny," Hansen said with a cool smile; but he was glad to see Ritter returning, glad not to have to check on the situation . . . gladder yet not to have checked and learned something that he didn't want to know, and then to act because he said he would act.

Hansen didn't want to die. Not really. Not most of the time.

Ritter shut off the engines and spread his blade pitch to maximum so that air would brake the drive fans to a halt in the least amount of time. Though the car rested solidly on the ground, it rocked when the engineer lifted his heavy body out of it.

He grinned at Hansen and said, "Tsk. Didn't think I'd stay away from a puzzle like this one just to screw, did you?"

Ritter raised his arms over his head, interlaced his fingers with the backs of his hands downward, and stretched up onto his tiptoes, still smiling. His clothing looked the same as that in which he had left with Penny, but Hansen's practiced eye noted that these garments were perfectly clean and of a softer fabric than the originals—though whatever synthetic Penny chose would certainly wear like iron despite its comfort.

Otherwise the engineer—otherwise *Ritter*—wouldn't have accepted the replacements.

Hansen smiled again, this time with more humor than before. "You're ready for work, then?" he asked.

"I'm always ready for work," Ritter replied, and he quite clearly meant it. They walked through the simple doorway into the observation level of the house.

Penny followed them. Her face was twisted into an expression too dismal to be described as a pout.

Penny's garb was normal enough for her: a macrame bra, briefs cut to expose rather than conceal, and net stockings. Her body, however, was unusual.

Penny now wore the form of a nineteen-year-old with vaguely blond hair, slightly overweight in a puppyish sort of way. She was neither stunningly beautiful nor strikingly grotesque. A mildly attractive young woman, but not the appearance someone would pick from an infinite choice of features and bodies.

Unless it was the way they had looked before they received the power to choose; and if so, that was a fact Penny had been working to conceal for as long as Hansen knew her.

"Unusual vehicle there," Hansen said. He gestured with his thumb, but he did not look back toward the aircar.

Ritter blinked. "You're joking!" he said. "It's dead standard. Besides, nothing could be unusual after that whatever-you-call-it pulled by all those birds."

"Swans," said Penny quietly.

"You'd be surprised what people will come up with when any whim works as well as the next," Hansen said. "It *does* all work, you know. When all times are the same time; and when any idea has power if a—"

Hansen swallowed but managed not to lose his calm expression. "If a god chooses to think it."

Penny stared morosely out a window. For the moment the view was only waving grass the aircar had overflown on its way here.

"Penny just . . . ," Ritter said, rubbing his chin and scowling at the memory. "She said, 'All right,' and there it was, a car like the ones we build for Duke Greville's scouts on campaign. I don't understand."

"It's a matter of arranging the correct point on the correct event wave to intersect with present reality," Hansen said.

Ritter turned in sudden fury—looked for a solid object within his reach—saw nothing. He slammed his right fist into his left palm with a tremendous smack.

"That's just words!" he shouted. "It means nothing!"

Penny flinched at the engineer's anger. She turned around.

"How would you," Hansen said coolly, "describe to a blind man the process of sorting red and yellow objects without touching them, Master Ritter?"

The engineer grimaced at his display of temper. Frustration carved his face into harsh angles like those of a tumbled wall. "Sorry," he muttered.

"Sorting event waves through the Matrix works in much of Northworld," Hansen continued, "for some people."

His voice had less of an edge than a moment before. "It didn't work where I came from, not that I knew about, anyway. And it doesn't work for *any*damnbody on the plane you come from. But that doesn't mean it isn't real."

"I remember when we put them on Plane Five," Penny said without emotion. "The first fleet the Consensus sent looking for us after we'd disappeared."

Ritter looked at the woman in fresh horror. "You *remember* the colonization?" he said. "That was—tens of thousands of years ago!"

Hansen put a hand on the engineer's shoulder and kept exerting pressure until the big man noticed and turned to face him.

"Time isn't the same here," Hansen said gently, though part of his mind noted that if Penny wanted to convince her latest stud that she was some kind of ageless monster, she couldn't have picked a better way. "And anyway, you're thinking of duration again. Besides—"

He grinned honestly, infectiously. "—you 'n me have got a job to do."

Ritter laughed, loose again. Whatever else Penny might be, Ritter knew she was a woman; and a woman was nothing to worry about when there was a uniquely challenging task to accomplish.

He looked around the observation room with a slight frown. "Ah," he asked. "Do you have a—"

"Toilet?" completed Hansen. "You bet. Down there—" He pointed to a drop shaft with a coaming of molded plastic "—and just to the right of the door."

"Back in a minute," the engineer muttered as he stepped into the shaft.

Now that they were alone, Hansen nodded a cautious greeting to Penny. "I guess things worked out for the two of you," he said.

It disturbed Hansen to see the woman acting . . . different. Hansen's fellow gods, who had the power to do virtually *anything*, always seemed to do the same thing again and again.

It was easy for Penny to create an aircar in place of the swan-drawn vehicle she always used. It was amazing to see her do something because of a man's whim.

Penny hugged herself, squeezing her full breasts almost out of their slight restraint. "Well enough," she said.

She looked at Hansen with the disconcerting intelligence that sometimes glinted from her brown eyes. *Out of place in a trollop who thought only of sex and her appearance.* "How much danger is there going to be?" she asked.

"On this?" Hansen said in surprise. He waved at a section of window. The clear surface suddenly showed a thicket of magnolia bushes and tall, scale-trunked trees.

Krita's dragonfly and those of her two companions nestled into the vegetation. Their spindly legs compensated automatically for the slope, keeping the saddles level.

Hansen's eyes went flat as he calculated. "Not a lot of risk," he said. "None at all, if things go as they should."

"You're armed," said Penny, nodding toward the cutaway holster high on Hansen's right hip.

Not stupid at all.

"Well, you know what they say," Hansen replied with a chuckle. "You carry a pistol when you *don't* expect trouble. When you know the shit's going to hit the fan, then you lug something serious along."

Except that pistols were Nils Hansen's weapon of choice, because he pointed handguns as though they were his own fingers. Not that he really expected trouble.

"And those damned things—" Penny turned and spat in the direction of the dragonflies "—are there with the Lomeri."

The spittle vanished in a puff of light at the surface of what was still a window, not a physical opening onto another plane of the Matrix.

"I can make you as many as you—" Penny said.

She spread her pudgy right hand. Five dragonflies, indistinguishable from those sitting in the magnolia scrub, appeared in the gazebo.

Hansen brushed them back into nonexistence with a flick of his own hand. "North and I have an agreement, Penny," he said mildly. "We're going to do a quick in-and-out, Ritter and me. We'll be gone before the Lomeri know we were there. No sweat."

"Easy for you!" the woman blazed. "He isn't a, isn't a killer like you, Hansen."

"Ritter isn't exactly a babe in arms, you know," Hansen said with the care he would have displayed if his dog began yelping and snapping at the air. "Besides, nobody's going to be doing any fighting. We're just going to pick up a piece of hardware."

The engineer rose through the shaft, hitching up his equipment belt and checking the flap of pistol holster dangling from it. He waved cheerfully toward Penny and Hansen.

Penny walked out of the observation room. She leaned against the aircar with her back to both men.

Hansen heard her mutter, "Bastard!"

Hansen supposed Penny meant the epithet for him; but he wasn't quite sure.

Chapter Seventeen

"What's the stupid bastard waiting for?" muttered King Hermann to Crowl, the nearest of the warriors hiding with him; but as the king spoke, Platt reappeared at the door of the lodge and began to walk back with an exaggerated care not to leave footprints.

"Are you really going to let Platt live?" Crowl asked. Instead of the external speaker, he used the radio built into his battlesuit's circuitry. Platt, wearing only the ragged jacket and fur trousers in which he had reappeared at court, could not overhear them.

"As long as he's useful," Hermann said.

The party consisted of six warriors including the king; a dozen freemen with bows or spears; and almost a hundred slaves. The slaves had been necessary to carry the battlesuits the last three kilometers to the lodge so that the sound of baggage animals would not alert the smith.

The warriors knelt in their armor, flanked by the freemen. The slaves huddled a kilometer away, keeping as silent as possible. If the overseer told Hermann that the slaves had made any commotion while they waited, they would all be killed.

Platt the outlaw entered the lodge alone to determine whether or not the householder was present. A part of Hermann's mind whispered to him that the best result would be for Platt's body to be flung back out the door in pieces . . .

But the smith was absent.

"It's empty, majesty," said Platt, wringing his hands nervously. He dipped as though he intended to kneel on the mold of leaves and needles. "We can wait now, and when he returns, we'll have him."

"Well, when *does* he come back?" Crowl demanded. "I don't want to sit in this damned suit for the next fortnight."

"There's no way to tell, milord Crowl," the outlaw mewled. His voice had the same choppy, high-pitched timbre as that of

331

the head-down squirrel complaining from a nearby tree trunk. "He may come back in minutes, or he may have just—"

"I want to see the interior," Hermann said abruptly.

Platt's face froze in a rictus. The king started forward.

"Milord!" the outlaw wailed, throwing himself flat on the ground as King Hermann's boot rose to crush forward with several hundredweight of armor behind it. "Milord, you'll leave marks and he's a hunter and he'll see and he'll, oh my lord we'll miss him!"

Platt was terrified. He knew that if the ambush failed for whatever cause, he would pay the price.

And he was right. A battlesuit's weight and the sputtering discharge wherever its forcefield touched a solid object left browned, deeply-impressed footprints on any surface but solid rock. If their quarry returned by daylight, he would have to be blind to miss the tracks.

The king sighed and stepped backward. Platt was scum, but he was cunning scum.

"All right," said Hermann, reaching for the catch of his armor. "I'll take this off."

"I'll go too," said Crowl.

The outlaw got up from the ground, dribbling flecks of forest debris. From the look in his eyes, he was doubtful about the safety of this course also.

But Platt knew there was no doubt at all as to what would happen to him if he tried to block his monarch's whim again.

The lodge had a breathy, lived-in-but-empty quality which worried Platt but only made Crowl's lip curl. Crowl hadn't seen the smith, moving with the power and arrogance of a bear.

King Hermann halted three steps into the long room. He was impressed despite himself by the unique objects scattered in careless profusion.

Crowl paused at the moving lights. He poked, then flailed his arms impatiently beneath them, trying to find the invisible pillar. "What in hell holds these up, Platt?" he demanded. Before the outlaw could answer, the warrior leaped into the air with his hands cupped.

"Don't!" Platt shrieked. "You'll—"

The air snapped like the popper of a drover's whip.

"YEOW!" Crowl bellowed. He came down in a crash, one hand gripping the other.

The air smelled of burned meat. The hole seared through the warrior's hand was as neat as could have been pierced with a white-hot wire.

The beads of light continued their slow, undimmed circles.

"—break something . . . ," Platt concluded.

The outlaw's voice trailed off. He maneuvered to put a tall silver spiral that sang like a waterfall between him and Crowl's angry reflex.

"Stop fooling around, Crowl," Hermann grunted, very possibly saving Platt's life for the moment.

The king stopped in front of the battlesuit. He fingered its lining of padded leather. It was a big suit, but Hermann was a big man himself. The jointed arms lifted and fell to his touch with a feeling of jeweled smoothness, as though inertia alone restrained the motion without any friction between segments.

"Did he *make* this suit?" Hermann wondered aloud.

"He must have done, majesty," Platt said, wringing his hands again. "And all this, must have made them because how else would they be here, one man and no baggage train?"

Crowl drifted across the hall to stare at a construction of gears and pivoting levers. Its purpose was beyond the warrior's imagination. He kept his hands thrust firmly through his back, though at intervals he withdrew the injured member and pressed it against his belly. The cauterized hole did not bleed.

Platt bent over the pile of scrap and ore beside a bench. He prodded with the point of his long knife. At the core of the heap was a section of tubing decorated with lightly-etched flowers.

"You see his work?" the outlaw said. "Have you ever seen a smith who could make *this*?"

"Toys," King Hermann grunted. "But this . . ."

His hand ran over the battlesuit's surface, a finish as smooth as that of a pool of black ice.

The king stepped back to see the armor complete. His eye caught a wink from the floor between the boots; he bent to retrieve the mirror. "What's this, do you suppose?" he asked.

Platt was covering the object in process more or less the way it had been when they arrived. "Oh, that's another wonderful thing, milord," he said, lifting a last pebble of ore onto the pile. "It shows you the owner, wherever he is."

"No it doesn't!" Hermann snarled; but as the king spoke, the reflective metal suddenly cleared into a vision as sharp as that in a diamond lens.

Platt looked over his shoulder and frowned. "That's not the smith . . . ," he muttered.

The mirror showed a scene in the royal hall. Princess Miriam sat at leisure in a chair inlaid with ivory and gold. A slavegirl teased out her long hair, and ladies in waiting played a soothing trio for lute, recorder, and solo voice.

"I just wondered what Miriam was doing, and there she is," the king murmured in an awestruck tone.

"Truly a marvel, majesty," Platt said in nervous approval. "Like all the objects here, treasures beyond imagining, just as I said."

Hermann stared into the mirror, which now showed his sons. They were in the palace kitchen. Bran tipped a ladleful of hot broth down the back of a scullery maid sleeping in a corner.

"But perhaps we should, ah . . . ," the outlaw murmured, "ah, go back into concealment so we don't lose our prey?"

The miniature image trembled again. Each scene had its own internal light, so even in the gloom of the lodge's interior the intruders could see every detail of the smith who strode through the forest, seemingly unaffected by his load.

"He's a mean-looking one," the king muttered.

"Stella said to chop him," Crowl said as he joined the other men at last.

"That's a whole stag," Platt said, unable to keep bitterness at the smith's strength and ease out of his tone. "That's a hundred kilos dressed out—besides what else he's carrying."

"And if he's carrying it like that," King Hermann said in sudden decision, "then he's probably coming home. We'd best get into position."

The mirror blanked suddenly into a circle of polished bronze again. The king hung its carrying loop around his neck.

Platt paused halfway to the back door of the lodge. "Ah . . . majesty?" he said.

"Well?" Hermann snapped.

Crowl was in the doorway. The tone of the king's voice turned the warrior around, his face tense with the chance he would be called on to finish Platt.

"Are you . . . milord, ah, going to take that mirror with you now?" Platt blurted in an agony of indecision.

"Yes," said King Hermann.

His lips pursed. "It's—" he went on with a hint of doubt, "—just one little thing, after all. He won't notice it, and . . . Anyway, we'll be waiting."

"Yes, majesty," the outlaw said, bowing and mopping in terror. "Yes, of course, majesty."

But instead of leaving immediately, Platt hopped back to the work in progress. His fingers poised for a moment. He removed a piece of flint no larger than a pea and carried it across the room to the battlesuit.

"What are you . . . ?" King Hermann said in wonder.

Platt set the chip of flint carefully in the joint of the lower hinge of the frontal plate.

He gave a great sigh as he straightened. "Now . . . ," he said. The polished surface of the battlesuit reflected his relief.

Chapter Eighteen

The House of Assembly was an echoing confusion of voices and battlesuits.

Warriors got into and out of their armor, clashing the frontal plates. Helmet speakers amplified their shouts in metallic dissonance.

The coffered ceiling was still decorated with a Pageant of Trade from the days when Frekka had been an independent trading port ruled by a syndicate of merchants. Frescoed Syndics frowned down on the warlike babble.

Occasionally one of the levies would light his cutting arc. That created a snarling dazzle and thunderous orders to, "*Shut it off or eat it, dickhead!*" from the armored professionals overseeing Marshal Maharg's examination.

Other warriors argued face to face with the staff officers who trailed along behind Maharg. The officers were hard-faced men who jotted down notes and explained what the marshal's cryptic remarks meant to the levy he had just examined.

Almost every warrior had a complaint. Some spoke in disbelief, some in anger; and not a few in a desperate hope that surely they could be raised a little in the roster, their suit was surely better than a *sixth* ranking (. . . fourth ranking . . . seventh ranking . . .) wasn't it?

The officers never raised their voices, except to be heard over some exceptional commotion; and they never took any notice of the complaints except to deny with the cool firmness of marble slabs that there would be any change in Marshal Maharg's dispositions.

Some men would have argued further, but the professionals following the staff officers wore battlesuits. These escorts gave every indication of being willing to end a problem within seconds of when it started.

The marshal finished with the warrior to the left of Arnor

and, beside him, Hansen. He looked at Arnor and asked, "Name?"

"I'm the Champion of Peace Rock," said Arnor with an obviously manufactured assurance. "Obviously I have the right to demand the front rank in the name of Lord Waldron, but in view of the circumstances, I'm willing to accept a s-sec—"

Arnor's flood of confidence waned under the pressure of the marshal's gaze. "Ah," Arnor concluded in a softer voice, "a third-rank posting."

Maharg's eyes were brown and as hard as polished chert.

"Buddy," he said with the air of a man repeating what he'd said to *every* damn warrior he'd examined this morning, "if you'll let me do my job, then you can get around to yours when the time comes at Colimore. Now, get in your suit but *don't* switch on the bloody arc."

"You ought to list the levies separately from the household," Hansen said.

He pitched his voice to carry, but he kept the tone as cool as that of Maharg's staffers. "People are going to get their backs up about ranking anyway. There's no reason to make it worse by maybe three steps each time."

The marshal turned with no more haste than the first boulder of an avalanche. "And just who the hell are you, buddy?" he asked.

One of the armored professionals stepped around the staff officers—in case of need.

"I'm the guy who just gave you good advice for the next time," Hansen said. His right arm was at his side. He leaned on his left hand against the thorax of his battlesuit.

Maharg was a tall man with broad shoulders. He wasn't paunchy, but his waist was thicker than that of his father.

Of course, I knew his father as a much younger man.

The marshal's complexion was just dark enough to suggest that his father Malcolm was an octoroon; his eyes hinted that his father's quirky intelligence had passed to the son as well.

"There won't be another time," Maharg said. "Not after what we're going to do at Colimore."

Hansen shook his head gently. "There's always another Colimore," he said. "Peace doesn't happen. It's something you make and keep."

Maharg turned away. "Close up your suit," he said to Arnor,

peering from his open battlesuit. "Take a couple steps forward."

An expert—Maharg was certainly an expert—could determine a battlesuit's quality from visual examination. If there were any doubts, the artificial intelligence of any battlesuit could provide either a relative or an absolute ranking of any other suit within an observation range of several kilometers.

Maharg wasn't examining the armor alone. He was checking the way each suit behaved when its owner was wearing it. Hesitation, awkwardness; overcompensation for the inertia which servo motors did not quite eliminate—all would be evident to the marshal's practiced eye in a matter of a few seconds and a few steps.

Hansen watched the current demonstration as critically as Maharg and his staff officers did.

Arnor had good armor. Had he wanted it to, his battlesuit would have earned him high rank in a household that was less of a backwater than Peace Rock.

But that was the point: Arnor *didn't* want to duel his way to a position, even if that meant bruising, half-power contests instead of arc weapons at their full lethal intensity.

The Peace Rock champion was skillful enough. He stepped forward, then pirouetted on one foot; a tricky maneuver even on a surface as solid as this floor. Despite that, each of Arnor's movements started with a jerkiness which indicated mental uncertainty rather than a power-train lag in his armor.

"All right," said the marshal wearily. "You're done for now."

He turned to an officer who carried a notebook made of boards planed thin and bound with leather thongs. "Call him a five and put him in White Section," Maharg said. "And get his damned name, will you?"

The officer flipped a board over and dipped his writing brush into the pot of oak-gall ink attached to his belt.

"And what," the marshal continued, sliding his eyes over Hansen and onto Hansen's armor, "do we have here, smart guy?"

"Put on your own suit, Marshal," Hansen said, still leaning on his armor, "and I'll show you exactly what we've got."

Maharg ran his fingers over the battlesuit's forearm, then worked the elbow joint from the outside. The bearing surfaces slid like fitted diamonds.

The marshal snapped his fingers and gestured, still concentrating on the suit's finish. Hansen moved his hand and stepped aside obediently so that Maharg could examine the frontal plate.

Maharg looked at Hansen. "I wonder, smart guy," the marshal said in a tone that would have brought the armored bodyguards to attention again if the words had not been spoken so softly, "just where you got this suit?"

"I took it from a rover who didn't need it any more," Hansen said evenly.

"That's right, Marshal," Arnor put in as he climbed from his battlesuit. "I saw him."

Everyone ignored the Peace Rock champion.

"He thought I was a smartass," Hansen continued, his eyes on Maharg's eyes and neither man blinked. "I thought he'd lived long enough already."

Maharg ran his fingers over the faceplate and thorax, the parts of a battlesuit that normally received damage in combat. He glanced down at the legs to be sure that neither of them had been burned off and patched with the inevitable scarring and degradation of performance.

He looked at Hansen again. "Were you wearing suits when you killed him?" the marshal asked.

"He was," said Hansen.

Maharg began to grin. "You *are* a smart sonuvabitch, aren't you?" he said, but this time there was a certain respect in the words.

He rang his knuckles off the thorax plate. It gave no more than the stone wall behind it would have done. "Pretty good piece of hardware," he said. "Pretty *damn* good, I'd say."

Hansen also relaxed. "Thing is . . . ," he said.

He ran his fingers across the epaulet plate, found the point he wanted. "Here," he went on. "Feel the join line? And the same just above the hip joints."

Maharg placed the tips of two long, shapely fingers at the point Hansen indicated. Arnor and the staff officers watched; Arnor in curiosity, the others in amazement.

Maharg's lips pursed. "That's not bad," he said.

"It's not bad," Hansen said, "but it's not in a class with the rest of the workmanship, believe me."

He gave the marshal a hard, professional smile. "But yeah, it's a good suit. It's a real good suit."

Maharg patted the battlesuit again while he continued to look at Hansen, curious now rather than challenging. "You wouldn't happen to know something about team tactics, would you, smart guy?" he asked at last.

"As much as anybody in this room does, I guess," Hansen said. He smiled, but he could feel all his muscles start to quiver with the prospect of imminent action.

"As much as any of the levies do, you mean," corrected the officer with the notebook.

Hansen raised an eyebrow. "*Is* that what I mean?" he said.

"Right," said the marshal in sudden decision. He nodded to the officer who had spoken. "Patchett," he said, "take over here. I may or may not be back before you're done."

"What?" said the staff officer. "Ah, yessir, but—"

Maharg had already switched his attention back to Hansen. "Do you have a name, smart guy?" he demanded.

"Hansen."

"Is that what it is?" Maharg said without particular emphasis. "Bring your suit, then, Hansen. You can wear it or I'll get a crew to carry it for you to the practice ground, it's all one with me. You and I will each lead a three-man team, and we'll see just what you do know."

"But sir!" Patchett interjected. "Where should we place this Hansen?"

Maharg scowled over his shoulder at his subordinate. "I'll know when I've seen him on the field, won't I, Patchett?"

He grimaced and added without enthusiasm, "After all, *somebody's* got to lead this lot of stumblebums we've levied."

Chapter Nineteen

"Well come on, Hansen," the engineer demanded, showing his nervousness in an excess of enthusiasm. "It's time to go!"

Ritter knew only that the next few minutes would involve a situation different from every situation of his past life—and that there would be some danger. Anybody sane would be nervous under those circumstances.

Hansen looked around one more time. The image of the dragonflies sat placidly in the image of their thicket.

Hansen scowled and changed the window back to normal viewing with a quick brush of his hand. The falsely innocent landscape irritated him.

"Don't worry," he said in a voice closer to a growl than he'd intended. "We'll get there."

Hansen was nervous also. He *did* know what to expect on a visit to the Lomeri.

The aircar squatted on the other side of the observation room's clear windows. Penny sat in the vehicle, her head raised and her back turned ostentatiously to the men.

If you looked carefully—and Hansen always looked carefully, even when his eyes swept and his expression stayed as flat as the finish on his pistol barrel—you could note that a plane of air formed a reflecting surface in front of the woman.

Penny might have been viewing her own appearance. That was probably the act she performed most often. But it rather seemed that her eyes followed the activities of the men she appeared to ignore. . . .

"Yeah, right," Hansen muttered to himself. "Look, stick close, do what I tell you to. This oughta go slicker 'n snot."

He put his left arm around Ritter's shoulders; checked the fit of his pistol in its breakaway holster; and—

The engineer reached down toward his own weapon in imitation.

—they inserted.

The air was warm and humid. Some of the flies buzzing among the pink magnolia blooms lighted on Hansen's cheeks. They flicked away and returned moments later as sweat popped out of his pores. The soil underfoot was pebbles and grit, well enough drained to keep the magnolias comfortable despite the horsetail marsh within twenty meters.

Hansen couldn't see the horsetails. He couldn't see jack shit because of the mass of blossoms and shiny green leaves in all directions including up. Some of the damned magnolia bushes were three meters high.

Especially, Hansen couldn't see any sign of the Searchers' vehicles which he knew had to be parked here.

Ritter fluffed his loose garment away from his chest without any sign of discomfort. The engineer kept the humidity of the controlled climate in which he lived at 50%. Static had been more of a problem to his tests than contaminating water vapor was.

"Which direction?" he asked Hansen. As he spoke, he took a small magnetometer from his sidepocket to answer his own question.

Ritter didn't realize anything was wrong.

Hansen was very calm. He didn't know what the *fuck* was going on, and you never let yourself get into a flap when it's that bad. That could get you killed.

Something bellowed a kilometer or so away. The sound seemed to come from the west, but in this tangle of branches ramifying to interweave like a puzzle there were no certain directions.

"That's funny . . . ," the engineer said as he peered at his magnetometer. The loops holding his pistol holster to his belt were long and flexible. He raised and lowered the holstered weapon, checking the motion against the read-out.

Hansen thought about the image he had seen from his house. He didn't know much about vegetation, but the shape of the surrounding magnolias seemed correct for the brush he'd glimpsed from the window's higher vantage. He put out his hand, his left hand, because Krita's vehicle *should* be—

It wasn't.

"Do you have the place and time correct?" the engineer asked as he frowned at his instrument. "Because I'm not getting—"

"Hell, that's it!" Hansen shouted.

Sparrow's instinctive understanding of the Matrix had led him to twist his concealment of the dragonflies one step further than Hansen had realized. When the smith lifted the dimensional vehicles from his plane to this one, he'd also set the time horizon a millisecond out of phase with the spatial controls.

Hansen's window conflated the partial spacetime realities, but that was an image and this—

A two-tonne megalosaur, long-jawed and carnivorous, crashed through the magnolias at a dead run.

Ritter bawled in surprise. He juggled his magnetometer from his right hand to his left so that he could draw his pistol.

Hansen's instincts were different—*nothing* is as important as clearing a weapon when a weapon is needed—and his gun was pointing within a quarter second at the eyes and yellow-white palate tearing into sight.

Hansen didn't fire. The megalosaur was fleeing, not charging, and it ripped past several meters away.

The beast's tail and spinal column were almost parallel to the ground as it ran. The hips, covered with flattened scutes in a leathery, bronze-on-brown hide, were higher than either man's head.

Fleeing. Which meant—

"What was that?" the engineer shouted.

Part of Hansen's mind was viewing a present concealed from Ritter. His left hand blurred out of sight. His fingers touched a dragonfly's controls.

—something was chasing it.

Hansen had reholstered his weapon. The practiced reflex of drawing and firing was actually quicker for Hansen than it would be for him to aim a weapon in his hand. Ritter waved his own pistol toward the flutter of quivering branches the megalosaur had left as it disappeared through the tangle.

A gun isn't a magic wand that you wave and hope something desirable happens.

The dimensional vehicle popped into sight. Magnolia branches wove through its angled legs.

In a gap through the upper foliage—

Hansen drew and fired. The thicket exploded in actinic radiation that crisped the nearest flies and stung the exposed skin of the men twenty meters away.

The Lomeri scout was mounted on a saddled iguanodont. The five-meter height advantage permitted the lizardman to look over the tops of the magnolia bushes. The Lomeri's instruments had warned it that the intruders were nearby—

But instinct and the fleeing carnivore had done the same for Hansen. He fired at sunlight winking through the foliage from the visored helmet that covered the Lomeri's flat skull.

"Get on the dragonfly!" Hansen screamed over the hissing echoes of his shot.

Hansen was carrying a directed-energy weapon. Though his bolt loaded the Lomeri's forcefield to a dazzling coruscance, it did not penetrate. The energy, rebroadcast all across the electro-optical spectrum, seared the iguanodont like a bath of live steam.

The bipedal beast honked and curvetted as it tried to paw its injured forequarters. The lizardman, thin as a wire armature, tried simultaneously to control his mount and point his short-barreled shoulder weapon in the direction of the shot.

Hansen fired again, down the track of foliage withered by his first bolt. The Lomeri forcefields were normally directional, convex bowls of protection which faced the front and danger.

The scout, broadside to Hansen as the iguanodont spun, took the shot in the middle of his ribcage. The creature's head and shoulders toppled backwards. His long feet retained the stirrups.

Reflex discharged the lizardman's weapon in a thunderclap of shredded vegetation.

"Get aboard!" Hansen shouted. *The engineer swung his leg over the dragonfly's saddle, but there were more Lomeri coming. He aimed at them instead of—*

Hansen shot again.

The scouts had seen what happened to their leading fellow. They dismounted with predatory grace, slapping their mounts aside to avoid being set up by the beasts' gyrations. Hansen's bolt re-radiated like a minuscule nova, but it did nothing to disrupt the attackers' movements.

One of the lizardmen managed to fire in the air, aiming along the ionized track of Hansen's bolts. He hit the injured iguanodont.

This time the explosion was accompanied by a mist of blood, scales, and bone fragments. The beast whooped a gout of lung tissue.

"Get—" Hansen said.

Ritter fired as his buttocks settled on the dragonfly's seat. There was a high-pressure *crack*! at his pistol's muzzle, doubled instantly by a *crack*! that cut through the shouts and echoes.

Hansen expected a ricochet from the forcefield of the arching lizardman. The duplex projectile struck the Lomeri shield with a blue spark at the point of impact and a tiny jet of radiance *through* the forcefield where kinetic energy had already loaded the unit to maximum output. There was nothing unsophisticated about Ritter's equipment.

And nothing wrong with his aim, though the way his miniature plasma beam pierced the target's slit-pupiled eye might have been luck.

Hansen's left hand slapped the dragonfly's engagement control, hoping that he'd set the coordinates correctly despite the confusion—

And certain as he followed Ritter through the Matrix that there was no worse place to be than the thicket detonating in orange fury as the humans fled.

The dragonfly's legs flexed as the vehicle settled in the center of Hansen's observation room. Penny stared from outside. Her moist palms were pressed against the crystal barrier.

Hansen's exposed skin prickled. It would peel in a few days unless he chose to cure the harm by manipulating reality—

Which he would not do, because he'd been so sure he could dodge the Lomeri that he'd gone underequipped. *When you screw up, a minor injury like a UV burn from your own weapon was maybe worth your life the next time. That made it a lesson to be treasured.*

Ritter was gasping. A twig or a fragment from an explosive projectile had gashed the engineer's sleeve into rags, but the skin beneath appeared unharmed.

"Were those—" he said and hacked to a stop.

Hansen tried to adjust the dragonfly's controls left-handed. Now that he and Ritter were safe, he was all thumbs.

"Those were the Lomeri," he said. The inside of his throat had been savaged by ions released when he fired. "Pray you never get a better look at the bastards."

The barrel of Hansen's pistol glowed. He laid the weapon on the floor and set the controls with his right hand.

Penny strode into the room radiating fury and sexual excitement. The men and the borrowed dimensional vehicle were already phasing back to Ritter's home.

Chapter Twenty

It was nearly midnight when Sparrow entered his home. He started to unsling his pack, then paused.

The betrothal gift he had given Krita was missing. His bride must have returned while he was hunting.

"Krita?" he called softly.

"K—" and his voice caught. "Krita?"

His pack slipped the rest of the way and thumped. Sparrow didn't notice it as he ran to where the mirror had been, like a bear making its short, unstoppable rush onto prey.

The crossbow was still in Sparrow's left hand. He flipped the uncocked weapon away with a motion that skidded it across the puncheons.

The crossbow could as easily have smashed to fragments on a wall. Sparrow didn't care.

The smith knelt on the bare floor and ran his fingers over the wood as if he could touch past events. For minutes he remained in that attitude of subjection.

Sparrow's body blocked light from the illuminating spiral which rotated in the center of the hall. There was nothing to see in light or shadow, only in the big man's memory.

A breeze made the door of the lodge creak on its leather hinges. The night air felt cold on the skin of a man who had hiked twenty kilometers with a heavy load.

Sparrow stood up. "Krita!" he called. "I've waited for you!"

A crow, wakened by the shouting, squawked from a pine tree.

"I'll still wait!"

Sparrow made a fireset of punk and kindling in the corner of the hearth beneath the smoker cage. He lighted the set with an object which looked like a silver salamander and spat a blue spark from its jaws when Sparrow moved its tail.

Sparrow went outside again. He looked tired but steadfast,

347

an ox near the end of the day's plowing. When he returned, he carried the stag's carcase and a large square of mammoth hide, stiff and reeking with old blood.

The smith tossed the hide on the floor with a clop like a wooden pallet falling; fed up the fire; and finished butchering the deer beneath the slowly turning lights. He used his belt knife for the job, a sturdy tool with deep fullers to keep the suction of raw flesh from gripping the blade on long cuts.

Occasionally a sound made Sparrow look up, but it was never more than wind or an animal scrabbling.

As he separated each strip of venison, the smith hung the piece on a hook in the smoker. The slatted cage was indoors to protect it from scavengers—which could include a bear. The low heat began to drive out meat juices in a tangy perfume that replaced the scent of death.

Sparrow wrapped the stripped bones in the deerhide and carried them outside with the butchering mat. He kept his offal in a safe of fieldstone and lime cement until he could dispose of it in a gorge two kilometers away.

A scavenger is almost any predator who's between meals. Sparrow was confident in his strength and agility; but he was a methodical man, and there was no reason to increase the risks he took. Logic, not immediate ease, governed his choices.

When he had finished the clean-up and washed his hands with a gourd of water from his cistern, Sparrow closed the lodge door. He called a harsh command. The beads of light darkened, though they continued to move in blackness relieved only by the coals beneath the smoker.

Though the night was cool rather than cold, the smith took a huge white bearskin from a chest and wrapped himself in it. For a time, he sat beside the fire, staring toward the shadowed emptiness between the feet of his battlesuit.

Then, eventually, Sparrow fell asleep.

The doorlatch clicked as it opened. Sparrow jumped like a bear awakened by hounds.

They were in battlesuits, fumbling through the front door. At the back, wood splintered as gauntleted hands failed to work the latch mechanism in their haste. The image-amplifying screens of the powered armor would turn scraps of moonlight to day, but Sparrow knew his home.

"He's—" bawled a warrior's amplified voice.

The intruder would have continued 'awake' or 'moving' or simply 'there,' but Sparrow *was* moving, toward his own battlesuit, and light glinted from steel as he flung his knife like a bolt from a catapult.

The darkness ignited in harsh, ripping light. The knifeblade struck the leading warrior and burned because it could not penetrate the battlesuit's forcefield.

Breaking through the back door were two warriors and a third. There were three more at the front, much closer to Sparrow, but the leader of that trio staggered backward from the white dazzle of the knife and blocked his fellows.

A man with a face like a jackal and no armor shouted as he ducked away from the afterimage and fading red sparks.

Sparrow was at his battlesuit and in it, launching himself and turning in the air with the grace of a dancer or a lunging wolverine.

Static discharges popped around the intruders' feet as they clomped forward in their armor. The gauntlets of several warriors glared with dense arcs to cut and kill.

"*Don't hurt him!*" squealed the little man without armor as Sparrow slammed the thorax of his battlesuit closed and—

The vision screens did not brighten into life. The suit's forcefield did not glow with a lambent aura that could block the weapon of any of the warriors, maybe of all six together.

And the arc which should have sprouted from Sparrow's right hand to shear forcefields, metal-ceramic substrate, and the blazing flesh of the intruders—

The arc did not light, because Sparrow's armor had not latched closed.

The leading intruder gripped the edge of the thorax plate and pulled. The smith resisted with all his strength; but Sparrow's strength was human, while his opponent's steel gauntlet was driven by the energy of the Matrix itself.

The smith let the frontal plate go. He tried to leap clear of his battlesuit. Armored hands gripped him before he could get his legs free. He was dragged into the center of the hall.

Freemen carrying torches and supple withies entered through both doors. While warriors held the smith firmly, the freemen wove the captive's limbs with bindings that could have hobbled a mammoth.

Only when that task was completed did the leading warrior open his armor and get out. He was a big man, almost as big as Sparrow, though his face held a hint of softness despite the cruelty of the lips.

Krita's mirror hung from its loop around his neck.

"Well," the intruder said. "I'm King Hermann, lord of this domain. Who are you who've been robbing me all these years?"

"My name's Sparrow," the smith said. "There's no king over this valley. Or over me."

His gaze touched but did not linger on the mirror. His face looked like a fragment of nature, a boulder or a wrack of clouds rising into a thunderhead.

The jackal-faced man spit on him. "Treat your master with respect, scum!" he shouted in a shrill voice.

"Move back, Platt," King Hermann warned without emotion. The little man scuttled away.

Hermann knelt beside his captive. "Of course I'm king here," he said. "And you're a thief, because it's only from me your king that you could have gotten treasures like these."

He gestured calmly, palm upward, at the wonders winking in the torchlight.

"I made everything here!" Sparrow shouted. "I've stolen nothing!"

A warrior who'd taken off his armor stepped forward. He raised his foot.

The captive twisted to glare at him. The man blinked and eased back without kicking.

Sparrow turned his face to the king again. "Why would I need to rob a poor princeling like you?" he demanded. His voice sounded like rocks sliding. "I'm a king's son myself!"

King Hermann straightened. "No," he said in a tone of finality, "you're a slave. And if it turns out that you really are a smith . . . then you'll use your craftsmanship for *me*, Sparrow."

Chapter Twenty-one

Ritter, sluicing the last of his cider around his mouth, turned from contemplating the craftsmanship of the dimensional vehicle on the central examination stand.

A woman had entered the workroom. She was watching him.

"Look, do I have to lock the damned door?" the engineer snarled. "When I want you, I'll call—"

He broke off. Though the woman's features were unfamiliar—pretty but rail-thin, scarcely sixty kilos on a height of a meter sixty-five—he recognized the jewel glowing on her transparent choker.

"I thought I'd pay you a visit at home, you know," Penny said.

She was dressed as though she were a concubine: her black hair teased high on a framework so that she seemed to be wearing a shako; groin and oxters depilated; gold sandals and belt; and a baggy blouse and trousers which were transparent except for the hundred-millimeter net of metallized fabric woven in to flash as she moved.

"Look, not here, Penny," Ritter said in irritation. "I'm busy, and—"

A chime over the suite's outer door rang, a cheerful sound only if you didn't know what it meant. The screen showed a procession of courtiers who wore brocade and weapons decorated to catch the light. They were coming down the hallway in respectful attendance on Lord Greville.

"It never rains but it fucking pours," the engineer snarled. "Look, Penny, just disappear again or you'll cause all damn sorts of—"

But he wasn't speaking to Penny any more; not speaking to a concubine, that is. The woman before him was stooped and old, a housemaid. Her gray smock hid the jewel around her neck. The electrostatic broom she held in her gnarled fingers was reasonable enough, but—

351

"Get that damned thing out of here!" Ritter said. "Don't you know what it could do to some of these instruments?"

The outer door opened. "All rise for noble Lord Greville!" caroled the four courtiers in front.

The engineer had added a secret interlock which could prevent even Lord Greville from keying the mechanism against Ritter's will. Ritter was saving that modification for a great need which he hoped would never come. When Lord Greville *did* manage to batter through, lock or no lock, it would be with the fixed intention of flaying his insubordinate servant alive.

Ritter waited a moment until the Lord of Keep Greville had entered and seen him, then bowed. Otherwise the engineer would have disappeared within his dense clutter of equipment, creating an absurd situation.

That was never a good idea when dealing with an arrogant master who held the power of life and death.

The slavey bowed also. She held a long-handled duster of feathers from cranes like those which fished the marsh beyond the keep.

"Ah, there you are, Ritter," Lord Greville said amiably as he wove a path through the banks of instruments and test pieces. "I've just come to congratulate you on those triplex charges of yours. They penetrated the forcefields of Lord Worrel's tanks almost every time we hit."

Greville was a young man, clean-limbed and extremely handsome except for the white scar trailing up his cheek and deforming his left ear. He'd gotten that ten years ago, in the same skirmish which put paid to his uncle and made a fifteen-year-old Lord of Keep Greville.

The new lord's first act had been to execute his uncle's chief engineer and put Ritter in the victim's place. Since then, Keep Greville had been uniformly successful in its squabbles with its neighbors.

"Very glad to hear that, milord," Ritter said, nodding where a commoner of lower status would have bowed.

"Yes, I took two of them myself," Greville continued. "And damaged Worrel's marshal. Thought I had him too, but—"

Lord Greville's handsome face darkened; frustration bit as deeply from memory as it had during the event. "But he managed to restart and back away. It was a *perfect* shot. I saw his hatches lift, but he drove away."

"Well, milord," Ritter said, "it's a trade-off. Penetration or punch. I'll see what—"

"I'll tell you, I don't much like this new shit," interjected Colonel Maynor, one of the courtiers. He was a grizzled man who'd reached his rank because he was a favored drinking companion of the previous lord. "The old ammo opened 'em a treat *every* time we got home."

Ritter looked at the man who'd spoken. In theory, any soldier was the superior of any commoner. In practice *here*—

"Yes," Ritter said coolly, "the duplex rounds did pack more of a punch inside the forcefields. When they got there, that is. Which would be about one time in twelve with the beefed-up armor of Worrel's current production."

The soldier glared at Ritter, then glanced aside in willingness to end the exchange.

"Of course," Ritter continued, became he *wasn't* willing to let challenges to his professional judgment end as draws, "having gone over your accuracy records, Colonel Maynor, I don't think your personal experience with hits is enough of a sample for any meaningful generalization."

Lord Greville smiled. Several courtiers guffawed openly. Maynor turned and kicked an instrument console.

The engineer chuckled. He built his equipment to last. From the sound the boot made on the console, Maynor had broken a toe.

Lord Greville's eyes wandered toward the dragonfly in the center of the lab. "What on earth is this, Ritter?" he asked.

One of the courtiers put his hand on the dragonfly's saddle. He pumped the vehicle up and down against the shock absorbers in the legs.

"Oh, that's just a notion, milord," the engineer said calmly. "It may or may not pan out."

Lord Greville pursed his lips. "Doesn't look very sturdy," he said. "But—"

His face brightened into a patronizing smile. "—I suppose we can let you have your little surprise. You don't let us down very often, Master Ritter."

The engineer bowed.

"Come along, you lot," Greville said to his entourage. "Maxwell's creating a moving diorama of yesterday's battle, and I want to see what he's chosen for his color scheme."

Ritter's visitors swept out of the laboratory. The engineer wiped his hands on his trousers, leaving sweaty streaks across the electric blue fabric.

"You're really good at your job, aren't you?" Penny said sadly. "I suppose I should have known that, or Hansen wouldn't have . . ."

Ritter turned. She was beautiful again. Perfectly formed, at least. The puzzle-solving part of his mind traced the network of gold accents in Penny's clothing back to sunbursts centered at her nipples and vulva.

"Good?" the engineer snapped. "Do you want to know how good? I could design weapons that would *vaporize* Lord Worrel's tanks. I could vaporize Keep Worrel from right here, give me a year and the budget. And he tells me that I'm doing pretty well, I can keep it up!"

Penny took Ritter's left hand. She slid the loose sleeve above his elbow, checking critically to be sure that the firefight with the Lomeri had not left a permanent injury.

"Why don't you, then?" she asked. "Build the weapons?"

Ritter snorted and turned to look at the dragonfly again. The motion pulled him away from the woman's hands.

"Because if they even dreamed I could do that," he said, "they'd shoot me before I had time to blink. They don't want to upset the balance, you see."

Penny snuggled close to Ritter's side. The pistol holster interfered with her attempt to press their hips together.

"They just want to blow up a few of their neighbors' tanks and have a few of their own blown up too," the engineer continued, oblivious to his companion except as a wall from which he could echo his frustration. "And then all the survivors go home to drink and brag and get ready for the next pointless skirmish!"

"Do you think I'm pretty this way?" Penny asked abruptly.

Ritter blinked and looked at her. She stepped back obligingly and did a pirouette.

"Yeah, you're fine," Ritter said. Actually, she was too thin for the squat ideal of beauty here on Earth—

On Northworld, as Hansen and the ancient colonists called it.

—but Ritter's interest was in function, not form, in sex as in all his other pursuits. No one was likely to object to Penny's ability to function in that category of activity.

"I mean," the woman pressed, "because you said you wanted me the way I was, the—way before we came to Northworld and I got this."

She clutched the jewel at her throat, hiding for a moment the brilliance that flashed like a sun's core.

"I told you I didn't care," Ritter said, frowning at her misquote. Penny took his hands. "I said I'd as soon see you the way you really were. This is fine."

"Come on," she said, tugging him toward the door to his living quarters.

He might as well. The first thing he had to do about the dragonfly was think, just think, and he wasn't going to be able to concentrate anyway after Lord Greville's interrupt—

Whoops.

"No," Ritter said, pulling back, but Penny was already within reach of the latchplate. "Don't—"

Penny opened the door. The concubine on the bedside chair was a sultry brunette. She had thrown back her robe while she did her toenails.

"Are there going to be two of us tonight, then?" she asked. Then, with a catty smile, she added, "Or one and a half, I should say, unless you've got another skinny one to come later."

"Look, you can leave—" Ritter began. *It was always this way when he wanted to get stuck into a project, one balls-up after another—*

Penny leaned forward, swept up the footstool, and went for the concubine.

Ritter didn't realize what was happening for an instant because the other woman—the woman who *belonged* in his bedroom—was twice Penny's size. The concubine raised her hand to keep Penny from clawing at her eyes and bleated, "What—"

Penny clouted the larger woman above the temple with the stool.

The concubine sprawled to the floor. Penny jerked the robe's sash of multicolored silk out of its loops and began to choke her rival with it.

Ritter grabbed Penny's wrists from behind. He squeezed and twisted until the garrote slipped out of her hands. He backed up, ignoring the way Penny kicked his shins with her slippered heels.

The concubine got slowly to her feet, rubbing her throat with her palms. She was wheezing.

"Go on, get out," Ritter snapped. "Next time, hold your smart remarks until somebody calls for them."

The concubine looked as though she might speak. Either her throat or the look in Penny's eyes convinced her to keep her mouth shut. She banged closed the door in the opposite wall.

Ritter let Penny go. He was breathing hard. She turned and struck at his face. He blocked the blow.

"Do you let her suck your cock?" Penny screamed. The puffed sleeve had torn loose from her left shoulder seam. It dangled around her wrist. "You do, don't you?"

"Look," said Ritter, "you better leave too. I should've listened to Hansen."

"Hansen?" the woman repeated, turning the name into a curse. "Oh, you think he'll save you, do you?"

She pointed her index finger at the engineer's chest.

"He never said he'd save me, Penny," Ritter said softly.

He wondered whether he would feel death. His mind clicked over and over like a tumbler lock. "But I guess he'll do what he did say."

Penny stood like a statue of Nemesis. "Do you think I'm afraid?" she shrilled.

"*I'm* afraid, Penny," Ritter said in a burst of dry-lipped honesty.

She lowered her hand.

Ritter took a deep breath.

"Look, lady," he said. "This doesn't make any sense. Pussy's cheap, so's dick, I suppose. You go find your Myron or whoever and we don't ever have to look at each other again. All right?"

Penny laced her fingers together like a knot of vipers. The dangling sleeve got in the way. She tugged at it. "What did Hansen say about me?" she demanded in a husky voice.

"Noth—" the engineer began, but he paused when he saw the spark ignite in her eyes.

"That you liked men," he continued flatly. "That you had a temper."

The woman lifted her chin in a brief nod of acceptance. Another time, she might have argued with the obvious.

"Look," Ritter went on, "I don't want trouble for you or him either. He didn't give me orders, he just . . ."

He smiled wryly. "Hansen treated me like a man," he said. "I don't get a lot of that from Lord Greville, you see."

"Or from me, you mean," Penny said bitterly.

Abruptly, she sobbed and threw herself against the engineer's chest. "Oh, darling," she said, "I'm sorry, I just—"

She leaned back so that she could meet Ritter's eyes. "Look," she went on, "I don't care who you fuck, just so you fuck me, all right? And, you know, you don't tell me about it . . . and I won't go looking."

As Penny spoke, she slid down Ritter's body and opened his trouser fly. She paused for a moment with his penis in her right hand, then began to lick it as she tore away the remnants of her blouse with the other hand.

"Does she take you up her ass, darling?" Penny murmured.

"For god's sake, woman!"

"Oh, darling, I'm sorry, I won't . . ."

Tears sparkled like jewels on her cheeks. "It doesn't matter."

Penny wiped her eyes quickly with her left wrist. "Look," she said, bright and controlled again. "I'll get you really good and slippery—"

She paused to engulf the shaft of his penis, then slide it back out and tongue it firmly.

"—and then I'll kneel on the bed and show you how much fun somebody who's *really* had practice can be!"

Chapter Twenty-two

Warriors already on the practice ground lit the air with the blue *c-c-crack!* of their arcs as Maharg led his group onto it.

The field outside the old walls of Frekka was roughly square and nearly five hundred meters on a side. More than sufficient room remained for six more men to hold a mock duel.

"All right," said the marshal. "Get kitted up and we'll start."

The boundary was marked by posts—and by the stumps which remained when a warrior tested his arc against a post. Eight slaves carried each battlesuit. The coffle set down its burdens gratefully at the margin of the field.

"It'll take a moment," Hansen said. "I need to talk with my troops, here."

He gave a terse, friendly smile to Culbreth and Lee, the warriors Maharg had picked for Hansen as they strode past the levies whom the marshal had already examined. The levies glared back at Hansen with flat-eyed insolence.

Culbreth turned deliberately to Maharg. "I came here," he said, "in response to the royal levy, to serve the king. I didn't come to take orders from some underling from Peace Rock, of all places."

Hansen's face smiled. His muscles quivered, and his vision blurred in a moment of red haze while he waited for Maharg to deal with the problem.

It was Maharg's problem. Until it became Nils Hansen's.

The marshal had chosen two professionals for his own team. They got into their armor without wasting motion, then ran preliminary checks of the sensors and displays.

"Yes, indeed, champion," Maharg said in a tone that might not have been mocking at all. "You came here on your lord's oath to serve the king and the king's officers . . . and I'm sure King Prandia is as grateful as I am that your lord is no oathbreaker."

He put his hand gently on Culbreth's shoulder. The levy was

no taller than Hansen and of a slimmer build, but he did not flinch at the marshal's touch. Culbreth's muscles were firm; his wrists bore the calluses of a man who had spent long hours inside a battlesuit.

" 'Serve' doesn't mean you rush off to die in single combat against Colimore," Maharg said, lowering his hand.

His voice had changed, hardened. Hansen's mind nodded approval because the other tone had been mocking. You might break a man by sarcasm, but that wouldn't make him a soldier; and Culbreth had too much potential to waste unless—

Hansen wiped his palms against his thighs.

—he *had* to be wasted.

"Look—" said Culbreth. The other levy, Lee, pretended to examine the exterior of his battlesuit.

The sky was gray-white. The clouds were too thin to mean rain, but they turned the sun into a milky blur which could not warm the wind gusting across the field.

"Your oath—and your lord's oath," Maharg said, his voice crackling like the arc which the professional beside him tested at that moment, "means that you obey orders. King Prandia's orders, my orders—anybody he or I put over you."

"Look—"

"Otherwise you're an oathbreaker!" the marshal said. "Otherwise you'll get better men killed. And I—"

"I—" said Culbreth, white-faced.

"—will have you executed *now* as an oathbreaker and leave your body for the dogs!"

"Marshal," said Nils Hansen.

Everyone stared at him. He heard his own voice from a distance.

"He's a man I want at my side," Hansen said. "We'll do fine. You don't need an army of people who don't have any balls."

Maharg stared at him. Hansen could almost hear the marshal wondering whether this was a clever variation on an interrogation technique: bonding the subject to a gentle questioner after the harsh member of the team had threatened—

Or whether Hansen really *was* trying to prevent Culbreth from making the wrong response and being executed as an example to the whole army.

Hansen grinned. He wasn't sure himself.

Maharg relaxed. "Yeah," he said. "Get into your armor. I've got work to do."

"Wait a sec," Hansen said, holding out his hands, palm down, to Lee and Culbreth to get their attention. "You both know the basics of team tactics? Everybody strikes at the target the leader designates. And *only* that target."

The levies nodded warily.

That was about as much as you could hope for. The warriors from scattered holdings might be as experienced as those of the Royal Household in individual combat, *but*—

There was no honor in group evolutions, and group training didn't help a man survive the lethal personal duels that occurred in the absence of war. Warriors would practice as teams only if a hard-fisted leader insisted that they do so. The few days before the army set off for Colimore weren't going to make the levies expert in the tactics that would multiply their effectiveness in war.

Though Duke Colimore's warriors weren't likely to be a damned bit better.

"Right," said Hansen. He grimaced unintentionally.

This was going to be a ratfuck, and the campaign that followed was going to be a bigger ratfuck . . . but that's what wars were, individual ratfucks multiplied by the number of combatants.

"I'm going to lead," he continued briskly. Maharg had already slammed his battlesuit closed. "They'll try to split us up, then concentrate to take us one at a time. Block cuts aimed at you, but don't strike till I mark the target."

Culbreth gave Hansen a tight grin and nodded. Lee looked blank, but he might do all right, as well as could be expected.

"If you don't get moving, Hansen," said the marshal coldly, "I'm going to see how long you last without armor."

Hansen made a chopping gesture with both hands. "Remember," he said to his men, "it's practice. And don't lose your cool, because that's the main thing these bastards want."

An arc snapped high from Maharg's right palm.

Hansen slid quickly into his battlesuit. It was quite possible the marshal *would* prod one of the levies if they delayed further. Even at practice power, the arc weapon would sear through flesh as easily as its blue lambency danced in the air.

When Hansen closed the frontal plate over him, his battlesuit switched on. The screens gave him a visual display both brighter and more clear than that of his unaided eyes.

The practice battle had attracted spectators besides the band of slaves who carried the battlesuits. Most of the warriors on the field interrupted their training sessions to watch. A surprising number of others—civilians and off-duty warriors alike—had come out of the city as well.

All right, they'd get something to look at.

"Suit, secure commo for Team White," Hansen ordered. His suit's artificial intelligence set up a lock-out channel for Hansen, Culbreth, and Lee—perhaps the first time the other levies had even heard of such a thing, though the capacity was built into every battlesuit. The AI also tagged the three of them with a white carat on the team's vision screens so that the friendly elements could identify one another instantly.

"Ready?" demanded Maharg. He used his external speaker rather than spread-frequency radio to communicate. Arcs quivered from both his gauntlets, crossing, without quite intersecting in front of his thorax.

Hansen stood in the center of his team with Culbreth to his right. No time now to talk.

"Practice," Hansen ordered his AI. "Cut." A low-power arc spluttered from Hansen's right gauntlet, extending and then condensing to a higher flux density as he scissored his thumb and forefinger.

Maharg and his two professionals stepped forward in unison. The teams were well matched in terms of equipment. The marshal himself wore a suit of royal quality, the creation of a master smith on a long series of good days. Its overall finish was flawless, though Hansen was confident that the armor he'd taken from the Solfygg rover could equal it in terms of offense and protection.

The other four battlesuits were clustered on the boundary between third class and fourth—better than 90% of the suits in the royal army, and inferior only by contrast to the nearly unique armor worn by the team leaders. Hansen doubted that there would be any advantage to his team if Culbreth and Lee swapped equipment with Maharg's two subordinates.

But equipment doesn't fight wars: men do. And these professionals were very fucking good.

"Mark!" Hansen shouted to his AI with his command field centered on the professional fronting Culbreth.

The warrior's image pulsed red in Hansen's display and those of the other levies, but Maharg wasn't waiting for Hansen to drill his subordinates in the fine points of teamwork. Each of the professionals moved against his opposite number.

Maharg slashed at Hansen with his arc extended two meters from his glove. The weapon was too attenuated at that distance to endanger a royal suit even if Hansen hadn't parried the stroke with his own dense flux.

The arcs crossed with a dazzle. Sparks flew and the air itself fluoresced for the instant before Maharg's overloaded weapon died with a sputter. The marshal stepped backward to relight it with a command.

Hansen's screen was set to a 120° wedge to his front. At the left margin of his vision, he saw Lee parry a stroke skillfully and step forward to chop at his opponent in turn. The professional locked arcs with him.

Maharg cut sideways. His weapon took Lee waist high while all the power of the levy's battlesuit was concentrated on beating down the arc of the warrior in front of him.

Circuit breakers tripped. Lee toppled, his battlesuit as cold and dead as a steel coffin. Had the combat been real instead of an exercise, the marshal's arc would lave cut Lee and his armor into a pair of smoldering pieces.

"Strike, Culbreth!" Hansen shouted as he cut at the warrior he'd marked on the displays.

There wasn't any good thinking about the ones who didn't make it through, not while the fighting was going on. Not afterward either, but Hansen did, he always did.

The professional backpedaled and parried, but Hansen's arc licked out three meters to soak up the power available to the lesser suit in a blaze of protective sparks. The man started to fall because his servo motors couldn't react at the expected speed, and Culbreth slashed across his ankles to trip the suit off-line.

One down from either side, but there wasn't any time to think about it because Maharg, an instant too late to save his subordinate, cut at the peak of Hansen's helmet. Hansen barely blocked the stroke with an arc from his left gauntlet.

The roaring *thrum* of the hostile weapon vibrated through Hansen's battlesuit. His displays broke into snow. He kicked, overcoming the inertia of drained servo motors with the strength of his thigh muscles.

Hansen felt but could not hear the clang of his boot striking something; Maharg's suit had been as near overload as his opponent's. The marshal staggered backward and broke the contact.

Hansen's vision display cleared in time to show Culbreth stepping in to stab Maharg—

Not now! Maharg was free!

—with a straight thrust to the belly which Maharg parried. The other professional cut Culbreth down while the levy focused, mind and battlesuit, like a gadfly eager to die so long as it can drink blood first.

Culbreth didn't get his drink of blood this time, but his depowered suit was still falling toward bruising contact with the ground when Hansen dropped the professional who had gotten between Hansen and the marshal.

Hansen stepped onto rather than over the professional and cut at his remaining opponent. This time it was Hansen's arc within a hundred millimeters before the marshal was able to block it.

Their suits crashed together. The physical shock was lost in the electrical roar that bathed both men. All the power the battlesuits sucked from the Matrix snarled out again through the locked right gauntlets as arc cut arc.

"Poplin and Branch!" the marshal shouted through the deafening static. "Reset and join me! You others, you stay where you are."

"Bastard!" Hansen wheezed and lurched sideways to break the contact.

One of Maharg's subordinates was already on his feet with his weapon lighted. The other warrior was getting up also.

Hansen's right arm was in an oven. As good as his battlesuit was, the amount of power being channeled through the gauntlet heated the current pathways and soaked into the flesh of the man inside.

The bastard Maharg was determined to win. He was going

to shut down Hansen's suit even if that meant changing the rules mid-way.

It wasn't dangerous to lose a practice round. You bounced around like the pea in a whistle when your suit hit the ground—bruises, pressure cuts; maybe a bloody nose.

Not really dangerous.

Hansen flashed the arc from his left gauntlet in a long stroke toward the marshal's face, then waved the other arc toward the subordinate on his right as if ready to parry an attack from that side.

Maharg laughed. The sound from his external speaker had a metallic cruelty. He strode in. His two fellows were a step behind to either side.

Hansen flicked the left-hand arc high, clamped it off, and lunged with all his suit's power toward the marshal's left knee.

Three arcs hit him simultaneously, overloading even Hansen's armor in a fingersnap.

And it didn't matter a damn, because of what Hansen's display showed him in the last instant before it went black: his thrust had gotten home. Maharg was dropping also, as sure as a barrel-rider in a waterfall.

Hansen hit face-down. His nose and forehead rapped the vision display. His eyes watered, but he didn't think he was bleeding anywhere from the impact.

He would have liked to rest where he lay, dragging air into his blazing lungs, but the heat cooking his arm was too much to bear.

"Reset," Hansen said to switch the battlesuit live.

The display flooded Hansen's world with light. He wasn't interested in that or even in getting to his feet. He used the suit's servos to roll him over on his back; then he unlatched the frontal plate and shut the power off again.

The outside air was cold and comforting, though it made him shiver uncontrollably. Hansen dragged both his arms from the battlesuit. He tried to lever his body clear and felt his muscles quiver uselessly under the strain.

"You there!" he shouted toward the slaves goggling at the edge of the field.

Hell, his voice was cracking also. He felt like death, like meat through a grinder.

"Come fucking help me out of this coffin!"

Lee and Culbreth had already taken off their battlesuits. They reached Hansen's side before the slaves did and supported him while he pulled his legs from the armor.

Maharg lay on his side. He opened his suit without having to power it up again. His subordinates stepped close, then backed away from the marshal when they saw his face.

"Smart guy," Maharg muttered. He'd cut his lip on a tooth when his suit hit the ground.

Hansen offered him a hand, though god only knew whether Hansen wouldn't just fall back down if the marshal put any weight on him. He hadn't hurt like this since . . .

Since the last time he'd been in action, and nothing had mattered except whether he nailed the ones he was after.

"Naw, that's all right," Maharg rasped. He set his palms on the ground to support his upper body. His biceps were trembling.

"Are you okay, sir?" asked one of his subordinates. Both of them were still suited up.

"Oh, I'm bloody wonderful," the marshal grunted. "Will you get out of that damned armor before you step on somebody?"

He looked at Hansen. "That's a pretty good battlesuit, buddy," he said; paused; and added, "And you're not so bad yourself."

Hansen managed to smile. "When I don't hurt all over," he said, "I'll thank you for the compliment."

Maharg swore and got to his feet in a series of determined movements that didn't quite overbalance and make him fall again.

"Think you can lead the left wing with all the levies when we meet Colimore, Hansen?" he asked.

Hansen nodded. "Yeah," he said. "I think so."

"Then I guess you got the job," the marshal said, as nonchalantly as if they had discussed the time till sunset. His eyes swept the crowd, then focused on Hansen again. "Where did you say you served before you came to Peace Rock, buddy?" he asked.

"I didn't say," said Hansen.

Maharg nodded. "Yeah," he agreed. "That's what I remembered too."

He laughed. "Come on," he said. "We've got three days to train these levies well enough to keep them alive."

Chapter Twenty-three

"Why is he still alive?" Stella demanded as she saw hate as cold as black ice glistening in the eyes of the prisoner bound in the palace courtyard. "Hermann, you're a fool!"

"Don't use that tone on me, woman," the king replied. His tone was too querulous to be an order. "Anyway, you don't understand. His work is—"

Sparrow smiled at the queen.

King Hermann saw the mirrored expressions on their faces, his wife's and the smith's, and looked away quickly. "Get the loot brought in at once!" he shouted to the servants already unloading the baggage mammoths.

The evening sky was pale and streaked by high clouds that threatened an early snow.

"You're the one who doesn't understand, Stella," Hermann resumed, drawing strength from the protectively-wrapped bundles which slaves lifted from the baggage nets. "He's too valuable to lose."

"What did you bring for *me*, Father?" asked Miriam. The princess wore an ermine cape, clasped at the throat with gold and garnets. She flared it open with her elbows to display the gown beneath, scarlet silk brocaded with gold.

"Oh, there'll be wonders for you, darling," Hermann said. "Wait till we get things in—Bran! Don't do—"

The king shouted too late, though the twins rarely paid attention to commands anyway. The twins had stretched a boot thong at ankle height between them, in the path of the burden bearers. A wizened slave in rags tripped, grunted as he tried to catch his balance—

—and crashed forward on his bundle. Metal tinkled into junk despite the layers of deerhide.

"Hell take you!" Crowl shouted as he kicked the fallen slave. The slave tried to rise. Crowl kicked him again.

"I want my things now!" cried the princess.

The remainder of the slaves had frozen. They resumed moving, but they stepped well off the usual path in order to skirt the incident.

The twins had run away. Their laughter chirped from an alcove of the stone-built palace.

"You're a fool, Hermann," Queen Stella repeated with her eyes still locked with the smith's, "if you think a few baubles are worth the risk of leaving this one alive."

"Bring that battlesuit over here at once!" the king shouted. "At once!"

"Daddy!"

"Darling," Hermann said to his daughter desperately, "you'll see it all, every bit of it very soon. And you can have—ah!"

Eight slaves approached, carrying the considerable deadweight load of Sparrow's battlesuit. Platt led them.

"Here is the suit I won for you, Your Excellency," said the outlaw with an unctuous bow.

"Well, open it up, then!" cried the king. He turned to his wife and continued, "You'll see, my dear; you'll see what I mean."

"I've seen armor before, Hermann," said his wife as she watched tight-lipped. The slaves carefully set the battlesuit down on its own legs and held it while Platt opened the frontal plate. "I'm sure it's very nice. It's this *man* that—"

"Mother," snapped Princess Miriam, "can't you make—"

"Hush, dear," said the queen.

While mother and daughter faced one another beneath the slowly darkening sky, King Hermann clambered into the undecorated battlesuit and closed it over him. The edges of the thorax and faceplate mated with the remainder of the suit like layers of rock in a cliff face.

The battlesuit's sensors gave a visual display sharper than the same scene by daylight. The suede lining was initially at air temperature but the suit's environmental control began quickly to warm the pads.

Hermann swung his arms. Normally there was inertia, a lag before the suit's servos converted the operator's motion into movements by the powered armor itself.

Not with this wonder. The whole mass of steel and circuitry

slid through the air as if it were Hermann's own skin.

The slaves who had been holding the armor ducked away. One of them slipped. The king pirouetted like a dancer and kicked out. The armored boot lifted the man a meter in the air, then dropped him like a burst grainsack.

Hermann laughed like a god.

"Look at me, Stella!" his amplified voice thundered. "Look at me!"

He raised his gauntlet and said, "Cut!" to the artificial intelligence controlling the battlesuit. A flaring arc ripped into the air, ten meters, twenty meters—

Hermann continued to narrow the angle between his thumb and index finger, controlling the flux that leaped from them and seared still higher without the arc breaking. "Is this a bauble, Stella?" he shouted. "Is this a—"

He swept the arc down across one of the palace's projecting roof drains, ten meters above him. The stone cracked. Rock fragments and a bright blazing spray of quicklime flew in all directions.

Onlookers flattened and cried out; even the queen flinched. A scullery maid watching from across the courtyard knelt with her eyes closed and her hands over her ears. She screamed like one of the damned until the cook clubbed her silent for fear that the maid would bring royal displeasure on his department.

"—a bauble?"

Stella looked upward. The fractured stone still glowed. Streaks of molten lead from the drainpipe had twisted a meter down the face of the wall before cooling.

"Hermann," said the queen in a distant voice, "get out of that armor before you hurt somebody."

The king unlatched his battlesuit. His face was flushed with the power he had worn. "You do see," he said with assurance. Platt and a slave—both of them hesitant—jumped to Hermann's side to help him out of the armor. "I know you do."

The mirror flashed against Hermann's chest as he was lifted from the battlesuit. Princess Miriam pointed toward it.

"Daddy, what's that?" she demanded. Her voice was thinner than usual because of the way her father's demonstration had frightened her.

"This?" said the king, lifting the loop over his head and showing it to her. "This is a wonder too. Just hold it in your hands and think of anything."

Miriam took the mirror. Her expression was a mix of her normal petulance with anger at the recent fear. Her face cleared. "Oh!" she said. For a moment she was truly beautiful.

"Oh, darling!" her father gasped. Even Queen Stella's face softened.

"It's my room!" Miriam squealed. "Oh! And it changes! It's my garden and it's springtime again! Oh!"

Suddenly a more normal emotion drew the princess' lips back, in a feral grimace. She pressed the mirror against her brocaded bosom. "This is mine, isn't it?" she insisted. "You *have* to give it to me!"

"Of course, darling," said the king, stroking his daughter's ermine shoulder.

"King Hermann," said a voice like a tree splitting with the cold, "don't do that."

They all glanced around. It took a moment to identify the speaker—the prisoner lying on the ground where the slaves had dropped him.

"Not that piece," Sparrow said. His eyes were the same color as the lead had been while it dripped over cold stone.

Miriam continued to clutch the mirror tightly. She backed a step, looking down with horror and disgust.

Hermann turned to his wife and said with the false brightness of unease, "You see, my dear, what a smith like this can mean to the kingdom?"

"He's too dangerous," Stella muttered. Her glance now vibrated between the mirror in Miriam's hand and the face of the man who had made it.

"There won't be any danger," the king wheedled. "We'll put him in the old tower, the citadel my grandfather built, and he'll work for *us*."

"If he has to live," said the queen slowly, "then at least be sure that he stays locked up forever. And—"

Her smile was as cold as winter dawn. "—why don't you just cut his hamstrings, too?"

"Of course, of course," said King Hermann, beaming. He

glanced at Platt and snapped, "Well, what are you waiting for, you?"

The outlaw drew his knife and knelt beside the prisoner. Sparrow tried to kick him. Withies bound the smith's thighs as well as his ankles.

Platt dodged back from the clumsy blow and gripped the prisoner's feet. "Hold him!" Platt shouted.

Half a dozen slaves piled onto the bound smith like dogs on a bear. Sparrow twisted in speechless fury, but Platt waited his time. The knife slid forward as smoothly as a viper's fang. It cut the backs of the supple deerhide boots and withdrew.

Blood followed the knife, but not much blood.

Platt sprang away; "All right," he said. "You can let him go."

Sparrow's muscles bunched like steel hawsers, but his feet lolled loose now that the tendons to them were cut.

Hermann looked at his prisoner in satisfaction—and looked away, because Sparrow's face was the face of a beast.

Chapter Twenty-four

The beast Saburo rode to Hansen's home was a dinohyid that looked like a huge pig. The slim god with oriental features sat doll-sized in his saddle on the creature's bristling, two-meter back.

Hansen waved from his crystal enclosure. When Saburo dropped the dinohyid's reins and sprang lightly from its back, the beast snorted and began to browse morosely. The grass that covered much of the rolling plain was of little interest to it.

"Just thought I'd visit and see how you were getting on," Saburo said as he entered the observation room.

The giant hog the young man rode was at variance with the fussy niceness Saburo projected in all other respects. His clothing was in muted taste, layers of translucent robes which were mostly shades of gray. The black-and-orange tiger stripes of the innermost garment were smothered into a suggestion, not a highlight.

The ensemble had been high fashion in Saburo's section of the Consensus of Worlds—before Saburo came to Northworld as part of an exploration unit and found godhead.

"Moving along," said Hansen. "Can't complain."

Hansen gestured to the image on part of the observation room's windows. There was no point in trying to hide the scene from his visitor. If Saburo was interested enough to come here, he had doubtless been following the events already.

To the east of the building, the dinohyid nuzzled soft-bodied flowers from among the grassblades. On the lower side, the view plunged toward the distant arroyo which was dry except when Hansen's whim brought the rains down in thunderclaps and sheets of sky-splitting lightning.

Between the landscapes, instead of a sideslope, an image of Ritter caressed instruments that probed Krita's dragonfly.

"What's he doing now?" Saburo asked.

Hansen shrugged. "I'm not sure," he said. "Just looking it over so far, I suppose."

He grinned at his visitor. Neither man was big, the way the bulky Ritter or North, almost two meters tall, were; but Saburo looked like a sparrow—

While Hansen was a sparrowhawk, blunt-featured and strong and assuredly a predator.

"After all," said Hansen, "if I knew what he was doing, I wouldn't need him to do it, would I?"

Saburo checked the hang of his robes critically, then smoothed the pleat of the fourth layer between his thumb and forefinger. His hands were slender but corded with sinew.

"That's rather the problem, isn't it?" he remarked as he returned his attention to the engineer. "Having the power to accomplish anything we want doesn't mean that we know what we should want."

Hansen had arranged the image to look down on Ritter from a slight angle, with a panorama of the entire engineering complex beyond as though the walls did not exist. A dozen under-engineers worked in separate alcoves or lounged, chatting or staring at the ceiling—which was very possibly work also. From the number of empty cubicles, as many more of Ritter's personnel were out on the shop floor, supervising construction.

Ritter touched his controls. A beam of cyan light vanished into the ultraviolet, then reappeared as pure magenta as it rotated about the surface of one of the dragonfly's legs. A greatly magnified hologram of the leg's internal structure appeared in the air behind the engineer and in a small screen inset into his console.

"You think that one's good, do you?" Saburo asked without looking at Hansen.

Hansen smiled at the indirection. "He is good, Saburo," he said mildly.

"I don't suppose you'll need him after your game with North is finished," his slender visitor said. "Will you?" Saburo pretended to watch intently as Ritter's console hummed and the holographic information dissolved into its central file for analysis.

Hansen's expression did not change, but his face was suddenly harder as all the muscles beneath the skin grew minusculely more taut. "It's not a game, Saburo," he said evenly.

Saburo fluttered a hand and met Hansen's direct gaze. "Not to you, I'm sure," he said.

"Not to North either," Hansen snapped. "And most particularly not to the people in the West Kingdom."

Saburo could not have been either a coward or a fool and still qualify for a place in an exploration unit. He straightened but he did not back away from his host's sudden cold anger. "Yes," he said, "of course, in the Open Lands. . . . But let's not argue, Commissioner. I wish you well, though—" neither his face nor his voice changed "—with our leader on the other side, I don't know how optimistic you can be about success."

Hansen relaxed with a chuckle. "Yeah, well," he said. "There aren't any guarantees in life, are there?"

Hansen continued to smile, but there was a slight edge in his voice as he went on, "Care to tell me what brought you here?"

"You're so very direct, Commissioner," Saburo said with a brittle laugh. "It's a wonder to me that you don't get along better with poor Penny."

He waved a dismissive hand, a flutter of gray robes, as he saw Hansen's face go cold again. "Please forgive me, we all have our ways. I came because I could use a servant who understood how to make things. I was rather hoping—"

Saburo turned aside, having forced himself as far as his personality could go into flat statement and direct eye contact.

Ritter's probe was now chrome yellow. It wriggled in a narrow line across the dragonfly's saddle. The mass of gray patterns in the engineer's hologram could have been a complex parking lot, but it was more probably a map of the vehicle's microcircuitry.

"I was rather hoping," Saburo continued to the image, "that you might give this servant of yours to me. When you're finished with him, of course."

"He's a human being, Saburo," Hansen said. There was just enough steel in his tone to make sure his visitor would listen and understand what he was being told. "I won't *give* him to anybody."

Robes fluttered.

"But if you want to cut your own deal with Ritter when he and I are through," Hansen continued more mildly, "then I won't have any objections, no."

He grinned and added, "Penny might have ideas of her own, of course. But that's between you two."

"Oh, I'm not worried about our Penny," Saburo said. He gave a high-pitched giggle. "At the rate she goes through men—even if duration mattered to us, I wouldn't be concerned about the wait."

He looked at the engineer and pursed his lips. "One can't really say that Penny has a type, of course. But it still seems a little odd that she'd have any real interest in a dwarf from the Fifth Plane, doesn't it?"

"Maybe she's more interested in what he is than in what body he comes wrapped in," Hansen suggested with no apparent emotional gloss over his words.

"Penny?" said Saburo in amazement.

He stared at Hansen, then giggled again. "Oh, you caught me that time, Commissioner. You see, I can never tell when you're making one of your little jokes."

Saburo looked back at the engineer. Ritter stood and stretched with his fingers locked behind his short, massive neck. His elbow blurred a portion of the hologram which continued to scroll upward in a dense array, meaningless to either Hansen or his visitor.

"The tricky part," said Saburo with a slight narrowing of the eyes, "will be to prevent Penny from disposing of Master Ritter in some final fashion when she gets tired of him. That would be such a waste! He makes things so well."

Chapter Twenty-five

"Well, Sparrow," boomed the king from the polished magnificence of his battlesuit, "what have you made this time?"

"What you asked for, Hermann . . . ," the smith said quietly. "What you expected. No more and no less."

"I wanted him to make something for me," said Princess Miriam. "Has he made something for me?"

Platt tripped near the outer door. The citadel's attendant—the smith's jailer—had been backing to prevent either of the twin boys from getting behind him. He had forgotten the slops bucket which he had yet to empty.

"Pee-ew!" Bran shouted as he scampered back to his parents in false innocence. "See what he did, Mommie?"

"Have him beaten, Mommie!" his brother cried. "Have him beaten!"

"Boys, be quiet," Stella said sharply, seizing each of the brothers by the hair. She held them for only a moment, but long enough for them to try to pull free and start to shriek.

"Platt, you whorespawn," she continued in a voice whose syllables crackled, "clean that up!"

"At once, lady," Platt murmured, bowing and looking around desperately for something to mop with.

"Now!" the queen shouted. "If you have to use your tongue!"

Platt pulled off his shirt and began to scrub. He scooped up the bigger chunks and wrung the rest out into the bucket.

"You see, darling," boasted the king from his armor. "The prison is perfectly safe."

Stella looked around in a mixture of distaste and disapproval. Though it was much as her husband said. . . .

The citadel seemed from the outside to be a large building, but its stone walls were three meters thick. The circular internal cavity was only half the outside diameter; it was bisected now by a barrier of close-set iron bars each of which was as thick as

375

a man's wrist. The ceiling—the floor of the upper level—was five meters high.

Sparrow crouched on a pile of furs on the other side of the bars. A dog whose hind legs were withered lay beside him. Sorted heaps of ore and scrap metals, the raw materials for the smith's work, filled almost all the remaining floorspace. "Well, open the gate, man!" Hermann snarled at the citadel's attendant.

Platt leaped up from his cleaning. There was a look of controlled desperation in his eyes. The key to Sparrow's cell was chained to his waist. Platt fumbled for it, then thrust it into the lock and twisted.

King Hermann used the powered strength of his armor to open the gate against the friction of its massive hinges. The metal shrieked, making everyone in the citadel wince—

Except for Sparrow.

The smith looked from the king, who wore the battlesuit Sparrow had fashioned for himself, to Princess Miriam, who wore the mirror Sparrow had given Krita as a betrothal gift. His face was as still as a broken cliff.

"Get on with it," Hermann ordered.

The six slaves accompanying the king entered the cell one by one, bent under wicker baskets of stone and metal. They knelt to deposit their burdens, then snatched up part of the finished work. This time Sparrow had formed the thorax plates of battlesuits.

The slaves watched the smith warily. They moved with a clumsy quickness, as though they were mucking out a sabertooth's cage. The dog whined softly.

"Not bad," King Hermann murmured as the slabs of armor passed under his protection, though he knew that the pieces were excellent rather than merely good.

Sparrow's work was always excellent.

King Hermann checked his prisoner every week. Any other smith would have required a month to accomplish the amount of work that the slaves were now removing. More important, the consistent quality of Sparrow's work was higher than virtually any rival could have managed no matter *how* long he took.

Princess Miriam watched the procession of slaves with increasing irritation. At last she shrilled, "Father! Why did you bring me here if there's nothing for me?"

"I just wanted you all to see how well I've—" Hermann said.

"Do you want gifts, lady princess?" the smith interrupted. His voice carried over the king's amplified words. "I'll make you a wonder, Princess Miriam. Give me back the mirror, and I'll make you any number of wonders."

Sparrow had calluses on both knees. A shod pair of sticks helped him to stump around his cell, but he could not have walked even with full-length crutches. He could balance for a moment, perhaps, on the crutch tips and the flopping baggage that had been his feet; but not walk.

Never again.

The princess crossed her hands reflexively over the mirror hanging from her neck. "What?" she said. "No! Make me things anyway. After all, this isn't any good to you. It would just show you where you can't go."

"This is what you have him making?" the queen asked Hermann in puzzlement.

"I have him making battlesuits," the king explained. "But not all the parts at one time. You—"

"Make him give me more jewelry, Father!" Miriam interrupted. "—see how careful I'm being."

"Will you let me go if I make a bauble for your daughter, King Hermann?" the smith asked. His voice was calm and his face still; but there was a gleam of frozen Hell in Sparrow's eyes.

The last of the slaves left the cell carrying the prisoner's slops bucket.

The king clashed the gate closed. "Don't be stupid," he muttered, quietly so that Princess Miriam would not hear him over the clang.

While the adults looked at Sparrow, Brech again overturned the bucket into which Platt had been mopping. The attendant grabbed the full bucket to prevent it from suffering the same fate. In theory, Platt was still a noble. In practice . . .

But he was alive; and he had his legs.

"I don't see why you worry, majesty," Platt said with a chuckle. "Even if Sparrow here did build an entire battlesuit, it still wouldn't help him walk!"

He laughed, and they all laughed at the despair on Sparrow's face.

Chapter Twenty-six

The only thing that kept Hansen from open despair was his knowledge that the Colimore army a kilometer away was no better prepared for battle than were the levies Hansen led.

Intellectual awareness wasn't the same as emotional belief. Hansen believed, whatever his mind told him, that warriors on royal left wing—his wing—were going to charge without any discipline at all and be sliced six ways from Sunday by a Colimore phalanx.

Freemen mounted on ponies galloped back from a sortie toward the Colimore lines. It had been more bravado than reconnaissance. One of the riders lifted his curved bronze horn from its neck sling and blew a trill of meaningless excitement.

"God help us all," Hansen muttered as he stood in his battlesuit with the frontal plate still open.

Culbreth was at Hansen's side, already suited up. "Sir?" he boomed. "The marshal says, ah, would you get into your armor so he could talk to you."

Maharg had said to tell his left wing commander to get his thumb out of his ass, there was a job to do—if the marshal had been so polite.

Maharg was right. Hansen swung his battlesuit closed.

"Suit," he ordered to switch on his artificial intelligence. "Schematic overlay, opposing forces." He paused, then added, "Thirty percent mask."

"Hansen," snapped the command frequency in Maharg's voice, "what do you make their numbers as being?"

The same thing your suit's AI does, Marshal.

"A hundred and forty-six, Maharg," Hansen said, keeping his voice cool. "We've got a clear margin of forty warriors. That's not the problem."

The normally diamond-sharp visual display of Hansen's battlesuit was now covered by a thin overlay which showed the two armies disposed across the terrain. At the edge of the screen, the artificial intelligence tabulated the relative strength of the forces, both total and by class of battlesuit.

"There's no possible way Colimore could hire more than fifty warriors!" Maharg said sharply. "Not if he sold the whole bloody duchy."

Maharg had chosen to let off steam with Hansen, a levy from nobody-knew-where, on a closed push where no one else could hear them. It was one of the greatest compliments anyone had ever paid Hansen.

It also spoke pretty well for the marshal's ability to judge men.

"We knew Solfygg was behind all this, Maharg," Hansen said. "We've still got them by numbers, and I think we're generally better man-for-man, even my crew."

Hansen kept his tone that of the calm advisor; a man whose guts *weren't* a gray turmoil at the thought of leading warriors whose idea of group action was persuading a scullery wench to pull a train before everybody was too drunk to stand up.

"Generally better, I'll grant," the marshal said. "But my read-out says there's twelve Class I suits on their left flank. *Twelve* royal suits."

"Yeah," said Hansen. "That's the thing that bothers me, too."

It was going to rain before the day was out. Earlier storms had beaten down the prairie's autumnal grasses, though tussocks of brown and gray and remembered green still remained. The field, a traditional battle area for the generations before the Peace of Golsingh, was nearly flat, but visibility would still be tricky.

The Solfygg armor was one of the things that bothered Hansen.

"It had better bother you," Maharg grumbled. His voice had lost the particular harshness of concern Hansen had noticed at the beginning of the discussion. "I was expecting to be able to give your wing some support. I don't know how quick I'll be able to take care of those royal suits."

"Look, my boys'll hold up their end, never fear," Hansen said, his voice sharp with pride despite himself. "You can call us levies if you want to, but if we weren't the damned-best warriors in our households, our lords would've sent somebody else!"

And that was flat truth.

Hansen suddenly realized how much he cared about the men he led . . . and how much he hoped they wouldn't let him down.

Horns and bugles blew across the field. Thirty or forty mounted freemen armed with lances and crossbows advanced through the Colimore line. The warriors in battlesuits remained motionless for the moment.

Hansen's overlay showed that the Colimore warriors were spaced irregularly, like beads strung by an infant. Duke Ontell was using his freemen to entice the royal forces to advance first.

The royal army wasn't in parade-ground order either, but its four-to-three advantage in numbers gave Hansen a feeling of comfort as he glanced through the overlay—

So long as he ignored the twelve Solfygg warriors who stood out from the Colimore left wing like the teeth of a saw. Those champions wore suits as good as Hansen's own . . . or just about anybody else's.

A hundred or more royal freemen charged to meet the Colimore riders. The latter immediately turned tail and galloped back toward their own lines.

"All right," said Maharg in a tone of calm determination. "This is as good a time as any, I suppose."

Hansen visualized the marshal as he stood in his armor at the center of the right wing. Maharg's face would be set, his eyes knowing. The marshal was betting numbers against quality, and he was perfectly aware of the casualties that always resulted from that trade-off.

"Hey, buddy," Hansen said softly.

"What, then?"

"That's a lot of royal suits," Hansen said. "More than you've seen in one place before, probably more than anybody has. Don't push. If they come to us, they'll get separated and you can handle them just like you did me on the practice ground."

Maharg snorted. "Who's the marshal?" he demanded. "You or me?"

And then he said, "Thanks. We're going to take care of these bastards."

Or die trying—

But that thought was lost in Maharg's command over the general frequency, "Warriors, remember to keep your line and hold your intervals. All forces, advance!"

Bellowing with amplified enthusiasm, the royal army strode forward. The warriors' battlesuits sizzled blue halos in the humid air as they went forth to kill and die.

Chapter Twenty-seven

Ritter was pacing back and forth behind his console when Hansen appeared in the workroom. The engineer took the staccato, frustrated strides of a caged carnivore.

"Thought I'd drop in and say hi," Hansen said.

His ultramarine trousers and cream-colored shirt made him look like one of Ritter's underlings. The pistol he carried was part of the uniform also. The weapon was in a heavy flap holster very different from the breakaway unit Hansen had worn against the Lomeri.

"Drop in and check up on me, you mean," the engineer snarled.

If I wanted to check on you—

Hansen waved his left hand. An image of Ritter in his laboratory hung in front of the man whom it pictured. The color was full and rich, the resolution crystalline. The image's face went blank, then grimaced in embarrassment as though it were a non-reversing mirror.

Hansen waved the image away. "Hi, Master Ritter," he said with a slight smile.

"Hell, I'm sorry," the engineer said.

He slapped the chair built into the console. It spun on its gimbals, but the blow wasn't a serious one, just a flick of irritation. "I'm not usually that dumb. Hell, maybe I'm just too dumb to do your job, Colonel Hansen."

Hansen shrugged. "I doubt that," he said.

He sat down on the bed of a milling machine, shifting a tray of jigs carefully so that they didn't fall onto the floor. "Anyway," he continued, "I'm no colonel. Just Hansen. Or—"

He smiled. "—Nils, if you want to, but that formation's not much in favor on Northworld, I've found."

Ritter gave a deep sigh, not so much relaxing as expressing a willingness to relax. He seated himself with his back to the console's screens and controls. "Penny calls you 'Commissioner' sometimes," he said. "It seemed to mean 'colonel,' in the ranks here."

" 'Commissioner' was . . . ," Hansen said.

He quirked a corner of his mouth, trying to hook the correct words. "That was before I came to Northworld. I was a . . . type of policeman. For oh, well; violence, I suppose you could say."

"You were Civic Patrol?" the engineer translated, cautiously trying to avoid contempt.

Hansen grinned. "Close enough," he said. "It wasn't a high-status job where I came from either, Master Ritter. But maybe not quite as low as it is here, where military elites run the keeps and the police only have authority over the laboring class."

Ritter shrugged. "Well," he said, "none of that stuff matters anyway, does it?"

"Status doesn't matter?" Hansen said. "Balls."

He laughed, stood up, and stretched. The knuckles of his left hand bumped the suction hood that would close over the workpiece during operations. "You wouldn't say that after you told Lord Greville to go piss up a slope."

Hansen's smile was as hard as the diamond cutters of the milling machine. "Or," he added, "if one of your party girls said the equivalent to you."

Ritter grimaced at the backs of his hands. "You know what I mean," he said. "*You* know that getting the job done is the only important thing. And I've hit a stone wall on your job."

"What's the problem?" Hansen asked equably. "I don't know jack shit about the hardware, but you do; and talking helps a lot of times."

The engineer shrugged. "Okay," he said. "I can't find the bloody power supply. And I know there is one, because I've seen the unit work."

"You made a liar out of me," Hansen said. "I *can* help there."

He got up again, smiling at an unexpected win. "The dragonflies draw their power direct from imbalances in the Matrix. Same with the battlesuits. You remember them?"

Hansen waved his hand. Men in armored suits weighing a hundred kilos and more moved uphill at a swift, staggering pace toward another similarly-equipped force. Blue radiance sprang from the warriors' gauntlets. The lines crashed together in a blaze of arcs on protective forcefields like the lightning-lit core of a tornado.

"The problem those men have running," Hansen continued, "isn't the weight, it's the control circuits. There's lag time between moving your leg and the servos obeying, especially in the cheap suits."

Ritter swore and pounded the console behind him. He used the side of his hand, but there was nothing petty about the blow. He stood up again and walked around the console to put his back to his visitor.

"Problem with that?" Hansen asked mildly. His lips were the only portion of his face that moved.

"Look," said the engineer, "I know the Matrix exists, I've, I've been in it. But—"

He turned. "It *doesn't* exist for me, do you see? It's bloody magic!"

"Oh, yeah," said Hansen. He stepped forward, almost gliding, and put his arm around the engineer's shoulders. "Yeah, I do know what you mean. But look, friend—"

He waited until Ritter met his eyes, then continued, "It's what we've got. Pretending reality doesn't exist can get you killed in my line of work. Or yours."

Ritter began to laugh. "Civic Patrol!" he said.

Hansen laughed also. "Hey, man, try me one-on-one with your Lord Greville and we'll see who has a better idea which end of a gun goes bang. Is it my fault that your cops only carry nets and clubs?"

"Okay," Ritter said, "I'll build your magic horse, now that I'm sure I've got all the pieces." The laughter had broken his mood into good humor. "Reverse engineering isn't as easy as it looks. People don't realize that."

"If it was easy," Hansen replied, "I wouldn't have had to come to you, right?"

"So you figure I'm the best, do you?" the engineer said, half mocking but half in justifiable certainty of his own worth.

"You're the best I could find," Hansen agreed. "Of what you do, I mean."

He waved an image to life in the air before them. "In the Open Lands," he went on, "there are smiths who use the Matrix to create things. Some of them might be as good in their way as you are in yours."

In the image, a big man in a filthy garment lay on a bed of furs. His legs were scabbed, and his feet sprawled like a seal's flippers.

The viewpoint slid downward to cut a slice through the pile of gravel and metal arranged beside the man. Solid matter shifted, then re-formed from chaos into intricate patterns of circuitry and sheathing.

Hansen rotated the image viewpoint to a close focus on the man's face. His mouth lolled open, and the pupils of his slitted eyes were rolled up out of sight.

"His name is Sparrow," Hansen said. "And he's probably as good as you are."

Chapter Twenty-eight

Platt clutched the flaccid wineskin in both hands and said, "You know, Sparrow, I don't see what good you get outa making all this for King Hermann."

The smith shuddered on his pallet of furs.

"Hey, you!" Platt shouted. He pounded his hand on a bar. The metal rang. The attendant cursed the pain in his hand. He picked up his stool.

Sparrow's dog lay with its head across its master's belly. The beast growled and bared its teeth without lifting its head. Sparrow was still in the outer fringes of his trance, but his hand stroked the dog back to silence.

The crippled animal tracked Platt with hate-filled eyes.

Platt rang his stool across the bars in a clatter like a bridge falling. "Hey!" he bellowed. "Hey, you legless bastard!"

Sparrow's eyes snapped fully open. For an instant, the smith's expression was the same as that of his dog. His face calmed in quick stages, as though control overlaid hatred in a series of nictitating membranes.

Platt stepped back from the bars and belched. He tried to squeeze another dribble from the stolen wineskin. Scarcely enough remained to wet the tip of his tongue. He threw the container down in anger.

Sparrow stroked the head and neck of his dog. "What are you doing with wine, Platt?" the smith asked. His tone held no more emotion than the sound of a distant landslide.

"None of your business, is it?" Platt shrilled. The question had surfaced fear in his drunken mind like a shark slicing up from murky seas.

He turned and picked up the wineskin, then paused for a moment to regain his balance. At last he plunged the container deep within his slops bucket. It would stay there unnoticed until he had a chance to empty the bucket unobserved in the community cesspool.

Platt stared again at the prisoner he attended. "What I wanna know . . ." he said.

He blinked and glanced down at his hands. After a moment, he wiped them on his breeches.

"What I wanna know," he resumed as he traced the thread of his intention, "is why you do it? Make the stuff. Seeings they treat you like shit."

Platt belched again. He caught the bars to keep from falling down.

The dog growled. Platt stared owlishly at his hand, then removed it with care from the metal.

You didn't cling to the bars of a bear's cage. Not even if the bear had been hamstrung.

"Seein' as they treat you worsen 'n they treat me," the attendant muttered. "And they treat *me* like shit."

Sparrow sat up; his dog perked sharply onto its haunches and front legs. It was not immediately obvious that either of them was crippled.

The smith smoothed the dross away from the piece on which he had been working in his trance. Some of the rocks crumbled to grit and dust as he touched them.

Bits of the crystals forming the rocks' structure had been rearranged into the core of a metal/ceramic/metal sandwich: the left calf of a battlesuit. Scrap metal—a broken scythe, a worn plow coulter, a grill from the palace kitchen which long use had warped and thinned—had been added to the pile. Most of the metal had vanished into the sheathing of the workpiece which Sparrow withdrew from the dross and eyed critically.

"You think I should refuse to work for King Hermann, do you?" the smith asked in a voice too flat to be calm.

"I didn't say that!" Platt cried.

He hadn't said it, the wine had been talking; and anyway, he'd deny the words with the experience born of a life of lying denials.

Sparrow set the workpiece down and laughed. It was not a pleasant sound. "Are you worried I'll tell the king?" he said. "Who would believe *me?*"

Of course, who would believe that crippled husk?

"And besides," the smith continued with a smile as brutal as his laughter, "you're too useful to be chopped for what you spew when you're drunk. A slave would run away if they kept him like they do you—"

The smile again. "—but the king knows that if you ever leave the protection of his palace, there's a hundred men waiting to kill you in the slowest way they can think of. See how useful you are?"

Sparrow's fingers caressed the upper ball of the armor's knee joint. He would form the thigh piece in a few hours. The join would be so perfect that only the creator himself would know where one section stopped and the other began.

But even Sparrow needed rest and food.

He looked in his bowl for the remainder of his noon feeding. The crust and porridge were only a memory.

A hog thighbone had arrived the night before with some fat and skin. The bone remained, lying between the dog's forepaws. The animal's jaws had worried but could not crack the dense bone. He whined hopefully as his master lifted the thighbone.

"Tell them I need more food," Sparrow said. "The Matrix is cold. . . ."

Sparrow's mouth trembled with the memory. He controlled it. "If they want the work out of me, they'll have to feed me better."

"You'll get whatever the king chooses to send you, crippled scum!" Platt cried in an attempt to assert the authority both men knew he lacked.

"They will send me more food," Sparrow said.

His right thumb pressed against the ball of the hog thigh which snapped like an arc breaking. The shaft of the bone splintered between his palm and fingers.

"Not because they love me," the smith continued with his eyes focused on his attendant's. "But because they want what I make."

Sparrow smiled. He opened his right palm and gave one of the bone fragments to his dog. He put another in his own mouth and began to suck the marrow.

"So they must feed me," he concluded.

"I . . ." Platt said. He was suddenly very queasy. He could steal wine only rarely, and there was no place to hide a part-finished container. He'd drunk his spoils too quickly.

"You tell them yourself when they come next," Platt said in the bitterness of sudden self-realization. "They won't listen to me, whatever I say."

Sparrow picked out another splinter for the dog. It growled in anticipation.

"You want to know why I work for King Hermann?" the smith said with his usual lack of affect. "Because in the Matrix—"

Platt knelt and began to vomit, onto the floor and onto the tumble of his own bedding. The spasms wracked him as though they were trying to bring his bowels up through his throat.

"—I'm not a slave any more, Platt," Sparrow continued.

The smith smiled, but his dog drew away from him with a sudden yelp of concern.

"In the Matrix, I'm free," said Sparrow in a harsh, terrible voice. "And there are no walls around me!"

Chapter Twenty-nine

"Hansen?" Ritter asked suddenly. "Can you take me outside the walls?"

The laboratory held numerous duplicated pieces from the dragonfly, though the only set obvious to an outsider was the four legs. They were mounted upside down on a testbed which flexed them rapidly in three planes. The hydraulic pump driving the test rig whined, but the articulated legs performed without complaint.

"Sure," Hansen said, shrugging in his loose blouse. The local fashion was so comfortable that he'd begun wearing similar garb back home. "The only thing is . . ."

Hansen's voice trembled. His mind reviewed the muzzle of the lizardman's weapon and the fireball enveloping the vegetation as he and Ritter shifted from the dimension. "We're going to be carrying more gear this time," he continued, "if you want to go back to visit the Lomeri. Forcefield projectors, for a start."

The engineer looked at him in honest surprise. "Why on earth would I want to do that?" he asked.

To prove you weren't really frightened by what scared the hell out of you and me both.

"Why does anybody do anything?" Hansen replied aloud.

Ritter shook his head in amazement. "Well," he said, "all I want to do is see what's out there—"

He reached behind him and touched a switch on the console. The control replaced laboratory walls with a panorama of lake and vegetation. A number of large animals sported in the shallow water.

Laboratory equipment and some feed lines had been run along rather than within the walls. They stood out in eerie contrast to the natural scene.

"—under an open sky."

"Sure, no problem," Hansen said, checking his holstered pistol by reflex to be sure that the flap was unsnapped. Hansen had been practicing with the clumsy rig, not that he expected ever to need the weapon. "Ah—it's raining out there just now."

"I won't shrink," Ritter said. He flipped up his armrest to access an array of hidden controls. "Just a minute while I seal the doors so that nobody stumbles in while we're gone."

"Don't bother," said Hansen. He put an arm around the engineer's shoulders. "I'll bring you back the same time we leave. Only you'll be—"

Reality became two-dimensional, then flip-flopped into infinite pathways—

And shifted back along a different plane of reality, into soft ground and the smell of living things.

"—a little damp," Hansen concluded. It wasn't so much rain as a mugginess so thick that droplets condensed out of the air.

"Oh . . . ," said Ritter. He looked around slowly.

Keep Greville rose behind them, a great blue hemisphere of force that hissed in the damp atmosphere. At its peak, the dome's vague glow merged with that of the mid-morning sun.

The red, gritty soil supported a knee-high cover of grasses and broad-leafed vegetation. There were many palm trees in clusters of two or three. Ritter walked over to the nearest. Something with long, fawn-colored fur scampered up the tree as the engineer approached; it chittered its irritation from among the fronds.

Ritter patted the treetrunk. The surface was as coarse as concrete, but where concrete would have been cool to the touch, the bark was warm.

"I used to spend a lot of time out here when I was a boy," he said. "I sneaked out with the creche leader's pistol in case I ran into any of the carnivores that hang around the keep's waste outlets. Shot a few of them too, though just when I had to."

The sky was clearing. When one of the hornless rhinos suddenly galloped from the lake, the spray its short legs stirred up made a sudden rainbow. The beast must have been playing, because it immediately plunged back in with its fellows.

"I was afraid the creche leader would notice the missing shells, you see," Ritter continued softly. He explored the bark with his fingertips while his eyes followed the rhino's antics. "But he never checked the magazine. Not once."

"Not many people go outside the keep, then?" Hansen asked.

He was keeping a careful watch around them. The carnivores of Plane Five weren't any great shakes compared to those on Plane Two with the Lomeri—or in the Open Lands, for that matter. But something that weighed upwards of fifty kilos, with long jaws and a nasty disposition, was worth blasting before it got within fang range.

"Not except for the soldiers," Ritter agreed.

He stepped around the palm, looking up toward the chittering. The animal making the sound retreated around the trunk. Hansen, standing still, got a good view of a little rodent with black rings on its slender tail.

"The soldiers are always in armored vehicles," the engineer added. He walked slowly in the direction of the lake. "So that isn't really getting outside either."

The rhinoceroses noticed Ritter's approach. One barked a challenge, then ducked under the surface. In a moment, all of the half-tonne animals had vanished. Regular wheezing from the beds of water hyacinth indicated that the rhinos had not gone far.

"There's no *need* to go out, after all, though it's not prohibited for most people," Ritter said. "There just isn't much reason to bother. The colonizing vessels had efficient hydroponic systems, and we've improved the technique since then."

Mud squished onto the uppers of the engineer's short boots. He changed direction slightly to parallel the shore. Hansen stayed a few steps inshore of Ritter, though even so there were occasional wet spots to hop over.

"But I liked the outside," Ritter continued.

He bent and plucked a spray of something fernlike, though Hansen wasn't sure it was really a fern. "And you know, Hansen, the Lords Greville—this one and his uncle—haven't allowed me out of the keep in twenty years. They were afraid—"

Ritter savagely stripped the leaves from the frond he held, leaving only the bare stem. "—that something might happen to me. Even a kidnapping attempt by another keep."

"You're good enough they need to worry about losing you," Hansen said evenly. "I guess you were good even twenty years ago."

Hansen felt uneasy. He slipped the pistol up and down in its holster, but it wasn't the approach of anything tangible that his subconscious feared.

"Oh, you bet I was," the engineer said. He squatted and poked at the soft sod, twisting until his finger had almost disappeared. "Do you know . . ."

Ritter's voice trailed off without completing the question. He rose and wiped the muck from his finger against the bole of a deciduous tree.

"I'm treated well," he continued harshly. "There's almost nothing in Keep Greville that I couldn't have if I demanded it. But do you know, Hansen . . . do you know what it's like to be unfree?"

The back of Hansen's neck prickled. He heard his voice saying, "I don't suppose I've ever been free, Ritter. Surely not before I came to Northworld . . . and even now. . . ."

Hansen gripped a sapling slender enough for him to close his hands about its trunk. He wasn't trying to experience its nature, the way the engineer had been doing ever since he left the constructed reality of the keep.

Hansen just needed something safe against which anger could work his muscles.

"Look, I'm . . ." he said. His hands went white and mottled with the sudden strain.

"I always did my job, the job right in front of me," he said. His voice sounded like gravel sliding through a sieve. "Now I can do anything, *anything*. And it scares me."

Hansen's whole body shuddered. He released the tree and hugged his arms to his body. His eyes focused on Ritter, but all that entered his conscious mind from the sight was a vague impression of the bigger man's concern.

"I look at the others," Hansen said, "the other *gods*, and they're caricatures, Ritter, they're warping themselves into one little slice of whatever they musta been when they came here. Look at Penny! She's got all the power there is, and look what she does with it."

"Ah, Hansen . . ." the engineer said.

"So what I do is pretend that nothing's changed for me, do you see?" Hansen went on. "Pretending that I'm no more than what I used to be when I, when, when they sent me here."

It had come on him unexpectedly, a combination of what the engineer meant as a rhetorical question and the process of watching the other man peel off the layers hiding his past life. Hansen knew he was speaking loudly, because dozens of birds exploded from the undergrowth in panic, their wingfeathers clattering. He couldn't stop.

He didn't want to be talking about this, he didn't want to think about this; but he couldn't stop.

"I pretend I'm just a cop," he said. "Just a troubleshooter. The one they call in when the job's going to mean serious violence, do you see? Because there's nobody in the human universe who's better at *that* than Commissioner Nils Hansen!"

His hands were shaking. His whole body was shaking.

Ritter wrapped Hansen in his muscular arms. He held him, gently but as firmly as a crash harness, until the multiple spasms passed.

Hansen drew a deep breath. He began to laugh. He felt the engineer's arms tighten again.

"No," he said, "no, it's all right, Master Ritter. I'm okay now."

Ritter released him cautiously, as though he were afraid that the slighter man would jump for his throat as soon the engineer's grip slackened.

Hansen squeezed Ritter's shoulder affectionately. "Hey, look," he said, "it's really all right. I'm as crazy as the rest of them, I guess . . . but I'm under control. That's all that really matters, isn't it?"

The sun blazed down, making the atmosphere even more humid as heat lifted water from the foliage and the surface of the lake. The rodent in the palm tree had at last grown silent.

"Let's get me back to my lab," said Ritter. "I've got a dragonfly to make."

Chapter Thirty

When he saw Bran and Brech at the citadel doorway, Sparrow took from beneath his bedding the piece he had made in anticipation.

"Hey!" cried Platt in alarm. "Nobody's supposed to come here unless the king brings them himself."

"Here, boys," Sparrow called from his cell. "You want me to make something for you. Isn't that right?"

King Hermann might or might not be trailing a few meters behind his sons. Even if the king was present and Sparrow's plan could go no further forward for the moment, a hint of wonderful toys would bring the twins back like dogs scenting a bitch in heat.

"Shut up, you!" snarled Platt.

The attendant snatched up his half-full slops bucket. He went on in a voice compounded of fear, hatred, and a horrible oily subservience, "Now, boys, you know your father wouldn't want you to be up here with this nasty man, would he?"

Light danced on Sparrow's right palm, within the cage of his fingers.

"Oh!" said Bran and kicked Platt on the ankle.

The attendant yelped. The bucket swung on its handle, splashing out a little of its contents.

The twins ran up to the bars. "He threw *shit* on us!" Brech caroled. "We'll tell Daddy he threw shit on us!"

The crippled dog edged back against the stone wall. It bared its teeth and growled at so deep a level that only a hand on the beast's chest would have disclosed the vibration.

"Yes . . ." Sparrow said. He rose to his knees and stumped a little closer to the bars. The barrier was still a hand's breadth beyond his reach. "Look what I made for you boys."

The smith opened his fingers. Two beads of yellow light began to rotate in separate figure-eight patterns around a common center.

Sparrow cupped his hand behind them as if to give the insubstantial display a push. The speed of rotation increased, and the beads drifted toward the twins.

"Ooh, no, please . . ." the attendant moaned. He clutched the bucket to his chest as if it were treasure being snatched from a holocaust.

"Ooh . . . ," said the twins together.

The spinning beads reached the barrier. Part of the diameter of the circle they described passed through a gap between bars, but the rest of their motion took them into the iron itself. The light vanished while the beads were within solid matter, but they reappeared unchanged on the other side of the bars. They continued to slide forward.

"Please," whimpered Platt. "Please, please. . . ."

Bran and Brech snatched simultaneously at Sparrow's creation. Neither of the twins quite touched it, though their hands collided where the thing of light had been a moment before. The object bounced a meter into the air and continued in roughly its previous direction, sinking slowly.

"There . . ." murmured Sparrow in satisfaction. "Isn't that a wonder, boys? Isn't that a marvel for you?"

The twins ignored him as they squealed in pursuit of the gleaming construct. Brech leaped high to grab the object. He only succeeded in swatting it toward Platt.

The attendant stutter-stepped to the right, then the left, and finally threw up one of his hands with a shriek. At the moment the spinning lights should have touched Platt's splayed fingers, the object's rotation increased to a blur and it shot straight up.

The lights vanished into the high wooden ceiling.

"He broke it!" Bran cried in genuine fury. "He *broke* it!"

Wailing in anger, both the young princes began to kick and pummel Platt. The terrified attendant yelped and broke for the outside door.

"I'll get it!" he called, instinctively reaching for an explanatory lie even in a moment of panic.

The slops bucket hit the doorframe and spilled half its contents. Platt dropped the container onto his bedding and continued to run. The children started to follow him.

"Here, boys!" Sparrow called.

Brech turned. His face was screwed into an expression of inhuman rage. Bran took another step and looked back also.

"I have things much lovelier than that, my royal darlings," the smith said. His husky whisper was as terrible as the arc ripping from a battlesuit.

"Show me!" Brech cried. He ran to the barrier and hammered at the gate with his bare hands. Iron rang on iron, nearly drowning out the boy's repeated, "Show me now!"

Sparrow's dog began to howl. The beast's eyes were slits; it thrashed its tail against the stone.

"Hush, lad," the smith said. He stepped forward on his knees, over a pile of brass and pewter scrap, and stroked Brech's head.

"Don't touch us, you slave!" Bran shrieked. He jumped to the barrier and clawed at Sparrow's hand where it lay on Brech's fine, fair hair.

"Ah, my error, darling boys," Sparrow said, snatching his hand away and raising it, palm outward in token of submission.

"Show us, then!" Bran demanded. "The toy!"

"Shh . . . ," Sparrow warned, gesturing toward the outer door with an index finger as solid as a pick handle. "Don't let him hear or he'll break the new toys too, don't you see?"

"My daddy will *fix* that dirty slavebastard," Brech said with grim certainty.

"No, we'll do better than that," the smith warned. The light in his eyes would have chilled any adult who saw it; but there were no adults to watch, only a dog and two young boys . . . and the crippled dog lolled its tongue out like that of a wolf closing on fawns.

"If you come back tonight, boys," Sparrow continued, "Platt will be asleep, and I'll show you things that not even your father and mother can yet imagine. But you'll have to do something for me, all right?"

Though he spoke without haste, Sparrow glanced frequently toward the door, afraid that his attendant would return at any moment.

"We don't have to do anything!" Bran announced shrilly.

"He wants us to let him out," his brother said. "He wants us to take the key from that old slavebastard."

"No, no-no, my lads," the smith said. "Where would I go—"

he gestured toward his feet, as loose as the tongue of his dog "—a cripple like me?"

"We could make Platt give us the key," Bran said to his brother. "We could have Daddy beat him if he didn't."

"Not the key, lads," Sparrow said with a face like vengeance become a god. "Only wine, only a little skin of wine, that you can hide in the kitchen midden at dusk, is that not so? You can steal a skin of wine and hide it?"

Brech sniffed with simulated maturity. "Sure," he said. "We can get through the ventilator into the buttery. We do it *lots* of times."

"Oh, I thought you might, lad," the smith whispered. "It was a thing I thought you might do. And then—"

There was shadow on the doorjamb. Platt was returning.

"—come to me at midnight," Sparrow concluded quickly. "Not before, but at midnight, and you'll see wonders."

Platt peeked around the jamb. "What are you doing?" he demanded. "You get away from those boys, you cripple!"

"Run along, lads," Sparrow said in a voice as bright as the sun on a glacier. "And remember what I told you."

"What?" the attendant demanded in renewed panic. "What did you tell them?"

The twins darted past him, gurgling their delight at a plot and the promise. Bran kicked at Platt as he went by, but the little boot only brushed the attendant's jerkin.

"What . . . ?" Platt repeated, looking out the door after the twins' disappearing forms.

"Oh, they're lovely lads, Platt," Sparrow said. "And so generous. Would you believe that they offered to me a skin of wine?"

Platt's head snapped around. "What?"

"Yes, a skin of wine," the smith continued. He spoke in nearly a falsetto, so high and thin was his voice. "They'll hide it at dusk in the kitchen midden, so that when you go to fetch my supper tonight you can bring that as well."

He gave the attendant a great, twisted smile. "Is that not generous, Platt?" he said. "To offer wine to a crippled slave like me?"

Platt laughed; first a sharp hark of sound, then cackling, echoing peels of mirth.

"Did the gods make you such a fool, Sparrow?" the attendant said after he regained control of his merriment. "Don't you know that stolen goods have no owner but the one who holds them?"

"Ah, but the lads mean the wine for me to drink, Platt," the smith said softly as his eyes gleamed with his own hellish laughter.

"Maybe they do," Platt announced. "But *I* mean it for my own throat!"

He began to bellow his amusement again.

"If that's what you really want, my deserving friend," Sparrow whispered as his hand stroked the ears of his crippled dog, "then I'll see that you get it."

Chapter Thirty-one

A Colimore warrior, chasing honor or pursued by it, got five meters ahead of his fellows and died as three arcs slashed his battlesuit to sparks and molten metal.

"An omen!" Hansen bellowed over the general push. "Peace and Prandia! An omen!"

Not because he believed in omens, but it was a good thing to shout to his troops. Anyway, it was one fewer opposing warrior and a champion besides—though his suit hadn't been good enough to absorb the simultaneous strokes of levies who had, after all, learned something about teamwork in the past few days.

And besides, anybody who needed luck to live knew that omens *did* count, at least when they were in your favor.

The battlefield stuttered into electrical brilliance. Clumps of sodden grass began to burn, sending drifts of smoke across the fighters like veils of dirty cobweb.

No one else on Hansen's wing of the army fell. Warriors probed one another at a few meters' distance, steeling themselves to lunge close to a range at which their arcs could be effective—

And where their opponents' weapons could gut them like trout, giving them just enough time to scream in sizzling agony as they died.

The lines eased together, as nearly parallel as the rolling prairie and variables of human nature allowed. Every third man or fourth stood a little in advance of his fellows, twitching his arc toward an enemy who was doing the same, just out of effective reach.

Hansen, with Culbreth to his right and Arnor on the left, followed three paces behind the center of his line. He was trying to keep the whole wing in view on his overlay while he continued to step forward. He paused when the warriors ahead of him stopped advancing. There were commanders, and there were leaders. Nils Hansen had never been very good at ordering other men to go die.

"Suit, straight visuals!" Hansen ordered his AI, clearing the display. "Team, follow me!" he added as he drove forward between two levies.

He wasn't really confident that Culbreth and Arnor would follow him. He was pretty sure that he could handle alone what was about to happen, pretty sure, but he'd seen too many men die in too many places to believe that he was invulnerable either.

A pair of Colimore champions met motion with motion, striding forward behind points of dense blue flame.

What happened didn't matter as much to Hansen as the fact he was moving now and not just watching.

The arc from Hansen's right gauntlet parried one stroke and started to burn back toward the helmet of the warrior who made it. Hansen's weapon paled to a fraction of its initial density as the other warrior slashed at his ribs and Hansen's suit redirected power to the defensive screen.

Culbreth thrust at the warrior whose arc Hansen was holding. The man's defenses fluoresced a microsecond before the angel painted over his thorax went black and the steel beneath burned.

Instead of doubling Culbreth's stroke, Arnor cut at the warrior whose arc lit a coruscant blaze from Hansen's screen. That wasn't the way Hansen had trained them, but it was all right, the Colimore man stepped back—

Hansen's left side burned like the wall of a furnace, but the servo motors had power again and the flux from his gauntlet was blue fury.

—and Hansen pivoted to follow him, slashing at the neck joint, shearing *it* and down through the *thorax* plate and *out*.

The body toppled. The head, still attached to the warrior's right arm, fell separately.

Real close. Real close to Hansen's final mistake.

Hansen's battlesuit was an oven, though the environmental control whined to cool it. There was a bubbled patch on the sheathing above his left ribs, and his vision display took a moment to regain its normal crystalline precision.

The less enthusiastic warriors formed a second half-line behind the Colimore champions. Six of them had surged forward when their leaders did. Now they were trying to retreat from the sudden carnage. Smudgy grass fires lapped at their feet like a flood of thick liquid.

This was the chance to turn local success into a sweeping rout.

"C'mon!" Hansen croaked. He lurched forward, hoping his team would follow.

Culbreth was already a stride ahead, cutting at a Colimore warrior who turned to run.

Culbreth's weapon sprayed the smoldering grass with bits from the victim's shoulder armor, violating the battlesuit's integrity and probably killing the man inside. Arnor followed with a quick downward cut which ended the latter doubt by burning a chin-deep wedge in the Colimore helmet.

Hansen had his footing and his suit at full power again, but the warriors he'd passed to break the hostile line were moving now also. Hansen almost slashed a royal warrior who stepped between him and a Colimore champion.

Both the suits were good and well-matched. The point-blank grapple created a spray of sparks and radiance, ending an instant later when Arnor stabbed the Colimore warrior under the arm and blew the victim's screens with a double load.

Warriors were down all across Hansen's end of the field. Some of them royal levies—half a dozen of them royal levies. *The people who talk about light casualties are the ones who've never had to mop a man's body from the interior of his equipment.*

But the Colimore line was unraveling like a knit garment. Twenty or more of the duke's warriors sizzled on the ground as power continued to short through their ruined armor. The remainder were backing in nervous desperation or had taken the risk of turning to run.

"Suit, overlay!" Hansen said, letting his men flare past him to right and left now that the wing needed an officer more than it did another shock troop.

What the 30% mask told Hansen was chilling. The battle *was* by god a rout on the left wing. It was damned close to a rout on the right also—but there it was the dozen Solfygg warriors in first-class armor who had hammered the Royal Household to the verge of cracking.

One of the Solfygg champions was down, but smoldering

fragments of five of Maharg's professionals lay around him. White carats on Hansen's display marked other friendly casualties, all along the original line of contact.

The surviving eleven champions strode forward. The remainder of the Colimore left wing followed rather than supported their splendidly armored leaders, stepping over the blackened armor of royal troops who failed to retreat in time from the Solfygg advance.

Hansen opened his mouth to shout an order. He remembered that his radio was still on White Band, the general frequency for the levies on the left wing.

"Blue push," he directed his AI. He jogged up the rolling slope to his right, behind and paralleling the triumphant line of his own troops. The last thing Hansen wanted to do was to drag those men along with him.

The levies would hunt their fleeing opponents until disaster slammed into them from behind. There was nothing they could do against the Solfygg champions except die . . . and they would do that soon enough if the right wing collapsed and left them unsupported.

"Aim at the hip and shoulder joints!" Hansen ordered as he saw—direct vision and the overlay as well, it was still blurring the sight he needed now—three of the royal professionals make a desperate sally against the champion on the right of the Solfygg line. "The suits have weak spots at the joins!"

Duke Ontell had deployed his shock troops against the Royal Household, discounting King Prandia's levies as no more than a match for his regular warriors. That had been a misjudgment—

But maybe not a fatal one.

The eleven champions were arrayed together on one wing of the army. Because they were concentrated, they supported one another even though they appeared to have no more notion of team tactics than so many snarling tigers.

Maharg's three men made a well-coordinated attack. It stalled when the Solfygg champion lashed the leader with an arc so powerful that it froze his suit at three meters' distance. The other two royal troops stepped in from either side. Their enemy's battlesuit held for the moment their weapons licked it; then another Solfygg warrior struck the man on the right.

"The joints!" Hansen screamed again.

Running in a battlesuit was like running in liquid: though the motors did the work, the massive inertia of over a hundred kilos of armor required soul-deadening effort to make it move quickly. Hansen's thigh muscles pumped, anesthetized by the adrenaline that would leave them pools of fire as soon as the crisis cooled.

Unless he died in the next few minutes.

Either the professional on the Solfygg champion's right heard Hansen call or else he got lucky. He shifted his arc from the champion's helmet to the line between arm and thorax where a lesser smith had mated the pieces.

The leader of the royal team died as the supporting Solfygg champion struck from the side. Everything between the victim's neck and diaphragm flared into saffron plasma in the powerful arc.

But in the instant the other Solfygg warrior's weapon was locked by the leader's, the surviving royal professional struck home. The Solfygg armor failed at the join line.

The arm of the Solfygg suit spun away in a devouring flash. The black stump of a humerus poked from the open end, but the muscles had shriveled in a current so hot that even the battlesuit's ceramic core burned.

The Solfygg champion who had killed the other two team members rushed the third at a lumbering run. The royal professional backed as quickly as he could, knowing that his suit could survive his opponent's weapon for only fractions of a second.

Hansen stepped between the hunter and his prey.

The royal army was falling back; Duke Ontell's forces pressed on faster. Two more of the champions from Solfygg moved up in support of the warrior on the right of their wing.

This was going to have to be fast.

Hansen was at close quarters before the Solfygg champion realized he had another opponent. The champion's arc was already extended several meters to lick the lesser suit of the man he was chasing.

Hansen held the Solfygg weapon with the merest flicker from his right gauntlet. His main blow was with his left, a thrust that ended only when the steel of his glove clanged on the sheathing of his opponent's hip. A white-hot collop exploded from the Solfygg battlesuit.

Another Solfygg warrior in top-quality armor slid to a startled halt a few meters away when he saw his fellow's blazing corpse topple into the smoldering grass.

"At the joints!" Hansen screamed.

Instead of pressing in against Hansen, the Solfygg champion shouted for another of his peers to join him. Hansen went for him, coldly careful to step between the armored legs of the man he had just killed.

The Solfygg warrior tilted his foot to retreat, then lunged forward in what was either desperation or fury. His arc was so dense it was nearly palpable. He thrust at the center of Hansen's chest.

Hansen blocked the stroke with his right hand. His gauntlet began to heat immediately. Blue-white discharges heated the air into sudden vortices, lifting ash from the ground. Colimore supports moved up behind a curtain of smoke and diffracted light.

Hansen's vision displays degraded as the AI diverted still more of his suit's power into the flux that protected his life. He twisted slowly against the mass of his armor and cold servos, shifting his torso and directing the arc from his gauntlet down rather than up as it continued to lock the Solfygg weapon.

Hammering vibration from the two full-power arcs overwhelmed any chance of Hansen's screaming fury being heard except by his artificial intelligence.

The tip of Hansen's arc touched the soil. Both discharges shorted to ground in a cataclysmic uproar.

Hansen switched most of his suit's power to his left gauntlet, leaving only a trickle to keep the current path open and his opponent's weapon safely grounded. He struck at the hip joint. The gout of flame in which the Solfygg champion died was less dazzling than the spouting effulgence a moment before as both battlesuits discharged at their full capacity.

There was another Solf—

There wasn't.

The third champion was down, a gaping wound in the shoulder of his armor. Two of Maharg's professionals were down also, one's helmet a molten ruin, but they'd got the bastard, they'd *got* him.

Eighty meters from where Hansen stood, brilliant light danced skyward as Maharg in his own royal suit faced two Solfygg champions. The marshal had been covering the retreat of the Royal Household. It was a miracle that he'd lasted so long, but now several of his warriors scrambled back to his aid.

"Peace and Prandia!" shouted somebody who ran past as Hansen gasped to breathe before he staggered on toward Maharg. *Arnor, and that was fucking Culbreth, they were going to get themselves—*

The nearest Colimore troops hadn't yet made up their minds what to do when their Solfygg leaders fell. Arnor and Culbreth, Hansen's *team*, hacked at an opponent together. He fell.

The next Colimore warrior wore a silver battlesuit, itself of nearly royal quality. He blocked Arnor's thrust, parried a stroke by Culbreth—

And died when the professional that Hansen saved as he rushed to the right wing struck between the two arcs and finished the job.

"Aim at the joints!" Hansen called as he stumbled forward. He couldn't feel his legs, just lances of fire into his groin every time he took a step, but that didn't matter as long as he moved.

A lightning storm snarled across the surface of the battlefield. Men died, and most of them were members of the Royal Household attempting to engage the Solfygg champions.

Six of the latter still stood. The Colimore line had wavered, but now the Solfygg warriors resumed their advance.

Hansen was under no illusions about the situation. He had dropped two of the Solfygg champions, but the only thing wrong with their armor was that it hadn't been worn by a killer as experienced as Nils Hansen. Hansen couldn't deal with six more of the bastards alone, and—

Death rippled in blue fire. Three professionals had run to Maharg's side. All were dead now. The legs of one man were intermixed with those of another; the torsos lay at a meter's distance.

—there weren't going to be many surviving friendlies to help him.

A Colimore warrior got in Hansen's way, not trying to stop him but caught in the flow of battle. Hansen swiped the enemy aside in two pieces, slowing his rush only for the moment his battlesuit reduced current to the servos.

It was suicide to go up against royal-quality armor while wearing a lesser suit.

"Maharg, I'm—" Hansen shouted.

The marshal, ten meters away, held a Solfygg champion at bay with either gauntlet. He stepped back, a grudging retreat that changed into a thrust as one Solfygg warrior slipped on a corpse's armored hand and Maharg shifted full power to his other weapon.

"—coming!"

The Solfygg battlesuit failed in a blaze of light. Maharg's remaining opponent turned his stumble into a lunge toward the small of the marshal's back. Maharg's suit exploded.

Hansen hacked from behind, severing the Solfygg champion's right leg. The warrior sprawled forward onto Maharg.

The ruined battlesuits of the marshal and the man who had killed him spluttered on soil which their struggle had burned to glass.

"C'mon," Hansen wheezed. "Come—"

He took a step and stumbled because his foot did not, *would not*, lift high enough to clear the body of a man Hansen didn't recognize.

"Oh god," he whispered on his knees. "We've gotta go on. We gotta finish. . . ."

The Colimore forces were in full retreat. Many of the levies Hansen led had scattered in pursuit of the Colimore right wing, and the Royal Household had been butchered in its attempt to stop the Solfygg champions.

The warriors who fled toward Colimore outnumbered the forces Hansen could bring against them. Three Solfygg champions survived to shepherd them home.

"We gotta finish them!" Hansen cried as he lurched upright and ran toward the enemy: two strides, ten strides.

Two or three royal warriors followed him. None of the rest were able to.

Hansen toppled forward. He lay among the dead until Culbreth and a pair of freemen managed to turn his suit over so that they could open it.

It had begun to drizzle. The rain settled ash from the air and washed the tears from Hansen's upturned face.

Chapter Thirty-two

Bran's face peeked around the edge of the outer door as they pushed it open. The massive hinges groaned so softly that the sound might have come from Platt, snoring as he sprawled on the floor.

Bran slipped through the opening. Brech grabbed his arm and tried to pull past. The twins struggled for a moment in whispered anger.

The attendant, dead to the world, continued to snore. Instead of ordinary wine, the boys had stolen a small cask of liquor made by freezing a portion of the water out of raw wine.

Platt had gulped down the whole contents, chortling to Sparrow in successful greed until drink stupefied him. He vomited in the night and now lay in his own spew, but his system had absorbed enough of the alcohol to keep him comatose till morning.

"Here, boys," called Sparrow softly as he spread his huge right hand.

This time the object that lifted from Sparrow's palm was material, a skein of silvery threads which wavered in slow undulations around a common center. The skein rose slowly as it moved toward the boys. When it neared the barrier, it hesitated as if it were repelled by the iron bars.

"Oh!" cried the twins together, forgetting the need for secrecy in their delight.

Their short capes, scarlet satin with fur linings, flared out like wings as they ran to the barrier. Brech trod on Platt's outflung hand, but the attendant was too drunk to twitch.

Sparrow's dog trembled like a motor straining against the brake. The dog's teeth were bared, but no sound came out of the jaws glistening with nervous drool.

"Here, lads, I'll help you," said the smith as he hitched himself closer to the bars and raised his hand toward the skein. The threads seemed to have a light of their own in addition to that of the tallow lamp guttering in the niche by the outside door.

Individual strands bowed farther out from the center. The skein lifted another twenty centimeters, but it would not approach the iron.

"Give me!" Bran cried as he pressed himself against the barrier. He flailed his right hand toward the object.

"Me!" shrieked his brother, waving also, his face red with effort and frustration.

Platt snored.

Sparrow reached out with both hands. The motion was as swift and perfectly gauged as that of a bear swiping trout from a stream. His fingers closed on the throats of both twins simultaneously.

The boys did not scream. Nothing, not even a burble of surprise, could pass the grip of fingers that could break limestone into powder.

Sparrow leaned forward so that the twins' thrashing feet did not ring against the bars. Death had been assured from the first instant in which he crushed the cartilage of the boys' windpipes, but he continued to squeeze with his full force.

If he let them go, they would wheeze and kick in a commotion that might arouse even Platt—

But the real reason Sparrow did not release his victims was that this act was the first he had done by his own choice since Hermann trapped him.

The boys' faces turned purple, then black. Their tongues protruded. The smith continued to squeeze. Increased pressure made drops of blood seep from the victims' ears.

When Brech's right eye started from its socket and hung by the optic nerve, Sparrow opened his hands. The bodies slumped to the angle of the floor and the barrier. The bars rang softly.

Sparrow took a deep, shuddering breath. He did not realize he was crying until a hot droplet splashed on the back of his wrist. He didn't know why his body—not his mind; certainly not his mind—was acting that way.

It didn't matter. . . .

The dog crept over to Sparrow and thrust its head onto his lap, whining softly. After a time, the smith began to stroke the animal's ear between his thumb and forefinger. His breathing returned to normal.

The silvery toy continued to spin in the air; just as it had when it decoyed the twins into reach. Sparrow pointed his forefinger at his creation.

The filaments drew in. The skein drifted purposefully, between the bars and across the outer room until it hovered low over the sleeping attendant.

The smith snapped his thumb and middle finger. The sound was like that of a treelimb cracking. Platt stirred but did not rise.

Threads extended from the skein. One of them hooked the guard of Platt's knife and tightened as a snake does when it seizes prey. The remainder of the toy spun at an increased rate until it drew back toward the barrier, dragging the knife along.

The blade dangled from the filament holding it, skittering just above the floor. Occasionally the point touched stone with a faint *tsk!*

Sparrow spread the twins' clothing on the floor and set the bodies on the garments. Their skin was smooth and white, except for the lividly swollen faces. Both the boys had fouled themselves as they died, but the smell was indistinguishable for the thick reek of Sparrow's cell and Platt.

The smith took the knife from the waiting toy and began to butcher the small bodies so that they would fit between the bars enclosing him. The job required very few cuts. The blood had not had time to extravasate, but the wadded clothing absorbed most of it.

Sparrow had already arranged hollow ovals of scrap and ores like a pair of shallow graves. As he cut away each portion of a body, he set it within a hollow.

The heads were a problem: they would neither pass entire nor could Sparrow section the skulls with a knife. But the skulls would crush between the palms of his two huge hands. . . .

When he completed the task, Sparrow sat back. He was crying again.

He wiped the knife and set it down, then used the least saturated of the boys' clothing to wipe down the bars. He laid the wet cloth on top of the bodies, then covered the fabric in turn with more chunks of metal and rock. The skein, its tasks complete, slid between the interstices of one of the mounds and disappeared.

The smith's last act of concealment was to upset his slops bucket over the scene of the murder and butchery. Platt would probably require the prisoner to clean up the mess with his bedding, but Sparrow's furs were already filthy anyway.

Sparrow lay on the floor between the two oval mounds. The corpses took up surprisingly little space when sectioned and piled part upon part.

The attendant continued to snore. Sparrow used the rhythm of Platt's rasping breaths to jog himself into a trance in which the Matrix opened its infinite series of pathways and patterns.

The dog was asleep also. Its belly was full, for perhaps the first time in the animal's life.

The mounds shifted and clicked as the structure of what was within them changed. Fluid soaked its way across the floor—demineralized water, a waste product beneath the notice of the most suspicious of observers.

The master smith was creating something again; but not a battlesuit this time. . . .

Chapter Thirty-three

"This time . . . ," Ritter said to himself in confidence and wonder. He stood up slowly from his chair as he stared at the two dragonflies rotating like mirror images in an all-angles view. *This* time I think I've got you where you'll work, you cunning little devil."

"So she's ready for a test—" said a voice from behind him where nobody was. The engineer turned and groped for the pistol slung over his chair back.

The fingertips of Hansen's left hand rested on Ritter's holster flap. "—ride, is she, Master Ritter?" the slim, cold-eyed man concluded.

"I don't like that," Ritter said flatly. "I wish you wouldn't do that."

"I'm sorry," Hansen said. "I—"

He didn't look away from Ritter, but his eyes were no longer staring into the same universe. He was wearing a suit of velvet dyed a muddy blue, breeches and a jerkin cinched with a broad leather belt. The garments were obviously handmade, and they seemed to have been cut for a bigger man.

"There's been some things going on," Hansen went on with no more emotion than a voice synthesizer could supply. "Nothing to do with you, friend. Not even going that bad—"

Hansen shuddered. His face changed and he attempted a smile. "For the survivors, at least, and that's about all you can ever say, isn't it?"

"Your work is going all right, then?" Ritter said. Given his own focus, that was the most positive thing he could suggest to the other man without seeming to pry.

"That *is* my work, Ritter," Hansen said. His smile was wistful for a moment. "And yeah, like I said, it's going pretty well."

That wasn't what Ritter's visitor had said before.

"But the main thing," Hansen continued, "is how your project's going. Think you've got a handle on it?"

"Why don't you ride what I've built?" the engineer suggested proudly. "Then you can tell me."

He touched a control on his console. The pair of dimensional vehicles stopped turning on their invisible pedestals.

Ritter continued to manipulate his joystick. An invisible overhead beam slid one of the dragonflies out of the examination area. When the engineer thumbed the control downward, the crane deposited the dragonfly on the floor of the laboratory between the two men.

Hansen ran his hand slowly over the dimensional vehicle. The saddle was smooth, but it had a slight tackiness to the touch. He rubbed his fingertips together and found no residue on them.

Ritter smiled with quiet pride. "There's a suction system that works through tiny pores to help the rider keep his seat," he explained. "I'll bet you couldn't tell mine from the original."

"*Her* seat mostly, friend," Hansen said as he checked the control panel. "But I take your meaning."

He looked at Ritter. "I'm really impressed. You built it all here?" He gestured around the huge workroom.

"Some of the smaller, one-off pieces," the engineer said with a shrug. "Most of it, though, I just piped the specs down to fabrication—"

He touched a switch. A wall became a full-scale window onto Keep Greville's manufacturing level.

Thousands of technicians and laborers worked in the interconnected bays. Occasional splotches of bright clothing marked Ritter's under-engineers, performing set-up or overseeing particularly complex operations.

"—as normal," Ritter concluded. "Does it matter?"

Hansen laughed. "I was worried somebody might find out what you were doing," he said. "For your sake, I mean. But I've always been told the best place to hide a needle is with a million other needles, not a haystack. Forgive me for trying to tell you your business."

Ritter shut off the wall image. "You didn't," he said. "And anyway, I'd have done what I pleased anyhow."

His smile was half humor, half challenge.

Hansen raised an eyebrow. "Like I say," he said. "It's your business, Master Ritter."

The slim man swung aboard the dragonfly.

At rest, he didn't look dangerous. It was only when Hansen moved that Ritter remembered the way the pistol was in the other man's hand and firing before the engineer knew an enemy had arrived.

"Are you going like that?" Ritter asked. His voice caught on the first syllable. He cleared his dry throat to finish the question.

Hansen plucked his jerkin between thumb and forefinger and peered at the material critically.

"Oh, this would fit in where I'm going," he said. He patted the saddlehorn. "The dragonfly would raise some eyebrows, but I'll hover just out of synchronous the way the Searchers themselves do over a battlefield. Anyway, it's just a quick test run."

"It . . . ," Ritter said.

He licked his lips. "Look," the engineer went on, "I'm good, but this is a complex sonuvabitch. I don't want you stuck in the middle of those lizardmen with no way to defend yourself."

He gave Hansen the holstered pistol which hung from his chair. "Take this at least. I'll find you a forcefield projector to go with it."

Hansen's mouth opened to protest.

Look, if I thought I needed hardware, I've got my own that'd make this look like a pop-gun.

Then he remembered Maharg standing within arm's length, and Hansen unable to save his life. Hansen *failing* to do what was necessary to save Maharg's life.

"Thanks," Hansen said. "Not the forcefield, though. An untuned unit might interfere with the dragonfly's own projector."

The belt was sized for Ritter's waist. Hansen hung it over his left shoulder like a bandolier. He adjusted the containers of spare magazines so that they did not chafe bone.

He gave Ritter a thumbs-up. "See you soon," he said.

"Good luck," said the engineer. He smiled tautly.

"I don't need luck, Master Ritter," Hansen said. "I've got you."

He stroked the dragonfly out of the present continuum, using the manual controls rather than voice operation.

To a Searcher, the Matrix was merely a blur of light. The dimensional vehicle shielded its user from the medium instead of merging her with it the way Hansen or even a smith on the Open Lands could do.

Dragonflies did not convey information about the Matrix, any more than a hovercar permitted its rider to levitate unaided—but that was beside the point. All a Searcher needed to know was that her vehicle would take her where North or her own whim decided she should be.

And that was all Hansen needed now as well.

The dragonfly shifted out of the veils of light. That was expected, a momentary pause on the next plane of the Matrix—

But this was Plane Four, which was Hell in truth as well as in appearance; and the dragonfly did not pause on the cold, milky ice sheath—

It stopped dead.

Hansen moved the thumb switch to its neutral setting, then rolled it forward again in case Ritter had simply failed to copy the original vehicle's repetitive-input setting. Nothing happened.

Nothing happened inside the dimensional vehicle's bubble of force. The ice was warted with milky stalagmites the height of men. They stretched to the blank horizon in all directions. The stalagmites were turning toward Hansen with glacial slowness.

"Control," said Hansen calmly, activating voice operation. "Shift to Plane Three."

The dragonfly was alive with the normal complement of electronic quivers; it had not depowered. The force bubble was at full strength. The nearest stalagmites began to press against the invisible barrier, deforming as exterior sections of a perfect sphere.

"Control," Hansen said, "Plane Two!"

The holstered pistol was in his way as he groped for the saddle-edge controls again. He swore and slung it behind him, then toggled the switch forward against its stop.

Nothing was bloody happening with the dragonfly. The sunless horizon humped up slowly and began to sag with cavities which hinted at the eyesockets of a skull.

Hansen swore by the god of his childhood. He gripped the vehicle's unified in-plane control, a wheel that moved in three dimensions as well as rotating on its axis.

He lifted the unified control on its column. He'd hover ten meters in the air—or a thousand meters up if the tumor growing on the horizon was what Hansen thought it was. Some safe altitude, so that he'd have time to figure out what the hell was going on with the bloody—

The dragonfly didn't lift.

Hansen spun the control column forward and gave it a vicious twist. The vehicle had plenty of power to smash through the wall of stalagmites—

But it didn't move, wouldn't move, and the milky peaks of the stalagmites were forming human features.

"Control!" Hansen shouted. "Plane One!"

He bumped the pistol butt again as he groped for the manual control because the dragonfly had done *nothing* this time either. The weapon was in his hand before he thought—

Nils Hansen never had to think about a weapon.

—but he didn't shoot because he knew the faces growing on ice colder than Death were the visages of dead men.

Men he had killed. Women—but only a few women, not many at all compared to the male faces, stretching to the horizon in every direction.

The skull at the edge of vision turned and cloaked itself in a milky semblance of flesh. Hansen stared at his own face.

He screamed then and—

His hand reholstered the pistol without conscious command.

—rocked the toggle switch back, to return the dragonfly to Plane Five.

If that control worked, while all the others had failed. It was Hansen's last resort.

The Matrix was magenta light as warm as love. Hansen caught the saddle with both hands as the dimensional vehicle purred and slipped from nowhere to rest on the floor of Ritter's workroom.

The dragonfly bobbed as its legs telescoped, accepting the pull of gravity that it had escaped in the Matrix.

"Oh my god," Hansen said. He was gasping.

He closed his eyes. "Oh my god."

"What is it?" the engineer demanded. "Come on, man! Are you all right? Tell me!"

"I'm all right," Hansen said in a voice that shuddered into normalcy. "Just keep the fuck away for a minute."

He opened his eyes and swung off the dragonfly. The vehicle's force bubble collapsed automatically as its rider's weight left the saddle. Condensate formed on all exposed surfaces.

The engineer's face was plastic; his need for information shimmered under a crust of rigid control. "Okay," Hansen said, "we've got a problem. Two problems. The unit switches to the next plane down, but it won't go farther."

He shuddered despite himself. "It does come back. That's a big one. It came back just fine."

"The other problem?" said Ritter.

"The in-plane controls, the physical movement ones," Hansen said. "They don't work either. Zip. Nada."

He could have abandoned the dimensional vehicle in Hell and entered the Matrix himself.

He thought he could have.

He had been safe all the time. He thought.

Hansen shuddered again. He unslung the gunbelt and handed it to Ritter.

"Right," said the engineer emotionlessly. "Well, there's full telemetry on the unit. I'll get to work on it right away."

"There's always glitches," Hansen said to his trembling hands.

"Sure," said Ritter. "We'll take care of it."

Then he turned and slammed his fist into the console, hard enough to crack the dense plastic top.

Chapter Thirty-four

Princess Miriam looked bored and angry; Queen Stella looked
cold and angry; King Hermann's expression was hidden by the
battlesuit he wore—but Hermann was so nearly blind with fear
that a stumble slammed him into the doorjamb as he entered
the citadel.

"Majesty, milady," Platt said, bowing to rise and bow again,
as quick and graceless as a bird drinking. "Milady princess—"

Stella trod on his foot without noticing the contact. The
attendant jumped out of the way with a stifled yelp. King
Hermann, equally oblivious, swept through the vacated space
like Juggernaut's carriage.

"Sparrow!" boomed the king's amplified voice.

"Where is he?" demanded the queen, though she was looking
at the cell rather than Sparrow's attendant. "Where's the
prisoner?"

"Why are you dragging me to *this* filthy place?" the princess
said in a tone as hot and clear as live steam.

"Your Majesties!" Sparrow cried in apparent amazement.

It was just after noon. Light through the door the king had
flung open was dazzling to eyes adapted for the citadel's normal
gloom. "What's the matter?"

An under-cellarer, one of the freemen now accompanying
the royal family, pointed toward the smith.

"When I came here searching for the boys this morning,"
the servant said/accused, "he told me he had to see all three of
you right away!"

"Where are Bran and Brech?" Stella asked in a glassy, echoing
tone. She would have stepped to the barrier, but her husband's
armored body blocked her away from the danger.

"Where are my sons?" Hermann shouted.

"*I* don't see why *I* have to be here!" Miriam said shrilly.

"Your Majesties?" the prisoner said. He clung to the bars to

418

hold his torso upright, blinking and apparently bewildered. "Has something happened to the boys? I only asked you to come because I've made wonderful presents for all of you."

"But I thought—" the queen said. The quivering distress of a moment before gave way to her more usual look of cruel anger as she stared at the under-cellarer.

"But he said—" the servant blurted before terror dried his voice in his throat. Other freemen in the entourage, most of them carrying bows or edged weapons, backed away from their fellow.

"I know nothing of this!" Platt cried from as far out of the way as he could cringe. "I didn't speak! I didn't see the boys!"

Platt had awakened this noon to sunlight, a pounding head, and the toe of the cellarer's boot kicking him. The freeman was demanding something about the boys—*might they freeze in Hell, wherever they were*—which Platt was too nauseously hung over to understand. Sparrow had called something to the questioner, but Platt hadn't caught that either.

"I didn't really notice what your servant said when he came here," apologized Sparrow, no longer the focus of his visitors' eyes. "I've spent the entire night in the Matrix, creating your presents. But of *course* I know nothing of your sons, King Hermann. Perhaps it's a prank of theirs."

"I said, 'Are the princes here?' and *he* said I must bring you at once!" the under-cellarer bleated.

He looked from the king to his wife. There was no more mercy in Stella's expression than there was on the steel faceplate of Hermann's battlesuit.

The queen drew a gold-toothed comb from her hair and raked it toward the freeman's face. He lurched sideways. The king's armored fist crushed his skull.

In the sudden silence, Princess Miriam said, "What's this present you made for me, prisoner?"

Before Sparrow could reply, the princess clutched the mirror against her heart and added, "But I'm not giving this up! It's mine!"

Platt's head rang with each beat of his pulse, but the death had set his mind to working again. He had seen Bran and Brech . . . *when?* A day ago, the previous noon; but they'd been their normal selves, vicious and cruel, when they left.

And they had hidden the liquor as Sparrow said they would, so above all things Platt must know *nothing* of what the boys did or thought or went. . . .

"Of course you won't, princess," Sparrow said.

He turned, rotating awkwardly on his buttocks. His legs swept aside the remains of the materials he had worked into his latest creations, merely powder and grit.

"This is for you," the smith continued, holding a glittering something to a gap between bars, "because so fine a lady as you deserves to have it."

Miriam stepped forward.

"No!" her mother said with a voice like a whiplash.

Hermann raised his hand. An arc licked from the gauntlet, out and back and out again in snarling threat.

Platt threw his forearms across his face so that he would not see Death come if it were coming for him.

"I ask your pardon, Majesties," said the smith calmly.

Sparrow raised his hands—one empty and the other holding a pattern of lights and motion between thumb and forefinger. He set the object on the floor between the bars and slid himself backward, away from the barrier.

The dog, brighter-eyed than usual, dragged itself to Sparrow and licked his great, calloused hand.

King Hermann switched off his arc weapon. He bent forward and picked up the thing the smith had made.

The object was a doubled loop of golden light. The circles tilted at a slight angle to one another along a hidden axis. They pulsed with increased brightness in a pattern like that of the surf, never quiet but never the same.

The loops encircled Hermann's armored forearm without touching the metal at any point.

"It's a necklace for the princess," Sparrow explained softly.

"It's mine!" Miriam cried and snatched at the object before either of her parents could stop her.

The necklace came away in her hand as if it were a material thing, but the golden light had slipped *through* the battlesuit.

Hermann flexed his gauntlet. He had felt nothing. He tested his arc. It snarled out with full lethal intensity.

Miriam raised the necklace over her head. Stella caught the

girl's arm, but the necklace dropped past and through the queen's flesh as easily as it had King Hermann's armored forearm.

The joined lights pulsed their perfect circles around Miriam's neck. They woke rich color from her complexion and the sable trim of the dress she wore.

"Oh!" the princess cried, delighted even before she saw the result. She lifted the mirror on its chain and used the polished bronze surface to view herself with still greater enthusiasm.

"And for you also, King Hermann," the smith said with a courtier's diffidence, "and your lady wife. Just call for it, Your Majesty. Call, 'Come, chair.' "

"What?" said the king.

" 'Come, chair,' " Sparrow repeated. "No more than that."

"Wha . . . ?" King Hermann began. After a pause, his voice grunted from the battlesuit, "All right: come, chair."

Dust stirred within Sparrow's cell. Stella screamed.

A network of silvery filaments rose through the filth and litter beyond the barrier. The wires were so fine that they looked for a moment like the sheen of oil on water. They spread into an interlocking pattern of lines describing a three-dimensional object, a chair with back and legs and curving arms. The creation slid toward the bars.

Hermann's arc blazed out in readiness.

Sparrow seized the object with one powerful hand. "Only a chair for your comfort, Your Majesty," he said. The chair tried to move away from him, but the smith's arm was too strong.

"Only a chair, Your Majesty," Sparrow repeated.

He levered his body onto the seat. The sketchy cushions sank and shifted, molding themselves to the heavy body they now supported. The chair resumed its motion toward the barrier and stopped only when it touched the bars.

The smith raised himself again and swung onto the floor. "A gift I think you will treasure," he said.

As he spoke, the chair's wire fabric tightened. The shimmering construct squeezed between the bars and halted expectantly behind King Hermann.

The king turned to look at the chair. It scuttled on hollow, castored feet to stay in back of him.

"Don't . . ." the queen said. Her eyes were on the chair also, and her voice trailed off without completing the warning.

"Hell take you, woman!" Hermann grunted. "I'm in my armor."

Hermann lowered himself cautiously. The chair remained motionless until the battlesuit touched it. Then it deformed into a perfect match for the armored curves, accepting the weight and holding it as easily as light lies on the surface of a pond.

King Hermann leaned back.

"It would carry you if you wanted it to," the smith said in an obsequious tone. "It was a pleasure to create it for you, Your Majesty. One of the greatest pleasures of my life."

The king jumped up in a sudden fit of terror. The chair helped him rise, lifting his torso and buttocks until he was planted firmly on his feet again.

"And another for you, my lady queen," Sparrow continued. "As fine as the first."

Stella licked her lips. "Come, chair," she said in what was little more than a whisper.

The ores and waste material shifted as a second chair surfaced and slid toward the barrier. The filaments were so fine that when the chairs were at rest, they quivered like pools of liquid rather than solid objects.

"You'll never sit in anything else so comfortable," the smith said. His voice was soft, and it trembled with unholy joy.

"I only ask, Your Majesties," he continued as those outside the iron barrier stared at the wonders that had taken their minds off the missing children, "that you think of the service I have done you every time you use these marvels."

A terrible blue light moved in Sparrow's eyes as he spoke.

Chapter Thirty-five

The trunks of mammoths moved ceaselessly to squeeze rain from the fur where their bodies were not covered by cargo nets. The slight sounds the huge animals made as they padded through the main gate of Frekka were lost in the human cries within the walls.

Hansen's pony whickered in irritation as it waited, unable to find even a twig to crop so close to the gate. Hansen stroked its neck absently. Life wasn't perfect, even for a horse.

But maybe it was better for a horse.

"Ah," said Culbreth, who had halted a cautious three meters away from his leader. "Ah, I think that's the lot of them, sir."

Rain had turned the sky black, though it was still an hour short of sundown. A lantern hung from a pole above the pack saddle of each mammoth, above and behind the driver. The red glow which marked the last animal in line swung into view.

"I'm not keeping you, Culbreth," Hansen snapped.

Culbreth did not reply.

Arnor began to hum a song that Hansen had taught him around the campfire two nights before the battle, when it was safe to be drunk and not so safe to think soberly about the future. Taught Arnor and Culbreth; and Maharg was there too, joining in the choruses. . . .

"Sorry, Culbreth," Hansen said. "I'm on edge. I thought maybe I'd let the crowd thin."

Maybe some of the tearful accusing faces would have gone back to their empty rooms by the time Hansen rode through the city gate.

"*Yet I've always sort of missed her*," Hansen murmured under his breath as Arnor hummed, "*Since that last wild night I kissed her. . . .*"

On the way to battle, the mammoths carried the army's provisions and the battlesuits to be worn by the royal army.

Now, on the road back, the cargo nets slung from the pack saddles were swollen with loads of booty besides: armor stripped from the enemy dead, often in separate pieces.

Virtually any damaged suit could be repaired more easily than complete new armor could be constructed. The result would be a battlesuit whose quality was lower than the virgin unit before high-amplitude currents surged through its circuitry; but it would do for somebody to wear.

There had been battles where the margin of victory was one warrior more or less in the line.

"Left her heart and lost my own," Hansen whispered as cold trickles of rain ran down his spine. " *'Adiós, mi corazón. . . .'* "

The red lantern swung under the archway at the mammoth's smooth, ground-devouring stride.

Much of the armor that had gone out of Frekka whole was returning gouged with molten fury, and freemen led strings of ponies whose riders had gone to North or Hell in a great pyre after the battle. The dead men's families waited inside the gate, hoping against hope. . . .

"You weren't responsible, sir. You weren't in charge."

"I was there, Arnor," Hansen said. "Don't tell me I wasn't responsible."

Fathers with stiff faces and dry eyes. Sons trying to copy the old men, succeeding well enough but not understanding why it had had to happen to *their* father.

Hansen knew why it had happened. It had happened because Nils Hansen hadn't been good enough to stop it from happening.

Culbreth laid his fingers on the back of Hansen's hand.

Hansen jumped. He hadn't heard Culbreth cluck his pony closer. He hadn't realized how hard he was gripping the saddlehorn until the other warrior touched him, either.

"Yeah," said Hansen. "Let's go"

He nudged the pony with his heels. "Somebody's got to explain to King Prandia why the Searchers took so many of his men," he muttered, "and it may as well be me."

Chapter Thirty-six

The walls of Ritter's workroom displayed a dozen views of the original dragonfly in action, ridden by the Searcher in her black battlesuit. It swooped, hovered—then faded through planes. Each scene was a computer simulation created from data in the vehicle's flight recorder.

On the examination stand in the center of the room rested Ritter's copy, which had done none of those things when Hansen rode it into danger.

Penny appeared on the other side of the examination stand. She was a leggy blond whose breasts, secured by a transparent bandeau, looked too large for her rib cage.

Ritter touched a key. Vertical sections through the original dragonfly and the copy appeared beside one another in front of the engineer, then merged. Colors highlighted the incongruities between the pairs; a sidebar tabulated those differences.

None of the colored masks was farther up the spectrum than bright red. At the sensitivity setting which Ritter had chosen, chips from the same production batch might vary into the green level, and a ten-thousandth's variation in wall diameter would make the image of tubing glow yellow.

Penny's jewel flashed. She became a brunette with broad hips and a small bosom, then a black-haired woman as squat as Ritter himself.

The paired sections slid through the dimensional vehicles from the front backward. The mask stayed within the red level. The engineer balled his fist silently.

Penny walked around the viewing stand. "What are you doing, then?" she asked.

"There's a control problem," Ritter said, still watching the holograms. "The software was copied directly, so that leaves the equipment itself, probably somewhere in the control circuits. But I'm *damned* if I know where."

"What, ah . . ." Penny said. She leaned against the engineer. Her nipple became erect when it brushed his triceps. "What sort of shape do you particularly like me in, darling?"

"Huh?" said Ritter. He glanced over at her. He put the display on pause reflexively for the moment he looked away from it. "Tall and thin's unusual, I suppose, but I've told you—I don't really care."

The images began to scroll forward again. "And look, Penny," he added. "Time may not mean anything to you, but it does to me. I really don't have time for recreation just now."

The woman's head jerked back as though Ritter had slapped her.

The engineer continued with his painstaking search. He had performed the operation several times already, slicing the vehicles at a different viewing plane for each attempt.

"It'll descend only one level of the Matrix from wherever you start it," the engineer said. "We've tried it from several planes, and it's the same each one. It'll go from here to Four, or Eight to Seven if Hansen lifts it up to his house to begin with. But not down to Six from Eight."

Penny brightened when Ritter first began to speak, but she soon realized that he was using her as a living wall from which to echo his own thoughts. One of the engineer's concubines would have done as well; or a skivvy.

"Now that wouldn't thrill me," Ritter continued. "It means there's something wrong in my set-up . . . but by this time I could live with that, because we can work around it. Hansen can take the vehicle to Plane Two and drop into the Open Lands from there. But the other thing is, the bird won't move *within* the dimension, and that means it's no good at all."

Penny shivered at mention of Plane Two. She was now a tall red-head, almost skeletally thin. She crossed her arms over small breasts with jewels depending from the nipples. "The Lomeri are too dangerous to interfere with," she said. "Hansen could have killed you when he took you there before."

Multiple images of the Searcher on her dragonfly raced over a battlefield on the walls of the laboratory, framed by conduits and fittings within the room. Below the Searcher, battlesuits shorted incandescently. Delicate antennae on the underside of the vehicle's saddle received and copied men's minds at the moment of their dissolution.

Ritter scowled at Penny in irritation. He resumed running the paired sections.

"We were there longer than we'd expected, that was all," he said. "The fellow who stashed the dragonflies there had set them a millisecond out of phase with the surroun—"

His body grew rigid. His mouth was suddenly dry.

"Ritter?" Penny asked. "Ritter? Are you—"

"Oh my *god!*" the engineer said.

He turned, seized Penny beneath the elbows, and lifted her tall form another half meter in the air without showing any strain. "That's it! Hansen fetched the unit back by using the override switch, but the software still thinks it's out of synchronous. It won't *let* any of the in-plane controls operate!"

Penny twisted her legs around the big man's waist and drew her groin tightly against his diaphragm. "You've fixed it, then?" she asked, reflecting his delight like the full moon.

"Well, next best," explained the engineer with a slight frown.

He set the woman down and returned to his keyboard. She barely got her feet beneath her in time to avoid dropping onto the smooth floor.

"There's no way to reprogram the software," Ritter continued, muttering in the direction of his console. "Not from what I have. But the override switch will work, I'm sure, so long as it's detached from the chassis and operated back on Plane Four!"

"Now that you've done that . . . ," Penny said. She knelt to fumble with the engineer's fly.

"Not now, for god's sake!" Ritter snapped. "I need to check this while it's still clear in my mind."

He shifted his groin. When the woman's hands tried to follow, he slapped them away.

Penny sat on the floor beside the console. She drew her knees up to her chin. Her body flickered through a series of forms before settling on a statuesque blond with an hourglass waist and high, firm breasts.

Holographic images, both schematics and solids, shifted in quick succession on Ritter's holographic display. Possible redesigns vanished into limbo or were lifted higher in the air for comparison with other ideas.

The engineer whistled between his teeth as he worked.

Silent tears ran down the cheeks of the woman at his feet.

Chapter Thirty-seven

"I would have come out to greet you at the gate, Lord Hansen," the king said in concern at the silent anger on Hansen's visage. "But I'd summoned another advisor when I received the first reports of the battle, and he just arrived. No disrespect was meant."

Hansen blinked. "Excuse me?" he said.

Why was the king apologizing?

Formal functions were held in the House of Audience. The houses of two of the Syndics who ruled Frekka in past times had been knocked together to form a royal residence across the square from it.

The entrance hall into which Prandia strode with a bustle of nervous menials was decorated for comfort rather than show. Clerks with parchment scrolls and tablets of wood peered from side corridors, whispering among themselves.

"Ah, I'm sorry about the delay, sir," Hansen resumed "I . . . wanted to be sure all the baggage train got in. It—"

He shrugged to loosen the words which tension held back. "We'll need the armor, even the suits that really got chopped up. We'll—that is, you'll want to get all the smiths in the kingdom working on repairs immediately. You'll need to gather warriors—and raise new ones or, or . . ."

Hansen's face twisted. "Or else the next defeat will be a lot worse than this one."

Two professionals in battlesuits guarded the door to the residence. Half the Royal Household had remained in Frekka when Maharg marched, a necessary reserve.

Between the surviving portion of the Royal Household and the much larger number of warriors available in an emergency from the kingdom's individual landholders, King Prandia had the makings of a very impressive army.

"You weren't defeated," said Prandia. "You won. The army won because of you, Lord Hansen."

429

Hansen's mind went white. "Balls," he said.

"Sir!" Culbreth hissed desperately as he gripped his leader's shoulder.

"Duke Ontell holds Colimore," Hansen continued harshly. "Our campaign objective was to remove him. We failed."

"But Lord Hansen—" the king said with a look of pained uncertainty.

"Look," Hansen said. "I don't mind giving things their right names! It makes it easier to change them."

"Lord Hansen?" said Arnor. "We killed Ontell. Me and Culbreth."

"And Tapper from the Household," Culbreth put in. "Ontell had silver armor."

"Why—" Hansen shouted in amazement. "—*didn't you tell me?*" died in his throat.

Because you didn't bloody ask, his mind sneered. *Because you were too deep in doom and guilt to behave like a commander and learn the facts.*

Hansen started to laugh. Prandia's jaw dropped. Culbreth thought his leader was going into hysterics and grabbed Hansen in a bear hug.

"No, no, it's all right," Hansen said. "I'm fine, Culbreth, I'm not going to go berserk."

Culbreth stepped back uncertainly.

"Your Excellency?" Hansen said to the king. "Could I trouble you for the loan of something dry to wear? My clothes're somewhere back at my billet. I'd like to discuss your future operations now—but without catching pneumonia."

Prandia snapped his fingers.

"See to it," he ordered. He didn't bother to look around at his train of servants, several of whom were already scrambling to obey. "For all three of the lords. Do forgive me, Lord Hansen. I'm not myself with, with the press of events."

Arnor reached behind Hansen to nudge Culbreth. "We don't need to stick around," he murmured.

"And I did indeed hope that you would join me and my new marshal immediately," King Prandia continued. "It was an emergency appointment, of course . . . but I think the right one. He just arrived."

Hansen reached out and hugged Arnor and Culbreth. "Thanks, troops," he said quietly. "There's worse things than a battlefield, sometimes."

He released his team and met the king's eyes. "Yes sir," he said. "I think that's just what we need to do. There isn't a lot of time."

Servants sprang away like startled quail as the king turned with Hansen beside him. Prandia strode into a large chamber behind the hall. He held a whispered conversation with a gorgeously-dressed usher.

A servant carrying a set of clothes pranced up to Hansen, who tossed his sodden cloak toward the floor to get rid of it. Another servant snatched it out of the air and disappeared down a side corridor.

Hansen began to change. He took clothing from the servant's pile every time he stripped off one of his present garments.

"We'll go to him, if that's acceptable with you, Lord Hansen," the king said. "He's very tired from his journey to Frekka."

"What?" Hansen said. "Hell, of course."

The servant held out soft slippers with pointed toes, velvet rather than fur. Hansen accepted them with a smile and patted her hand. She was only about eighteen, pretty in a frightened sort of way.

Hansen padded behind the king barefoot rather than spend the time to pull the slippers on.

The usher threw open the door to a luxuriously appointed chamber. There was a separate hearth; a curtained bed in place of the bed closet normal in communities less sophisticated than Frekka; and a high-backed armchair in which huddled a shrunken, aged figure swathed in quilts.

"Foster father," the king said, "Lord Hansen has arrived. Lord Hansen, this is Malcolm, Duke of Thrasey and marshal of my armies in place of his son."

Hansen froze.

"Ex-duke," said the man in the chair. "Glad of that, too."

His vote was cracked, but his brown eyes were as bright as they had been two generations before, when Hansen first met the man.

"And as for marshal, we'll talk about—"

"You agreed, foster father!"

Malcolm looked straight at the king. "Another outburst, Your Royal Majesty," the old man said, "and I'll tell you to leave the room while the grown men speak."

Prandia opened his mouth, then turned his head with an expression of frustration and chagrin. After a moment, the king began to smile.

Malcolm grinned also. "Hansen . . ." he said, rolling the name across his tongue. "I knew a man of your name once, Hansen. He was older than you."

The room was illuminated by the hearth and a flaring rushlight, a lighted reed whose pith was soaked in tallow. It made Hansen nervous to watch the rushlight's tongue of pale, tremulous flame; but these walls were stone rather than wattle, and the plastered ceiling was high enough to be out of danger.

Hansen and the king stood in front of the door. Servants huddled in the hall, unable to enter the room with their superiors in the way.

Two of the servants carried extra chairs. Hansen glanced over his shoulder at them, then stepped close to Malcolm and sat cross-legged at the old man's feet.

Malcolm looked down at him. "I can't marshal the kingdom's troops," he said. "You know that, don't you, Hansen? I can't even walk."

"You can be carried, foster father," Prandia said.

The king waved away the servants with their chairs, but he squatted instead of sitting on the rush-strewn floor. "It's your counsel I need, not your legs."

"You, Hansen," Malcolm said as if he had not heard his king speak. "My son put you in charge of the left wing. Why did you leave your post?"

"Our side of the fight was under control," Hansen said. He met the bright brown eyes squarely. He avoided blinking, because blinking looked shifty, and you never wanted to look shifty when you reported to a superior.

God, how old was Malcolm now?

"The right wing was having problems," Hansen went on, "because of the, of the champions from Solfygg."

"Alone though?" Malcolm demanded. "You left your men and went haring off by yourself?"

"My men were levies," Hansen replied deliberately. "I knew what the weak points of the opposition's suits were. All my men could have done was die, a little faster even than the Household troops were doing already."

"Ah, foster father?" Prandia said. "Lord Hansen restored the—"

Hansen gestured at him with a spread left hand. He did not look away from Malcolm.

"—right wing," Prandia continued, ignoring an attempt to silence him in his own residence, "and won the battle for us. All reports agree on that."

"And at the end, then, Hansen?" the old man said in his cracked, piercing voice. "When you decided to charge the Colimore rear guard alone?"

Hansen licked his dry lips. "Yeah," he said. "I screwed up."

The king jumped to his feet. "Marshal Malcolm!" he said hotly. "All the men talk about that charge. Lord Hansen is a hero!"

"Do they talk about it—*son*?" Malcolm said. "The man *I* knew, *Lord* Hansen—he would have said that was a fool's act. The sort of trick a warrior pulls, not a trained soldier who wins battles for his liege."

"If—" the king said.

Hansen turned to the king. "If I'd managed to get myself killed," he said harshly, his voice full of the power that Malcolm's had lost with age, "we might have lost the field and all the armor there to salvage. And that would have been our ass."

He chuckled without humor. "Your asses, milords."

Malcolm cackled in delight. "Not mine either, Lord Hansen. I have nothing to lose."

He reached out with the care old bones require. Hansen opened his hand and clasped Malcolm's gently.

"I'm supposed to know things, Malcolm," Hansen whispered. "I should have seen it coming and warned him."

"My son wouldn't have lived forever," Malcolm said. "If the gods were good to him, he wouldn't have lived—" Hansen felt the wizened fingers tighten in senile fury "—as long as I have."

The rushlight beat like a slow pulse, stroke and stroke and stroke, while the two men gripped one another's hand.

"Maharg has a son, you know," Malcolm added. "Named after me, he was. Only ten years old now, but a fine lad . . . and the only immortality that *men* find, my friend."

"Have you two met before?" Prandia said uncertainly.

"In a matter of speaking, Your Excellency," Malcolm said.

He lifted his hand free and made a peremptory gesture at Hansen. "Get up, get up," he said. "I'm not a god that you should be sitting at my feet."

Malcolm turned to the king. "Make Lord Hansen your marshal, lad," he said. "Your grandfather had a warchief of that name. Perhaps it's an omen."

He cackled until a fit of coughing interrupted his laughter.

"Ah, foster father?" King Prandia said. He was careful not to let his eyes fall on Hansen as his lips formed the words of disapproval.

Malcolm shook his head sharply. "No," he said. "Your Excellency. Son. You said you wanted my counsel. Look at me."

Prandia met the old man's eyes. He nodded.

"Sometimes the gods give men one chance," Malcolm said softly. "The survivors are the ones who are smart enough to take it when it's offered."

The king sighed, then straightened his shoulders and turned to Hansen.

"Lord Hansen," he said formally. "I ask that you accept your duty to your liege and your kingdom by becoming Marshal of the Royal Army."

"If you've got any women around that you feel personally about, lad," Malcolm said to the king, "then you'd better keep them locked away tight." He laughed.

Hansen looked at the old man flat-eyed. "We still may not win," he said. "If they had twelve royal suits to send to Colimore, then they've got a lot more besides."

"Oh, I've got faith in you, Marshal," Malcolm said.

The flame of the rushlight was so pale that the texture of the stone was visible through it. It gave Malcolm's *café au lait* complexion a patina like that of old ivory.

"And it may be, Marshal," he went on, "that you're not really younger than the Hansen I knew in times past after all."

Chapter Thirty-eight

The young woman opened the door suddenly and spilled light past the barrier in the middle of the citadel. Glare turned the black iron into a grid of silvery reflection. The smith's dog whined.

Platt sneezed and jumped to his feet in surprise. "P-princess!" he blurted and sneezed again. "I—that is, is your father here?"

"Phew!" Miriam said, wrinkling her nose.

She waved dismissively to the attendant. "I don't want to talk to you. Go stand outside."

The princess carried a sable muff and wore a short sable cape over a coat of creamy silk brocade which covered her to the ankles. The ornament of light which Sparrow had made for her oscillated around her neck in golden radiance.

The mirror that Sparrow had given Krita was a bulge beneath Miriam's cape instead of being worn in plain view as was her wont.

"Lady princess," Platt said as he knelt with his head bowed. He peered up at Miriam from the corner of one bright, cunning eye. "Your father the king was most speci—"

"Shut up!" Miriam said. "I told you to go outside. I don't like the way you smell."

"But I mustn't—" the attendant whined.

He raised his head as the princess strode toward the barrier. A quick glance through the open door proved that she had come by herself. To her back Platt continued, "Anyway, you can't talk to the prisoner now, lady. He's in a trance. His mind's lost in the Matrix."

Miriam turned like the nut of a crossbow rotating to loose the string.

"Then we'll have to wake him up, won't we?" she snapped. One of her perfect hands slid out of the muff and snatched the empty bowl from Platt's three-legged table.

Miriam's ring twined like a snake on her middle finger. Its

gold scales and garnet eyes quivered on the pewter as she rang the bowl along the barrier. The racket was as loud as the gates of Hell crashing open.

Sparrow woke up. His body rose upright before the mind returned to light his pale eyes. The event was more similar to a glacier calving icebergs than it was to the movement of a living thing.

Princess Miriam stepped backward. Her shoulder bumped Platt, who had approached behind her.

Miriam screamed and struck the attendant with the bowl. "Get out!" she shrieked at him. "I told you to get—"

Platt scuttled to the outside door with the graceless haste of a frightened spider. Miriam hurled the bowl at his head.

"—out of here, Hell take you!"

The pewter dented on the transom instead.

She turned back, recovering her aplomb with a shiver like the motion of a fore-edge book being thumbed to release its hidden scene. Sparrow smiled at her.

The princess blinked. Whatever expression she thought she had seen on the prisoner's face was gone as suddenly as it appeared. It could have been a trick of the light. . . .

"You," she said haughtily. "Prisoner! I need you to do something."

The smith rubbed the spot between the dog's eyes. The animal licked his huge calloused hand.

"What can I do for you, lady princess?" Sparrow asked. His voice was a rasping caress.

"I—" Miriam said.

She paused to look back at the door. Platt's shadow was visible, though the attendant himself was concealed behind the stone doorpost.

The princess stepped up to the bars again. She unpinned her cape and held it with one hand as she lifted the mirror from around her neck. The ornament of light quivered as Miriam's hand and the gold cord slid through it, but the helix continued its dual track unimpeded.

"It's my mirror," Miriam whispered. She waggled its face toward Sparrow. Since the light was behind her, the reflection was never more than a pale blur. "It doesn't work any more."

The smith locked his hands behind his neck and stretched.

"I see myself in it, lady princess," Sparrow said. Cords of sinew stood out on his neck. "What could be wrong with that?"

"You fool!" the girl snapped. "I mean it's *only* a mirror! It doesn't show me the places I want to see, the way it should."

"Ah," said Sparrow wisely. "Show it to me, then, lady."

He pointed to the filthy floor between the bars. "Set it there and step back while I take it," he said. "We can't have my jailor telling King Hermann that I put you at risk, now can we?"

Miriam spun on her heel. "You!" she cried to the eye that slid aside an instant too late to go unseen. "Get out into the courtyard, you little foulness! Or I'll have Daddy flay you!"

The attendant's shadow bobbed away from the doorjamb. Platt was mumbling something exculpatory.

The princess set the object down. She did not move back. Sparrow leaned only as close as necessary to pinch the cord between his thumb and forefinger, then rocked to his former position as he inspected the mirror.

"Ah," he said. "Ah, I see what the problem is."

The mirror had stopped working because the ornaments Sparrow had made for Princess Miriam interfered with its ability to take power from the Matrix.

Just as the smith had intended.

"You can fix it, then?" Miriam said, unable to keep a tone of concern from her voice. The mirror was unique and uniquely wonderful. Even the princess in her arrogance had realized that.

"Very difficult, lady princess," the smith lied solemnly. He closed the mirror again and set it where Miriam had placed it. "But I think . . . yes. But in two weeks, at the new moon. Not during daylight. And not now."

"I don't understand!" Miriam said, making the words an accusation rather than a confession of ignorance.

"The Matrix, lady princess," the smith said. He waved his hand dismissively. The dog smelled the hormones Sparrow was exuding and growled in anticipation.

"Well—" said the princess. She drew herself up in a regal pretense that her will had not been thwarted.

"One thing, lady princess . . . ?" Sparrow added.

"What?" she snapped.

"For this particular task," the smith said, his voice rasping softly like a dog's tongue, "I'll need a skin of strong wine. Can you bring that when you return with the piece that I will repair?"

"I don't see why I should bring you anything!" the princess said. "You're only a slave."

"Ah, not for me, lady," Sparrow said. "For the task. Only for the task."

"We'll see," she said coldly; turned, and swept out of the citadel. She paused on the threshold for a moment and called back over her shoulder, "You'd *better* fix it!"

When the princess was gone, Platt slunk back inside.

"What was that all about?" the attendant asked spitefully. He did not expect an answer.

Sparrow smiled at him. "Oh, she's a fine girl," he said. "She came to thank me for the ornaments I made her."

"*She* did?" said Platt in puzzlement.

"Oh, yes, a fine girl and worthy of her family," Sparrow said. "And to prove how grateful she is, she'll come back when the moon is dark and bring a skin of wine for us. Is that not a fine girl?"

Platt shook his head. He found his bowl. He morosely attempted to press out the dents, using the butt of his knife as a mallet.

The smith lowered himself onto his furs and slipped back into his trance. Platt glanced through the bars, then returned to his own task.

He supposed that Sparrow was making some piece of a battlesuit.

Chapter Thirty-nine

Somewhere in the ruck of hundreds of men exercising on the plain below Hansen, Culbreth wore Hansen's own battlesuit.

The warriors of the royal army were going through tactical evolutions in small groups. The troops particularly needed experience in how to deal with armor of exceptional quality. When Hansen was too exhausted to go on, another trusted warrior took his place in the suit.

The skin was raw over Hansen's joints, the places where his body first touched the interior of the battlesuit as he moved. He was wrung out physically and mentally. Though he trained his eyes in the direction of the troops as he chewed a grassblade on the bluff above the exercise field, he wasn't really seeing the men.

He had been this tired before. He was sure he must have been, sometime or other.

Black wings beat through the Matrix. He could feel Searchers coming closer. . . .

On the field sunlit below, warriors fell battered—their armor stunned, their bodies bruised by hitting the ground.

But they weren't dying—and as with ravens, little but death would summon the Searchers.

Hansen turned without rising as the dragonflies, two of them, changed from shadows to matter more solid than that of the scrub grass on which they landed—

And vanished again a millisecond out of temporal phase, leaving their riders behind. The Searchers wore linen rather than their powered armor.

"Race," Hansen said. He crossed his legs beneath him, then straightened them like the arms of a scissors bridge to lift him upright. "Julia."

He gave the women a smile that was not so much careful as ready for whatever came next. The Searchers were North's minions, but Hansen had the powers of a god. . . .

439

"Does North have a message for me," Hansen said, "that he doesn't choose to bring himself?"

"Who knows what North does?" Race said.

"We came for ourselves, Lord Hansen," Julia added in a gentler tone. "Nobody sent us."

The women were like enough to be sisters, though not twins. Race's nose was a little higher than that of her companion. Her eyes were blue rather than gray, and her body looked vaguely more taut than Julia's—though Julia moved like a cat, while Race had more of a birdlike jerkiness.

Both of the Searchers were beautiful; and both were hard, by the standards of the warriors battering one another in training below.

"Look, we . . ." Race said.

Thanks did not come easily to her tongue. She paused to watch the movements on the practice field, her hair flying in the breeze that came up the bluff and broke in turbulence.

"Look, we may as well sit," said Hansen, indicating the ground.

Herds being driven to slaughter in Frekka pastured often enough in the area to keep the grass on the overlook cropped. Neither beasts nor herdsmen were in sight at the moment.

"You gave us our dragonflies back," Julia said. "We came to thank you."

"I liked Sledd well enough," Race said. "But I'd been *free* before. You don't know what it's like to be . . . held. When you've been free."

"You may like having the wind blow in your face . . . ," Hansen said. He sat, recrossing his legs and lowering himself in the same fashion as he had gotten up "But I don't. And—"

His tone became softer, partly because he was below the level of the constant breeze and no longer had to speak over its keening. "—I really didn't do anything that requires thanks."

The Searchers settled also. Race squatted; Julia sat on one hip, curling her feet behind her and supporting part of her weight an her left arm.

"Krita said she wouldn't come unless you ordered her to," Race said, scowling at her interlaced fingers. She wore rabbit-leather slippers and a chemise that fell to mid-thigh when she stood but hiked up to the hip joint in her present position.

"I did nothing important," Hansen said in a sharper voice. "I showed Krita that her mirror was a doorway as well as a window—that she could touch anything she could see through it. That's nothing."

Julia said, "You are a god, Lord Hansen. We're only servants. For you to think of us at all was an honor."

Unlike her companion, Julia wore a loose shirtwaist belted over a pair of trousers. The belt was of gold worked into a broad strap and clasped by a sapphire-eyed dragon swallowing its tail.

Hansen laughed. He was amazed at how bitter he felt at the images called up by the Searcher's words, "Be thankful you at least know who you serve, Julia. And don't—"

He stared critically at the rubbed spot over his left wrist-bone, then patted it with his fingertips. "Don't ever think that I'm not still human."

"Your warriors are pretty good," Race said neutrally as she watched the practice field. "Are they the whole army?"

"About a third of it," Hansen said, turning sideways to look over the bluff. "Every warrior in the kingdom has been mustered. It costs Prandia a fortune just to feed and maintain them, but it's the only way that they're going to get the training they need."

Julia eased forward so that she also could see the field. Viewed from the bluff, the arcs and glowing forcefields were a work of art; but all three of the watchers could add the reality of their own experience to the distance-blurred portrait.

Dust, sweat; the bitterness of lactic acid cramping muscles. Ozone scouring mouths and nasal passages, making eyes water even before the tears of fatigue started. Blood from pressure cuts and lips bitten in the shock of falling. Bruises and raw skin.

And above all, pain. The same constant, enervating pain which was as certain a concomitant of battle as death, and which practice trained warriors to accept until death or victory released them.

Hansen shivered.

"It's going to be a slaughter," Race said. Her voice held no loading but that of professional experience. "If all your men are as good as these—"

"More or less," Hansen said.

He turned to squat beside the Searcher, facing the practice

field. "This is Wolf Battalion, but Bear and Eagle started with personnel as nearly equal as my staff and I could pick."

"Then you may win," Race continued. "But the Solfygg champions in royal suits will cut your lines to ribbons, no matter how good your training is."

"North will be pleased," said Julia. They now perched on the bluff like the three wise monkeys. "There will be a slaughter like the world has never known."

Hansen turned to her. "Do you think I don't know that, Julia?" he said very softly. He was shivering again.

Race cleared her throat. She continued to face over the edge of the bluff. "Krita learned that the mirror was open to what it showed," she said. "Because she kissed your image through it, Lord Hansen."

Hansen's head rotated. "She can do as she pleases!" he snapped. "That's none of my business!"

"Lord Hansen?" Julia said. She put her right hand softly on his shoulder. "This is what we please, Race and I."

"I'm jumpy," Hansen said in embarrassment. He backed into a sitting position a little farther from the edge of the bluff. "I'm sorry. I—"

Julia was smiling. Her free hand released her dragon-clasped belt. She stood up for a moment to let her trousers slip down about her ankles, then stepped out of them.

Race tossed her crumpled singlet on top of the trousers while Julia was still lifting her shirtwaist over her head.

"We could try spreading clothes to cover the ground," she said. Her pubic wedge was light red, almost orange. "If the grass bothers you."

"It never has yet," said Hansen as he and Julia reached together for the waist tie of his shirt.

Hansen started to laugh with real humor for the first time in too long. He laughed several times more in the next hour and a quarter.

Chapter Forty

Ritter had become used to seeing visitors appear from the air before him, but the laughter in Hansen's eyes was a surprise to the engineer. Hansen was always grimly purposeful. For that matter, Penny had more often than not been sullenly gloomy the past several times she visited.

If he made her so miserable, why the hell didn't she stay away?

"How are we doing, Master Ritter?" Hansen asked, hitching his felt trousers around to a more comfortable position.

Hansen was not dressed to fit in with the personnel of Keep Greville, though Ritter knew he could vanish again into the Matrix as quickly as he appeared. Besides the obviously hand-sewn trousers, the slim man wore a shirt of coarse gray wool with bits of dry grass clinging to it—and a belt of flexible gold with a dragon-head buckle which combined function and artistry in a fashion that Ritter approved.

Still, the combination of coarse garments and intricate belt was as unexpected as Hansen's cheerfulness.

"I've completed the modifications," Ritter said.

Normally it didn't make him nervous to turn hardware over to users—the soldiers of Keep Greville—for testing. Ritter knew, and Lord Greville knew, that there would always be flaws in new equipment. Field testing was the only way that designs could be refined to meet actual needs—or be scrapped as certainly useless because the flaws uncovered were insuperable.

But Lord Greville didn't personally test new equipment against the weapons of his neighbors . . . and that was just what this thin, cold-eyed god intended to do.

"That was your job," Hansen said, raising a quizzical eyebrow. "That makes it a win, friend. What's the problem?"

"I wish . . . ," said the engineer.

He touched his console, idly rotating an image of the dragonfly directly above the unit itself. "I wish that someone else could test its operation. Especially after the last time. Don't you have servants?"

Hansen's face was briefly immobile. A tiny smile played at the corners of his mouth and his nostrils were flared.

Ritter had seen the look before on his visitor's face. That time it had been directed at the Lomeri, not at him.

"Send somebody where it's too dangerous for me to go, Master Ritter?" Hansen said in a whisper like whetted steel. "It was always me that they sent."

He licked his dry lips. "I'd rather die than be one of *them*, Master Ritter."

The engineer lowered himself to one knee and bowed his head. "Forgive me, my lord," he said.

"Hey," said Hansen, stepping around a rack of testing equipment. He gave Ritter's arm a friendly tug upward. "You're doing your job to warn of the risks. But, you know, I'll carry out my end my own way."

Ritter stood and nodded appreciatively. He gestured toward the dimensional vehicle. "Well . . . ," he said.

Hansen was lost within his memories again. "I've lived a lot longer than I ever thought I would, Ritter," the slim man said as he stared into the past. "Maybe longer than I should have, too."

His hand still lay on Ritter's left shoulder. The engineer clasped it with his right hand and said jovially, "Well, just watch yourself on your end, and I'll keep my thumb on the override button here."

Hansen's eyes focused again. "You bet," he said. "But not *here*, exactly. We're going to do this safely this time. I'll run you and the hardware up to Plane Seven and drop the dragonfly back to Six where there won't be any, ah, problems besides what may happen with the equipment."

"Glad to hear it," said Ritter, relieved at more than the plan of operation. He followed his visitor through the aisle and onto the examination stand where the dimensional vehicle waited.

"Climb into the saddle," said Hansen, "but don't fool with the controls. I'll take it and you both with me."

The engineer obeyed his instructions. Hansen's mouth quirked into a lopsided smile and he added, "You know, I made a pretty good choice in you."

Ritter guffawed. "I've pulled in my horns since the screw-up the last time," he said. "But—" serious again "—I don't think you were going to find a better engineer within a thousand kilometers of Keep Greville."

Hansen spread his fingers to touch the saddle and Ritter simultaneously. "Yeah," he said. "That too."

The Matrix hardened around them, turning the workroom into a memory as slight as chaff drifting through a steel cage.

Only illumination surrounded Ritter. Bars of light branched in infinite directions, each a pure color and different from every other.

His guide had vanished. The dragonfly had vanished. The light had form and power and—

The dragonfly rocked under Ritter's weight. Its feet ground into the sandy loam of a ridge above the tide line. Large-headed grass waved to the height of Hansen's chest, and a line of palms leaned their coconuts out toward the surf.

"Oh!" said the engineer, reacting to the Matrix world he now overlooked.

The atmosphere was alive in a fashion that the air of Ritter's own countryside lacked. Near the horizon, the sea changed color, gray-green replaced the inshore gray-blue.

For as far as Ritter could see from twenty meters above sea level, a great circular storm arced around the horizon. Lightning crackled silently, back-lighting the clouds, and slanted bars of rain joined clouds and sea at intervals. The sparkling tang to the air was more likely ozone from the storm than salt alone.

"Where are we?" Ritter asked.

"This was the plane that the original exploration team under Captain Rolls found," Hansen explained. "Thousands of islands but no large continents. When Rolls vanished, the Consensus of Worlds sent North and his troubleshooters to find out what had gone wrong."

The engineer shook his head. "I heard all that when I was little," he said. "And a colony was sent—"

"To the Open Lands," his guide agreed. "To Plane One, where all the other planes impinge without going through the Matrix."

It appeared that a great wave was swelling at the juncture of blue water and green. The mass grew still further; streaming seawater in all directions to assume its own dense black color.

The thing was alive. It spouted a double plume of spray which hung in the air after the beast itself had resubmerged.

"And the colony vanished too," Ritter said. He was beginning to shiver. "And we were sent, my ancestors, ten thousand years ago, in a fleet to find them."

"After you, a fleet of androids," Hansen agreed softly. "And after the androids, a fleet crewed by machine intelligences. They're all here, each on its own plane; and the Lomeri, who came before there were humans in the greater universe."

He laid his hand on the engineer's hand. After a moment, Ritter stopped trembling.

Last of all, the Lords of the Consensus sent Commissioner Nils Hansen alone, to go where fleets had disappeared to no avail. But the engineer didn't have to know about that. . . .

"But that's mythology!" Ritter shouted. "That isn't real!"

Hansen bent down and pinched up a portion of soil. He turned Ritter's hand palm-up with his own free hand and dribbled the sand and dirt into it.

Ritter rubbed the grit between his palms.

"Yeah," he said. " 'What?' is more important than 'Why?' isn't it? Sorry."

Hansen chuckled. "For people like you and me it is, friend," he said. "Now, trade me places and let's see how our noble steed—" he patted the dimensional vehicle "—handles in a nice, safe pasture like Plane Six."

Ritter swung himself off the dragonfly. His mass dwarfed that of the vehicle, but its spindly legs barely twitched when his weight came off them.

The engineer detached the control panel from the saddle. "I'm ready, my lord," he said.

Hansen waved from the saddle—left-handed by instinct, though he wasn't wearing a pistol that his right hand had to be free to grasp. "Let's do it," he said.

Ritter pressed the override switch. The vehicle and its jewel-hard rider shrank out of sight.

❖   ❖   ❖

The veils of color that surrounded Hansen were identical when he slid down into Hell. They were not a description of the Matrix, merely an artifact of the dragonfly's passage.

Even so, Hansen flicked his eyes around him like a beast which suspects that it may be in the slaughter chute. . . .

The vehicle touched down on a gravel beach, rocking gently. The landing was soundless because there was no air here, only rock; and, motionless in the sky, a huge red sun.

So far, so good.

"Control," Hansen ordered. "Drop to Plane Five."

The dragonfly's mechanisms whirred softly within themselves, but the vehicle remained where it had been.

As expected. Ritter hadn't thought he'd be able to cure that part of the unit's problem.

Light winked on a distant corniche. There was life of a sort on Plane Six: the great crystalline descendants of machine intelligences which the Consensus had sent to Northworld within Hansen's lifetime—

Or in the unimaginably distant past, depending on the vantage from which one viewed temporal duration.

The creature on the cliff edge was too far away for Hansen to see it directly, but light striking the myriad facets of its body amplified the slightest motion.

Hansen drew a deep breath. The force bubble surrounding the dragonfly was firm. Even if that protection failed, Hansen could walk unaffected across this airless waste chilled to within a degree of absolute zero. He had the powers of a god. . . .

Hansen lifted the in-plane controls. The dragonfly lifted also, as smoothly as water spouting from a fountain.

Hansen cocked the column forward and sailed over the gravel, speeding or slowing as he chose. The bloody light transmuted all colors into shades of red and gray, but bands of texture paralleled the ancient shoreline to mark the stages by which the sea had vanished.

The skeleton of something terrifyingly huge lay on a bed of ooze which had frozen to the hardness of basalt. Most of the bones were scattered on the ground, but toothless jawplates gaped upward like some work of man. Hansen thought of the spouting creature he had watched from the beach where Ritter now waited.

The in-plane controls worked. He had learned what he came for.

Hansen sighed and swung the dragonfly back the way he had come.

"Control," he said as the frozen waste blurred past beneath him. "Plane Seven."

Hansen swam through color into sunlight that seemed brighter became there was an atmosphere to scatter it. He drew back on the control column when the surf foamed to fleck his legs.

With a dragonfly, apparent duration was the same at either end of the dimensional contact. While Hansen maneuvered over the waterless sea, the storm had swept closer to the beach on Plane Seven. The first big drops pocked the sand like miniature asteroid impacts.

The engineer released the override switch. "How did it go?" he asked anxiously.

Hansen grounded squarely on the marks from which the vehicle had lifted. "Like a charm!" he said. He hopped out of the saddle. "Now, let's get you home before we get soaked."

Ritter climbed aboard the dragonfly. His movements were graceless but adequate to his need. "So there won't be any problem with the actual operation?" he pressed.

"No hardware problem at all," Hansen said cheerfully.

But because of the limited dimensional control, the insertion would have to be made from Plane Two . . . and whoever operated the override switch from the Lomeri's home risked more than the chance of being soaked by a storm.

Chapter Forty-one

The storm had banged the shutters of the royal residence throughout the night, but a part of Hansen's subconscious must have heard the pattern of outer door, inner door, and nervous voices. He was up and dressed when someone rapped on his bedroom door.

"Lord marshal?" a servant called. "L—oh!"

Hansen pulled the door open from the inside swiftly enough that the servant's lantern guttered. The man's knuckles, raised to knock again, almost struck Hansen instead of the doorpanel.

"Oh, I'm sorry, m-m-m," the servant stuttered. "M-milord!"

There was a crisis. Prandia would want Malcolm in crisis discussions, and Hansen's old friend didn't move very quickly any more. Therefore—

"In Malcolm's suite?" Hansen demanded.

The servant nodded.

Hansen was already trotting down the corridor toward the other wing of the residence.

"Alert my battalion commanders!" he threw over his shoulder, though he couldn't take time to be sure that the servant knew where those warriors were billeted. If the fellow did, it might save a little time.

The message that spurred this crisis almost certainly meant war. That was good. During the past several days, Hansen had been waiting for an excuse for war.

For the last twenty meters to Malcolm's door, Hansen could have followed the trail of wet footprints on the flagstones. Prandia's major domo stood outside the suite with a handful of flunkies carrying lanterns.

"Yes, milord marshal," he called. "His Majesty is waiting for you!"

The major domo had managed to pull on a velvet robe and cinch it with his sash of office, proving that it wasn't only military men who could move quickly in a crisis.

Malcolm had gotten up from his bed. He sat in one of the chimney seats. Servants had built up the hearth fire before they scurried out of the way.

With Malcolm when Hansen entered were the king and another man, both standing. The stranger was of middle height and had a facial scar which showed as a white worm across his dark beard. He wore rain-soaked leather garments. There was a crude bandage on his left hand. It was leaking blood.

"This is Kraft," said King Prandia. "He's, ah, a scout from the Solfygg border."

Hansen looked at the spy. "Your hand?" he asked.

"It'll wait," Kraft grunted. "I took a forest shortcut I shouldn't have. Wolves got my pony."

"The Duke of Gennt is about to switch his allegiance from my foster son to the King of Solfygg," Malcolm said. He looked like a bedroll in the corner of the hearth—unless you noticed the glitter of his eyes. "If our friend here is correct."

Kraft grinned at the old man. The expression suggested that not all of the wolves had survived to eat Kraft's pony.

Hansen said, "Yeah, let's operate on that assumption."

The spy had risked his life to deliver the information. That didn't *prove* he was right about Gennt's intentions, but it sure-hell predisposed Hansen to believe him.

"Well, then," said the king crisply. "I don't think this is any time for half measures. Lord Hansen, all the forces available to the kingdom have been mustered for the past month. Have they not?"

"Yessir," Hansen said, nodding.

His eye caught on Kraft. The spy was losing the nervous energy which had sustained him thus far; he looked all in. Hansen gestured to him, then pointed at the other chimney seat, opposite Malcolm.

Kraft hesitated. He glanced at the king. Prandia was still standing.

"Sit," ordered Hansen. "We've been asleep while you rode." *And fought the wolves. And god knew what all else.*

"What's the state of training, Marshal Hansen?" Malcolm asked. He ended with a sound somewhere between a cough and a giggle.

Hansen shrugged. "You've seen them, Malcolm," he said.

"They're a hell of a lot better overall than they were a month ago when we pushed the training."

Malcolm wore a stocking cap of wool dyed red. The pompon on the end of it bobbed as he nodded. "They're at a plateau, though?" he said in his cracked voice.

"Yeah, that's right," Hansen agreed. "I don't think we can expect any significant further improvement in less than another six months. And we don't have six months."

"Because Solfygg will invade us before that?" Prandia asked with a frown. The king's head shifted from his former marshal to the current one and back.

"It's their royal suits that're the problem," Hansen explained, drawing Prandia's attention again. "At the rate Solfygg is getting them, they'll have hundreds in six months' time."

"I don't understand that," the king said, shaking his head. "A royal suit is a year's work for a master smith!"

"It doesn't matter whe—" Malcolm said. He subsided in a fit of coughing.

Hansen stepped over to the fireplace and ducked under the mantel. He put an arm around the old man and held him gently.

Malcolm thrust a crabbed hand out of the quilts and clasped Hansen with it. "We don't have to understand, lad," he said to the king. "The world does what it pleases, whether we understand or not."

"Kraft," said Hansen. "Will the King of Solfygg be sending warriors to Gennt?"

The spy nodded. "That's how I learned what was going to happen," he said from his seat. "There's a party of fifty warriors on the way now. Ten of them have the new armor."

Kraft was shivering from reaction. The fire on the hearth cooked moisture out of his leather garments in a miasma of sweat and the chemicals used in tanning.

"Solfygg can't have that many good warriors!" Prandia snapped. "They may have armor, yes. But warriors of the first rank are just as rare as royal suits, and I haven't heard that Solfygg has gotten around *that*."

"They don't have to be good, Your Majesty," Hansen explained wearily. "You're thinking of a battle like you're used to, where the top warriors fight one another and the rest of the armies hack around. When there's this many first-class suits . . . it's slaughter. I've seen it, and it's bloody slaughter."

He rubbed his eyes, trying to erase the memory.

"A god couldn't have done better with your warriors than Marshal Hansen has," Malcolm mumbled from Hansen's arms. "But that won't keep them from dying, lad. Ten for every one they kill, that'll be the way the battle goes."

"All right!" Prandia said harshly. "All right. We'll take the full army to Gennt except for a guard detachment here. At least Thurmond of Gennt will regret his treachery."

"No," said Hansen, "Your Majesty."

"How *dare* you!" the king shouted.

Kraft shifted in his corner. The knife handle projecting from the top of his right boot was suddenly close to the spy's uninjured hand.

"Listen to him, lad," Malcolm cackled. "*This* one doesn't threaten any better than a dying old man does."

"King Prandia," Hansen said. He cleared his throat. He'd *always* made a horse's ass of himself in situations that required tact.

"Ah, Your Majesty," he resumed, "I think it's time to win. We don't go to Gennt—we go to Solfygg. And we finish this instead of letting those bastards nibble you down till there's only a nub to swallow."

Prandia made a moue of apology for his outburst. "Ah, can we win against the main Solfygg army, Marshal Hansen?" he asked. "I understood from what you said . . ."

"Easier now than later, lad," Malcolm whispered.

"And the contingent split off and sent to Gennt is a bonus," Hansen added. "But—what Malcolm said is the truth. There'll never be a better time to try."

"Very well," said the king. "Give the orders, Marshal Hansen. I will accompany the army, but it will be under your command."

Prandia shivered. "And may North be with us!" he added.

"No, lad," Malcolm said. "Pray that Hansen be with us."

He giggled. "The god, I mean. Of course."

Hansen held his old friend while the laughter turned into spasms of coughing; but in every pause, Malcolm's laughter resumed.

Chapter Forty-two

One panel of the observation room showed a vehicle speeding toward Hansen. The panels to either side gave close-ups of an aircar driven by a lone woman.

The driver's features were unfamiliar, but the jewel between the full breasts left no doubt of Penny's identity.

The three-quarter frontal angles in the magnified images showed Penny's face was set with grim determination. That would have been normal enough for North—or Rolls, or almost any other member of their teams, the men and women who had become gods when they came to Northworld. But not Penny.

Perhaps the expression, like the visage itself, was merely a shape formed by her necklace.

The sky behind the aircar turned black. A squall swept across the plain.

Rain-cooled air slammed down in a column, then spread over the pond as a fierce wind which flattened grass. In the far distance, black-backed grazing animals the size of the aircar faced the storm. Their Y-shaped nasal horns lifted as they bellowed challenges to the lightning.

Hansen smiled as he stepped out into the wind. The titanotheres were as stupid as the aircar, and the vehicle had no brain at all.

But then, Hansen's own recent behavior had a lot in common with what the beasts were doing now.

Penny pulled up hard and let the vehicle fall twenty centimeters with the fans cut off. Its shock absorbers protested. The driver herself hung inertialess in the air for the time it took for the results of her lack of skill to settle down; then she got out of the car.

Penny had grace and—which was harder to recognize—intelligence. She drove badly because nothing, either animate or machine, mattered to her except for her own appearance and her own lust.

At least until now.

"I have a favor to ask you, Hansen," she said.

The squall hit.

The huge drops of the leading edge were massive enough to batter through layers of warm air and chill it so that the rest of the storm could follow. They smashed and splattered silently on the bubble of protection covering the aircar and the two gods beside it.

There was no thunder, but lightning rippled every few seconds. Penny's face looked terrible in its blue-white glare.

Hansen said, "Let's go inside, then," and led the way into his home.

Penny looked with distaste at the extruded furniture and blank walls of the lower chamber, not because the decor would have been cheap on any of the 1,200 planets of the Consensus of Worlds, but rather because it was austere to the point of asceticism.

Hansen smiled. The walls became a mass of pink, gold, and mirrors, while the furniture sprouted carvings so florid that they almost hid the underlying purpose of the items.

"Oh, I don't care about any of that!" said Penny with a wave of her jeweled hand. She sounded as if she meant it . . . but if she did, it was for the first time since Hansen had met her. "I came about—something else."

"All right," said Hansen.

He'd wait for her to get to the point . . . but this was his home. He wasn't going to hop around in it like a nervous client in a fancy cathouse.

"I know that duration doesn't mean anything to us," Hansen said. "But . . . ?"

He sat on the floor, not a chair, and stretched out on his left hip and elbow. The surface looked hard, but it gave slightly under his weight.

"Yes, well," said Penny, making washing movements with her hands. She turned almost instinctively to one of the mirrors now adorning the walls and checked her appearance "I, ah . . ."

Penny's right hand touched the beehive of red hair she

currently wore. She was full-bodied with a dusting of freckles on her shoulders and cheekbones. Her skirt and scoop-necked blouse were made of tiny gemstones, strung rather than attached like sequins to a fabric backing. They rustled minutely as she moved.

The woman realized what she was doing. Her face contorted into an expression Hansen would have described as self-loathing on anyone but Penny.

She turned and snapped to Hansen, "I don't want you to take Ritter with you against the Lomeri. That's what I came for."

"Oh . . . ," said Hansen as he got to his feet again.

Lying down was about as awkward a position as you could find for drawing a pistol. Intellectually that made no difference here, where the two parties controlled the Matrix and powers which dwarfed the destructive capabilities of any artifacts.

But Hansen's subconscious knew it was going to be the kind of conversation that had made Hansen very thankful for guns in the days when he was no more than human.

"We aren't attacking the Lomeri, Penny," he said. He looked at a Cupid-decorated pilaster instead of his visitor, who stood near it. "It's just that we need to launch from Plane Two to get where, ah, I need to be in the Open Lands."

"The lizardmen think you're attacking," Penny said coldly. "And anyway, they wouldn't care. They *like* to kill, just the way you and North do!"

I don't like to—

Hansen grimaced. "I guess if I didn't like killing . . ." he muttered, aloud to himself, "I'd do something else. Other people manage, most of them."

"All I'm asking is that you not take Ritter with you," Penny said with careful precision. "I can give you any number of servants, thousands of them if you like."

Hansen snorted. "That *would* convince the Lomeri that the Final Day had come, wouldn't it?" he said. "Look, Penny, I didn't tell Ritter he had to come along and mind the override. He *wants* to come."

"Because he thinks it's his fault that the damned machine doesn't work!" the woman blazed. "Anybody could do that! Anybody!"

"Not anybody," Hansen said, clipping the syllables. "And—"

There were a few of the West Kingdom warriors Hansen could train into the job; Culbreth certainly, and maybe Arnor. They had the courage, but the technology of war outside the Open Lands was alien to them.

That technology was crucial. On Plane Two, the Matrix was only a gateway—not a weapon to turn against the lizardmen, who would swarm toward any intrusion they detected.

"—if it comes to that, it *is* Ritter's fault that the dragonfly won't work unless somebody minds the shop on Plane Two for a couple minutes."

"So for that you make him—!"

"No!" Hansen snapped. "He did everything a human can who doesn't work in the Matrix. But for that I *let* him volunteer to help me. Because I sure-hell need the help."

Penny looked at him. Her gaze was as smooth and opaque as polished granite. Instead of speaking, she lifted the jewel on her breast by its transparent neck band and held it out to Hansen.

"Go ahead," she said at last. "Take it."

"I don't understand, Penny," Hansen said. His voice was thinned by the truth of the statement. He kept his hands at his sides.

Without the necklace to transform her appearance, the woman before him was what genetics and about nineteen standard years had made her: soft though not fat; blondish hair, but not blond by several shades. Her areolae were small and very pale. Despite her youth, her breasts sagged, and there was a mole near the left nipple.

"I'm giving it to you!" she shouted. Her eyes were clamped shut, but tears streamed out beneath the lids anyway. "Only give me Ritter! That's all I ask, just give me Ritter."

"Penny," Hansen said. He didn't know what to do with his hands. "Penny, listen, it's not like that."

He put one arm around her plump shoulder. She collapsed against his chest, sobbing.

"Please," she whispered. "Please, Commissioner. . . ."

Hansen eased the woman's head back and guided her hand so that the necklace dropped around her neck, where it belonged.

"Penny," he said, "listen to me. Ritter thinks he's responsible for the problem. I don't think he's responsible; there's just so much you can do working back from a piece of hardware."

The woman stepped away from him. Her form shifted reflexively through a number of choices before settling into someone with black hair and austere, aristocratic features.

Someone as different from the real Penny as Hansen could imagine meeting.

"Ritter says it's his duty to back me up," Hansen went on, knowing that she didn't—*couldn't*—understand what he was saying. "I can't tell him he's wrong, because I'd feel the same way myself if I stood where he does. And I'm going to let him do what he wants to do, because I like him well enough to let him make his own decisions."

He swallowed, then added the rest of the truth: "And because I need him."

"You're a bastard, Hansen," Penny said distinctly but without raising her voice. "You're doing this because you hate me. I don't know why, but you hate me."

She turned and walked with stately grace to the lift shaft which would return her to the upper level where her vehicle waited.

"I don't hate you, Penny," Hansen called to her back. "I don't hate anybody."

Except myself. And that's never stopped me doing whatever was necessary.

Chapter Forty-three

The sky was clear and windless, and the bright sunlight was all that was necessary to raise the spirits of the Eagle Battalion. It would be bitterly cold tonight in the lean-tos of leather and brushwood—and colder still for the slaves stoking the fires around which the warriors' lean-tos would cluster; but this was now.

The three battalions of the West Kingdom army were spaced across a ten-kilometer front. Hansen didn't like to divide his forces, but the need for haste made a multi-pronged advance necessary.

A dozen warriors and a larger contingent of freemen trotted by on ponies. They were going off to hunt, both for pleasure and to supplement the expedition's rations. The hunters would have no difficulty rejoining, since the main column was limited to the stolid pacing of the draft mammoths.

"Hey, Marshal Hansen!" called Tapper from the hunting party. "Why don't you tell Wolf and Bear to go home and whittle by the fire? We'll take care of Solfygg ourself!"

Hansen waved to them cheerfully from the back of his pony.

"Damn it, Malcolm," he muttered. "I'm leading lambs to the slaughter."

A mammoth carried the one-time Duke of Thrasey in a modified baggage basket rather than a howdah on the beast's back. The trails beneath the huge conifers were broad, free from undergrowth that might scrape off the cargo. And the low-hanging basket permitted Hansen to ride alongside Malcolm, the only person alive in the Open Lands with whom Hansen shared enough background to think of as a friend.

"Not children, Hansen," Malcolm replied. "They're all old enough to know what they're doing. We were, when we were their age."

Hansen clucked his pony on a wide circuit around a tree.

When he closed with the mammoth again, he said, "They're well trained, but the West Kingdom's had peace for—"

His tongue stumbled. He'd almost said, "too long"; but that was the whole point of what he was trying to do.

Wasn't it?

"For a long time, Malcolm," he said. "They don't know what a real war's like, the way w-w-you do."

Malcolm gave a cracked, crippled laugh. It sounded much like the squirrels who occasionally chattered from out of sight in the branches; but the squirrels were louder and vibrant with health.

"Colimore wasn't war, then, laddie?" Malcolm said.

"Colimore was war," Hansen replied grimly. "But most of these men—" he waved his hand in the direction of the hunting party and the head of the column "—weren't there."

"You're always looking for a stick to beat yourself with, laddie," the old man said. "I didn't understand it before, and I don't understand it now."

"I—" Hansen said.

Another giant tree separated them. As he rode around it, Hansen realized he didn't know what he had been going to say next.

"How many of the men who served at Colimore," Malcolm asked in a voice as jagged and cutting as broken glass, "deserted after you got back, Marshal?"

"We lost a couple," Hansen admitted.

"And we didn't lose a hundred and some others," the old man said, "who knew sure as *hell* what a real war was like. We didn't lose Tapper, for one."

"Yeah," Hansen said. "That's true."

Ravens flew silently down the column.

Hansen started. The birds' broad wings made them seem shockingly huge, more like aircraft than their lesser relatives the crows.

"You made Tapper the sub-commander of Eagle Battalion," Malcolm continued. "Good choice, that. He's twice the man his father ever was. . . . But what are his chances of surviving Solfygg, Marshal Hansen?"

"Right," said Hansen.

Malcolm's formal phrasing brought up the coldly analytical part of Hansen's mind, much the way a code word switched on a battlesuit's artificial intelligence. Hansen weighed variables— the terrain, the Solfygg array; and then factored in the certainties, the way Tapper had fought at Colimore and the way he would behave now that Marshal Hansen had honored him by promotion for his skill and courage.

"I've upgraded his armor," Hansen said. "He's got the least damaged of the suits we took off Solfygg bodies at Colimore."

He wet his lips. "But the odds aren't good. Tapper has as much chance of surviving a full-scale battle at Solfygg as you do of living another century."

The wicker container rattled softly. Malcolm shifted within it to look squarely at the man riding beside him. "And you think he doesn't know it, laddie?" he asked.

Hansen said nothing.

"Go on," the cracked voice demanded. "You know the answer. I've told you the answer."

"I lead them to *die*, Malcolm!" Hansen cried bitterly.

"No friend," Malcolm said. "You lead the lucky ones to die."

The basket creaked again. The old man was working a hand out of his fur wrappings with the stolid determination of a butterfly emerging from its cocoon.

"Some of us grow old and useless," Malcolm continued in the whisper that was all the voice which age had left him. "But none of us get so old that we forget we were led by Lord Hansen—back when we were men."

Hansen did not reply. He reached out and held Malcolm's hand until another tree parted them.

Chapter Forty-four

When he saw Hansen, Ritter clapped his hands in amazement. "Don't tell me you're wearing *that* when we go see your lizardmen!" he said.

A thought crossed the big engineer's mind. He added, "Unless you want me to kit you up? I can, you know—weapons and a force screen as good as anything you're going to find anywhere."

Hansen grinned slightly, absently. "Almost as good," he said.

Hansen wore hand-loomed wool trousers, a knitted wool pullover, and a short cape. A resident of the Open Lands would have exclaimed at the costly scarlet and indigo dyes, then noted that the cape was sewn from prime sables. To Ritter, the cloth was coarse, the colors muddy, and furs of any sort unhygienic and unsuited for the climate with which he was familiar.

More important, the short dagger slung from Hansen's belt wasn't a weapon in the engineer's technologically sophisticated terms.

"But, ah . . . ," Hansen mumbled. "I thought you and I ought to talk before, ah, I insert."

He looked around the workroom. There were tools and materials in such profusion that the huge expanse looked crowded. It looked like a junkyard.

There'd been a firefight in a junkyard once while Hansen was still in the Civic Patrol. Him carrying a needle stunner, and three villains with energy weapons.

This room was probably home to the engineer, but it depressed the hell out of Hansen.

"Look," he said, "why don't we go for a walk? Would you like to see somebody else's swamp?"

Ritter raised an eyebrow. "Sure," he said. "You over to Keep Worrel?"

"A little farther that that," Hansen said with a smile. "I'm

461

thinking of visiting Plane Three where the androids that followed your ancestors' fleet wound up."

He grinned more broadly. "And though I don't intend to meet any of their descendants, I *will* borrow a pistol and personal forcefield."

They landed on what looked like solid ground. It was so soft that Hansen sank in to his ankles. Muck rolled almost to the top of Ritter's half-boots under his greater weight.

They were on a spit of land between shallow water-courses. Reedlike horsetails sprouted around them, growing only waist-high or less. There was no grass, but the mud itself showed the green tinge of algae between the bases of larger vegetation.

Ritter wrapped the stems of several spike-branched horsetails together in one broad hand and tried to use the plants as an anchor as he walked up the gentle slope. Their shallow roots pulled out with a squelching sound as soon as he put tension on them. Muttering under his breath, the engineer stepped upward unaided.

"You can clean off at my place before we go back," Hansen said. "Never fear."

He stared at the similar mud shoreline across the water. The bank was less than fifty meters away, but mist drawn from the swamp by the red sun overhead was almost thick enough to turn all its features into a blur.

"See?" Hansen said, pointing.

Ritter followed the gesture. The flicker of eyelids made a lump of mud coalesce into something alive: stumpy legs, a barrel-shaped body, and a head that seemed huge even for the size of the body.

The creature was several meters long. It was hard to be certain about the length, because the tail merged with mud, mist, and vegetation.

"A crocodile?" Ritter asked.

"Nothing so advanced," said Hansen. "An amphibian. A big salamander."

He cleared his throat. "You know," he resumed, "I've been thinking. There really isn't any need for you to come along on this project. You've done your—"

"Like hell I've done my job!" said Ritter, anticipating the next word. "If I'd *done* my job you wouldn't need somebody manning the control panel while the vehicle shifts planes!"

"One of the Searchers can handle that," said Hansen. "They're used to hardware, it won't be a problem."

"No," said Ritter. "We had a deal, you and I. I'm going to do my end of it, and I damn well expect you to do yours."

The giant amphibian emitted a great burp of noise. It sounded as though a truck had skidded to a hard stop. The beast slid into the water with unexpected grace, leaving behind only a roiled patch on the surface.

Hansen sheepishly reholstered his borrowed pistol. "Look," he said, "there's no question about you getting the freedom you want. I can set you up with a keep on your own plane, if that's what you like—"

The engineer grimaced. "I don't like taking orders from fools," he said. "That doesn't mean I want to act like a fool myself."

"—or," Hansen continued with a nod of approval, "you can take service with any of a number of . . ."

He cleared his throat. "Of gods," he said. "Me—I would be honored. Saburo has asked after you. I think you would find him undemanding and . . . not a fool, in most fashions."

Hansen bent as if to examine the large millipede crawling over the algal mat. "And of course there's Penny."

The engineer touched Hansen's elbow. Hansen met his eyes again.

"I told you I'd make your dragonfly work," Ritter said. "I figured that I could manage that in the lab, but I was wrong. I *will* do what I said."

Hansen slapped the engineer's hand away. "Do you *want* to die?" he snarled.

Ritter's left fingertips massaged the red mark Hansen had raised on the back of the other hand. "No, I don't," he said mildly. "Do *you* want to die, Master Hansen?"

"Sorry," Hansen whispered. "Yeah, that's a fair question."

He managed a wry smile. "It's just, you know . . . There's nothing in this that requires somebody of your talent. There's no point in you risking yourself for nothing."

Ritter squatted and tweezered up the millipede between the

thumb and forefinger of his hand. The animal twisted its shiny black body furiously while its legs quivered in the air.

"Not for nothing," he muttered to the arthropod. "Sure, I'm scared, but I . . ."

Ritter put the millipede back on the ground carefully and stood up again. "I wasn't as good an engineer as I thought I was," he said. "Don't make me think I've failed as a man too, my friend."

Hansen squeezed the web of the engineer's hand where the red patch was still fading. "If you're not a man," he said, "then I'm sure-hell not fit to meet somebody who is."

He cleared his throat. "Like I said, there's no need for you to come. But if you want to—I'd be honored to have you covering my back. Friend."

Chapter Forty-five

Two warriors with short blond hair accompanied King Prandia and a guard of honor to where Hansen sat on a camp stool in his open tent.

"This is my marshal," the king said. "He'll formally enroll you in our forces."

Hansen held in one hand a dispatch from Wolf Battalion which he was reading while he sipped broth from the wooden bowl in the other. Arnor and Culbreth were nearby on a felled log. They rose, and the coterie of lounging servants and freemen jumped to attention.

Hansen put down the tablet of planed wood. He continued to drink his soup, watching his visitors over the edge of the bowl.

"Marshal Hansen!" Prandia called. "Excellent luck! Even in this near wasteland there's a pair of warriors who want to join us against Solfygg. And better yet—"

"They both have royal suits," Hansen supplied.

His sidemen, Arnor and Culbreth, looked at him.

King Prandia blinked in amazement. "How did you know that?" he asked. "Did you see them come in?"

"I'd been expecting them," Hansen said dryly. "Though I thought they might have tried to join one of the other battalions."

"Then you know them?" the king said, increasingly puzzled in finding his marshal knowledgeable—and cold when Prandia expected enthusiasm.

Hansen finished his broth and stood up. "I'll deal with them, Your Majesty," he said. His voice was quiet, but the anger underlying it made all those in earshot blink.

The two warriors were stocky. They wore heavy fur cloaks, wolfskin and wolverine. Though their features were regular enough to be conventionally handsome, their eyes were hard.

Nearly as hard as Hansen's own.

"Lord Marshal," said the warrior in wolverine fur, "my name is Race."

"And your companion is Julius, I suppose," Hansen said grimly. Julia nodded meek assent.

Hansen glanced up at the sky. It still lacked an hour of sundown, though the ground among the great trees was in shadow.

"Let's the three of us go walk in the woods," he said in a neutral voice. He looked at his sidemen and said, "I'll be back in good time."

"Milord marshal?" called a courier, probably the man bearing Bear Battalion's situation report. "Later!" Hansen snapped.

Hansen walked for more than a minute in silence. The Searchers followed him, one to either side and a step behind.

A squirrel called nervously. Hansen stopped. A moment later the animal's chattering stopped also.

Confident that the rodent would warn them if anyone crept close enough to overhear, Hansen turned and said, "I appreciate what you two are trying to do, but you've got no business here. I hope you'll leave quietly. You *will* leave."

Race opened her mouth to object loudly. Julia touched her arm to silence her.

"We've been watching the Solfygg army," Julia said. "The state of training isn't nearly as good as yours, Lord Hansen—"

"Not as much difference in numbers as I would've thought, though," interjected Race, calm and professional again. "Solfygg has been planning for this war."

She grinned a hawk's grin. "But they didn't expect you to strike first, that I'll bet. They don't have all their levies in yet."

Julia nodded the interruption away. "They have seventy-three battlesuits as good or better than the ones you faced at Colimore."

Hansen winced despite himself. He felt as though he'd been punched in the pit of the stomach.

"We thought," Julia continued, "that you could use a pair of warriors with first-class armor."

"I really appreciate it," Hansen said. "But I can't accept your help. My arrangement with North—"

"This is no action of yours, Lord Hansen," Race said. "This is *our* choice, with nothing of you or any god to do with it.

The squirrel began to click and yammer in response to the Searcher's harsh tone.

"Well, let me put it another way," Hansen said coldly. "When North learns that you're fighting against his interests, he will punish you—rightly, to my way of thinking, because you've taken his service."

"That's our—" Race began.

"I won't have that happen on my account," Hansen continued, trampling her voice beneath the steel in his own.

"Lord Hansen," Julia said. She bit her lower lip, then reached out and took Hansen's right hand in hers. After a moment, he returned the pressure, then patted her and broke away.

"Milord," Julia continued, "at the end of the battle—and I expect you to win it, I would never bet against your ability, milord . . . but there won't be enough survivors to burn the dead. It will be like nothing until the Final Day."

"Lord Hansen," Race said softly. "Let us stand beside you. Please."

"No," said Hansen.

He stepped forward and put an arm around the hard shoulders of each woman to embrace them.

"But I won't forget," he whispered. "Some day you'll learn how much your offer meant to me."

Hansen walked back to the encampment alone. No one asked him about the two warriors.

No one who saw the controlled look on Hansen's face asked him anything at all until well after sunset.

Chapter Forty-six

Hansen used the manual controls rather than the aircar's artificial intelligence to settle them in front of the palace's gold-barred gate. String instruments inside played lushly.

"I feel," said Ritter acidly, "like a load of protein being delivered to the commissary."

Penny's palace was a gingerbread creation of marble and gold. It sprouted upward from a dozen turrets and a great, onion-domed tower in the center. Now, close on to midnight, lights concealed in the machicolations illuminated swathes of the pink stone. The creation seemed even more of a fairytale castle than it did by daylight.

"I need to talk with her," Hansen said mildly. "When I've done that, I'm going to leave. You can come straight back with me if that's really what you want to do."

The gates opened. A dozen male servants in pink and white livery marched out carrying trumpets festooned with pennons. The servants did not step in close unison, and a few of them did not seem to realize that they were even supposed to.

"I don't owe her anything, you know," the engineer said truculently. "I never asked anything from her, and I never promised anything either."

Hansen got out of the car. "I'm not arguing with you," he said. "I just need to talk to the lady."

Penny's servants raised their instruments to their lips. Instead of crashing peals of brass, sophisticated electronics within the seeming trumpets sang like harps and violins.

Trumpets *looked* right, but Penny was not to be balked of her saccharine string music.

Hansen strode between the two lines of musicians. The engineer was still in the aircar. Hansen didn't look back.

Penny's reception hall had a thirty-meter ceiling. The walls were of mirrors; gold panels—antiqued bronze would have been far more attractive—with love scenes in low relief; and internally-lighted sconces of frosted glass.

More liveried servants lined the walls. They serenaded the visitor with music that might have been Wagnerian before being transmuted through the tastes of the palace's mistress.

Six red-plush steps rose to another portal at the far end of the hall. The doors were closed, and no one stood on the upper landing where Penny normally greeted male visitors.

Hansen paused, just within the outer set of doors. Penny's major domo scurried to his side. The man was plump, balding, and ridiculous in his costume: pink tights and body stocking, with white pompons on his toes, shorts, and sleeves.

For all that, the major domo looked less harried than most of the other male servants, probably because his duties to his mistress were unlikely to include the most basic one. Penny was quite particular about the performance of her lovers, and a fit of godlike pique could have horrifying results for the victim.

The major domo bowed to Hansen. "The mistress has asked me to conduct you to her in the garden, sir," he said over the murmur of the music. "If you'll follow me . . . ?"

They went out through a side door concealed in the paneling. Behind them, servants continued to play, but the walls thankfully muted the sound.

The walls of the service corridor were pink stucco, decorated with swags and Cupids and highlighted in gold. Neither the walls nor the floor were particularly clean. The building could have been constructed to maintain itself—as Hansen's utilitarian home did—but Penny cared too little about such details to bother.

A couple was making love in an alcove. When the woman suddenly realized that Hansen wasn't just another servant, she shrieked and knocked over a potted fern in trying to rise. By the time her partner looked around, Hansen and the major domo were out of sight around a corner.

Hansen heard the chuckle of water even before his guide unlocked the wrought-gold wicket gate and ushered him through. "Milady," the major domo called. "Your visitor is here."

Warm twilight hung over the garden, though there was deep night beyond the palace walls. Bowered roses and wisteria perfumed the air, lotuses bloomed in the spring-fed pond.

There was a gazebo in the center of the pond. A bridge of gold bars led to it. Penny stood hipshot in the gazebo's doorway, wearing her own form and draped in a single off-the-shoulder length of translucent silk.

For the first time since he met her, Hansen felt a touch of desire for Penny.

Her half-closed eyes opened. "Hansen!" she cried. "What are *you* doing here?"

The major domo staggered as though shot. "B-but milady!" he whimpered. "You said to show your visitor—"

"Not *him*!" the woman shouted. She pointed her finger.

Hansen stepped between Penny and the servant.

"Wait, for god's sake, Penny!" he snapped, thinking as he did so that his choice of words was as unfortunate as everything else about this situation. "He just did what you told him."

The woman remained poised to send her major domo to death or a worse fate . . . and there assuredly were fates worse than simple death at Penny's godlike command.

"Ritter came along, Penny," Hansen said in a calmer voice. "He's out in the car for the moment, but I think he'll come in later, after I talk to you."

Penny lowered her arm and turned away. After a moment, her figure changed to that of a tall, slim woman with a skullcap of blond hair. She was dressed in a high-necked black chemise.

Hansen stepped onto the bridge. It creaked softly, making him wonder how it would perform under the engineer's great weight. Behind him, he heard the wicket click as the major domo fled, safe at least for the moment.

"You won't give him up, will you?" the woman said sadly. Her back was straight, but she dabbed at her eyes with one hand.

Carp with streaming fins and scales of mottled gold and silver stared open-mouthed from either side of the walkway, hoping for scraps of food.

Hansen reached the gazebo. "*Ritter* won't give up," he said. "And I won't order him not to go."

Penny walked across the octagonal building and sat on one of the ermine-fur couches. She crossed her legs at the knee and said brightly, "Ritter doesn't love me, you know. Isn't that amusing? I love a man, and he doesn't love me."

"People are different, Penny," Hansen said. He licked his lips, hoping to find words that would help him—

Explain? Apologize? He didn't know. Maybe just show sympathy.

"Look," he said aloud, "I asked him to come along so you could, you know, see him off. All I want is that you bring him back in good shape, because he's got a tough job to do."

Penny flared her aquiline nostrils. "Very magnanimous, aren't you, Commissioner?"

"Look, Penny," Hansen snapped. "If you treated him like a man instead of the latest goody in the candy store, it might be that he liked you better than he does!"

He paused and grimaced. In a softer tone he continued, "You might find that you liked him better, too."

The wicket squeaked open. Ritter stood in the gateway, filling it with his massive body.

"Guess I'll leave now," Hansen murmured as he turned.

He heard Penny get to her feet. "Like him better, Hansen?" she said. "That's the biggest joke of all. I *couldn't* like him better than I already do. The bastard."

The engineer waited at the gate until Hansen reached it.

Hansen nodded. "Thanks," he said to Ritter. "She's not a bad kid."

Ritter snorted. "The hell she's not," he said. "But she's a human being. And it's not as though it costs me anything I can't afford."

Hansen closed the gate behind him. He took one last look over his shoulder at Ritter crossing to the gazebo.

The engineer was doing his duty, because he was a responsible man.

Chapter Forty-seven

Hansen settled his commo helmet and grinned like a death's head at the engineer. "Still time to change your mind," he offered with a lilt.

"Screw you," Ritter muttered.

Ritter's heavy form was as lumpy as the deck of a warship. Hansen had offered to equip him for the insertion, but Ritter preferred to carry hardware of his own design and construction. Hansen's forcefield and weapons might have been superior in some absolute sense—

"Ah, you're not my type, Master Ritter," Hansen said. He wore close-fitting coveralls with a flat forcefield generator that looked like a breastplate. His pistol rode in a cutaway holster high on his right hip, and a stocked, short-barreled energy weapon was slung muzzle-down over his left shoulder.

Hansen's voice trembled as if with laughter or madness, but that was only the adrenaline coursing through his blood.

—but in a firefight, the shooter was more important than his equipment. Hansen was too experienced to choose to send somebody into combat with hardware that the user didn't know by instinct.

Ritter's laboratory clicked and sizzled with the sound of ongoing processes, tests and experiments and computer-directed refining steps; mechanical life which continued whether its creator was present or not.

"Well," Hansen said softly. He lifted himself onto the dragonfly's saddle. "Let's do it."

The engineer stepped close to his mounted guide and touched his hands, skin to bare skin; but in the moment before Hansen took them into the infinite perfection of the Matrix, Ritter's mouth opened.

"Yeah?" said Hansen.

His voice was calm, his face calm. His hands shivered with hot fury.

"You're going to carry us to Plane Two," Ritter said. "This isn't going to—be a problem with North?"

Hansen's face glared ice through the mask of his smile. "I *have* powers," he said with brutal calm. "I've agreed not to use them for a time in the Open Lands. Period."

For a moment, Hansen's smile was touched with humor. "If North has a problem with what we're doing with the Lomeri," he said, "then he can come visit us on Plane Two. This is one time I wouldn't mind his company."

Ritter managed a grin which the taut muscles of his face turned to blocks and angles. His body's response to tension differed from Hansen's. "We don't need North," he said. "You and I can handle any trouble the lizards start."

Both of them knew that if the Lomeri managed to react in time to the brief intrusion, Ritter would have to face them alone.

"Hang on," said Hansen.

The walls became sharper, clearer. The network of reinforcing rods expanded in all directions until—

Ritter hung in a void at the base of an enormous tree. The roots spread to borderless infinity, forking again and again into hair-fine tendrils that split still further as Ritter surged along their pathways, dragged by a touch he could not feel toward—

They landed in a magnolia thicket. The ground was black with charcoal from the fire which had cleared the hill a few years before. Limbless stumps up to five meters high remained as grave markers for the forest that had once existed here.

Ritter stepped away from the dragonfly and took the separate control panel from one of his cargo pockets. The color-coded read-out was in the middle of the green zone, as expected.

"Ready!" he said to Hansen. He thought his voice sounded thin.

Horns sounded, clear and terrible in the humans' ears. The Lomeri were already on the trail.

Hansen nodded curtly. He and the dimensional vehicle started to fade.

"Good hunting!" the engineer shouted.

The read-out started to edge toward the upper yellow zone. Ritter thumbed the roller switch to center it again, then concentrated on his own defense.

There was low ground to the north and west of the hill. At the moment it was a band of lush meadow. There must have been standing water in it when fire swept past where Ritter now stood, since the forest on the other side was undamaged.

The trees were conifers. On the side facing the meadow and full sunlight, the trunks were lapped in lesser vegetation, brush and vines and white-blossomed dogwoods. Only a few meters deeper into the forest's heart, the gloom of great trees would open paths as broad as cathedral aisles among the pillared boles.

That was the direction from which the horns had called.

Ritter pushed his way downhill. Where possible he squeezed through or ducked under the tangled, odorous branches. When necessary, his powerful arms tore a passage. He was used to moving swiftly in the complex passages of his own workroom.

On standby status at present, none of the engineer's equipment had an electromagnetic signature on which the lizardmen could home, but their instruments had obviously registered the intrusion itself. He needed to put some distance between himself and the insertion site.

A cloud of insects, flies or dull-colored bees, rose from the magnolia stems and swarmed around Ritter's face. Some of them settled on his skin, drinking his sweat or sticking to it. He squinted, hoping the insects would stay out of his eyes.

The dragonfly read-out was sliding toward the low end of functional. Ritter corrected it.

If he'd done his job, there wouldn't have been any need for the override switch.

Ritter had coupled his passive sensors to a mechanical plotting table because he didn't want to risk the electronic signature of even a liquid crystal display. Three styluses jolted suddenly onto a positive bearing.

Ritter unslung his shoulder weapon and pumped the fore-end to chamber the first round. The *click-clack*, scarcely louder than the insects' buzzing, made him wince.

A horn sounded its brassy challenge from the forest margin. Three Lomeri scouts riding ceratosaurs strode into view. Vines and bits of undergrowth fluttered behind their powerful bipedal mounts.

Ritter held his breath. The leading scout clucked. The trio

charged across the meadow in line abreast, aiming their short carbines one-handed as if they were lances.

The lizardmen were headed for the hilltop. They would not pass within twenty meters of where the engineer huddled near the lower edge of the magnolia thicket.

Ritter moved only his head, trying to keep the Lomeri in sight through gaps in the branches and dark green leaves. He hadn't had time to deploy the miniature optical periscope he'd brought along. Anyway, it might have gotten in his way if he needed to snap off a shot. . . .

For a moment the engineer wondered what would happen if the dragonfly reappeared just as the lizardmen reached the hilltop.

He'd seen Hansen move when it was time to kill. Ritter would bet on him again.

Muddy dirt splashed up beneath the ceratosaurs' great clawed feet. The ten-meter-long carnivores moved with birdlike jerkiness. Each beast had a short, blunt nose horn and a mouthful of daggerlike teeth.

They were passing him by. . . .

The nearest of the ceratosaurs paused. Its Lomeri rider snarled and kicked it with spike-roweled spurs. The carnivore ignored the punishment and twisted its head toward Ritter's hiding place. Its rider tugged on the reins.

The beast flared its nostrils. It had scented warm-blooded prey.

The Lomeri leader turned to chirrup up a complaint to the lagging scout. Nictitating membranes clouded and cleared as the slit-pupiled lizard eyes followed the line of the ceratosaur's interest.

Ritter fired at the nearest scout.

A magnolia branch caught the muzzle of his rifle as he swung it on target; the powerful duplex round struck low, in the carnosaur's haunch behind the protective hemisphere of the Lomeri force screen. The initial explosion blew a hole the size of a washtub in the beast's hide, and the follower projectile smashed the pelvis like a dropped glass before exiting on the other side.

The Lomeri leader swung his weapon past the crests of his

mount and fired. A bolt of saffron energy crisped ten square meters of bushes, halfway between Ritter and the lizardman.

Ritter aimed and squeezed the trigger. There was a blue flash on the Lomeri forcefield, a second flash in the center of the lizardman's chest, and a spray of bright blood in the air as the creature went over the crupper of its saddle while its mount curvetted.

Though Ritter had missed the nearest scout, the lizardman's crippled, dying mount thrashed on the ground where it had thrown its rider under the bullet's goad. The beast's slashing legs flung leaves, magnolia branches, and bloody dirt in the air.

The third scout was aiming his—

The air in a spherical section around Ritter went bright yellow.

The engineer could see nothing but the enveloping afterimage. The back and breast pods of his forcefield generator glowed white with the overload, searing Ritter despite their thick asbestos padding. Deflected radiance blasted a ten-meter semicircle from the thicket, reducing the thick stems to carbon skeletons and completely vaporizing the foliage.

But the forcefield which Ritter designed and wore held against the direct hit.

He couldn't see the Lomeri scout because his retinas still pulsed from the lizardman's bolt. The engineer fired twice, aiming roughly along the radius of the blackened arc.

His bullets snapped blue sparks against the blur of light. As vision returned, he saw the third ceratosaur running riderless across the meadow.

The dragonfly's control read-out had risen into the red zone. Ritter screamed a curse and thrust it back into the green with the rotary switch.

He stumbled deeper into the magnolias. The thicket which had sheltered him was a charred waste that would draw the attention of every lizardman on this side of the planet. Of course, now that his forcefield generator was live, Lomeri instruments could home on it.

Three steps into the undisturbed magnolias, Ritter ran head on into another Lomeri on a ceratosaur.

The lizardman shrilled a curse and tried to aim his energy

weapon over the head of his mount. The ceratosaur's gullet was mottled black and yellow; its breath stank like an abattoir.

Ritter pointed his short rifle as if it were a pistol and fired reflexively. The heavy recoil would have torn the weapon from the hand of a weaker man. The engineer noticed only the flash of heat as his initial projectile struck the Lomeri force screen and vaporized.

Metal plasma recondensed on the nearest solid objects, plating Ritter's gun muzzle and freezing in black microcrystals over his leading hand and wrist. The back of the ceratosaur's high-domed head blew away.

The dinosaur leaped high in an autonomic spasm. One of its legs flung Ritter backward, though the engineer's own forcefield prevented the black claws from rending him.

The lizardman spun out of his saddle, his weapon flying in an opposing parabola. Magnolias crackled when the Lomeri hit, then continued to rustle as the disarmed scout fled in panic.

Ritter got to his feet and ran toward the hilltop. The dragonfly's read-out was still in the green zone.

Bellowing and the calls of brass trumpets sounded from the forest. The Lomeri main force was coming up swiftly. From the sound the draft animals made, they were much larger than those the scouts had ridden.

Ritter wondered how far he could run before they caught him.

And he wondered when the dragonfly would return.

Chapter Forty-eight

Hansen felt his dragonfly struggle as though the Matrix had
material substance instead of being a skein of possibility.

The wash of surrounding light should have been monochrome.
Instead, the enveloping blur shaded from yellow straight ahead
of him into green at the corners of his eyes.

Hansen's face was calm, but his brow was cold with sweat.
Like being stuffed in a garbage can and rolled into a firefight.

The dimensional vehicle broke into a realtime universe with
the suddenness of an equatorial sunset.

It was night. He floated twenty meters above the roofs of a
walled city. Torches flared yellow and a dull, smoky red. Men
walked the streets between dwellings and taverns. No one seemed
to be looking up, but—

Hansen touched the temporal trim control, adjusting for the
microsecond advance which would permit him to see without
being seen. The vernier rolled easily beneath his thumb.

The dragonfly's electronics did not obey. If Hansen looked
carefully, he could see his shadow thrown across the slate roofs
by the quarter moon. A dog began to howl.

Hansen swore softly. While the meaningless syllables tripped
off his tongue, his vehicle lurched at if it were being hauled
through a wire-puller's template. Time drew a faint mask over
the scene below.

Hansen drew a deep breath. He couldn't really be said to
have relaxed, because his eyes kept flicking in one direction,
then another, as though a gunman was waiting, might be
waiting . . . but he knew that the first trial was over.

"Control, locator," he ordered the vehicle's AI. The holographic
display that sprang to life above the in-plane controls was as
crisp as that of the unit Ritter had copied. It gave a vector and
a distance, 837 meters, wobbling between .44 and .50 as Sparrow
moved within the confines of his cell.

Hansen pivoted the column forward. He could already see the dark mass of the citadel ahead of him.

The controls moved as easily as if they were disconnected. For a moment, Hansen thought that might be the case, but the dragonfly was moving, very slightly, slower than the smoke drifting from chimney pots.

Instinct made Hansen want to push the column harder. His conscious mind told him that the problem was in the override panel, not any of the controls over which the rider had mastery here in the Open Lands. He waited, moving only to scan the terrain—and to switch his left hand onto the control column, though he had no intention of clearing his weapons.

The dragonfly began to slide through the air at the speed of a man running. The force bubble protected its rider from the wash of winter air.

He kept a light grip on the control column, avoiding any input so long as his vehicle proceeded more or less as he wanted it to do. He was overflying the waste of rubble and rubbish between the modern part of the city and his destination.

The wall of the ancient citadel loomed. Hansen drew the column back—no change in velocity; pulled the column straight up on its axis and felt the dragonfly respond instantly by swooping higher than the brutal, lichen-splotched stone an instant before the vehicle's forward motion trembled to a halt.

The time lag was irritating.

The time lag was damned dangerous; but then, so were most of the things Nils Hansen had found himself doing with his life.

He pushed the control column slowly into the pommel. The dragonfly dropped in obedience to the controls. The distance read-out was still operating—6.59/6.60/6.61—so Hansen decided to trust it.

He edged the vernier clockwise another three clicks of the detent. The city faded. The Matrix's foggy illumination returned.

The dragonfly was no longer *quite* a part of Plane One. Hansen tilted the control column forward again, only a hair, and watched the metered distance to Sparrow reel down the holographic digits.

He was sweating again. There were judgments, uncertainties;

none of them serious if his vehicle performed as it should, but—

Ritter's copy worked flawlessly. Hansen centered the in-plane controls at three meters and brought the vernier back three clicks, a fourth. The only light was moonglow through a high slit window, but Hansen could see well enough by it.

He could smell the interior of the cell also. The dragonfly hovered just across the iron barrier from Sparrow. The attendant, Platt, snored in filth as complete as that in which he compelled the prisoner to live.

Hansen's fingers tightened on the grip of his pistol; but he remembered his plan. He was not here for vengeance, only from necessity.

He smiled like a shark killing.

Hansen rotated the vernier one last point to bring the dimensional vehicle into perfect synchrony with the Open Lands.

"Master Sparrow," he called in a low voice. "I have an offer for you."

A dog growled low. The smith touched the beast's throat with huge, gentle hands and stilled the threat. "Krita?" he whispered into the dark. "Have you come for me at last?"

"Not Krita," Hansen said. He would kill the attendant if necessary, but even the flies walking over Platt's face seemed unable to rouse him. "There are gods who would employ you, Master Sparrow. All you have to do is leave your prison."

"I *can't* leave, you fool!" the smith snarled. "I'm—"

His voice changed. "But you could take me on your vehicle. It will pass through the bars. Take me and I'll—"

"I won't take you, Sparrow," Hansen interrupted. "But if you're the master smith you claim, you could find the template in the Matrix yourself, couldn't you?"

Hansen felt it buzz in the dragonfly's saddle, sure sign that the override control had slipped out of the safe zone. The vehicle began to sink, almost imperceptibly.

There was a tiny metallic sound. The crippled prisoner had gripped the bars with both hands and was squeezing them in an access of emotion. The particular cause was uncertain in the darkness.

"Why did you tell me that?" he asked.

"Because you didn't think of it for yourself," Hansen replied.

"I didn't think of it . . . ," Sparrow said in a tone of mingled wonder and fury.

"Control, Plane Two," Hansen ordered his dragonfly.

Nothing happened for seconds, tens of seconds.

It gave Hansen far too long to wonder whether he would come back to Ritter in time.

Chapter Forty-nine

"I wonder if she's coming," Platt muttered as he stared out the citadel door.

He rubbed his hands together nervously. The backs of his fingers were ulcerated from poor diet and poor hygiene. "The moon's dark tonight," he added.

He turned around. "That's what you said, isn't it?" he demanded. The only light in the citadel came from the small lamp near the doorway. "At the new moon?"

Gravel ticked as a pile collapsed on itself. Its internal structure had been modified by the template into which Sparrow's mind forced it.

"Sparrow, damn you!" the attendant shouted. He strode toward the barrier. "Answer me, you half-man!"

The smith's dog backed against the stone wall, growling. Sparrow rose onto the support of his hands. "Wha . . . ?" he muttered. "Wh . . ."

"Where is she?" Platt said.

Sparrow chuckled like a falling tree.

The crackling, crunching sound went on too long for the attendant's temper. Platt tried to shout over the laughter, but the smith's deep lungs were too powerful.

"I want to know what you're making these past nights," Platt demanded in the final silence. "It's not armor. I know it's not armor."

"It's a gift," Sparrow said. "Aren't the king and queen happy with the gifts I made them?"

The smith's hand hovered over the pile of material on which he had been working in his trance. For the moment he did not disturb the covering of excess material to check his progress.

"How the hell would I know?" the attendant muttered sullenly. "D'ye think they talk to me except to curse?"

Platt's weasel eyes focused on the prisoner again. "Anyway,

it doesn't matter. I'm to make sure you don't do anything but what the king tells you. You'll stop it now, or—"

Sparrow smiled. "Our guest is here, Lord Platt," he said.

Platt turned. "The hell she is," he snarled.

As he spoke, Princess Miriam flung back the half-closed door and cried, "Platt, you filthy fool! Why didn't you put a lamp outside the door? Did you think I was going to come here with a train of linkmen?"

"M-m-m princess!" the attendant blurted. "I didn't—"

"Close and bolt the door, Platt," Sparrow said/ordered. "The city's full of warriors tonight. We don't want them disturbing us while I provide for the lady princess."

"Yes, that's right," the young woman agreed haughtily.

Instead of dealing with the door herself, Miriam stepped aside so that Platt could get by to accomplish the menial task. She wore white suede boots. They were muddy to the ankles. "And you—Sparrow. Be quick about it. I don't want to spend any longer in this disgusting place than I have to."

Miriam was wrapped in an ankle-length cloak of mottled sealskin; a matching shako covered her head. Although she wanted to avoid attention in the dark streets of the city, she still wore the glowing ornaments Sparrow had made for her. Every time the princess tried to remove the loops of light, they slipped back through her fingers to continue their slow, lovely spirals around her neck.

"Put more fuel on the hearth, Platt," the smith ordered. "The lady princess wants to be comfortable while she waits."

"I want—" Miriam snapped.

"The wait," Sparrow continued with an easy power that overwhelmed the girl's sharper accents, "will be only as long as necessary."

He smiled again. "You brought the mirror, lady?" he asked.

"Of course I brought the mirror!" Miriam said. "Why else would I be here? And I brought—"

She swept back the sealskin. She wore a jumper of scarlet linen over a blue silk tunic which showed its sleeves, high neckline, and hem. The mirror was on its neck chain.

A skin of wine hung from a broad shoulder strap, waist-high where the princess' cloak had concealed it.

"—this," Miriam continued. "As if I were some sort of servant!"

She slung the wineskin toward Sparrow. It struck the bars with a squishy sound and flopped to the floor. The stopper remained seated in the wooden mouthpiece.

The attendant knelt by the hearth on one wall of the building. It had no hood or chimney. Fagots of pine popped and sizzled, multiplying the amount of light within the citadel but throwing shadows in ghastly patterns as well.

Platt stared at the wine with eyes turned orange by the reflection.

Sparrow grinned. "It's necessary, lady princess," he said. "Now, give me the mirror."

The attendant jumped to his feet. "I'll take it to him!" he said sharply. His eyes were still on the wineskin.

Miriam made a moue of distaste. She lifted the mirror over her head and headgear, then held it out to her side without looking to see Platt's scabrous hands take it from her.

Platt minced toward the barrier and knelt so that his body was between the princess and sight of the wineskin. As the attendant slid the mirror through the barrier, his free hand slipped toward the wineskin.

Sparrow took the mirror. "Why don't you open the wine and try it, Master Platt?" he said in a playful voice.

"What?" Miriam cried. "I didn't bring—"

She broke off. The attendant was already guzzling at the mouthpiece. A drop of the strong red wine spurted across his cheek. He squeezed the fluid out of his whiskers and licked the edge of his hand to lose as little as possible.

"It's all right, lady princess," the smith said. His voice was gentle, but there was a current underlying it that made his dog's hackles rise. "You will see."

Sparrow removed rods and small wedges of less definable shape from their concealment among his piles of raw materials. He began to arrange them into a linked pattern on the floor of his cell.

"What are you doing?" Princess Miriam demanded. She looked at the attendant, then glanced in the direction of the door. Platt had barred it securely.

"I have everything under control now, lady princess," Sparrow said. "You will see."

The smith shuffled purposefully around the confines of his cell. He had made himself thick leather kneepads for walking. Gravel between the pads and the stone floor must still have been painful, but he showed no sign of discomfort.

Platt noticed that the princess was no longer watching him. He lifted the wineskin surreptitiously to his mouth.

Sparrow put the mirror in the center of the partial objects he had already arranged. He covered the array with carefully-chosen bits of ore and scrap metal.

"What are you *doing*?" the princess demanded. She stepped closer to the bars and tried to peer past her own shadow.

"What is necessary, lady princess," the smith said flatly. "When I have completed it, then you can tell me how much to your taste the result is."

"You'd better make my mirror work again!" Miriam said in a venomous whisper.

Sparrow smiled at her. He lay back on his bed of furs. His eyes remained open, but after a moment they glazed as the master smith's mind slipped into the Matrix.

The man and woman on the other side of the bars watched Sparrow. Platt glanced sidelong as he squirted more wine down his throat.

Though the rekindled hearth was warming the room quickly, Princess Miriam shivered and pulled her sealskin cloak more tightly around her.

Chapter Fifty

The colored ambiance surrounding Hansen shivered like glass struck by a brick. Sunlight and the glare of energy weapons made the hillside quiver.

The dragonfly emerged at the edge of the unburned forest, half a klick north of where Hansen had inserted. The undergrowth was torn. Facing away from Hansen were six lizardmen.

The Lomeri were mounted in pairs on blocky, broad-frilled triceratops. The beasts were in line abreast with about fifty meters separating each from the next. Containers with black, gray, and bright shimmering copper finishes were slung to their flanks.

The modules carried defensive electronics—and fed the wrist-thick barrel of the energy weapon which protruded above each triceratops' own triple horns.

The nearest Lomeri had reached the low ground between the forest and the magnolia-covered hill. They were the reserve line. Five more pairs of their fellows, also on heavily-burdened ceratopsians, had blasted their way through the brush to the hilltop.

The dragonfly's force bubble was made for general protection, not combat. Its controls would not spin an opening automatically when Hansen fired out. Hansen shut the bubble down, trusting in the lighter personal screen projected from his breastplate. His left hand swept the dragonfly toward the middle triceratops.

Hansen's right hand held the pistol he'd drawn as naturally as he breathed. He opened fire.

The ceratopsians carried forcefield projectors powerful enough to provide all-round protection against bolts from Hansen's pistol. Because the Lomeri thought they had only one intruder to deal with, they had shifted their defensive arrays so that the frontal arc facing Ritter was nearly opaque even to the optical spectrum.

Hansen shot the nearest pair from behind. The second lizardman died before his brain registered the actinic dazzle which had killed his fellow mounted at the console on the rear saddle.

The triceratops trundled on. It was not disturbed by the fact one of its riders had fallen to the ground and the other was slumped over his control console with a hole in his flat skull.

The instrument crewmen of the flanking teams both noticed the spike on their screens as a second intruder entered their plane almost on top of them.

Hansen shot at both ceratopsians, flicking his pistol barrel from one side to the other like a conductor's baton. He aimed at the large copper modules containing the power supplies.

One unit collapsed silently when the white bolt punched through its center. The shell of light distorted by the forcefield vanished from in front of the triceratops. Hansen fired twice more to finish the screaming riders before they could clear their personal weapons.

He didn't have to worry about the crew of the other beast. The power supply exploded in a sun-bright flash which devoured the lizardmen as well as the rear half of their mount.

The dragonfly skimmed past the tail of the beast whose electronics were intact. "Control," Hansen shouted. "Stop!"

The dragonfly was inertialess; its rider was not. Hansen slammed forward against the locked control column, bruising his palm.

He jumped off and ran to the triceratops. The mounting ladder which hung from its saddle was designed for longer, narrower feet than Hansen's. He snatched at it with his free hand, then holstered his pistol to get a better grip with his right. The beast continued to walk forward.

The pistol's ceramic barrel was white hot. The holster was extruded from refractory material which withstood the heat, but the fabric of Hansen's coveralls began to melt.

A volley of explosive projectiles raked across the dragonfly, sending up spouts of dirt. The little vehicle disintegrated.

Hansen pulled himself into the forward lobe of the saddle and swung the pintle-mounted energy weapon.

The magnolia thicket burned sluggishly wherever the Lomeri had not blasted it away as their mounts advanced deliberately on Ritter. The underlying soil had a great deal of silica in it. In some places the lizardmen had melted the ground to cups of glass around which even the triceratops' horny feet had to detour.

The air stank. The basic odors were of smoke and ash, but those were underlain by the complex, sickening molecular by-products of explosives through which stabbed ozone and other ions.

One of the lizardmen stood on his saddle and fired at Hansen with a shoulder weapon while his fellow tried desperately to turn their beast so that the forward-mounted main gun would bear.

The force screen of Hansen's ceratopsian muted to gray the flash of bullets hitting it. Even the *cracks* of the bursting charges were pillowed into thumps.

Hansen centered the sights of his hijacked energy weapon on the flank of the shooter's mount. *The trigger guard is meant for slender, scaly fingers, but that isn't a serious problem.*

Hansen's weapon jetted a line of blue radiance for as long as he held the trigger back. The target's forcefield held for a millisecond, then overloaded. Both power supply modules vanished in a huge green fireball, leaving a crater where eight tonnes of flesh and equipment had been a moment before.

Hansen didn't know how to control his mount, but the rate at which the beast plodded forward was faster than a man would walk. He didn't bother asking his helmet AI for a vector on his companion. He could be quite sure that the lizardmen had already pointed the triceratops in the right direction.

Two of the leading Lomeri teams had disappeared over the hill before they realized they were under attack from the rear, but the other pair were an immediate danger. One lizardman fired his main gun before it could bear an Hansen.

The Lomeri's blast raked the swale twenty meters away into a hell of smoke and steam, making himself the human's next target. Hansen aimed and fired at the sphere of protection.

Because the Lomeri was shooting out, there was already a hole in the forcefield. Hansen's bolt licked across the weapon and both riders, crisping them.

The triceratops squealed and lurched up on its hind legs alone. The top ten centimeters of its frill burned off in a razor-sharp line, but the beast was essentially uninjured. When its forefeet hit the ground again, it galloped away at racehorse speed.

The remaining driver had spun his mount to three-quarters frontal by the time Hansen rotated his weapon on target. The rear-seat crewman remained at the controls of his defensive electronics instead of jumping up to fire useless shots with his personal weapon at Hansen's full-density forcefield.

Hansen triggered a long burst anyway, lighting up the opposing armor just in case a portal opened as the lizardmen tried to shoot out. The forcefield remained solid. It pulsed across the spectrum, easily reradiating the energy Hansen's weapon poured into it.

The hostile ceratopsian now faced Hansen squarely. It strode forward. At any moment, one or both of the other Lomeri teams would trot back over the hill. Hansen would have to stop shooting or be caught in a crossfire while there was an aperture in his own forcefield.

Hansen lowered the muzzle of his weapon and blew a trench in the soil beneath the forefeet of his opponent's mount.

The triceratops lunged knee-deep in a pit of bubbling glass.

The beast screamed like the earth splitting. It threw itself backward and lifted its front legs into the air. Hansen ripped the triceratops' uncovered belly, killing the animal instantly before cutting upward into the module which controlled the forcefield.

When the protective hemisphere vanished, the Lomeri riders leaped from the saddle in opposite directions. Hansen's stream of blue fire turned them both to ash in midair.

The world around Hansen had slowed, but his body could not keep up with the kaleidoscopic impressions filling his mind. His triceratops continued to stride uphill, unconcerned by nearby bolts and burning flesh.

Hansen drew a slim-bladed knife from his boot and rammed it through the trigger guard of the pintle-mounted weapon, jamming the weapon to fire continuously. Then he jumped from the saddle and ran for the hilltop at an angle diverging from that of the triceratops. As he moved, he unslung his shoulder weapon.

The hillside was a smoldering, ash-strewn waste. It was hard to remember that this had been an expanse of magnolia flowers and the exuberant life which buzzed around them. Sparks stung Hansen's bare skin and melted speckles into his coveralls. The corpse of a saddled dinosaur lay on its side with one stiffening leg in the air. It was a carnosaur of some sort, not a ceratopsian like those the present Lomeri rode. Ritter had been busy.

A laden triceratops strode over the hilltop ten meters from Hansen. The lizardmen riding the beast were concentrating on the animal Hansen had hijacked, then abandoned. The Lomeri force screen was a narrow wedge, dark as a moon in eclipse, facing what they thought to be the threat.

Hansen shot from the flank and killed both crewmen with a single bolt. He continued to run.

Horns sounded from the forest. Another troop of lizardmen was arriving.

The hill's farther slope had not been stripped by energy weapons, though the crew Hansen just killed had blackened a tunnel through the gorgeous foliage. A knob of higher ground to the left protected Hansen from the surviving Lomeri fire team.

That was also the direction toward Ritter, according to Hansen's AI.

A projectile weapon fired nearby. It was either semiautomatic or set to cycle very slowly. Despite the muffling vegetation, the muzzle blasts seemed sharper than those of Lomeri carbines, and Hansen was sure the impacts had the characteristic *cr-crack!* of the engineer's duplex rounds.

A triceratops blundered through the brush just in front of Hansen. He had to jump aside to avoid its hooves. The force screen was a hemisphere of smoky crystal shadowed by the animal's beak and black-tipped horns.

Hansen poised with his weapon aimed up at a 45° angle, waiting for the discontinuity behind which he could hope to penetrate the lizardmen's front-focused protection.

If the lizardmen didn't fire first, through an aperture they could form by pointing a gun.

One of the Lomeri lay slumped over his console. Most of his skull was missing. His fellow had fallen out of the saddle. They had turned away from Ritter to meet the sudden threat of Hansen's arrival, but the engineer was not a toothless victim. . . .

"Ritter!" Hansen bellowed. "It's me! Don't shoot!"

He wondered if the engineer could hear after firing his

high-powered rifle repeatedly. If Ritter shot at any movement, Hansen's personal forcefield might block the impact, but the damage Ritter had done was convincing proof of the effectiveness of his duplex ammunition.

"Ritter, I'm—" Hansen shouted and almost fired by reflex into the figure that loomed in front of him. A squat troll of a man, singed and blackened except where perspiration had runneled paths through the soot—

But a man. Ritter was alive.

Hansen threw down his weapon and stretched out his hand to touch the engineer. A lizardman mounted on a ceratosaurus crashed through the thicket five meters to Hansen's left. The creature's carbine was already aimed.

Ritter turned and brought up his own weapon.

"*No!*" Hansen screamed.

He was too late. The *crack!* of the engineer's shot merged with the devouring radiance of the Lomeri bolt which streamed through the hole in Ritter's force screen.

Hansen threw his arms around his friend and hurtled out of the plane with him. In the cold radiance of the Matrix, he could not hear the engineer screaming.

But black wings hovered nearby, a Searcher whom North had sent to carry away the soul of a dying hero.

Chapter Fifty-one

Dawn was a pale warning, and the waning moon was a sliver on the black western horizon.

"Milord!" the voice demanded again. "Marshal Hansen! They're coming!"

Several trumpets sounded together from near Hansen's tent and the field headquarters.

Hansen shrugged out of his cocoon of furs and pulled on an additional linen sweater. He'd slept in shirt, breeches, and felt boots, suitable for either light use around the camp or for wearing within powered armor.

"*Who's* coming?" Hansen demanded as he slipped into his battlesuit. It would begin to warm up as soon as he closed it over him, but for the moment the suit's interior was at the ambient temperature of a night in late fall.

"A Solfygg army!" said Culbreth. He was already in his armor. "Ah, Baron Vandemann of Ice Ford and some of the other local lords!"

Hansen slammed his battlesuit closed. He was already shivering, but that was partly in reaction to the news. He'd counted on avoiding battle until he encamped beneath the walls of Solfygg, but the enemy wasn't obeying the West Kingdom's war plan. . . .

"Suit," Hansen ordered. "Hostile forces in red, map location."

Hansen's servants had thrown open the tent flap to admit Culbreth. The marshal stepped outside as a dozen high-ranking warriors including King Prandia arrived in their armor. Brightly-painted battlesuits gave the bustling throng the look of giant insects.

The suit's AI overlaid Hansen's immediate surroundings with a terrain map and three groups of tiny red dots converging on the blue pip at center. The nearest of the Solfygg forces were within a kilometer of the Eagle Battalion camp.

The artificial intelligence provided a numerical read-out in the upper left corner of the screen without being asked. According to that sidebar, the attackers totaled ninety-seven warriors. Roughly half of them were in the central group, with the remainder evenly divided among the flanking forces.

"The chief baron in these parts is attacking," the king said. "I can't imagine what he's thinking. We have twice his numbers in this battalion alone."

The three West Kingdom battalions were almost within mutual supporting range now that the invasion had penetrated so close to the enemy capital. That shouldn't be necessary, but Hansen was more concerned than King Prandia appeared to be.

Hansen had fought more battles than King Prandia had.

"They were trying to surprise us," grumbled Wood, a warrior from Prandia's combat team. "That's ungentlemanly!"

"Suit," Hansen muttered. Part of his mind listened to the words his officers spoke, but he had more important things to do at the moment than join pointless conversations. "Rank hostile suits on the map by color code."

Parties of mounted freemen were bivouacked along the approaches a kilometer or so from each battalion's camp. Inside the camps, at least six warriors were on duty throughout the night, watching through their battlesuit sensors for the enemy.

The entire battalion was in armor by now. Ponies and draft mammoths added their separate brands of noise to the confusion. Hansen hadn't *expected* an attack any more than Wood had; but Hansen had made sure his forces were prepared for the unlikely.

"Section leaders," Hansen ordered, "this is the marshal. Deploy your troops to meet attack from the west. Odd sections by the north gate, even numbers by the south. Sections Nine and Ten are the reserve. Out."

"Baron Vandemann must be mad," Prandia muttered. "What can he hope to achieve with so few men?"

The sections were units of eighteen or twenty-one men. Hansen's AI reduced the responses of their leaders to a bar of green light across the top of the marshal's screen. There was certainly a great deal of chatter as the troops advanced to meet the unexpected threat, but again the marshal's artificial intelligence protected him from the distraction.

Hansen concentrated on the new overlay the AI provided at his request. He swore softly.

Ten of the forty-four pips in Baron Vandemann's central formation shone pure white: suits of royal quality. The flanking formations were probably conglomerations of lesser nobles from the neighborhood. None of them were marked higher in the spectrum than a dull blue, the AI's shorthand for third-class armor.

"What Vandemann's counting on, Your Majesty . . . ," Hansen said.

All the section leaders and the high-ranking warriors in Hansen's immediate vicinity could hear him. That was fine.

". . . is that his ten champions wearing royal suits will slice straight through our line, kill you and me, and panic the rest of the battalion."

Which they just might have been able to do if we hadn't been keeping a good watch.

"Also," Hansen added aloud, "it's because he's a jackass. Our foragers drove off most of Ice Ford's herds yesterday. Instead of abandoning his own lands and joining his king like he ought to do, Vandemann's going to teach us a lesson personally."

"Instead of which we're going to teach him one, hey?" suggested Arnor.

"No," said Hansen. "We're just going to kill him."

He took one last look at the map, then said, "Suit, straight visuals. Your Majesty, gentlemen—let's go do it."

As Hansen led the command group out of the camp, he noticed an ancient, wizened face peering from a fur cloak by the south gate. He waved his armored hand.

Malcolm waved back. The despair in the old man's eyes was pitiful to see.

Chapter Fifty-two

Hansen's eyes were slitted when he burst into Plane Five on the examination stand of Ritter's laboratory, as though what he couldn't see clearly had not really happened. He was too numb to realize that he carried a hundred-and-fifty-kilo body, almost double his own weight.

The laboratory should have been empty. Instead, a woman waited. "Is he—" she called.

The smell was as sickening as it was familiar to Hansen. "For god's sake, Penny!" he shouted. *"Don't look!"*

He placed Ritter on the stand. The engineer's left forearm was burned to a stump. His ribs were showing, except where lung tissue had bubbled out through the gaps, and he no longer had a face.

Penny screamed as she stumbled toward the men. That was good, because otherwise Hansen would have had to scream for himself.

Ritter went into convulsions. The blast had seared open his esophagus. His dying breath wheezed through the gap, blowing out charred flecks of cartilage as the engineer's muscles contracted in their final spasms.

"Get away from him," Penny said.

Hansen looked up. "Penny, we can't—" he said.

Can't bring the dead to life. Can't modify events embedded in the Matrix.

Can't change the will of a woman named Unn or a man named Ritter, though a god's powers could have forced their bodies into any slavery the god desired. . . .

"Get away from him, Hansen," the woman said as she knelt beside the body. "Or I'll kill you. If I have to collapse the Matrix to do it."

Hansen nodded and backed away. He knew the feeling too well himself to doubt the truth of her words.

He hadn't noticed Penny's appearance when he entered the plane; now she wore her own form. Her body was naked except for the jewel hanging between her breasts.

She lifted Ritter's head onto her thighs, ignoring the blood and ash which smeared her skin:

Penny turned her head. "Will you leave us, please, Hansen?" she said in a cold, regal tone.

Hansen looked at her. Penny had the face and body of a teenage girl, but her eyes were as old as death.

"I'm sorry," he muttered.

There's nothing you can say, but you've got to say something.

Hansen let himself slide into the Matrix. The icy terror of the transition was almost pleasurable, a bath to wash away the stench of death and failure.

For a time, Hansen watched the scene from the observation room of his dwelling. He'd thought Penny would immediately carry the body of her lover back to her palace. Instead, she remained in the darkened workroom until Ritter's assistants entered at dawn to receive instructions for the day's work.

Penny set her jewel on the corpse's ruined chest, but the engineer had no mind to direct its activities. The body remained as life had left it, cooling slowly and congealing.

Penny kissed it repeatedly, though her lips touched only blood and charred bone.

Chapter Fifty-three

Sunrise turned the Solfygg battlesuits blood red, whatever the underlying markings might be, when the Vandemann contingent strode out of the morning haze half a kilometer away.

The attackers were not preceded by the usual screen of freemen mounted on ponies. Baron Vandemann was an innovator, a rare thing on Northworld. It was his fatally bad luck that he had chosen to experiment against a force led by Nils Hansen.

A few of the Solfygg warriors hesitated when they saw Eagle Battalion was not only aroused but that most of Prandia's greatly superior numbers were already deployed outside the palisaded camp. Vandemann, a scarlet-suited warrior in the center of the line, turned and shouted a command. He used the battlesuit's speaker instead of its radio. The sound echoed to the camp, though distance robbed the words of meaning.

The central body resumed its advance.

"The courage of them!" Arnor said.

Because Arnor stood beside Hansen, the marshal heard his fatuous words even though the artificial intelligence cut them out of the radio net.

They're idiots!

The Solfygg flanking forces straggled into sight. Each of the smaller bodies was separated from Vandemann's force by nearly a half kilometer of flattened yellow pasture. When *they* saw the West Kingdom array, they stopped in their tracks and began to edge backward.

Arnor's job was to cover Hansen's back, not to deploy troops. Hansen didn't need to correct his sideman's words, and he had no time now for anything unnecessary.

"Suit," Hansen said, "display schematic. Undermarshal Tapper, advance at double-time with Sections Three, Five, and Seven toward the northernmost hostile force."

As Hansen spoke, his AI drew a pale blue arrow from Tapper's right flank units toward the clot of red beads. The Solfygg warriors were already retreating to put a rolling hill between them and the battalion they were supposed to attack.

"Undermarshal Patchett," Hansen continued, "advance at double-time—" another blue arrow "—with Sections Four, Six, and Eight toward the southernmost hostile force. Both undermarshals, screen the hostile flanking forces with one section—"

The blue arrows flattened into lines which were slightly concave in the direction of the hesitant Solfygg flanking units.

"—and hit the hostile main body in the rear as soon as it's fully engaged with our center."

The forces under Vandemann's personal control became a red arrow that flattened against the blue line of Hansen's remaining sections. Blue arrows curved back in from the flanks and squeezed the red patch into electronic limbo.

Reality wasn't going to be nearly that clean.

"Suit, send schematic," Hansen ordered. He'd learned not to trust words alone when trying to get across a complex, utterly vital concept. "Undermarshals, move out!"

Vandemann's main body was within three hundred meters. A warrior directly in front of Hansen turned. "What about *us?*" the man demanded in a voice that would have growled even without amplification.

The undermarshals' sections streamed forward at a jog. The lines lost cohesion almost immediately, but for the current purpose that wasn't crucial.

"Suit," Hansen said. "Straight visuals. Sections Nine and Ten, remain in reserve under King Prandia."

Because Vandemann's troops were concentrated on a narrow front, Hansen could use no more than two sections effectively in the front line himself.

"Sections One and Two, advance under my command. *Peace and Prandia!*"

Hansen stepped forward. He slapped the warrior who'd spoken on the shoulder to move him sideways so that his marshal could stride by. The fellow yelped, but he must have sensed that it would be a very bad time to get in Hansen's way.

Arnor and Culbreth were to either side and a pace behind.

Sections One and Two were in motion. Hansen had intended to advance at a walk, but sight of the undermarshals' forces jogging drew the center into the same gait.

And hell, he was leading the line himself.

"Marshal Hansen!" yelped the king's voice over the command frequency. "You can't leave me—"

Behind with the reserves, Prandia no doubt continued, but Hansen's artificial intelligence cut him off. The AI knew the marshal didn't care squat what the king or anybody else felt about his deployments; and Prandia himself had put Hansen in command.

"Cut," Hansen ordered, forming his right gauntlet into a scissors which quivered with blue fire.

His hand tingled pleasurably. All along the lines, Hansen's and that of the Solfygg force, arc weapons sawed through dawn's slow brightening. The opposing numbers were roughly equal, but the quality of the armor was—

The lines crashed together. Vandemann's ten champions strode onward with none of the hesitation which warriors normally showed just before the moment of impact.

Hansen parried Baron Vandemann's high cut. The blaze of light paralyzed both men in their overloaded battlesuits. Culbreth thrust at Vandemann's left shoulder. Arnor stepped close and hacked at his right ankle.

Vandemann's suit failed with a loud bang. Arnor's arc blackened all the paint from toes to knee. The baron's right foot flew away from a ball of plasma.

The baron toppled. "I got him!" shouted Arnor.

The Solfygg champion beside Vandemann cut Arnor's head off.

Hansen's battlesuit was hot and reeked of ozone. He switched his arc to his left gauntlet and stabbed at the killer's helmet. He had to pull the blow when a second champion pressed from his right. He didn't know where Culbreth was.

Hansen backpedaled, waggling a three-meter arc in the face of each opponent. Several of the Solfygg champions had fallen. The survivors of Hansen's front line stumbled in retreat.

One of Hansen's immediate opponents slashed through his arc. Hansen relighted his weapon and tried to step backward. It was like trying to push a dreadnought.

Hansen's suit was using all its power to defend against the hostile arcs. The joints of his armor were stiff, and if he stumbled—

His heel clanged against a battlesuit. He guessed he'd found Culbreth.

—Hansen was dead.

King Prandia's battlesuit was bright gold. He and his sideman Wood struck together, chopping the opponent on Hansen's right into three pieces.

Hansen transferred full power to the arc from his left gauntlet. When he tried to lunge into the blow, his legs trembled instead of obeying smoothly. The king and another warrior, the left-side member of his team, stepped around the marshal and finished that Solfygg champion also.

The battle area shrank into a dazzle like that of a megawatt transformer shorting out. It was over almost immediately. The undermarshals' forces had swept in behind Vandemann's troops and hammered them to scrap metal.

Just like it was supposed to happen. . . .

Hansen unlatched his battlesuit and opened it wide to the morning breeze. The wind was already dispersing ionization products in the air, but the smell of charred flesh would remain for months.

Hansen tried to get out of his armor. His muscles wouldn't obey. He wasn't sure he could have stood upright had not the legs of his battlesuit been firmly planted on the soil. He began to sob.

Two of Hansen's freemen ran over to lift the marshal out of his suit. On their second attempt, they succeeded.

King Prandia had stripped off his battlesuit. He walked toward Hansen, taking short, precise steps.

There was a windrow of armored bodies where the lines met. The remainder of the dead all lay in the direction of the West Kingdom encampment.

Even as they died, Baron Vandemann's warriors continued driving their opponents back.

"How . . . ?" the king mumbled. "Marshal Hansen, how many men did we lose?"

"We won the battle, Your Majesty," Hansen said. His eyes were closed. "That's all history's going to care."

He opened his eyes again. The smell and the memories behind his closed lids were worse than viewing the carnage.

Prandia put his arm around Hansen's shoulders, "I don't mean to seem ungrateful for your—your wisdom and your courage, Lord Hansen," he said. "But their battlesuits were, were . . ."

The king swallowed. "Were what you warned me they would be. What if the rest of the troops had supported Vandemann the way they were supposed to?"

"They didn't," Hansen said harshly. "They won't. You have a kingdom, Your Majesty. Solfygg has only a conglomeration of barons. They mostly hate each other worse than they hate you."

"Yes, but—" Prandia said.

A man stumbled toward them, through the wandering freemen and blank-eyed warriors who muttered about what had just happened.

Culbreth! Hansen's sideman wore a numb expression and his forelock was shriveled by the arc that slashed into his helmet, but he was still alive.

"What could've happened doesn't matter, Your Majesty!" Hansen said. "All that matters is that we've won!"

The ranks of silent dead threw the lie back in his face.

Chapter Fifty-four

Sparrow moaned, breaking the silence. His dog licked his
face while it stared watchfully at Platt and the princess beyond
the bars.

The smith had stacked ore and pieces of metal over his partial
construct. The arrangement shivered. Bits fell to either side,
and a puff of dust spurted from the interior.

Miriam turned from the barrier. "What's he *doing*?" she hissed,
an apostrophe to her own frustration rather than a question
for the attendant.

Platt lowered the wineskin. He stared goggle-eyed at the
princess. The skin had been empty for more than an hour, but
at intervals the feral attendant lifted it again to his lips.

Miriam grimaced in disgust. She spun on her heel and cried,
"You! Prisoner! What are you doing?"

Sparrow had been dipping in and out of his working trance.
Now he awoke slowly but completely. He rose into a sitting
position and stretched his mighty arms—straight out from his
sides; back as far as they would go; and then forward, crossing
in front of him.

The smith's blue eyes snapped with the lively humor which
had been lacking since his capture.

"What are you doing?" Princess Miriam repeated in a less
assured tone.

"I'll show you, lady princess," Sparrow said. He reached into
the slag and lifted out his workpiece.

"What the bloody hell is it?" Platt mumbled.

The attendant rose from his stool and stepped heavily toward
the barrier. Drink had not impaired his coordination, but his
face was a mask of truculent evil.

Sparrow lifted the broad saddle with his left hand until it
was more than a meter in the air. The four legs dangled loosely.

"Don't you recognize it?" the smith asked with patronizing

amusement. "But then, I don't suppose you've ever been on precisely the same timeline as one before."

His right index finger made an adjustment at the base of each leg. Mechanisms clicked into place. The leg joints locked into self-supporting springiness.

Sparrow lowered the dragonfly. He brushed bits of rock dust from the saddle.

There was no sign of the mirror in the pile of slag. Its material had provided elements necessary to create the dimensional vehicle.

Sparrow's dog whined in curiosity and concern.

"I'm leaving!" shrilled the princess. She turned and collided with Platt.

The attendant cursed and grabbed at the girl reflexively. When he realized what he had done, he snatched his hands away as though they had touched hot metal.

Sparrow chuckled. "She's the nicest piece *you'll* ever have in your life, Platt," he said. "Why are you letting her go?"

Miriam broke for the door.

Platt snatched at her. He caught a handful of the sealskin cloak. Miriam clutched convulsively at her throat and bent open the pin of her gold clasp. The cloak fell away and tangled the attendant's legs.

Miriam took two steps and tripped over the slops bucket. Her head and right shoulder crashed into the heavy doorpanel. The shako fell off.

As the princess crouched on her knees half-stunned, Platt gripped her shoulder and flung her onto her back on the floor. The necklace of light winked on steel as Platt slit Miriam's clothing from hem to neckline.

The princess began to scream. Platt's clenched fist knocked her head against the stone floor. Her eyes unfocused.

Sparrow used the strength of his arms to pull himself onto the dragonfly's saddle. His dog whimpered and tried to climb up with him. The animal's scarred hind legs would not support it; it could only nuzzle its master's feet.

Platt had lowered his leather breeches. The half-rotten tie-string parted under his desperate enthusiasm. He knelt between the woman's legs.

Princess Miriam turned her face away from the attendant. Her eyes followed without understanding the smith's activities beyond the bars.

Sparrow leaned over and scooped up his dog with one hand under its rib cage. The animal whined and thrashed its limbs, but it settled again when Sparrow rested it on the saddle ahead of him.

"Prisoner!" Princess Miriam whined. "Help me! You've got to—"

Platt hit the princess again, bloodying her mouth. He attempted to enter her. In his excitement, he instead ejaculated across her white belly. He screamed a curse and slapped her, front and backhand.

"I would rather leave on my own legs, princess," Sparrow said in a tone of inexorable calm. "But your parents denied that to me."

Miriam sobbed at a pain so intense that it penetrated her state of borderline consciousness.

Sparrow touched a control. The dimensional vehicle faded from sight, then reappeared on the other side of the barrier, hovering in the air as Hansen had done when he visited the smith.

Platt did not look up. He removed the knife hilt with which he had forced the virgin and bent to his work again.

The dog looked around brightly. It gave no sign that it was concerned at what was happening to it.

Sparrow slid into the curtains of the Matrix again. The light was sharp and pure, perfect. He had duplicated the dimensional vehicle with a skill that no other smith in the Open Lands could have imagined.

The dragonfly returned to synchrony with the world around it. The waste ground between the citadel and the modern city was dark and silent. The eastern sky lacked an hour of dawn, and the stars were feeble tremblings, above the haze of smoke that trickled from chimney pots.

Sparrow slid the in-plane controls forward, heading for the stone mass of the palace. The dragonfly rose as he proceeded. It climbed until the vehicle was almost two hundred meters in the air and the great gargoyles carven on the palace roof were insect-sized blotches.

"King Hermann!" the smith shouted. "Queen Stella!"

Sparrow's words were little more than a suggestion in the cold night. From within, the walls echoed, *"King Hermann! Queen Stella!"* in childish voices, terrible and terribly loud.

"King Hermann!" Sparrow cried. "Run to the citadel to find your children!"

The voices from the palace repeated Sparrow's words. Lights winked through the cracks in shutters as servants ignited rushlights on the hearths.

King Hermann and a dozen of his barons in battlesuits poured out of the front door of the palace. The king wore the armor he had stolen when he captured Sparrow. Stella, throwing a cloak over her night dress, ran after the men.

"Quickly!" the smith urged. "To the citadel!"

His dog howled. Sparrow began to laugh.

The two mobile chairs the smith had built for the royal couple slid through the palace gates behind them.

The chairs had voices. They echoed Sparrow's laughter, but they did so in the cruel, childish tones of Bran and Brech.

Chapter Fifty-five

In the hour before dawn, a cruel wind blew from the West Kingdom army toward the walls of Solfygg. Warriors in battlesuits kept watch from the walls, but Hansen had no intention of committing his forces to unfamiliar streets in the face of a hostile army.

"They'll be marching out soon," said King Prandia. He let his voice trail off as his mind considered what would happen next.

"We've got to assume that," Hansen said. He thought he could hear shouting from within the city, but it might have been the wind which skirled around the rooftops.

"We're ready for them," said Wood, the king's sideman. He used his helmet speaker rather than the radio, so only the two teams—the king's and the marshal's—could hear his words.

"Marshal, this is Tapper," said Hansen's earphones. "Eagle Battalion is fully arrayed. Over."

"Report accepted," said Hansen, knowing his AI would do the rest.

Just like a good secretary.

"Ready to die, you mean?" said Culbreth in what seemed to be no more than a tone of idle question. Culbreth hadn't been *right* since the morning Arnor killed Baron Vandemann, but there was nothing physically wrong with him.

Hansen had offered to remove Culbreth from the line on the grounds that the army had no time to repair his damaged battlesuit. Culbreth refused. He now wore an equally good suit, one abandoned by a Solfygg warrior in one of the units which had failed to support the baron.

"Marshal Hansen," the king said formally over the channel to which only the pair of them had access, "this time I will not be left with the reserve. You'll need my armor in the front rank."

"Marshal, this is Sears," said the right wing commandant over

506

the general command channel. "Wolf Battalion is fully arrayed. Over."

"Of course I'm ready to die," responded Wood in a tone of wonderment. "I'm a warrior. We're all warriors."

"Report accepted," Hansen said. Then, "Your Majesty, I'll need first-class warriors in the reserve also. Without you at Ice Ford—"

"We lost twenty-five men from the front rank at Ice Ford!" Prandia interrupted angrily.

"We won!" Hansen said. "Your Majesty, your job today is to do what I tell you to do. Dig *latrines* if I tell you to do it!"

The net passed a spurt of sound, a brief snippet before the AI realized that it was a shocked intake of breath rather than a syllable.

"They'll be coming out anytime now," said Culbreth softly. "I can feel the Searchers gathering. Can't you?"

"Marshal, this is Epson. Bear Battalion is fully arrayed."

There was definitely an uproar within the walls of Solfygg. It might have been warriors jockeying for the order in which they would march from the city and fall upon the West Kingdom attackers.

"Report accepted," Hansen said.

The eastern sky hinted dawn. Arc weapons quivered in Solfygg, lighting the battlements into momentary silhouette like summer clouds in a distant storm.

And the black wings of Searchers trembled just out of sight, waiting for the slaughter to begin.

Chapter Fifty-six

Warriors armed for slaughter stamped from the houses of Solfygg in which they had been billeted. Shouts from the palace area had aroused the Solfygg forces before dawn, the hour of assembly which King Hermann had set.

Arcs flashed in the confusion. Warriors were testing their equipment nervously. The streets of the city were too narrow for arc weapons, even when used cautiously.

Sparrow watched in cold amusement as a warrior brushed the lower edge of a house with his arc. The stone footings shattered, causing the building front to sag.

Roof tiles slid into the street. Some of them broke on the battlesuit of another warrior who wheeled about, cursing and flailing his arms.

The warrior's armored right hand smashed plaster from the half-timbered facade of a house. He lit his arc in shock at the impact. The dense flux blew a hole completely through the wall, igniting both the wattlework core and tapestries inside the structure.

Sparrow surveyed the city. Dense blue sparks marked a dozen repetitions of the same scene. He didn't care about the Solfygg warriors, not even those champions who wore armor the smith had been enslaved to create. They could live their lives without his let or hindrance.

The royal family, though. . . .

Hermann and his entourage stumbled across the rubbish tip toward the citadel, lighted by several torchbearing servants. Besides the queen and the armored barons, there was a score of freemen with lights or weapons.

The chairs followed.

The chairs glided behind the humans as if drawn by cords. Their wire bodies gleamed softly in the torchlight and the occasional snap of a distant arc weapon. Servants and even warriors glanced sidelong at Sparrow's eerie gifts, but the royal couple were oblivious of everything save their goal.

A freeman tried the door. The inner bar was shot through its staples. King Hermann raised his right gauntlet. The servant barely had time to leap aside before Hermann's arc shattered both panel and bar.

Iron—the bars and studs within the doorpanel—burned white when the flux touched it, but the glow faded as soon as the weapon sliced away. Splintered wood flew out in a blazing five-meter circle, causing servants to yelp and swat at the sparks on their garments.

Queen Stella's cloak smoldered. She ignored it and pushed past her armored husband in the narrow doorway.

Sparrow twisted his in-plane controls. The dragonfly slid through black air toward the citadel.

"Are you pleased to have robbed me, King Hermann?" the smith shouted. Cradled in his left arm, the dog shivered and whined.

The interior of the citadel blazed and echoed with the arc Hermann swept across it. Platt had started to rise. Blue fire from the battlesuit Sparrow had crafted for himself ripped the attendant's torso into vapor and glowing carbon.

Platt's severed head bounced on the stones. His mouth was open, but the intended curse had burned away with his lungs. His legs and dangling genitalia toppled in the opposite direction.

The king continued to slash the citadel's interior, severing the iron barrier in fire and deafening noise. His weapon melted the piles of slag and ignited the bedding on which the master smith had lain.

Queen Stella stumbled out the door. She carried her daughter. Miriam's head dangled, mindless or lifeless. After a moment, the king followed them.

"Do you remember telling them to cripple me, Queen Stella?" Sparrow called. "*I* remember, lady."

King Hermann looked at Sparrow, three meters above his head. He slashed his arc upward.

The vehicle's protective systems resisted easily. An opalescent globe surrounded the dragonfly and defied Hermann's efforts for over a minute.

The king shut off his weapon. His right gauntlet shimmered, glowing from the current it had carried in its failed attempt.

"Would I had killed you in your lodge," King Hermann whispered.

"Would you had killed me in my lodge," the crippled smith whispered back.

Queen Stella looked up from her silent daughter.

"Sparrow," she said on a rising inflection. "Sparrow? Where are my sons?"

"With you now, lady queen," Sparrow said.

He pointed with the first and second fingers of his right hand. The chairs shifted into wire simulacra of small boys.

"Hello, Mother," squeaked one in Bran's voice, stretching out its arms to the queen.

"I'm here, Father," said the other as its wire legs walked toward Hermann. "It's me, Brech."

Stella began screaming. She buried her face in the mud, but even that was unable to stifle her shrieks.

King Hermann cut the approaching wire figure in half at the waist. Until the arc weapon had completely devoured the creature, the legs continued to walk and the mouth to chirp, "It's me, Father!"

The eastern sky was lemon-colored. Fires were breaking out all over the city. Some conflagrations had grown to the point of showing open flames rather than just a rosy glow.

Metal clanged as Baron Tealer gripped the king's forearm. "Your Majesty," Tealer said, "it's almost dawn. The West King—"

Hermann shrugged away. He spread his right gauntlet and wiped the remaining wire figure away in a hissing electrical fan.

"I'm getting out of here," Baron Salem said. He spoke softly despite the suit's amplification. Three more of the armored warriors slipped away from the group when he did.

"Your Majest—" Tealer attempted.

King Hermann stabbed his vassal in the thorax. The unexpected, point-blank attack burned a hole the size of a fist through Tealer's own excellent armor.

Tealer toppled backward from the force of the blow. Other barons lurched away, then jogged at their suits' best speed toward the safety of their own retainers.

The king turned. He began methodically to erase his daughter's body as he had the armatures which spoke in his sons' voices.

Queen Stella babbled hysterically. Her face was turned toward the sky. Neither her eyes nor her mind held any image.

The dragonfly rose higher in the air. If there was an expression on Sparrow's face, it was pity; but there may have been no expression at all. His great, capable hands petted the crippled dog.

Below them, battle and chaos raged within the walls of Solfygg.

Chapter Fifty-seven

The sounds of battle from within the city were unmistakable. Arc weapons were a constant nervous flickering The guards on Solfygg's battlements turned to watch what was happening behind them. Some deserted their posts.

"Marshal?" said Blaney, the warrior who had replaced Arnor on Hansen's left side. "What the hell is going on in Solfygg?"

"Marshal," said Hansen's earphones, "this is Tapper. Do you know what's going on in the city?"

"Hold one," Hansen said. His artificial intelligence correctly keyed the response both over the command channel and through his battlesuit's speaker, answering both men's question.

"Suit," Hansen said, "patch the vision inputs from King Hermann's battlesuit into the left half of my screen."

This wouldn't work if Hermann had secured his inputs . . . but the AIs did *that* only if their operators told them to do so. Very few warriors in the Open Lands understood that their battlesuit's artificial intelligence was as valuable—if properly used—as the forcefield or arc weapon.

"But—" said Blaney.

King Prandia touched a finger to Blaney's vision pick-ups. "Silence," he said.

The left half of Hansen's viewpoint was the interior of Solfygg:

The ancient citadel blazed like a chimney. Wind ripped through the doorway and slit windows. The draft fed flames fueled by everything inside the stone walls, including the floor joists.

A body lay sprawled in what had been a first-class battlesuit before an arc destroyed the breastplate and the heart of the man wearing it.

An empty-eyed woman screamed hysterically beside a trench burned into the broken ground. Her body was uninjured, but her mind had shattered like a lightning-struck cliff.

"Montage view," Hansen directed his AI. "Four top Solfygg leaders, your pick."

The center of the vision screen remained a view of Hansen's immediate surroundings. King Prandia and the other West Kingdom warriors, faceless in their battlesuits, stared at their marshal.

The four corners of Hansen's screen each flashed with a different scene of panic and strife. *The Solfygg barons hate each other more than they hate you,* Hansen had told King Prandia. Now that central control had disintegrated, those hatreds flowered.

A major battle with at least twenty warriors on either side was taking place in the square in front of Solfygg's royal palace. Two of the viewpoints Hansen's AI had chosen were reverse images—barons hacking at one another, while beside them their retainers did the same.

In another quadrant, the viewpoint was a sea of flames. A Solfygg baron turned and turned again, looking for safe passage between buildings which had blazed until they collapsed across the street. The screens degraded as the battlesuit heated. Even if the images had been perfectly clear, they would have been images of death.

The fourth corner was a scene of flight. Servants quickly loaded their lord's movable possessions—and a quantity of obvious loot—onto baggage mammoths near the east gate of Solfygg, the side opposite King Prandia's drawn-up army. The baron and his warriors watched and guarded them.

"Suit," Hansen said. "Set all the friendly suits to receive these images unless overridden."

He took a deep breath. The warriors around him began gasping in wonderment.

"All units," Hansen said. "This is the marshal. Hold your lines until your section leaders re-form you. We've won, gentlemen. There will be no battle. We've won."

His teeth were chattering violently. It was with difficulty that he managed to add, "Out."

He'd won. Now there was nothing to save Hansen from the memory of what victory had cost.

The sky was growing brighter. As if in reaction, smoke from

the burning city rose into the clear air. West Kingdom warriors cheered to watch chaos through the eyes of their enemies.

Hansen unlatched his battlesuit. He lifted himself out of it. A freeman jumped to Hansen's side and offered his shoulder for support.

"Shall I have the armor carried to your tent, milord?" the man asked.

Hansen blinked. The freeman was Kraft, the spy who had brought Prandia warning of Gennt's treachery. Kraft's left hand was no longer bandaged, but there were angry pink scars where a dire wolf had chewed until Kraft severed the beast's throat to the backbone.

"What are you doing here?" Hansen asked.

Kraft shrugged. "I like to go where it's interesting," he said. "When I met you, I thought I'd stick close till my arm healed."

He smiled tightly. "As I said—are you finished with your armor for today?"

"I'm finished with it forever," Hansen said. "It's yours. I give it to you."

"Marshal Hansen?" said the king. Like all the other warriors, Prandia still wore his battlesuit. "Shouldn't we attack now? While the enemy is confused, I mean."

"No!" said Hansen more sharply than he intended. "No, Your Majesty. March back home as quick as you can, so that you don't get caught up in the fighting."

"But they're ripe for finishing, milord!" the king protested. "Even I can see that."

"No, Your Majesty," Hansen said. "Anything that needs to be done, they'll do themselves—Hermann's barons and their own vassals."

"But—"

"Go home and enjoy your peace, King Prandia!" Hansen said. He had to shout to interrupt Prandia's amplified voice.

"God knows we've paid enough for it," he added bitterly.

Hansen strode back toward the West Kingdom camp. The crackle of Solfygg burning had mounted into a dull roar.

"Marshal Hansen!" the king called.

He turned only his head. "Just 'Hansen,' Your Majesty. You don't need a marshal any more."

"But where are you going?" Prandia called to Hansen's back.

"To see Malcolm," Hansen replied. "To say goodbye."

Wind drove a curl of smoke westward. It wrapped Prandia's army in smoke and the stench of death.

Nils Hansen had done his job.

Again.

Chapter Fifty-eight

Sparrow sat in the saddle of the dragonfly he had built, looking down on the rest of what he had done. The smoke was so general that only strong gusts swept it from the roofs of Solfygg, and those same winds whipped flames across the tiles.

The army arrayed to the west of the city was disengaging cautiously. Servants had struck the tents. Warriors, a score at a time, handed over their battlesuits to be loaded on draft mammoths.

The sky around Sparrow darkened. His dog wormed into the fold of the smith's tunic. The beast opened its mouth as if to howl, but its jaws closed again each time with a dry smack.

Sparrow thought for a moment that a column of smoke had enveloped him, but the dragonfly did not respond when he lifted the control wheel on its axis.

He—they; he stroked the dog, to reassure it and to assure himself of its presence—were in a globe of deep amber light. Sparrow could see hints of motion through the surface in one direction.

It was a tunnel, not a globe. A figure appeared, walking toward the dragonfly and its riders. A woman—

Not a woman. A man with fine oriental features, wearing flowing robes.

The hem of each sheer garment showed beneath the hem of the next above. There were at least a dozen robes. All of them were basically green, but the shades were graduated by what seemed to be no more than a few hundred angstroms.

The dog shivered.

"Who are you?" the smith demanded.

"My name is Saburo," the slender man said. "I'll guide you. You're to be my servant now."

"Am I, milord . . . ?" Sparrow said. He had no feeling of motion, but striations in the wall of the tunnel suggested that something

516

was happening. The color slipped down through the spectrum into orange.

"I was recently in the service of the King of Solfygg . . . ," Sparrow's tongue added.

Saburo looked into the smith's eyes and jerked back from what he saw there.

"Of course, of course," Saburo muttered. "I should have known, given where the recommendation came from."

He smiled formally at Sparrow.

"Nothing like that, master smith," Saburo explained. "You do, after all, have to go somewhere now. I am offering you a home with me, with better conditions and services than you could possibly find anywhere in the Open Lands. In return, you would be expected to act for me in those instances when I need a skillful craftsman."

He cleared his throat. "And you could leave my service at any time," he added with his face slightly averted.

"You said 'recommendation,'" Sparrow said. "Whose?"

Saburo smiled again, minutely looser than the first time. "From Commissioner Hansen," he explained. "He says that you are as skillful as the servant he recently lost himself. I trust his judgment implicitly on anything of this sort."

"Actually," Saburo added with a frown at the memory, "Hansen said the *friend* he recently lost. But he meant servant, I'm sure."

Sparrow still said nothing. His face was opaque. His fingers moved, gently massaging the fur of the dog huddled to his warmth.

"Ah . . . ," said Saburo. "Ah, Master Sparrow, you would honor me if you accepted my offer of employment."

"All right," Sparrow said at last. "We'll come with you willingly. My lord."

The walls of the tunnel now were a streaky red, as bright as the flames which devoured Solfygg.

Chapter Fifty-nine

As Nils Hansen lay on the dead grass of Unn's grave mound, watching the red sun set beyond the silhouetted pines, he felt the subliminal tremor of black wings behind him.

The dragonfly halted with a soft *pouf* of displaced air. Hansen waited for the second vehicle to land, but this time there was only one. He rose to a sitting position and turned.

Krita walked toward him. The sunset deepened and enriched the color of her lips and long, lustrous hair.

Hansen nodded, then looked back toward the west again.

The woman sat down beside him. She raised her knees and locked them with her forearms, holding her torso upright.

Krita wore a suede singlet. It was a light garment for the season, but Hansen himself was dressed in only the linen shirt and breeches he had worn at Solfygg that morning in his battlesuit.

The flattened ball of the sun disappeared. The ragged pines stood out sharply against the red and purple light it bled across the sky.

"Do you come here often?" Krita asked.

An owl banked close to the humans, hunting for voles. The bird's soft-feathered wings were soundless, but it made a *krk-krk-krk* sound deep in its throat as it passed.

"Yeah," Hansen said. "I . . ."

After a moment, he added, "I should've come more often before. While she was still alive."

"I miss her too," Krita said. "But I couldn't stay in the palace, knowing she had you."

Hansen looked at the woman. "Nobody *has* anybody," he said harshly. "Nobody *owns* anybody."

Krita reached out and touched his cheek, brushing her fingertips down the whiskers Hansen had allowed to grow while he lived as a warrior in the Open Lands.

"I miss her too," the woman repeated.

Hansen put a hand on Krita's shoulder, then leaned forward to kiss her as the first stars came out in the sky behind them.

Finské and the writing provided the Northworld series.
Haven gut à road on Kirja's shadow, then learned toward
gothics has while it makes clear on the the the inhibit illum

Afterword

The *Volundarkvida* is one of the oldest, finest, and most
grim of the poems of The Poetic Edda, but the tale of Volund
the Smith can be traced back well before the Eddas. Probably
the earliest extant account of the legend is non-literary: a
seventh-century Frankish casket shows the crippled smith
hiding the corpses of twin boys beneath his hearth.

The themes of *Northworld: Vengeance*, like those of its
predecessor in this series, are largely drawn from the compilations
of Norse myth in The Poetic Edda and The Snorri (or Prose)
Edda. *The Lay of Volund* provides the core episode for the novel.

The remaining strands of *Vengeance* have come from quite
a number of sources within the Eddas. The structure of
Northworld is that of the *Alvissmal*. This short lay is of no interest
as literature, but it provides tabular data (which the stunning,
magnificent *Voluspa* lacks). Perhaps because of my eight years
as a practicing attorney, I feel a manic need for structure in
the fictions that I create.

Alvis himself is one of the Black Dwarfs, the cunning craftsmen
who do work for the gods of Asgarth—and generally have time
to regret the fact before they die.

The *Hyndluljoth*, a source that surprised me, provided the
circumstances to which Penny's behavior leads.

The Peace of Frothi is an incident of the *Grottasongr*, a very
powerful lay which I expect to figure largely in the next novel
I set on Northworld.

One major incident was imported from outside the Eddas.
The scene within Waldron's hall was borrowed/researched/stolen
(you pick your own verb) from *Killer Glum's Saga*, an anonymous
work written in Iceland at about the time The Poetic Edda was
taking its final form.

Let me emphasize that the sensibilities of the Eddas are in
large measure those of Dark Age warriors in some of the bleakest

terrain that humans have chosen to inhabit. Volund was not a civilized figure even at the time his legend was created: he was a force as stark and implacable as the rivers of ice which crush their way downward until they calve icebergs into the sea.

But it is well for those of us living in the soft lands of our own day to remember that there are still cultures to whom vengeance is a way of life, and to whom an enemy's women and children are targets as acceptable as they were to a red-handed Viking.

Dave Drake
Chatham County, N.C.

Justice

To Beth Fleisher
My once and future editor

Chapter One

The guard standing beside the four steps to King Venkatna's throne was probably bored beneath the smooth faceplate of his battlesuit. The armor's black-and-yellow striping which made the soldier look like a giant bumblebee.

Memory danced in the mind of Nils Hansen: *Shill, Hansen's sideman in battered armor with black and yellow stripes, strikes home and crows his triumph. A hostile warrior turns. The arc springing from the enemy's right gauntlet rips Shill's legs off at the knees.*

Shill topples. The air is full of the stench of burned meat. Hansen screams as his own arc lashes out in a deadly curve. . . .

To the folk here in the Open Lands of Northworld, that event had occurred more than a century ago. Duration no longer mattered to Nils Hansen. The dead of ages crowded in on him, and he shivered in the warm hall.

The craggy trader who stood before the throne claimed his name was Grey. "Your majesty," he said, "the device I offer you—the *Web*, the folk who sold it to me called it—can change the whole course of your reign."

Venkatna's father had built a new palace on the outskirts of Frekka. Rooms surrounding courtyards within the palace complex provided space for the West Kingdom's growing bureaucracy. Previously, the court offices had been scattered within the Old City over a number of buildings which dated from long before Frekka became the kingdom's capital.

Before Nils Hansen made Frekka the capital of the West Kingdom.

The city continued to expand. Already shanties and a stockyard lapped the exterior walls of the palace, and the king was erecting additional barracks for his army nearby.

"We are not displeased with the present course of our reign, Grey," King Venkatna said. The coolness of his voice left uncertain whether he believed the trader's statement was merely unfortunately worded—or was a subtle curse.

Venkatna was a tall man, but willowy rather than massive. His dark eyes glinted with a determination just short of fanaticism. His father had replaced the old linen diadem of the West Kingdom with a circlet of gold, but Venkatna himself affected a jeweled platinum helix which added timeless majesty to his thirty-two years.

"Forgive me, your majesty," said Grey. He bowed so low that his forehead almost touched the ground. "The course of your reign is already splendid. This device, this Web, has the capacity to build from that splendor into an era which will live in memory for all time."

The petitioner who crowded against Hansen's right side appeared to be a rural lordling. He wore imported finery for this court appearance: hose, a jerkin, and a peaked cap. The garments were dyed three shades of green which should have been mutually exclusive. His belt was of aurochs leather, while his boots were cut from the hide of giant peccaries. The materials had reacted in wildly different fashions to the russet stain applied during the tanning process.

He nudged Hansen and whispered, "I think those roofbeams up there are *stone*."

Hansen glanced upward at the coffered dome over the audience hall. The lower band of decoration, ten meters above the inlaid floor, was mosaic. The portraits and vine tendrils running higher to the lens of clear glass at the peak of the vault were painters' work which tried to mimic the stiffness of the mosaics.

"Concrete, I'd guess, under the stucco," Hansen murmured back. "But very impressive, I agree."

"The Web shapes the course of events," explained the trader at the front of the hall. "There is any number of ways that— dice can fall, let us say."

Grey's left hand came from beneath his cloak with a pair of six-sided dice between his thumb and bony forefinger. "This device thrusts possibilities to one side or the other of the event curve. The Web doesn't make things happen, your majesty, but it encourages the occurrence of possible events that *you* choose."

Grey dropped the dice. They clicked and chittered repeatedly on the stone floor before coming to rest, five pips and one, in front of the throne.

"Can you see?" whispered Hansen's neighbor. He craned his neck, pointlessly given that there were several rows of restive petitioners standing ahead of him.

"No," Hansen said.

Not quite a lie. He couldn't *see*, but he felt the Matrix warping to a particular result.

A five-meter semicircle was marked on the floor with white tesserae which stood out brilliantly from the mottled gray marble of the remainder of the room. The white band was a deadline, literally. Except for the highest members of Venkatna's court—with permission—and Queen Esme herself, anyone who stepped across the boundary would be killed by the guard.

"I'm Salles of Peace Rock," the stranger said, offering his arm to shake. "Are you here to get your district's tribute reduced too?"

"Now, your majesty," the trader said. "Throw the dice yourself while your chamberlain here sits within the Web and controls the fall to come up six each time."

"I'll throw them, my dear," said Queen Esme. She rose from the top step of the throne where she regularly sat, leaning against the leg of her husband.

Though the seat was one of highest honor, it cannot have been particularly comfortable. Esme moved stiffly in her garments of silk brocade. The wimple which framed her face also concealed the gray of her hair, but the queen looked very old. She was her husband's senior by a dozen years; a casual observer might have thought her Venkatna's mother rather than his wife.

"No," said Hansen. "My name's Hansen and I'm from far away. Just visiting the court I've heard so much about."

He locked his grip with that of Salles. A warrior's salute, forearm to forearm; either man's hand grasping the other near the elbow. The calluses on Salles' joints had been rubbed by years of exercise wearing a battlesuit.

Hansen remembered: *locked together with a better-armed warrior named Zieborn. Sweat in Hansen's eyes, his muscles straining, and his skin rubbed raw by the inner surface of his*

*shoddy battlesuit. Zieborn's blazing, blue-white arc edging
inexorably toward Hansen's face. . . .*

"N-n-n . . . ," Hansen whispered inaudibly.

*Zieborn's face afterward. Tongue protruding. Hair and
moustache out straight with the ends still smoldering from
Hansen's fatal bolt.*

"What's that?" Salles asked in puzzlement. He released
Hansen's arm and stepped back.

"I wish you luck," Hansen said.

"Hope your namesake hears you," Salles muttered. "The god
Hansen is a warrior's friend. We'll have need of him at Peace
Rock if something isn't done about these new demands. My
neighbors and I, we've about run out of patience with these
slave-bailiffs the king's sending around."

The chamberlain wore cloth-of-gold and a scarlet sash of office,
but he was a slave himself. Slaves made suitable instruments
for the will of a powerful monarch like Venkatna. Slaves knew
that their wealth and influence depended solely on their master—
and that if the king were overthrown, they would not long survive
him.

A minor noble like Salles had a tendency to think that he
was every bit as good as the next man, even a king. Particularly
when he'd locked down the chest plate of his battlesuit and a
live arc quivered from his gauntlet. . . .

The chamberlain gingerly took the position to which Grey
directed him in the center of the Web. The device was a
framework of thin wires with wide gaps between them. It was
not so much a structure as the silvery sketch of a structure.

Within the tracery were two couches of bare wood. The
chamberlain lay down on one of them.

"It's *cold*," he objected in surprise and pique.

"Concentrate on the dice," the trader ordered. His voice was
suddenly as harsh as an ice fall. "That they should fall as a six."

Queen Esme knelt and threw the dice before her. "Three
and . . . three!" she called.

The chamberlain screamed. He sat bolt upright on the bench.
His complexion had gone pale and his cheeks had drawn in.

"It's *cold*!" he cried. He squeezed his temples. "It's like frozen
rock in my, in my . . ."

"Boardman," said Venkatna in a thin voice, "if you no longer choose to carry out the duties I give my chamberlain, I will find another place for you."

The chamberlain lay back down. His whole body trembled.

"Throw the dice again, my dear," the king said. "Six is not a fall to be remarked."

The chamberlain moaned as the dice clicked, first against each other, then onto the floor. "Four and two," Esme said. Her voice was a melodious contralto.

"And again, I think," Venkatna remarked judiciously. "Though I don't see that a toy which turns dice in the air will make my reign—"

"Six!" called Esme. "And—"

The front rank of petitioners gave out a collective gasp. Whispered comments rose and rebounded from the vaulting like distant surf.

"The second die fell on top of the first," Esme said in a controlled tone that was loud enough to be heard over the babble of lesser folk. "It is also a six."

Boardman lay on the bench breathing hoarsely. His face was ashen except for the trickle of blood from his bitten lip.

"With the right operators, your majesty," said Grey. "Two operators, that would be—this device can impose peace over the whole of your domains. *Your* peace, so that you never need to worry about internal dissent when you face enemies across your borders."

Queen Esme gave the dice to her husband and seated herself again beneath him. Venkatna stared at the dice in his palm. His free hand stroked the back of Esme's neck.

"How will I find the operators?" the king said as if to the ivory cubes which clicked softly as they rolled against his callused palm.

"By searching," said the trader. "You are a great king, your majesty. Somewhere you will find the right two slaves to make you the greatest king who will ever live on Northworld."

Venkatna looked up. "Eh?" he said.

"An old name for the Earth, your majesty," the trader explained. Grey was turning slowly. "We use it occasionally where I came from."

The crowd of petitioners shuffled. The ranks between Hansen and the front parted as though Grey had drawn a weapon.

Hansen met the trader's gaze. Grey had only one eye. It glittered, pale and as threatening as the arc ripping from a battlesuit.

He smiled, and Hansen smiled . . . and the trader faced back to the king.

"Is the Web to your satisfaction, your majesty?" Grey asked from behind the screen of petitioners who had crowded back as soon as the trader's cold eye had been shifted in another direction.

"My, my . . . ," Salles muttered. "I don't mind telling you, Hansen, I'd watch my back around that boy. Besides, one-eyed men remind me of North the War God. He's nobody even a warrior wants to think on much."

King Venkatna nodded curtly. "Boardman," he ordered. "See to it that Master Grey here is paid his price." He paused, then repeated, "Boardman?"

Two lesser functionaries were lifting the chamberlain's recumbent body from the bench, being careful not to touch the tracery of wires. A line of drool and blood trailed from Boardman's chin.

"I'll see, to it, y-your majesty," volunteered one of the servants between gasps caused by nervousness and the chamberlain's weight.

"You've got that right, Lord Salles," Hansen muttered. "North can be a bad man to know. . . ."

Chapter Two

From his ice palace on a high peak, Fortin watched North in the guise of a trader offer a device to King Venkatna in the Open Lands. Fortin hated his father, North, almost as much as Fortin hated himself; but then, Fortin hated all things.

The view through the faceted discontinuity around which Fortin had built his palace was flawed, like that through windows frosted and glittering with reflected light. Nonetheless, the images were real, not electronic constructs. If Fortin wished, he could step through the field and enter the plane of the Matrix which he viewed.

There were eight worlds in the Matrix, and the Matrix was a world. Those who could walk between the planes unaided, shaping the event waves, were gods; but there were discontinuities where planes rubbed close to one another and beings unaided could step between them.

Fortin was a god, but the existence of this natural discontinuity was the reason he had chosen the site for his palace. The multiple images—eight simultaneous impingements, unique within the universe of the Matrix—permitted him to watch and move without leaving a ripple among folk whose lives appeared to have purpose and happiness. . . .

In the audience hall in the Open Lands, North spoke to a king as a plump underling suffered on a bench between them. Fortin couldn't tell the purpose of his father's activities; and even North's son by an android female thought twice before interfering with North's plans.

Several of Fortin's servants watched their master furtively. They were afraid to be seen looking directly at him, but terrified to be late in obeying if Fortin suddenly turned and snapped out an order. Fortin was not usually a bad master . . . but occasionally he was a very bad master indeed.

Fortin stepped slowly around the discontinuity to the next

facet, which looked onto a geodesic dome built in a swamp. Mist rose from black water, draping the serpentine trees into the semblance of monsters.

In the far distance was a range of sharp-edged hills. The rocks bore scarcely enough vegetation to mark their ruddy surfaces, much less break the force of the rains which cascaded across them and glutted the lowlands.

The woman in the dwelling's doorway was too perfectly beautiful to be human. Plane Three had been settled by survivors of a fleet crewed by androids, sent by the Consensus to investigate when Northworld vanished from the universe around it. Some of the androids were misshapen creatures whose body plans departed far from the human norm, but that was by no means universal: the same batch could give forth monsters and visages as fine and delicate as that of the woman in the dome.

Her complexion was white as chalk; as white as Fortin's own skin, the genetic gift of his android mother.

Fortin moved to the next facet. He stared with a fascination just short of sexual release. Stretching from an interminable horizon was a plain, broken by a single hill and peopled by stumpy columns like stalagmites of ice. There was no evident source of light, but the stark terrain was blotched by shadows nevertheless.

If Fortin looked with particular care, it seemed to him that the columns bore the faces of humans in the icy agony of Hell, and the hill looming above them had a face as well.

After a long pause, Fortin walked on.

Plane Five had been settled by a Consensus fleet also, one of three sent to determine how Northworld had disappeared. Gone with the planet were a colony, an exploration unit, and the team of troubleshooters headed by Captain North, who had named the world after himself when he cleared it for colonization. . . .

Trembling with memory and expectation, Fortin stepped to the fifth facet. The sun in its final days hung—huge, red and immobile—over a landscape of rock and desolation. There was intelligent life of a sort here, the crystalline machines which had crewed the last of the Consensus fleets. None of those glittering forms were at present visible through the discontinuity.

The only remaining life native to the plane was the patch of lichen on the face of a corniche above a shingle beach. For long ages, the lichen had been dying. Its minute roots had exhausted the nutriments they could reach in the rock, and the utter airless cold prevented the lichen from expanding outward to gain further sustenance.

To the extent that a creature so crude had feeling, the lichen was in pain. A smile touched Fortin's lips again; then his thought and his expression changed together.

The fourth time the Lords of the Consensus tried to investigate Northworld, they sent not a fleet but a man. His name was Nils Hansen. Hansen now had the powers of a god, but Fortin knew he would kill even a fellow god; though he knew the fabric of the Matrix would tear and all that was Northworld would collapse into a singularity, a black hole in spacetime.

Hansen, if he chose, would kill Fortin with the same cold certainty as Samson brought the temple down on himself and his tormentors.

Fortin's smile was a tight rictus. He walked on.

In a forest of giant conifers, six Lomeri prepared to make a slaving raid into the Open Lands. The Lomeri were lizard-featured bipeds with jaws full of cruel teeth, but the weapons and personal force-screens with which they were armed were smoothly efficient in design and execution.

The lizardmen rode ceratosaurs, bipedal carnivores with blunt nose horns and spiky brows that suggested horns as well. The beasts would eat during the raid, snatching a fifty-kilo gobbet from the flanks of a human's draft animal or bolting whole a screaming child, whichever came first to hand. Half the potential slaves would probably be killed by the lizardmen's mounts; a form of inefficiency which bothered the Lomeri as little as it did Fortin.

Dimly visible, as though a mirrored mirror, the Lomeri's target shimmered across a separate discontinuity. Despite the dark blurring of the image, Fortin recognized the thatched hall and houses of Peace Rock, perched on a low plateau.

Commissioner Hansen had a long association with Peace Rock. The disaster would distress him. Fortin smiled as he moved on.

Saburo, a member of the exploration unit that first discovered the planet, had built his palace on a basalt spire that pointed like a black finger from the surface of the sea. Surf crashed on all sides, kicking froth upward to be torn by the winds into smoky streamers.

On the roof of the palace, three gas-cratered lumps of volcanic rock rested on a sand table. The surface awaited the contemplation of the palace's master, but he was not present now.

The eighth face of the discontinuity was an image of Fortin's own central hall. He wondered what would happen if he reached through the frost-webbed surface and throttled the figure who sneered back at him with perfect android features. . . .

Moving with decision, Fortin walked back to the window onto Plane Five. In the distance rose Keep Starnes, the massive city/building of one of the lords descended from the humans of the first fleet the Consensus had sent to investigate Northworld's disappearance.

Outside, primitive mammals prowled a landscape of palms and cypresses, but few of the keep's teeming inhabitants had either the need or desire to leave the armored fastness. For all the ages since the settlement, the populace of Keep Starnes labored to equip armored squadrons which skirmished, pointlessly and interminably, with the forces of its neighbors. The soldiers ruled the keep, and the count ruled the soldiers.

In one particular only did Keep Starnes differ from similar keeps on Plane Five: the core of the installation was APEX, the Fleet Battle Director which had controlled all the Consensus ships. In the past, that had not mattered. Now there was a mind in Keep Starnes willing and able to use the capabilities of APEX against other keeps.

War in the neighborhood of Keep Starnes had ceased to be a gentleman's sport fought without direct involvement by the civilian establishment which supported the armies. As the walls and forcefields of other keeps crumbled, the territory under the sway of Count Starnes' self-sufficient city-state expanded proportionately.

Fortin smiled coldly as he unfurled his cloak. Its gossamer fabric bent radiation, so that a would-be observer looked *around* the wearer but thought he saw *through* a patch of empty air.

When Fortin donned the garment, he vanished from the sight of his servants. They trembled, even more fearful now than they had been before.

Within the cloak's protection, Fortin put on a pair of goggles. A hair-fine filament extended from either lens. The filaments extended through the cloak and served as the god's periscopes to the outer world.

In the center of Fortin's back and chest, supported by cross-belts, were active jammers. They could explode in dazzling radiance across the whole electro-optical spectrum. If Fortin activated the paired units, no scanner could operate in the signal flooding from them.

The half-android's most important tool of defense was not a piece of equipment: it was his ability to flee through the Matrix at need, leaving Plane Five and whatever was arrayed there against him. There would be no need for that, though. Fortin had visited Keep Starnes frequently. He liked to watch in person as the count's armies ground through the defenses of keep after keep.

Starnes enslaved specialists among the population before turning the remainder out into the wild. Invariably the refugees starved, because they were unable to recognize any food except that which had been grown in hydroponic tanks before being formed into flavored bricks.

If anyone could have seen him beneath his cloak, Fortin would have looked like an angel with a beatific smile. He vanished into the Matrix, unseen and unseeable—

And Karring, Chief Engineer of Keep Starnes, watched a telltale on APEX's console begin to blink.

"Sir!" called Karring to his master. "He's slipped in again!"

Chapter Three

"I didn't know you'd be here, North," Hansen said to the man who walked up behind him on the stone-railed loggia of the palace, overlooking Frekka's expanding suburbs.

North chuckled. "I'm selling my wares, Commissioner Hansen. Why are you here?"

"The only thing you have to sell," Hansen said as he turned to face the taller man, "is ways to die. What are you *doing* here?"

The breeze held a crackling undertone of warriors at battle practice in the near distance, cutting at one another with arcs on reduced settings. Occasionally, suits clashed together like anvils in collision.

Closer at hand, workmen hammered and shouted to one another during the construction of a long two-story building. Snow overlaying the job site had been trampled into muddy slush. The surface swallowed fallen tools and made the footing treacherous for folk carrying heavy loads, but the work continued.

The building would provide another barracks for the Royal Army. Every time King Venkatna advanced the borders of the West Kingdom, he gained an additional number of paid soldiers—for whom he would assuredly have need during the next campaigning season.

"I'm admiring your handiwork, Kommissar," North said coolly. "I may have encouraged warriors to battle, but *you've* taught the rulers here to conquer and crush their neighbors with an iron fist. My way, it was mostly warriors who died."

He laughed again. "You must be proud of the way you've improved things," he added.

Neither man was heavily built, but North was both taller and older than Nils Hansen. Where North's lanky build was obvious even under the cloak which he now wore in the guise of a trader, Hansen was close-coupled. Planes of muscle stretched over

536

prominent bones framed the younger man's face, while North's visage was all crags and a hooked nose.

No one would have seen a similarity between the two men—unless he looked at their eyes. The certainty that glared from beneath North's deep brow was no colder than that which flashed back in Hansen's fierce gaze.

One eye and two; but both men killers, and both of them very sure in their actions, come what might.

"*I* didn't—" Hansen said.

The denial died on his lips. He turned and faced out over the city again. He knew what he'd done. . . .

Tooley comes at Hansen over the bodies of the slain. The hostile warrior's battlesuit is striped white and red as blood. No single warrior can stop him, but when Hansen grapples with Tooley, the sidemen strike as Hansen has taught them. Tooley's spluttering armor topples, streaming the black smoke of burning flesh.

It was a cold afternoon. No one came out to share the loggia with the two men, a trader and a warrior traveling from somewhere distant called Annunciation, perhaps in the far south. Clouds lowered from the middle heights of the sky, but the snow had not yet begun for the day.

Down on the practice field, soldiers were trained in the team tactics which were Hansen's gift to Northworld. An army of professionals who fought in groups of three was unanswerably superior to feudal levies whose honor baulked at the subordination needed for the new style of war.

"I wanted them to have peace," Hansen said softly. Construction work was pretty much the same everywhere. That wasn't true about every sort of job, though.

Sometimes when Hansen closed his eyes, he could remember the former life in which he was merely Commissioner of Special Units—the armed fist of the planetary security forces on Annunciation. Then the rules were simple and straightforward: the Commissioner didn't make policy, he only enforced it; and he enforced it with a harsh certainty that left no one in any doubt as to what had been decided.

Now. . . .

"There had to be a central government to keep every lord and fifty-hectare kinglet from fighting his neighbor six days out of seven," Hansen said, speaking to North and to himself at the same time. "But it could have been a just government. It *was* a just government for years, North."

He glared at the other man. "You know that!"

North shrugged. "I know what I see, Commissioner," he said. He spread a hand idly in the direction of the slave gang unfastening a forty-meter centerpole from the draft mammoth which had dragged it to the site.

"They were from the Thrasey community, I believe," North went on. "The community fell behind with its tribute. A battalion of the royal army swept them all up to work off the debt over the next three years—those who survive."

His eye swept critically over the slave gang. A woman slipped in the slush, but she managed to slide clear before the heavy beam crushed down.

"They didn't have a prayer of resisting, of course," North said. "Not against the army *you* trained."

The Thrasey warrior has the better armor. Hansen has bitten his tongue and his muscles burn with fatigue poisons, but his arc holds his opponent for the moment it takes.

Hansen's sideman strikes. The already-extended Thrasey battlesuit fails with a bang and a shower of sparks. An arm decorated with black and white checks flies to the side. The paint is seared at the shoulder end, and the limb is no longer attached to the warrior's torso. A stump of bone protrudes as the arm spins away.

"Are you laughing at me, North?" Hansen whispered to the air.

"Yes, Commissioner," North said. "I am laughing at you. How *do* you like the changes you've made here?"

The woman who had slipped fell again. An overseer uncoiled his whip. The guard watched the proceedings with mild interest. The battlesuit he wore was of poor quality, but it would do against a coffle of unarmed slaves if they chose to object to discipline.

Hansen gripped the railing before him. He squeezed as if he were trying to grind the brown-mottled stone into sand with his bare hands.

"Nobody cares but you and me, Hansen," North said. "You

know that, don't you? The others are too wrapped up in their own affairs to notice what goes on among men."

"*Those* people care!" Hansen snapped, indicating the slave gang with a jerk of his chin.

"The other gods," North said. "As you well know. . . . And if you care so much about the folk here in the West Kingdom, Hansen—perhaps you should undo what you've created?"

Hansen looked at him. North stared off into the distance. The clouds over the practice field occasionally flickered with the light of the arc weapons spluttering beneath.

"The fellow you were talking to in the audience hall," North asked, careful not to catch Hansen's eye. "Salles. . . . Do you suppose he'll get the tax burden for Peace Rock reduced?"

"He won't get his petition heard," Hansen said flatly.

North hadn't picked up Salles' name and seat during the hubbub within the hall. He'd checked on Salles, as surely as he'd known the answer to the question he'd just asked Hansen.

"A moment . . . ," North murmured.

The tall man stepped to the door into the interior of the palace and snapped his fingers to bring a footman to him. The two held a brief, low-voiced conversation. At the end of it, coins clinked from North's purse and the palace servant scurried off on an errand.

Hansen's mind remained wrapped around the question, though he knew North had asked it only to goad him. "They'll fight, though, Salles and his neighbors," he said in a tone of cold analysis. His job on Annunciation had been a reactive one. He wasn't a strategist, but he was very good at predicting what somebody else would do next—so that he could smash them down with overwhelming force.

"They've seen what happened to Thrasey, so they won't be taken by surprise." Hansen took his hands from the railing and dusted the palms softly together. He was clearing them of the grit that might cause a slip if he needed suddenly to draw a pistol.

Not here, not now; but when Hansen's conscious mind moved on these paths, his reflexes ran down their checklist of actions that had kept him alive in former days and places.

"It won't help," his hard, emotionless voice continued.

"Venkatna knows they'll be waiting, so he'll send sufficient force to deal with anything a bunch of yokels can raise. But they'll fight anyway, long odds on that."

Their three opponents wear suits as good as any on Northworld. Hansen's armor glows with the charges that are about to overload its circuits. His lungs burn and his right arm swells as though he had thrust it into an oven.

Arnor, Hansen's sideman, cuts home. An enemy falls. Another of the hostile warriors swipes sideways, slashing through the neck of Arnor's tan-and-gray battlesuit.

"If you really cared . . . ," came North's voice from somewhere in the world outside of memory. ". . . you could change it all back, Kommissar. You do know that, don't you?"

"I can't unteach team tactics!" Hansen snapped. "Or do you want me to collapse the whole continent in an earthquake, North? Swallow up everybody who knows anything or even *might* know anything? Is that what you'd do?"

"I wouldn't have caused the problem in the first place, Kommissar," the taller man said. All the play, all the mockery, had left his voice. His tones were as gray and certain as the promise of snow in the clouds above. "*I* was satisfied when my Searchers gleaned only the souls of warriors killed in skirmishes which hurt no one but those involved."

"You—" Hansen began.

North overrode his protest. "It's not a joke, Hansen. I've seen it! When the Day comes, we'll need all the warriors we can get—and even *that* won't be enough to stop the hordes that come from other planes when the walls of the Matrix grow too thin to prevent them."

North swallowed, forcing his mouth to close against its own dryness. He stared in Hansen's direction, but he was looking at something much farther away.

Captain North had led the foremost team of troubleshooters in the Exploration Service of the Consensus of Worlds. The expression that Hansen saw flash across the other man's face was fear or bleak despair. Either emotion was as out of place as love in the grin of a leopard.

There were rumors among the gods about what it was North had seen in the Matrix that cost him his left eye.

The wind skirled through the stone railing, reaching under Hansen's short dress cape and tugging the fastenings of North's heavier traveling garment. The taller man grinned, fully himself again in his smirking assumption of what *he* knew that others didn't.

"If you're asking me for advice, though, Kommissar . . . ," North resumed. "As a friend and fellow, that is . . . the way men fight isn't the—cause of this."

He pointed deliberately toward the job site. The woman who had fallen was managing to stay upright only by clinging to a naked doorpost. She was obviously either sick or malnourished.

"It's the state you created to impose peace," North said. "There's where the trouble is. Bring down the West Kingdom and you'll end the worst of *that*."

At the job site, the overseer who had lashed the woman to her feet was about to administer another whipping.

"Go back to constant wars, each lord against his neighbor, you mean?" Hansen asked harshly.

Unexpected movement caught the corner of Hansen's eye; he looked back at the construction site. A man in the ruffed livery of Venkatna's footmen was talking earnestly with the overseer and the battlesuited guard.

"They'll still be human beings, Hansen," North said softly. "They just won't be ground into the dirt by a single tyrant. . . . But *I* don't care."

"What's going on down there?" Hansen demanded.

The footman left with the sick woman in tow. Gold winked in the overseer's palm and the armored gauntlet of the guard.

North shrugged. "A little bribe," he said. "Enough that she'll be reported dead—not so very unlikely an outcome, is it, given her condition. The servant will send her on to Peace Rock, where she'll be safe for a time. She has relatives there."

He laughed. North's smile was like the crags of a cliff face, and his laughter was the surf hitting those rocks.

"You imposed this on the Open Lands against *my* will," North said. "Now we'll see if you're man enough to do something about it."

Snow began to fall onto the roofs of Venkatna's palace, but it was no colder than the ice in Hansen's glare.

Chapter Four

In an object which could have been a small bronze handmirror, Sparrow the Smith considered the device in the audience hall of Venkatna's palace. His left hand stroked his dog's neck, where a darker ruff marked the generally tan fur. The dog sighed comfortably. She twisted to lick her master's palm.

None of the other servants came near the open door of Sparrow's suite—cell, it might have been called, deep in the rock-cut sub-basements of Saburo's dwelling. Early on, a pair of delicate, silk-clad favorites had tittered pointedly behind raised fingers at the hulking newcomer who still wore bearskin in a place of such sophistication.

They hadn't realized how long Sparrow's arms were, or that the smith would act with no more hesitation than a white bear making its kill on the ice.

Not that he killed them. Sparrow held his victims out over the sea crashing hundreds of meters below, one wrist of either gripped in his huge left hand. Sparrow plucked off their garments, seven layers each and color-coordinated according to rules so complex that they required years to understand. The bits of silk lifted in updrafts, then disappeared into the spume trailing downwind from the spire of rock.

The smith's dog was terrified by heights and the surf roaring below. She ran back and forth, yammering her concern for her master. The braces of living metal which permitted the beast to walk on her withered hind legs clicked against the limestone surface of the terrace.

Similar braces replaced Sparrow's severed hamstrings. The hard metal sharpened the shock of his heels through the rawhide boots.

When the servants were naked except for the paint on their finger- and toenails, Sparrow set them back on the terrace. One of them gripped the stones, screaming uncontrollably. The other

542

hurled himself into the sea with a blank look in his eyes. The act might have been either suicide or a convulsion as meaningless as the kicking legs of a pithed frog.

Saburo pretended he knew nothing of what the smith had done. No one troubled Sparrow after that. The other servants learned quickly that the smith saw things and heard things; and they already knew that he was willing to act with ruthless certainty.

Sparrow acted as if he were a god rather than a god's servant.

Tonight the smith's dog perked up suddenly in awareness at a change so subtle that it had escaped even Sparrow's senses. The bitch whined, hoping for direction; willing to fight or flee, willing to do almost anything but leave her master.

Sparrow touched the side of the object in his hand. It became no more than it had seemed at a glance before, a bronze mirror in a frame chased with delicately-fashioned serpents, each swallowing the tail of the snake before it in the frieze.

He got to his feet. He wore a long-bladed knife in a belt sheath, but the idea of a weapon was lost against the image of Sparrow's massive, careless strength.

The walls of Sparrow's suite shook as they always did with the shock and counter-shock of waves hitting the rock and shivering up the spire in dazzling harmonies. The vibrations made dust hang in the air above bins of ore and metals, stockpiles waiting for the moment that the smith needed some particular property to shape and smelt through the Matrix into—

Anything at all. There were great smiths in the Open Lands, but there was only one Sparrow.

There was an additional component to the quivering. Something was occurring, not on *this* plane of the Matrix but through the Matrix itself.

Sparrow stood, facing the apparent source and flexing his hands. The bitch crept between her master's outspread legs and bared her teeth in a silent growl.

The walls fell into a series of geometric shards.

Man and dog stood in a wormhole of octagonal sheets. Sparrow had no sense of motion, but the faceted walls/ceiling/floor rotated about him as though he were in the tailings of a spiral-cut drill, being lifted inexorably to—

❖   ❖   ❖

They were in a glade of bamboo. In the bower before them, a young woman lounged. She had oriental features and a look of godlike hauteur.

Her name was Miyoko. She was Saburo's sister, and her mere whim would scatter the atoms of the smith's being across the eight worlds of the Matrix. Sparrow watched her without expression.

For a moment, neither of the humans spoke. Sparrow's dog, released from the trembling terror of moments before, began to take an active interest in her surroundings. Birds hopped among the tops of the tall, jointed grass, flaunting their brilliant plumage. Sparrow knelt to knead his fingers into the dog's ruff, his eyes still on those of the woman.

"I have a task for you, Sparrow," Miyoko said a heartbeat after she realized that the big smith did not intend to speak first. Pretending she had not studied the man carefully, she added, "That is your name, isn't it?"

"I've willingly performed every task my master set me, lady," Sparrow said. He spoke in a low rumble with a catch in it, as though his voice had known little use of late.

If Miyoko had been stupid, she would not have been navigating officer for an Consensus exploration unit. Her nostrils flared at what she correctly understood was not refusal—but a threat, as surely as the hideous doom that Sparrow had inflicted on those who once had forced him to their will when he lived in the Open Lands. The dog stiffened at the dangerous atmosphere.

But Miyoko was not stupid . . . and she had summoned this skin-clad *animal* because she was afraid no one else could accomplish what she required.

"Yes," she said coolly. "It's because of Saburo that I need you. My brother is acting oddly, and I want to know why."

"Have you asked *him* why?" Sparrow said. His fingers continued to play with the dog, controlling the beast and providing an outlet for the smith's own nervousness. He didn't want to die, that one, despite his demeanor. . . .

"Of course I asked him!" Miyoko snapped. "He denies that there's anything wrong. I'm sure that he would tell the same foolish lie to any of the rest of us who asked him."

Not that any of the other gods would have come so far from their own self-willed purposes as to interest themselves in someone else . . . except perhaps for Hansen, and Hansen would refuse to intrude into another human's personal life.

"Anyway," Miyoko continued more calmly, "I want you to talk with him. I know Saburo *does* talk to you sometimes."

Though I can't imagine why, she thought; and as the thought formed, she *did* know why. This hulking brute would listen to Saburo, as another god would not; and he would still speak flat blunt truths to his master, as if he were unaware that a god's mere fingersnap could doom a mortal like Sparrow to death or eternal torture.

A smith spent much of his time in the Matrix. The Matrix took and gave according to immutable laws, and there was something of the same attitude in Sparrow himself.

"My brother is . . . ," Miyoko said with a gentleness which had been missing from her tone previously. "Moody. Angry. Withdrawn. I don't like to see him so unhappy, and he won't let me help him."

"Stay, girl," Sparrow murmured as he stood up.

The smith's motions were deliberate. Miyoko's eyes narrowed as she realized that the big man was not slow, only perfectly controlled. If he wanted to, he could lunge across the space between the two of them almost before the woman could form the thought that would blast Sparrow into nonexistence.

Almost. . . .

A weaver bird with a black head and brilliantly-yellow body fluttered onto Sparrow's right shoulder. It tugged at a lock of his hair. "He might not thank *me* for interfering either, lady," the smith said as if oblivious of the bird's strong, curved beak.

"If you're afraid—" Miyoko said.

Sparrow shook his head. The bird squawked and flung itself back into the air. "No, lady," he said. "I'm not afraid to do my duty. Aiding Saburo is a duty I've undertaken."

He smiled, gently enough, but his eyes were focused inward. "He's not a bad man, Saburo," Sparrow said softly. "I don't think he understands me, but we get along well enough."

The dog began edging to the side, pretending not to be disobeying her master's orders to stay. Sparrow stretched out a leg as solid as a treetrunk. He rubbed the beast's belly with his toe. When the smith's leg was extended, the leg brace glittered in the green-lit ambiance of the bower.

"I . . . ," said Miyoko. "You will not find me ungrateful. I've—noticed—that you appear to lack regular female companionship. If you would—"

"No, lady," Sparrow said. He was still smiling, but it was a very different expression now. "My master sees to it that my needs are taken care of whenever I require it." His visage softened. "That isn't a matter of great concern to me anyway. I have the Matrix and my work."

"But there was a woman when you lived in the Open Lands . . . ?" Miyoko said, intrigued despite herself.

"There was a woman," Sparrow agreed. His voice was without emotion and his eyes stared at a memory in the infinite distance. "Her name was Krita, and she left me. But that's no concern of yours, lady."

The dog began to whine. She sat up and pawed at the smith's thigh to break the mood that suddenly reeked in his sweat.

Sparrow smiled and bent to scratch the back of the dog's head. "Krita is a Searcher," he said without looking up at the god who had summoned him. "You would not force Krita to your will any more than you would force . . ."

He straightened; the smile slight but real enough, the rest of the sentence left unsaid.

"But I'll talk to your brother," Sparrow went on. "If he needs help—"

The smith locked his hands behind his neck and stretched, causing his biceps to swell mountainously "—then I'll help him to the limits of my strength."

His tone was as flat and certain as the approach of death.

Chapter Five

Five warriors closed in while a sixth waited for his death, standing on a knoll with his back to an ice-slicked outcrop. The individual warrior wore armor with silver limbs and a plastron of royal blue. Servants drove his caravan of clopping pack-ponies along the muddy trail in the direction of Peace Rock and safety.

Twenty or so of the mounted freemen who accompanied the five warriors paced the caravan from a safe distance, but they did not dare close in. Two Peace Rock warriors stumbled along beside the ponies. Their armor was of low quality and wouldn't have lasted a heartbeat in close-quarters action against the group of five, but freemen without battlesuits were no more than cheese for their slicing arcs.

Salles of Peace Rock stood on the knoll in a battlesuit nearly of royal quality. His armor was better than that of any of the band sent to fetch him back to Frekka, in chains or in pieces—it was all one to King Venkatna; but they were five and he was alone, and North had sent a pair of Searchers to gather Salles' soul when the arcs seared it out.

Race and Julia held their dragonflies in one of the interstices between planes of the Matrix, watching the battle shape on the knoll beneath them. If any of the warriors chanced to look up, he would see no more than the quiver of refraction, as though a mirage had been disturbed by the rustle of black wings.

But the warriors had more pressing business than the question of what waited in the sky.

The five advanced in a shallow vee. The apex pointed away from Salles while the wings moved to envelope him. The slope was steep enough to make the footing awkward, but it was no real protection to the trapped man.

"Why don't they get it over with?" Race muttered angrily. She twisted a vernier control on her saddle, bringing the tracery of slim booms which she rode through the Matrix closer temporally to the Open Lands.

Race hung in a curtain of colored light. Dimly visible across the pastel shimmer was her companion in a separate bubble of reality, bounded by the tips of wands stretching from her dragonfly's saddle. Below, through a screen of slight asynchrony, warriors and the bleak landscape appeared in shades of gray.

Venkatna's men were in no hurry. The caravan would get away, which was a pity; but Peace Rock would be no refuge in the long run, and Salles was too dangerous an opponent to take lightly.

Salles lighted the arc from his right gauntlet, burning harsh highlights from the icy rocks behind him. His opponents paused, less than three meters away. Salles feinted to his right, watching Venkatna's warriors bunch reflexively.

Julia snorted in derision. She and Race wore battlesuits of better quality than those of the men below. The Searchers had seen more war than any warrior, and they had only scorn for the folk the king had sent to do his bidding.

Salles, on the other hand . . .

Salles lunged, not to his side but for the man in the center. Salles' legs moved stiffly. He had concentrated into his cutting arc the power that would normally have been driving the servos in his limbs.

The slope aided him. Salles' target got his own weapon up, but none of his sidemen were in time to strike with him and drain the attack's power into the defenses of Salles' battlesuit.

No single opponent could meet Salles' rush and live.

Light blazed as the arcs crossed, burning air to a plasma. The Frekka warrior's overloaded weapon failed. Salles cut home. For a fraction of a second, his opponent's suit was shrouded in a corona that boiled snow to steam and cracked the rock underneath with transmitted heat.

The suit's defenses overloaded. Salles' arc tore a deep wedge into his opponent's shoulder. Metal sheathing burned and peeled back. The short-circuited victim collapsed, a dead man in dead armor.

In the saddle of Race's dragonfly, a delicate electronic package clucked. It was recording every nuance of the warrior's mind at the moment of his death. On the Searchers' return, their master North would turn that data to his own purposes. . . .

A Frekka warrior wheeled in time to cut as the Lord of Peace Rock crashed through the line. His extended weapon lighted the carapace of Salles' armor. The arc was too diffuse to kill, but it made Salles' servos stutter as power fed the defenses.

Salles doubled over in a somersault and rolled free. He came to his feet, facing Venkatna's men as they hesitated on the slope above him. He switched his arc off, planted his arms akimbo, and laughed.

"Race!" Julia called across the blur of nothingness. There was grim joy in her voice. "My armor to your hairband that North isn't going to get the Lord of Peace Rock *this* day!"

She brought her dragonfly closer to the plane they were observing. The Searchers were shadowy outlines to the men on the ground, while the warriors' arcs burned blue-white and vivid to the women above.

One of the Frekka warriors lunged forward as though Salles' laughter had goaded him into movement. He took two gravity-lengthened strides before his companions realized what was happening.

Salles lighted the arc in his left hand. He slashed through his opponent's ankles so swiftly that the crippling shock was his victim's first warning. The depowered battlesuit skidded downslope on its plastron, spluttering and steaming. The warrior inside screamed.

Race began to laugh. "North sent us for the wrong man," she cried to her companion. "He won't be pleased!"

Salles took a step toward his three remaining opponents. Arcs sprang like corpse candles from Salles' right gauntlet, then his left.

The Frekka warriors moved as well, this time as a trained unit—

Until the man in the center, concentrating on his opponent, missed his footing. He shrieked as he skidded downslope on his back. His legs were splayed outward.

Salles stabbed through the man's groin. He stepped back from the smoking corpse before the other two warriors could interfere.

Venkatna's surviving men eased away also. They put their backs against the outcrop at which Salles had awaited them only minutes before. Turf smoldered on the face of the knoll where there was organic material for the arcs to ignite.

Five fresh warriors trotted down the trail. The men had decorated their battlesuits with their personal colors, but each helmet bore the crimson-in-gold rosette of Venkatna's royal army. They spread out as they closed on the Lord of Peace Rock from behind.

"It's not fair!" Julia cried.

"Since when was North fair?" Race replied bitterly. "He wants the souls of warriors, and he'll have his way no matter what."

Julia twisted a control. "Not Salles," she said simply. "Not this time."

The Searcher and her dragonfly sprang into perfect focus with the landscape beneath them. Julia slid forward the joystick on her pommel, sending the vehicle downward at a sharp slant. Its four jointed legs flexed as the feet touched down. The booms folded and telescoped as the dragonfly came to rest. Julia sprang from the saddle.

Race landed beside her companion. The dragonflies trailed tendrils of ozone as their electronics meshed with the new temporal ambiance. That ionized harshness was lost in the effluvium of the arc weapons of the oncoming warriors.

The fresh squad of Venkatna's men hesitated at the Searchers' sudden appearance. Race and Julia gave them no time to consider their course of action.

Race, wearing a battlesuit colored orange with bronze highlights, stepped forward—struck with her right hand—and switched the power instantly to her left gauntlet. Her arc doubled Julia's stroke at the leading warrior's sideman.

The Searchers' armor was of the highest quality attainable, the ideal within the Matrix which smiths in the Open Lands attempted to replicate. The chest of the man struck by the paired blow exploded in a yellow blast like that of raw sodium dropped into water. His helmet and both arms separated as the mangled suit toppled backwards.

Race strode forward and cut into the hip of the warrior at whom she had feinted initially. Julia, clad in a scale-patterned suit of scarlet, silver and mauve, ran down the man who fled screaming that the gods fought against them.

Not the gods. . . .

Julia's powerful arc licked out and caught her opponent three meters away. His suit concentrated all its energies on defense; the warrior fell over because the servos in his leg armor froze while he was in an unstable position. Julia stepped forward, a pace and then a second. The defensive screen overloaded and the victim's carapace burst into a fountain of burning steel and shorted electronics.

Salles looked over his shoulder; but only for an instant, because the survivors of the group he'd fought started the rush they'd intended to coordinate with the newcomers' attack. Salles parried one slash with his right hand, then pivoted as he tried to keep the second warrior at a distance with a dangerously-weak arc from the other gauntlet.

Race and Julia attacked their remaining opponents. Venkatna's men stood, but they made only the feeblest of attempts to defend themselves. The sudden turn of events had left them with no more volition than calves in the slaughter chute.

Behind the Searchers, the Lord of Peace Rock swiveled to put both royal warriors in line before him. He struck high at the nearer with the full power of his arc, then leaped the headless battlesuit to meet the sole survivor before the man could decide whether to lunge or backpedal.

The two warriors grappled. The long shadows cast by the sun through the pines danced with discharges from the straining battlesuits.

Salles got his left arm into the position he wanted. He directed a full-power arc from that gauntlet into his opponent's throat. Circuits blew out with a bang.

Venkatna's man fell backward. For a moment, currents played across the blackened surface of his armor in fluctuating patterns. One of the dragonflies chuckled as it drank another soul.

The Lord of Peace Rock swayed. Paint had blistered from his plastron and right forearm, but all his opponents were down.

Freemen rode east along the trail. They carried word to King Venkatna, who had tried to forestall a rebellion by assassinating its leader. Venkatna would try again, but for now the fighting was over.

"Who are you?" Salles called to the figures, faceless in their battlesuits. "Why did you—"

The figure in orange and bronze raised a hand. It might have been about to speak. Before it could do so, the shadow of a great hand blurred across the landscape and gathered Salles' rescuers into the Matrix.

Chapter Six

Fortin slipped through the Matrix like a silverfish crawling between the pages of a book. His soft, cling-soled footgear stepped without a tremor onto the floor of a corridor within Count Starnes' fortress.

Fortin was on one of the lower levels of Keep Starnes, beneath many layers of shielding. Except for one of the cleaning personnel in an orange uniform, sucking grit from the thin carpet with a static broom, the men and women in the corridor wore blue serge outfits. They belonged to units which directly supported the army.

Fortin in his light-bending cape was completely invisible to them.

A colonel in magenta and gold strode down the hall like a battleship under way, looking neither to his right nor his left. He had a train of six subordinates—all of them in blue. Even the lowliest of the elite who crewed Count Starnes' war vehicles was too grand a personage to perform in a servile capacity within the keep.

Civilians stood at attention against the sides of the corridor. The cleaner knelt and pressed his forehead to the dull green carpet. His broom whined unattended. The cleaner's hand patted the floor in tiny arcs, hoping to find the off switch. He was afraid to open his eyes to guide his movements.

Fortin fell into line at the end of the colonel's entourage.

They came to a rotunda. Armored doors hung ready to seal any or all the corridors which starred off from this center. The civilians present were in the retinues of the score or more soldiers striding along on their business. This deep within Keep Starnes, each corridor was a community from which civilian staff members moved only upon direct orders of the military.

There were six sets of paired elevators in the center of the rotunda. The colonel stepped into one cage; his servants got into the other half of the pair.

Fortin, grinning with the spice of near-danger, hopped into the cage behind the colonel.

This side of the elevator had a full set of controls, but the colonel did not deign to touch them. The cages dropped together, under the direction of one of the servants.

The elevator stopped four levels down, just above the Citadel. The atmosphere pulsed with the life of the keep itself: relays which clicked like beetles mating; the soft susurrus of the ventilation system; the hollow echo of water which had seeped through the rock walls of the enormous structure, being pumped up to the surface for disposal with the sewage.

The tremble of the Fleet Battle Director operating in the Citadel beneath was omnipresent.

The colonel got off and strode down an empty corridor. He didn't bother to look to see that his entourage had fallen into place behind him.

Fortin tapped the control for Citadel level as the elevator door began to close. The cameras which peered from all four corners of the cage ceiling could not see his smile of superiority.

The elevator resumed its descent. Fortin prepared to slip out quickly when the cage stopped.

Fortin knew he was the cleverest of all those who lived in Northworld. There was no situation from which his cunning would not extricate him; and anyway, he could always escape through the Matrix.

But there was no point in taking risks. . . .

"He's entered Elevator Four with Colonel Markesan," said Karring. "He's coming here, as we expected."

The Citadel was the lowest inhabited level of Keep Starnes. Its rotunda had a forty-meter ceiling, but a far greater mass of metal and crystalline armor separated the Citadel from the nearest portion of the keep above it.

The single corridor that led off from the rotunda held the nodular immensity of APEX, a computer capable of controlling the largest battle fleets of the Consensus of Worlds. It was now the domain of Karring, Count Starnes' chief engineer.

"Why doesn't Markesan see him?" Count Starnes asked. He was stocky and very broad; a physically-powerful man whose uniform was tailored to conceal the extra weight of middle age.

Starnes' build ran true to the dominant genotype on Plane Five—on Earth, Starnes would have said, though there were still folk who used the name Northworld. Northworld was a term from the distant past, associated with the myth that humans had come from a wholly different planet to settle here. . . .

Lena, Starnes' elder daughter, operated from one of the four remote consoles in the rotunda. She reclined like a huge spider at the heart of a web formed by all the systems of Keep Starnes which fed into her semi-circular workstation. "Markesan couldn't find his ass with both hands," she said. "Or," she added with a giggle, "his prick."

The pair of lovers standing behind Lena's contoured chair chuckled with practiced appreciation. Both wore leather briefs; one of them had added a studded leather cross-belt and balanced pistol holsters as ornamentation. The men were as thick-set as their mistress, but their bodies were densely muscular while Lena was fat. A sheen of oil glistened on their skins.

"The intruder is shielding himself from all normal observation," Karring explained. At his mental direction, APEX projected a holographic image of the elevator's interior in the air above Count Starnes. "We can't see him either."

Colonel Markesan stood in a formal at-ease posture, even though he must have believed himself to be unobserved. There was nothing near him but the walls of the descending elevator.

"It might not be *him*," said Lisa, Starnes' other daughter. "It might be *her*."

Lena guffawed. The count turned away to conceal a smile.

Lisa was a sport, a throwback to a body type which had become increasingly rare in Plane Five's limited gene pool. She was as tall as her father, but she weighed less than a third of his hundred-and-sixty kilograms. Where her elder sister wore a net bra and crotchless briefs, Lisa affected the uniform of a private soldier.

"We'll know soon enough," Karring said mildly. "I'm going to Bay 20 to prepare for our visitor."

"Well, it *might* be," Lisa muttered.

She lifted the bulky helmet fabricated to Karring's specifications. The face of the helmet was solid and featureless. A ten-centimeter tube stuck out to either side, like the periscopic lenses of a range-finder hood. She put the helmet on.

Air began to sigh in the single elevator shaft which penetrated the Citadel's cap.

"And I'll get ready too," said Count Starnes with a tone of satisfaction. At last he would face a new kind of enemy; an enemy who *might* provide the challenge which he no longer found in grinding to dust the neighboring keeps on Earth.

The squat master of Keep Starnes opened the hatch in the rear face of his personal war vehicle, a miniaturized tank three meters long and almost equally broad. The tank's frontal armor of collapsed uranium sloped at a 70° angle. It was thick enough to resist even a slug of the same material fired from a railgun like the tank's own weapon.

The interior of the vehicle fitted Count Starnes like a glove. All the available space was filled by the operator, the railgun, or the fusion powerplant on which the tank's weapon and repulsion drive depended. Additional internal volume would require additional armor to protect it. The present defensive load was at the limits of what a magnetic flux could raise a workable distance above the surface.

The hatch clanged shut. The vehicle quivered as Starnes brought its systems to life.

In the huge curving screen in front of Lena, a three-dimensional schematic of Keep Starnes spread with the complexity of a taproot's microstructure. Passages were color-coded as to purpose and level. There were almost a hundred shades in the pattern, and Lena recognized every one of them.

The display changed as APEX responded to the huge woman's mental directions. Her lovers preened and posed behind her couch, waiting patiently for the next demand on their particular skills. They knew from experience that their mistress' requirements would not be long in coming.

The Fleet Battle Director extended over twenty bays, offset from one another so that the corridor between them jogged like a series of square waves. Though Karring walked quickly, it took him over a minute to reach his destination.

A tracery of wires hung in the air above the entrance to Bay 20 without physical connection to any other solid object. Karring looked at it in grim satisfaction. The object's existence was only partly within the dimension in which it had been built. APEX converted into a map display the changes in potential which the device recognized.

If ordered, APEX could modulate the device that looked like no more than a wire cage; and through the device, the fabric of spacetime. . . .

looked at it in grim satisfaction. The object's existence was only partly within the dimension in which it had been built. APEX converted into a map display the data sets of potential which the device recognized.

If entered, APEX would modulate the device that formed five

Chapter Seven

Sparrow settled his mount at the edge of a plain so flat that an optical illusion made it seem to rise in the far distance. The setting sun cast long shadows.

For as far as the eye could see, the ground was covered with warriors battling.

Duration meant nothing to immortals like Miyoko and her brother. They might choose to walk or might slip through the Matrix to their destination in a nerve-freezing flash; it was all the same to the gods.

Sparrow was a man. He rode to North's battleplain to find Saburo.

The vehicle was one the smith had built himself. It was a dragonfly in general form, capable of travel between the planes of the Matrix as well as flying at speeds high enough that its forcefield glowed with the collisions with air molecules. Sparrow had modified the vehicle so that the pressure of his knees and bootheels controlled speed and direction in-plane, as he would control a pony.

Sparrow could use dials and rocker switches, just as he was comfortable with either a crossbow or a battlesuit. He had chosen a unique design for *his* dragonfly because he was the greatest smith in the eight planes of Northworld.

To the gods, creation was a thought or a fingersnap; but they did not understand the process by which they controlled event waves. Sparrow entered the Matrix in a trance; found the pattern of his desire; and reformed piles of ore and rubble into smooth crystalline machines in which atoms were spaced and arranged just as they were in the ideal he dreamed.

Other smiths built battlesuits. Sparrow built anything he chose. He was the master of all patterns within the Matrix, and the Matrix was the pattern of all existence on Northworld.

Saburo stood alone, a silent figure in layers of peach-colored silk. Before him, battle clashed into the observable distance.

The combatants could be identified by the colors and flashings which each warrior had worn when he died. Now, however, their battlesuits were uniformly of the highest quality: armor that only Sparrow or a handful of other smiths could have duplicated, and that with great effort. The air between the two opposing lines glowed as arc weapons shorted against one another.

Sparrow watched with critical interest for a moment. Though the battlesuits were all ideal, there were variations among the warriors. Neither side had been able to advance since combat began at dawn, but suits lay dead and blackened all along the line of conflict.

Turtle-backed machines slid across the plain, gathering limbs and helmets to the torsos from which they had been sheared. When the machines moved on, the armor they left behind was perfect again, though it lacked the sheen that indicated its systems were alive.

"Good evening, lord," Sparrow said.

Saburo spun around. At once a bubble of silence surrounded the two men, isolating them from the arcs' continuous snarl and an occasional crash as a forcefield was loaded to the point of failure.

"Ah," said Saburo. "Master Sparrow. I—didn't expect to see you here."

His tone might have been one of disapproval, if Sparrow has chosen to take it that way.

Sparrow smiled. Saburo could blast him into atoms—but he could not control *this* servant by subtleties of intonation. "One wouldn't expect to find you here, either, milord," he said bluntly. "It's Lord North's domain, one would say."

He glanced past his master toward the continuing battle. "Or Lord Hansen's, perhaps."

"Commissioner Hansen never visits the battleplain," Saburo remarked. He turned to view the fighting again himself.

Saburo was a slight man with delicate features, though Sparrow had never made the mistake of thinking that his master was soft. They were very different in personality; but Sparrow would never have taken service with someone he did not respect.

"They're quite splendid in their way, aren't they?" Saburo

said. "There's a poetry of sorts in their motion. It's all a matter of understanding the idiom."

Sparrow snorted, though he could see that his master's observation had a certain validity—

For someone who had never worn a battlesuit. Who hadn't chafed his limbs in long hours of practice, straining against the delay before the suit's servos translated the wearer's motion into the swing of an armored leg. Who hadn't felt the heat build up during battle, until the interior of the suit was an oven which burned the wearers lungs and boiled the juices from his cramping limbs.

Who hadn't seen his vision displays break up into multicolored snow which meant the battlesuit was about to explode in coruscating flames, carbonizing all portions of the wearer near the point of failure.

The warriors still on their feet at evening on the battleplain were the best of the best. Their movements of attack and defense were so skillful that they might have been dancers.

But every one of them had died in battle in the Open Lands, or they would not be fighting again here.

"No one could stand against them, don't you think?" Saburo said. Despite his phrasing, the slight man was speaking to himself rather than his servant. "One could lead a group of them on a raid into another of the planes and—whisk off a slave very easily. If one wished."

"*And* tear a hole in the fabric of the Matrix," Sparrow said. "*And* start the Final Day, when the armies of the other planes come through the hole you've torn."

Saburo turned. "It might not do that," he said sharply. "If perhaps only a few of the—of the warriors crossed. There needn't be a serious disruption of the Matrix."

"Which plane?" said Sparrow.

"This is purely an intellectual problem of the sort your crude—"

"*Which* plane, milord?" Sparrow repeated. He did not bother to raise his voice, but no one who knew the smith could doubt that he would continue pressing until he had an answer—or Saburo gave him his death for asking.

"Say—as an intellectual exercise," Saburo said. "Say Plane

Three. The androids would be easily surprised. In and out. And no repercussions. There very likely wouldn't be any repercussions."

"The androids," the smith said, "aren't defenseless, milord . . . but that wouldn't really matter. Seeings that the holds on Plane Three are all within the swamps, the androids wouldn't need to defend themselves. That lot—"

Sparrow jerked his bushy, cinnamon beard to indicate the warriors struggling in the last moments of full daylight.

"—would sink out of sight on the first piece of soft ground, which they'd find the first step they took out of the Matrix."

He fixed Saburo with eyes as frosty as metal burned in the casting crucible. "What is it that you really want, milord?" Sparrow asked.

Saburo tented his hands. "You can't help me," he said to his fingertips.

"I can't help you until you tell me what you want," the smith replied.

The sun dipped below the horizon, though refracted light continued to brighten the sky: lemon yellow in the west, a rich and saturated blue on the opposite horizon. The warriors still on their feet froze in position. Their arc weapons vanished like the visual aftershocks of a myriad lightning bolts, and the luster of the battlesuits dulled.

"All right," said Saburo with a calm that belied the struggle before he permitted himself to speak. "I'll show you, Master Sparrow."

He waved a hand. Master and servant vanished together from the battleplain as though they had never been.

The turtle-backed repair vehicles continued to crawl among the casualties as yet unrepaired.

The severed limbs were hollow. The battlesuits fought without anyone inside them.

Chapter Eight

The rising sun cast North's shadow across the island toward Race and Julia. Though the sea was calm, waves slid far up the slimy surface which could not be more than a hundred meters in diameter at this stage of the tide.

Gulls wheeled a half kilometer upwind, calling shrilly and occasionally diving into the pale green water. Scales flashed in their beaks as the birds climbed back to altitude, and the odors of salt and fish mingled in the air.

"So . . . ," said North in a voice as bitter and reptilian as the shrieks of the gulls. "My will is nothing to you?"

Race fell to her knees; Julia was trembling despite herself.

There was nothing in North's physical appearance to demand respect: he was merely a tall, craggy man past middle age, wearing Exploration Service coveralls. An expert might have noted that the butt of North's holstered pistol was worn and that he wore his rank badges on the underside of his collar where they would not target him for a distant marksman—

But Race and Julia dealt almost exclusively with men of war, and they had themselves faced death many times. The power of all Northworld emanated from the space where this man stood, as though he were a window for its majesty.

Julia covered her face with her hands. "F-father . . . ," she whispered. "Father, forgive me."

The Searchers' armor had vanished along with their dragonflies. The two women stood in the garments which they had worn under their battlesuits, a linen shift for Julia and Race in a singlet of thin suede, sweat-stained and rumpled. They were both big, both of them strawberry blondes, and—though they were not related—similar enough in appearance to have been sisters.

The gulls and the chuckling sea were the only speakers for moments that stretched toward a lifetime.

"Why should I forgive you . . . ," said North at last, ". . . ladies?"

He spoke mildly. The whip-sting was in the epithet rather than in the tone with which he delivered it.

"You took my service of your own free will," he continued. "And you laughed when you played me false. My will and your oath were *nothing* to you."

The horizon was without shore in any direction. In a broad arc to the west, a gray slant of rain joined the darker gray of clouds to the sea. The breeze picked up. Thunder became an undertone without noticeable peaks.

"He was so brave, m-majesty," Race whispered. She didn't fear death, but the power that wore North like a garment was greater than life and death.

"It was my sin, master," Julia said. She lowered her hands slowly. "He was strong and brave, and I didn't want to see him murdered like a dog."

She swallowed. Tears were streaming down her broad cheeks. "Forgive me, master. I . . ."

"Oh," said North in bitter derision. "I won't punish you, ladies. You're beneath my contempt, aren't you? Oathbreakers? I'll simply set you down in the Open Lands and be shut of you."

A sheet of lightning leaped across peaks of the oncoming storm. The flash glinted from North's strong teeth and deep-set right eye.

"Your kin are long dead, but I couldn't do anything about that even if I chose," North said. "The sense of honor you displayed to me fits you admirably to live as whores."

Thunder from the storm front rolled across the island. Julia knelt as though an unbearable weight had crushed her down. Her eyes were closed, and her mouth drooped open.

"Slay us, master," Race said. "Or give us leave to kill ourselves. . . ."

The Searcher wrung her hands together, rasping callus against callus where her body rubbed in her battlesuit. She tried to recall the feeling of bravado with which she had plunged into the skirmish in the Open Lands. Her only fear *then* had been of arc weapons, of the skill and numbers of Venkatna's troops; and that was less fear than a thrill of excitement. The will of North the War God was the farthest thing from her mind—

Then.

"Are you truly contrite?" North asked. His voice seemed softer, though it was hard to say just what the change in timbre had been. His words were audible through the now-constant thunder. "Do you truly wish to redeem yourselves? Though I warn you, the task I will set you, *if* you choose, will be a hard one."

"Anything, master," Julia whispered. She opened her eyes.

"Anything . . . ," Race said. She spoke so softly that the word was in the form of her lips and tongue rather than sound.

"Good Searchers," the god in gray coveralls mused, "are too valuable to waste. So . . ."

Water sluicing over the ridged surface of the island licked unnoticed at the Searchers' toes. The ground began to rock with the rhythm of the thunder.

"It is my *will*," continued North, "that you serve the human I choose for as long as he lives and requires you. That you carry out his orders with abject obedience. And if you do so—"

The lightning flash was so bright that it dimmed the risen sun for the instant of the discharge. The thunder was nearly simultaneous, and it echoed from the dome of the sky.

"—then it may be that you will become Searchers again," North continued through the pulsing roar, his tone audible and awful. "But I promise you nothing except the chance to live as the slaves of the man to whom I give you!"

"As you will," Race murmured.

She linked her right hand with Julia's left. They rose to their feet. A sullen wave broke over them from behind. The water was warm.

"As you will, your majesty!" the Searchers cried in unison to the figure of North which swelled from the sea's surface to the heavens without losing solidity.

The rays of the sun streamed from the clear eastern horizon. The light, polarized between the sea and the overhanging cloudbank, tinged the women green. The storm broke over them in blast of huge cold drops.

"Do you think it will be Salles we serve?" Race shouted into the ear of her companion.

The figure of the god disappeared. His laughter boomed across Race and Julia, louder than the thunder and more terrible than the scintillant ropes of lightning above them.

The island humped upward, ridge after green-black ridge, tumorous with barnacles and streaming ropes of seaweed. Almost a kilometer away, great flukes rose to hide the sun.

The beast dived. The storm-lashed sea swept over the place the Searchers had stood, but Race and Julia were no longer on this plane of the Matrix.

Chapter Nine

The cage of Fortin's elevator opened into the armored heart of APEX.

With the right will and mind controlling it, a Fleet Battle Director could design weapons and draft tactics superior by an order of magnitude to those of any other keep on the planet. Count Starnes' was the will, Karring's the subtle mind. Together they could succeed within their generation in reducing all hostile keeps—all civilization on Plane Five outside Keep Starnes itself—to smoking ruin.

Fortin had observed the beginning of their destruction with a pleasure greater than any he achieved during brief moments of sexual climax. He grinned as he stepped once more into the Citadel, concealed in his wrapper of bent light. The keep's technicians would spend days tracing the fault in the elevator system which had caused a pair of cages to descend to Citadel level, but they would find nothing. . . .

A high-pitched alarm signal began to warble. The sound was not loud, but it cut through the vibration which funnelled from the corridor containing APEX.

Fortin frowned. The alarm was new, and so were other aspects of the Citadel. . . .

Four remote consoles were spaced around the periphery of the rotunda. In the center of the circular room was the bank of elevators. The figure walking toward the elevators—toward Fortin—must be Lisa, because there was virtually no one else in Keep Starnes so thin.

A bulbous helmet with horns and shoulder braces covered her head. It was apparently opaque, because she moved with the care of a blind man in an unfamiliar room. Lisa swivelled her torso, back and forth like a scythe stroke, every time she placed her foot.

Her sister, Lena, lay as usual in the center of a huge console.

566

She concentrated on a display which, to Fortin's cursory glance and lack of interest, appeared to be a palette of blurred pastels. Her body gleamed with a thin film of sweat.

The huge woman's current pair of lovers stood—or posed—behind her couch. They flexed muscles and plucked nervously at their harness as they watched Lisa's deliberate progress across the rotunda. The lovers had no part in present events, but they obviously felt they were at risk.

Karring wasn't in the rotunda, but that was no surprise. The Chief Engineer's normal lair was Bay 20, at the far end of the APEX corridor. Others were not barred from entering that sanctum—Starnes and his daughters would have flayed alive anyone, even Karring, who presumed to dictate where they could or could not go in their own keep. Nonetheless, Karring was important enough to be allowed his privacy, so long as it didn't become a point of honor. Keep Starnes was a huge place, and its rulers had no desire to visit every cranny of their domain.

Count Starnes was not visible either, but the tank across the rotunda from Lena's console was alive and ready for action. The elevator shafts had been cleared so that the massive vehicle could be lowered into the Citadel. It was always parked here, where it provided Starnes last refuge against an enemy who had penetrated the myriad lines of defense above.

Fortin had never before seen the tank with its systems up.

The railgun's fat barrel was pointed only generally in the intruder's direction. A slug from *that* weapon could penetrate a hundred meters into living rock. A human as close to the muzzle as Fortin was would splash if the meteor-swift projectile struck him. Even a human with the powers of a god. . . .

Fortin smiled and shivered. He pretended to himself that he was unaware of the danger, but the danger itself was what brought him to this place of war.

"Try to your right," Lena called. She could pivot her couch to watch her sister, but she didn't choose to do so.

Lisa obediently turned and took another step—toward Fortin. She was still about ten meters away.

Real concern blanked the frown from the half-android's face. He walked across the rotunda with the quick, stiff steps of a dog in a modest hurry.

Fortin understood the operation of Lisa's helmet now. The short booms to either side projected coherent light. The interference pattern the beams should form where they crossed five meters from the source was calibrated to within angstroms. The slightest variation in the path of one of the beams would disrupt the pattern—

And locate the intruder, despite the near perfection of his light-bending suit, with precision.

"He's heading for APEX!" Lena shouted. She leaned forward in the heat of excitement; her couch rolled up to follow her, continuing to cradle the woman's head and shoulders.

Fortin did *not* understand where Lena's console got its input. It seemed to be only an approximation, but not even that should have been possible to Starnes' daughter. They were using the Fleet Battle Director to track him. Fortin needed to learn how.

His heart was beating fast, though there was no real risk. The elevators were too dangerous for Fortin to attempt again, but he could escape directly into the Matrix.

Not, however, before he learned how Karring had detected his presence. It had to be Karring.

Lisa followed Fortin down the corridor at a quicker shuffle. The two of them were playing a game of blind-man's buff, but the quarry could move. There was no risk, even though Lisa wore the pistol holster that was a badge of rank on Plane Five.

The corridor was five meters broad, but it jogged repeatedly where the banks of equipment projected farthest into it. APEX lowered over its surroundings like a giant carnivore bearing down on prey.

The Fleet Battle Director was constructed in twenty linked nodes. The designers' intention was both to minimize battle damage from a single hit and to provide shielding between segments so that sets of operations would not interfere fratricidally with one another. The armored bays contained individual input and output hardware. Input was via the operator's mental command, if so desired, or through a number of physical options. Primary output came in the form of holographic images which glowed in the air above each terminal.

Meter-thick conduits cross-connected the nodes and snaked

through the walls of the Citadel, putting APEX in uninterruptible touch with every aspect of Keep Starnes. High overhead, the corridor ceiling crowded with a maze of lesser lines and the girders which supported them.

So close to APEX, the air was alive with a chittering like that of myriad goats, gnawing at the fabric of the universe.

Fortin walked on. His smile was becoming fixed. There was only a dim glow in the unoccupied bays he passed. Lisa's grotesquely distorted silhouette followed, backlit by the faint ambiance reflecting in from the rotunda.

The terminal at the far end of APEX was lighted. Rapidly-changing holographic displays modulated the pool of radiance which spilled from the bay into the corridor.

Karring was responsible. . . .

"He's still ahead of you," Lena directed her sister. Her throaty contralto rang from the speakers in the ceiling of each alcove. Their varying distance from Fortin blurred the words into reptilian menace.

Fortin reached Bay 20. Behind him, Lisa began to jog forward.

Karring sat upright at a terminal not dissimilar from the outstation at which Lena performed in the rotunda. Between the bald, aging engineer and the display hung a one-meter globe. Only careful study showed that it was constructed of matter rather than light. It glittered as it spun unsupported.

On the display—

Fortin squinted as his eyes tried to focus on holographic lines that seemed to be not quite in the same plane of existence. It was a pattern of translucent octohedrons with mass and depth that went beyond the three spacial dimensions; they were distorted, and as APEX twisted the globe in response to a silent order from Karring—

"I see—" Lisa cried from the mouth of the bay.

Fortin's jamming pods fired a blast of radiance matched to the helmet's input frequency. He ran back down the corridor, past Lisa.

Six of Count Starnes' soldiers poised in the shadows above Bay 18. In preparation for this moment, the cables had been removed from the conduit feeding that node and two others. The armored tubes now provided secret paths into the Citadel.

Special troops crawled into position while Lisa drew the intruder's attention.

A mesh as fine as spidersilk drifted down onto Fortin from the maze of pipes and wires in the corridor ceiling. The strands were monomolecular. Any one of them was strong enough to serve as the tow-rope of a truck.

The pattern on Karring's display slipped over itself, torquing and rotating until one of the octohedrons was crushed almost to non-existence. The Chief engineer turned. He smiled.

The net tightened.

Fortin's brain was ice cold. He shifted himself into the Matrix, conscious only of his need to escape.

He couldn't move in the Matrix, either. Fortin's right hand clutched and wriggled in the free ambiance that was all eight planes and the paths between them—but only his hand. The vent that should have sucked the god in as the surface of a pool does a diver did not form.

Karring's globe spun faster as it distorted. The grip of the Matrix on Fortin's wrist was fiercer yet. He began to scream.

Glowing with the nimbus created by induced magnetic fields, moving at a walking pace, Count Starnes' tank slid down the corridor.

The bore of its railgun was centered on Fortin's chest.

Chapter Ten

The room's eight windows were so clear, and the scenes they displayed were so diverse, that Sparrow doubted for a moment that he was inside a building after all. He reached out toward the image of courtiers and petitioners gathered in King Venkatna's audience hall to see if he could—

Saburo's nostrils pinched. Seven of the windows, including that displaying the Open Lands, went a gray as solid as stone and featureless as vacuum.

In the remaining window, a black geodesic dome squatted on a mud island in a swamp. Around the stagnant lake, tree-ferns reached through the mists to spread the feathery fronds which sprouted from the sides of their trunks.

"Who made this place, milord?" Sparrow asked. He looked around with undisguised interest.

The windows met, edge to edge, in a complete circuit, but the room had no door. It was only accessible in the fashion by which Saburo had brought his servant here: through the Matrix.

"Why do you say 'made'?" Saburo asked. There was a touch of asperity in his voice. "Discontinuities between planes exist throughout the eight worlds. North as our leader could of course choose to place his dwelling around the best of those natural sports."

Saburo knew that his own palace—perfectly sited and balanced with its surroundings though it was—had not impressed Sparrow. The opinion of an artisan, scarcely better than a savage, was of course of no importance; but still. . . .

Sparrow snorted. "I've seen nature," he said. "Don't tell me I can't recognize craftsmanship."

He ran his index and middle fingers down the edge of the unclouded window, where the frame would be if it had a physical frame. The material was without temperature, neither hot nor cold. The only property it imparted to Sparrow's touch was the feeling of adamantine solidity.

"North built this himself, did he?" the smith said in marvel.

"I believe that is the case, yes," his guide and master replied. Saburo's voice was as colorless as the seven windows he had closed.

"I give him best, then," Sparrow said softly. His hand worked slowly up and down the gray, as though polishing a surface already smoother than matter could be. "*I* couldn't have built this, and I never thought I'd say that of a thing I could see."

"Master Sparrow—"

"I wonder what it cost him," the smith said. He wasn't interrupting Saburo; he was simply oblivious to everything except wonder at the construct in which he stood. "I know what it costs to turn the Matrix on itself, and to do it on this scale—"

"*Master* Sparrow," Saburo hissed in a towering fury.

The smith blinked, then immediately knelt—in contrition rather than fear. "Milord," he said, "Lord Saburo—I was inattentive when my duty was to you. It will not happen again."

"I—" Saburo said. He was startled to receive a sincere apology from this man. The smith's stiff-necked honor and controlled violence were as much a part of him as his cinnamon beard and hair. "I should have realized that this room would be of interest to someone of your—talents. But rise, please rise."

Sparrow stood and turned again to the window. This time he examined the scene rather than the structure which displayed it.

The water which surrounded the dome looked silver where sunlight glanced from it, deep black with dissolved tannin outside the angle of reflection. Meter-tall horsetails grew at the margins of the pool, wearing their branches like successive crowns sprouting at each joint of their stems.

Trees rose from the humps and ridges of higher ground nearby. The soil even of the hillocks was almost liquid, so that roots had to spread broadly across the surface in order to support modest thirty-meter trunks.

"Not battlesuits," Sparrow muttered, smug to see his off-hand assessment borne out by further evidence. "Not unless they're on stilts. Which I suppose I could . . ."

Saburo brought the image in the window nearer without giving an audible command. A wall of the same black plastic as the dome encircled the small island. The vertical corrugations every few meters looked at first to be structural stiffeners, but closer observation showed that each rib had a narrow shutter. The posts supporting the wall's single gate were thicker than the remaining ribs.

Because of the swamp's flat terrain, the ports the shutters masked could sweep for almost a kilometer in every direction. That judgment assumed the wall's defensive weapons were sufficiently powerful, of course; but the smith had a high opinion of the products of the androids' craft.

"The place *could* be captured . . . ," Sparrow murmured; considering ways and means, considering the tools he would build for the task.

He turned to his master again. "I don't know how long it could be held, though," he added.

"It wouldn't have to be held," said Saburo. "However . . ."

The image closed nearer yet and slid through the faceted dome of the structure. In the center of an open room knelt a woman—

An android, this was Plane Three—

A *girl* with perfect features. Her hair was in a tight bun, and she had painted her face chalk white over the naturally pallid android complexion. Black makeup emphasized her eyes, and her lips and spots high on either cheek were brilliant carmine.

She was arranging a spray of ferns and seed pods on the low table before her.

"She is . . . ," Saburo whispered.

Sparrow expected his master to continue with '*perfect*,' because that was the word which glowed from Saburo's eyes as he spoke.

Instead, Saburo said, ". . . Mala. She is the daughter of King Nainfari. She is—"

Saburo's voice strengthened as he spoke, until it crashed out with godlike force, "—the woman whom I have wanted for my wife ever since I amused myself here in North's vantage point."

His face tightened. The image drew back with the suddenness of a crossbow releasing. Mud, black plastic, and dozing armaments filled the window.

"Amused myself like a fool," Saburo continued harshly. "And

saw her by chance, whom I could never have. Because for me to enter Plane Three with the necessary force would mean . . ."

The slim god's eyes stared at a day, a Day, that he had been unable to prevent himself from seeing. The Final Day, seen once in the Matrix and forever after in memory.

Sparrow smiled coldly. "You swim in the Matrix, my lord," he said mildly, "and you still believe in Chance?"

The smith had memories too. . . .

Sparrow shook himself like a bear dragging itself onto an ice floe. "So . . . ," he said, rotating the dome and its defenses in his mind. "You want the girl."

He focused again on his master. "All right," he said. "I'll bring her to you."

For a moment, Saburo's face looked beatific. Then he frowned and said colorlessly, "Master Sparrow, I have the greatest respect for your abilities, as an artisan and as a . . ."

His voice trailed off. Perhaps he would have said 'man,' had he continued in that vein. Instead, Saburo resumed with, "The terrain is swamp, and the temperatures there are very high. Not the sort of climate to which you are accustomed. Also—"

Saburo's voice returned by imperceptible stages to that of the technical expert he had been in an exploration unit. "—the defenses are strong, extremely strong. I've examined them at length. I don't believe one man, however equipped . . ."

He broke off when he realized that the smith was smiling at him. The expression had humor in it, but the underlying emotion was quite different.

"Lord Saburo," Sparrow said to the smaller man, "we both know that I serve you—"

"Serve me very well," Saburo broke in, afraid of what the smith might say next.

"—on my own terms," Sparrow continued without deigning to notice the interruption. "Which is all right, so long as neither of us makes a point of it . . . very often."

He paused.

"Go on," Saburo said. His voice was like the blue heart of a glacier.

"My terms are, milord . . . ," Sparrow continued softly, ". . . that I will serve your need to the best of my ability, and that you will permit me to do so. I *will* do this thing for you, Lord Saburo."

"Then do so," Saburo said. His eyes were focused on the memory of the slim figure to whom his heart belonged. "And if you succeed . . . your will shall be my will, Master Smith."

Chapter Eleven

Marketday crowds swept by the entrance, but a hush filled the interior of the shop of the merchant prince.

It was even cool—by the standards of southern sweatboxes like the port of Simplain. Brett, the underchamberlain, lowered the dampened linen kerchief with which he had been patting his face since an hour before sunrise.

D'Auber, the warrior who was both Brett's escort and his fellow envoy, continued to flap the throat of his tunic. The warrior insisted on wearing wool, no matter what the temperature was. Brett suspected that D'Auber would report the underchamberlain's switch to local materials as treason against Venkatna.

"Well, where's the guy with the slaves?" D'Auber demanded. "Where's Guest?"

The guards at the door were a pair of dark men wearing baggy white shirts and pantaloons. They carried broad-bladed halberds for show. Warriors in battlesuits stood in alcoves nearby where potted ferns discreetly camouflaged them.

Guest's entrance hall was a circular room whose high alabaster ceiling imitated the sag and folding of a tent roof. The clerestory level was a screen of filigreed stone. It and the vaguely-translucent ceiling provided adequate illumination, once the envoys' eyes had readapted from the dazzling blaze outside.

Water trickled down the steps of an artificial rill at the rear of the hall. It smoothed the raucous street cries from outside and contributed significantly to the room's coolness.

"Where's *Guest?*" D'Auber repeated, since everyone within hearing had ignored him the first time. "And what's the matter with that damned water? Does the place leak?"

Another white-suited servant entered the hall. This fellow was nearly two meters tall. "Lord Guest will join you now," the servant declaimed in a loud voice without looking at either of the envoys.

He stepped aside. A whole line of additional servants bustled in with an ivory stool, peacock-feather fans, and—incongruous within a masonry building—a parasol of either cloth-of-gold or gold foil on a thin backing.

Two servants ceremonially unfolded the stool. The man who sat on it seemed to appear from nowhere.

He was tall, almost as tall as his annunciator, but the gray silk he wore had been concealed behind his servants' shimmering garments. Fans waved, the parasol extended above his head, and the white-clad entourage made a formal bow to their master.

"So . . . ," said Guest. His voice was deep and powerful, that of a younger man than Brett had expected from the merchant prince's gray beard. "You are the couriers from the West Kingdom, responding to my offer."

"*I'm* a warrior," D'Auber rejoined harshly. "Not some messenger. And we've come from the Empire of Venkatna the First to escort back his slaves."

A train of heavy beasts passed in the street outside. They hooted at the city crowds and clanked the chains which some of them dragged to permit their mahouts to snub them up if they failed to respond to direction. The elephants of the region of Simplain had straight tusks and bare gray hides, unlike the black-wooled mammoths familiar to the northern envoys. The beasts, like the dark-skinned humans, were just close enough to familiar models that their *wrongness* was all the more disturbing.

Guest's complexion appeared to be as pale as Brett's own. It was hard to be certain as the fans moved in the dim light.

The merchant prince chuckled. "Ah, styles change faster than I can keep up with them. So long as your master's gold assays to the required purity, he has my leave to call himself whatever he pleases."

"The gold is of course being checked by your clerks, ah, Lord Guest," Brett said. "But there'll be no difficulty with its purity."

The underchamberlain had jumped in quickly because he was concerned about where D'Auber's temper was going to lead the conversation. It was all well and good to say in the privacy of your tent that Guest was nothing but a mere trader, of less account than a royal—than an imperial—slave.

In Simplain, though, Guest was a person of obvious importance.

The battlesuits in which his guards watched from the edge of the hall were as good as the one which D'Auber had left perforce in the envoys' quarters. And Frekka was very far away . . .

"Even down in this hellhole," D'Auber said, mopping his face with the end of his sash, "you ought to be careful about what you say about the emperor. North the War God stands behind him, you know."

Perhaps the warrior was concerned about the risk also, because his neutral tone robbed his words of the threatening implications which they might otherwise have held.

"Ah, well," said Guest without obvious offense. "We in Simplain have many gods, and I fear that your North isn't widely worshipped here. Still, I wish Emperor Venkatna well, as I hope to do much business with him in the future."

"When may we hope to see the present merchandise?" Brett said brightly, another desperate attempt to turn the discussion into safer fields.

Guest clapped his left fingertips into his right palm. "At once, good sirs, at once," he said.

The curtains behind the merchant prince billowed again. Male servants entered, guiding a pair of women. To Brett's surprise, the females were not from the Simplain region at all. Both of them were pale and blond. They weren't fat, but they were larger than the local women—and indeed, larger than most of the local men.

"Step forward, girls," Guest said. "Give the gentlemen a good look at you."

He smiled as he added to the envoys, "They will meet your master's requirements perfectly, good sirs. In the lands where they come from, the use of such devices is well known and they are experts in it."

"They'd better be," D'Auber growled. "At what the emperor is paying for them."

"Half now," said Guest easily. "Half when they have proved their abilities. What could be more fair?"

Brett stepped closer to the new slaves. Something about them was—not right, though the underchamberlain couldn't put his finger on precisely what it was.

The expression with which they met his eyes was not so much

cowed as resigned. Certainly there was no indication of rebelliousness or danger.

"It's only . . . ," D'Auber went on angrily, ". . . that some folk, I don't mean you, Gues—*Lord* Guest. Some folk down here to Simplain, that is—"

Brett turned. "D'Auber, stop it *now*," he hissed with as much authority as he could assert without making the situation worse than it already was.

"What's a palace flunky think he's doing," D'Auber snarled, "tryin' to give orders to a front-rank warrior, anyhow?"

Guest laughed with unexpected relish. "That's telling him, Lord D'Auber!" he said.

D'Auber, not in the least mollified by the support, snapped his attention back to the merchant prince. "Like I was saying," he said, "folk down here might think they could cheat us and not worry about it. Well, you can laugh at North if you like, but he's the chief of gods in Simplain as well—and before he's done, he'll have brought the whole world under the Peace of King Venkatna!"

Brett saw his chance. "*Emperor* Venkatna!" he said. "Now shut up, D'Auber, before you blurt *more* treason."

The warrior backed a step in shock. He opened his mouth like a gaffed fish. D'Auber had drunk enough of the local wine this morning to stain his tongue and palate dark.

"I envy your friend his certainty," Guest said to the underchamberlain in a conversational tone. "Few of us here in the southern lands are so sure of the gods' will."

Brett stepped to the side to put his body between D'Auber and the merchant prince. "The emperor looks forward to paying the remainder of the purchase price," he said. "If these are the experts you say, milord, there might well be a bonus."

Flummery, soap to lubricate the path of commerce—though it was by no means impossible that Venkatna would add a bonus. If the Web performed to its claimed capacity, the emperor could well afford to do so.

The underchamberlain frowned. He suddenly realized what was unusual about these slaves. They had calluses on all their visible joints, just as if they were warriors who practiced regularly in their battlesuits.

"I assure you," said Guest, "that this pair will be your master's most dutiful slaves. They will carry out his orders as though they were the injunctions of a god."

He laughed again.

Brett shivered despite himself. The particular sort of humor that suffused the sound was more disquieting than another man's rage.

"Do they have names?" he asked to break the spell.

"Race," said Guest, pointing, "and Julia."

Guest rose abruptly. Though the action was sudden, servants whisked the fans and parasol clear. He was scarcely upright before other servants were refolding the ivory stool.

"They will bring your master the fortune he deserves," Guest added before he vanished again through the curtains.

Until Guest stood up again, Brett had not noticed that the merchant prince had only one eye.

Chapter Twelve

The man hanging in the center of the white bottle babbled. Count Starnes watched the image of Lena's console with a smile of accomplishment.

"... *anything you want* ...," the prisoner's voice whispered through a console speaker. His haggard face, the only non-white object in the containment facility, filled the huge curved screen. "... *only let me go ... power ... wealth ... anything, I swear by the Matrix, only let me go ...*"

"About ready, I would say, Karring," Starnes said complacently.

Lena split the screen to add a full-length view of the prisoner. She giggled like heavy soup bubbling. "He's so skinny," she said. "Just right for you, hey, Lisa?"

Her sister colored and turned away from the screen.

One of Lena's lovers smirked. When he saw Lisa's expression, his face blanked. He shifted so that his partner stood between him and the count's younger daughter. Lena could not protect her lovers from fury like *that* if it were unleashed.

Not, in all likelihood, that Lena would care. The men who serviced her were fungible goods.

"... *all the power in the world ... only ...*"

"As you say, milord," Karring agreed coolly. "Though had you permitted me to try, I'm confident that APEX could have sucked from him all the information that you could wish."

Starnes shook his head. "No, Karring," he said. "The old ways are best. For old problems, at least."

The bottle which held the prisoner sat in Bay 20, at the focus of the device by which Karring closed the escape route through dimensions. The chief engineer was more at home in the heart of APEX than anywhere else; but the others, even Count Starnes, found the inner recesses of the Fleet Battle Director to be as disquieting as a crocodile's den. They observed the bottle's internal pick-ups at Lena's outstation in the rotunda rather than on Bay 20's integral displays.

The internal security squad which captured the prisoner had stripped him through the meshes and inserted intravenous drips into his arms. Then they hung the intruder, still trussed, within the containment bottle.

In the three months since the capture, the prisoner had been without sensory input. The inner walls of the bottle maintained an even white glow. Even the water that flushed his wastes was held at precisely blood temperature.

After a time, the prisoner began to talk . . .

"In a way," Starnes said, "I'm sorry we've captured him. For a time, there, when we knew he was entering the keep . . . there was a new challenge, a *real* challenge again."

"There are the other keeps to conquer, father," Lisa said. She was still dressed—she was invariably dressed—as a common soldier. She spoke without emotion, but her eyes feasted on the pale, slender body of the man on the screen.

"Pft!" Count Starnes said. "That's gotten to be like kicking over anthills now. Oh, I'll go through with it, eliminate the rest of them, because I've started. But there's none of them that'll give me a fight . . . and when I'm done, what *then?*"

"*. . . a god . . . power beyond your dreams, just . . .*"

"There will be others where he came from, milord," Karring said. His voice held the same wistfulness as his master's had a moment earlier. "Dangerous opponents, perhaps, though we will defeat them. You and I and APEX . . ."

Lena blanked the screens. She reached down the front of her briefs and began to masturbate herself idly. Without looking back at the others around the console, she said, "All right, you've broken him. Are you going to go on from here? Because if you're not, father dear, I have better things to do with my time than watch a thin stick like him drool."

Count Starnes looked down at his daughter without expression. "Yes," he said after a moment. "All right, I'll speak with him."

The images blinked back onto the screen. "Prisoner!" the count ordered sharply. "What is your name?"

"*. . . gold and jewels and slaves for torture for any pleasure . . .*"

"Prisoner!"

The prisoner's eyes were open. They snapped shut, and he

said in a cracked whisper with no hint of inflection, "My name is Fortin and I am a god and I will make you—"

"Prisoner!" Starnes repeated, slapping off the chain of syllables. "Fortin. Who sent you here?"

"No one sent me, your majesty," Fortin replied. His eyes reopened. A chilling intelligence had returned to their amber depths. Karring, perhaps the only one of the observers to notice, frowned. "I came as a visitor, meaning no harm and harming nothing of your wonderful power."

The close-up image smiled vastly. "I can make you still more powerful, if you only release me."

Karring shrugged. "He has nothing we need, milord," the chief engineer said.

Starnes pursed his lips. "The fabric that concealed him was interesting," he said.

"It took time to analyze," Karring agreed. "But it only conceals someone who isn't using any active sensors himself, much less weapons. Frippery, and anyway, we can duplicate it now ourselves."

"He's not even a soldier," Lisa said abruptly. "Give him to me, father. I might have use for a servant."

Lena chuckled. She was now toying with both her lovers as they stood to either side of her couch. Her eyes were on the holographic display.

"I could bring you an expert in war," Fortin said with an ingratiating smile. "Someone who could teach you to fight even better, who—"

"We don't need to be *taught* war," snapped the count. "We need an opponent worthy of our mettle."

He sniffed and added, "As *you* certainly were not."

"Though for a time, milord," Karring said, "it looked as if . . ."

"I can bring you an opponent, Count Starnes," the prisoner said. His face twisted into a look of horrible anticipation. "I can bring you a . . . soldier of my own people, to challenge you, if you like."

"No," said Karring abruptly. "I don't think that would be safe."

"Safe?" the count said. He looked at his chief engineer. "I don't see the danger."

"He may be a scout, milord," Karring explained. "He could return with an army of—I can only guess. We don't *know* the size of the keeps and their armies where he comes from."

"I'll bring him alone, your majesty," Fortin said, reverting to inflated address. "I'll send him, and he'll come without weapons, just as I did. No army, only one man, and you can run him like a rat in your maze. I swear by the Matrix!"

He licked his lips to keep from drooling again.

"His word's worth nothing, of course," Count Starnes said. His eyes were narrow with calculation.

"The Matrix . . ." repeated the chief engineer. "Prisoner: this Matrix is the medium through which you entered Keep Starnes?"

"Yes, yes," Fortin said. "And the oath has power, power to bind even me, even a god, milord."

He bobbed his head as he hung, still wrapped in unbreakable meshes. Fortin didn't know what Karring intended by the question, but he knew that anything was better than an eternity of white silence. . . .

"Is it alive, the Matrix?" Starnes asked his chief engineer.

"No," said Fortin.

"Y—" Karring began. He looked curiously at Fortin's expanded image.

"From what APEX tells me, milord," Karring continued when he saw that the prisoner had nothing to add, "I rather think that this Matrix may be alive in some fashion. But I don't see that it matters to us at present."

"You don't have anything to gain from me, your majesty," Fortin said quickly. "But I can bring you an opponent, a *safe* challenge. A game worthy of your skill and powers."

"We've caught him," Lisa said. "There's no reason to let him go. I'll take him for—for a time."

Lena chortled. "Just because you're skinny, you don't have to make do with *that*," she said.

She roused herself in the couch. It obediently shaped to continue supporting her as she twisted to look directly at her younger sister. "Here, take one of the boys. Take them both, child, it'll do you a *world* of good."

"Shut up," said Lisa distinctly, "or I'll—"

"Daughters!" snapped Count Starnes.

The women ostentatiously turned away, from one another and from their father as well.

"*I* say," Lena murmured, "let's send him back, and see if the next one is full grown."

"There's a risk, Count Starnes," the chief engineer said simply. "Even to us."

For a moment, Starnes pursed his lips. Then he shrugged and said, "If they can send one scout, they can send another. Keeping this one or killing him, that won't change anything."

Count Starnes reached past Lena and touched a mechanical switch for certainty. "The prisoner can't hear us now," the count said. "Karring, can you take our forces through this Matrix?"

"N—" the chief engineer began. He pursed his lips, then continued, "Not as yet, milord. Every time this one comes or goes, APEX gathers more data. Very shortly, I—we—might be able to do that."

Count Starnes smiled, a look very like that of the prisoner when he started to drool with anticipation. He opened the audio channel to the exclusion bottle again. "If this one can send us a single soldier . . . then that might be an interesting game, don't you think, Karring?"

"I'll send him, your majesty," Fortin's voice pleaded from the console. "One man, a soldier."

"Unarmed!" said the chief engineer. "Swear by your Matrix that he will come without any weapon."

"I swear by the Matrix . . ." Fortin whispered. "His name will be Hansen."

Starnes looked at Karring. "All right," Starnes ordered.

The globe in Bay 20 ceased abruptly to spin. As it did so, the net within the containment bottle fell limp as the prisoner vanished into the Matrix.

APEX murmured to itself, waiting as it had waited through the eons since the settlement of Plane Five.

Chapter Thirteen

Some of the chaotic crowd eyed Hansen, but that was normal interest rather than doubt about his presence here in Heimrtal.

Kings Lukanov, Wenceslas, and Young had come as envoys of the Mirala District to treat with Emperor Venkatna. None of the three knew every member of the other entourages, and there were hundreds of warriors from the imperial army besides.

No one thought that Hansen was out of place. The short wolfskin cape which he wore over gray velvet emphasized the breadth of his shoulders and compact strength. His thick wrists bore the calluses of long practice in a battlesuit, and he moved with the stiff-legged arrogance of a warrior.

A warrior, or a mammoth-killing sabertooth.

No, he wasn't out of place. Heimr Town was a scene of blood and destruction; precisely where Nils Hansen belonged . . . especially since Hansen was the root cause of the desolation himself.

An imperial servant blew notice on his twisted brass horn. Warriors in the crowd moved closer to the court Venkatna had set up in the marketplace on Water Street, where merchants bartered with the citizenry of Heimrtal in former days.

No more. Though the houses surrounding the marketplace had burned, the heavy timbers of the ground floors still remained. Imperial troops had nailed Heimrtal's warriors there, bodies dragged from the battlefield dead as well as men who had surrendered when the Heimrtal line collapsed.

Some of the latter were still alive. Night would take care of that, when the air dropped below freezing. The only warmth the victims had was that of the posts smoldering at their backs.

"Lord Nettley, step forward!" called a strong-lunged usher, one of the bureaucratic entourage which accompanied Venkatna even on campaign.

Not bureaucrats alone, however. The only warriors in armor

in Heimr Town now were imperial troops, and there were enough of them to handle any trouble the Mirala delegation might want to start.

Venkatna wore red silk brocade and a puff-sleeved jacket rich with gold embroidery. Six champions in battlesuits stood beside and behind the emperor where they could protect him from sudden attack. More warriors were stationed along the rear of the marketplace and at the edge of the circle cleared in front of Venkatna.

The imperial troops had reverted to painting their battlesuits with personal colors. A generation before, the professionals of the West Kingdom buffed their armor to bare metal and went to battle in the white, with only the rank badges flashed on their helmets to differentiate the units of their disciplined mass. . . .

Marshal Maharg's helmet is marked with seven chevrons, alternating black and yellow. His gauntlets glow dull red with the weight of current flowing through them as he withstands the attack of two Solfygg champions.

The servos in the joints of Maharg's armor have been robbed of power to feed the defenses. He steps backward anyway, fighting the whole mass of his battlesuit. He is a true champion; worthy of his father, worthy of Nils Hansen, his father's greatest friend.

"Maharg, I'm—" Hansen shouts. Breath flays Hansen's lungs with knives of ozone. The skin of his right arm feels as though it has melted into the charred suede lining of his battlesuit. His legs stride forward in slow motion.

Maharg moves like a cat killing. He shunts full power into a thrust that blows one opponent's circuitry in a dazzling fireball. The remaining Solfygg warrior carves through Maharg's backplate.

"—coming!" shouts Hansen as he strikes, too late for anything but revenge.

A man jostled Hansen's left elbow.

When the horn sounded, the delegation from the Mirala District came out of the shock to which Heimr Town had reduced it. Warriors pushed to the front of the crowd. Hansen sat on an overturned wagon from which one could see over the armored bulk of the imperial guards. King Wenceslas and his entourage determined to take the wagon as a vantage point.

Hansen was still in a waking trance as he turned toward the warrior who pushed him. Whatever was on Hansen's face was enough to throw the other man back like a hammerblow. Wenceslas and his warriors settled around Hansen like snow drifting across a waiting lynx.

"Lord Nettley," Venkatna said. "You have proved yourself our faithful servant many times in the past."

The emperor's voice lacked the deep-chested fullness that his usher had shown a moment before, but it snapped with stone-hard authority. He sat on a stool. Though the piece was light and could be folded for travel, Hansen noticed that it had five short steps below the seat.

"Nettley? *That* little booger?" grumbled the warrior who'd bumped Hansen. "Bloody traitor, that's what *he* is."

"Left his rightful lord two summers back," agreed another of Wenceslas' attendant warriors. "Then led Venkatna back t' his home here to gut it, he did."

Nettley was a solid-looking man in his thirties. He moved well. If Hansen had been putting together an army, he would have hired Nettley without concern . . . so far as competence went. Nettley was very much the sort that a wise leader kept an eye on.

Venkatna was smart enough to know the risk of treachery. The ruins of Heimr Town proved the emperor was ruthless enough to obviate the risk as well.

"Kneel, Lord Nettley," Venkatna ordered. "In the name of the powers which the gods have vested in me as their vicar on Earth—"

The immediate crowd hushed so thoroughly that the cries of women in the background soughed through the marketplace. Over a hundred of them—freeborn, not slaves until disaster engulfed the Heimrtal levy the previous afternoon—were being marched off toward Frekka in chains.

"—and before the assembly of the people, I name you Duke of Heimrtal and Mayor of Heimr Town, with the rights of high and low justice without reference to custom or the authority of the elders—"

The crowd gasped. The man beside Hansen blurted to Wenceslas, "*You* don't have that authority, Vince, and you're a king!"

"I don't have a thousand warriors to call from Frekka when the freeholders get up in arms against me, either, Blood," King Wenceslas replied bluntly.

"—and the right to administer all land within the district as imperial land, beneath my authority," Venkatna concluded. "Rise, Duke Nettley."

Imperial troops cheered. Battlesuit speakers amplified the voices of armored warriors into terrifying threats. No one else in the crowd made a sound. When the shouts died away, the keening of the women could be heard again.

A warrior near Hansen mumbled a curse.

Hansen absorbed the scene as if none of it touched him emotionally. He was gathering data. The way his hands flexed as if toward a gun butt when the women cried meant nothing to the men around him.

"Isn't a bloody lot left t' be duke *of*," the warrior called Blood whispered.

Most of the district's freemen were unharmed; even some of the warriors would have fled to the woods and escaped instead of trying to face Venkatna's professionals. Nettley would have no difficulty finding willing tools to promote into the seats of the fallen lords, just as the emperor had found Nettley to replace the late King of Heimrtal. . . .

The new-made duke stepped out of the circle. His face was smug and gleaming with sweat.

"I have here," the emperor continued, waving a document from whose wax seal fluttered ribbons of blue and crimson, "a petition from the Mirala District, in the names of Lukanov, Wenceslas, and Young—"

"Bloody well about time!" said a warrior under his breath.

"—requesting, I should almost say *demanding*, a meeting with me," Venkatna said. "Regarding what they term 'the traditionally free relations of their district with the West Kingdom.' "

King Lukanov, an old man and so fat that he seemed to balance his weight on a briar-root walking stick, tried to enter the cleared circle. An imperial warrior stretched out his arm to block the aged monarch.

Lukanov squawked. Wenceslas cursed under his breath, but

he'd had the judgment not to move before he was invited to do so.

Venkatna tossed the document behind him. An aide caught it in the air, but the meaning was clear.

"Their petition is denied," the emperor said flatly. "The gods have appointed me vicar of *all* the Earth."

He stood up and continued in a sharp, carrying voice, "My friends from Mirala can see around them how I deal with those who oppose the gods' will. They can talk to Duke Nettley to learn how I treat those who support me in North's great enterprise, the bringing of peace to all corners of the Earth. Next spring, my armies and I will meet them in Mirala, and we will see whether they have learned the lesson from others, or whether I will have to teach them myself."

Venkatna clapped his hands.

"This council is dismissed!" the usher cried. Horns blew a raucous discord.

Wenceslas turned and stalked off through the dispersing crowd, his face white with rage.

"That stuck-up sonuvabitch!" growled one of the warriors tagging along in the petty king's wake. "Who does he think he is!"

Hansen's face was as still as a cocked gunlock. That *question was an easy one to answer. Where you might get an argument was over whether the sonuvabitch was right.*

He wasn't right if Nils Hansen had anything to do with it.

Venkatna spoke briefly with his aides. A courier handed him a document tied with the crimson ribbon of the chamberlain's office, and a pair of body servants folded the portable throne. The emperor's bodyguards spaced themselves in a circle around him; more alert, not less, in the clamor of the thinning crowd.

Queen—it would be Empress now—Esme, flanked by a pair of armored warriors, walked past the overturned wagon on her way to her husband. Behind her followed a mixed group of male slaves and well-dressed young women. A hitch in Esme's step reminded Hansen of King Lukanov a few minutes earlier.

Venkatna broke off his discussion and strode over to his wife. "Darling!" he said as he gripped Esme's arms. He kissed her on the forehead, just beneath her wimple. "You shouldn't be walking around like this. You should have waited in the tent."

Esme indeed looked slight and cold, despite the bright sunshine and the cloak of white bearskin which she wore. She smiled toward her husband with genuine happiness and said, "No, no, dearest. It does me good to get out. And—"

She half-turned and gestured toward the women whom the slaves were herding into a line abreast, facing the emperor.

"—I wanted you to see the selection of girls I've made while it's still daylight," Esme continued. "Only the six on the left are virgins, but I thought the other four were too interesting not to include. Lamps and torches do so blur the finer points, don't you think?"

One of the women was sobbing. The others stood silent. Their faces reflected a range of expressions from interest to wide-eyed shock like that which Hansen had seen on a man he'd gut-shot.

"Well, they're all very nice, Esme," Venkatna said with a cursory glance toward the women. "Very nice, I do appreciate it. But actually, I think I'll start back immediately with the vanguard. You see—"

"You won't be riding all night, dearest," the empress said sharply. "You'll sleep somewhere, won't you?"

Venkatna flashed a perfunctory smile. "Yes, quite right, my darling."

He looked past Esme's shoulder again. "The two in the middle, shall we say? They'll do nicely."

He stepped back from his wife and waved the document from his chancellor. "What I wanted to tell you, though," he said, "is that Saxtorph says he's succeeded in finding slaves who can work the Web as it should be worked! He's waiting for my return before he gives them a serious test, though."

Esme turned her head. She looked at the envoys from Mirala, already striking their tents and loading impedimenta onto draft mammoths. "As you think right, dear," she said. "But those fellows over there mean you no good, and you know it."

Venkatna laughed in loud triumph. "I *want* them to get home, dearest. Fear defeats more enemies for me than I've had to face in open battle. And it saves me potential subjects, recruits for—"

He looked at the bodies nailed to ruined walls, stiffening and still moaning.

"—my armies."

"As you say, dear," Esme said. "But I don't think the Mirala District will come without a fight."

The empress glanced around the marketplace. Her eyes met those of Nils Hansen, sitting alone now on the wrecked wagon. He smiled at her.

A smart woman. Hansen didn't think Mirala would give up without a fight either.

If he could arrange it, that would be a fight the imperial forces lost. . . .

Chapter Fourteen

Sparrow's dog thrust her nose under the smith's hand and joggled him, because he'd been concentrating too hard to pet her willingly. He muttered a curse, but his fingers were gently firm as they flexed to scratch the animal's ruff.

Sparrow had said—Sparrow had boasted—that he would bring Saburo his bride; and so he would.

But precisely how was another matter.

Sparrow's handmirror held a tiny image of Plane Three; raw swamp, not Mala's dome kilometers to the west of where the smith now focused. He would enter the plane through a discontinuity rather than by forcing a hole in the Matrix. To do otherwise would be to alert the entire android defense structure, and Sparrow was under no illusions as to his ability to battle through *that*.

He had nothing against kidnapping the princess against her will. Saburo had directed him to bring the girl; if Saburo felt there should be limitations on the methods his servant chose to use, then he should have said so from the start. But Sparrow had no intention of getting into a biting match with a sabertooth, either.

So . . . Sparrow would have to enter Plane Three at some distance from his objective and travel through the swamp to Mala's outlying bower. The terrain was unpleasant; and, while the wildlife didn't include sabertooths, there were some hazards of a similar line.

The beast which Sparrow studied through his window on other realities was a dimetrodon several meters long. It would weigh several hundred kilos after a good meal. It lay on a rock, sideways to the dawn. The sail arching high on the dimetrodon's back would warm its blood more quickly to splay-foot after its prey. Such beasts wouldn't be the real danger of the journey, but they weren't negligible either.

The dog peered at the dimetrodon's reduced image. She

growled from the back of her throat, uncertain of what she saw but disquieted by it. Sparrow stroked his pet.

The smith adjusted the handmirror, returning—for he had stared at this during three hours of the past four—to a scene in the Open Lands. In the palace of the Emperor Venkatna, a tracery of metal and silk-fine semi-conductor crystals waited for operators who could drive it to capacity.

Sparrow shifted his viewpoint down into the Web's microstructure. He did not understand the mechanism by which the construct channeled event waves, but he could *use* one. . . .

There were, of course, risks.

The big man stood up in sudden decision. He switched off the viewing mirror which he had built according to shadows in the Matrix that no one but he could have seen.

What Sparrow built now would be a still greater triumph of his craft.

The bitch rubbed against her master's legs. The braces of living metal which Sparrow had made for both of them clicked together. She could sense his excitement, and she felt it was too long since they had hunted together. . . .

It took the smith over an hour to gather the raw materials which he needed, then to array them precisely to the side of the split-log bench. Any surface would do when he entered the Matrix, but the old symbols were best.

The dog waited, alert but patient. The smith lay down on the bench and closed his eyes. After a moment, the pile of raw materials began to shift. Stones grew webs of gossamer crystals, doped with traces of other elements at the necessary points in the silicon lattice.

Chance *could* have brought the molecules together in this fashion. Somewhere in the infinite universes, chance had done so.

The will of Sparrow the Smith picked atoms from the pile he had prepared and shifted them in accordance with the pattern only *he* could have discerned in the Matrix. From the ores and scraps of metal grew a delicate object—small, but in every other respect a duplicate of the probability generator in Venkatna's audience hall.

Chapter Fifteen

Hansen turned when he heard a mechanical sound over the snorts and murmurs of the Y-horned titanotheres browsing around him on the plateau.

A high-powered unicycle was headed his way. Its hub-mounted motor howled every time the wheel bounced into the air from a pothole. The rider sat easily erect, dressed in black leathers. His mirror-polished visor was a reflective ball. On it a medial horizon separated the rich azure sky from a distorted panorama of the rough terrain.

On *that* vehicle, the visitor could only be Fortin; and in Hansen's book, there was never a good time to see Fortin.

The unicycle slowed as it neared the titanotheres. The multitonne beasts were loosely spread over the landscape; calves, generally in pairs, close to their mothers, and a huge male stationed downwind of the herd he dominated.

Fortin picked the last thousand meters of his way carefully, trying to reach Hansen at the center of the herd without approaching any of the titanotheres. The ball of his helmet spun from side to side as he tried to look in all directions at once.

A young male titanothere bellowed and did a sudden curvette, snapping at its haunches. Apparently the beast had mistaken the sound of the unicycle for that of a horsefly about to light. Fortin wobbled and almost fell: though the dim-sighted browser was unaware of the vehicle's presence, the titanothere's circular rush nearly trampled unicycle and rider accidentally.

Fortin pulled up beside Hansen and switched off his engine. He stepped to the ground. The sidestand bit into the friable soil, and the unicycle fell over beside its rider.

The drive motor was hydraulic. The smell of hot oil made Hansen's nose wrinkle.

Fortin touched his helmet. The front half snicked back and merged with the rear. His white android features were no paler than usual in the near dusk. "What a bloody place!" he snarled. "Can't you find somewhere decent to be, Commissioner?"

"I suppose if I felt like human company just now," Hansen said, "I'd be back in the Open Lands with Lord Salles."

Hansen smiled. It was not a particularly-pleasant expression, but there was enough humor in it to raise a question of how pointed he meant the insult to be when he added, "Human company or yours, Fortin."

The android laughed. "And here I came to do you a favor, Hansen," he said.

The two men—the man and the android—were close to the same height, but Hansen's build was much solider without being heavy. Despite that, Fortin had a wiry strength—as a weasel does, and it was coupled with a weasel's mad urge to slaughter.

Well, Hansen hadn't always needed much of a reason to kill either; though sometimes he dreamed about it afterward, nightmares in which all the faces became one face with glazing eyes. . . .

"You never did anybody a favor, Fortin," Hansen said without overt emotion. He stepped over to the unicycle and raised it, since its rider wasn't about to.

The little vehicle was extremely dense. Hansen grunted, letting his knees do the work to save his back. His toe teased closer a broad, fibrous chip of titanothere dung, years and perhaps decades old. He slid it under the stand. The chip spread the weight enough to keep the unicycle from toppling when he let go of the handlebars.

Fortin's face hardened as it had not at the verbal insult. "Perhaps," he said to Hansen's back, "you'd rather that I just go away and not bother you with what I've learned?"

"Don't play games, Fortin," Hansen said. He turned and met his visitor's eyes. "I know, duration doesn't matter to us any more . . . but I don't have much taste for silly games."

A titanothere forty meters away drew Hansen's attention when it flopped down. Its ribs boomed a drumbeat against the ground.

The beast rolled on the light soil, kicking its four-toed forefeet in the air and gouging the dirt with its nose horn. Small birds hopped in and out of the dust cloud, snapping at insects the titanothere roused.

Fortin watched, frowning as he tried to divine what it was that Hansen saw in the spectacle to hold his rapt attention. If Hansen had hunted the huge beasts—

—had blasted the animals to gobbets of flesh which lost life and then even the semblance of life—

—the android could have understood; but instead Hansen merely observed. He was so gentle with beasts that Fortin could almost forget the lethal violence gleaming at the back of the ex-policeman's green eyes.

"All right . . . ," Fortin said aloud. "It's simple enough, really. You came here to learn how Captain North made this world vanish from the outside universe, did you not?"

"That's why the Consensus sent me to Northworld, yes," Hansen said. He looked over his shoulder at Fortin. "Do you know the answer?" he added without emotion.

Fortin quirked an ingratiating smile. "I know who does," he said. "Or more accurately, I know where the information is. But I don't suppose you consider that you have a duty to the Consensus of Worlds any longer, now that you've become a god . . . ?"

"I'll worry about my duty, friend," Hansen said softly. "Why don't you tell me what you think you know?"

"The folk on Plane Five are descended from the human crews of the fleet the Consensus sent first to search for Northworld," Fortin said. "When Captain North made us vanish. They're settled in keeps, and they fight each other."

Hansen nodded. "Fight each other within limitations," he corrected. "Armies fight each other, but they pretty much leave each other's homes alone so they don't spoil the game for the future."

He grinned harshly and added, "God forbid that anybody decides to live in peace anywhere on Northworld."

"It used to be that way on Plane Five," Fortin said. "All the millennia since the settlement. But the current Count Starnes is destroying all his neighbors, one by one. So I went to see how."

The dust-bathing titanothere rolled to its feet and woofed like a huge dog. It ambled toward another young male, then charged. The beasts thudded together in a mock courtship battle.

"You *would* like that, wouldn't you, Fortin?" Hansen said. His eyes were on the great herbivores and his voice was controlled, but the android noticed Hansen's fingers twitched as though reaching for a pistol. "People killed, people left to starve; people chained in labor gangs, all for no reason. . . ."

"I'm *trying* to do you a favor, Commissioner," Fortin said sharply.

Hansen turned. He was dressed in Open Lands style, a leather jerkin over his wool blouse and breeches. He wore no weapon, but the threat of murder was in his eyes.

"Then do it, Fortin, and get out," Hansen said. He spoke with difficulty, as though his throat were choked with dust. "I decided a long time ago that I shouldn't kill people just because they were evil little bastards . . . but I've been known to make exceptions."

"If you kill me, Hansen . . . ," the android whispered. "If you kill any of us gods, the whole Matrix collapses and there's *nothing* left."

"Yep," said Hansen. "I've been told that."

Fortin's mind turned inward to a vision of nothingness so icy and perfect that his body shivered in rapture. The very motion drew him back to where he stood, on a plateau on Plane Eight, where titanotheres gamboled in the dusk.

"Yes," the android said to clear his throat and mind.

"All the keeps on Plane Five have powerful computers," he resumed in a voice as light as the breeze. "That of Keep Starnes is the original Fleet Battle Director, an APEX system, that came with the settlement. It outclasses the other systems as the sun does a candle. That's how Count Starnes is able to overwhelm his neighbors."

"Go on," Hansen said. His voice had lost its edge. He didn't see Fortin's point as yet, but he was now sure there was a point.

"Don't you see, Commissioner?" the android crowed. "APEX is powerful enough to determine how North took us beyond the outside universe. But in all the time the unit has sat on Plane Five, nobody bothered to ask it the question!"

The titanotheres began to move off in the direction of the setting sun. The odor of their bodies and the alkaline bite of the dust they stirred filled the muttering gloom. A big female passed within a few meters of the humans, unaware or unconcerned.

Fortin could no longer make out Hansen's features. "I'm telling you this because I thought you'd want to know," the android went on. "But I advise you not to attempt to access the data. It's too dangerous."

He tried to conceal his anxiety that Hansen wasn't going to react; that the ex-Commissioner would ignore the duty that had sent him to Northworld in the first place.

But—when the Matrix gave humans power that made them gods, it also accentuated the primary traits of each human's underlying personality. Duty must have been important to Commissioner Nils Hansen long before the Consensus sent him to Northworld.

Whereas Fortin's personality—

"Count Starnes says he'll let you use APEX," Fortin said, "but it's not really safe to visit Plane Five, is it? Since we can draw power from the Matrix only here and in the Open Lands."

Hansen did not appear to be listening. His eyes followed the titanotheres, black humps against a crimson sky. The fingers of his left hand played across the seat of Fortin's unicycle.

"Besides," the android added, desperate in his fear and his evil, "Starnes says he'll see you only if you come to him unarmed. He's not to be trusted. I'm afraid that if he has you in the center of his keep, he'll strike you down."

Hansen stretched his arms out to the sides, then twisted them behind him and craned his neck back as well. "Will he just?" he murmured. "Quite a boy that Starnes, hey?"

"Look," said Fortin. "I've told you what I surmise and I've given you my recommendation: stay away, it's too dangerous for you. I have nothing more to do with it."

His voice rose without his being aware of it. A titanothere straggling behind the rest of the herd broke into a snorting trot in the direction of the sound.

Fortin's left hand splayed out. A ball of orange sparks devoured a section of the landscape, expanding until it struck a vertical plane separating it from the titanothere. The ball winked out with the hollow *whoomp* of an implosion.

The titanothere skidded, then galloped off in the opposite direction.

Hansen lowered his own left hand. "He wasn't going to do any harm," he said to the android. "Usually they don't charge home; and anyway, they're too clumsy to chase you down if you dodge."

"I have better things to do than play games with mindless beef!" Fortin snarled. He threw his leg over the saddle of the unicycle and locked his face shield down.

"I'd feel naked, going into a place like Keep Starnes without a pistol," Hansen said conversationally. "'T' tell the truth, I feel naked even out here without a pistol. Maybe that's why I come, d'ye think?"

"I think nothing!" the android snapped. "What you do is your own affair, Commissioner Hansen."

He touched a switch on the left handgrip. White radiance fanned across the landscape from the unicycle's headlamp. The wheel spun in the light soil, tilting the saddle forward despite the stabilized suspension. The little vehicle tore off into the night in the direction the titanotheres had gone.

Hansen dusted his palms absently over his thighs, brushing away grit that the unicycle had thrown onto him. He could return to the Open Lands at the moment of his departure, so that he would seem never to have been gone.

He could as easily travel through the Matrix to the dwelling he kept here on Plane Eight, a dozen kilometers in less than an eyeblink.

But duration no longer mattered to him, and he needed to think. He started to walk through the gathering dark, an easy pace that would get him where he was going in the short term . . .

And perhaps by then he would know what he intended to do in the larger sense.

Chapter Sixteen

The legs of Sparrow's dragonfly clicked delicately as he set the vehicle down on the shingle beach. Jade-green waters swelled in the sunlight, bubbling over the pebbles. Similar white ruffs in the distance marked other islets.

Above the surf lapping toward the dragonfly hung the image of a swamp, glimpsed as though through a frosty mirror: a discontinuity into Plane Three.

Sparrow's dog leaped from the cradle of his arm. She darted forward and yapped at the waves, then ran back with a curve of foam pursuing her. The omnipresent rustle of water against air and stone thinned the barking to chirps indistinguishable from those of distant gulls.

Sparrow opened his vehicle's side compartments. Ordinary dragonflies were fitted with the electronics necessary for them to carry out the tasks North set his Searchers. Sparrow used the space to haul limited amounts of cargo.

Birds circling the island dropped lower. Their wings were jointed crescents against the clear sky. The metal braces which gleamed like fishscales as the smith and his dog moved drew their interest.

The dog hopped up on her hind legs, snapping at the gulls as opponents she could understand. The big birds shrieked disdainfully, then flared their wings to rise again.

Sparrow laid a ground sheet over the shingle. He took out the first parcel and unwrapped the soft leather covering of a bell-muzzled energy weapon, a mob gun. It had a sling and a short stock, but it could be fired as easily with one hand.

When Sparrow asked Hansen for advice about weapons which were not in use in the Open Lands, the god had suggested this one. Hansen's careful neutrality cloaked obvious doubts about anybody who chose to enter a dangerous situation carrying arms which—however effective in themselves—were not natural to him.

Sparrow set the mob gun on the ground sheet. The second parcel contained a pair of gauntlets. He tried them on. They were massive, heavier even than they would have been if the smith had fashioned them entirely from steel. The wrist flares covered half the length of his forearms.

The gauntlets' thumb and finger joints slid like miniature waterfalls when Sparrow clenched his fists and opened them. He could pick an egg out of a nest and not break its shell.

Sparrow clashed the gauntlets together and laughed. His dog sprinted toward him from where she had been chasing waves. Her feet spurned pebbles as she barked in concern.

Hansen was right. Sparrow had practiced with the mob gun. He'd been impressed by the way its discharge converted cubic meters of landscape into a fireball . . . but the mob gun would stay here, and Sparrow would wear the gauntlets into Plane Three.

The smith wore a sleeveless shirt and short breeches of undyed wool. His sandals were laced halfway up his calves. They had heavy soles with hobnails, though he didn't suppose the studs would help his footing in the soup to which he was headed.

He'd been in swamps before. He'd killed a bogged mammoth once, moving cautiously because he was as much at risk as the beast which screamed and tried to twist enough to wrap the tiny human in its trunk. The water had been cool, even though it was midsummer when the sun set for less than an hour. Gnats had covered Sparrow like a black skin as he eased forward with his spear poised. . . .

The dog jumped up, barking worriedly as she clawed Sparrow through his thin breeches.

"North gut you!" the smith swore by habit and reached down; but the mass of the gauntlet slowed and reminded him. He rubbed the base of the animal's ears with his armored fingertip, then patted its flank in reassurance before he stepped to the compartment on the other side of the dragonfly.

There was only one object in this compartment. Because of its delicacy, Sparrow had fastened it with dozens of flexible restraints instead of trusting a padded wrapper. Now he undid the clips one by one until finally he removed the ovoid construct of metals and semi-metals grown as monocrystals rather than being pulled through a drawplate.

The wire egg was about twenty centimeters through the long axis and some fifteen across the center of the swell. It flexed slightly and began to glow in the violet-magenta range as the smith held it by the ends.

A pattern of water droplets shimmered above the breaking waves. As Sparrow concentrated, Brownian motion drew a corridor through the mist. Merely a pocket in the fabric of random chance. . . .

Sparrow sighed and hung the probability generator from the pair of hooks he had worked through his supple bearskin belt. The device was as sturdy as he could make it and still retain its powers. It that wasn't sufficient for field use, then Sparrow would succeed without it.

He grimaced. When he used the device, it felt as though a cat drew icy claws across the surface of his mind.

Through the discontinuity, heat bent horizontal waves across horsetails growing from the mud of the swamp. Sparrow flexed his gauntlets. It was tempting to consider letting the dragonfly carry him across the muggy wasteland to his destination—

But the dragonfly would trip alarms all over Plane Three's single continental land mass. They would come for him, the androids, with force he could not withstand.

The discomfort of the trek would be only an incident. Sparrow's face and arms had swollen to twice their normal size from gnat bites after he slew the mammoth in the bog, but he hadn't noticed the insects until after his spear thrust home. . . .

Sparrow stepped into the surf. It foamed suddenly to knee height, then dropped back. The dog ran back and forth along the tide line, yapping frantically.

Sparrow turned. "Come on, then!" he shouted. "Or stay, I don't care. I'll be back for you."

The dog tested the salt water with a paw. A wave licked forward. The animal tumbled over herself scrambling backward. She sat on her haunches and yowled piteously.

"You damned fool," the big smith said. To an outsider, he appeared to be talking to his dog.

He waded back onto the shingle and scooped the animal up in his left arm, cradling her carefully so that she didn't kick the wire egg on his belt. The bitch raised her muzzle and began to lick Sparrow's ear. Her canines were white and powerful.

Sparrow splashed into the surf, carrying the thirty-kilo animal as though she weighed no more than the sunlight on his cinnamon-gold hair. As he neared the discontinuity, frost thickened across its surface. The scene beyond was lost in diffracted light.

Sparrow lurched forward. The waves advanced to meet him, but when they drew back, the man and his dog were gone.

Chapter Seventeen

The point of black light in front of Hansen lost itself for a moment, then twitched inside out like an origami sculpture. The light became the figure of a black-haired woman on a dragonfly, landing in the courtyard of the Searcher Barracks.

A whiff of ozone dissipated quickly in the fresh breeze; the substrate of heated resins and polymers, the spoor of electronics seeing hard use, remained somewhat longer.

"A manual touch-down, Krita?" Hansen said in amusement. "As smooth as the automatic systems could have managed, I'll grant."

"Hello, Nils!" the Searcher said brightly as she swung off the saddle of her dragonfly. The dimensional vehicle's four legs were jointed into V-struts like the hind limbs of jumping insects. They bobbed when the rider's weight came off them.

Krita was a small woman, coming to a little above the shoulder of Hansen, who was of only average height for a man. Like Hansen, she was densely muscled and callused from battle practice; but she was a woman beyond doubt.

She wore soft boots and a white linen shift which had embroidered borders at the hem, armholes, and deeply-scooped neckline. Her breasts were wide-set on a broad chest, much more prominent when she was nude than through even a thin garment. The shift was cut to mid-thigh so that she could wear it comfortably in a battlesuit; her legs as she dismounted were smooth and tanned all the way to the black pubic wedge.

Krita put her arms around Hansen and kissed him. She smelled faintly of female sweat, modified by the fruit-oil soap with which she had recently washed her hair.

The barracks were apartments on three sides of a courtyard whose fourth face was closed by the towering majesty of North's palace. Dragonflies waited before many of the twenty-seven units. Another Searcher opened the door beside Krita's, noticed the couple embracing—

Recognized Hansen and jumped back so quickly that the panel of carved light shivered in its frame as it slammed.

Krita chuckled. "Come on in," she said, tugging at the edge of Hansen's marten-fur cape. "Seeing the gods here—"

She laughed again.

"—disturbs some of the girls."

"I've offered you a place of your own," Hansen said somberly as he stepped into Krita's suite.

If one looked carefully at the walls, one could see they were created of points of light disappearing into the infinite distance, like a clear winter sky compressed into a few centimeters. The design was North's business and that of those who chose to live in the War God's outbuildings. It reminded Hansen of Plane Four, where souls existed in ice and torture. . . .

Maybe that was what it reminded North of also.

Krita lifted on tiptoe to kiss Hansen again. She paused and said, "You know I won't do that."

"Sure," he agreed, looking around him. The walls were hung with tapestries, finely-wrought drinking horns, and the bows and spears of the chase. Very like a lord's hall in the Open Lands, but without the soot and bustle and *life* of that other plane. "No strings, though."

"I said *no*," Krita snapped. "You heard me the first time, and all the times since."

Hansen sucked his lips in. "Yeah, sorry," he said. "It's just I—"

He sat on a bench covered with a bearskin. As if changing the subject, he said, "There's something I'm thinking of doing."

Hansen gestured. In the air appeared a simulacrum of Keep Starnes, a dome a meter across glowing with the pale blue aura of a magnetic screen.

"On Plane Five?" the Searcher asked. Her anger was gone. The tone of her voice was cautious. Her mind had run ahead of what her lover was saying to what she knew he *was*: the most accomplished man of violence that she or Northworld had ever seen.

Krita sat down on the bench, an arm's length from the man.

"Right," Hansen said. "Count Starnes' keep. Fortin says there's a Fleet Battle Director there, a computer from the settlement."

As Hansen spoke, layers stripped one by one from the image. First the glow faded, exposing the underlying surface of collapsed metal and crystals grown in seamless, refractory sheets.

"A unit like that," Hansen continued in a tone half playful, half appraising, "might have the data I was sent to Northworld to find. Fortin says Count Starnes claims he'd let me access it."

The uppermost layers of the keep were given over to huge plasma weapons and missile batteries, artillery that could scar the face of the moon—but which could be used only if ports were opened in the defenses. For all their seeming power, an attempt to use the banks of weapons would be next to suicidal.

"That's nonsense!" Krita snapped. "You can't possibly trust him."

Hansen raised an eyebrow. "You know Count Starnes?" he asked.

"*You* know Fortin," she retorted. "Everybody knows Fortin! Whatever he says is a lie."

"Yeah," Hansen agreed/said. "There's that."

The living spaces and the workshops of Keep Starnes appeared as the plane of vision sliced deeper. The warrens of the lower classes near the top; deeper in, technicians' apartments, scarcely more spacious.

The overwhelming majority of the production lines that opened, layer by layer, were given over to armaments.

"Whoever sent you here has no authority now," Krita said. "You're a *god*, Lord Hansen. Nobody can force you to do anything!"

Hansen's face hardened from its neutral set. "Nobody *ever* had to order me to do my job," he said, more harshly than perhaps he had intended.

Krita's lips parted to let her breath hiss in.

The Searcher's eyes focused on the image of Keep Starnes. The lower levels, where Count Starnes' soldiers and their dependents lived, were laid out on a more spacious floorplan than those of civilians. Even so, the suites were harsh concretions of straight lines and right angles.

After a moment Krita said, "Yes, I see. I've . . . always wanted to see the Fifth Plane. Maybe I can arrange for Etienne—"

Hansen shook his head.

"—and Sula to take over my—"

"*No*, Krita," he said softly. He took her by the shoulders and deliberately met her eyes squarely.

"Why not?" she demanded. She shook herself violently, so that Hansen jerked his hands away. "Tell me why you can go but I can't?"

"Because," he said, his voice low, his words as precise as the clicking of a weapon coming to battery, "because if I go, there'll be problems enough—"

"Danger, damn you!" the woman shouted. "Say the word, *danger*."

"There'll be *danger* enough," Hansen said. "Without me having to nursemaid somebody raised in the Open Lands without a clue about how to conduct herself in a technological environment."

He got to his feet.

Krita closed her eyes. She said, "You could be killed, Nils. You c-could very possibly be killed."

"*If* I go. And I told you . . . ," Hansen added with intended tenderness as he stepped to the woman's side, "I'd like to make you a place of your own before I leave."

The woman jumped up and slapped his hand away as though it were a snake. "D'ye think I'm a whore?" she shouted. "Is that what you think?"

Hansen swallowed, massaging the red mark on the back of his right hand with the lean, strong fingers of his left. "I think," he said quietly, "that every time I try to do something with people, I fuck up."

He turned to the door muttering, almost under his breath, "Except when I've got a gun in my hand."

"Wait," Krita said.

Hansen looked back over his shoulder. Krita was rummaging among a pile of furs in an alcove, rich skins marked like red fox but the size of oxhides. Her short garment rode up over the curve of her buttocks.

"I have someth . . . here it is."

She straightened and turned, holding in her hands a low helmet of black plastic. There was a frosty jewel the size of Hansen's thumbnail in the center of the forehead.

"Here," Krita said. "Take it."

Hansen obeyed. The plastic was colder than the air around it. "Where did you get this, then?" he asked, his intonations faintly sing-song.

"North gave it to me when he brought me here," the Searcher said flatly. "Before you were a god. But he said—"

Hansen lowered the helmet carefully over his head. He continued to hold the rim as though he expected the material to burn his scalp.

"—that I should give it to you when the time came," Krita continued. "That I would know—"

"To *me?*" Hansen said in amazement.

"*My name is Third,*" said/thought the artificial intelligence in the helmet.

"Bloody hell!" Hansen snarled as he snatched the helmet off.

"What's the matter?" Krita asked, concern breaking through the cold visage of a moment before. "Did it . . . ?"

She didn't know how to complete the sentence. The helmet had shaped itself to her skull when she once had tried it on; but it was otherwise cold and dead to her, a construct of dense black plastic.

"Nothing's wrong," said Hansen. "I've used . . . one of these before. It's a command helmet."

His thumb rubbed the bezel which clamped the jewel. "Yeah," he added, "it might come in handy."

Krita tossed her head. Her hair hung down to the middle of her back. When she shook it, it rolled like a black waterfall.

"I may not be here when you get back," she said in a distant voice. Her eyes were focused on a patch of wall slightly above Hansen's left shoulder. "I'm going to arrange with some of the others to handle my duties for a time. I need a break—"

She turned her back.

"And I have business. Of my own."

"Right," said Hansen. "Ah, sure. We'll get together again soon."

He started to don the helmet, then thought the better of it. With the object in his left hand, he took a step toward the door.

"Is that all?" Krita demanded on a rising note. When Hansen looked around, she was facing a sidewall of black light.

"Aren't we going to make love, Nils?" she went on stumblingly. "For old times' sake at least?"

"Oh, love," Hansen said.

He tossed the helmet onto the pile of furs and put his arms around the woman. She was crying silently, but her hands uncinched the hooks of her waistbelt when Hansen fumbled them.

They made rough, passionate love on the bearskin Hansen slid from the bench beside them. The jewel in the command helmet gleamed down on them like a cold gray star.

Chapter Eighteen

Brett, the Searchers' escort, stepped into the audience hall between Race and Julia. He came to a dead halt when he realized that the throne was empty. No one was present except guards in battlesuits at the room's three sets of doors.

"I was told . . . ," the underchamberlain said to the warrior in black-and-silver armor at the door giving onto the imperial apartments. "Ah, that the emperor wished to see me at once?"

The volume of the large-domed room turned Brett's voice into a pattern of cicada raspings. Without the usual crowd to give it life, the audience hall was a tomb.

"Don't get your bowels in 'n uproar, pretty-boy," the guard boomed harshly through his suit speaker. "Himself'll be here when he chooses t' be, don't you worry."

Julia grinned at Brett. "Little toad," she said distinctly. The Searchers were sworn to obey Venkatna in all things . . . but the underchamberlain had attempted to turn imperial authority into personal favors from the new slaves on the road back from Simplain.

Race held Brett while Julia singed the hairs off Brett's scrotum with a candleflame. It had taken the underchamberlain some time and a serious blister to realize that he would be much better off if he held absolutely still. . . .

"I wouldn't mind a piece of that, though," Race said, nodding toward the black-and-silver guard.

Julia laughed. Their uninhibited voices rang clearly from the ceiling vaults. "You don't know what there is inside," she said. "Might be like an oyster, all gray and shriveled up."

"I know," said Race, as though the object of their discussion were on another planet instead of listening in amazement from a few meters away, "that if he's got armor that good—"

The black-and-silver suit was at least third-class, maybe second.

"—then he's worth my time to see how he handles himself shucked."

The warrior at the staff entrance, through which Brett had brought the Searchers, rumbled a peal of amplified laughter.

Julia walked over to the Web and ran her hand through the air, just above one of the crystalline struts. "This must be what they want us for," she said.

"For North's sake!" the underchamberlain blurted. "Don't *touch* that."

"Says who, sonny?" Race snapped. She giggled. "Baldie, I mean."

"Like a maze," Julia said, leaning with her hands on her thighs to peer toward the benches within the apparatus. The rearward thrust of her hips to balance drew the eyes of the four men in the room. "You know what it looks like . . . ?"

"Something Sparrow night have done," Race agreed, suddenly sober. "I hear he's—"

She shrugged. "Up there, now, you know? Serving Saburo."

Brett and the nearest guard stiffened to hear a god's name in this context. Though children were named for gods, and the slaves might have meant—

"Saburo's a brave man, then," Julia said without irony. The men overhearing her relaxed.

The tall Searcher knelt. Someone her size would have to hunch forward like a gnome to reach the benches.

"Yeah," agreed Race. "Giving orders to Sparrow would be like giving orders to Lord Hansen: they better be the right orders. Those two have got tempers as cold as North's heart."

The warrior and underchamberlain looked at one another. They stood very still.

Servants pulled open the door behind the black-and-silver guard, then hopped aside. Emperor Venkatna stepped through with his right arm around Esme and a worried look on his face. "Really, my dear," he said. "There's no need for you to be up at all."

His wife patted his hand. Her face beneath the heavy makeup had a grayish pallor. "Nonsense," she said. "Nonsense. A little touch of indigestion isn't going to keep me down."

Esme straightened with an effort, but her voice gained strength as she did so. "These are the slaves, then? I hadn't realized they'd be so attractive. Do you suppose . . . ?"

"No, no," Venkatna said with a touch of peevishness. "They're far too valuable to waste warming my bed."

He frowned. "If they have the skills they're supposed to, that is."

"I only want you happy, dearest," Esme said.

Race looked at Julia. Julia rocked her left hand in the air, palm down. Venkatna wasn't a badly set-up man. A bit on the soft side, but athletic ability on the battlefield didn't necessarily translate to skill on a good, firm mattress.

Anyway; the Searchers would perform whatever tasks their master required, for as long as he lived. . . .

Venkatna tried to support Esme up the low steps of the throne, but she now resisted the coddling. "Go on," she said crisply, gesturing to the seat. "I'll not sit down before you, you know that."

The emperor made a moue that flexed the tips of his moustache, then settled himself on the throne. His wife lowered herself primly to the top step. She put her hand affectionately on Venkatna's knee.

Venkatna patted Esme's hand. "All right," he said, looking from one Searcher to the other. I understand you are skilled in the use of the Web?"

"Yes, that's right, your majesty," Brett interjected. Old Saxtorph, who had replaced the brain-dead Boardman as chamberlain, couldn't last long. Brett's risk in calling himself to the emperor's attention was—possibly, very possibly—worth the chance of being remembered when it came time to appoint another chamberlain.

"Be silent, fool," Esme said without bothering to look at him.

Race pursed her lips. "Ah . . . ," she said. "What is it that your majesty wishes us to do, exactly?"

"Get into the Web and use it," Venkatna said with a flash of anger. "The merchant who sold it to me said that it could affect my whole domains. I want you to do that. I want you to bring peace to my entire Empire!"

Julia glanced at her companion, then back to the emperor. "Peace, your majesty? When you say peace, do you mean . . . ?"

Venkatna lunged up from his throne. "I mean peace!" he

shouted. "I mean that no one in the Empire takes up arms against my orders. Peace!"

Race looked at the Web. The benches were to lie on, that was clear enough. For the rest, the device was an amalgam of nodes and shimmers almost too delicate to be material. It was as incomprehensible as North's purpose in sending her here to Venkatna.

But North *had* a purpose, of that she and Julia could be sure.

"Your orders are our fate, your majesty," the tall Searcher said. She bent and crawled within the Web through a gap— not an entrance, there was no proper entrance. Julia found another opening across the Web's humped form.

The bench felt cool to Race's back. The glimmering pattern of which the Web was woven did not so much illuminate the Searchers inside as it distorted the humans and architecture when Race tried to look beyond it. She closed her eyes because she could think of nothing else to do—

There was a globe of infinite vastness, and she had no being. It was colder than thought, and her not-self trembled.

Peace . . . boomed a voice/memory.

She concentrated. Tiny figures skittered across a landscape dwarfed by the hugeness of the frame on which it appeared. Arc weapons flashed, spikes in the limitless dark.

Race *pushed* as she would move the controls of her dragonfly. The cold gnawed at her heart and marrow. In the distance she heard moaning; Julia, or it might have been Race's own voice.

The arcs vanished . . . sprang up elsewhere in emptiness and winked out . . . elsewhere. . . . Nothing was constant but the cold that sucked away life and juices.

Your orders are our fate.

She thought she heard North's titanic laughter trail across the black sky.

Chapter Nineteen

"This one says he come t' fight the tax men with us, Lord Salles," called the guard stumbling down the trail behind Hansen. "But I don't know."

The response lag of servos in the guard's battlesuit was so long that the fellow was lucky not to fall on his face. If he'd survived even a single battle in armor so shoddy, he was either lucky or improbably skillful.

"He knows," said Hansen as he dismounted in the center of the neat bivouac, "that I'm carrying the best battlesuit he's ever seen in his life. And he hasn't figured out that a man who owns armor like mine might just be more use to rebels like yourselves than his hardware is."

"This man's a friend of mine, Bosey," Salles said, exaggerating a brief meeting in Venkatna's audience hall. He clasped the newcomer, forearm to forearm. "Glad to have you with us, Lord Hansen. We'll need all the help we can get to defend our ancestral rights."

You'll need more than that, with an imperial battalion on its way. You'll need a bloody miracle. . . .

Wood smoke drifted through the roofs of the stick-built hutments and hung in a vaguely-sickening layer above the cold ground. A dozen warriors were at battle practice behind the circle of dwellings. About a hundred other folk could be seen in the small camp; some of them probably warriors, but the bulk freemen and slaves.

Salles released Hansen's arm and stepped to the side to view the trio of ponies which were the newcomer's only companions. "Where are your servants?" he asked in surprise.

Hansen smiled wryly. "Just me," he said. "I never much cared for folks poking around me when I'm trying to get dressed, and I figured I could dip my own stew out of the dinner pot if I had to."

"He could still be a spy," Bosey objected. His battlesuit was a black-and-green plaid. The paint was fresh but it had been applied by an amateur, probably Bosey himself. Even an expert would have been hard put to conceal the ragged welds which joined the portions of Bosey's battlesuit into a wretched whole.

"Bosey, get back to your position," Salles ordered sharply. To Hansen he added apologetically, "From high ground, suit sensors—even Bosey's suit sensors—can give us three kilometers' warning of any force approaching from the east. Assuming they move with a least a few guards suited up in live armor, that is."

"I'll give you more warning than that," Hansen said coldly as he surveyed the encampment. "Venkatna's troops are about two days out. Less if they push, but they won't bother to."

Salles swallowed, then nodded crisply. "How many?" he asked in a nonchalant tone.

Hansen stretched his head backward and kneaded his buttocks with his fingertips. Not a lot of fat there, which was as it should be; but not a lot of padding for a pony's saddle, either.

"A battalion," he said, looking toward the tops of the pine trees. The latest snowfall had slipped from the upper branches. There were collars of half ice, half crusted snow, on the shadowed needles partway down the trunk.

Before the next snow fell, most of the people in this camp would be dead.

"About a hundred battlesuits," Hansen continued to the sky. "The co-commanders are named Ashley and D'Auber, I'm told."

"D'Auber's a butcher," Bosey said. The cracking of his voice was accentuated by the bad reproduction in his battlesuit amplifiers. "He'll kill every damned thing down t' the rats in the garbage, he will."

Hansen turned like a hawk stooping. "If you're not back to your post in two minutes," he shouted at Bosey, "I'll stuff your head up your worthless asshole and save D'Auber the trouble! *Move*, you scut!"

Bosey stumbled back a step, turned, and made off toward his vantage point at the best speed his battlesuit could manage. Warriors playing chess in front of the nearest hut jumped to their feet. The freemen leading away Hansen's ponies stopped; one of them dropped the reins in his hand. A woman, very possibly a noble from the quality of her fur-trimmed cloak, watched Hansen with particular intensity.

Hansen knelt, rubbing his forehead with his fingertips and kneading his cheeks hard with his thumbs. From a great distance he heard Salles say gently, "He's loyal, you know. He didn't leave my service when he realized we were going to fight the tyrant in Frekka."

Hansen's arc cuts off the warrior's head and the man's outstretched left forearm. The legs and brown-mottled torso of the battlesuit fall front down, away from the surprise attack.

The men at the back of the enemy line do not expect close-quarters battle. They cannot survive more than a few seconds when battle finds them. Warriors in red and green and an ill-painted pattern of silver stars try to turn. Their battlesuits, like that of the first victim, are scarred by frequent repairs. Each sequence of damage and repair further degrades the armor's capabilities.

Hansen slices through both men at chest level. He doesn't have time to pick weak points for his arc, nor is there any need to do so with this caliber of opponent. The sectioned battlesuits topple into the mud, sparking modestly. The victims' armor does not carry enough power to create an impressive display, even when it is vented in a dead short. . . .

"All they're good for is to die," Hansen muttered. The pressure of his hands on his cheeks slurred his voice. "I' say that they're warriors, 'n' t' die the first time they happen t' get in the way of somebody with a real suit."

"Bosey can keep watch for us," Salles said. "Him and Aldo and a couple of the others. And they can keep Venkatna's freemen out of our camp while, while the battle's still going on."

His voice was thinner than before and had an artificial lilt. Salles had been badly shaken by Hansen's news.

What the hell had he *expected* was going to happen? That Venkatna would ignore a rebellion just because the rebel warriors had moved out of their keeps?

Hansen got to his feet. His back was to Salles. He didn't turn. A warrior in a black battlesuit had left the practice field and was walking toward Salles and the newcomer.

"Got any more troops than these?" Hansen asked mildly.

"About this many more, three kilometers west with Lord Richtig," Salles replied. "Thirty-one all told. Thirty-two with— if you join us."

"I've joined," Hansen said. "I'm fucking here, aren't I?"

On bivouac Salles wore rough garments, homespun wool without embroidered designs. They suited him much better than court clothes. He moved well, too. Hansen didn't doubt that he'd be a tough opponent with anything like parity of equipment.

"I rather thought . . . ," Salles said. "That perhaps they'd send a smaller force initially, and we could overwhelm it. Of course, there'd be a battalion the next time. . . ."

Hansen turned. "What are you going to do now?" he demanded harshly. "Surrender?"

Salles met his glare. "If we surrendered," said the Lord of Peace Rock, "they'd execute us anyway. It won't make any difference to the civilians back at the keeps, since they'll be enslaved in either event."

"As they would have been in any case when the district was unable to meet its autumn tribute," said the woman in the fur-trimmed cloak. She had walked up behind Hansen. "As I well know."

"Lucille is my cousin," Salles said without looking at the woman. "She was married to the Lord of Thrasey . . . who failed to pay his tribute last year. I thought she'd been killed when the keep was sacked, until she escaped to me last month."

"What are you going to *do?*" Hansen repeated.

"Fight," Salles said flatly. "Die in battle if that's the will of North . . . but battles have been won against the odds before."

Hansen snorted.

"Why are you here, then, Lord Hansen?" Salles said sharply. "This isn't your fight, and you've obviously formed an opinion about our chances of establishing our rights against Frekka."

"What do *you* think your chances are, b-b—milord?" Hansen retorted.

He grimaced. Before the Lord of Peace Rock could snap out the dismissal that the barely-swallowed '*boyo*' demanded, Hansen knelt and said, "Sorry, Lord Salles. The injustice of the situation bothers me, and I, I'm taking it out on the victims."

"For the gods' sweet sake," said Lucille calmly, "get out of that mud, milord. We have better use for you than that you should catch your death of cold."

She touched Salles' forearm. "This is the man who bought me out of the labor gang, cousin. The usher who carried the bribe said the money came from a warrior named Hansen, a stranger."

Which explained Lucille's pallor. Quite an attractive woman, if you liked them thin and with hair colored something between brown and blond.

It didn't explain the game North was playing; but you could never be sure about that. . . .

"Gods, I'm sorry!" blurted Salles, clasping Hansen's arm again. "I didn't realize! I—"

"You thought I was some prick come to laugh at you when you were about to die," Hansen said wryly. "Reasonable guess, the way I was acting."

His face sobered. "I knew some folk from this district a long time since," he added. *About a hundred years ago, as time runs in the Open Lands.* "Nobody you'd know, but—I figure they wouldn't want me to walk away from this fight if they were still around."

Aubray wears armor decorated with black-and-cream rosettes. Hansen doesn't remember the sideman's features. The Colimore arc shears off the front of Aubray's helmet, igniting Aubray's hair and beard in an orange frame for the warrior's screaming face.

The blow was meant for Hansen. . . .

"Hansen?" Lucille said from very close by. "Milord?"

Hansen shook himself. "I'm all right," he said before his eyes had focused again. Lucille stood beside him, ready to grab him if he started to fall.

"Maybe the gods will slay Venkatna," muttered the Lord of Peace Rock. "His exactions are an affront to them, surely."

"The gods don't interfere that way," said the warrior in black armor who had finally reached them from the practice ground. "Events have a balance. Trying to bend them by brute force means that they'll snap back in a way you won't much like."

"Let me introduce you to our other new recruit," Salles said. "Like you, he says he used to have friends in this area. Lord Hansen, this is—"

The warrior gripped the latch of the battlesuit and pulled open the frontal plate.

"—Lord Kriton."

Even though her hair is cropped short and she wears a quilted jacket, how could they think Krita was a man? But they saw only the hard eyes, and skill with a battlesuit that not even Salles himself could overmatch.

"I've met Kriton before, Lord Salles," Hansen said. "With warriors of his quality and yours—and mine . . . I think maybe we can survive the present problem. Then we can reach the Mirala District in time to do some real good."

Hansen offered his arm for Krita to grip as she got out of her battlesuit. She swayed against him. *Breasts as firm as apples, with dark nipples extending as he kissed them. . . .*

"I'm glad to see you here also, Lord Hansen," the Searcher said as she met her lover's eyes.

Chapter Twenty

Hansen sensed a presence in North's palace of carved light, though the owner himself was not in his gleaming hall. Someone waited in the sheets and columns of material radiance. . . .

"Dowson?" called Nils Hansen. "I'd like to talk to you."

A plane of light dissolved, uncovering a wall niche. In it were a stalagmite of multi-hued ice and a tank of clear crystal—

Which held a human brain.

The outermost layer of the stalagmite scaled away like dry ice subliming. A lilac bubble, almost too pale to be called pastel, expanded from the stalagmite. When the bubble's edge intersected Hansen, he heard Dowson's voice say, "I'm always glad to help you, Commissioner Hansen."

The cold equivalent of laughter swept from the cone as a hint of yellow. "I'm always glad," Dowson added, "to interact with any of you who still have flesh."

Hansen walked closer to the tank, though there was no need to do so. The floor beneath his feet appeared to be parquetry of black and white slabs. Closer observation showed that the black was absolute void, while the white shimmered like sections from the heart of a sun.

"I may visit Plane Five," Hansen said. Gas beaded at the bottom of the tank and rose sluggishly through the fluid in which the brain was suspended. "I wanted to know about the Fleet Battle Director that I'm told is there."

Mauve and blue-violet sprang from the ice cone. Dowson's voice was cool and dry, but that had probably been true when the speaker was a man and not a disembodied brain.

"Fortin told you that APEX is in Keep Starnes," said the voice in Hansen's mind. "Which is true. And he told you that APEX knows how North took us out of the universe, how he stole all Northworld from the Consensus. . . ."

"Is *that* true?" Hansen demanded. He couldn't help staring

at the once-man when he spoke to him/it, but he kept his face rigidly blank. "Does APEX . . . have that information?"

"I don't know, Commissioner," whispered the moss-green scales which drifted past Hansen. "I would tell you if I knew, but I do not know."

If the voice were fully human, Hansen would have said there was a wistful quality to it.

He turned from the encased brain and looked across the hall. When North wished, the lines of congealed light could reach infinitely high, and there were a thousand bright gates in the walls.

When North wished.

"Commissioner," Dowson's voice said. "You came to me because I live in the Matrix—"

"Because you see it all," Hansen said with the harshness of disappointment. "Because I can look here or look there, but I'll miss the context. And the context is everything."

His voice echoed from the distant wall with a sound like that of keys turning in a tumbler lock, inhuman and inanimate. *He'd wanted a simple answer, This Is or This Is Not, so that he wouldn't have to make a decision himself. So that Commissioner Nils Hansen could just follow orders without being responsible for whatever resulted from his actions.*

"I live all that exists in the Matrix," Dowson corrected gently. "But Plane Five has its own rules, Commissioner; as you know."

Hansen spread his arms. He felt the bubble of tawny thought tingle through them on its way across the hall's expanse. He turned again and crooked a smile to the crystal tank.

"I'm afraid, you see," Hansen said quietly. He had been twenty-nine years old when he entered Northworld; a powerfully built man who was even quicker than he was strong.

His body was still that of the man he had been, but his eyes were ageless and terrible.

"If APEX knows how North took the planet . . . ," he said. He squatted down, resting his forearms on his knees. He stared at the floor beneath the tank as he used Dowson as a mental sounding board. "Then I'll go there and get the information. But I don't trust Fortin—"

"Not even a madman would trust Fortin, Commissioner," said a dusting of blue light.

"—and Fortin himself says that Count Starnes isn't to be trusted."

"You're afraid to die?" Dowson asked, as though he were compiling emotional data to add to his complete knowledge of objects and events.

Hansen looked up, still balanced on he balls of his feet. He smiled again.

"No, Dowson," he said. The lilt in his voice was a defense mechanism, an instinctive trick to prevent listeners from believing the truth that they were about to hear. "I'm afraid that I want to die, because—"

Hansen laughed. The sound was as humorless as chains rattling.

"Because so many other people have, you see?" he went on. "Either because they tried to help when I got in over my head, or because they were in my way and I was, I was . . . ."

"APEX may have been able to analyze Captain North's actions," Dowson said. His words were olive and soothing in their emotionlessness. "But no one can command you now, Nils Hansen. Not the Consensus, not North himself. You have free will."

A drift of thought so faint that it was gray by default trailed Dowson's voice across Hansen. "As those who followed you and faced you had free will."

Hansen stood up in a single smooth motion. "When *I* choose to do something," he said, "It makes things worse! Have you seen what the West Kingdom is like, Dowson?"

"I live all things in the Matrix, Commissioner," the brain responded in a shower of sublimed azure. "You see here and see there; and you miss the context, as you say. Don't—"

"I—" shouted Hansen.

A wash of orange thought swept over Hansen with the force of the surf combing a beach. "You pretend that until you have all knowledge, you are unable to act on your own decision, Nils Hansen. I tell you now: when you have all knowledge, you will be like me—unable to act at all."

Another bead of gas lifted from the bottom of the tank. It began to crawl upward, hugging the convoluted surface of Dowson's brain.

Hansen stretched and laughed cleanly. When he bent

backward, he closed his eyes so that the saturated radiance of the hall's high arches wouldn't dazzle him.

"Guess I'll go talk to Count Starnes in a little while, then," he said as he straightened. "Thank'ee, my friend."

He grinned, wondering if Dowson could see the expression; whether Dowson could actually *see* anything at all. There was humor in the smile, and in Hansen's tone as he added, "Not because the Consensus ordered me to do it. I'm going because I'm curious to see what I'll learn, and—"

Although Hansen's expression did not precisely change, the planes of solid muscle drew taut over his cheekbones. They formed a visage more terrible than a grinning skull.

"—from what I hear, there are some things that ought to be fixed on Plane Five. Nobody's paying me to fix things nowadays, but if Fortin's little friend the count wants to make it my business . . ."

Hansen's words blurred off into savage laughter, echoing from the vaults and niches.

"Then you will oblige him," said Dowson in a thought of pure blood red.

"Nobody better," Hansen agreed. He flexed his supple, gunman's hands and grinned. "Nobody better at fixing *that* sort in the twelve hundred fucking worlds of the Consensus."

"Hansen . . . ?" Dowson asked as his visitor started to leave. The curtain of light was in place again, so the scales of ultramarine seemed to expand from a solid wall.

"Yeah?"

"When you say 'friend,' as you did," Dowson's voice continued, "that is a mere form of address, is it not?"

"It can be," Hansen said. "That's not how I meant it this time, though."

The trim, cat-muscled killer turned toward the portal leading out of the enormous hall. As he left, he called over his shoulder, "I'll be back to see you when I get back, friend!"

Chapter Twenty-one

Smoke from imperial cookfires formed a haze where land met the sky. Hansen began counting the bell tents which stood in a straggling circuit of the hilltop. Each was pennoned according to the rank of the quartet of warriors to which it was assigned.

The freemen and slaves serving Venkatna's troops were now seeing to their own shelter: ground sheets, tarpaulins laid across bushes on the gentle sideslopes, or nothing at all. The day had been clear. Though the temperature tonight would probably drop to freezing, the air was dry. A blanket roll was sufficient for men hardened to campaign.

Some of them wouldn't be around long enough to worry about the pre-dawn chill.

The imperial servants weren't a problem, not even the freemen who scouted for the armored warriors when the battleline advanced; but there were going to be some of them who got in the way. Salles' rebels—*Hansen's* rebels now, in all but name— didn't have time to pick and choose. When they went in, anything imperial that moved would be a target. . . .

A single armored warrior stood at the edge of the imperial camp. He was probably bored, but that would change quickly enough when his battlesuit display indicated the presence of thirty-two rebel warriors.

At the moment, the sentinel saw nothing except a birch-shaded covert a hundred meters east of the campsite. The battlesuits of Salles and his men stood empty behind the ambush line. Until the rebels closed the frontal plates over themselves, the suits remained unpowered. Cold, the armor provided no emanations for Venkatna's sensors to receive and report.

Soon dusk would cloak the lower slopes of the hill. Warriors using the image intensifiers of their battlesuits would not be affected.

The imperial troops, relaxing over their meals, wouldn't be

625

sure what was happening until the line of armored rebels burst into the camp with their arc weapons lighting the way.

Very soon. . . .

Lord Salles stood beside Hansen on the right flank. A courier, panting from having run the length of the rebel line, gasped a message to him. When the courier finished speaking, he darted his head back as though he feared a blow.

The man probably did. Nobles were not permitted by law and custom to kill out of hand freemen like the courier . . . but a courier who brought a haughty message from one warrior to another couldn't assume mere law would be sufficient protection.

Salles laughed harshly. The Lord of Peace Rock had been moving ever since his rebels reached their ambush site; but he was restive, not nervous, like a thoroughbred which curvettes at the starting line.

"*Tell* your master," Salles said, "that he will await our signal— as he agreed under oath. Tell him!"

"It won't be long," Hansen added in a mild tone. He wondered if *he* sounded nervous. His mouth was dry and he wanted to piss, but at the moment he didn't like the thought of having his dick bare and unprotected. . . .

The courier nodded gloomily and started back toward Lord Richtig. His boots popped and rustled through the litter. The noise wasn't audible for any distance—certainly not the fifty meters to the nearest imperial servants—but it was unnecessary. . . .

"I'm worried about Richtig," Salles muttered to Hansen. "He's likely to suit up and attack on his own."

Servants behind the ambush line edged closer. They turned their faces away, so that they could hear the leaders without being obvious about it. It wasn't just warriors who were in this, particularly if the attack failed.

"That's all right," Hansen said. "He won't."

He looked at the sky through the tracery of bare branches. Still pale blue. After another few minutes, though. . . .

"You don't know Richtig!" Salles snapped.

"I know his type," Hansen said calmly. *Didn't he just!* "That's why I put Kri-Kriton beside him."

Bells chimed from the imperial baggage mammoths which grazed on the lush meadow west of the camp. The location of the grass had determined where Hansen's force could lie in wait. The beasts would not have been fooled by a screen of trees and the lack of electronic warning; but all they cared for now was to fill their vast rumbling bellies.

"Eh?" said Salles.

"If Richtig tries to get an early start," Hansen explained, "Kriton'll stick a knife into the seam of his battlesuit so that it won't close and show up on our friend's—" he nodded toward the imperial sentinel "—sensors."

Hansen smiled in bleak humor. "If sh—Kriton's in a good mood, he won't put the point a centimeter into Richtig's side t' remind him about orders."

Lord Salles blanked his face as he considered the statement. "You know Kriton well, then?" he asked in a neutral tone.

"You bet," Hansen said.

Black hair so short that it scarcely brushes his cheek when she bends over him on the couch. Her dark nipples on his chest, the taut muscles over her ribs and under the swell of her buttocks as he pulls her down to engulf him. . . .

The slope to the imperial camp was a rich purple-blue.

"Mount up," Hansen, ordered as he turned to his own battlesuit. "But nobody close their suits till the gong sounds."

There was a freeman standing behind each warrior with orders to jam a stick into the seam of any suit whose owner tried to close up early. Venkatna's forces would certainly torture to death *everyone* they captured if the surprise assault failed. It was just possible that some of the freemen would obey Hansen's orders, though they knew how angry any warrior so treated would be.

The motion of warriors getting into their battlesuits shifted down the line like a wave. The act itself was a visual signal to the next man over, though trees hid each rebel from all but a few of his fellows in either direction. A gong signal would warn the imperial forces early, and each battlesuit's frequency-hopping radio was shut down with the rest of its electronics until the plastron latched into the backplate.

The suede lining of Hansen's armor felt cold, but its pressure encircling his legs and arms was a relief. The plastron, including the front portion of the helmet, remained open. He laced his gauntleted hands over it, ready to slam the piece closed and

bring up the suit's systems as soon as the whole force was ready.
He waited.

His hand fumbling with Krita's sash for the first time, so clumsy that she chuckles and slips the tie herself. . . .

"Lord Kriton says they're ready on our end, sir!" gasped a puffing runner.

"Sound the gong," said Hansen as he slammed shut his frontal plate. He'd forgotten that the Lord of Peace Rock was in titular command, but the waiting slave forgot also and hammered the fat bronze tube.

"Suit!" Hansen shouted to switch on his armor's artificial intelligence as he pounded uphill. "Full daylight equivalent—" the display became a clear window before his eyes as the AI enhanced the scene to what it would have been at noon "—and carat friendlies white in all displays!"

"Hansen the War God!" Kriton shouted as a battlecry as she burst from the woods on the opposite end of the line.

Little minx.

A battlesuit weighed in the order of a hundred kilos. Servo motors in the joints amplified the wearer's movements, but the speed and strength of the response depended on the suit's quality. Running in a suit as poor as that of Bosey or those of several other rebel warriors was only marginally less punishing than jogging with an anvil.

The diverse rebel force couldn't possibly hit the imperial camp as a unit unless all the troops governed the speed of their charge to that of the men with the poorest equipment—

In which case the enemy would have most of his triply superior numbers armed and ready to meet them. Hansen had arrayed the rebels with the best battlesuits on the flanks—he and Salles on the right, Krita and Lord Richtig on the left. The rest were spaced inward in declining order of their armor's quality. That way the attack would, with luck, display a smoothly concave front to Venkatna's startled men.

"Alarm!" the imperial sentinel cried. "We're attacked! Alarm!"

He was using his radio, not the loudspeaker in his helmet. None of his unsuited fellows could hear him.

An imperial freeman tried to run from Hansen's approach. The man slipped and curled into a screaming ball. Hansen would have spared him, but a slave behind the line of rebel warriors smashed the fellow's skull with the mallet which had just rung the gong.

A slave with a club was a better man than a warrior caught halfway into his armor. This was no time to be choosy about technique.

Hansen sucked air in through his open mouth, but his lungs hadn't begun to burn yet. Ten meters before he reached the imperial camp, he glanced to his left. Salles was a pace behind him, handicapped by having lighted his arc weapon. The discharge drained some power that would otherwise have fed his servos.

Krita's black battlesuit was parallel to Hansen's and a hundred meters away, while Richtig was several strides behind her.

The rest of the force . . . was coming at its best speed, with only a few drop-outs, for a wonder. Even Bosey, though he had sprawled and was just picking himself up again. Hansen's artificial intelligence—and that of all the other rebels, if the order had passed as it should on the suit-to-suit data link—inserted a white plume above the helmet of every friendly figure glimpsed on the display.

It was time.

"Cut!" Hansen shouted with his right thumb and forefinger spread wide. His AI obeyed by switching on his weapon for a long looping cut.

Three tents ignited at the arc's touch. The wool burned orange with sparklings from the strands of metal woven into the pennons.

"Hansen the War God!" shouted a rebel other than Krita.

There were half a dozen men in the tents, relaxing warriors or those serving them. They had only enough time to leap to their feet. Hansen's blue-white arc slashed across their unarmored bodies. Flesh exploded into steam and droplets of blazing fat.

Hansen strode into the inferno, clearing his path with quick blind slashes of his arc. The stench of burning wool was overpowering despite his battlesuit's filters. A long bandage of tent-flap swaddled Hansen's helmet when he stepped into what should have been the clear area in the camp's center. He flailed his arms to rid himself of the encumbrance.

The sentinel was the only imperial warrior wearing a battlesuit. The man rushed Hansen with a cry of fury.

Lord Salles stepped through the gap between two tents. He flicked the sentinel with an arc extended to three meters. Salles' weapon was too attenuated to cut, but it licked like a serpent's tongue over the defensive screens of the imperial battlesuit—draining so much power from the servos that the sentinel froze in mid-step.

Hansen thrust through the sentinel's plastron. The victim fell onto his back. There was a black hole in his chest and a rim of molten metal bubbling around the edges of the cut.

"Hansen the War God!" Hansen screamed, why not, as he charged a group of imperial warriors desperately trying to get into their battlesuits.

It was going to work. They'd caught Venkatna's men completely unaware. There'd be casualties, sure, at the end when they had to deal with the few imperials who managed to arm themselves, but all the rebels were engaged and half the camp was already aflame.

He felt it change.

The Matrix shrugged; that was the only word Hansen could think of to describe the sensation. He wasn't affected himself—his arc ripped a pair of empty battlesuits and the screaming imperial warrior who changed his mind too late about getting into one—

But the other rebels switched off their weapons and began opening their battlesuits.

"Don't!" Hansen cried incredulously. *The probability generator, the Web, that North had sold Venkatna. It was now operating.* "For pity's sake, don't stop now!"

An imperial warrior slammed his plastron closed. He cut Bosey in half. Bosey's black-and-green armor was poor stuff to begin with, but the young rebel—*sixteen and he'd never see seventeen now*—had started to climb out even as the arc swept toward him.

"Take them prisoner!" ordered a steely voice on what Hansen's display noted was the imperial command channel. His AI decoded even the lock-out push of lesser battlesuits. "Don't kill them till we learn what's happened!"

Half a dozen of Venkatna's troops, wearing their armor, approached Hansen in a tight group. He backed away.

Lord Salles stepped clear of his battlesuit. He looked at Hansen in surprise. "What are you doing, Lord Hansen?" demanded the one-time rebel leader. "We shouldn't take up arms against Emperor Venkatna."

Krita got out of her armor. She was not immune to the forces twisting through the Web.

"Get him!" cried an imperial warrior as he started for the only rebel still in armor.

Hansen's arc touched the man as he started his rush from several meters away. The imperial was off-balance when his servos lost power. His shout turned to a squawk. He fell forward, tripping the pair of warriors following him most closely.

Hansen plunged into the smoky flames of the tent behind him.

Imperial warriors surrounded the tent immediately. The only things they found when the fire died down were the corpses of their fellows, killed in the rebel onrush.

Chapter Twenty-two

The air which Sparrow drew into his lungs was as humid as the contents of a warm bath; the tang of salt was gone.

The dog yipped in startlement. The smith set her down. She ran from one plant to another, snuffling furiously at their spreading roots. There was no true ground cover; thin, russet mud splashed the dog's feet and belly, though the muck slid from her leg braces like grease from heated iron.

Sparrow shrugged to loosen his woolen blouse. A streak of sweat between his shoulderblades already glued the fabric to his back. He could see the tops of trees kilometers away; some of them spiked, others with ribbons of foliage clumped into pompons. Closer to hand grew horsetails and low cycads like scaly balls tufted with fronds. They disappeared into the mist within a hundred meters.

Sparrow didn't bother to sigh. He was a hunter, long used to the punishment of climate and terrain: bitter cold, sleet storms, or this muggy swamp—it was all the same, and all to be accepted.

Besides, he knew what Hell was. On a plain so cold that metal cracked, frozen souls oozed forward like slime molds; infinitely slowly and forever, until the Final Day ended time. This was not Hell.

When Sparrow opened his small mirror to determine his course, the face immediately beaded with condensate. He took off one gauntlet and wiped the screen with the edge of his palm; then repeated the motion. The difference in temperature across the discontinuity—and the saturated atmosphere here—had blurred the surface a second time.

Mala's fortress bower squatted on the screen. Part of the haze fogging the image was on the far side of the view. A red bead on the mirror's bronze frame gave Sparrow a vector to his destination.

"C'mon, you fool dog!" the smith called as he set off. Mud

swelled over his feet at every step, but the high laces would prevent the sandals from being stripped off. Not that Sparrow couldn't go on barefoot—or naked and weaponless—but he didn't intend to do so.

The dog could find her master by scent easily enough, but Sparrow was worried about the sorts of things he knew lurked in this swamp. Not worried for himself, but the fool dog didn't have any sense at all. . . .

When there was something like firm ground running in the proper direction, they followed it. When open water crossed their path, Sparrow waded and the dog swam. The warm, sluggish waters didn't disturb the bitch the way living surf had done.

The dog barked in a high-pitched, enthusiastic tone and with the regularity of a metronome while she paddled. Sparrow glowered until there was a sudden commotion on the far bank of the stream they were crossing. The unfamiliar yapping had panicked a fat-bodied amphibian, three meters long and far too big to prey on fish. It bolted through the marsh in the opposite direction.

The dog hopped onto the bank and shook herself violently. "Fool animal . . . ," Sparrow murmured as he climbed out beside her. He scratched between her ears, his touch as delicate as a delivering midwife's despite his gauntlets.

They passed numbers of sail-backed edaphosaurs chewing vegetation with peglike teeth. For the most part, the herbivores ignored the human and his dog, though one—a male with scarlet wattles—grunted a challenge. All the edaphosaurs wore collars of black plastic: control devices, marking these beasts as members of a herd.

Nainfari's cattle; so Nainfari's hold would not be far distant.

After three hours of slogging, Sparrow paused and sat on a cycad. Fronds, squashed outward by the smith's weight, tickled the backs of his calves. Insects were lured by pink flowers growing from the cycad's scaly hunk. They buzzed around Sparrow in confusion at his mammalian odor.

The smith and his dog had just crossed from a headland between a pair of streams emptying into a pond. It had been deep wading, and for a moment Sparrow thought he too would have to swim. His equipment was waterproof, and the smith wouldn't shrink either; but it was a reasonable time to settle for a moment and wring some of the muck from his blouse and breeches.

Edaphosaurs browsed the horsetails on the margins of the pond. A swimming reptile, scarcely the length of the smith's forearm, surfaced in the center of the standing water. A fish glittered in its tiny jaws. It vanished again as suddenly into the black fluid again.

Sparrow rose to his feet. His dog, panting and mud-stained except for her nose and forehead, remained sprawled on the ground with only her head lifted. "All right, dog," the smith grumbled. "You wanted to come, so I brought—"

The dog jumped up with a snarl.

Sparrow turned, quick as a baited bear. The dimetrodon, ten meters from them and poised to rush, hunched back in surprise. Its jaws of large, ragged teeth gaped wider, but the blush darkening the big carnivore's fin indicated fear and consternation rather than anger.

The dimetrodon grunted. The dog backed between Sparrow's legs. Her growl sounded like a saw cutting rock many kilometers away.

"There's no need for trouble," Sparrow murmured. His arms were splayed at his sides. He began to edge away. The pond was to his right.

The herd of edaphosaurs shuddered into a slow-motion stampede. Those nearest to the dimetrodon waddled off, and their motion warned the next rank of the beasts. The edaphosaurs' sails wobbled with the sinuous motion of their lizardlike bodies.

"No trouble at all . . . ," the smith said.

The dimetrodon rocked forward and back on its four splayed legs. It wasn't likely to charge now; but there was limited room for reflexes in the sail-backed carnivore's small brain. You couldn't be sure which one was going to trip the beast into motion.

Spray like the base of a waterfall lifted from the far edge of the pond. A dozen figures on repulsion skimmers tore through the horsetails, heading across the surface of the black water. Edaphosaurs which had splashed midway into the pond for fear of the carnivore now swam in terrified circles.

The leader of the band on skimmers was a four-armed android,

but the remainder of his party wore slave collars. The bulk of
them were either humans from the Open Lands or Lomeri,
the scaled, bipedal lizardmen who inhabited Plane Two. One
female had the squat somatotype of Plane Five.

The newcomers were dressed in leather harnesses and rags
which they wore for their brilliant hues rather than protection
or modesty. Knives, handguns, and shoulder weapons on slings
bounced and jangled as the party crossed the water.

The android held his skimmer's controls with one pair of
hands and aimed a multibarreled weapon with the other. The
gun belched a white flash and a hypersonic *c-crack-k-k* from
its twenty muzzles. A volley of fléchettes spewed toward the
dimetrodon.

The beast blatted in surprise. At least a half dozen of the
miniature projectiles punched out scales or made bloody dimples
in the thin fabric of the carnivore's sail. The animal sound was
submerged by the slave gang's roaring weapons.

Bullets, laser light, a sulphurous bolt of plasma, and a sheaf
of thumb-sized rockets raked the area of the dimetrodon in a
deafening salvo. Most missed their intended target. A human's
laser sheared through the control column of a Lomeri's skimmer,
sending the latter tumbling wildly across the water.

Enough of the salvo hit to rip the carnivore to bloody rags.
Explosive projectiles sawed almost through the dimetrodon's
short neck, while the plasma bolt reduced the beast's sail to
blackened spines from which the connecting tissue had burned.

The reptile thrashed in the mud. Individual muscles retained
vitality which the entity as a whole had lost.

The hunters swept up onto the bank. They grounded their
skimmers, then got off and formed a semicircle around Sparrow
at the distance of two or three meters. The Fifth Plane female
scooped up the lizardman from the disabled skimmer. She tossed
him negligently to the mud at the edge of the pond.

The band's weapons smoked or glowed from the recent firing.
They pointed in various directions, but most of them pointed
at Sparrow. The dog crouched between the smith's legs, growling
below the range of audibility.

"Hey, Morfari," the squat female called to her android leader.
"Give him t' me, hey? He's just about the right size."

"Balls to that!" snorted the human male with the laser. He was grinning. "*I'm* not getting sloppy tenths again!"

"You can share, can't you, Lilius?" Morfari said. He broke open his volley gun, ejecting the fired casings so that he could reload with another bundle of fléchettes from a belt pouch. "You don't need the same part, after all."

"Use the Chewer," chittered a Lomeri slave, pointing his snub-nosed rocket launcher at the quivering dimetrodon.

"Naw, it's a female. That rules it out for Lilius."

Morfari's arms were muscular and well-shaped. He waggled his reloaded volley gun in a one-handed arc that lifted the weapon's point of aim over Sparrow's head and lowered it again to the other side.

"Greetings, stranger," the android said. "I'm Morfari. My father, Nainfari, is the king hereabouts, and me 'n the crew guard his cattle."

The big female chuckled. One of the Lomeri began to pick his pointed teeth theatrically with a dagger.

"Now . . . ," Morfari continued. "Just who might *you* be?"

The smith shrugged. "My name's Sparrow," he said. "I'm passing through your father's domains, but I'll do no hurt to his herds."

"You can say that again, sweetie," said a human slave whose automatic rifle was pointed at Sparrow's belly. The slave ran a finger around his collar in a habitual action. The plastic had chafed a callus on his neck.

"We saved his life," said the Fifth Plane female, more than half serious. "He owes us a little entertainment at least."

"Lady . . . ," said the smith in a voice as detached as distant lightning. "My master sent a man who could fight his own battles."

He opened his iron-shod hands. Sparrow's grip would span the trunk of the largest tree on this island. "I thank you for killing the monster, but I would have avoided it had you not arrived . . . and if the beast would not be avoided, then I would have torn its head off—"

He smiled, an expression of power and implacable determination. "—as you have done yourselves, with your weapons."

Sparrow cocked his right hip so that he could scratch his dog behind the ears with his left fingertips. The touch wouldn't calm her, but it would keep her steady . . . and it would keep the smith steady also, at a time when death could come as easily as when the rock of a sheer cliff began to flake under the weight of the climber.

Three of the lizardmen chirped to one another in their own language. A human said, "You know, he just mighta done that thing," as his thumb polished a worn place on the receiver of his grenade launcher.

"I'm a courier," Sparrow said as he straightened. "My master sent me with a message for the Princess Mala. I'll deliver it and leave."

The slave gang responded with hoots and guffaws. Their collars were control devices. A signal, from the lavaliere bouncing on Morfari's chest or from the base unit at Nainfari's hold, would inject pain or even death through the collars.

But Morfari and his hunting party were clearly united in enthusiasm for what they did—and the ways they were permitted to do it.

The android chuckled. He rubbed his chin with one hand and scratched his back with another. All the time, his remaining pair of arms kept the volley gun aimed at Sparrow's belly.

"Well, Master Sparrow," Morfari said. "I don't think that's a good idea at all. Even if you got past—and I grant you might, big fellow—the Chewers—"

He nodded toward the dimetrodon; one of the beast's hind legs still clawed the air slowly.

"—and the Gulpers, there's what my sister's put up to keep her privacy."

To the side, a joke between a pair of Lomeri turned ugly. One of the lizardmen snatched out a knife. The Fifth Plane human, apparently Morfari's adjutant, knocked the knife-wielder down with a clout across the temple.

"The outer ring," Morfari continued, seemingly oblivious to the fuss among his slaves, "that'll cut you apart while you're still a kilometer away, even if you—"

His pale, perfect face smiled.

"—slide on your belly through the mud. Inside her walls, nothing bigger than a roach can live, without dear Mala gives it special dispensation. That's pretty good defenses, don't you think?"

Sparrow shrugged. His eyes were on Morfari; his expression calm, almost bovine.

"And besides *that* . . . ," the android continued.

His tone was sharper from irritation at the smith's placidity. The slaves stopped their japes and looked to their weapons.

". . . my father's told his cattle guards to slay all vagabonds they find in the neighborhood of Mala's bower. What do you think of that, Master Vagabond?"

Sparrow shrugged again. "My master sent me with a message," he said calmly. "I have to deliver it."

"What would you say," Morfari snarled, "if I told you that we were going to kill you right here in the mud?"

"Gloves," said Sparrow as he spread the thumbs and forefingers of his arc gauntlets. "Cut!"

Chapter Twenty-three

Venkatna's dozen top advisors stood, each man shoulder-to-shoulder with two fellows, in the audience hall at Frekka. Torches flaring from wall sconces lighted the gathering.

Venkatna enthroned was the diamond mounted on the ring of his advisors.

"There's no question now," said old Bontempo. "The Mirala kings are getting aid from outside the district."

"Hiring mercenaries!" snorted Weast. "Everybody does it when they know war's coming."

"Heimrtal did it," another laughed.

The women in the Web behind the council circle moaned softly, but the sound had been going on for hours. No one took notice of it or of them. The bands of soft light moved so slowly across the surface of the device that the patterns appeared to be static.

"I don't mean mercenaries!" Bontempo protested. Anger made him wheeze, but he couldn't raise the volume of his voice. "They're being *joined* by others, some from as far away as the deep South—just to stop us!"

"And by rebels from within our borders . . . ," added Kleber in a tone of dry concern. Kleber viewed battlesuits with disdain. His cold competence in combat—as in all things—had gained him respect though not affection.

A quick knock and the creak of the outer door drew Venkatna's eyes. Several of his advisors glanced around also. The armored guard at the door talked with an usher, then turned and boomed over his loudspeaker, "Your majesty? Lord D'Auber is here."

"Send him in, then!" the emperor said curtly. In a slightly warmer tone he added toward the council, "Since we're discussing rebels."

D'Auber had ridden hard and hastened to the council without bothering to dress or change. His breeches were black with

639

the sweat of his ponies. The warrior's effluvium made the advisors in court dress blink at two meters' distance.

"Another failure with Salles, is it?" Kleber said, guessing aloud from D'Auber's haste and anger.

"Like bloody hell!" the warrior snapped. He raised his eyes to Venkatna. "Your majesty, we've captured the whole lot of them—Salles, Richtig, everydamnbody but a couple got killed. And that pussy bastard Ashley you sent with me, *he* says not to execute 'em without you say so! *He* says you gave him the right to overrule my decisions even though we're supposed t' be co-commanders!"

"Too bloody right, we did," Weast muttered.

"I want you t' give me a chit says—" D'Auber continued.

"One moment!" Venkatna said. He leaned forward on the five-step throne. "You captured the rebel warriors alive? You surprised them in bivouac, then?"

"Ah—" D'Auber said. The question shocked him back to a memory of Lord Ashley's nattering after the battle. This was obviously on the way to becoming the same discussion: *'You idiot, D'Auber! We can't kill them until we know what's going on. Don't you even wonder why this happened?'*

D'Auber *didn't* wonder about that at all. He just knew that the best time to kick an enemy was when he was down. When you had the chance to execute thirty rebels, you didn't stand around talking about it.

Other people, particularly ranking people, didn't always see the things that appeared obvious to D'Auber.

"Ah," he repeated. "Actually, it was a battle. They, ah, kind of surprised us, but then they gave up."

In sudden anger at a question which none of the advisors had enough information to ask, D'Auber shouted, "We'd have beat 'em anyway! I was getting things organized!"

"Ashley did well," Venkatna said.

The emperor stood up slowly. Reflected torchlight made his cloth-of-gold robe gleam and turned its ermine trim into a serpent of lambent flame. "Gentlemen!" Venkatna cried. "Let us give thanks to North who rules men's fate! The Web works!"

As if the word were a signal, the women on their benches within the device moaned in unison. They shook themselves, like people awakening from nightmare. All the advisors turned. Even D'Auber was shocked enough out of his confusion to glance around.

The internal lights faded from the Web. The two slaves sat up, shivering. They grasped one another instinctively as they rose to their feet.

The women's eyes were closed or slitted, but they walked out of the maze of wire with the slow grace of a fluid flowing past barriers in a lighter medium. It was as though the location of each portion of the Web was burned into their very cells.

"Who the hell are they, then?" D'Auber asked.

"Your majesty," Race said. "We must rest."

"Food . . . ," Julia whimpered.

"We've done your task," Race continued. She managed to open her eyes. The Searchers huddled together, shuddering uncontrollably though the room was reasonably warm and sealed against drafts. "The Matrix stretches. It will hold its present shape without us f-f-forcing it."

Her eyes scrunched shut again. "For a time."

"Food. . . ."

"Saxtorph!" the emperor shouted. He sat down again. The chamberlain and all of his staff had been excluded from the chamber before the council of war began.

"You at the door," Venkatna said, amending his address to summon the guard. "Get in somebody to take care of these girls. Set up one of the antechambers for them to eat and rest."

He looked at the Searchers, still huddled together. "One of you—Bontempo, your cloak would do for a tent. Put it over them, will you?"

"They're slaves!" cried Weast, not Bontempo himself.

"They are doing my will," said Venkatna in a thin voice. "See to it that you do the same, Count Weast. . . ."

Bontempo draped his garment of foxfur and red velvet over the women. For a moment, they appeared unaware of what was happening. Then Julia raised a trembling hand to grip the garment and hold it in place.

"But the prisoners?" D'Auber said. He hadn't understood what was going on, and it wouldn't have interested him if someone had bothered to explain. "Ashley says—"

"We don't have to kill them now," mused young Trigane; blond, handsome, and as ambitious as he was unprincipled.

"They're still rebels!" snapped Weast. He was angry at his rebuke and determined to take it out on a relatively-safe target.

"They *were* rebels," the emperor said mildly.

Weast winced and formed his mouth into a tight line, his back to the throne.

"Now they're . . . I wonder just how loyal they are?" Venkatna said/asked.

Race replied with her eyes closed, "Perfectly loyal, your majesty. All those subject to you within your empire will do your will."

Brett and four slaves bustled into the chamber with food and bedclothes. The underchamberlain watched Venkatna out of the corner of his eye. He was afraid to cross the emperor, but the message which the guard had shouted down the hall could have been misconstrued a dozen different—potentially fatal—ways.

"They're warriors, your majesty," Trigane said. "*Use* them as warriors."

"Yes, use them as the front line against Mirala," the emperor agreed. With growing enthusiasm he went on, "Yes, and against all the other enemies of the peace North chose me to impose on his world! And—"

Venkatna rose to his feet again.

"—those who survive when Earth is united, then they too shall have peace!"

"They'll mostly have found peace before that, your majesty," Kleber said with a tight smile. "The peace of North's battleplain."

The emperor began to laugh. The others joined in, both from inclination and a desire not to stand out; all but D'Auber, who still didn't understand.

The door to the royal apartments opened, so slowly that for a moment no one noticed it. Esme stepped into the large hall, walking carefully.

Venkatna jumped directly to the stone floor and strode to her. "Darling!" he said. "You shouldn't be up when you don't feel well."

"I'm fine, dearest," said Esme, but she took his offered hand with more than conventional ardor. The empress looked as gray and drawn as the two Searchers. "Just a touch of indigestion. And I do like to be with you, you know."

Venkatna's advisors formed small groups, each man with his face turned determinedly away from the imperial couple. D'Auber started to interrupt, but Kleber and Trigane took the warrior firmly aside and spoke to him urgently.

"The Web has done just what . . . ," Venkatna said as he walked his wife toward the throne, his left arm around her and both of her cold hands in his.

He looked at Esme more carefully and his voice softened. "Darling," Venkatna said, "you really *don't* look well."

"If I can just sit down for a moment, I'll be fine," the empress insisted with forced good cheer.

Venkatna set her on the top step, lifting the slight woman despite her protests that she wasn't a cripple. "Dearest?" he asked. "Would you like me to share your bed tonight? It's been far too long, what with—"

Esme looked beatified. "Oh, darling," she said. "When you're under such strain, you should have someone young and pretty to relax you. I don't need—"

"Nonsense!" said the emperor. The conversations beyond the throne buzzed pointedly louder. "You know you're the only woman I could ever love."

"Oh, darling," Esme murmured as she nestled her face against Venkatna's broad, gold-clad shoulder.

Chapter Twenty-four

The red-bearded warrior to Hansen's right in the broad, sunlit bowl of Mirala's Assembly Valley turned and stared.

"Got a problem, friend?" Hansen asked in a voice as emotionless as stone. He was uneasily aware that the fellow was a member of King Wenceslas' household, with a dozen battle comrades within spitting distance . . . while Hansen was alone.

As usual, and more or less as he chose, he guessed.

"Naw, no problem," said the other warrior. He was a little taller than Hansen and a little bulkier, though he carried no more flesh than was necessary to clothe his heavy bones. "Only I saw you before. At Heimr Town."

"I was there," Hansen agreed. *The guy who'd shouldered him on the cart, then backed off.*

Redbeard wasn't looking for a fight, but he too knew that he had a lot of friends around him. He was going to get answers. The best way for Hansen to respond was openly, as a friendly stranger who didn't notice the threat implied by the situation itself.

A petty chieftain on the Speaker's Rock droned about the traditional freedoms of Mirala. There were over a thousand men in the valley. The whole male population of the district, slave and free, was summoned to a war assembly. Only a few hundred of the crowd were warriors, though, on whose skill and arc weapons the speaker's 'traditional freedoms' would depend when Venkatna came.

There would be more slaves than warriors present if the Mirala District marched to meet the Empire. Feeding and dressing the warriors; setting up shelters and polishing battlesuits.

Not infrequently rushing into the battleline if their master fell, trying to succor him in a whirl of carnage where the accidental touch of an arc weapon would be instantly fatal to a

rag-clad slave. Hansen could never figure out why they did it,
why anybody followed anybody.

Least of all why anybody followed Commissioner Nils Hansen;
though they did, and though they'd died in windrows following
him. . . .

"Right, I thought so," Redbeard said. His tone lost a trifle of
the cautious veneer. "Only I thought you was with King Young . . .
and he decided he'd rather be a baron for Venkatna than a king
on his own, didn't he?"

Hansen smiled. Denying a former place in Young's entourage
would lead to other questions—and there wasn't any need for
it. Redbeard had just given Hansen a background that he didn't
even have to lie to claim.

"If Young didn't want t' fight those bastards in Frekka, then
I figure there's people who do," Hansen said. "I joined Lord
Salles and then *he* went over. So I came here."

"You came the right place," Redbeard said after a brief pause.
"I guess they'll get done jawin' sometime soon."

He thrust on his right hand. "I'm King Wenceslas' sideman,"
he said. "My name's Weatherhill, but ever'body calls me
Blood."

Hansen clasped Blood's proffered forearm. He remembered
doing the same thing with Lord Salles in the timeless present.

A different speaker was prating now, a king of fifty hectares
named Kawalec. He looked the same as the previous man; his
words were the same mush of nonsense and braggadocio; and
if there was a distinction at all, it was that Kawalec's voice had
a nasal twang which made it even more unpleasant than was
guaranteed by the pointlessness of his words.

In the north of the continent was a watercourse called the
Assembly River. It meandered through sands and stagnant
marshes without ever getting anywhere.

"My name's Hansen," Hansen said. At Blood's raised eyebrow,
he added, "The name's been in my family a long time. It doesn't
mean my parents thought I was a god."

If they thought anything at all. Nils Hansen had been raised
in a State Creche, but no one in the Open Lands would
understand that.

Hansen didn't really understand it himself. If you were going to create a child, you didn't throw it away like a lump of wet clay for the State to mold . . . did you?

Blood pursed his lips. "How good's your armor?" he asked.

"The best," Hansen said; knowing that Blood would discount the flat truth of the statement by one or even two levels. "It's a royal-quality piece."

Blood smiled slightly. *Every guy lies about how good his battlesuit is, and how good he is in bed.* "Right," he said. "But if you left King Young and then got out of Peace Rock in a hurry besides, I don't guess you've got much of a personal train, do you?"

"Too true," Hansen agreed. "I'm here with two ponies, my armor, and my traps. Not so much as a slave t' boil my breakfast."

Blood pursed his lips again. "No fooling?" he said, mentally knocking the quality of Hansen's battlesuit down another couple stages. "Well, when all this bumf is over, I'll take you over and interduce you t' the king. He's not a bad guy t' fight for . . . though ye mustn't worry much about what he says after a couple cups in the evening, he don't mean nothing by it."

Hansen smiled slightly at the assumption that everybody had to have a formal place in the structure. There couldn't be individual do-gooders who just wanted to help remove a tyrant. People had to be fitted into place, for their own good and for society's.

Aloud he said, "I wouldn't mind that."

Blood, having just recruited another warrior for his master's entourage, looked around him in satisfaction. The places immediately beneath the Speaker's Rock were held by warriors. The score or so of nobles attending the assembly sat on stools on the rock itself.

"I'd take you t' see Vince right now," Blood said, "only he's waiting t' speak himself. All this talk is bullshit, but it's like putting on your best clothes on assembly day, y' see. Somethin' you gotta do."

He grinned at the ranks of warriors. "We're going t' stuff this empire bullshit right up Venkatna's ass. We'll roll right over them Frekka nancy-boys."

"I'd like to think that," Hansen said soberly. He'd seen armies of individuals like this meet trained soldiers before. . . .

Hansen faces a Syndic in gold armor and a pair of his bodyguards. Three meters separate the lines. Men to either side of Hansen shout and wave their arcs, but they do not close and the Syndics wait also, trusting in their greater numbers.

To Hansen's right flank, the shouts have given way to screams and the rip of battlesuits failing under the onslaught of multiple arcs. The shock troops which Hansen trained are rolling down the enemy line like a scythe through wheat.

The Syndic turns to run. Hansen lunges. A bodyguard in pale green stripes blocks his path. Hansen's arc shears through the bodyguard's chest. Blood and metal bubble away from the cut. . . .

"Hey?" said Blood, his voice a mix between anger and surprised fear. "What . . . ?"

Hansen forced a smile. Memory had frozen his visage. He felt as though the skin over his cheekbones should crack like icebergs calving from the face of a glacier.

"Sorry," he said. "Just thinking."

"I guess you were . . . ," Blood said in something more than agreement. "Look, you don't like our chances? *Look* at these guys. And there'll be more when we march, not less. They're comin' from all over, just like you. Ever'body who hates the West Kingdom."

Another speaker rose on the flat prow of rock overlooking Assembly Valley. He was thin and abnormally tall, wearing a cloak of gray fox skins as lustrous as the seas of the far north.

"There's good men here," Hansen said, "and a lot of them. But they'll fight as so many men, and Venkatna's troops will fight like one man. And that'll be all she wrote. . . ."

There was a commotion on the Speaker's Rock. Kawalec, the kinglet who had just spoken, was refusing to give way. "I'll not be followed by a merchant!" he shouted nasally. "And a foreigner besides!"

Two of the other nobles assisted King Lukanov to his feet. Lukanov led the district because of his age. No member of Mirala's nobility had a real edge on the others by wealth or number of retainers. Nobody was sure how far seniority alone would go in a highly-charged situation like the present, but there wasn't a better alternative to the fat, wheezing old king.

"I come from far away, that is true," the tall outlander said.

His voice rang from the distant rim of the bowl. "But I am a prince among princes in my home, and if I buy and sell there—"

The Mirala kinglet scrunched away from the full shock of the foreigner's glare.

"—then some of the things I bought are the fifty warriors I've brought with me here. Can you say the same, *Master*—" the civilian honorific a deliberate insult "—Kawalec?"

A claque of warriors shouted bloodthirsty approval from the base of the Speaker's Rock. Kawalec must have had retainers present in the crowd, but none of them were foolish enough to call attention to themselves.

Lukanov waddled to the front of the rock. "I arranged, the order, of the speakers," he said. His shortness of breath broke the statement into three portions, but they were clearly audible.

He waved his heavy walking stick in the direction of the local kinglet, while the stranger stood coldly aloof. "Kawalec, milord," Lukanov said. "You've had your say and we've listened. Now be seated while others speak."

Kawalec nodded curtly to Lukanov and quickly took his stool again. He pointedly ignored the foreigner, but the incident had shaken a sense of self-worth Hansen would have judged to be impregnable. The mercenary claque had called for Kawalec's skull as a drinking cup, but the glance of the bearded stranger had an even greater impact.

"Lords of Mirala," the tall man said. "Lovers of freedom. I didn't journey from far Simplain to tell you of your rights, or of the wrongs that this upstart Venkatna has done others and plans to do to us. We all know that—that's why we're here."

He looked behind him at the seated nobles, then swept the crowd in the valley dished out of the mountainside by an ancient glacier. "I will tell you instead what we must do to safeguard our rights and end Venkatna's wrongs. If we wait here for the *emperor* to come in the spring, then we will win the battle or he will win—"

King Wenceslas leaped up from his stool. "We will win!" he shouted. "We will win!"

"And we will win *nothing*," the stranger continued. His voice carried over the shouts of a hundred warriors mouthing responses of rote pride and rote patriotism.

The shocked crowd quieted. "Because he will come again," the tall man resumed. "And again, milords and princes; and again, until finally he gains the day and we are all as dead as the defenders of Heimrtal. *That* is what will happen if we let Venkatna fight his war."

The Assembly Valley buzzed like bees swarming. The emotions were mixed, but no one cried a denial of what they all, warrior or civilian, knew in their hearts to be true.

"What we must do," the stranger continued, "is carry the war *to* Venkatna. Defeat his army beneath the walls of Frekka. Raze his palace, kill him before he can call upon the resources of his subject states to raise an army twice the size the next time. Venkatna has no son. If we break him and his army *now*, we break the West Kingdom back into a score of small states like our own."

"What's Simplain know about what *we* got to do?" Blood shouted unexpectedly from beside Hansen.

The tall man turned and looked down at Blood.

"What do I know?" he asked in a voice that crackled like a crown fire. "Then ask a warrior who has fought against Venkatna already, as none of you in Mirala have done."

He pointed into the crowd like a sniper aiming. "What do you think we should do, Lord Hansen?" he boomed.

Hansen met the cold gray eye of the figure on the rock above him.

"We should strike straight for Frekka," Hansen said. His voice seemed to fill the bowl of the valley. "Just as you suggest, Lord Guest."

Chapter Twenty-five

Sparrow's arc weapons, optimized for range rather than flux density, cut through Morfari and his crew like surf hitting a sand castle.

The arc from the right gauntlet caught the android at pelvis level. Morfari's bones were black from their stiffening of carbon fiber, but his blood was as red as a man's. His torso collapsed forward. The volley gun blew a crater in the mud, a centimeter short of the dog's forepaws.

There were risks to any endeavor.

Sparrow swept his gloves left to left, right to right, simultaneously, completing between them the semicircle of his unprepared opponents. The powerpack of a Lomeri laser exploded, spraying the molten plastic stock in all directions. Rifle ammunition, detonated by the arcs' fluctuating currents, crackled in bandoliers.

The squabble among the lizardmen had diverted the Fifth Plane female at the crucial instant. She tried to bring her plasma weapon to bear on Sparrow. A whipping arc sawed through her massive body at belt level, cutting to the spine.

Incredibly, the woman managed to squeeze the trigger. Her toppling body swung the muzzle so that the saffron fireball engulfed instead the lizardman she had just disciplined.

One of the slaves wore concussion grenades alternating with knives on his cross-belts. Three of the grenades went off in quick succession. The multiple blast staggered Sparrow and turned the slave's upper body into a soup distinguishable only by color from the thin mud of the swamp.

Sparrow's ears rang. Between his legs, the dog's mouth opened and closed as if barking. The sound, if there was one, did not reach the smith's shocked senses.

Two lizardmen still moved, but that was merely galvanic response to the high voltage which had lopped their bodies apart.

The stench—of voided bowels and body cavities ripped open by the arcs—quivered over the scene like a bubble of green putrescence.

Sparrow sank to his knees. The dog leaped around him yapping silently as she pawed muddy streaks onto her master's arms and shoulders.

The thumbs and forefingers of Sparrow's gauntlets glowed yellow; even the wrist flares had been heated to dull red. The smith tried to pull the overloaded weapons off with his hands. The heat and pain of closing his fingers to grip were too great, even for him.

At last Sparrow put his right hand on the ground. He stood on the gauntlet as steam spurted over him and the mud baked to terra cotta. He dragged his hand out of the metal by the strength of his arm. The relief was so dizzying that it was a moment before he was able to strip his left glove the same way.

The smith's hands were red and already beginning to swell. All the hair had been singed off them.

The smith laughed bitterly. He was used to pain, but he knew that pain didn't strengthen anything. Pain ripped a soul down to a desperate core in which the will blazed—if the will were strong enough.

Sparrow thrust his hands into the water, working his fingers into the mud past the horsetail roots. The cool fluids soothed his dry, throbbing skin.

Insects buzzed over the windrow of corpses. A pinkish slime overlaid the normal hues of the swamp. The arcs cauterized as they cut, but flash-heated blood ruptured vessels at some distance above and below the wound channels. Exploding ammunition, especially the grenades, did further damage.

Sparrow had butchered out mammoths. The aftermath of battle did not concern him; only the fact that he had survived.

He walked over to Morfari's body. The android lay face-down. His legs were beside the torso. The black-booted feet were planted firmly together, but the severed thighs splayed out to either side.

Sparrow rolled the body over. Morfari's muscles were rigid; the arms held their set as though they were welded steel. The smith wasn't sure whether that had something to do with the android's physiology, or if it was simply a freak result of high voltages blasting the central nervous system.

The dog, now confident that her master was well, sniffed the bodies. She bounced frequently as though threatened by some aspect of the cooling flesh. Sparrow could hear her barking again.

Morfari's mouth was drawn into a tight rictus. The lavaliere on his breast was undamaged. Sparrow let out the breath that he had held without realizing it. He needed the android's control device for the next stage of his mission . . . but in a wide-open battle that left a dozen dead, there was a limit to how much care Sparrow had been able to show.

The lavaliere hung on a ribbon of lustrous green synthetic. The material was non-conductive, which was lucky. Otherwise, the currents surging over Morfari's skin might have blown the circuits of the control device.

Sparrow activated the device in pre-set mode by keying one of the dozen buttons on its small control pad. A Lomeri corpse bent like a bow. The lizardman was dead, but his nerve pathways still passed the jolt of current which his slave collar applied.

So. The lavaliere was functional. More complex actions could be programmed through the keypad, but Sparrow had no need of those. What he needed . . .

He looked around him at mud and blood and stench. He would prefer a bench to lie on as he worked; but nothing outside the Matrix really mattered when the smith was working.

He lay down on the bank. The lavaliere was clasped in his huge right hand. The dog, familiar with the process, perked up her ears, but she didn't interfere with the smith's concentration.

Sparrow was a hunter and a warrior; and once, when he was a young man in the Open Lands, he had been a prince. Above all, and encompassing all, Sparrow was a smith. He slid into a state of half-sleep, half-hypnosis.

His eyes were open but glazed. The ball of the sun glowing through the mists swelled until its sanguine light filled all the universe. . . .

Sparrow's mind ranged the Matrix, searching through ideals without number, the basic substance of all objects existing in all times in the eight worlds of Northworld. Each a template, a mold from which a master smith could strike copies into matter in realtime.

The master of *all* smiths could strike copies: Sparrow alone.

Nothing changed visibly in the swamp where Sparrow's body lay, but crystals within the control device shifted their electronic pathways. A chip now resonated in tune with the smith's brainwaves rather than those of the android, who was slowly reaching equilibrium with the ambient temperature.

Sparrow blinked twice as his mind returned from the Matrix. He rubbed his eyes with the back of his hand, forgetful of the swollen flesh and the mud in which he had cooled it. The gritty shock brought him fully alert. He rose to a scene from a hotter Hell than Northworld's.

Dimetrodons—not a pack but rather a score of individuals lured by the reek of slaughter—swarmed over the recent corpses. A huge male, easily four meters long and a half tonne in weight, stood on the chewed remnant of Morfari's body and threatened the smith.

Sparrow's dog, snarling like a saw in knotted wood, stood between her master and the reptile's ragged jaws. She snapped every time the dimetrodon's tongue lapped the air. The big carnivore twitched out with a clawed forepaw, but the bitch dodged its clumsy blows easily. The dimetrodon was so disconcerted by the violent opposition that it didn't use its weight and scaly hide to brush past the dog.

Sparrow got to his feet. He was dizzy. His skin was cold and clammy in reaction to the time his mind had spent in the Matrix, but the swamp's oven temperatures and saturated humidity covered him like an avalanche of sodden clay.

The dog noticed that her master was up. She continued to snap and snarl at the monster. Her leg braces flashed like knives in the bloody sunlight.

There was an easy path of retreat along the stream bank. The other dimetrodons were wholly occupied with carrion, including the smoking carcase of their own fellow killed by Morfari's gang. The nearest beast would lose interest when its intended meal moved off with mammalian quickness.

"Dog!" Sparrow called. "Come away, you bloody fool!"

The carnivore lunged. The dog met the motion instead of

retreating. Her canines scored two long gouges across the dimetrodon's snout.

"*Dog!*" Sparrow shouted, but the bitch's blood was up. If he tried to drag her off by main force, the carnivore would take them both while they struggled. The gauntlets lay beneath the dimetrodon trampling feet, and even the thought of donning them again made Sparrow's punished flesh crawl.

He drew the knife from his belt sheath. It had a broad, 30-cm blade with a single edge and blood grooves to keep the suction of flesh from binding the steel during deep cuts.

Sparrow moved within a meter of the dimetrodon, then paused while the monster switched its attention from the dog to the dog's master. As if this were a planned maneuver, the dog leaped in and tore at the dimetrodon's ear hole. The dimetrodon snapped sideways with a wobbling undulation of its backfin.

Sparrow stepped forward. He slammed his knife home to the hilt in the dimetrodon's neck. Reflexively, the smith tried to throw his left leg astride the creature's back as his right arm ripped the knife downward against the resistance of flesh and scaly hide.

The sail blocked his motion. The tip of a spine jabbed his knee, and the creature's foreclaws tore the sandal straps and the flesh beneath. The reptile's stricken body writhed; Sparrow let the motion fling him away.

The dimetrodon waddled off, spewing blood and arping. The knifehilt wobbled in a wound that pierced the beast's throat and gaped to the breadth of the smith's own huge hand.

The injured animal blundered into one of its fellows which was snuffling at a lizardman's disjointed foot. With the suddenness of a trap springing, the second dimetrodon clamped its jaws on the other's neck wound. Three more of the big lizards immediately piled into the slaughter, ripping huge chunks out of their injured fellow.

Sparrow's dog turned and began to whine in delight as she licked her master's hand. The dog's rough tongue felt like a rasp against the swollen flesh.

Sparrow picked up the lavaliere, which he had dropped to draw his knife. He hung the ribbon over his own thick neck. The control device rode higher than it had on the android, who was classically proportioned except for his extra set of arms. That shouldn't make any difference to the unit's operation.

The killing frenzy directed at one of their own kind had dragged most of the carnivores twenty meters through the swamp before the victim finally collapsed to be devoured alive. They left Sparrow free to examine the cattle guard's paraphernalia.

Morfari's skimmer had been knocked over, but it appeared to be essentially undamaged. The vehicle was a control column on a circular plate a meter in diameter. It generated an electromagnetic field in the surface over which it rode and repelled that field by one of identical polarity in the plate itself.

The whole unit weighed only thirty kilograms or so. Sparrow righted it easily.

One of the knives scattered in the kill zone among the charred equipment and bits of meat—the dimetrodons were messy eaters—was the length and width at the hilt of the blade Sparrow had carried. The cattle guard's weapon was double-edged and tapered to a sharp point, but it fit the smith's sheath snugly enough.

Sparrow kept the knife. The rest of the weapons and equipment, including the arc gauntlets, he left for mud and the tannin-bitter waters to reclaim.

He touched the skimmer's controls. The little vehicle wobbled obediently.

"C'mon, dog," Sparrow said. When the animal stepped onto the plate with him, he reached down and tousled her ears again. "You're not so bad to have around, you know?"

The dog barked. Sparrow rolled a handgrip, and the skimmer slid off toward the bower of Princess Mala, deeper in the swamp.

Chapter Twenty-six

"If you'll step this way, milady," suggested the voice of Kumiswari, Hansen's new servant. "The tent with the *gold* battlesuit before it. And no finer suit in the host, not the armor of King Wenceslas himself."

Lamplight gleamed through the stitches of the pony-leather tent. Hansen bumped his head on the ridgepole while pulling on his linen breeches. The tent was twenty centimeters shorter than Hansen was, a hard fact to remember when he was in a hurry. He swore quietly.

Krita must have escaped.

The flap rustled as Kumiswari undid the upper set of ties. "Lord Hansen?" the servant called. He was one of the pair of slaves Wenceslas had assigned to Hansen—like the tent itself—from his own establishment. "There's a lady to see you, sir."

"All right," Hansen said, checking—not that there was the least danger—that the dagger with the spiked handguard was unobtrusively available in the sheath hanging from the head of his cot. A 'lady' looking for Hansen here had to be Krita—or a messenger from North, and North would not send an assassin.

Would North send an assassin?

The only light in the tent was a candle of mammoth tallow, held at reading height by a meter-long spike jabbed into the ground beside the cot. The wavering yellow flame had an animal odor which Hansen found surprisingly pleasant when he'd gotten used to it.

Kumiswari opened the tent with a flourish degraded by the fact that the woman still had to stoop to step past the end pole. This was too big a tent for one man's field use, but that didn't make it a palace reception room.

Backlit by the servant's lantern, the woman's hair glowed red/blond. She wasn't Krita, and she wasn't anybody Hansen knew—

Until she turned and said to Kumiswari, "You may go now—and if you know your master as well as you should, you won't linger too close."

Lucille. Lord Salles' . . . cousin, hadn't he said?

"Of course, milady," Kumiswari murmured. The light behind Lucille quivered as the servant bowed. His voice faded as he added, "Milord? If you call loudly, I will come."

She had only been around him for a few days, in the rebels' camp. Why had she put her threat to the servant in that particular way, as if she knew Commissioner Nils Hansen?

"Fine, that's fine," Hansen agreed. The woman bent forward to refasten the ties, reaching between the flaps.

He looked around the tent and grimaced, not that he'd asked for a visitor.

He wasn't really a hard-handed bastard like his reputation. He didn't lose his temper very often; and when he did, it was always a cold passion. As cold as Death himself.

The only furniture within the tent was the cot and the round of treetrunk that Hansen used as a stool. He'd been sitting on the wood, wrapped in a black bearskin and staring through the Matrix at distant places, when he was interrupted. A notebook made from thin plates of beechwood lay on the cot beside him, to explain to a servant or visitor what Lord Hansen was doing in his tent.

Lucille turned. Her head cleared the ridgepole by the thickness of the cowl which she had thrown back over her shoulders. Hansen, awkward because he had to hunch until he sat down again, gestured toward the stool and cot in a single sweep. "Please," he offered. "I'm not set up for this."

She settled, like a cat curling onto the end of the bed. There was no obvious hesitation. Hansen thankfully sat on the stool. He thought of flipping the bearskin over his legs again; but thought better of it.

"I . . . hoped you might know whether any of the others escaped from the—the attack," Lucille asked. She was minutely less self-possessed than she had been a moment before.

"Your cousin, you mean?" Hansen said. "No, lady. They all opened their suits and surrendered. I ran."

True enough, though not on his legs.

"Lord Salles was beside me when it happened," he said aloud.

Candid ignorance was the best choice. She could denounce him, if she chose.

"He shouted that we mustn't fight against the emperor," Hansen continued. "And he surrendered. I thought the servants and dependents had been captured also."

Lucille nodded curtly. "Most of them were," she said. "My sister is a lord's wife here in Mirala, and I—"

Her face was warmer and more textured than it had been when Hansen met her in the rebels' camp, but it suddenly went gray even in the candle's tawny light.

"—have had as much of the emperor's hospitality as my body could stand." She forced a smile. "Or my soul."

"I'm sorry," Hansen said truthfully. "I wish I could give you better news."

The woman wore a scarlet-lined cape of heavy blue wool. The dress beneath was brown and cream, with lace at the throat and bodice seams. Either her brother-in-law was wealthy as well as being noble, or Lucille had escaped from the wreck of the rebel cause with an unlikely quantity of belongings.

She had escaped because she had kin outside the West Kingdom. It was no treason to Venkatna that a woman visit her sister. The Web—and the slaves controlling the Web—carried out the emperor's instructions as precisely as a crossbow slammed its bolt down a trajectory determined by aim and physics when the trigger was pulled.

"It was the Web," Lucille said, correctly and to Hansen's surprise. Her fingers toyed with the bearskin Hansen had tossed onto the cot. "The thing in that demon's palace. There are rumors—"

She stared at Hansen, as if expecting confirmation or denial. "—and they're true."

He shrugged. *He was just here to fight.* "I'm sorry," he repeated.

"Did—" something changed in the woman's expression, though Hansen wasn't sure what "—Kriton escape also?"

"No," Hansen said flatly.

He'd been watching Krita when Kumiswari announced the visitor. She and the remainder of the Peace Rock rebels were imperial troops now. For the time being they carried out evolutions and battle training on the practice fields outside Frekka, but the real fight would come soon enough. . . .

"I asked . . . ," Lucille said to her hands. The fingers were so thin that the knuckles seemed unusually prominent, although they were not enlarged. "Because I know that she's a woman."

"I think," Hansen said quietly, "that you're mistaken."

"Oh, it's all right," the woman said hastily. "I won't tell anyone—I haven't, after all. But if Kriton was here, I wouldn't have . . ."

She looked up and met Hansen's eyes. He cleared his throat.

Lucille leaned forward and took his hands in hers. Her fingers felt cold even to him, sitting in breeches and a shirt of thin gray wool. "Will we defeat him?" she demanded. "The devil Venkatna?"

"I'm not the comman—" Hansen began.

"Don't!" Lucille snapped. "Milord, I don't know who you are, but you *know* things. I saw you in the camp, I *watched* you. You should be commanding this army and you're not, but you can tell me the truth!"

Hansen grimaced. At the direction of one part of his conscious mind, he began rubbing the woman's hands. "We've got enough troops to do it," he said. "A quick, straight shot at Frekka like we're planning—"

Thanks to the 'merchant prince from Simplain.'

"—could do the job."

"But," Lucille said. She shifted slightly, so that Hansen's right hand lay on her thigh and her own hand held it there.

He was a man, God knew. Whatever else he was, he was a man. . . .

"But," Hansen agreed, staring at the soft wool that bunched as his fingers kneaded gently, "we won't move fast. We've got twice the baggage and a quarter the speed of the same number of Venkatna's troops. We won't take them by surprise, and when we join battle—"

He raised his eyes.

"—*they'll* fight like an army, and we'll fight like a mob."

"Why are you here, Lord Hansen?" she asked softly.

Because I'm responsible for the problem. Because if I can't cure it, I can—

Die trying.

Die.

"I've fought enough battles," he said aloud, "to know that there's always a chance the other guy's going to fuck up bigtime. Let's hope, shall we?"

"I hope you survive, Lord Hansen," Lucille said as if she were replying to the words he spoke only in his mind. "But you may not—"

She lifted his right hand. He started to draw back, surprised and embarrassed, but the woman swept her skirt waist-high with her free hand.

"—and I've wanted you from the first time I saw you in camp." She smiled. Her eyes were unfocused. "It was like watching a leopard around those poor housecats my cousin led."

Her lips half-parted as she pulled Hansen toward her.

He wondered why he had thought her hair was brown. It gleamed golden in the candlelight, and the down above her thighs was pure blond.

Chapter Twenty-seven

For a moment, nothing reflected back from the pool except cypresses and the stars above them. Planes shifted with the suddenness of prisms flashing. Nils Hansen stood on the bank. He wore boots, a jumpsuit, and a close-fitting helmet.

The smooth khaki surface of Hansen's garment was not broken, as it normally would have been, by a weapons belt.

A large, short-snouted tapir honked in surprise at the human's arrival, then galloped off through the forest. The beast vanished quickly among the undergrowth and the trees' outflung buttress roots. Its primitive hooves could be heard for another twenty seconds, splashing in the low spots and thudding heavily through the leaf mold on drier ground.

Bats chittered.

Hansen turned. The northern sky burned a cold blue, the corona discharge from the horizon-filling dome of Keep Starnes.

"You could have inserted closer to our objective," said the artificial intelligence in what Hansen's mind heard as a waspish voice. *"You could have inserted* within *our objective."*

"I could do anything I please, Third," Hansen said. "I'm a god, remember?"

As Hansen studied the huge fortress, he wiped his hands on his thighs to dry the sweat, then rubbed the palms together. The degree of care was worthy of volitional action.

"Besides, it's my legs that'll be getting the exercise." His fingers kept brushing back to where the pistol holster should have ridden, high on his right hip. "Maybe I wanted the exercise."

Sky glow penetrated the conifer needles and pin-leafed cypress foliage. The light illuminated the forest floor once Hansen's eyes adapted. Keep Starnes was its own beacon.

Maybe he *should* have entered Plane Five nearer to his objective. He'd always operated on instinct in a tense situation, though. This was tense, the good lord knew. Instinct warned Hansen to leave room for maneuver.

"Find us a good place to get in, Third," Hansen directed as he started walking north. "I kinda doubt they're going to roll out the red carpet for us."

The warning signal undulated through the Citadel like the tentacles of an octopus swimming.

Count Starnes lifted his head. "He's come?" he asked.

"He's come!" said Karring from an outstation in the rotunda. He shut off the alarm. "At any rate . . ."

The chief engineer paused to give APEX mental instructions. The numerical display above his console shifted to a panorama as it might be glimpsed from the exterior of Keep Starnes, hundreds of meters above their heads.

The trees were supported by bulbous bases or roots flung out from halfway up their boles. They grew on a surface that was as much shallow water as treacherous land. Over the next fifty million years, the present landscape would decay to peat and brown coal. For the moment, the site was notable for a stagnant purulence of vegetable life in which browsing animals seemed interlopers despite their considerable size.

Keep Starnes' sensor array extended kilometers into the sodden forest, but the thick growth shielded a man-sized target on many spectra. APEX formed the hints of mass, shape, and infra-red distribution into a figure on the display. The computer could have given it a face and mimicked expressions besides, but such details would have been wholly fanciful.

Karring limited the construct to what was supportable on the evidence: a male of moderate height and a compactly-powerful build.

"He isn't armed," he called to the others. "Lena, seal all the keep's orifices as though we were under massive attack."

"Use proper respect when you address the lady!" bellowed one of the big woman's lovers. His hourglass shape was accentuated by a broad belt decorated with studs of electrum. The frames of his two holstered pistols were plated with the same rich, silvery metal; the black onyx of the weapons' grips matched the leather harness.

"Shut up, Plaid," Lena said as she watched her own display. "You're useless when you're using your tongue to talk."

Plaid straightened with an incredulous expression. His companion, Voightman, sneered and began to pose to set off his muscles. No one bothered to look at him, but the polished metal surfaces of the console provided a mirror.

"But Karring, dear," Lena continued, her tone smoother but far from agreeable. "I don't want to keep him out, this Hansen or whoever Fortin sent us. I want him inside where I can play with him."

Lena's display showed the network of all systems within Keep Starnes, overlaid in forty hues distinguishable only by an expert. As she spoke, the image rotated. The visual result suggested the peristaltic motion of an intestine digesting the animal's last meal.

"I want him inside also," Karring explained. "But for me to close his escape route properly—as I did that of his fellow— it's necessary that he enter through what Fortin called the Matrix."

"Oh, all right," Lena said. The pattern on her display changed. Sounds rang through the fabric of Keep Starnes, penetrating even to the Citadel. Shutters dropped; valves closed. The hum of the ventilation fans changed note as the system switched over to recycle the atmosphere, scrubbing poisons instead of sucking in large quantities of outside air to replace what was dumped in normal, total-loss, operation.

"I hear water," said Count Starnes. He lifted his helmet and rubbed his cropped hair.

"Back-pressure in the sewage lines," his daughter said with satisfaction. "Waste is being pumped into the holding tank at ground level instead of being voided through the main siphon. We can go for three days this way."

Lena turned on her couch to look at Count Starnes. She moved like a whale basking. "Unless you want me to shut off water to everybody higher than Level K17? Or hold them to two liters a day? Then we could—"

"This will be fine, I'm sure, milady," Karring interrupted as he worked his manual keyboard.

He spoke more crisply than he should have done. Lena rotated her head, this time to look at the engineer. She did nothing further, but Plaid lost his pout and smiled again.

The external sensor trunks were conduits a meter in diameter. Lena's shutdown had severed them, so Karring shifted to induction input to regain data on the world outside the keep. The initial results were badly degraded compared to the images which passed through optical cables, but APEX used the baseline information gathered previously to enhance the new material to a similar standard.

"He's coming toward us," Karring said. He frowned. "But he's still walking."

"Some soldier," Lena said. "There's no more of this one than there was of the other. I've got room for his whole head."

She giggled and added, "Which might just be fun."

"Where's Lisa?" Count Starnes asked suddenly. He glanced toward the elevators as if expecting to see his younger daughter appearing from one of the cages.

"She is . . ." said Karring.

His screen split. On the left half of the display, the blur-faced figure of the stranger walked among cypresses and bog conifers. On the right was a one-man armored vehicle gliding through the same forest on an air cushion pressurized by eight fans. From the center of the tank's turret projected the short, tapering barrel of a charged-particle weapon with a co-axial machinegun beside it.

"Lisa is outside the keep in her personal scout tank," the chief engineer resumed. A topographic overlay glowed in the air beneath the images of the two contestants, the man in khaki and the tank surrounding a woman. "She's moving to intercept our visitor."

"I didn't tell her to do that," Starnes muttered. There was both pride and concern in his tone. His hand idly caressed the bow slope of his own repulsion-drive tank. The frontal armor was of almost stellar density.

"She puts pressure on him," Karring said with satisfaction. "He'll have to do something, enter or flee back where he came from. Since he's come this far, I think we can expect him to come the rest of the way to where we want him."

Voightman and Plaid lounged and posed, bored by what was

going on beyond their immediate presence. The other three humans in the Citadel watched the ill-matched contestants avidly.

In the corridor beyond, the Fleet Battle Director hummed as it gathered and analyzed and . . . waited.

Chapter Twenty-eight

Venkatna flung the door open so violently that the single lamp in the audience hall guttered, stirring golden ripples across the brightwork of the Web.

The device was silent, the benches within its framework empty. No one was present in the hall except the armored guard at the entrance to the imperial suite.

"Where are they?" Venkatna shouted. His voice rang from the dome, rebounding like the raucous anger of crows. "Why aren't they here, the slaves?"

"S—your ma—" the guard stammered in surprise.

To stay awake, the guard had been watching the procession of ants moving under a leaded transom on the other side of the hall. His battlesuit optics were at $\times 300$ magnification, giving him an unintelligible view of whiskers when he spun to face the emperor.

"Here they are, your majesty!" bleated the terrified underchamberlain responsible for the care and feeding of Venkatna's most cherished slaves. "Come along, you bitches, for North's sake!"

The guard muttered under his breath to the suit's AI, dropping the magnification to 1:1 while retaining a degree of light enhancement. What he saw *now* was even more of a shock.

Venkatna wore his night garb, a long linen gown with flowing sleeves and a quilted cap. He was barefoot.

He held his wife in his arms. Esme's cap had fallen off, her face was gray. Her arms were stiff at her sides instead of hanging down as gravity should have drawn them.

Race and Julia stumbled from the alcove at the back of the audience hall where they slept and lived during the few hours a day they were not within the Web. Their tunics were clean enough, though rumpled, and they had been able to sponge their bodies off recently, but the women's hair was a dull mass of knots and matting.

Brett, the underchamberlain, wore court dress. His duties primarily involved the period the women were not entranced in the Web. The demands for his presence were uncertain, however, and the imperial focus was so close that Brett looked almost as worn as his charges.

"Here they are, your majesty!" he repeated. He tugged at the sleeve of Julia's shift. The Searcher, only half awake and ten kilos lighter than her normal weight, slapped Brett's hand away without being fully aware of the contact.

"She's sick!" the emperor cried, hugging Esme's stiff body closer to him. "I woke up and she felt—she felt—"

She felt cold as ice.

"—she didn't feel right. Make her *well,* damn you!"

Servants and officials in various stages of undress banged through the door leading to the apartments of the general household. Slaves began lighting additional wall lamps, adding to the illumination of the torches and lanterns the newcomers had brought with them.

"Let me see her," Race ordered, wakeful now if not entirely aware of her surroundings. She reached toward Esme's neck to check the carotid pulse.

Venkatna jerked back instinctively.

"Let me *see*—" Race snarled through waves of fatigue which corroded away the normal desire for self-preservation.

Race's fingertips brushed a cheek instead of the empress' throat. The temperature of the flesh, easily 15° below that of life, told the Searcher as much as she could have learned by searching for a heartbeat. "Forget it, she's dead."

"Make her well!" the emperor screamed.

Several of Venkatna's top advisors entered the hall. Baron Trigane saw what the emperor held, judged the potentials of the situation, and slipped back out hoping that he had gone unobserved.

"Your majesty," said Julia, "we can't do that. North himself, our master, can't bring the dead to life, not as flesh and blood. The Web affects only what is, not what once was."

"Your majesty!" Brett babbled. "It isn't my fault. Please, I'll have them whipped until—"

Kleber struck the underchamberlain with the butt of his dagger.

Brett went boneless. He fell backward instead of on his face because Kleber's free hand tugged the back of the servant's collar.

Kleber flicked a smile of embarrassment toward the emperor. The advisor regretted that he hadn't acted more quickly, but he still hoped that Venkatna would not, in what was clearly an irrational moment, order the death of everyone in the audience hall.

"Your majesty," said Race with the power of simple honesty. "We will carry out your every order that we can. This we cannot do."

Venkatna's lips brushed the cheek of his wife. "Keep her, then," he said in a ragged whisper. His voice strengthened. "You say you can preserve what is, so preserve her! I'll dress her in silks, I'll build her a couch here in the hall—but you preserve her!"

Advisors looked at one another and tried to wipe all expression from their faces.

"Your majesty, we've been in the Web all—" Julia began.

"Get in there!" the emperor shouted. "You bitch, you could have saved her but you didn't! I should have you—"

"You didn't tell—" Julia said, but Race gripped her shoulder with hard fingers and shocked her mind back to present realities.

"Your orders are our fate," Race murmured softly as she led her companion into the net of curves and crystal.

"What are you waiting for?" Venkatna demanded of the nearest servant, a night-duty usher. "Bring a couch! And where are my darling's maids? They should be dressing her!"

"Does this mean that your majesty will delay plans to bring Mirala within the Empire?" asked Bontempo from the open doorway. His age had delayed him, and he wore a full-length cloak over his nightdress and slippers.

"No!" the emperor said. "I'll rule Mirala or I'll kill every living thing in the district! I'll make my darling the queen of all the earth, and those pair—"

He glared at the Searchers as they settled themselves on the benches within the Web. Lamplight gleamed in his eyes like the fires of madness.

"—will preserve my peace and my Esme both, without fail!"

Race sighed softly. The universe trembled as internal lights began to play across the surface of the Web.

Chapter Twenty-nine

Sparrow's dog growled deep in her throat. She was responding to the ultrasonics which, along with probes in a dozen other spectra, painted their skimmer.

"Steady . . . ," the smith murmured as he eased off the throttle. The skimmer slowed and dropped minusculy closer to the ground. "Steady now. . . ."

They curved around a spit where the land rose higher than most. It was covered densely with trees whose trunks were slender cones and whose branches flared into pompon tufts. Beyond the trees was a pond over which the sun drew mist like a bloody shroud. Across the water stood the stark black walls surrounding Princess Mala's bower, three meters high.

"Gee-*up*," Sparrow muttered reflexively as he dialed on more power and adjusted the skimmer's angle of attack. The little platform needed more speed to cross the pond. Open water dissipated the supporting charge more swiftly than dry soil would.

From the walls and the dome whose faceted curve could be dimly glimpsed beyond, scores and perhaps hundreds of weapons aimed at the skimmer. The lavaliere prickled on Sparrow's chest, seeming to burn him through the fabric. That was all in his mind—but Sparrow the Smith knew better than most the reality of a mind's images.

A large amphibian rose from the center of the pond with a fish in its jaws. The broad skull turned. One of the beast's separate-focusing eyes started to rotate toward the skimmer a hundred meters away.

The motion brought the amphibian within the area protected against targets of that mass. The walls' automatic defenses went into action.

Vertical rods every two meters stiffened the black wall the way a bat's fingerbones brace its wings. Gun muzzles unmasked at mid-height on three of the miniature bastions.

669

A laser howled, pulsing its indigo beam across the amphibian's broad neck like a bandsaw. Explosive shells from an automatic cannon blew fist-sized chunks out of the creature's skull. Fléchettes from the third bastion drilled through the pond surface to the calculated location of the amphibian's body.

The shattered head sank and the beast's torso curved up convulsively. High explosive and the laser worked over the blotchy gray hide, while fléchettes now sought what was left of the skull. The weapons stopped hammering only when the largest piece of the luckless amphibian was the size of Sparrow's hand.

The reformatted identification chip in the lavaliere had properly matched the brainwave patterns of Sparrow and his dog. Otherwise, similar weapons would have ripped them to patches of red mammalian pulp.

Spray lifted from beneath the skimmer. The spewing water caused further batteries to unmask and track the intruders, but none of them fired.

In order to reach the courtyard's single gate, Sparrow had to curve near the weapons which had destroyed the amphibian. The stomach-turning miasma of propellant permeated the humid atmosphere, mixed with the scaly odor of air the laser had burned to plasma.

The bitch rubbed herself against her master's legs, reassuring herself of Sparrow's presence and solidity. Her body trembled.

The gates were as wide as the wall was high. The double leaves were inset slightly between a pair of thick towers supporting multi-barrel plasma dischargers for high-altitude defense. Sparrow pulled up before them.

The strip of mud in front of the gates was the only bare earth on the island outside the walls. It was broad enough, if barely, and Sparrow would have lain down in the muddy water if necessary. There was no discomfort that Sparrow would not accept if it was a necessary step in his path.

The smith arranged his equipment so that the weight of his body would not damage it. He settled full-length in front of the portal. One mark of a smith's skill was the distance from his entranced body at which he could affect the structure of molecules through the Matrix. Sparrow's powers of extension were unexcelled—but closer was better, and he wasn't involved in a contest.

The dog snuffled up along the smooth walls for a few meters, finding nothing of particular interest. The dense black plastic had no taste or odor, and the debris of years had been unable to cling to its waxy surface.

Insects hummed in clouds over the pond, settling on bits of the amphibian. Occasionally fish lifted through the greasy sheen to suck down carrion and carrion-flies together. The dog eyed the froth and the activity it drew, but she remained close to her master.

Sparrow closed his eyes. He slid into the Matrix like one of the pond's lungfish diving back for its burrow in the mud . . . but the water was warm and the Matrix was a slime of cold light which froze the minds of those who entered it.

All templates, all realities, all time.

Princess Mala's dwelling had two layers of defense. The external band destroyed all targets which came within range. The targeting array plotted mass and proximity on a graph of death. Nothing larger than a thumb-sized beetle would be permitted to live within a meter of the black walls unless the creature was correctly keyed into the bower's identification system.

Within the gates, the defenses were simpler and still more stringent. Only if someone inside deliberately imprinted the visitor onto the system could that visitor enter and survive. Otherwise, blasting radiance would fill the courtyard, fusing the mud to glass and ripping all protoplasm into a haze which spewed upward toward the clouds.

But the controls were electronic, and their crystalline pathways clicked into new forms under the smith's instinctual touch. Sparrow's body shivered on the warm mudbank, but there was never such a smith as he, never in the measureless eons of Northworld. . . .

Sparrow awoke from a shuddering nightmare in which he was one of the damned souls on Plane Four and crawled motionlessly across the endless ice. The dog barked fiercely as she pranced beside him, turning from Sparrow to the gates and back again.

The gate leaves were open. Their lower edges had planed

arcs across the mud of the courtyard. The interior was virtually undisturbed, except by the daily rainstorms.

Sparrow started to get to his feet. He had to pause for a moment on all fours. His knees and knuckles sank into the wet soil.

The smith was still trembling from the cold of the Matrix, entered twice in an hour and either time on a task of utmost precision. His head ached from the grenade explosions, and his hands and forearms were swollen. He inhaled deeply, expelled the breath, and drew in another without yet attempting to rise further.

A fly, bloated with the meal it had made on the amphibian's remains, burred past Sparrow. The dog made a half-hearted snap at the little creature.

The insect zigzagged through the portal. When it was three centimeters into the enclosure, a spear of light from the inner surface of the wall made the fly vanish completely. Only the echoing thunderclap proved that the insect had ever existed.

Sparrow smiled. He rose to his feet. "Time for us to go, dog," he said, slurring the initial words slightly. "Inside, we will ask as guest rights that they feed us."

Dog and master stepped into the courtyard together. Their feet left deep prints in the bare mud.

Sparrow's stride was unsteady for the first few paces. For the rest of the way to the dome, his legs obeyed as though the smith were a creation of his own unsurpassed craftsmanship.

Chapter Thirty

"They aren't going to wait for us to come to them," said the voice in Hansen's mind with what sounded like satisfaction. *"One of them is headed for us from the other side of the keep."*

Hansen jumped an open patch that be suspected was bottomless mud under a treacherous skin of cypress leaves. He was trying to pretend that the warning had not startled him, but he pushed off too hard and had to twist in the air to keep from falling.

"One?" he asked. He didn't have to vocalize questions to the AI, but it was natural to treat the command helmet as a person.

"One," agreed the helmet. It projected the ghostly monochrome of a hovertank into an apparent 20-cm circle a meter ahead of Hansen.

The image rotated, displaying the traditional three views. The hologram was bright enough for Hansen to pick out details if he so desired, but it didn't block his normal vision. He could continue moving forward if he wished.

"She is female," Third added. The tank was replaced by a view of a youngish woman in uniform. She had no particularly-distinguishing features, except that for Plane Five, she was very slender.

"Enough," Hansen muttered gruffly. Even as the image vanished from his field of view, he went on, "Vector and ETA?"

When he listened carefully, he could hear the roar of the tank's eight fans . . . or maybe that was his imagination.

The blue glow of Keep Starnes' protective field was occasionally visible through the trees three hundred meters away. The magnetic barrier didn't mean safety, but it was safety of a sort. The tank's co-axial machinegun wouldn't be affected, but the plasma weapon couldn't be discharged from or through that shield.

Third projected a schematic map of the immediate area.

Hansen's position was a pulsing dot. A broken line worked around from the other side of the keep's huge bulk.

"*Several minutes,*" the artificial intelligence said, "*but I cannot be precise. She is more constrained by the forest than you are, though of course the vehicle is much faster when it has a clear run.*"

Hansen jumped, slipped, and dropped to mid-thigh in a pool so clear that he could see the bottom. He swore under his breath as he dragged himself out by a dangling tree root.

He *did* hear the fans.

"*You could have entered the keep directly,*" the command helmet noted smugly.

"That's what they fucking expect me to do!" Hansen snapped.

Except that the woman in the tank either expected *this*, or somebody was playing a hunch. Fortin? That was possible.

"*You are afraid that APEX will teach Karring how to use the Matrix and precipitate the Final Day?*" the command helmet asked.

Hansen frowned. He hopped onto a fallen log. Rotten wood sagged beneath his boots. "Should I be?" he asked.

"*Oh, yes, Commissioner,*" Third said. "*You should certainly fear that—if you care.*"

The soil was firmer. Hansen could see the keep's shield regularly now. A pair of creatures with long, bushy tails chattered from a tree. Their slender bodies dipped forward and rose as part of their display behavior, while their forepaws continued to grip half-shredded pinecones.

"Are you ready?" Hansen shouted. He was three strides from the blue haze, light diffracted by the intense magnetic flux. If Third's electronics needed longer than an eyeblink to come into phase with the field, the command helmet was shit outa luck.

"*I am always ready.*"

Hansen sprinted between a cypress and a pine standing on gnarled black roots like a gigantic spider. His skin tingled at the field's plane of demarcation. The tank must be very close now.

"*To the right,*" the helmet ordered. "*There's a gully. Get into it.*"

"I can't hide from a damned thing with sensors like that bitch'll have!" Hansen shouted. He angled right anyway, running flat out though it meant he stumbled twice. He burst through a tangle of saplings—

And hurtled into a gully, all right, a fucking *river*bed—twenty meters across and five meters down. The bottom was soft mud, gleaming like black pearls because of water standing in low spots.

Hansen tucked and rolled. He was so pumped that he hadn't time to worry that a rock was going to smash his ribs.

You mighta warned me, he thought; but there wasn't much time, not for him or the command helmet. If they both survived, they could chew it over later.

Hansen used the momentum of his fall to fling him upright and running again toward the far bank. It was a perfect maneuver that he couldn't have duplicated in a thousand years on a gymnasium floor.

"*No!*" Third ordered. "*Follow the gully toward the keep. She has lost us for the moment, if you stay out of sight.*"

Hansen grimaced, but he obeyed. He felt as though he were jogging down a main highway on Annunciation at rush hour. The broad gully made him a perfect target if the tank forced its way through the screen of pines as Hansen himself had done.

"*Her sensors are not registering you,*" the command helmet explained in a tone of self-satisfaction. "*I can do nothing with simple optics.*"

Before Hansen could frame the next question—or as he did, thought replacing speech with the AI—Third admitted, "*If she realized what has happened, her vehicle's computer—*" the pejorative overtones the artificial intelligence gave to 'computer' were obvious "*—will be able to predict our course.*"

"Slick work," said Hansen aloud. If the tank driver had gotten this far, she *would* figure out where her quarry had gone; but at least he—he and Third—now had a chance to reach the keep before she caught up with them.

The gully had drained only recently. The bottom was soggy where it wasn't standing water. Rivulets flowed into the main channel from what had obviously been the overflow pools of previous periods.

"What the hell is this place?" Hansen asked.

"The waste outlet for all of Keep Starnes," Third explained. *"They closed the gates when you appeared."*

"Is that so . . . ?" Hansen murmured. Well, you expect a swamp to stink like a sewer. He had more important things on his mind just now than the muck clinging to his boots and the back of his jumpsuit.

For instance, the footprints crossing the gully ahead of him, left to right. They might have been bear prints, though they probably weren't.

For one thing, there weren't any bears on Plane Five. For another, bears didn't get this big.

Sewers meant nutrients . . . which meant life of all sorts in a concentrated food chain. The top of the chain here seemed to be a mesonychid carnivore. It was five or six meters long, with claws to match the size of its huge feet.

Hansen leaped for a root dangling down into the gully. He raised his grip with the other hand, then used the strength of his shoulders to twist his body back up onto the left bank. He vectored off at an angle to the left.

"She is coming again," Third warned, but the remark was informational rather than a comment on the human's judgment. *"She is following the gully now."*

They reached the outer skin of the dome. Hansen was breathing through his mouth. The humid air felt soothing to the roughness in his throat.

"There is a personnel hatch twenty meters to our right," Third said. *"Or a vehicle hatch one hundred and seventy meters to the left."*

Hansen jogged toward the right along the curving wall. Mosses and small plants grew in the detritus that had accumulated on the surface of the armor, but they did nothing to detract from the solidity of the dense metal beneath.

The air vibrated with the sound of the tank's lift fans, amplified by the gully walls. It was going to be close.

"Can she—" Hansen started to ask, then shut off the remainder of the question. Of *course* the tank could climb a five-meter bank. It had gotten down into there to begin with, hadn't it?

"The fans swivel," his command helmet explained without being asked to do so. *"They have sufficient excess power to lift*

the vehicle at a 70° angle, so long as there is a surface against which the plenum chamber can seal."

He found the hatch, which was too fucking near the edge of the gully. Within what Hansen judged was a year or so, a maintenance crew had used defoliant spray to clear the immediate area. That looked like the last time the portal had been opened.

The hatch was sealed, as expected, a rectangle with radiused corners two meters by one.

There was no external latch or key plate.

"Put me against the power jack," Third directed crisply. *"At ground level beside the door."*

If the words had been human speech instead of thoughts generated by a machine, Hansen would have said Third was tense. Perhaps that was the listener's projection. . . .

The power jack was a three-prong outlet beneath a sprung cover, intended for the use of maintenance crews. Hansen tore off the command helmet. He felt naked without it.

The jewel on the helmet's forehead winked. Jointed arms extended the way iron filings grow into spikes in a magnetic field. The crystal appendages entered the jack. Hansen expected sparks, but there was no immediate response.

Hansen's body was trembling with adrenaline, but he had nothing to do except wait. A conifer uprooted in a storm lay tilted against several of its fellows nearby. Its sprays of needles were prickly brown; the bark had dried to a fungus-shot gray.

Hansen gripped a wrist-thick branch with both hands. The wood resisted, though fibers crackled as the branch bent. Hansen shouted and tore the limb away.

He turned, flushed with effort and triumph, to see how the helmet was coming with whatever it was doing.

The carnivore whose tracks they had noted lurched up from the gully. Its meter-long skull was almost all jaw. The beast straightened like a cat on a countertop, facing Hansen.

The beast had a brindled coat and legs that seemed rather short for its huge body. Its canines, upper and lower both, were the length of Hansen's index fingers.

Its snarl bathed the human with the effluvia of ancient death.

"Third," Hansen said in a lilting voice pitched to be heard

over the predator's threat. "You'd best get that hatch open, or—"

He shouted and thrust out with the brush of dried needles. The beast, startled an instant before its own attack, snapped and caught the branch. Hansen tried to hold on. A quick jerk of the long jaws flung him sideways into the fallen tree.

The mesonychid worried the dead limb for an instant. Despite the size of its skull, the brain box was of reptilian proportions. Hansen staggered upright. The beast—

The beast turned in its own length and lunged toward the bow of the hovertank lifting up from the gully floor at a skew angle.

The carnivore weighed tonnes. The shock of its sudden mass overbalanced the vehicle and sent it skidding down the bank again. The tank's driver fought expertly to keep her vehicle from turning turtle. Her co-ax ripped the unexpected attacker.

Machinery shuddered somewhere in the dome. Third had penetrated the keep's control circuits by sending signals through the disused power jack, but the door was still set as firmly as if it had been cast in one piece with the armored dome around it.

"Third, damn you!" Hansen screamed as he tore off another treelimb, *useless*, even against the carnivore. He could flee through the Matrix and Starnes would win, evil would win, and that wasn't going to happen. Fuck 'em all!

The tank's co-ax used chemical propellant to fire ring penetrators, hollow tubes the size of a man's little finger that punched through armor more effectively than long-rod projectiles of similar mass and velocity. Continuous bursts raked whatever part of the mesonychid was in front of the gun muzzle at the moment. Some of them drilled the body the long way.

The beast continued to snap and struggle. Its snarls were as loud as the roar of the tank's eight lift fans.

The gate at the gully's head, twenty meters broad, rose majestically. Beneath it foamed the stored backlog of Keep Starnes' waste water. Hundreds of thousands of liters emptied into the gully as fast as the huge outlet could dump them.

The first onrush swept the predator's tattered corpse down the gully, biting at the foam. The tank lifted momentarily. When the flood poured over the vehicle's upper deck, the overloaded fans failed in a series of loud reports.

Hansen stared in amazement. Water boiled briefly over the tank's turret; then the flow sank back to a broad stream no more than a meter deep as the storage tanks emptied.

Hansen dropped the treelimb. He rubbed his palms against his thighs. They were sticky with pitch. He reached down for the command helmet and put it back on.

"*I thought,*" said Third, "*that it might be better to deal with what was behind us before we went inside.*"

"I don't second-guess my people," Hansen said. He rubbed his hands again, this time against one another. "So long as it works."

The tank's controls had fried when the drive motors shorted out. As Hansen watched, the turret hatch began to turn slowly open under the operator's muscle power.

Chapter Thirty-one

"Duration exists only in the eight worlds on the surface of the Matrix, Hansen," said Dowson in a sparkle of violet light. His curtained jar sat on the table at the head of the Prince of Simplain's couch. "Within, all times are one time."

Outside the richly-appointed tent, a draft mammoth shrieked to the moon and a dozen of her fellows echoed the call. From a lesser distance came another of the normal noises of an army in its marching camp: two gangs of servants raised their voices in a violent argument. There would be a riot unless nobles intervened quickly to damp down the anger.

"There aren't any guards posted," Hansen said glumly. "Venkatna could hit us with a hundred men, and there wouldn't be a Mirala Confederation left."

"Have some wine, Kommissar," North said, offering a ewer of agate glass. "Anyway, I've set guards. You needn't fear that we won't be able to escape into the Matrix if there's a surprise attack."

Because Dowson was present at this dinner in 'Lord Guest's' tent, North and Hansen served themselves. The chirp of female voices beyond a double curtain indicated that North traveled in the full state of a prince of the Southlands, with a harem as well as servants for all other bodily needs.

"What I'm afraid of," Hansen said, "is that there's no way this bunch of clowns can beat the imperial army."

His finger slid his cup of gold-mounted crystal a finger's breadth closer to his dinner companion, signaling North to pour. The serving table between the two dining couches was a round of mountain cedar; polished to bring out the prominent markings.

Very pretty if you liked that sort of thing; and Hansen did, more or less, though his mind didn't dwell on natural luxuries even when he didn't have a fight to prepare for.

"Win or lose," North said with harsh gusto. "It's more souls for us on the Final Day. We'll need them, Hansen."

"We will need," Dowson said in thoughts as cold as the Matrix, "more than we have. More than we can ever have, Captain."

"Excellent wine, this," North said as he swallowed the sip he had been savoring in his mouth. North wore the flowing silk robes suitable for a southern magnate and he reclined while dining, though there was gray ice in his eye wherever it fell. "It comes from estates of mine near Simplain."

Hansen drank without finesse. Wine and beer were generally safer than water in the inhabited regions of the Open Lands. And they had alcohol in them, which was usually a bad thing . . . but not always, and not just now.

"Are you afraid of it?" he asked abruptly. "Of the end?"

"Not necessarily the end, Commissioner," corrected lime-green thoughts expanding from beside the shrouded container. "The end for us, perhaps, and we see no farther than we live . . . but the Matrix may exist beyond the Final Day, though we no longer observe it."

The sizzle of an arc weapon brought the men to attention. Flickers of light beat through the tent's silken weave.

The light died. An amplified voice shouted. A camp marshal was putting down the servants' quarrel, using his arc as a baton of office to get attention.

North chuckled. "Have you viewed your own death, Hansen?" he asked playfully.

"I don't look forward," Hansen said. He slugged down the rest of his wine, then refilled the cup.

"There is no forward or back in the Matrix," Dowson said in a soft mauve whisper. "There is no duration, Commissioner."

"You're a god," North said harshly. He fixed Hansen with his good eye and the milky globe of the other. "You can either accept that—"

"I'm a man, Captain," Hansen said. "I live life as it *comes*, because the line of it's important even if duration isn't!"

"Yes, you're a man," North sneered. "And by acting like a *man*, you've brought to life the monster that Venkatna's empire now is, haven't you?"

Hansen suddenly relaxed and sank back on his couch. There was a bowl of fruit on the table. He took a peach from the bowl. He toyed with it instead of biting through the soft skin.

"I'm not denying my responsibility, North," Hansen said softly. "I'm here."

North laughed. "You've come here to die, Hansen," he gibed. "You don't think these *clowns* can win. You've said it yourself!"

"You're here too, North," Hansen replied. His voice was toneless and still soft, but his face muscles were settling into planes.

"Oh, I'm here, Kommissar," the one-eyed man said lightly. "And my arc will lift souls from Venkatna's army for my Searchers to reap, never fear. But I won't stand and die when the battle is hopelessly lost."

"You'll stand on the Day, Captain North," Dowson said.

Hansen quirked a smile toward the curtained brain.

"You could bring down Venkatna, Hansen," North offered persuasively.

He lifted the ewer and noted from the weight that it was empty. A wine-thief hung from the flared lip of a footed forty-liter jar behind him, but for the moment the tall god remained on his couch.

"You could tumble the whole kingdom—the *Empire*—into the sea," North continued. "Flood it, shatter it with earthquakes, scour it clean with volcanos. I'd let you, you know. There'll be other battles, other souls than these."

"Never souls enough, Captain . . . ," murmured a bubble of tangerine yellow from the jar.

"When I do what a man does . . . ," Hansen said. He spoke slowly because he was articulating a judgment that he had never before formed in words, even within his own mind. "I make mistakes, I misjudge side-effects. But I can't not act."

He took a bite of the peach and chewed it carefully. Juice ran from the corner of his mouth; he wasn't used to lying on his side as he ate.

North watched him, half smiling.

"If I use the powers that I have *now*," Hansen continued "my judgment doesn't get better. I do more harm, and more harm yet if I try to straighten out *that* mess. So I won't do that I'll use what I know."

He set the peach down on the table and flexed his right hand as if there were a gun in it. He smiled back, a wolf to North' craggy eagle, and stood up.

North's laughter boomed out.

"Very well, Kommissar," he said as he rose also. He looked even taller than usual as his head brushed the lamplit expanse of the tent roof. "You follow your devices, and I'll follow mine. Who knows? We may find ourselves at a similar point in the future—"

North stepped toward the room's internal wall.

"—if you survive," he added.

"Thanks for dinner," Hansen said. He considered a moment, then picked up the peach again to finish on his way to his own quarters.

"Unless . . . ," North said as he paused with the silk brocade curtain half-raised ". . . you'd perhaps like another sort of hospitality also? I have one along who looks a great deal like Krita, I believe."

Hansen looked at the taller man; and, very deliberately, took another bite of peach instead of answering. He walked out of the tent, past the pair of guards in battlesuits.

"Surely," North said musingly, "he doesn't think he can correct *all* injustice here on Northworld?"

"He thinks," replied a shimmer of peach-colored light, "that a man could do worse than try."

North thought of Hansen's expression as he left. His face had been composed, his mouth vaguely smiling.

But Hansen's eyes were pits of molten fury.

Chapter Thirty-two

Hansen didn't have to speak aloud to the command helmet, but under the spur of tension he shouted, "Third! Hook to the antennas and take the bastard over!"

Then he jumped to the hovertank's back deck.

The vehicle was disabled; it wouldn't move anywhere under its own power until the burned-out drive fans were replaced. The tank's general systems were another matter.

The surge from shorting motors had tripped breakers and perhaps destroyed some of the circuitry itself, but a vehicle this sophisticated had redundant pathways. If the woman inside reset a switch or two, the automatic weapon which had sawed apart the mesonychid would be ready to repeat the process on Nils Hansen.

The tank was stranded in the gully. Hansen could avoid becoming a target simply by entering the dome through the personnel hatch—

But those who ran Keep Starnes would expect their visitor by that route. Avoiding the obvious was a survival ploy.

"Staying home in bed is another survival ploy, Commissioner Hansen," Third commented acidly.

Hansen's boots hit and skidded sideways, both of them. Slime and water from the flood still pooled on the back deck, making the armor slick as glass.

Hansen snatched at the grab-rail welded to the turret side for the convenience of the crewman boarding through the single turret-roof hatch. His left-handed grip kept him from sliding completely off the tank, but his hip slammed the deck. The impact would have been disabling if his bloodstream hadn't been so charged with adrenaline.

"Sonuvabitch!" Hansen wheezed as he pulled himself up. He seized the hatch's outer undogging handle with his right hand. It rotated the last eighth of a turn to unlatch beneath his palm.

684

"Put me down, then," Third ordered.

Hansen hung the command helmet from the stub antenna projecting from the top of the turret. He'd obeyed the artificial intelligence's directions without thinking about anything except how he was going to take out the tank crewman.

The club with which Hansen had faced the predator was up the bank, and he hadn't brought a gun or even knife through the Matrix with him. The hatch was a pretty good weapon itself for *this* purpose.

The armored disk started to rise. Hansen poised behind it. When the forward lip was twenty centimeters above the rim, he would slam it back down with the shock of all his weight. The armored bludgeon would crush the crewman's hands and maybe dish his skull—

"I surrender!" called a woman's clear voice through the part-open hatch.

Right. The crew *woman*, Third had said.

"You've beaten me! I'm completely at your mercy! I'm coming out!"

Hansen glared. The hatch was now vertical, his last chance to use it as a weapon, and he *ought* to . . . but instead he straightened and said, "Keep your hands high, and if you've got a gun, so help me—"

He swallowed the rest of the words. She didn't have a gun. She was stark naked.

"To prove that I'm no threat to you," the woman said demurely.

The command helmet clicked and sputtered. Antennas are designed to accept data and transmit it through a distribution apparatus. Third used the tank's common link to enter the vehicle's information processing network. The helmet now reset the operating system to suit Hansen's purposes. The tank was as thoroughly disarmed as if the component parts of its guns were slung out into the gully.

"I am Lisa, Lady Starnes," the woman said. "My father is the count."

Lisa looked like a parody of *The Birth of Venus* as she climbed from the hatch. She was a slight woman for Plane Five, though she would have passed for stocky in the Open Lands. Cropped brown hair, small breasts; pale lips and nipples.

A look of anticipation rather than fear, but maybe fear.

Hair-fine crystalline probes withdrew into the command helmet. Hansen donned Third again.

"*I have dealt with it,*" stated the cold machine thoughts.

"I'm at your mercy," Lisa Starnes repeated forcefully. "I can't prevent you from raping me. The others are waiting for you inside, but they won't be able to interfere with you here."

Hansen shivered. He'd once met—very briefly—a man who liked the bodies of those he'd freshly killed. That acquaintance had lasted little longer than the time it took to take up three kilos of trigger pressure.

Lisa turned Hansen's stomach about as bad, though he didn't guess she was hurting anybody else. . . .

"Let's go," he said mentally to Third. He jumped down from the vehicle's deck.

Waste water gurgled thirty or forty centimeters up the skirts of the disabled tank. It was a hindrance for walking but not a problem. Hansen could see an inspection way built into the side of the outfall line, above the current flow level. He'd follow that for a distance, then have Third find him an access hatch well inside the keep.

"Wait!" the woman shouted. "Where are you going?"

"Find somebody else, lady," Hansen muttered. "I'm not interested even a little bit."

The echoing pipe slurred and deepened his words; he doubted that Starnes' daughter could hear him.

"*You should take the opportunity, Commissioner,*" the AI said. "*You may not get another one if you persist in this endeavor.*"

"I'll want you to find us a way out of here in a hundred meters or so," Hansen said instead of responding to the—joke? Was the machine making jokes? "I don't want them to figure a way to flood—"

The tank's hatch clanged shut again. A mechanical whine indicated that the vehicle's systems had been reset.

"You *did* disconnect the armament controls, didn't you?" Hansen said.

He jumped onto the slimy metal ladder leading to the walkway. A blind man couldn't miss a target in a tunnel, even a tunnel this big. The walls would channel shots until they found flesh.

"Not exactly," said Third.

A breechblock rang as Lisa charged the tank's co-ax.

"Shit!" Hansen shouted and vaulted to the walkway. If he lay flat, he might be covered until ring penetrators chewed away the—

There was a flood of orange light and a huge explosion. The shockwave flung Hansen down, but he was already diving and the walkway's slickly-wet surface saved him from the pavement rash he would otherwise have acquired.

He looked over his shoulder. The tank's hull spewed flame from the turret ring and all eight fan ducts. The turret was gone, blown somewhere beyond Hansen's present field of view.

"I set it so that the whole power supply would short through the hull if anyone tried to close a gunswitch, Commissioner," Third said. *"Are you satisfied?"*

Hansen's ears rang. He got to his feet. "Any one you walk away from," he muttered.

He thought he smelled burning pork; but that might have been his imagination.

Chapter Thirty-three

"Hello the house!" roared Sparrow in a voice loud enough to wake the stones from their rest. He waited.

The smith had regained his strength from proximity to his goal—and the momentary likelihood of action. He was living on his nerves and he knew it; but he knew also knew he could go on like this with no degradation in his performance until he dropped.

For now, Sparrow stood with his muscular arms akimbo and his chin slightly raised. The dagger in his belt had scales carved from dimetrodon canine and wound with gold wire. The hilt made a show in the sunlight to rival the ovoid glitter of the probability generator on the other side.

Sparrow looked strong and smart and utterly confident. He was all those things, and ruthless besides.

The smith's dog walked an aimless figure-8 in the vicinity of the dome's entrance. She sniffed determinedly, but the mud was absolutely barren.

The door was pentagonal, a facet of the dome rather than a section of a facet. It opened abruptly, inward and down at a 30° angle because the side forming the jamb wasn't vertical.

The maid with her hand on the door switch stared open-mouthed at Sparrow. "Who are—" she began. Then she gasped and blurted instead, "You don't have a collar!"

She was a tall woman, only a hand's breadth shorter than the smith. Her black hair was caught up with pins and ivory combs, and her fingers touched the black plastic ring around her own neck.

"I'm not a slave," Sparrow said. He stepped through the angled doorway before the maid took it into her mind to close the panel again. "My name is Sparrow, and I'm the son of a king. Who are you?"

"No!" the maid said and put her foot out. The dog followed

Sparrow anyway, tracking footprints. Her tail wagged further speckles of mud across the antiseptically-white anteroom.

The woman grimaced in amazement, then looked at Sparrow. "I'm Olrun," she said. "I was captured when I was a child. But you're from the Open Lands and you're not a slave?"

"I'm a messenger," the smith said as he looked around him. "From my master Saburo to the Princess Mala."

The anteroom was featureless—except for the mud, the dog's and that from Sparrow's own sandals. The ceiling and walls were of a thin material. It looked translucent, but it probably generated a soft illumination of its own rather than transmitting light from another source. For the room to stay this clean, most visitors must ride their skimmers directly to the dome's entrance.

Though mostly, Mala must not have visitors.

"Saburo?" Olrun said. "The *god* Saburo? But you—I mean, I don't dare disturb milady now, she's meditating."

Sparrow snorted. "Is she so harsh a mistress, then? Never mind. I'll protect you."

"No, she's very . . . ," the maid said. She patted a curl already precisely skewered by a pin of dark-veined wood. "She couldn't be nicer, really. Much gentler than anyone I knew before the slavers came . . . though I was very young."

Sparrow guessed Olrun was about thirty now, though it was hard to tell in the present context. She wore a robe of brown silk with a white sash, a careful centimeter or two shorter than her white undergarment. The fabric was of excellent quality, but its softness was out of place on a big-boned, strong-featured woman like her.

Olrun could have come from the kingdom of Sparrow's father. . . .

"It's just . . . ," the maid said musingly. Her eyes were on the visitor, but she hadn't fully comprehended his presence yet. "When we were at Nainfari's hold, there were lots of people around—and I was Princess Mala's maid, so nobody bothered me if I—"

Her smile was briefly tender.

"Unless I wanted it." The woman truly focused on Sparrow as a person. The smile that coalesced on her lips was frankly speculative. "But since milady had her bower built out here, three years and more, I . . . haven't seen many people."

The smith returned the smile, but anyone who could read his expression could hear a tree thinking. "That will change," he said and started for the rectangular doorway into the dome's interior.

"But—" Olrun objected. She stepped in front of Sparrow. The bitch barked happily at the movement. She trotted through the door, her nails clicking on the hard floor.

"Oh, North and Penny save us!" the maid cried as she turned to catch the dog.

Sparrow followed the bitch and the woman. He was smiling faintly again.

The center of the dome was a large room suffused with gentle light. A slender woman was seated cross-legged on a mat of russet fibers. She scrambled to her feet as the dog tried to lick her cheek. The dog's tail no longer slung mud, but its furious wagging knocked over foliage arranged in a vase on the low table.

"What?" Princess Mala cried. She looked shocked to the point of fainting. Her eyes stared from their black make-up like aiming circles on the pure white skin.

"Oh, milady—" Olrun said.

"Princess," Sparrow said in a rumbling voice that overwhelmed those of the women, "I bring you the greetings of my master, the god Saburo."

Mala straightened. The room's only furnishings were the mat, the table, and a featureless white cabinet behind the princess. Odd angles and the lack of shadows on the internally-lighted walls made it difficult to judge the room's size and shape.

"How did you get here?" Mala demanded in a shrill voice. The fabric of her robes grew brighter, layer by layer, from the olive-drab coloration of the outermost.

"I walked, princess, and I rode," Sparrow said. "My master sent me to bring you to his palace so that he can honor you by making you his wife."

Sparrow stood like a bear on its hind legs. His visage was neither angry nor threatening, but it was as coldly relentless as the advance of a glacier.

Olrun watched the big man without expression of her own. She knelt by the door, holding the dog with an arm around its chest. The dog licked the maid's wrist as Olrun picked dried mud from the animal's fur with her free hand.

"I don't want a husband!" Mala blazed. "Certainly not—"

Her face blanked. "Where did you get that knife?" she asked softly.

"I found it on the way," Sparrow said. His voice rumbled like steam building deep in the earth. By contrast, the android female chirped like a wren on the geyser's sulphurous rim. "Princess—"

"That knife was my brother's! You've killed my brother, haven't you?"

"Princess," the smith went on, "my master would like me to bring you willingly to him. But my *duty* is to bring you . . . and so I shall."

"How could you have killed Morfari?" Mala whispered in wonder. "And his whole band?"

"Saburo offers you wealth and power beyond your dreams, princess," Sparrow said. Her questions weren't really directed to him, and he had no intention of departing from the grinding certainty of his demands anyway. "He will—"

Olrun continued to stroke the dog as she watched Sparrow. The slight, crooked smile on the maid's face may have been unconscious.

"I don't want any man!" the princess said. "I'm happy here!"

She added with a vindictive glare at her visitor, "My father will kill you, you realize. You'll die in the way you deserve!"

Sparrow laced his fingers together and stretched his arms toward the princess. The calluses on his palms were as coarse as treebark.

"Lady princess," the smith said, "my master is a *god*. The emissary a god sends will accomplish his task no matter what must be done along the way. Slave killed or prince, or—"

Sparrow smiled. His expression was not a threat, any more than the maelstrom threatens as it sweeps down a ship for all the screams and prayers of the crew.

"Or the king himself, princess."

Mala stared at the big man. The only sound in the room was the skritch of the maid's fingers on the dog's hide.

"*Watch*—" Olrun cried.

Mala turned like fluff spinning in the breeze. The cabinet behind her was the size and shape of a coffin on end. She stepped *through* its face—

And vanished, woman and cabinet together, as if there had never been anything between Sparrow and the white space of the wall beyond.

Chapter Thirty-four

The courier, passed by the guard and Venkatna's advisors, eyed the emperor hesitantly.

"Well, go on!" Kleber whispered hoarsely. "Deliver your message!"

"Your majesty," the courier said, running his words together as if he hoped they would prevent him from seeing what he thought he saw. "Duke Justin informs you that the Mirala kings are marching with hundreds of warriors maybe a thousand they're looting as they pass but they seem to be making for the capital Duke Justin thinks six days maybe less."

The man was no court messenger. He wore back-country garb, the cape of a dire wolf and aurochs-hide chaps stained by the froth of the ponies he had ridden hard enough to reach Frekka in a day and a half.

Venkatna's audience hall was like nothing the courier had ever imagined.

The Web's sweeping curves were meaningless to anyone who hadn't been told of the device's purpose. The courier's first thought was that it was a cage, a prison, for the two emaciated women who sat on benches within the construct. They were being fed milk and soup by palace slaves who reached within the glimmering loops. Though the Web had gaps through which those within could exit, the women looked barely able to stand, much less flee.

Other slaves cleaned with mops and rags the women and the benches on which they sat. The women had not been permitted to leave the enclosed area to relieve themselves.

That was disconcerting to find in a palace . . . and the fear which marked the imperial advisors made the courier uncomfortable too, though it was a normal enough attitude among those forced to stand very close to the great. Neither of those things bothered the courier as much as the emperor and his companion did.

"Your majesty," said Duke Bontempo. The fat old man faced Venkatna, but his eyes were almost closed. The clerestory windows had faded to gray bars and the lamps were as yet unlit. "Do you wish to accompany your forces to meet these . . . ?"

Bontempo spoke softly, as though afraid of rousing the emperor from his—reverie?

Venkatna sat in a cushioned armchair. A robe of marmot skins lay over his legs. His hair had been left untrimmed longer than had the courier's own, and the stringiness of the imperial beard indicated why Venkatna had always before gone clean-shaven.

He held his wife's hand and stroked it gently. The Empress Esme's cheeks were sunken and there was a bluish pallor to her skin. She was obviously dead.

Venkatna's eyes focused on Bontempo, then flicked to the courier with a frown, as if wondering who he was. The courier stood perfectly still. He stared at a point on the far wall, just above the emperor's shoulder.

The audience hall contained three broad fireplaces connected to flues and chimneys. No fires were lighted. The courier began to tremble at his first experience of the imperial court.

Venkatna looked at Duke Bontempo and said, "We'll meet them here at Frekka. Order the forces to marshal at the palace barracks."

"They're in poor order, the Mirala troops," Trigane offered. He based his statement as much on past experience as on his hurried questions to the courier at the door to the hall. "A bunch of farmers, really. I could lead the frontier levies in a night attack and settle matters quickly."

"No!" shouted Venkatna with unexpected violence. He half rose from his chair, and his left hand tightened on that of his dead wife. "I'll lead the army. It was while meeting that Mirala scum at Heimrtal that my Esme took cold, you know. She hasn't been right since."

Duke Bontempo's eyes squeezed firmly shut. From his expression, one might have thought the old man was being disemboweled.

The emperor settled again on his seat. A look of ordinary concern passed quickly across his face. He glanced—barely an eye-flick—toward the corpse on the bed beside him.

"That will give us the greatest time to gather our forces," Venkatna went on in normal tones. "We shouldn't be over-confident, even against Mirala farmers—"

His voice rose. Tendons began to show in his throat.

"—who will die to the *man* and the *slave*—"

He was shouting.

"—and the very beasts that they bring against me in their pack train! Die! And I will kill them!"

No one spoke or moved.

Venkatna relaxed again. He even managed a faint smile. "I . . . ," he said mildly. "Well, there's no advantage to us in stunts and night attacks. We will win as we've always won, through training and discipline. Until I've fulfilled my destiny. And laid the whole world at my darling's feet."

His hand stroked Esme's cold cheek, but he did not look at her.

Duke Bontempo bowed. "I'll see to gathering our forces, your majesty," he said. He strode out of the room, calling for his aides before he was through the doorway.

The courier winced. If he had been ready for it, he could have left the hall in Bontempo's wake. Now he wasn't sure if he dared walk out without asking permission. He was *absolutely* sure that he didn't want to open his mouth without a direct order to do so.

Venkatna suddenly lifted his hand and stared at the fingertips. He looked over at Esme. His complexion sank through sullen pallor before flooding back in an apoplectic flush. "Mold!" he shouted. "They've let mold grow!"

The emperor jumped to his feet. The fur slipped, tangling his legs but ignored. For the first time Venkatna seemed to notice that the women within the Web were awake and the device's fabric did not glow with its own power.

"Get back!" Venkatna screamed. "You're letting her—you're—*get back!*"

"Excellency . . . ?" one of the women begged. Some of the milk she had drunk dribbled from the corner of her mouth. "Please, we must have rest, just a little rest."

"So cold . . . ," whispered the other woman. Her eyes were glazed and unfocused.

"Get back to your work!" the emperor cried. "I order you! I *order* you!"

The face of the woman who had been able to plead slackened. "Your orders are our fate," she said. Her voice was so soft that the courier would not have been able to hear except for the breathless silence in which all others in the hall held themselves.

"Your orders are our fate," repeated her companion. They lay down on the benches as though they were entering their tombs.

Chapter Thirty-five

"Who would have thought it?" Lena murmured in a glutinous, good-humored voice.

The image of Lisa's vehicle exploding rolled in looped slow motion on a corner of Lena's screen. The tank's outline brightened and blurred as current surged through it. Steam bubbled from the water flowing around the skirts.

"Karring!" Count Starnes snarled. "Did Lisa get out? She had plenty of time to get out, didn't she?"

The image of the hatch blew off, puffing a perfect smoke ring into the sky. A heavier explosion bulged the hull's armored flanks. The turret lifted a hundred meters in the air, spinning like a flipped coin. The solid casting came down in the distant forest, while steam roared to cool and shroud the glowing hull.

"Who'd have thought it?" Lena repeated, chuckling over the utter dissolution of her sister.

"Milord," said be chief engineer in a distant voice, "we'll be able to determine casualties when we've accomplished our purpose. For the moment, the target is still loose."

Karring sat at an outstation in the Citadel's rotunda instead of his normal lair deep within APEX. The device he had created to modulate the Matrix hung in the air above him. On the chief engineer's console, the Fleet Battle Director used color and three dimensions to simulate the greater ambiance in which the intruder could move whenever he chose—

But he *didn't* choose. Without further data, not even APEX could make Karring's trap perfect.

"Another skinny one," Lena said. "But a clever little bastard, isn't he, boys?"

Her console displayed a full groundplan of Keep Starnes at the intruder's present level. Overlaid on the schematic were visuals of Lisa's death and—across the main screen—an image of Hansen in the waste outlet. The fabric of Keep Starnes was woven with sensors to determine the health and status of every portion of the keep's systems. A Fleet Battle Director was capable of converting heat, pressure and vibration into a three-dimensional picture—

So Lena could watch a stocky, filth-smeared man advancing relentlessly into the heart of the keep.

"I'm sure she got out before the—the explosion," Count Starnes muttered.

"What's he doing now, Lena?" whispered Voightman, the lover in iridescent posing briefs, in the ear of the count's surviving daughter.

"What are you going to do to *him*?" asked Plaid from Lena's other side. As usual, his costume involved studded leather and decorated pistols.

"Watch and see, dearie," Lena said as she reached up without looking to massage Plaid's bulging groin. "First we close the outflow again . . ."

Plaid hooked his thumbs in his groin cup to evert it and display himself to his mistress, but Lena's attention had returned fully to her workstation. The shudder of the waste gate slamming at the woman's direction could be felt through bedrock to the Citadel if one knew what to expect.

"I don't see why it opened in the first place," said Count Starnes. Starnes shook his head at memories which replayed as surely in his mind as they did on Lena's console.

"Because . . . ," said Karring. The chief engineer was so concentrated on his own screen that he didn't recognize his master's question as rhetorical. "All the keep's systems are interconnected. A power cable, a door control—APEX itself, though APEX is protected. He's using the system's own pathways to introduce commands."

The intruder stopped. He leaned his helmeted forehead against the tunnel's dripping wall. The waterlevel in the main channel was rising, though it was still well below the walkway.

"What's he doing?" Lena muttered. "There's nothing there but blank concrete."

Voightman preened and nuzzled closer to his mistress. Lena appeared oblivious of Voightman and the fact she had echoed his words of a moment before. Sweat gleamed on his body, from anticipation and the heat which radiated when the console worked at full capacity. Droplets splashed onto the gleaming rhodium plate of the workstation.

APEX threw the answer across Lena's display as a line of lime-green block letters which contrasted with both underlayers:

SUBJECT'S COMMAND HELMET IS EMITTING ULTRASONICS AT THE SYMPATHETIC FREQUENCY OF

Hansen's image stepped back. He kicked the tunnel wall with a bootheel. A one-by-two-meter section of cast plastic collapsed into powder.

"What?" cried Starnes' daughter.

THE POLYMER PLUG WHICH WAS INSERTED INTO THE OUTFLOW PIPE AT THE CLOSE OF KEEP CONSTRUCTION.

"That's not on my plans!" Lena shouted. "How did he know that there was a sealed tunnel there? His plans can't be better than mine!"

"Perhaps he's echo-sounding," Karring murmured as the shape and colors on his display changed almost imperceptibly.

THE SUBJECT IS NOT ECHO-SOUNDING, replied the Fleet Battle Director.

Lena angrily stabbed at her manual controls. She was too angry to limit herself to mental input. Though her wrists were bloated white sausages, her fingers were surprisingly delicate. They shifted the layers of schematic and simulacrum to follow the intruder through the ancient construction boring. Hansen's image lost some definition.

Karring's face suddenly froze. "For god's sake, woman!" he blurted.

He caught himself and resumed, "That is—milady? You've opened the outlet gate again, haven't you? If the level in the tunnel rises much further while this hole is open, it will drain down. We don't know precisely down *where*."

Lena swore. A fleck of light on her schematic switched from yellow to green, lost in the mass of detail to anyone but an expert like the huge woman herself. The vague ringing of the pumps changed.

GATE IS OPEN, APEX responded across Karring's display in response to the chief engineer's surreptitious question.

The emotional temperature in the Citadel had changed. Plaid

and Voightman were nervous. They didn't understand what was happening, only that something had gone wrong for their mistress; and they knew Lena well enough to understand how dangerous she could be when she was angry.

"I don't see how you can raise a door through a power socket," Count Starnes muttered as he wrung his hands together. "And Lisa . . . "

"If there weren't a connection between the electrical system and the gate motors, the motors wouldn't work, would they?" Karring snapped. Only the fact that his master listened with no more of his brain free than the chief engineer spoke saved Karring's life at that moment.

"Now, the computing power that can trace the pathway and counterfeit the proper instructions, *that* is very interesting," the chief engineer added more calmly.

"He's reached Level FF," Lena announced. "He's coming out through a ceiling vent in the main auditorium on that level. Now I'll get him."

"Now!" Voightman repeated in a husky whisper. Plaid didn't speak. He was slowly masturbating himself through his leather briefs.

The image above Lena's schematic sharpened: there were visual inputs in the large room as well as the wide variety of other sensors by which APEX had tracked the intruder thus far.

A grating fell away. Hansen followed it. He landed on his toes and kept his balance after the drop.

Moving swiftly but with no sign of panic, the intruder crossed to a door and left the auditorium. The cameras tracked him down a corridor of closed doors.

"Where are the personnel?" Count Starnes asked in surprise. "FF40 is troop leaders' quarters. There should be someone out, surely?"

For a moment, no one answered. Lena hissed a curse and made a manual correction with her controls.

"Ah . . . ," said Karring. He nodded cautiously toward Lena. "Your daughter has ordered all personnel to their quarters and locked them in. I'm not sure . . . ?"

"Now!" Lena snarled. Blast doors slammed down to seal off

the hundred-meter section of corridor through which Hansen strode. The ceiling vents pivoted shut. Dense yellow gas poured from the floor louvers.

"Halons to suffocate flame," the fat woman chortled. "They'll suffocate him, too!"

"His helmet has provided him with filters," Karring noted in a distant voice.

The intruder rested his helmeted forehead against a switch-plate controlling the corridor lights.

"He won't be able to—" Lena said. The blast door slid sideways, delayed only by the inertia of its great mass.

The Fleet Battle Director followed Hansen as he slipped through before the barrier was fully open. Water gurgled from a 10-cm wall outlet, onto the floor of the next section of corridor.

"What are you doing, Lena?" Count Starnes asked in puzzlement.

"I'm not doing it!" his daughter replied. "This *bastard* has opened the standpipe valves! The vents will flood if I don't keep them closed. I'll kill him for what he's doing to my system!"

The intruder entered an elevator, then brought his helmet in contact with the controls. The cage began to drop. It wasn't coupled, as it should have been, to another cage. This bank of elevators stopped two levels up from the Citadel.

"Wait," the count said sharply. "He's coming this way. That's what we want him to do. We'll simply let him come."

"I want him to come here through his *Matrix*," Karring objected. "Remember, we haven't had half a dozen visits from this one to refine our calculations, as we did with Fortin."

The chief engineer licked his lips nervously. "I think we need to release the personnel and set the mechanical locks. No matter how powerful his command helmet's computing capability, it won't be able to work a manually-set bolt on the opposite side of a barrier."

"No," said Lena as her schematic shifted to a new level.

"Milady, we *must*—" Karring began.

Lena moved with the sudden smoothness of a whale broaching. She drew the pistol from the holster slung to her couch and sent a bolt of charged particles toward Karring's head.

The chief engineer ducked at the first motion. A bank of

imaging controls behind him went white and slumped as the bolt's thunderclap rocked the Citadel.

"Daughter!" the count snapped.

Lena dropped her pistol onto the floor of her console. The weapon's glowing muzzle discolored a patch of the plating. The air was sulphurous with the reek of the discharge.

Lena resumed tracking her target. "*I will kill him*," she growled to herself. "When he leaves the elevator. I will!"

"Yes . . . ," Voightman purred as he rubbed his groin against the back of his mistress' couch.

Chapter Thirty-six

Olrun's face went white when her mistress disappeared. Sparrow began to chuckle.

The maid was already on her knees. She bowed her forehead to the floor and said, "Milord, milord! I wasn't a part of that. I didn't help her to, to . . ."

Sparrow's dog whined. She licked the woman's cheek and ear in concern.

The smith bent and touched Olrun's shoulder to guide her upright. "I didn't think it was your doing, lady. Do you—"

He smiled as Olrun rose at his touch. She was very nearly as tall as he was; and solidly built for a woman—though Sparrow was massive for a man.

"—know where it is your mistress might have gone, though?"

The maid shook her head miserably. "I'd never asked about the cabinet," she said. "It came from Nainfari's palace with us, but I'd never seen it do anything. It was just—"

She waved at the blank white walls and the overturned foliage. "Just decoration, I thought. I don't understand why she lives in a place so bleak when she's a princess."

Sparrow laughed again with grim amusement "She'll get along well with my master."

Olrun raised an eyebrow.

"Oh, yes," Sparrow said. "She'll come to my master. I was sent to arrange that."

The maid smiled minusculy. "That will be a change for Princess Mala," she said with a perfect absence of inflexion. "She has always done what she wishes . . . and only what she wishes."

Sparrow touched Olrun's shoulder again, the way he might have petted his dog in affection or for reassurance. "Do you think you could find us some food, lady?" he asked.

"Of course," Olrun said as she started out of the room. She

paused. "But it won't be real food like you're used to," she warned. "The meat hasn't any proper fat to it."

"That's all right," the smith replied. "In hot lands like these, you couldn't keep rich food down anyway. You'll learn that when you travel more."

The maid left the room with a vague smile playing over her lips. The dog followed her to the open doorway, then turned back to Sparrow and whined.

Sparrow got out his mirror. After a moment, the bronze face clouded. It cleared in a view of Princess Mala, huddled against a background of gray mist.

The vectoring bead on the mirror's rim was green. The smith walked slowly around the spot where Mala had vanished. The bead rotated around the metal rim, indicating a point in the center of the empty floor.

Sparrow chuckled again. He lowered his bulk onto the table carefully to be sure that the flimsy-looking piece of furniture would support him. The legs and paper-thin surface were stronger than they appeared. It was like sitting on a solid block of glass.

There was nothing wrong with the craftsmen here on Plane Three, though their techniques were not those the smith himself used.

Olrun bustled back with a platter. On it were a stew of boiled roots and a rack of edaphosaur ribs from which ladylike portions had already been carved. "What sort of utensils do you want, milord?" she asked.

"Nothing wrong with my fingers the last I checked," the big man replied. "You've been living among frogs in a swamp for too long, my girl."

The maid blushed and set the platter down beside him.

Sparrow gripped adjacent ribs with either hand and broke off the endmost. He tossed the smaller portion to his dog, then began gnawing the remainder of the roast himself. "It's hungry work, the job I've been doing," he commented to Olrun.

The maid's eye fell on the seeming handmirror which rested on Sparrow's lap. Mala's face stared from the bronze surface. The black eyes of the princess were calm but unfocused.

"Oh," Olrun cried. "You've found the mistress! Where was she?"

Sparrow cracked the rack's chine with a thrust of his thumbs. He dropped the rib that he had mostly cleared. The dog sniffed the new offering, then returned to the meatier portion she had started on.

"The princess is in the Matrix," the smith said. "Between planes. She hasn't traveled anywhere, she's just crawled into a hole."

He snorted. "To think that anybody would try to hide from *me* in the Matrix! Me, Sparrow the Smith!"

A tag of flesh hung down from the end of the roast Sparrow was worrying. Olrun tugged the bit of meat loose between her thumb and forefinger then dropped it into her mouth.

"Would you like to bathe?" she asked without looking at the smith directly.

Sparrow shrugged. "It'll be the same mud going in the opposite direction. There'll be time enough to clean off when I have the princess in my master's hands."

He glanced sidelong toward Olrun. "There'll be time enough for a lot of things, I think."

Olrun smiled without meeting the smith's eyes. "You'll go after her, then, Master Sparrow?" she asked.

Sparrow set the meat back on the planter and picked up the container of vegetables. They were still hot, hotter than comfortable. He slurped a little of the broth from the edge of the container.

He grimed at the maid. "No," he said judiciously. "I'll bring her back here. In good time. But first I'll give the princess a lesson about running from *me*."

The bitch looked up at the note she heard in Sparrow's voice. When she was sure nothing was intended for the immediate present, she went back to her bone. Her back teeth splintered the edaphosaur rib with a series of short, crunching sounds, like the *clock/clock* of a mason's hammer.

When Sparrow had finished his meal and washed it down with drafts of brandy distilled from cycad hearts, he lay on the cold stone floor. His eyes glazed.

Beside him, Olrun began to groom the dog.

Time meant nothing to Mala *here*. Often she entered this state to meditate in perfect nothingness. Some day, she thought, she would decide to remain forever in this gray perfection, free of the nagging asymmetries of present existence.

The stranger's intrusion, the *smith's* intrusion, was intolerable. It should not have happened, so here in the featureless realm of the ideal it had not happened. Nothing could touch her. Nothing existed outside herself, nothing moved—

Something moved.

At first Mala thought it was her hammering heart that caused the sensation. Nothing *could*—

But the grayness had shape now; beyond the strait confines of her cabinet was a plain of stark outlines.

Icy stalagmites rising from an icy floor. Slime molds the size of men, motionless all around her. Mala stared. On all sides the same.

Her feet edged to the center of her immaterial enclosure so that no part of her body was closer to the edge than any other.

The figures shifted at the infinite slowness with which constellations wheel in the heavens, turning their faces toward the girl in their midst.

A mountain loomed on the distant horizon. Mala stared at it for an unimaginable time in order to avoid watching the nearer figures; but as she looked, the crags and fissures ceased to be geological occurrences. The mountain wore the lineaments of a human face.

She gasped and spun around. A stalagmite of blue ice was pressed toward her. She started backward.

It was her brother, Morfari. Half his skull had been burned away.

Mala shrieked and closed her eyes. Her universe dived, then spun vertiginously. Light flashed. She threw herself forward, screaming, and sprawled onto the floor of her bower on Plane Three.

Olrun, her fingers tangled in the neck ruff of a brown dog, stared at her mistress, while Sparrow the Smith groaned as he returned from another frozen plunge into the Matrix.

Chapter Thirty-seven

Hansen paused a half second after the elevator door purred open. The air was muggy—warmer than expected in the climate-controlled keep, and very humid.

He stepped into the corridor. It was empty, as usual.

"Wait," Third ordered.

Hansen's feet held in place as though tack-welded to the dull blue carpet. His mind was balanced on a glass spike, tilting at the weight of a thought and prepared to free-fall if the support shattered. Hansen's head continued to swivel as he absorbed sensory cues.

All the hard surfaces within Keep Starnes vibrated to a single frequency, as though they were parts of a living cell. The residents must grow used to it; Hansen, coming from outside with his senses stropped to a fine edge on adrenaline, was constantly aware of the greasy quiver.

Air moved up from the floor vents and down again through intakes offset in the ceiling. The ventilation system was working normally, so the raised humidity didn't result from a malfunction there.

Hansen wasn't about to believe in a normal glitch in the keep's infrastructure anyway. Not now.

There wasn't a soul walking the halls. A child's ball lay near the edge of the carpet, abandoned in the owner's haste to get under cover.

"She is raising the humidity to provide a proper ground," Third said with obvious satisfaction. *"The door at the end of the corridor is connected to a high-amperage four-kilovolt line."*

Hansen sauntered forward. The rotunda and the elevators that served the Citadel were on the other side of that door. "Suggestions?" he asked.

"She expects me to enter the control system through the switchplate at the end of the corridor," the artificial intelligence

replied. *"It is electrified also. Bring that toy ball close to me."*

Hansen obeyed without comment. The ball was hollow plastic and the size of a grapefruit. Swirls of pale green and pale blue patterned its surface. The toy was the first sign of frivolity he had seen within the arid corridors of Keep Starnes.

"She?" he asked.

A crystalline blade, as narrow as a hair, extended from the jewel over Hansen's forehead. Its tip probed the ball. *"Her name is Lena,"* Third said. The mental voice lacked any of the overtones which would have suggested interest. *"She is a daughter of Count Starnes."*

The helmet offered at the corner of Hansen's view the hologram image of a woman. Lena did not so much look fat as she appeared to be a sea creature, rolling on a self-shaping couch which supplied the support of a fluid medium.

The blade finished its operations. The ball was slit two-thirds of the way around its circumference. The halves flopped loosely, though they were still joined.

Hansen suddenly laughed. "Are you a weapon, Third?" he asked. "Did I cheat the terms Count Starnes set?"

"Is your brain a weapon, Commissioner Hansen?" the artificial intelligence responded tartly.

"On a good day, Third," Hansen said. "On a good day."

He bent down and added, "Help me get this floor vent loose. It's graphite. It'll conduct just fine."

Hansen tugged against the louvers to stress the patches of hardened adhesive which attached the vent to the ducting. The command helmet extended a probe to touch the composite material, then fed in pulses of high-amplitude ultrasound. As the harmonics reached critical frequency, the adhesive vibrated into dust motes. The tacks failed one after another.

Hansen lifted the grate. It was rectangular, a meter by twenty centimeters. Long enough to reach from the door to the switchplate, and massive enough to carry the current for at least a time.

Hansen shifted so that he held the grating with his right hand alone. He gripped the graphite composite between insulating layers of the sectioned ball.

With that much current connected to the switchplate, Third

couldn't use it for access to the door controls. The AI hadn't explained its plan to Hansen; but as Hansen had said, *on a good day*, and this was a day that had waited too long.

Using the ball as an insulating mitt, Hansen extended one corner of the grating so that it touched the metal-faced blast door. The fat blue spark and *pop!* made Hansen jump even though he knew to expect it. He swung forward to bring the far corner of the meter-long plate in contact with the switchplate on the corridor wall.

Electricity roared like the sky tearing open.

Hansen stepped back. His hair stood on end.

The grating remained in place. Current had welded the ends into the structure of the door and wall. The remains of the plastic ball stuck to the louvers, melted there by resistance-generated heat in the first fraction of a second. The graphite fibers glowed white, and the epoxy which they stiffened sublimed off in the black curls.

There was a bang from inside the heavy door. A rectangle of foul-smelling smoke spurted from around the panel. It mushroomed upward.

The snarl of electricity died as suddenly as if a switch had been thrown—as, in a manner of speaking, one had. The enormous wattage had burned through its conductor in a fashion that neither Third nor Starnes' daughter could bridge.

A yellow-orange ball about the size of a man's head sprang from the switchplate. It rolled down the center of the corridor, hissing and emitting faint blue sparks. After a few seconds, the ball turned 90° and vanished through a closed door.

Hansen let his breath out. The circulation system was running at full capacity, but the hall was gray with bitter smoke.

"*You'll have to slide the door open manually, Commissioner Hansen,*" Third said.

Hansen gripped the handle and braced himself. "Don't s'pose you've welded it shut, do you?" he muttered.

"*I do not. Anyway, we could go around.*"

Hansen straightened the leg he had braced against the corridor wall. The blast door moved suddenly. Only inertia had held it in place. The grate, burned to ash and hairs of graphite, fell to the carpet when its corner broke free of the door.

A gush of air from the rotunda—scrubbed and textured by machines, but fresh as a sea breeze compared to the throbbing hallway behind—massaged Hansen's lungs. His legs felt suddenly weak.

"Have you had enough of this gaming, Commissioner?" Third asked coolly.

Hansen leaned against the wall of the rotunda. A stench of ozone and superheated polymers drifted from the corridor. He hadn't had enough ambition to slide the blast door shut behind him.

He walked toward the elevators in the center of the circular room. Every step away from the poisoned atmosphere brightened his mood and strengthened him.

"Yeah," Hansen said. "End it now."

He didn't have to be told the drill. He knelt with his head close to the elevator call-pad. His eyes roved around the empty room.

There was nothing to see. The carpet had been replaced in sections, leaving some patches brighter than others. The walls' luster had dimmed from ages of use and washing.

Above Hansen's eyes, limbs extended from the gray jewel and passed signals into the controls of Keep Starnes.

The elevator cage opened. *"Time to go, Commissioner Hansen,"* the command helmet said.

Hansen got into the cage. "What did you do?" he asked as the elevator began its long drop to the Citadel.

"What you said to do, Kommissar," replied Third. *"Precisely what you said."*

The display above Lena's couch showed the ball lightning trundling away from the intruder before disappearing into a residential suite. Hansen entered the rotunda, paused for a moment, and then strolled toward the elevators.

"How did he make the fire go down the hallway?" Plaid asked, staring at his memory of the *Kugelblitz*.

"Shut up!" Lena snarled as she stabbed at the manual controls. "If anyone says another word, I'll *kill him!*"

Count Starnes opened his mouth, then closed it. He walked toward the tank that fitted his powerful body like a glove. With its mass between him and his daughter, Starnes said, "I'm going to get ready. Karring, see to it that you're ready also."

The chief engineer nodded without taking his eyes off the display before him.

The intruder's image bent down beside the elevators. "Fine, that's fine . . . ," Lena hissed. "I'll let him get halfway, and then we'll see how well he eats his way through—"

The display above her console went fluorescent white and vanished. A blue aura played over all the workstation's conductive surfaces. Lena and her two lovers froze in the postures they occupied when the current gripped them. The woman's mouth was open to scream, but her paralyzed diaphragm couldn't force the sound out.

Components within the console banged loudly as they failed one after the other. A panel blew open but stuck midway when its hinges welded. Rapid puffs of smoke poured out of the console's interior.

Plaid fell sideways onto the concrete floor of the rotunda. His legs from the knees down remained stuck to the console's metal floor. They had burned to matchsticks of carbon. Voightman's body twisted in on itself. No human features remained. He looked like an outcrop of coal.

Count Starnes and Karring watched with amazement that was too shocked for horror.

"APEX is protected . . . ," the chief engineer repeated to himself in a whisper.

The current roaring through Lena's workstation cut off abruptly, but smoke continued to stream through the seams and connectors.

The grease fire on Lena's couch continued to burn as well.

Chapter Thirty-eight

"Now, let me scout the lay of the land," Blood said, pausing at the edge of servants and retainers around King Wenceslas, "before you shoot your mouth off."

"Fine with me," Hansen agreed mildly. The sun was well up, but the king's tent had not yet been struck—and Wenceslas' contingent was farther along than were some of the others in the Confederate forces.

"A' course," Blood admitted, "I don't really understand the crap myself. But fuck it, I guess it's a good idea. Let's go."

The red-haired warrior strode forward, muscling servants aside. Two senior warriors, Garces and Hopewell, discussed with the king the prospects for hawking this close to Frekka. They, with Blood, were Wenceslas' chief aides—bodyguards—and drinking companions.

"Vince," Blood said to the king, "I need t' talk to you without all these chickenshits around, okay?"

"Who you calling chickenshit, buddy?" said Garces, a black-bearded man whose beer gut did not keep him from looking both powerful and dangerous.

"Hey, not you guys," Blood explained hastily. He pushed at Wenceslas' secretary, a freeman wearing a cloak trimmed with beaver fur. "You know, the *other* guys."

Wenceslas looked around the chaotic camp. The Simplain mercenaries under Lord Guest had marched off an hour earlier. Some of the smaller contingents had followed, in no particular order; though by this time in the invasion, an order of march had been established in practice if not by formal agreement.

"Oh, all right," the king said. "Go on, give us some room, you all!"

Hopewell looked hard at Hansen.

"Not him," Blood said. "Look, it's his idea. It's about—"

He looked around. The servants moved away, chattering among

themselves. A few of the more cultured—the secretary among them—glared disdainfully at the crude warriors whose inferiority was a secret article of faith in the servants' hearts.

"Right," Blood said. "Look, Hansen, you understand it better 'n me, so you tell them. It's about winning the battle."

"Damn right we're going to win the battle!" Garces growled. "Assuming they come out 'n fight us, leastways."

"I don't think there'll be a problem with that," murmured Wenceslas.

It struck Hansen that the king was by no means a stupid man. It was even possible that he was smart enough to agree to Hansen's plan. . . .

"When we meet the imperial army, your majesty," Hansen said, "they'll be better disciplined than our troops. We'll have some edge in—"

Hopewell, a blond man in his twenties, built like a demigod, spat noisily to the side. "Discipline is a lot of bullshit," he said. "What wins battles is good armor and good men—and *we* got that. Venkatna's pussies, they have t' ask permission to wipe their ass. Fighting's for one man at a time—if he's a *man*."

Hansen remembered:

The Easterner's armor is dark green, with chevrons of lighter green across his back and chest. His battlesuit is of royal quality. It absorbs all the power Hansen can pour into it, while the Easterner forces his own arc inexorably down toward Malcolm's helmet.

Needles of ozone jab Hansen's lungs. He stretches out his left hand slowly, fighting the drag of his battlesuit's sticky joints. The stress of the duel has drawn all power away from the suit's servos. The soil under the combatants' feet has been cooked to brick.

Hansen's groping fingers jerk open the Easterner's suit latch. The armor switches off. Malcolm strikes upward with the fury of a man who saw his own death in an arc weapon approaching millimeters at a time. He burns away the chest of the opponent whom Hansen's trick has left defenseless.

The Easterner's intestines balloon for an instant before they burst. . . .

"You need men and armor, no argument . . . ," Hansen said

softly. His eyes took a moment to refocus on the present. The king was looking at him in surprise, while Garces blinked with a new respect.

What the hell did his face look like when he lost himself in a past he'd rather have forgotten?

"Right, okay," he resumed. "I want to lead off a good chunk of Venkatna's army. Enough to give the rest of our people the margin they need to crush what's left. If you'll give me ten men, I think I can do it."

"Give *you* ten men?" Wenceslas said in puzzlement. "And why should *I* do anything like this?"

The king looked from Hansen to Blood. Blood grimaced fiercely as though he hoped by wrinkling his face to squeeze understanding of Hansen's lengthy explanation the night before back into his awareness.

"Me, because I know how to work the identification circuits in the battlesuits to give a false report," Hansen said. "I'll tell them that there's a hundred-man battalion working around their flank, and they'll send out a force to block us."

He raised a finger to forestall the question none of his listeners were sophisticated enough to ask.

"I know," he went on. "If Venkatna's people go beyond the IFF signals—which they can—then they'll realize it's a trick; but I'm betting that they don't *understand* their hardware, they'll just say, 'Mark hostiles,' and not check they're getting suit locations instead of just identification codes."

"But they'll see you," Hopewell said. "Can't they count?"

"Negative," Hansen explained. "We'll keep behind cover with a good screen of horsemen. They'll have to hit us with warriors to learn that there's nothing there to hit."

He grinned. He saw in the king's eyes the realization that when fifty or a hundred imperial warriors realized they'd been duped by a handful of the enemy, it was going to be very hard on that handful.

"And it's you," Hansen went on, "because you're my liege . . . and because you're smart enough to make a decision. If I tried to bring this up to the Confederation council, nobody'd listen. And there's not a snowball's chance in Hell that word wouldn't get out to Venkatna besides."

Only Hell wasn't hot on Northworld . . . and it wasn't just a theological concept. Not to someone like Nils Hansen, who had seen the damned souls frozen to the ice of Plane Four. . . .

"We never done this sorta crap," said Garces. He wasn't so much hostile to the idea as baffled by it.

"No, it's a ruse," Wenceslas said with a frown of concentration. "Ruses are proper. Only—"

He stared very hard at Hansen. "You can make ten men look like a hundred?"

"Yes," said Hansen. He'd qualified his statement before. Now it was time to state probabilities as facts.

A female mammoth began to bleat in high, piteous notes. She'd made a friend among the baggage train of another princeling. She was not yet loaded, but her friend was padding out of the camp, carrying heavy battlesuits in rope slings on either flank.

. . . good night, Irene, Hansen thought inanely, *I'll see you in my dreams. . . .*

Maybe not so inane.

"Then why don't other people do it?" Wenceslas pressed.

Because I didn't teach them how when I put the West Kingdom army together four generations ago. "Because nobody thinks about it," Hansen said aloud. "But I do."

"Look, is he just trying to stay outa the fight?" Hopewell said to the king in genuine puzzlement.

"Are you questioning my honor, friend . . . ?" Hansen heard his voice lilt, as lightly as a nightingale calling from a distant hedge.

Hopewell turned and looked at him. Hopewell was the larger man by 10% in height, 20% in bulk; and Hopewell's bulk was muscle also. But a duel in battlesuits wasn't muscle against muscle; and anyway, Hansen wasn't the sort of fellow you chose to fight under *any* circumstances.

"Naw, that's not what I meant," the bigger warrior said. "Look, I just don't figure it, all right? Why don't we just, you know, fight 'em? That's what we come t' do."

"What about five?" the king asked. "All told."

Kingship, business—and love, however you defined it. They all required trade-offs, and you never had all the data that you needed for a decision. Like Dowson had said in another district of All Times. . . .

"Five should work," Hansen said aloud. "Ten would work better, and it wouldn't be much degradation of the Mirala main force."

"But it would degrade *my* contingent, Lord Hansen," Wenceslas said with a tone of equality that the king would never have used to address one of his bodyguards on a point of strategy. "I've brought seventy-three warriors to the fight . . . counting yourself."

Hansen understood the implication. "As you are right to do, your majesty," he said.

His mind spun in a montage of kings and slashing arcs and the way the Lord of Thrasey's battlesuit lost its gleam an instant before Golsingh's weapon ripped off the head in bubbles of glass and blazing metal and blood, blood flashing up as steam.

"If you so order," Hansen's voice continued, "I will stand by you as I have sworn; and fight in such a way that when Venkatna's men put us both down, as they surely will, you will say with your last breath that never did a warrior die better for his liege. . . ."

King Wenceslas touched the back of Hansen's wrist. When he saw that Hansen was alert in the present again, he said, "You're sure of yourself, aren't you, Hansen?"

Hansen managed a poor smile. "Of nothing else, your majesty," he replied. "But of that, yeah. I'm—all I've got."

"All right," Wenceslas said. "I'll give you three men, they won't be much but that shouldn't matter for your purpose."

He raised an eyebrow in query. Hansen nodded agreement.

"And I'll give you Blood," the king continued. "You'll need somebody that the back-rankers'll take orders from. They know Blood, and Blood knows you—"

The king grinned harshly. "As I hope that *I* know you, Lord Hansen."

The lovesick mammoth, laden at last, jingled past at a pace in advance of what the mahout on the beast's humped neck desired. He cursed, but the mammoth gurgled and strode on.

Hard to quantify emotional factors; hard to *identify* emotional factors. But they were what made the world work like it did, not the hardware and not even skill.

"You know the important part, your majesty," Hansen said. *You know as much as I do; and what the hell, it might work. Surely nothing* else *could possibly work.*

Blood clapped Hansen on the shoulder. "I told you he'd explain it!" the bodyguard caroled to his king and companions.

Blood didn't understand a thing about Hansen's plan or the necessity for it in the coming battle . . . but as King Wenceslas had said, Blood knew his man, and nothing else mattered.

Chapter Thirty-nine

Hansen stepped from the elevator with a smile and the nonchalance of a cat entering a familiar room, but his eyes were wells of green fury.

"*Hel*-lo, Count Starnes," he called to the Citadel. No human being moved within Hansen's line of sight, unless you counted the curl of smoke rising from Lena's couch. "You know, I could complain about the hospitality you show your guests, if I had a mind to."

Besides Lena's shattered console, one of the three outstations in the rotunda was live. The unit's seat had been spun to the rear when the user left in a hurry. The display was full of colors flowing in patterns. It could have been abstract art, for all it meant to Hansen.

"*Chief Engineer Karring is trying to display the Matrix in three dimensions,*" Third explained with a hint of mechanical amusement. "*When the power surged in Lena's workstation, Karring decided that he would be safe only in one of the bays of APEX proper.*"

"*Could* you get to him there?" Hansen asked as his eyes searched the portion of the rotunda he could see from where he stood. The haze of burned insulation and burned meat was familiar, God knew; but familiarity didn't make the reek less sickening, mentally as well as physically.

He'd known what he was doing when he gave Third the order. Not the technique, not exactly; but Hansen had ordered enough killings that he didn't kid himself when he had to—*chose* to—do it again.

"*I haven't had occasion to determine that,*" the AI responded coolly.

Hansen sauntered around the column of elevators in the center of the rotunda. "Count Starnes!" he called. "Hey, Count. Come out, come out, wherever you are!"

He could see the single corridor which led off the rotunda at this level. The mass of the Fleet Battle Director almost filled it, and Hansen knew the installation led back hundreds of meters into the bedrock.

A short man, balding and powerfully built (as were virtually all the inhabitants of Plane Five), sat in the nearest bay. He was dwarfed by the mass of the computer on three sides and above him. The device hanging over the mouth of the alcove had a noticeable similarity to the Web North gave King Venkatna; but the Web was static, and this unsupported ovoid spun in a pattern more complex than Hansen had thought at first glance.

"Count Starnes?" Hansen asked as he walked toward the corridor.

"That is Karring," Third said.

"I am Count Starnes!" boomed an amplified voice.

"Welladay!" said Hansen brightly. He turned to face the repulsion-drive tank a hundred meters away across to rotunda.

Despite the vehicle's mass, it was as much an article of dress as the battlesuits of the Open Lands were. The operator reclined in a couch with all the tank's controls at his fingertips—and no room to move more than those fingers. There was no rotating turret: the tube of a railgun extended from the frontal armor like the blade of a push dagger in an assassin's fist.

"Good to see you at last, Count. I was worried that I'd come all this way and missed you," Hansen said.

"Are you mad?" clicked the icy thoughts of the command helmet.

"Very, Third," Hansen said in a clear voice. "Very angry indeed. But I don't think he'll shoot when his computer's behind us, will he? How far through APEX do you suppose a slug from that gun would travel, eh?"

"He's right, milord!" Karring shouted from the bay. "There needn't be violence."

"Don't tell me what I need to do," snarled the speaker on the tank's roof. "Either of you!"

"They expected you to slink in here the way Fortin did," Third commented. *"They don't know how to react to Nils Hansen."*

"They'll know soon enough," Hansen said/thought.

The tank shuddered into motion. It slid forward at a barely-perceptible pace, the railgun centered on Hansen's chest. The hum of the vehicle's drive was almost hidden by the subliminal hugeness of the Fleet Battle Director, poised like a couching lion.

"You invited me to use APEX," Hansen said. He grinned and put his hands on his hips with the elbows flared out. "That's what I was told, anyhow. I think you ought to know that when I was Commissioner of Special Units back home, no place you ever heard of . . . but back on Annunciation—when I ran into somebody like you, Count Starnes, I kinda made it my job t' take care of things."

"Milord!" the chief engineer called desperately. "He can vanish faster than the bolt even!"

"Why would I want to do that?" Hansen lilted. "Now, you've nothing to fear, milord, not from me, so long as you keep your part of the bargain. I came to you unarmed . . . and you'll let me ask a question of APEX, now, won't you?"

"What question?" the tank demanded.

"Nothing to affect you," Hansen said. "Nothing to affect Plane Five, not really. I'll take off my helmet here—"

He touched the black plastic case above his temple with the pad of his right forefinger.

"—and it'll connect itself to APEX. Then I'll go home, and you'll go on with your—"

The air of mocking insouciance slipped. "—nasty little games that somebody oughta stop. But it won't be me. Unless."

"The locked sectors can't possibly be breached!" said Karring. The chief engineer was too aware that he was in the line of potential fire to listen to the nuances in the intruder's voice, nor was he in position to see the threat in Hansen's eyes. "Let him bring his helmet over here."

"He wants to bring you close to the device he built to control the Matrix," the command helmet observed.

"I know what it's like to have a new toy," said Hansen, pivoting smoothly though not particularly fast. "With me, it was mostly a gun, though, or a battlesuit later on. Let's go give Karring something to play with."

He walked across the rotunda with his back to Count Starnes.

He could hear the tank behind him. Its drive sputtered like bacon frying, though the vehicle had stopped and was merely hovering a hair's breadth above the concrete floor.

The chief engineer's expression was a mixture of fear and exaltation. Karring remained in his seat, but he looked ready to jump up and run. His hand dipped occasionally toward the pistol he wore as insignia of his rank within Keep Starnes' hierarchy, but that was just a sign of nervousness.

"*Karring is summoning additional troops,*" Third warned. "*Count Starnes is not aware of this.*"

Karring was no gunman. He perceived war as a chess game, while Nils Hansen saw it as muzzle blasts and men's eyes rolling up into the whites as their bodies toppled backward.

Hansen smiled. The chief engineer squeezed against the back of his chair. He spread his hands at the level of his mid-chest. The posture was an unconscious attempt to prove that he was harmless, no threat at all to the predator who walked toward him, grinning like a skull.

The twenty bays were inset 90° to the right or left from the axis of the corridor which APEX occupied. Hansen walked under the spinning ovoid at the head of the first one. He looked up and winked.

This close, the Fleet Battle Director was a lowering presence, not a machine.

"Have fun, Third," Hansen said. He took off the command helmet. "Karring, isn't it?" he went on. "And your APEX takes mental input?"

The chief engineer nodded tightly. A skein of colored fibers showed on the display which covered the inner face of the bay. The strands knotted down to opalescent white. Karring was afraid to look at the pattern lest Hansen understand and attack while he and Karring were within arm's length.

"Then it'll take mine, I'm sure," Hansen said. He stepped past Karring and placed the command helmet on the coaming in front of the holographic display.

"Purty thing, isn't it?" he said to the chief engineer as he walked back out of the bay. Probes extended from the moonstone-gray crystal on Third's forehead.

Hansen sauntered back across the rotunda without looking

behind. The tank swiveled to track him with its railgun. Hansen was headed toward the wrecked console and the corpses still smoldering on and around it.

"It's worked, milord!" Karring shouted. "He can't flee into his Matrix now, I'm sure of it!"

"Tsk!" said Hansen. "I just got here, Karring m'boy. Why would I want to leave?"

"Try it!" Karring said. "You're so sure of yourself, you bastard— but *try* your Matrix!"

Hansen shrugged. He continued strolling toward the destroyed workstation. His fingertips, then his right hand, vanished into a shimmer not of Plane Five.

"Not much of a trick, is it?" he said with a supercilious frown. His hand reappeared. The fingers, long and tanned and callused, flexed as though they held a weapon.

"He's yours, Count Starnes!" the chief engineer cried. "He's your slave, completely at your mercy!"

Hansen bent down and drew one of Plaid's pistols. The leather bolster had insulated the weapon from the current which burned off the owner's legs.

"The man who killed my daughters," boomed the speaker on Count Starnes' tank, "can scarcely expect mercy!"

The railgun fired.

Chapter Forty

"Princess," said Sparrow the Smith. His face was as bleak as cliffs at sunrise, and his voice rasped like tangled briars. "You will do. What I say. Or I will punish you in ways you will never forget."

"Kill me, then," Mala whispered, sprawled face-down at the feet of the huge, implacable man. "If that's your will."

The dog growled softly in Olrun's arms. The bitch's claws clicked on the floor, but the stone was too smooth to give her purchase. She felt the tension rising, and she wanted to be close to her master.

"Death would be a release, lady," Sparrow said.

He unhooked the small probability generator from his belt. It began to spin between the tips of his forefingers. When the ovoid settled into a rhythm, it hung in the air unsupported.

Sparrow's expression was too tight for certainty, but there might have been pity in the set of his mouth. "And *my* will," he went on, "is only that you do my master's bidding. I am the tool of my lord Saburo. But you *will* do as he requests."

The probability generator continued to spin at the same moderate velocity. The coils of its structure changed from wire and fine-drawn crystal to bands of rich indigo light.

"No," Mala said. She raised her face from the pale stone. "No, I will not."

Sparrow smiled. The ball of spinning light expanded away from him to engulf the princess in a web of alternate probabilities.

Reality shifted.

"Have you got the rest of the prisoners?" demanded King Stengard's two outer heads together. His middle head twisted to look into the hold his forces had just captured.

Stengard's androids and armed slaves wandered across the courtyard. The defensive wall was half melted, half blasted, into a thirty-meter gap, but the attackers had then opened the main gate for King Stengard to enter.

The party sent to the outlying hold dismounted from their individual skimmers and the heavy truck which carried the wall-breaching armament as well as a dozen personnel. The slaves, Lomeri and humans both, chattered with delight as they described to one another their recent victory.

"Got one," said the leader, Stengard's son Stenred. "The other, she was too close to the door. When it went west, so did she . . . but that was just the maid."

"Fishfood, that's all she was!" chortled a human slave who had been burned horribly some time in the past. His eyes winked out of masses of keloid, and his nostrils were slits in a smooth, pink surface. "But we got the main one!"

He jerked his electronic noose. The prisoner writhed at the jolt of fluctuating current applied to her tender throat.

"What you want done with her?" Stenred asked.

Stenred's head and torso were those of an ordinary human, save for their android pallor, but he walked on four legs. Because of the limbs' close placement on his modified pelvis, the prince looked less like a centaur than he did a spider lurching upright on two hind pairs of legs.

His genitalia hung down beneath a tasseled fringe intended for emphasis rather than concealment.

In the courtyard, the victors played with the control devices they had found in the hold. The game was to punch in random settings, then twist the control to full power. Each time, a captured slave bent backward, screaming until contraction of his or her muscles choked the throat silent. Occasionally, the victim's neck broke during the convulsions.

Stengard's troops were placing bets on which captive would die next. Whoever won crowed and demanded payment from the others. Occasionally, vicious fights broke out among Stengard's personnel, but those were minor incidents in the general bloody apathy.

"You captured her," said the king's left head.

"Whatever you please," agreed the center head.

"Though if you don't have an idea," leered the right head, "I sure do. Tasty little morsel, isn't she?"

Stenred grinned. "Hold her down!" he ordered.

"Seconds!" cried the slave with a face of scar tissue.

Princess Mala tried to struggle despite the pain that surged from the noose. It was no use. Slaves gripped her limbs and spread-eagled her on mud reeking with slaughter.

King Nainfari had been impaled on a stake in the gate of his hold. He stared through sightless eyes as Stenred knelt on his four knees to be the first of the conquerors to rape Nainfari's daughter.

Reality shifted.

"Where have you been?" croaked Mala as her husband's figure darkened the mouth of the cave. Behind him, red sand skirled on the wind. It filtered the light and made each breath taste dry.

"Keep your pants on!" snarled Offut in reply. He laughed at his own accidental joke.

The male android set down a container made from the hollow stem of a giant horsetail, a meter long and a quarter meter in diameter. He began to unwind the scarf with which he protected his face from the omnipresent wind.

"You've been gone all day!" Mala shrilled. Her fingers twitched, remembering the pain of weaving the coarse, cycad-leaf fibers into cloth. "And where's the water?"

"I brought water," Offut said, "but I had to go nearly five klicks to get it. Both the nearer holes were clogged deeper than I could dig."

Offut's left leg was shorter than his right. Both his left arms were withered, and the left side of his face looked as though it had been poured from wax which was still too hot when the mold was removed. He leered at Mala.

"Food?" Mala asked, trying to keep the desperation out of her voice.

Offut grimaced and turned aside. "There's still some of the Gulper hide, isn't there?" he said apologetically.

"That had been dead weeks before you found it!" Mala shrilled. "That's all we've had to eat for three days, and it's almost gone!"

"Well, tomorrow I'll find something better," her husband promised without confidence. He poured water from the pipe into a slab of rock polished concave by the wind. It was the cave's only furnishing. "Here, drink some water and you'll feel better."

Mala's stomach growled. She muttered a curse, but she knew from long experience that water really was better than nothing. She pulled herself to the rock with the fingers of her four hands. Her legless hindquarters dragged behind her.

"It's not, well, the clearest water I've ever seen," Offut admitted with his face turned away.

The brackish fluid stank, even in the dense fug of the cave.

Mala closed her eyes as she bent to slurp water from the hollow. Otherwise, she might catch sight of her own hideous reflection.

"And then," said Offut, limping around behind her, "we'll fuck before we finish eating the hide."

His misshapen hands gripped her. Mala whined in familiar desperation.

Reality shifted.

There was light but no sun and no movement, and the cold cut Mala like a thousand knives.

The plain might either be endless or straitly bounded, but all she could see was a single stalagmite of ice like those she had glimpsed when Sparrow sent her cabinet briefly to Plane Four.

This time Mala was one of them, and 'this time' was eternity.

She felt tides at her frozen core, but if there was any change in the round of her existence, she was not conscious of it. Pressed against Mala's being was the rigid soul of her brother Morfari. His mouth was twisted in an echo of her own eternal silent scream.

Reality shifted.

Princess Mala's gang yipped in delight. They grounded their skimmers in a circle around their quarry, a desperate male slave.

One of the cattle guards snapped his electronic noose about the escapee's neck from behind. The captive was naked except for smeared mud. His throat bore the calluses of servitude but not the collar itself.

"Hey, how did he cut the collar off?" demanded one of Mala's crew.

The princess shrugged. "How the fuck would I know?" she said. "I figure somebody fucked up welding it on, but it don't much matter. *He's* not gonna tell anybody else how t' do it."

She prodded the captive in the belly with her volley gun. "Is he, now?"

"Lookit that!" cried the Fifth Plane female who acted as adjutant of the cattle guards. "Lilius! Give 'im another jolt!"

The captive was sitting on the ground. "P-p-plea—" he whimpered uselessly.

The guard holding the noose twitched his end, sending surges of electricity through the captive. At each fresh shock, the victim's legs splayed and his penis pumped erect.

A Lomeri female chirped in her own language. She stepped toward the captive and started to crouch.

Mala knocked her reptilian subordinate sideways. "Who died and made *you* queen, Ssadzeril?" she demanded. The princess tugged down the sweat-blackened elastic briefs which were the only garment she wore apart from her harness.

"Nexties!" the Fifth Plane female cried in delight.

The princess stepped forward and squatted over the captive. The knives dangling from her harness jingled as the cattle guards cheered.

Reality shifted.

Princess Mala lay on the floor of her bower. The probability generator was a cold ball of wire hanging from Sparrow's belt, but the reflection of its blue glow colored Mala's memory of possible truths.

"Please . . . ," Mala whispered. Her eyes were open but glazed. "Please. Don't."

"Princess," said the smith, mildly for a man so big and so relentless, "my master Saburo is a gentle man. He loves you as ever a man could love a woman, and he will treat you as a goddess yourself."

Sparrow cleared his throat. He did not raise his voice as he continued, "But lady, *I* am sworn to bring you to my master. I wish you no harm, but there is nothing to which I will not subject you in order to gain your agreement to wed my master."

The menace was not in the statement but rather in the flat certainty with which Sparrow delivered it.

Mala began to sob. Olrun looked from her mistress to Sparrow. The maid's face revealed nothing. Her fingers continued to hold and stroke the dog.

"Lady," said the smith, "Saburo would never put you through tortures and misery to bring you to his palace. But I am not my master, and I will do whatever I need to do."

"Mistress," Olrun said quietly. "Go with him. This one will do whatever he says."

"I will go with you," Mala said, her lips so close to the floor that her breath fogged the cool stone.

Chapter Forty-one

The drop of clear matter oozing from Esme's right eye twinkled as the opening door made the lamps gutter.

There was a brief discussion. Baron Weast turned from the messenger. "Your majesty?" he said. "Lord D'Auber is here. He says that the Mirala forces are marshaling and the battle will surely begin at dawn."

Venkatna made no response. The only sound in the audience hall was the hiss of the lamps and D'Auber's harsh breathing. Rather than send a courier with this warning, D'Auber had run from the palisade marking Frekka's municipal limits.

Weast's face twisted into a caricature of pleasantry. "Lord D'Auber is of course concerned that your majesty be with his armies during the battle. . . ."

No response. It was like talking at a *pair* of corpses. The emperor's chief aides rotated night duty in the audience hall among themselves, but each further exposure to silence and the glittering Web was a closer approach to Hell.

"Or that you depute the command to, ah, one of your companions, your majesty."

He heard low voices out in the corridor, Bontempo and Kleber and the rest—being careful not to enter the presence unless they were summoned.

The presences. Weast wondered how the guards stood it. Perhaps their battlesuits protected them from the miasma that permeated the audience hall. More than death and madness; but certainly *including* death and madness.

Emperor Venkatna roused suddenly. His eyes had been open, but he blinked to clear them. Venkatna's cheeks were hollow and his eyesockets looked bruised. "No," he said wearily. "I'll—"

He shook himself and stood up, kicking aside the rug that lumped at his feet.

"But perhaps we won't have to fight," Venkatna resumed. He

729

spoke in the strong, determined voice of past years. That was the part that Weast found most disconcerting: the real man, the king and emperor, was still present—the way a skeleton lurks within a liquescent corpse.

The emperor walked over to the Web. Instead of boots, he wore felt slippers, like those a warrior dons before getting into his armor. "You there!" Venkatna called. "Slaves! Rouse and listen to me!"

An underchamberlain sat on the stone floor beside the Web, cradling his head in his hands. "Race and Julia," the man muttered in a sing-song. "They have names. Julia and Race."

Nobody paid any attention to him. The guards and councilors rotated night duty in the audience hall. This underchamberlain, Brett, had somehow gotten a permanent assignment, and by now he was quite mad.

Despite that, Brett's plight was less horrific than that of the slaves within the Web.

"Your orders are our fate . . . ," Race whispered from her bench as light faded from the device she used and which used her up. She had been a tall, muscular woman. Now she looked like something found in an unsealed sarcophagus. Her joints stood out from spindly limbs, and for some moments she was unable to lift herself upright.

Servants with milk and sponges scuttled to the women's sides. Brett watched the activities apathetically. Julia did not speak or rise. The violent shudders which shook her emaciated frame indicated that she too had returned from her trance within the probability generator.

Weast could not keep from glancing toward Empress Esme's bier. He trembled and locked his attention back on Venkatna.

The Empire had remained in perfect internal peace since the two slaves were put to work in the Web. The processes of corporeal decay, however, were more difficult to chain than those which afflicted political entities.

"This will be simpler than fighting them," Venkatna said confidingly—to Esme. "I won't need to leave you after all, my dearest."

Venkatna's expression hardened as he returned his attention to Race and Julia. "You two," he said crisply. "I want you to pacify the Mirala confederates. They're right outside the city. Make them all surrender."

"We can't do that, your majesty," Julia said. She managed to wipe her mouth. A palace servant, his fear overcome by pity, reached through the series of looped crystals. He held the woman upright while another servant fed her spoonfuls of thick gruel.

"You must do it!" Venkatna shouted. "I order you to do it!"

"M-m-mirala isn't part of your domains, majesty," Race whispered. Her tongue slurred through a mouthful of warm milk. She seemed unaware that droplets spattered as she spoke. "We cannot affect that which is beyond your rule."

"What use are you, then?" the emperor screamed. He spun on his heel. "Go on back to your work. I'll take care of these scum another way. Somebody bring my armor, but—"

A look of forceful cunning claimed his pallid face.

"But I won't leave here, ah, just now," he continued. "I'll stay with, with, *here,* until later. Weast, you take care of the army."

"*Him?*" blurted D'Auber, the first words the warrior had uttered since his whispered conversation with Weast at the door to the hall.

"Please, your majesty," Julia said. Her eyes were closed. Servants held a bison robe around her, but its thickness could not prevent the tremors shaking her wasted body. "We will do your work, but give us a little peace, just an hour . . . ?"

The clerestory windows of the dome brightened with a hint of dawn, though they did not yet illuminate the hall below.

"We are your slaves," Race echoed, "but give us peace. . . ."

"You'll have no peace, none!" shouted the emperor. "You let my darling *die,* you bitches!"

"Your majesty, you didn't tell—" Julia said. Her voice was too weak and toneless to be called a protest.

"No peace!" Venkatna cried. "Get back to your work, I order you! No peace!"

The slave women sighed together. The sound was like that of the last breath oozing from a dead ox.

Servants scrambled to get out of the hemisphere of the Web. Race and Julia lay back down on their filthy benches.

And there, in accordance with the orders of Emperor Venkatna the First, the two Searchers began to grind out No Peace.

Chapter Forty-two

"Ambush battalion, fall in!" Hansen ordered on the general frequency as the eastern sky hinted the first pale warning of dawn. As far north as Frekka, the sun made a long production of rising.

'Ambush Battalion' was boast and a chance of confusing the enemy, in the unlikely event that Venkatna's forces monitored enemy transmissions. Mostly it was a boast, a proud name with which to encourage Hansen's own four underlings.

They needed encouragement. They sure needed something.

Blood had a good battlesuit, about second class, decorated with large red drops on a silver field. It wasn't quite true that a warrior was only as good as his armor; but the armor was important and in this case there was a good match between the man and his hardware.

Blood was better equipped than nineteen out of twenty men he would meet on the field of battle. After sparring with him repeatedly in the past several weeks, Hansen knew Wenceslas' bodyguard was a man he would be happy to have backing him in any fight.

The other three were named al-Hauk, Empey, and Brownow. They were warriors by virtue of the fact they wore battlesuits. Hansen wouldn't trust the armor any of the three wore against a shower of crossbow bolts, much less the cutting arc which sprang from the gauntlet of another battlesuit.

The men were what he'd expected the king would give him; and for present purposes, they would do.

"Suit," Hansen said, switching on his AI, "battalion push."

Using encrypted transmission that could be heard only by the other members of the Ambush Battalion, he continued, "Boys, what we're going to do is win the battle if it can be won. It's absolutely necessary that you follow me and that you keep your intervals. I'll lead, Blood brings up the rear. Ten meters between each man and the next."

Hansen looked over the four faceless battlesuits that were his force. Empey's must have been made by an apprentice smith who never rose to journeyman status. Brownow and al-Hauk wore armor compiled from bits hacked off various suits in battle. The parts fit poorly together. Even when the welds were done expertly—most of these were not—there would be a noticeable degradation of performance compared to that of a battlesuit whose parts retained their integrity.

"Now, I realize you don't understand what all's happening," Hansen continued grimly. "But you can understand this: if any of you hangs back or runs away, I'll kill him. No matter what I'm doing at the time, I'll manage to kill him. Understood?"

"Less'n I get there first," Blood boomed, using his external speaker instead of the spread-transmission radio. "Then *I'll* kill ye."

The Confederate army marshaled around them with shouts and clashing. Warriors tested their arcs. The weapons picked threads of static from the radios despite the work of suit AIs to synthesize perfect reception.

"One more thing," Hansen said slowly. He hadn't meant to go on, but the words came out nonetheless. "I don't know that it matters to you—I don't know that it *ought* to matter. But if you follow me, boys, I'll make you heroes. They'll sing about us around banquet tables for generations to come."

He smiled. The other warriors couldn't see his expression, and they probably wouldn't have been encouraged if they *could* see.

Hansen's battlesuit was gold and of royal quality. The suit was as good as any armor in either army, and it was an article of Hansen's faith that he was better than any other man of war. He couldn't fight a whole army himself, or even two first-class men, not and hope to win; but Nils Hansen would do what he could, as he had always done. . . .

"Let's go, troops," Hansen said. "Let's kick some ass."

He led his four men out of the camp in a wide sweep to the left, moving at a fast walk. The pace would be bruising to his subordinates, since there was considerable lag time before their suit servos responded to the movements of the users' legs and bodies.

That wasn't the worst punishment the poor bastards were going to get this day.

Forty pony-mounted freemen conformed to the warriors' movements as Wenceslas had ordered them to do. It was crucial that Venkatna be forced to send armored warriors to develop the threat to his flank. The crossbows and lances of these Mirala freemen would keep imperial scouts at a distance.

On the map overlaid across Hansen's electronic visor, Venkatna's army was a mass of red specks falling into line at the edge of the built-up area. There were many hundreds of them, though still fewer than the amorphous blue mass of the Confederates rousing themselves for battle. Numbers weren't the whole story. The sharp-edged imperial divisions would punch through the Mirala army like an awl through leather.

Hansen headed out of the camp along a swale so slight as to go unnoticed by a strolling pedestrian. A slope of two meters in a thousand would hide a suited warrior from sight; that was all that Hansen needed. There were no trees within fifty klicks of Frekka, not with the population increase the capital had seen and the slow growth of vegetation in these latitudes.

"Suit," Hansen ordered as he moved. "Project a battalion IFF by ten times. Scatter the unit distribution according to friendly forces, plus ten—plus *twenty* percent in quality."

He couldn't pretend to be a force of a hundred warriors: the suits' Identification, Friend or Foe, circuits couldn't achieve the necessary separation to make more than a plus-ten magnification believable. Hansen was doing the next best thing by pretending to be a picked unit: fifty men wearing battlesuits of unusually high average quality, but of *believable* quality nonetheless.

The battalion's outriders reached the squatter dwellings on the outskirts of the Mirala encampment. Whores, gamblers, thieving traders—trading thieves; but of the low-level sort who preyed on the servants. They were debarred from entering the camp proper, as did the better sort of grifter who dealt with the nobles.

Hansen's freemen yipped and charged, knocking down leather tilts and swinging lance butts and sword flats at whoever got in the way.

The technique wasn't as mindlessly brutal as it looked. The mounted men cleared a path for the warriors; and most warriors would use their arcs as quickly on a slave as they would a clump of brambles that got in their way.

"Hey, Hansen," Blood called. "Boss."

"Go ahead," Hansen said. He had to watch the deployment of imperial forces, but the map overlay was a serious distraction. Not because he couldn't see his footing through a 30% mask. Rather, it was because the perfect discipline of Venkatna's troops drew Hansen's eyes the way he had once seen a victim staring at his blown-off foot.

"We gonna get any fighting ourself?"

"You bet your ass." Literally.

"That's good," Blood said.

And meant it, the damned fool . . . except he *wasn't* a fool. Blood was a warrior, and this was what he did.

Hansen barked out a laugh that the compressed transmission made even harsher than it sounded in his own ears. This was what Nils Hansen did too; and he did it very well.

"Hey, boss?" Blood again. The other three didn't have the breath to talk at the present pace, and chances were that they didn't have the stomach for it either.

"Go ahead."

"That girl of yours. The blond bint? I haven't seen her in camp."

Lucille.

Nils Hansen had been a fighting man in two cultures over a lot of time. Men whose business is death don't have a lot of delicacy about the various life-affirming activities in which they indulge.

"She's got kin in Peace Rock," Hansen said. "I sent her back there to them. She's a good lady. I don't need a piece so bad I want her t' get hurt."

"You sent her into the *Empire*?" gasped one of the other three; Brownow, Hansen thought it was.

"If we take Venkatna out," Hansen said, "then there's no problem. If we don't, the bastard's going to kill everything in Mirala down to the mice."

Blood chuckled. "My old mom's back t' the farm, not ten klicks from the valley mouth. Guess we better win this one for her, huh?"

Hansen's breath quickened. "Keep moving," he said. He hoped he sounded calm. "There's an imperial section changing front. I think we're going to have company soon."

They passed a trio of small houses with separate stables, built around a spring-fed pond. Perhaps the rural retreat of some court officials; as probably, one of Venkatna's marcher dukes lived in this isolated setting during his infrequent visits to the capital. The buildings were empty now.

Empey switched on his arc. The sudden power drain made the warrior stumble. He slashed his weapon across the shingled front of the nearest house anyway. Before Hansen could object, Blood got the stables of that house and extended his arc an impressive four meters to torch the next dwelling as well.

"*Hold* your fucking formation!" Hansen snarled. "Move!" He increased the pace by a half beat as punishment.

His bloodstream was already roiling with hormones. The surge he got from the vandalism made him almost sick. Nils Hansen, *Commissioner* Hansen, had spent his former life putting down— literally—the forces of destruction. He hadn't been choosy about his methods, preferring something fast even if it made a lot of noise to letting a situation drag on; but his long-term purpose was always to lessen destruction and stress on the society he was paid to protect.

Now he was leading a gang whose first thought when they passed a wooden house was that they could make it burn like a box of matches.

"Hey, boss?"

Blood. "Go ahead."

"If we're s'posed to look like an army all by ourse'f, then we gotta do what an army does, right?"

Blood was either smarter than Hansen had thought . . . or he was psychic. "Right," said Hansen. "There's a stock barn or some damn thing up ahead. The walls're stone, but there'll be fodder and the roof'll burn."

Some of the Ambush Battalion's outriders were engaged with imperial freemen half a kilometer to the right. A number of the riders nearer Hansen's warriors spurred their ponies to join the fight, though others hung back.

Nobles tended to ignore the mounted scouts. It was a wonder that the freemen had the amount of discipline and élan which they regularly displayed.

The main armies were moving. Hansen needed more than dots on a topographic display.

"Suit," he said. "Upper right quadrant. Remote me the view from K—"

He'd started to request that his suit echo the images from King Wenceslas' visor.

"The view from Lord Guest," Hansen finished instead.

Better see what a real professional was looking at. Captain North was that, the good lord knew.

The stockyard was on the outskirts of Frekka proper. Immediately beyond it were the new barracks whose construction Hansen had watched from a loggia of the imperial palace.

"Suit," he ordered, "*cut!*"

He slashed his arc, drawn thin as a king's honor, across the roof trusses projecting from the loft eight meters above. Masonry cracked under the tongue of high voltage. The building's roof of ancient thatch burped flame.

I am the best!

The viewpoint in the upper right quarter of Hansen's visor advanced by long, powerful strides. North was leading his Simplain contingent toward the imperial flank exposed when a section marched off to meet Hansen.

The Confederate army was ill-organized, but it was composed of *fighting* men. At the present juncture, the Mirala warriors' instinct was precisely correct. The whole mass swept forward to support North's calculated attack.

North was the point of the wedge into which he had formed his mercenaries. The front rank of Venkatna's troops had extended to the right to cover the detached section. The imperial warriors were featureless within their battlesuits, but their line bunched and gapped nervously.

It momentarily occurred to Hansen that his plan, his *feint*, might just succeed as a real thrust. What would the imperial forces do if the palace exploded into flame behind them? Were they disciplined enough to hold their impeccable formation and win the real battle before worrying about events among the civilian installations in their rear?

Probably; and anyhow, the question was moot. An imperial section fifty warriors strong was bearing down on Hansen's poor handful like the Wrath of God.

Chapter Forty-three

The railgun's collapsed uranium slug was invisible, but behind it followed a track of fluorescing plasma: the driving skirt, stripped of electrons and heated sun-heart white by the jolt of electricity which powered the bolt.

The streak ended a centimeter from Hansen's smiling face. There was an almost-visible blotch at the point the hypervelocity shot vanished, the hint of a fracture in reality. The shimmer was no larger than a hole that would permit a man Nils Hansen's size to thrust his hand through to the wrist—

But that gap in normal spacetime was more than large enough to engulf the railgun slug. The projectile snapped across the Matrix with its velocity and momentum unimpaired.

A fluting, birdlike cry burbled up the ten-meter throat of a distant sauropod. The call rang through the forest. The carnivorous mounts of the Lomeri turned their heads toward the sound like six questing gun turrets. Lizardmen spurred the beasts' off-side flanks and tugged fiercely at their reins.

After brief struggles, the ceratosaurs settled down again. Under other circumstances the carnivores might have been more difficult to control. Now, poised on the edge of the Open Lands, they knew they would soon have ample opportunity to kill and feed.

The Lomeri captain chirped a sharp order to his subordinates. One at a time the lizardmen racked back the bolts of their weapons to load them; switched on, then off again, the force screens which would protect them against both arcs and projectile weapons in the event that the victims mounted a defense; and held up the bundle of self-looping nooses that each slaver was to bring.

The nooses were metal fiber and extended ten meters when thrown. They goaded their victims with low-amperage shocks and attached the fresh-caught slaves securely to the lizardmen's saddles.

The Lomeri carried twenty nooses apiece, but a ceratosaur dragging such an entourage was likely to turn and rend half the slaves before the rider could whip the beast off.

Smoke drifted from the eave openings of the houses in Peace Rock. It was midmorning across the shifting discontinuity. Folk sat on the benches in front of their dwellings and enjoyed the winter sunshine while they knitted or worked on harness.

A woman with brown-blond hair wove on a hand loom in front of the lord's thatched hall. She was working the figure of a warrior in gold armor onto a white field.

The humans were not consciously aware of the disaster being prepared for them across the Matrix, but occasionally a child or an old woman stared at the sky and frowned. Hobbled mammoths blatted nervously to one another as they foraged among the stubble in the fields.

The Lomeri captain gave another order. His team jockeyed their mounts into line facing the discontinuity. Even at this juncture, the lizardmen snapped and kicked at one another with clawed, narrow feet over questions of precedence and perceived insult.

When the captain was satisfied, he took his place at the head of the line. He gave the final command and spurred his mount forward.

The railgun slug, moving at a substantial fraction of the speed of light, entered and exited Plane Two a millisecond later. The bodies of the six Lomeri, decapitated in a fluorescent streak, pitched out of their saddles.

The ceratosaurs, maddened by the spray of blood, began to fight as they devoured their late riders.

On a plain that stretched without curvature or horizon, cones of wrinkled ice crept with sidereal sluggishness. Light bathed them from a point source that was not a sun. It penetrated the crawling figures and drove the utter cold still deeper.

A streak of excited plasma appeared and vanished across the waste in front of the hill that was the only terrain feature for as far as an eye could see.

The hill suggested a human face: a man with prominent cheekbones and a mouth as ruthless as a bullet from his gun.

If one spent long enough staring at the stalagmites which crawled across the plain on their damned rounds, one might imagine that many bore the distorted visages of those whom Nils Hansen had slain.

A lichen stared up at the red, swollen sun which could no longer bring it comfort. The corniche cracked away, sliver by sliver. There was no other movement in the airless void overlooking what had been a beach.

The lichen had endured, starving more slowly than the rock eroded around it. In the ordinary course of existence, the lichen would continue to endure for countless eons; helpless in the grip of entropy and a pain no less real for being visited on a lifeform little more complex than a bacterium.

A streak, especially vivid for occurring in a void where no gases diffused its light, flashed across the landscape. Rock smashed to vapor at the touch of the hypervelocity slug. A patch of corniche vanished in the cleansing flare.

The glow faded, leaving the scene much as it had been before. The sun's dull red eye remained—

But the lichen had found peace at last.

Saburo knelt on the roof courtyard of his palace, facing a table. On the table's surface were sand ridges and three irregular bits of tuff—ash blown from the vent of a volcano to harden in the air. The eyes of the slim god were open, but his expression was blank. His mind was fading to gray void.

Above the crag-top palace, clouds boiled in a storm lighted opalescent by internal lightning strokes. The rain lashed down to within meters of the courtyard, then sluiced sideways against an invisible barrier. Droplets from the heavens mingled with spray kicked up against the rocks; fresh water with salt, neither penetrating the limpid perfection of Saburo's mind.

If he could clear his mind completely, then he would be above existence—even the existence of a god. He would be worthy of the Princess Mala. When he had made himself worthy, then Mala would come. When—

A lambent streak ripped across a short distance of the courtyard. The sand table shattered.

Saburo shouted and hurled himself backward. Servants poked their heads up the staircase, then ran to help their master.

Saburo stroked his tingling face in wonder. His fingers felt gritty and glittered when he stared at them.

His cheeks were covered with microbeads, like the tektites formed by a meteor strike. The uranium slug on its track through Plane Seven had friction-heated the sand on the table to glass.

Fortin stood in the hall of his ice palace. His upper lip quivered with ecstasy. He stared through the milk-streaked discontinuity toward the lowering splendor of Keep Starnes.

Fortin could not see what was happening within the keep, but he could guess. Hansen had gone straight ahead in his pride, in arrogant *certainty* that he was better than all the forces Count Starnes could range against him.

That he was better than Fortin . . . though Fortin knew a truth that Nils Hansen would die rather than learn. Fortin was as low as the algal slime on stagnant pools—but for all that, Fortin was as good as any *man*, human or android or self-loathing halfling like himself. . . .

Because of Hansen's pride, Hansen would die. Was dying *now*.

Fortin quivered before the dark mirror of the discontinuity. If he dared, he could watch the event rather than the exterior of the city/building in which the event occurred. He could see the vain struggles, the blood; the *screams*, perhaps, as the victim learned there was truly no escape.

To become a spectator meant becoming a victim as well. Fortin understood perfectly how Count Starnes' mind worked, and how little mercy Starnes would show if Fortin returned to the keep. But it would almost be worth that to watch Nils Hansen humiliated in the final degree.

The handsome half android paced by habit around the facets of the discontinuity, but his mind was caught in the vision of what he could not see. *The pain, the terror.* . . .

Fortin's servants stood in plain sight at the arched entrances to the central court. They were afraid to be accused of hiding if their master needed them, but they desperately avoided looking at the court. When Fortin was in this mood, he was less predictable and far more dangerous than a wounded sabertooth.

"What are you doing now, Commissioner?" Fortin whispered as he stared toward the facet showing Keep Starnes. His voice was thick with gloating and self-disgust.

The discontinuity shattered. Eight simultaneously co-existing images of the same uranium slug ruptured its fabric from within. The mirror through which Fortin viewed life vanished with the slap of air rushing to fill hard vacuum.

Eight glowing tracks hung in the courtyard for a moment before they dissipated.

Fortin stared at empty air.

And began to scream.

The Citadel of Keep Starnes rocked with the whiplash *crack!* of the railgun.

The track that vanished a finger's breadth from Hansen's face reappeared a meter to the rear of Count Starnes' vehicle. The projectile retained the same heading and virtually the same velocity as when it left the muzzle of the count's gun. The only difference was that it now was behind him.

The slug hit the tank with the sound of a hammer on an anvil, magnified to cataclysm by the velocity and densities involved.

The vehicle lurched forward despite its mass. The frontal slope bulged. A white glow marked where it took the slug's impact on its inner face. The side and roof armor, relatively thin, ballooned outward.

Everything in the projectile's path inside the tank had been converted to gas at a propagation rate faster than that of high explosive.

The hatch through which Count Starnes had entered his vehicle flew back across the rotunda. The slug's entry hole was a neat punch-mark in the center of the panel. Orange flame, then a perfect ring of black smoke, spouted from the opening.

All the tank's systems were destroyed. The vehicle's carcase crashed to the concrete in a dim echo of the impact which had gutted it. Anything flammable within the tank began to burn.

Hansen grinned. He held Plaid's pistol in his right hand. "Your turn, Karring," he called in a clear, terrible voice as he sauntered toward the Fleet Battle Director.

Chapter Forty-four

Olrun focused her gaze on a corner of the white wall beyond Sparrow. She asked coolly, "How will you take us to your master's home?"

At the word 'us,' Sparrow quirked a taut grin at the kneeling maid. "The way I came," he said. "A place where the worlds rub together, yours and Saburo's; a discontinuity."

He looked down at Mala. The princess lay limp as a sea creature brought from such depths that its cells burst from internal pressure. "You'll ride with me on the skimmer, princess," he said gently. "There may be some mud and discomfort. But as soon as you reach my master, he will dress you in gold and diamonds—or in flowers, if that's what you wish."

Mala groaned. "I *wish*," she murmured, "to stay here and live the life I choose to live."

"When we get back, Mistress Olrun," Sparrow said, as if apropos nothing, "I'll remove your slave collar."

Olrun released Sparrow's dog and stood up. The bitch ran to her master, yapping excitedly. She calmed almost at once when she had sniffed the backs of his knees.

Sparrow reached down to scratch her ears, but the dog had already trotted off to resume the course of exploration interrupted by the events in the bower's central room.

As she passed the theatrically-sprawled princess, the dog snuffled Mala's outflung hand. Mala shrieked in despair and flailed blindly. The dog woofed and left the room, her claws clicking.

Sparrow's face was without emotion. Once he too had hidden himself from the world . . . but the world had found him. As if idly, the smith's fingers touched the top of the leg brace he had made with such cunning that he could walk almost as well as a man with uncut hamstrings.

He hadn't made the world; he only acted a part in it. If

745

sometimes he regretted that part, well, there were many things he regretted in life.

Mala got up from the floor. She had no taste for playing a role in a farce.

"What sort of transportation do you have here?" Sparrow asked Olrun.

The maid grimaced. "None," she said. "We never go out. Sometimes Prince Morfari comes by, or the king. . . ."

She let her voice trail off, glancing with concern at her mistress. Mala did not appear to have heard the accidental reference to her brother.

Or perhaps she had. "I want time to see my fam—my father," the princess said with her face averted. Her right index finger stroked the perfect, pumpkinseed nails of her left hand. They were painted a green identical to her innermost garment in hue and metallic luster.

"No, lady," the smith said quietly. "You will come with me to Saburo. My master may allow your kin to attend the wedding—I don't know. When I've delivered you to Saburo, he will choose how you are to be kept. Until then . . ."

Mala covered her face with her hands.

"Why?" asked the maid unexpectedly. "Why don't you let her see Nainfari? You'd bring her back again, wouldn't you, whether he let or no?"

Olrun's face was expressionless, but her eyes reflected the vibrant animation Sparrow heard in her voice. He didn't answer for a moment. The dog returned to the central room, brushed by the maid in friendly fashion, and tapped over to her master to be stroked.

"I would find her if she hid," the smith said carefully. He watched Mala from the corner of his eye.

"I would bring her though she resisted," he continued. His voice was taking on the harsh sense of purpose that Sparrow could not avoid when his mind turned toward contingencies and the ruthless certainty with which he would deal, had always dealt, with obstacles.

"If others tried to stop me—"

His hand played, perhaps unknowingly, on the ivory pommel of the dagger he had taken from a waste of muck and blood.

"—then I would take her anyway. But not even the gods, milady, can bring the dead to life. And that . . ."

He looked squarely, appraisingly, at the princess.

". . . is why I do not choose to leave your mistress to her own devices. Until I've accomplished the task my master set me."

"Your *duty*," Mala sneered. "A slave's duty!"

"My task, lady," Sparrow said. He smiled, a slowly-mounted expression which finally enveloped his whole bearded face. "A man's task."

Mala turned abruptly away.

The dog whined softly. Sparrow reached down and rubbed the animal's ears.

"We'd best go, now," he said in a detached voice. "I have no wish to harm your kin."

"What should I pack?" asked Olrun. She forced a bright smile to meet Sparrow's eyes, but the smith knew the maid was still afraid that he was going to leave her behind.

His smile and face softened. "All will be provided. There's nothing you'll need, Olrun, you or your mistress either. And besides, the skimmer that we have for transport won't carry but two as it is."

Sparrow gestured abruptly with his chin. "Come," he said. "We need to be going."

Mala said nothing. She remained stiff as a statue, facing the empty wall. Olrun looked from her to the smith.

"Shall I take your arm, lady?" Sparrow asked in a voice as soft as the creak of a catapult being twisted to lock.

The princess turned like a marionette and walked toward the dome's entrance. She took short, precisely-measured steps.

"She will find that Saburo shares a heart and soul with her," the smith said conversationally to Olrun as the two of them followed the princess. "She'll actually be happier than she is now—"

Mala, moving like an automaton, touched the door switch. The panel began to swing down from its housing.

"—but I don't expect anyone to like being coerced," Sparrow continued. "Any more than I did, in my time."

Warm, fetid swamp air oozed through the open doorway. Mala shuddered uncontrollably. She tried to force herself to step into the muddy courtyard. Her dainty foot hung, quivering above the surface.

"I'll fetch the skimmer, lady," Sparrow said with a certain degree of pity. "You and I will ride."

The princess edged aside so that Sparrow could get past her without contact. The dog brushed between the man and android, barking joyfully to be outside again.

"When we reach my master's palace," Sparrow continued over his shoulder, "you'll have luxury that you've never dreamed of."

"I am a king's daughter!" Mala said.

"Ah, but there'll be flowers," said Sparrow from the courtyard gate. "You'll like them."

He got onto the skimmer and lifted it from where it had settled. Mud curled and spattered from the repulsion surfaces. When the vehicle had cleaned itself, Sparrow guided it through the gateposts and up to the dome where the princess waited.

"Milady," he said, grounding the vehicle again.

Mala broke from the doorway. She ran around Sparrow, headed toward the gate. The dog barked and gamboled alongside her.

"Lady!" Sparrow cried. He blipped the twistgrip, lifting the skimmer again. It would be hard to chase the girl down on the vehicle without injuring her, but she was too fleet for him to catch on foot. . . .

"Sparrow!" Olrun screamed. "Get out of the courtyard! She's going to clear the defense controller!"

Mala snatched open the access plate in the back of the left gatepost. Within were banks of touch-sensitive switches and two large red handles.

The upper handle disconnected all the weaponry which defended the courtyard. The second handle, intended for use after the first one had been pulled, cleared the defensive unit's memory completely.

Mala looked at Sparrow. Her face was a skull mask. She reached for the lower switch, knowing that the blast would vaporize her even if Sparrow and the maid managed to fling themselves back into the enforced exile of the dome.

Sparrow's hands were on the ends of his probability generator. It pivoted between his index fingers, glowing indigo and violet.

Mala touched the switch.

A slug of collapsed uranium, moving at the speed of a meteorite, ripped across the courtyard. The gatepost disintegrated with an electrical crash that echoed the thunderclap of the railgun bolt's own passage.

The blast hurled Princess Mala onto her back in the mud. The wall's tough plastic drank the energy from multiple shorts within the weapon-control circuits and melted in on itself.

The black wall lost the threatening glimmer which bespoke weapons live and prepared to rend intruders. The dog was angry and frightened. She barked and feinted attacks in the direction of the smoking, spluttering gatepost.

Sparrow began to laugh. He grounded the skimmer. Olrun looked at him in a mixture of fear and wonder.

"I think . . . ," he said, ". . . that we'll go in a different fashion for safety."

He put his broad right hand on Olrun's waist and guided her onto the skimmer.

Chapter Forty-five

The corral fences were of strong posts on masonry foundations a meter high. They were meant to hold aurochs and, in a pinch, herds of half-tamed mammoths. The barriers weren't proof against men whose battlesuits could shatter rock and sheer through any weight of wood. Even so, the rubble and flaming debris would be some protection for the outnumbered defenders.

Better than nothing.

"Battalion!" Hansen said. He lumbered through a gate left open. Stockmen had driven their herds to yards near the port, safer when the Confederate army arrived. "Hold up here and form close order!"

Five men in close order. Well, you did what you could.

Horsemen bolted past the gate. Hansen's men had been overborne by imperial riders backed by the section of battlesuited warriors. A few scouts carried crossbows that they weren't delaying to reload.

Blood paused at the entrance to the corral. His weapon licked out to its maximum length and touched a lancer wearing a quilted jack. The shock threw the man off his mount. His linen armor was aflame. The arc didn't have the amperage at five meters' range to detonate the victim's own body fluids, but he was certainly dead for his presumption in coming too close to a warrior.

Hansen wasn't absolutely sure that the rider was one of Venkatna's troops. *What the hell, he wouldn't be the last man to die this day.*

"Ever'body take it easy," Blood said calmly. "The boss, he's the left end and I'm the right. You other three, you just stay in the middle 'n back us the best ye can."

"How many of 'em are there?" gasped al-Hauk. Jogging in a poor-quality battlesuit left the user feeling like he'd run the gauntlet. Hansen knew that very well.

"Don't ye worry about it," Blood said. "When they see the whole army eat up behind them they'll run like lizard slavers're on their tails."

Did Blood believe that? Did he even care?

The images echoed from North's battlesuit were a-dance with the light of arc weapons. Three imperial warriors braced themselves to stop 'the Simplain prince.'

Hansen had never measured himself against North in a battlesuit. Captain North had seen his share of hard places before he came to this world and to godhead. His battlesuit was the template from which smiths forged other armor in the Matrix, and North was an artist in its use.

The center man of the imperial trio thrust. North stopped dead. Instead of crossing his arc with the threatening one, he slashed left-handed at a sideman and cut off the fellow's feet at the ankles.

The leading imperial glanced reflexively toward the toppling victim. *Then* North thrust home, striking at the junction of helmet and plastron. The remaining sideman bellowed in rage and stepped into the sparks streaming in ropes from his leader's short-circuited armor. North's backhand cut was almost contemptuous in the way it ripped the third victim's arm off at the shoulder.

Three men were dead in dazzle and fury, and North was through Venkatna's front line. The defensive screen of his battlesuit had not been required to block a single hostile arc.

"They're coming by the gate," Brownow noted in a high-pitched voice.

He must be using an order-of-battle display like the 30% mask across Hansen's own field of view. That was more initiative than Hansen would have expected from somebody wearing a piece of junk like Brownow's suit. If he survived this fight, Hansen would see to it that Brownow went into the next one better equipped; but there wasn't a chance in hell of that happening so fuck it. . . .

"They're coming *to* the gate," Hansen said aloud. "Back me, boys, I'm going to handle this one myself."

Imperial warriors had swept around the corral in both directions. Nobody'd cut a path through the fence; a facet of

Hansen's mind realized that they must still think there were fifty hostiles within the 500-meter stone and timber circuit.

The gate was wide enough to pass two bull aurochs side by side, but the beasts would be rubbing against one another. The four armored warriors who burst through together were cramped as well, to a slight but fatal degree.

Hansen stepped forward. He thrust high at the cerulean-armored man on the left of the line. The fellow wore a royal suit, and his nearest companion was nearly as well equipped.

Cerulean blocked Hansen's arc expertly. His companion's nervous slash flicked Cerulean's helmet in a hasty attempt to strike Hansen. Cerulean's armor failed under the double load. His voice screamed through a last blast of static on his external speaker.

Hansen used the upright dead man as a shield to block the imperial warriors pressing from behind. He stabbed Cerulean's companion in the groin, toppling him against the men bound by the right gatepost. Hansen's arc extended across their plastrons.

The armor of the last pair was of only moderate quality. It failed with two quick *cracks* and a gout of orange sparks.

Hansen stepped back. High-density arcs had burned air to ozone. His lungs throbbed as though he had been breathing vitriol. His gauntlets were hot, both of them. He hadn't been conscious that he was striking the last pair with his left hand until after they died. *Something unplanned, something instinct had suggested and reflex had put to lethal effect.* . . .

"Mine," said Blood. He lunged forward to meet an imperial warrior trying to clear the sudden windrow of bodies with a desperate leap.

Hansen swung to back his man, but Blood didn't need the help. His arc crossed the imperial's while the latter had both feet in the air. The power draining to the arc weapon froze the imperial's knee joints. He crashed down on his face with his limbs splayed.

Blood hacked off his head. The three other members of the Ambush Battalion ripped the legs and belly armor. The victim didn't need it, but perhaps Hansen's men did.

"They're breaking through the sides of the corral," wheezed Brownow.

"Right," said Hansen with the exalted calm he always got at the killing times, *as he ought to know by now.*

Venkatna's men bunched outside the open gateway. Cerulean had probably been the section leader. Dust swirled over the scene like a stripper's last veil, drawing attention to the bloody tangle that it did not conceal. "Not yet, when I tell you to move."

The Order of Battle display showed a blue wedge cutting into a red block, and a smaller red block shifting from the reserve to meet the point of the wedge. On the visuals relayed from Captain North's suit, twenty imperial troops double-timed to stop the Simplain charge—

And Krita was one of the imperials.

Arcs sawed into the corral fence at a dozen locations around the circumference. Blue-white electrical flux flickered viciously through the orange flames springing from the wood. Where imperial weapons touched the masonry, rock shattered and the yellow-white glare of superheated lime dimmed the rising sun.

An imperial stepped toward the gate. Hansen spread the thumb and forefinger of his right hand. His arc leaped out between the gateposts and kissed the imperial's frontal armor.

Defensive screens flared but withstood the arc. The imperial staggered; his fellows wavered back with him.

"Now!" Hansen shouted as he wheeled toward the most serious of the assaults on the corral fence.

A three-meter section of wall collapsed in a heap of blazing timbers. The imperials had severed tie-beams at the top of the fence as well as carving through the uprights. Some of the poles fell into the corral. The shattered foundations were a sea of white fire.

Hansen had thirty meters to run. He reached the gap in the fence as the first two imperial warriors struggled out of the flames. They swept their arcs widely in order to drive back opponents for the instant they were blinded by the inferno of their own creation.

Hansen thrust like a surgeon lancing a boil. His arc ripped the inside knee of the left man of the pair. The second warrior stumbled over the toppling body of his companion. Hansen stabbed through his backplate, where the neck joined the shoulders.

Another warrior bulled through. His arc met Hansen's, held for a moment. Two more imperials crashed into him from behind. Hansen and Blood—*only a stride behind, but so much heat and glare and fresh, stinking death*—cut the trio apart before they could disentangle.

The wood fire roared, supercharged by misdirected arcs.

"They're behind us!" Brownow said/screamed.

Hansen drew a deep breath. His arms to the shoulders felt as though they were being squeezed in red-hot iron. He turned.

Venkatna's warriors had rushed the gate after Hansen's force withdrew. Other imperials straggled through gaps they'd blasted in the fence at points the defenders couldn't reach.

Empey, Brownow, and al-Hauk lunged at the nearest of the oncoming enemy. They struck simultaneously, luck aiding desperation. The imperial warrior threw up his arc to block Empey's cut, but al-Hauk's thrust sizzled on the fellow's helmet. The paired arcs drew enough power that when Brownow slashed low an instant later, the imperial's suit failed in a spurt of glass, steel, and pelvis burned to carbon.

Other imperials hit the Confederates from both sides and the front. Brownow's cry of triumph was a one-syllable squawk as all three of Hansen's men died. Hansen took an imperial from behind while the fellow concentrated on Empey, but then he and Blood were back-to-back in a ring of hostile warriors.

The main Mirala onslaught was drowning in its own blood against Venkatna's army.

North's viewpoint danced like a dervish. Each shift was accompanied by a cut from one hand or the other. Many of the cuts went home.

It wasn't enough, just as North's disciplined wedge of mercenaries hadn't been enough—quite—to rip the fabric of the imperial line. His force had melted away under assault from all sides, as soon as the imperial reserves managed to slow the initial impetus.

The Mirala Confederates had started the battle with superior numbers, but their opponents fought as three-man units instead of being a mob of individuals. Trebled strokes would overload any battlesuit, even the best. Trying to overwhelm with mere numbers a force so disciplined was like trying to quench a fire with naphtha.

Captain North was almost alone, but his opponents gave him a wide berth. One of the suits at North's feet had a blue plastron and silver limbs. The helmet lay a meter away, burned black by the arc that had severed it.

Lord Salles had met his match at last.

"Try *that* again, fuckhead!" Blood shouted as he thrust at an imperial who'd made a distant pass at him. The man lurched back to the safety of his companions; but it wouldn't be long now.

"Hey, boss?" Blood gasped.

They were both breathing through their mouths, gasping in deep lungfuls that still weren't enough to fuel the needs of battle. The mucous lining of Hansen's nose and throat had been eroded by the trickle of ozone which leaked through his battlesuit's filters.

"Go ahead."

"D'jew see the way Brownow sold that bastid a farm? Suit as good as mine, too! You know, I—"

Two imperials came at Hansen's front while a third poised to the left. Hansen feinted left with his arc a long whip. One of Venkatna's men lunged a half-step ahead of his comrade, just in time to catch the full density of Hansen's weapon switched to the right hand.

Hansen's thrust penetrated the plastron. The latch gave. The whole frontal plate flew open, driven by the victim's exploding chest.

"—didn't think they'd keep *up* with us, let—"

Both the surviving imperials hopped back into the circle.

"—alone fight. But they sure—"

On the remote display, Krita in her black armor stepped forward. Her arc crossed North's. That quadrant of Hansen's visor flared into white static. The roar of the huge outrush of power made the air quiver even in the corral half a kilometer distant.

The Searcher's suit was as good as that of the master she long had served—

North's viewpoint suddenly cleared. Krita fell backward. Her helmet was the gray and black of fiery disaster instead of paint.

Should have been as good.

"—did that bastid up a treat!" Blood concluded as six of Venkatna's men rushed him together and he lunged a pace forward to meet them unexpectedly.

The remote transmission disappeared from Hansen's visor. North had vanished—into the Matrix, and into the legend of the Open Lands. His godlike laughter boomed in Hansen's ears; then it too was gone.

Blood's attack caught the imperials off-balance. They fouled one another. One went down and a second, arcs and overloading defensive screens tearing across the sonic and visual spectra. Hansen's quick pivot and swipe cut an imperial's legs off at the knees.

The man fell forward, covering the corpse of King Wenceslas' bodyguard. The backplate of Blood's garish armor had been blasted by the weapons of at least three opponents. Both his gauntlets glowed from the arcs they had been directing till the moment he died.

If Blood's mother was anything like her son, she'd tear the throat out of the first of Venkatna's men to come to her farm. But they would come. . . .

For a moment, only the crash of the burning fence broke the silence within the corral.

Nils Hansen knew that even gods had to die some day.

And he knew that he wasn't going to run from the battle in which Krita had fallen.

Chapter Forty-six

Deep in the Web, Race and Julia ran the figures of warriors through the icy fingers of their minds. Sorting, choosing; plucking one here, another there.

The terrible weight and chill of the Matrix impinged upon the Searchers, but they no longer felt its crushing burden as they had on their previous journeys into the frozen heart of probability.

Race and Julia were carrying out orders, as they were sworn to do. If the results were not what Venkatna desired, then he should have thought of that before he screamed his orders. This day he would get precisely what he asked for—

To the hilt.

Figures moved in two discrete settings, dwarfed by the vastness of infinity. The Searchers merged portions of one parcel with the shrinking remainder of the other; picking and choosing; using the power of the Web, but working with a subtlety that only the knowledge they had gained as humans made possible.

No peace? Then war would continue.

Warriors disappeared from North's battleplain. Their figures reappeared in the stinking, smoke-shrouded corral outside Frekka, at the side of Nils Hansen.

A warrior in red-and-gold armor, a warrior in horizontal stripes of black and yellow, a warrior in armor burnished to the bare metal, save for the chevrons of a marshal on the sides of his helmet. . . .

There were not so very many of the warriors who joined Hansen: a handful, a score; perhaps as many as a hundred at the end.

A warrior in lime green with a gold phoenix on his breast, a warrior in red and white; a warrior whose battlesuit had a blue torso and limbs of gleaming silver. . . .

757

Not so very many warriors; but they all wore armor of royal quality, and they were all very good men.

A pirate with bronze wings welded to the sides of his helmet, a warrior in orange swirls; a warrior in gleaming silver with no other marking. . . .

Or they had been good men, in the days they lived and walked the Open Lands.

Chapter Forty-seven

Life was good, now that it was about to end, but Nils Hansen stepped forward anyway.

Imperials in front of him retreated, but he heard the rasp of weapons at his back—

And knew that he was dead—

And charged the clot of hostile warriors, watching them shout and stumble over Blood's body. Hansen's arc flicked like a viper's fang and lopped off an imperial's wrist.

He wasn't alone any more. Taddeusz strode at Hansen's right hand in red-and-gold armor.

Whatever you said about Marshal Taddeusz—Hansen had said plenty—no one had ever denied he was a bad man with whom to cross arcs. A pair of imperials were too startled by Taddeusz' sudden appearance to react intelligently.

They see-sawed. One of them backed a step, then lunged forward to support his fellow who had tried for a moment to guard himself but retreated a heartbeat later.

Both imperials wore decent armor, suits in the third- or fourth-class range. There was no armor better than that of the dead warriors on North's battleplain, and few warriors ever with more experience than Taddeusz had of killing in a battlesuit.

The red-and-gold figure stuck alternately, right gauntlet and left; into one opponent's hip joint, through the other's guard and into his throat with fireworks of molten metal.

"Follow me!" boomed Taddeusz' amplified voice, but only because that was the sort of thing leaders were supposed to say. The warrior who had in life been warchief of Peace Rock didn't care if others followed him, so long as he himself was able to stride into the midst of blaze and slaughter.

"I'm closing your left, Lord Hansen!" called a once-familiar voice over the Ambush Battalion push. Hansen cut at an imperial. The man parried Hansen's arc, but the power drain froze the

joints of the fellow's armor and heated the outer skin of his
gauntlet bright red with the current of only a fraction of a second.

Shill, painted like a bumblebee—

Shill, who had closed Hansen's flank until he died, doing his
job—

Shill stepped forward to lop off the imperial's head. He used
the training Hansen had hammered into him, and the splendid
battlesuit his soul wore since Nils Hansen got him killed. . . .

There were a dozen beads of gold light on Hansen's Order
of Battle overlay, covering the sides and back of his own solitary
blue pip. More joined every moment, though he didn't—
couldn't—didn't *dare*—look around to be sure there was hard
metal and ceramic backing the signals on his helmet screen.

"All friendly units!" Hansen ordered. He didn't know what
to call the force now at his disposal. *Men he had killed, men he
had gotten killed . . . and men no more.* "Rush the gate!"

He didn't want his troops to struggle over walls reduced to
blazing rubble, the way the imperials had done. These were
Nils Hansen's men *now*, for whatever reason. He would spend
them if he had to, but he wouldn't throw them away.

Taddeusz was in front of the line, the way the self-willed bastard
always was. For a change the big warrior's lack of discipline
worked better than any plan could have done. His berserk fury
hit the clump of six imperials—half-arrayed, half-retreating—
in front of the gate. Taddeusz shattered them.

Hansen's screen blanked the sparks and purple coruscance
to save his vision. He paused, then lunged forward seconds later
when the glare of arcs and screens faded.

Four of Venkatna's men were down. Two got through the
gateway ahead of Taddeusz' ravening arcs, but the red-and-gold
figure was right behind them. He cleared the gateway that would
have been too strait for even a pair of warriors advancing
deliberately—

And Hansen was behind *him*, with Hansen's two sidemen
following at a half-step's distance.

*He'd never known the name of the warrior on his right. He'd
been bodyguard to one of Frekka's Syndics—a century ago when
Nils Hansen killed him.*

The imperial section didn't know what had hit it. For that

matter, neither did Hansen, but he'd learned long since not to slack off when his opponent stumbled. He crossed arcs right-handed with the nearest of Venkatna's troops. Even as Hansen spread his left gauntlet to stab home from an unexpected direction, Shill took the fellow's knees from under him.

"Suit!" Hansen said. He was gasping, but it didn't seem to slow him down. He was burning adrenaline in place of oxygen, he guessed. "Where the fuck's Venkatna? Gimme a—"

His right sideman engaged an imperial warrior. Hansen spun and slashed by instinct, overloading the enemy's carapace armor with a bang that blew the dead man forward in a cloud of steam and vaporized steel.

"—vector!"

A bead of imperial purple gleamed on Hansen's map overlay, amid the other Order of Battle information. "In his palace," said the suit AI.

It spoke in a sweetly feminine voice that Hansen hadn't heard it synthesize before. A comment on Hansen's lack of courtesy or he missed his bet. Even the machines were getting smart-ass.

"All units," he called. "Toward the palace!"

He doubled Shill's stroke on a warrior in green and blue—needless, the imperial was already toppling, his suit dead and the man too almost certainly. The rhythm was the thing, though, get into the rhythm of slash and lunge and the fighting would take care of itself.

Taddeusz' suit failed with a thunderclap.

There had been at least six of Venkatna's men surrounding Taddeusz. It was possible that every one of them had managed to get an arc home simultaneously. No battlesuit was capable of withstanding such abuse. The shockwave of ceramic components converted to gas lifted dust from the trampled soil.

Nothing remained where Taddeusz had been. No ashes charred from blood and bone, not even an empty battlesuit.

"Let's go!" Hansen shouted as his arc rocked an imperial whom his sidemen lopped to collops.

Taddeusz had done them another favor in his last instants by concentrating the attention of Venkatna's nearby troops on himself. When Hansen and the rest of his line hit the enemy, they went down like barley before a scythe.

There was nothing closer than the main imperial army that could stop Hansen now—

And the main army wasn't going to do the job either. Almost a hundred warriors followed Hansen, spreading out to either flank. Enough when they were as good as they were . . . and as well equipped as they were . . . and when Nils Hansen was leading them toward the spot the enemy was most vulnerable, as he always did.

The straight line toward Venkatna's palace led through a jumble of shanties and cribs which had serviced drovers and troops from the nearby barracks. The Strip had caught fire earlier in the day—earlier in the *morning*, it was still morning, even though a thousand men or more had died since the sun rose.

The flimsy buildings had too little substance to long sustain a fire, but as Hansen's armored boots stirred the ashes, they kicked orange tongues to life.

"Golsingh and Victory!" Shill called, a battlecry dead almost as long as the man who shouted it.

"Frekka and Freedom!" boomed Hansen's other sideman. Top-ranked warriors were by definition competitive. From the way they'd sliced through Venkatna's men, Hansen knew the troops he now led were the best.

From their performance today, and from their performance in the days that Nils Hansen watched them die.

The palace was in sight. Half a dozen imperial warriors braced themselves across its entrance. Their arc weapons licked in and out to maximum distention.

The display was probably meant to be threatening. Instead, it painted Venkatna's men with a look of nervous indecision. That emotion was just what the poor bastards were feeling, if they had the sense God gave a goose.

The buzzsaw shriek of arc weapons sounded to the east. What had been the imperial right flank stumbled down onto the right flank of Hansen's force. Venkatna's men were confused and shaken already by hard fighting, but they were professionals and still three hundred strong.

The imperials in the palace entrance hunched instinctively

lower. They knew that if they held for as little as three minutes, the weight of their fellows could win the battle for Venkatna after all—

And incidentally, save the lives of the remaining guards.

The threat was the imperial main body. If Hansen ignored that mass of troops to crush the entrance guards, the chances were very good that his whole force would be cut down from behind.

He opened his mouth.

"Maharg to Hansen!" crackled a voice on the command channel. "Take what you need, buddy, and let me handle the rear guard. Over!"

"Suit," Hansen ordered because there wasn't time for hesitation, wasn't *ever* time to look gift horses in the mouth, "pick six, they're Blue Group. Other units, form on Marshal Maharg."

He was gasping, but the air his lungs dragged in burned and his arms burned back as far as the shoulders while his gauntlets glowed. Pain wouldn't matter until afterward.

"Blue Group, *follow me!*"

The seven warriors hit the entrance guards like a broad-headed arrow; six warriors who had been men, and Nils Hansen at the point. Light ripped across the sky and the building's facade of colored marble.

Two of Venkatna's men hacked together. Hansen's right sideman vanished with a blue-white glare and a dull implosion. The men who—killed?—him were dead, and their fellows were dead.

Sections of battlesuit bubbled white and jounced to the flagged courtyard. The larger chunks of torso, some still attached to armored legs, fell more slowly because of their greater inertia.

"Up Wenceslas!" bawled the warrior now guarding Hansen's right side. "Gut the bastards!" His suit had a silver ground, decorated with painted drops of blood.

The palace doors exploded. Arc weapons shorted one another in their wielders' enthusiasm to slash through the obstacle. Gilt straps riveted to the wood as decoration curled back like honeysuckle, burning green and purple.

On Hansen's schematic overlay, seventy-odd gold dots met

the rush of three hundred red markers. The red mass recoiled. The scattered Mirala army was streaming back to catch the imperials, now, in the rear.

God have mercy on any poor bastard who thought he could power through a force Maharg led.

And God have mercy on Emperor Venkatna, for Hansen would show him none.

"Follow me!" he shouted through a throat rasped raw by ozone and more subtle poisons.

The stride of Nils Hansen's armored boots cracked delicate mosaics as he ran to bring an emperor the reward his actions had earned him.

Chapter Forty-eight

Chief engineer Karring leaped from his seat in the nearest bay and turned to run down the corridor housing the rest of the enormous mass that was APEX.

"Help!" Karring screamed as he rounded a corner that hid him from Hansen. "All troops to the Citadel! We've been—"

His direct voice faded. Speakers in the rotunda—speakers in every room and hallway in Keep Starnes—relayed the chief engineer's commands.

"—invaded!"

Hansen's head rang from the impact which had demolished Count Starnes' vehicle, and afterimages from the flash still danced across his retinas. His throat burned with combustion products of both organic and synthetic origin, fused at near-solar temperatures—

But he felt alive in a way that happened only in battle. He viewed his surroundings in crystal perfection through a template of experience and adrenaline and instinct.

Especially instinct. Without that killer instinct, Nils Hansen would not have been the man who could exist *here*.

Did Karring think to run from *him*? At fifty meters, Hansen could have emptied the pistol into the back of Karring's skull, and the tenth shot would hit before the shattered body slumped to the floor.

Hansen whistled between his teeth as he entered the bay the chief engineer had just vacated. *"This hard-liquor place, it's a lowdown disgrace. . . ."*

APEX was above and around him on all sides. Three-meter displays looked huge when attached to the outstations in the rotunda. The one in the alcove was dwarfed by the Fleet Battle Director. Lines of shifting color knotted themselves on the holographic screen.

"The meanest damn place in the town. . . ."

Karring's device spun above the entrance to the bay. Hansen swatted the hollow ovoid casually with the barrel of his pistol. Fragile connections shattered. The construct's off-balance rotation spun it across the corridor to flatten against the wall.

There was a green flash. The remnants of the delicate object drifted away as fine dust. The holographic screen blanked to an expectant pearl gray.

In the ambiance of the bay, Hansen understood better why Count Starnes—and Karring, still more Karring—had tried to trample down everything around. Living within APEX would be much like being immersed in the Matrix. Here were powers beyond the conception of a normal human; powers that could mold a human mind into something inhumane that thought itself above humanity.

Hansen understood; but he'd never been good at pity, and mercy was for after the job had been completed to full, ruthless perfection.

The Citadel trembled with unfamiliar stresses. Karring's alert— the words were little enough, but the Fleet Battle Director had certainly amplified them—had stirred up this anthill, no mistake.

Hansen's smile was instinctive. He hadn't come here to kill Count Starnes' common soldiers—

But he didn't have any objection to doing that too.

Third remained on the console. The helmet was connected through the jewel on its forehead to APEX. Hansen reached for Third with his left hand. As he did so, the huge display lighted with violet letters: NO DATA TO YOUR QUESTION.

Hansen lifted the command helmet. Crystal fetters reabsorbed themselves into the jewel with series of jerky movements, the way lightning moves across the sky when viewed in slow motion.

He settled the helmet onto his head. *"You took your time about it,"* Third commented acidly.

"Are we in a hurry?" replied Hansen in a mild voice. His eyes were as restless as wood flames, flickering across the bay and the corridor beyond, searching for dangers.

"They'll attack us, you know," said Third.

Hansen snorted. "They'll do wonders!"

He dodged out into the corridor. His eyes swept left—toward the rotunda—to right, while his body moved right to follow

Karring. The bays of the Fleet Battle Director alternated like
the teeth in a crocodile's jaws, ready to scissor together and
trap whatever entered them. . . .

"*Karring dropped the Citadel's defenses when he summoned
help,*" the helmet said with electronic smugness. "*He was in
too much of a hurry to be careful. He lifted the interlocks from
APEX, as well. I now have full access to APEX.*"

Hansen spun into the second bay, offset from the first on
the left side of the corridor. It was empty. The holographic display
showed a schematic of the Citadel. Blue carats marked the
elevator bank, the drain beneath the elevators in the center of
the rotunda, and three of the Fleet Battle Director's twenty
bays.

"You've blocked the elevators?" Hansen asked as he scanned
the vast cable trunks in the shadowed darkness above him.

"*Of course,*" Third replied. There was a click of thought that
would have been a sniff were there nostrils to deliver it. "*I sealed
them to the shaft walls by firing the safety girdle intended to
prevent the cages from free-falling.*"

Something crashed loudly in Bay 1. Hansen swung back into
the corridor. As he moved, his gunhand stretched upward like
the trunk of an elephant sniffing for danger.

Part of the base section had fallen from the meter-thick conduit
which normally fed Bay 1 with sensory data. The edges of the
metal glowed from the saws which had cut the opening. A soldier
was crawling out of the hole with a short-stocked energy weapon
in his hand.

*Quick work, that, even though the conduits had already been
gutted to trap Fortin.*

Hansen fired at the soldier ten meters above him. The pistol's
blam! and the *snap!* of its explosive bullet were almost
simultaneous.

Hansen's finger twitched a second round to follow the first
by reflex, but the target's chest had already vanished in a dazzling
flash. The bullet had struck one of the spare energy cells in
the soldier's bandolier. The cell shorted and set off at least a
dozen additional charges.

The command helmet blinked to save Hansen's sight. When
the visor cleared an instant later, he could see that the conduit

was bulged and wrinkled all the way to the dense cap of the Citadel roof. The chain explosion had traveled up the tube like powder flashing across the ready charges in an artillery magazine. It had wiped out the whole attacking force.

You have to be good; but it helps to be lucky.

"They're cutting through by way of the elevators as well," said Third, *"but I'll see to it that it takes them some time. Did they think we came here without knowing how to use a Fleet Battle Director?"*

Hansen ran back past Bay 2 and around Bay 3 on his right again. They were not among those by which the keep's defenders were entering the Citadel.

A tremendous explosion from the rotunda shook Hansen despite the corridor's baffling. Third giggled obscenely in Hansen's mind. *"I detonated the safety charges in only one of each pair of cages. I held the rest until the fools lowered an assault gun and its caisson through the hole they'd cut in the cage floor."*

Bay 4 was another of—

Gunfire ripped and ravened in Bay 4. Hansen's command helmet projected a miniature image of what he would see when he swung into the alcove behind his gun. A dozen of the keep's soldiers had spilled out of a hole in the data feed conduit. They were shooting down into the empty bay.

Hansen moved. One shot per target, not great because they were in body armor, so he was aiming for heads and he wished he had a mob gun or a back-pack laser, something to *sweep*, but they were going down, four of them, six, and the last was the only one who saw Hansen and aimed but it was too late and the soldier's cheeks bulged as the bullet exploded in the spongy bone behind where his nose had been.

The console was slashed and punctured by the volume of fire the soldiers had directed down into it. The holographic display was still live. On it capered a life-sized image of Nils Hansen. The hologram winked and thumbed its nose at the real gunman, then vanished into electronic limbo.

Equipment and bodies dribbled from the top of the bay like water overflowing a sink. Hansen thrust the pistol's smoking barrel through his belt. He snatched up a grenade launcher.

NO DATA TO YOUR QUESTION, said the display in blocky saffron type before it went blank.

Hansen fired two grenades into the hole from which the soldiers had entered the Citadel, angling the bombs upward. They burst within the conduit. There were no secondary explosions or sign of further attackers. The weapon's original owner had already expended the other three rounds in the magazine.

Hansen tossed the launcher away. He took an energy weapon from the hands of a soldier who'd been too nervous to slide up the safety before he squeezed the trigger in vain.

Keep Starnes rocked.

"I'm firing the main missile batteries," Third explained. The helmet's titter/giggle/electronic squeal scraped its nails across Hansen's mind again. *"But I haven't raised the shutters of the launch tubes. Karring really should have thought before he dropped the interlocks."*

Fallen soldiers lay on the floor of the bay like piles of old clothes. One of the men was on his back. His eyes were glazed, but the lids blinked and blinked again, despite the bullet hole in the middle of the forehead.

Stick grenades hung from the bandoliers crossing the victim's chest. Hansen pulled two grenades off and stuffed them into his left cargo pocket.

"What type are they, Third?" he asked. The folk of Plane Five fought in armored vehicles, so standard-issue grenades were likely to be smoke for marking rather than anti-personnel.

"Non-fragmenting assault," the helmet responded promptly. *"You're dealing with internal security teams. Until Fortin arrived, they hadn't been deployed operationally in the past three generations."*

"They sure kept their fucking training up," Hansen grunted. He looked at the weapon in his hands, still on Safe when its owner died. He smiled a shark's smile. *Mostly* they'd kept their training up.

The display had showed another team entering the Citadel through Bay 18. They were going to have plenty of time to prepare before the intruder reached them.

"Six men have entered the rotunda from the drain system,"

Third noted with thin exasperation. *"More are making their way through the elevator shafts."*

"No rest for the wicked," Nils Hansen said. He bent and took a third grenade from the bandolier. Aiming his energy weapon toward the crook in the corridor, Hansen held the grenade against the floor. He stepped on the safety ring, holding it while he drew the bomb away, armed.

"They're fanning out in the rotunda," Third reported.

Hansen threaded the corridor quickly, back to the edge of the first alcove. He tossed the grenade into the rotunda and darted back.

He wasn't left-handed, and the throw had to be side-arm anyway. For this purpose it didn't matter—and the bastards *were* good; a streak of focused plasma released its snarling fury against the corner of the bay only a fraction of a second after Hansen's hand curled back to cover.

A series of six rhythmic shocks made the whole fabric of Keep Starnes vibrate.

"Mine," the command helmet noted with cold pride. *"I overloaded the magnetic shield generators one by one. Next I will short the keep's power supply into the dome itself. It will glow like the sun before it weakens enough to collapse, Commissioner."*

The stick grenade went off in the rotunda with a triple *crack!* and a series of white reflections down the corridor instead of a unitary explosion. The bomb was designed to blind and stun defenders without fragments to endanger the assault force running toward the blast.

Hansen jogged back down the corridor. He ignored the ruin and corpses in the bays he had cleared. That was the past, that was over.

The massive Fifth Plane bodies looked utterly inhuman in death. . . .

Hansen didn't expect the ill-flung grenade to kill or injure any of the Keep Starnes troops. It *was* likely to hold them in the rotunda for a time, though. Heavy gunfire—some of it from an automatic cannon like the one Third had blown up earlier—ripped the mouth of the corridor in confirmation of Hansen's assumption.

Ghostly holograms, a 20% mask, glowed at the lower left of Hansen's field of view. They showed a schematic of Bay 18 from which advanced six rosy beads: Keep Starnes soldiers. They were rushing in pairs.

Hansen jogged past Bay 10. He'd meet them at about 14. *They* would meet Nils Hansen, because he knew exactly how his opponents were deployed. To the soldiers, the intruder they sought was only a lethal ghost.

"You're not bad backup to have in a firefight, Third," Hansen said/gasped. He didn't notice how his lungs were burning until he tried to speak.

"I was thinking the same thing of you, Kommissar," the helmet replied.

Hansen paused in Bay 12. He dragged in breaths as deep as his lungs could hold. His legs trembled. He sat in the console's chair for a moment and let his feet dangle as the muscles cleared themselves of fatigue poisons.

The trouble with living on nerves and hormones was that you could never be quite sure when you were about to exceed the mechanical limits of your body's framework.

Hansen didn't want that to happen five meters in the air.

Out of the line of Hansen's necessary vision, beads representing two soldiers flung themselves into the schematic of Bay 15. The Keep Starnes troops were alternating at point. They knew that the pair who first contacted the intruder had no purpose but to target Hansen for their fellows as they died.

Hansen slung his energy weapon. He jumped onto the console and groped within the pale glow of the holographic screen. Hansen's arms cast dark streaks when they interrupted one component of the three which gave the display solidity and color. He found the projection head and used the wrist-thick conduit which fed it as a pipe up which to shinny to the top of the alcove.

Soldiers rushed Bay 14.

"They're trying not to damage APEX," Third noted in amusement. *"Karring warned them not to."*

"Karring's a fool," Hansen gasped as he lifted himself to the platform where the thick sensor duct spread its optical cables throughout the alcove.

He unslung the energy weapon, then took the grenade sticks

from his cargo pocket. There was no cover on the platform, but the shadows were thick.

The pistol barrel was so hot from rapid fire that he'd burned a blister where the muzzle lay against his thigh. He hadn't noticed it till now; and anyway, it didn't matter.

"*Karring thinks he faces only a gunman, Kommissar*," the helmet said.

"*Though I admit . . .* ," the mental voice added judiciously, "*he faces that too.*"

NO DATA TO YOUR QUESTION, glowed the display in orange as soldiers threw themselves around the corner into Bay 13. Their weapons swept, side to side and upward, trying to cover every nook before the intruder's snake-swift trigger finger cut them down.

Hansen pulled the safety ring from a grenade. The other four members of the Keep Starnes team joined the two scouts. A new pair poised on the edge of Bay 12.

Hansen threw the grenade stick back the way he had come. It bounced off the corridor wall and detonated within Bay 11.

The blast jolted the pair picked to clear Bay 12 into action an instant faster than they otherwise would have moved. That broke their rhythm and robbed them of concentration on the task in hand. The first two men flopped onto the floor of the alcove beneath Hansen. Two of their fellows rushed past them screaming and shooting—at Bay 10, from which they assumed the bomb had come.

The remaining pair of soldiers were also drawn off-balance by the break in routine. They jumped from cover and hesitated. Their gun muzzles were lifted so as not to aim at the backs of their enthusiastic teammates.

One carried a grenade launcher, the other an energy weapon like the gun Hansen had appropriated. Hansen shot them, then shot the pair rising from the floor of Bay 12.

His gun fired bolts of saturated white, like bits clipped from a stellar corona. The weapon had considerable recoil. Though the plasma released could be measured in micrograms, it was accelerated to light speed by a miniature thermonuclear explosion.

The two standing soldiers flopped backward when their chests vaporized. The other pair were on their knees and twisting to scan the top of the bay as they had failed—to their cost—to do initially. The bolts slapped them against the floor again.

Hansen drew the safety ring of his remaining grenade. He lobbed it into Bay 10. The two soldiers who had rushed ahead of their companions launched themselves into the corridor before the bomb went off. They were trying to look everywhere, but the ten-meter height advantage gave Hansen the fraction of a second he needed. He dropped the men with two dazzling bolts.

One of the victims flew back into Bay 10 just as the grenade stick went off. It couldn't have mattered much to him. The bolt didn't penetrate his body armor, but its cataclysmic energy dished in what remained of the breastplate so that it was virtually a coating on the inner side of the back piece.

There were still four charges in the energy weapon's magazine, but its barrel glowed white. If Hansen tried to climb down with the gun slung, it would burn him to the bone as it oscillated on the sling. He tossed the weapon to the alcove floor.

"Karring has a pistol," Third warned.

"Karring doesn't have any balls," Hansen grunted. "Not for this."

He lowered himself hand over hand through the blank screen. His soles gripped the conduit until they swung free. "How about the guys from the other end, from the drains?"

The command helmet flashed him an image. A gang of twenty or more red beads clumped together in Bay 4. From the look of the schematic, the Keep Starnes soldiers were gnawing their way through, straightening the corridor with heavy weapons.

"Tsk," chirped Third. *"They needn't destroy APEX."*

Hansen stepped over a headless body and trotted toward Bay 20. He didn't bother to rearm himself. There were ten rounds or so in the pistol's magazine; that would be quite enough.

"I'm not going to leave APEX for another Karring to conquer the world," he said.

"That is correct, Kommissar," the command helmet said. *"We are not going to leave APEX."*

Keep Starnes shook.

"The dome is sagging," Third explained. *"Its weight is buckling the internal structures of the keep. I don't believe that even the*

Citadel will survive. Still, I've initiated the self-destruct sequence implanted in all Fleet Battle Directors to prevent them from being captured by an enemy."

Hansen reached the corner of Bay 20. He paused, breathing deeply. He was not so much catching his breath as controlling it.

Hansen laughed at his own vanity; the command helmet echoed the human sound with a trill of thought.

Pistol still thrust through his belt, coveralls torn and muddy, face blackened by metal vaporized from the energy weapon's bore and recondensed on the shooter's face—Nils Hansen strode into Bay 20.

"Hello, Karring," he said. Some of the syllables caught in his throat, making them a crazy half stammer, half lilt. "Not much point in running, you know. Not from me."

The chief engineer backed against the console. The display behind him writhed in an iridescent maelstrom. Hansen couldn't guess the question which APEX was trying to answer in its last moments of existence.

Karring's pistol was in his right hand, but the muzzle trembled toward the floor. This was a man to whom war was a game won by cunning strategy and superior weapons. Not a gunman; not a killer to face Nils Hansen.

"Go away . . . ," whispered the squat, bald man.

"You *brought* me here, Karring," Hansen said as he walked closer. "I would've told myself you were none of my business, but you and your boss insisted that I *make* you my business."

The air was hot. The cable ducts feeding Bay 20 were red where they passed through the ceiling. The glow brightened the alcove.

Karring looked upward despairingly. He let the pistol drop from his fingers. "Please," he begged. "Please. Take me away with you."

"You made your bed, friend," Hansen said. "Now lie in it."

The cable duct ruptured. It began to spurt smoke or steam across the ceiling of the alcove. "Time to go, I think, Third," Hansen said.

"Yes," agreed the command helmet. *"But I'll make my own way back, Kommissar."*

Hot, dry air puffed across Hansen's bare scalp. "Goodbye, Karring," he said and vanished into the Matrix himself.

NO DATA ON YOUR QUESTION, read the vermilion letters which crawled across the bottom of the huge display.

Karring's eyes opened wide. "You think you're gods!" he screamed to the empty bay. "You're not, you know? The *world* is a god and you're only its pawns! Paw—"

The roar of the ceiling's collapse drowned the last of Karring's words an instant before it crushed him into the ruins of APEX.

Chapter Forty-nine

The metal facing ran as Hansen's arc licked the doorleaves ahead of him. The audience hall's barred entrance tore apart in a blast of fire, charcoal, oak splinters, and the blue-white electrical tongue which flashed the portal into an orgy of self-destruction.

"There's troops comin' down the hallway towards us!" warned Shill behind him.

Hansen kicked at the center of the shattered doorleaves, where he thought the bar ought to be. He hoped Shill wouldn't decide to give the door an extra slash and get Hansen's boot instead, but at this point most actions had to be reflexive and you took your chances.

Something clanged away from the kick, an arc-severed bar or twists of decorative strap. Nothing that would have hindered the onrush of Hansen's close-coupled body wrapped in a hundred kilos of armor, but he was back on trained reflex. He hadn't worn a battlesuit until he arrived on Northworld—

A couple lifetimes ago.

Hansen crashed into the hall in a cloud of sparks and splinters. His AI instantly adjusted the visual displays to a preset 100% of normal daylight intensity, brightening the dim room.

"Blue Group," ordered Nils Hansen, "keep the rest of them off my back. I'll handle what's in here."

"Who are you?" boomed the Emperor Venkatna. His battlesuit was decorated in royal blue with ermine trim.

Venkatna stood at the right side of his wife's bier; behind him, Race and Julia stirred from their trances within the Web. Half a dozen slaves and palace functionaries cowered where the irruption had caught them in the large room, but there were no armored warriors except the emperor.

"I'm the guy who's come for you," said Nils Hansen as he eased forward. Arcs sputtered between his thumbs and forefingers. The flux was so dense that its color verged on the ultraviolet. "I'm what you earned for yourself."

"I earned glory!" Venkatna shouted. "I earned honor and worship!"

"Oh, no," Hansen said. His amplified voice rasped like a tiger's tongue. "That's not at all what *I* bring you, Venkatna."

The arc from Hansen's right gauntlet flicked four meters toward the emperor's helmet. Venkatna parried expertly. Madness hadn't destroyed his warrior's skills, and his suit was of royal quality.

Illumination by the snarling discharges lighted Esme's face deeper into the bluish glaze of death. Venkatna glanced aside at the corpse. As if the sight shocked him back to memory and reality, the emperor shouted, "Slaves! Make my enemies go away!"

Race's mouth gaped as she settled back. Julia had not risen from her bench. Her eyes closed, but her lips murmured, "Your orders are . . ."

Hansen lunged. He had to get past Venkatna to disrupt the Web before—

A railgun bolt, invisible save as a track of fluorescent plasma, lighted ten meters of the audience hall. The bier and the empress' corpse disintegrated under the impact and hypersonic shockwave.

Bits of the Web, shattered when the slug clipped through them, danced down on the Searchers like crystal rain.

"I wanted peace for the West Kingdom," Hansen said as he advanced slowly. "You turned it into a cancer."

His paired arcs extended twenty centimeters or so, killing range against anything short of another royal suit. When he struck home, it would be with one gauntlet or the other, not both.

The weapons pulsed slightly, forming a wave like the kerf of a metal-cutting saw.

"Who *are* you?" Venkatna screamed. He lunged, his arc extending in a sudden thrust.

Hansen parried with his left hand. He swiped at the emperor's helmet with his right. Venkatna's screens held in a roar and a momentary nimbus filling much of the hall. Paint scorched; bits of plaster dropped from the decorated vaults.

The emperor stumbled backward. Hansen continued his slow advance. The kill to come shimmered in Hansen's mind.

"I can't bring back the ones you starved to death," Hansen said. He spoke with the care of a man talking in a foreign language. All the animal parts of his brain were concerned with the animal processes of staying alive in combat; only the deeply-buried intellect formed words. "Worked to death. Killed."

Race and Julia stood against the wall, hugging one another for support. Neither woman looked capable of casting a shadow. They watched the battle with a hungry avidity, their eyes as bright as hawks'.

The probability generator had disintegrated when its integrity was broken. Its remnants lay on the floor like colored sand. Venkatna's boots streaked the granules as he backed between the benches on which the Searchers had lain.

Hansen feinted left, struck with his right. Venkatna threw himself backward from another crash and blue corona. Clerestory windows popped with the transient currents surging through them.

"But I'll send you the same place, Venkatna," Hansen promised softly. "Or a worse one."

"*Watch*—" Race warned in a shrill voice.

In Hansen's mind: *the emperor dived toward his opponent. Venkatna's body was a spearshaft and the arc from his right glove the spear's cutting head.*

In Hansen's mind.

Hansen leaped into the air as Venkatna dived forward. He didn't bother to block the emperor's thrust. Venkatna's weapon blasted a trench half a meter deep in the stone floor.

Hansen's boots crashed down on the emperor's back. His arc chopped. His gauntlet blazed in direct contact with its target. The flooring shuddered again as it drank the residual impact of Hansen's weapon.

The helmet of the Emperor Venkatna rolled away from the remainder of the battlesuit. It came to rest against the fungus-tinted cheek of his empress. The slug that smashed Esme's body had spared as much of her head as survived decay.

Hansen rose from the corpse of his opponent. The air

shimmered like stress cracks deep within black ice. A pair of dragonflies appeared before Race and Julia.

"Bless you, Lord Hansen!" the emaciated women whispered. They threw themselves aboard their mounts.

Air popped in the place they had been. Freed by Venkatna's death, the Searchers rode home through the Matrix.

The doorway to the audience hall had been blasted ten meters wide and as high as the ceiling vaults. The armored carcases of at least a score of Venkatna's troops lay beyond in desperate profusion. It would be difficult to count the dead with certainty, because of the number of lopped limbs and torsos.

Body cavities still steamed from the arcs that had seared them open. Blazing draperies and lathes from the plaster work softened the carnage with gray smoke.

Only one member of Hansen's Blue Group remained: Shill, still upright though his bumblebee battle colors were blistered in a dozen places by cuts that missed lethality by a hair.

He turned and saluted Hansen with his arc. "Until the Final Day, milord," he cried.

Even as his armored soul vanished back to North's round of death and slaughter, Shill added, "We did 'em up proper this time! Didn't we, buddy?"

Hansen was almost too exhausted to stand. His arms throbbed from the oven heat of his gauntlets. His lungs felt as though they had been torn out and used to scour paving-stones.

But that was all right, that would pass.

Not even gods could bring the dead to life.

Swearing through his tears, Nils Hansen hurled himself into the icy Matrix, on his way to an empty home.

Chapter Fifty

Saburo's giant hog, saddled and caparisoned in cloth-of-gold, snuffed its broad snout along the gravel beach. The beast was two and a half meters at the shoulder. Sparrow's dog eyed it watchfully.

Miyoko led the party which had already carried Mala and Olrun to the palace in pomp and splendor. Gulls screamed above the surf, recalling the unaccustomed display to one another.

Saburo remained, and the smith who served him.

"I, ah . . . ," said the slim god. For all Saburo's power, his nervousness quivered like a flame in dry twigs.

Sparrow stood stolidly. The cat's cradle of crystal and metal spun between the smith's index fingers, wrapped in a soft purple haze.

"You did perfectly, Master Sparrow," Saburo resumed. "I—your wishes will of course be fulfilled, whatever they may be . . . within reason."

Sparrow smiled. "The princess will need a new maid," he said. "I intend to marry the current one, if she'll have me. As I think she will."

"What?" said Saburo. "Oh. Well, of course. I've—you know, I've always wished you might find some companionship among my other servants. I—I rather feared you might be lonely, to tell the truth."

The sea breeze ruffled the god's robes of layered gossamer. The undermost was the same hue as the gold saddle-blanket and had the same metallic sheen.

The hog had found something dead at the tide line a few hundred meters down the strand. It snorted and began to bolt the carrion while gulls complained above.

"I'm not lonely," said Sparrow. "I have my work. But Olrun is a . . . worthy person. And I hope I prove worthy of her."

For the first time in Saburo's recollection, he saw what he read as softness on Sparrow's visage.

"Yes," said Saburo. He had given the maid no more notice than he had the gulls overhead. "She, ah, seemed very suitable." With his face and tone carefully blank, the god went on, "I notice that she didn't appear to have waded through mud, the way . . . ?"

The smith nodded. "I thought that I'd better keep my attention on the princess, not the skimmer controls. Mala and I walked. The others—"

The shadow of a laugh tinged Sparrow's voice, though nothing showed on his face. His toes rubbed the flank of his dog, leaving streaks of dry mud against the animal's clean black hide.

"—rode, since we had a vehicle for them."

"I," said his master, "see."

Saburo spent indeterminate moments staring at the water. The sea was gray almost to the horizon, where it changed to deep mauve.

"I was startled when the railgun projectile disrupted my sand table," Saburo said with consummate care. His eyes were focused on the horizon. "As soon as I—looked into the matter, though, I realized that it resulted from Commissioner Hansen's sense of humor. Reckless humor, I must say. But no harm done."

Sparrow shrugged. "Lord Hansen isn't reckless, milord," he said mildly. "He always thinks through his actions. As Lord North thinks through his actions . . . and I do also, milord, sometimes."

He waited for Saburo to turn and face him before adding, "Only we act anyway, after we've thought matters through. And no doubt that will some day cost us our lives, the three of us."

Saburo blinked. The remainder of his face was tight as he listened to a servant refer to himself on terms of equality with two gods. After a moment, Saburo shaped his mouth into a minute smile and said, "Yes, of course."

He glanced down the beach. The giant pig was half a kilometer away, scavenging the edge of the surf. Saburo frowned and pointed. A blue spark snapped from his finger. The animal arched up on its hindquarters like a dog which has run full-tilt to the end of its chain. It turned and galloped back, huffing and pounding the shingle with its cloven hooves.

"There's one other thing, Master Sparrow," Saburo said. His

manner was no longer hesitant, and his voice rang like thunder on the hilltops. "Though I took you into my service because of your ability to create things, I'm still amazed at the quality of the illusion you were able to project in the Princess Mala's bower."

"Illusion, milord?" the smith said. His eyes had been checking for the dog's location as the giant hog rushed toward them, but now his attention was back on Saburo.

"Yes," said the slim god. "The illusion that you had created a device to modify event waves."

A tick of Saburo's eyebrow indicated the ovoid rotating slowly between Sparrow's fingers. "That would constitute . . . godlike . . . powers. Which of course could not be permitted."

Saburo's huge mount braked to a halt, hunching its hindquarters beneath it and gouging trenches in the strand with all four hooves. Loose gravel hopped and danced. Some of it ricocheted from Sparrow's legs. The dog barked in sharp fury from behind her master.

None of the flying stones touched Saburo, though some of them rebounded from a hair's breadth short of his perfectly-shaded garments.

"I see," said Sparrow neutrally.

"There's not a problem with me, of course," Saburo continued. "But if anything of the sort should happen again, one of my colleagues might—misunderstand. And act hastily."

All the while the two men spoke, a freak of the weather caused a tiny breeze to course from the general vicinity of the device in Sparrow's hands. The wind had scoured the smith's legs clean of the mud which caked them.

Sparrow eyed his legs critically, then hung the probability generator on his belt. He reached down absently to polish his leg brace with the callused fingers of his right hand.

Gulls screamed above the surf, and the giant hog drew in snorting breaths to recover from its gallop. Sparrow's dog rubbed back and forth against her master's thighs, whining softly.

"Things like that happen," the smith said. "I couldn't prevent King Hermann from crippling me, either. Though it might have been as well for him if he hadn't."

Sparrow straightened.

Saburo gave a quick nod. "So long as we understand each

other," he said. He paused, no longer imperious, and added, "Captain North is quite ruthless, you know."

Sparrow smiled. "Yes, milord," he said. "As is Lord Hansen. And I would not have brought your bride to you if I were not ruthless as well."

"You are indeed a perfect servant," the god said in a voice without any emotional loading whatsoever.

He cleared his throat. "Ah . . . ," he said. "We should be getting back. I, ah, appreciate your . . ."

The dog skipped from the shelter of her master. She made short rushes in the direction of the giant pig, now that the huge beast stood cowed and blowing.

"Shall I take you to the palace myself?" Saburo asked, changing the subject brightly.

"Thank you, milord," said Sparrow. "But my dragonfly is here—"

He gestured curtly towards the spindle-legged vehicle at the edge of the high-tide line.

"—and anyway," Sparrow continued, "I think I'll walk along the beach for a while. It feels good to walk, sometimes."

He nodded, then turned and strode away at a moderate pace. Gravel crunched beneath his ponderous steps. There was nothing in front of him but weed and spume kicked onto the tumbled stones by the waves.

After a moment, the dog noticed her master's absence and gamboled after him. She barked each time her high-flung forefeet hit the strand again.

Saburo mounted his squatting hog and took its reins in his hand. The beast rose expectantly, but Saburo waited until Sparrow was almost out of sight before he wrenched his mount and himself into the Matrix.

Sunlight on the crippled smith and his crippled dog turned their leg braces into jeweled adornments.

Chapter Fifty-one

North rose in the center of his hall, shuddering like a man dragged from drowning in the frozen waters of the Matrix.

In his own form, he was a tall, craggy man with a gray beard and one eye as gray as sea ice. There were old scars on his body, lines and puckers and a dent the size of a maul's head in the side of his left thigh.

"Welcome home, Third," said Dowson's brain in a wash of tawny light. "Were you amused by your expedition with Commissioner Hansen?"

North snorted. He made a gesture with his right hand. Loose velvet garments clothed him, very different from the Consensus Exploration Authority coveralls which he ordinarily wore in private.

"As interesting as that?" Dowson gibed. The shower of light that brought his words was as pale as dry sand. A listener who knew Dowson as well as North did could hear the regret of a disembodied brain for the days in which it could act as well as be.

North barked out a harsh, false laugh. "I'll tell you this about our kommissar," he said. "In the old days, I'd have given him a job as scout for just as long as he lasted."

He laughed again. "Which wouldn't be long at all."

Thoughts with the sheen of hydrated turquoise scaled from the pillar before Dowson's tank. "When you look to *your* end on the Final Day," the brain noted, "as Commissioner Hansen does not . . . do you not see him still fighting as the hordes sweep you under? *I* see that, Captain."

"Oh, I never said he couldn't fight," North said. His tone was so coolly unemotional that a listener could almost ignore the fact that he was changing the subject.

North stretched high in the air. The garment's loose sleeves piled on his shoulders while his scarred, knobby arms wavered above them. "That's all he knows how to do, though, the commissioner. He brought down Keep Starnes, all right, but he got nothing at all out of APEX."

North dropped his heels to the floor and lowered his arms again. "Nothing!" he repeated forcefully toward the floating brain. "It was just an excuse for him to kill. He hasn't learned that we *gods* don't need excuses to do as we wish."

Dowson's laughter was as cold as the horizon-blue light that carried it in an expanding sphere across the hall. The lower edge sparkled and vanished as it rubbed against the floor, blocks of dense white laid in intricate marquetry with blocks of void in which distant galaxies gleamed.

"I don't think Hansen will ever learn that lesson," Dowson said, drawing an the final word into a mental sneer. "But as for what he learned from APEX—"

"Nothing!" snapped North. "APEX *had* no data on how I took Northworld out of the universe of the Consensus."

"That isn't what Commissioner Hansen asked while you were coupled to the Fleet Battle Director," Dowson explained. "He asked APEX to determine what *you* knew about how Northworld was removed from the universe of the Consensus."

North made a minuscule gesture. At the end of it, he was dressed again in gray coveralls with an equipment belt and a command helmet—the utility uniform he wore when he first arrived on the planet to determine why the original exploration unit had disappeared.

"He knows that you didn't steal Northworld at all, Captain," the brain continued in a shower of faded rose. "That you accepted the powers you had been given, but that you don't have the least idea yourself of who gave them to you."

"Do you know, Dowson?" North demanded. His voice was edged steel. North had never needed rank insignia to convey his authority.

"Karring did at the end, I think," Dowson replied/half-replied. "The Fleet Battle Director was the correct tool to correlate external data with what *Third* knew and to synthesize an answer. And I suspect Commissioner Hansen—"

From the pillar shimmered icy laughter the color of rotted bronze.

"—has guessed the answer as well. Did you think the Consensus of Worlds had chosen a mere gunman as their investigator, Captain North?"

For a time without measure, the tall man stared at the brain in the tank before him. At last North began to laugh—booming, godlike mirth that echoed from the mighty vaults of his palace.

Chapter Fifty-two

Reaction hit home fully when Nils Hansen climbed out of his battlesuit and stood in his undergarments in the dwelling he had created for himself.

He began to tremble. When he realized that he might vomit, he tried to reach the bathroom off the main hall. Spasms caught him too soon, doubling him up on the pale, resilient flooring.

Outside the clear panels which encircled the room, morning breezes combed a landscape of grassland and brush. The boulder-huge lumps silhouetted on the eastern horizon were a herd of titanotheres.

After a few minutes, Hansen started to get to his feet. His stomach lurched again sourly, but he managed to wait the moment out. There was nothing else in his guts to lose, anyway.

The synthetic floor purred as it cleaned itself, sucking in all traces of vomit through micropores in its surface. Hansen's idea of a palace was a utilitarian structure which took care of itself and which never intruded on its master's existence the way a human servant might do.

Hansen didn't want humans watching him puke his guts up because he wasn't perfect, even though he was a god. . . .

"Sometimes I live in the country . . . ," Hansen sang in a monotone as he looked down at his garments. His shirt of gray homespun was black with sweat, and he'd managed somehow to tear the right sleeve half loose from the body as well.

And the vomit.

He loosed the gold-clasped belt a woman had given him, then pulled the shirt over his head and tossed it away. The floor would take care of it and of the breeches of naturally black wool. They'd been well-made garments at the start of the battle. Hours of sweat and straining had felted the fabric and left it reeking like a goat in rut.

"Sometimes I live in the town," Hansen sang as he stepped

787

the rest of the way into the shower. His presence summoned a firm spray of water, two degrees above blood temperature, without need for a command.

The filth would wash away quickly. Fatigue would pass in time. Both his arms were bright red and tingling at the water's touch, but Hansen hadn't done himself permanent injury by loading his arc gauntlets so heavily for so long. . . .

"Sometimes I take a great notion . . . ," Hansen gurgled as he closed his eyes and opened his mouth to water that could not sluice the bile from his soul.

He had watched through North's screen as Krita's battlesuit lost its luster in a cyan fireball. That memory would never heal. Nils Hansen had enough deaths in his soul to be quite sure of that.

". . . to jump in the river and drown," chorused a woman in a throaty contralto; an attractive voice, but untrained and off-key.

Hansen's eyes opened. Krita stood outside the bathroom. She looked thin and worn. A patch of skin had rubbed from the edge of her right wrist, and the hair on the crown of her head was kinked and discolored.

She was all the beauty in the world.

"What . . . ?" Hansen said. He gestured, shutting off the water that had almost choked him.

"The door was open," Krita said. She crooked him a tired smile. Her suede singlet was polished smooth where it rubbed the inside of her battlesuit. "My lord North brought me here. After the battle."

"But you were . . . ?"

Hansen reached a hand out and drew the woman to him. She came willingly. Her normally-taut body was almost boneless in its present exhaustion.

"Not killed," she murmured into Hansen's shoulder. Her burned hair stank and cracked away as he nuzzled her. "His arc, my lord North's, it tore the top off my helmet. But not *me*."

Hansen began to laugh in a complex of emotions which he couldn't have untangled himself.

"He told me to say to you . . . ," Krita continued. She paused, desperate to get the quote precisely correct, despite her fatigue.

"He said, 'You aren't the only one who could handle a weapon. . . .' He called you 'Kommissar.' And he said—"

She raised her eyes to Hansen's and gave a half sob, half chuckle. "My lord North said that good Searchers were too valuable to waste; and that anyway, you might appreciate the favor. Was he right, my lord?"

Hansen was crying. He kissed her. Her mouth was as soft as a ripe peach.

Krita giggled in relief. "Do you mind company when you shower, my love?" she murmured.

"I don't mind you," Hansen said. The water sluiced down, and outside the sun rose in a crimson, purple splendor.

Author's Note

Two of the finest and most evocative of the poems of The Elder Edda, and a tale from The Younger Edda whose poetic form has not survived, became the core of *Justice*. These are:

1. The *Grottasongr*, in which Othin gives King Frothi, a ruler who has imposed absolute peace on his kingdom, a mill which will grind out exactly what the king asks for;

2. The *Skirnismal*, in which the human servant—and friend— of the god Frey goes to fetch his master a wife from Giantland; and

3. The journey of Thor to the hall of the Giant Geirroth, for sports that the giant and his daughters plan to end with Thor's death.

The *Grottasongr* appears to have been put in its present form around the middle of the tenth century. The poet knew and probably survived the unification of Norway by Harald the Fairhaired, who died in A.D. 933.

It appears to me beyond question that when the poet spoke of the Peace of Frothi, he had in mind (rather than some soft, modern vision) the iron-shod peace that Harald imposed on the squabbling petty kings who were his neighbors. Therefore, I've based the background of the novel on the techniques which King Harald used in cold fact.

Reinhard Heydrich employed similar methods when he governed Czechoslovakia on behalf of Hitler. The technique works perfectly—if the person wielding power is both smart and absolutely ruthless. Harald differed from his red-handed fellow Vikings only because he was smarter than the rest of them.

Despite modern impressions to the contrary, there was a highly-developed legal system in Dark Age Scandinavia, from which these Edda tales spring. Courts, compromise, and the reduction of injuries to money payments were the tools of the Law.

But that was the Law. Laws are made by society and applied by society. It's the Law that puts a killer back on the street because he was of unsound mind when he raped and slowly murdered the child selling Girl Scout cookies. Unlike our own civilized place and time, the Vikings also had a system of Justice.

Justice carried a sword.

Dave Drake
Chatham County, N.C.

DAVID WEBER

The Honor Harrington series: *(cont.)*

Field of Dishonor

Honor goes home to Manticore—and fights for her life on a battlefield she never trained for, in a private war that offers just two choices: death—or a "victory" that can end only in dishonor and the loss of all she loves....

Flag in Exile

Hounded into retirement and disgrace by political enemies, Honor Harrington has retreated to planet Grayson, where powerful men plot to reverse the changes she has brought to their world. And for their plans to suceed, Honor Harrington must die!

Honor Among Enemies

Offered a chance to end her exile and again command a ship, Honor Harrington must use a crew drawn from the dregs of the service to stop pirates who are plundering commerce. Her enemies have chosen the mission carefully, thinking that either she will stop the raiders or they will kill her . . . and either way, her enemies will win. . . .

In Enemy Hands

After being ambushed, Honor finds herself aboard an enemy cruiser, bound for her scheduled execution. But one lesson Honor has never learned is how to give up! One way or another, she and her crew are going home—even if they have to conquer Hell to get there!

continued ☞